2012
PUSHCART PRIZE XXXVI
BEST OF THE SMALL PRESSES

EDITED BY BILL HENDERSON
WITH THE PUSHCART PRIZE EDITORS

Note: nominations for this series are invited from any small, independent, literary book press or magazine in the world, print or online. Up to six nominations—tear sheets or copies, selected from work published, or about to be published, in the calendar year—are accepted by our December 1 deadline each year. Write to Pushcart Fellowships, P.O. Box 380, Wainscott, N.Y. 11975 for more information or consult our websites www.pushcartprize.com. or pushcart press.org.

Acknowledgments
Selections for The Pushcart Prize are reprinted with the permission of authors and presses cited. Copyright reverts to authors and presses immediately after publication.

Distributed by W. W. Norton & Co.
500 Fifth Ave., New York, N.Y. 10110

Library of Congress Card Number: 76-58675
ISBN (hardcover): 978-1-888889-64-2
ISBN (paperback): 978-1-888889-63-5
ISSN: 0149-7863

INTRODUCTION

I WAS BLESSED TO HAVE known Reynolds Price, who sadly died in January of 2011. He was a Pushcart Prize Founding Editor.

Way back in 1975 I wrote to Reynolds asking for his help in starting a new series celebrating the small and the beautiful. I'd never met him and I had no credentials for such an enterprise beyond publishing my first novel myself from a press dubbed Nautilus Books. (The nautilus you see, grows its shell gracefully year after year — our press collapsed in six months.) Reynolds replied that he would be happy to be listed as a Founding Editor of the Pushcart Prize — as did dozens of other distinguished writers — and with their backing, and only because of it, we produced PPI and over the past decades made a dent in literary history.

Reynolds Price wrote thirteen novels, many short stories, poetry, essays, a translation of The Bible and three volumes of memoirs starting with *A Whole New Life* in 1994. That memoir of his struggle with an eight-inch malignant tumor that had wrapped itself around his spinal column just below his neck and left him a paraplegic, in constant pain, inspired me and thousands of others to face a potentially fatal disease with humor and determination. (Personal note: this winter a slip on the ice brought me a broken ankle, surgery and a nasty pulmonary embolism. I was bed, wheelchair and housebound for three months. Reynolds's memoir of his survival and many years in a wheelchair was burned into my soul and helped me endure far lesser complaints.) At Duke University where he taught Milton's works for more than a half a century, Reynolds was an inspiration to generations of students. Anne Tyler recalls "I can still see him sitting Taylor fashion on top of his desk reading to the class from his own work or one of his students' papers. He seemed genuinely joyous when we did the slightest thing right."

I admired his determination, faith and daring — not only as "the gray eel" entwined his spine but also in creating that first sentence for his universally acclaimed first novel, *A Long and Happy Life*, 1962. The sentence stands as an inspiration to writers bound by too frequent timidity and the worship of mere competence, the curse of our MFA courses. I quote from his debut sentence in full. Take a deep breath.

> *Just with his body and from inside like a snake, leaning that black motorcycle side to side, cutting in and out of the slow line of cars to get there first, staring due north through goggles towards Mt. Moriah and switching coon tails in everybody's face was Wesley Beavers, and laid against his back like sleep, spraddle-legged on the sheepskin seat behind him was Rosacoke Mustian who was maybe his girlfriend and who had given up looking into the wind and trying to nod at every sad car in the line, and when he even speeded up and passed the truck (lent for the afternoon by Mr. Isaac Alston and driven by Sammy, his man, hauling one pine box and one black boy dressed in all he could borrow, set up in a ladder backed chair with flowers banked round him and a foot on the box to steady it) — when he even passed that, Rosacoke said once into his back "Don't" and rested in humiliation, not thinking but with her hands on his hips for dear life and her white blouse blown out behind her like a banner in defeat.*

It took courage for a young author to write that sentence, courage to teach John Milton for decades in a faithless age, courage to endure "the gray eel", to announce himself a homosexual in the less tolerant 60's, and to stand as an unorthodox, non-churchgoing believer and not be shy about his Christian faith. He told *The Georgia Review* in 1993, "the whole point of learning about the human race is to give it mercy." I am honored that he helped start this series.

∘ ∘ ∘

E.F. Schumacher was chief economist of the British National Coal Board when he reached the startling conclusion in the 1950's that big is not better. There simply wasn't enough coal to provide constant growth of the gross national product. His book *Small Is Beautiful* — at the time an unthinkable proclamation — is today not only thinkable but quite obvious.

In the publication industry, just like in big coal, small is beautiful as was evident in last year's awarding of the Pulitzer Prize for fiction to Paul Harding's novel *Tinkers*, rejected by the big pubs as "too slow, contemplative, meditative and quiet" and finally after years in a desk drawer published by Bellevue Literary Press, a small press of suitable daring.

Recently small was beautiful again when the commercially excluded novel by Jaimy Gordon, *Lord of Misrule*, won the National Book Award for fiction. It was published by Bruce McPherson, the one-man band behind McPherson & Co. who cares not a fig for the commercial but a whole basket of figs for what is worthy.

McPherson & Co first published Jaimy Gordon's underground classic novel, *Shamp of the City-Solo* in 1974. He and Gordon met as students at Brown University. The novel became a cornerstone of his press. For years McPherson has labored in relative obscurity in Kingston, New York keeping the faith with lovingly produced books.

Jaimy Gordon too has worked quietly for the past three decades as a writing teacher at Western Michigan University publishing several novels with small presses including *Bogeywoman* (1999) and *She Drove Without Stopping* (1990). She spent her early years working at various obscure horseracing tracks — the subject of *Lord of Misrule*. A New York *Times* feature describes her: "she has a huge corona of springy, tightly curled hair that suggests prolonged exposure to a light socket, and personality to match — forthright, disarming, uncensored." Like her novels.

The *Times* also noted the astonishing fact that McPherson printed *Lord of Misrule* with fine endpapers, a full cloth cover and stitched binding "practically unheard of in these days." (Except by the presses that care about such details.)

❖   ❖   ❖

Pushcart's offices — a backyard shack on Long island and a summer cabin in Maine — are annually deluged with mail from our 200 plus Contributing Editors and 650 small press nominators (the regular, substantial kind of mail — hardcopy if you will.)

Now and then a letter arrives that states the case. I have long railed against the e-book and instant Internet publication as damaging to writers. Instant anything is dangerous — great writing takes time. You should long to be as good as John Milton and Reynolds Price not just barf into the electronic void. But I repeat myself.

Here is an edited portion of that letter from Dr. Clay Reynolds, honored author and director of Creative Writing at the University of Texas, Dallas.

> *University presses are being told to convert or die, only this time the threat does not come from some bearded religious fanatic with an armored horse and gun power but in the form of the e-reader, the digitized book, the unvetted, unwarranted, unwanted and soon to be unread volume that everyone demands and to which no one will pay the least attention. In your previous Pushcart introduction you mentioned that you once attended a party given by George Plimpton for Pushcart . . . the scene took place in a New York apartment. It was a cramped space, jammed with people. Every wall was lined with books on shelves making hallways and passages around furniture so narrow people had to turn sideways to get by. Music was loud, smoke was thick and booze was flowing. Conversation was informed, erudite and serious.*
>
> *Now literary parties are peopled by crushing bores talking about iPads and Nooks, bragging about the number of volumes they've downloaded and comparing computers. There is no booze, certainly no smoking. And there are no books.*

Only books that require batteries — go figure. Thank you Clay.

*   *   *

Despite difficulties with broken bones and vagrant blood clots, this past year was fragrant with Pushcart celebrations.

The reviews for last year's PPXXXV were astonishing. "A monumental year," said *Publishers Weekly*. "As always essential, period," declared *Kirkus Reviews*. "An exciting overview of American literature," exclaimed *Booklist's* Donna Seaman. Hundreds of letters to Pushcart echoed these sentiments. A response like that keeps us going.

Poet and founder of New York's Writers Studio, Philip Schultz, staged a reading for Pushcart by Jayne Anne Phillips, C.K. Williams, Phil himself and Mary Gaitskill at New York's Le Poisson Rouge, a "hot spot" I'm told. The place was packed.

Best of all the Board of Directors of Pushcart Prize Fellowships, our endowment, plus my wife Genie and daughter Lily gathered a party for Pushcart Press' 40th anniversary (and my 70th). Lily, a brilliant documentary filmmaker, in secret contacted Pushcart's friends from years past and asked for testimonials — Joyce Carol Oates, Andre DuBus III, Harvey Shapiro, Grace Schulman, Phil Schultz, Gordon Lish, Rick Moody, Jim Charlton, Brad Morrow, Bill and Pat Strachan, Frank Stiffel and John Baker. From that failed Nautilus Books episode, through a stint at Doubleday to Pushcart's initial offer in *The Publish It Yourself Handbook*, through the first PP edition in 1976 and 60 books later Lily presented her dad with a film tribute that took my breath away — an approval of a flawed life that somehow meant something to others. I was suffused in mercy.

❋ ❋ ❋

Every year I ask our guest poetry editors to reveal what they have observed in sifting through approximately 4000 nominated poems. This year Laura Kasischke and Michael Waters did the impossible.

Laura Kasischke has published eight collections of poetry, most recently *Space, In Chains* (Copper Canyon 2011). She has also published seven novels and has a collection of short stories coming.

> *Every day for three months of this winter I had the nearly unbearable pleasure of casting myself into the vastness of the year's poetry in an attempt to winnow it down to the best. If it hadn't felt like such a sacred task, it would have seemed laughable. There was so much that anyone looking at the boxes and the pages would have assumed there could be no shape, nothing about it as a whole that one could say. In fact, that's not the case, and one of the poems I chose, (because how could I not?) manages to say it for them all: "I hold you like a hole holds light". (Maria Hummel's "Station.") Not one poem did not speak of the burden of so much freedom to speak, and of the limited time we have here on earth, and in this place to do so. A lucky, terrible time and place to be a poet, a child, a parent, a lover, these poems say. So much pain and ecstasy the paper doesn't contain it — but, finally, I came away with these astonishing poems, snatched from the multitudes, to offer up as proof of how much our poetry has to say.*

❋ ❋ ❋

Michael Waters' recent books include *Gospel Night* (2011) and *Darling Vulgarity* (2006) — a finalist for the Los Angeles *Times* Book Prize. He is editor of *Contemporary American Poetry* (2006) and has been the recipient of fellowships from the National Endowment For the Arts and The Fulbright Foundation. In 2004, he chaired the poetry panel for the National Book Award.

> *Having left home for college in 1967, I wound up at a school — SUNY Brockport — where a poetry or fiction reading took place every Wednesday night. In three years there I heard, among other poets, W.S. Merwin, W. D. Snodgrass, Diane Wakoski, Richard Wilbur, Robert Bly, Patricia Goedicke, Galway Kinnell, William Stafford and others (the series was weighted heavily towards men, a bias any woman who taught or attended college then will recognize). I was not yet 21. Each week, impressionable, I thought I want to write like him. Then the next week No, I want to write like her. Hearing these poets provided an education that deepened beyond my classroom experience. Reading through the nominated Pushcart poems that arrived on my doorstep in seemingly bottomless boxes, I was reminded of the excited and fluid loyalties of my undergraduate years. I wish I'd written this poem I thought, then, soon enough No, I wish I'd written this one. What surprised and pleased me was the number of terrific poems, by poets of whom I'd never heard, that appeared in journals unfamiliar to me. Many of the poems, beyond those included here or given special mention, have lodged themselves within me, so I'll remain grateful for having been asked to do what Bill called, more than once, "an impossible job."*

My profound thanks to Laura and Michael and to all our Contributing Editors and prose readers — you will find them listed on the masthead. This book is their gift to you — 67 stories, essays, memoirs and poems from 52 presses including 15 presses new to this series, — among the most generous selections we have gathered in 36 blessed years. Evidence anew, as Reynolds Price put it, of giving mercy to the human race.

B.H.

THE PEOPLE WHO HELPED

FOUNDING EDITORS—Anaïs Nin (1903-1977), Buckminster Fuller (1895-1983), Charles Newman (1938-2006), Daniel Halpern, Gordon Lish, Harry Smith, Hugh Fox, Ishmael Reed, Joyce Carol Oates, Len Fulton, Leonard Randolph, Leslie Fiedler (1917-2003), Nona Balakian (1918-1991), Paul Bowles (1910-1999), Paul Engle (1908-1991), Ralph Ellison (1914-1994), Reynolds Price (1933-2011), Rhoda Schwartz, Richard Morris, Ted Wilentz (1915-2001), Tom Montag, William Phillips (1907-2002). Poetry editor: H. L. Van Brunt

CONTRIBUTING EDITORS FOR THIS EDITION—*Kim Addonizio, Dan Albergotti, Dick Allen, John Allman, Idris Anderson, Antler, Philip Appleman, Tony Ardizzone, L. S. Asekoff, Renee Ashley, David Baker, Mary Jo Bang, Kim Barnes, Tony Barnstone, Ellen Bass, Rick Bass, Claire Bateman, Charles Baxter, Bruce Beasley, Marvin Bell, Molly Bendall, Karen E. Bender, Pinckney Benedict, Ciaran Berry, Marie-Helene Bertino, Linda Bierds, Diann Blakely, Michael Bowden, Betsy Boyd, John Bradley, Krista Bremer, Geoffrey Brock, Fleda Brown, Kurt Brown, Rosellen Brown, Michael Dennis Browne, Christopher Buckley, Andrea Hollander Budy, E. S. Bumas, Richard Burgin, Shannon Cain, Kathy J. Callaway, Bonnie Jo Campbell, Colin Cheney, Kim Chinquee, Jane Ciabattari, Suzanne Geary, Michael Collier, Billy Collins, Jeremy Collins, Martha Collins, Robert Cording, Stephen Corey, Michael Czyzniejewski, Phil Dacey, Claire Davis, Chard deNiord, Sharon Dilworth, Sharon Dolin, Sharon Doubiago, Rita Dove, Jack Driscoll, John Drury, Andre Dubus III, Nancy Eimers, Sarah Einstein, Karl Elder, Angie Estes, Ed Falco, Gary Fincke, Ben Fountain, Hugh Fox, H. E. Francis, Seth Fried, Joanna Fuhrman, John Fulton, Richard Garcia, David Gessner, Reginald Gibbons, Gary Gildner, William Giraldi, Herbert Gold, Linda Gregerson, Marilyn Hacker, Susan Hahn, Mark Hal-*

11

liday, *Jeffrey Hammond, James Harms, Jeffrey Harrison, Michael Heffernan, Daniel L. Henry, William Heyen, Bob Hicok, Kathleen Hill, Jane Hirshfield, Jen Hirt, Ted Hoagland, Tony Hoagland, Christie Hodgen, Daniel Hoffman, Elliot Holt, Caitlin Horrocks, Joe Hurka, Colette Inez, Mark Irwin, Laura Kasischke, Deborah Keenan, George Keithley, Brigit Pegeen Kelly, Thomas E. Kennedy, Kristin King, David Kirby, John Kistner, Judith Kitchen, Richard Kostelanetz, Maxine Kumin, Wally Lamb, Dorianne Laux, Fred Leebron, David Lehman, Dana Levin, Philip Levine, Daniel S. Libman, Gerald Locklin, Rachel Loden, William Lychack, Amos Magliocco, Paul Maliszewski, Kathryn Maris, Anthony Marra, Dan Masterson, Tracy Mayor, Robert McBrearty, Nancy McCabe, Rebecca McClanahan, Erin McGraw, Elizabeth McKenzie, Charles McLeod, Wesley McNair, Joseph Millar, Jim Moore, Joan Murray, Kirk Nesset, Michael Newirth, Aimee Nezhukumatathil, Joyce Carol Oates, Lance Olsen, William Olsen, Dzvinia Orlowsky, Peter Orner, Alan Michael Parker, Edith Pearlman, Lydia Peelle, Benjamin Percy, Lucia Perillo, Donald Platt, Andrew Porter, Joe Ashby Porter, C. E. Poverman, Sara Pritchard, Kevin Prufer, Lia Purpura, Amanda Rea, James Reiss, Donald Revell, Nancy Richard, Atsuro Riley, Katrina Roberts, Jessica Roeder, Jay Rogoff, Gibbons Ruark, Vern Rutsala, Kay Ryan, Maxine Scates, Alice Schell, Grace Schulman, Philip Schultz, Lloyd Schwartz, Salvatore Scibona, Maureen Seaton, Patty Seyburn, Ravi Shankar, Gerald Shapiro, Floyd Skloot, Arthur Smith, Harrison Solow, Debra Spark, Elizabeth Spires, David St. John, Maura Stanton, Maureen Stanton, Patricia Staton, Gerald Stern, Pamela Stewart, Cheryl Strayed, Terese Svoboda, Jennifer K. Sweeney, Janet Sylvester, Arthur Sze, Ron Tanner, Katherine Taylor, Susan Terris, Robert Thomas, Jean Thompson, Melanie Rae Thon, Pauls Toutonghi, Chase Twichell, Deb Olin Unferth, Lee Upton, Laura van den Berg, Dennis Vannatta, G.C. Waldrep, B. J. Ward, Rosanna Warren, Sylvia Watanabe, Don Waters, Michael Waters, Marc Watkins, Charles Harper Webb, Roger Weingarten, William Wenthe, Philip White, Dara Wier, Naomi J. Williams, Eleanor Wilner, S.L. Wisenberg (Sandi), Mark Wisniewski, David Wojahn, Carolyne Wright, Robert Wrigley, Christina Zawadiwsky, Paul Zimmer,*

PAST POETRY EDITORS—*H.L. Van Brunt, Naomi Lazard, Lynne Spaulding, Herb Leibowitz, Jon Galassi, Grace Schulman, Carolyn Forché, Gerald Stern, Stanley Plumly, William Stafford, Philip Levine, David Wojahn, Jorie Graham, Robert Hass, Philip Booth, Jay Meek,*

CONTENTS

PHANTOMS

fiction by STEVEN MILLHAUSER

from MCSWEENEY'S

THE PHENOMENON

THE PHANTOMS OF our town do not, as some think, appear only in the dark. Often we come upon them in full sunlight, when shadows lie sharp on the lawns and streets. The encounters take place for very short periods, ranging from two or three seconds to perhaps half a minute, though longer episodes are sometimes reported. So many of us have seen them that it's uncommon to meet someone who has not; of this minority, only a small number deny that phantoms exist. Sometimes an encounter occurs more than once in the course of a single day; sometimes six months pass, or a year. The phantoms, which some call Presences, are not easy to distinguish from ordinary citizens: they are not translucent, or smoke-like, or hazy, they do not ripple like heat waves, nor are they in any way unusual in figure or dress. Indeed they are so much like us that it sometimes happens we mistake them for someone we know. Such errors are rare, and never last for more than a moment. They themselves appear to be uneasy during an encounter and swiftly withdraw. They always look at us before turning away. They never speak. They are wary, elusive, secretive, haughty, unfriendly, remote.

EXPLANATION #1

One explanation has it that our phantoms are the auras, or visible traces, of earlier inhabitants of our town, which was settled in 1636.

Our atmosphere, saturated with the energy of all those who have preceded us, preserves them and permits them, under certain conditions, to become visible to us. This explanation, often fitted out with a pseudoscientific vocabulary, strikes most of us as unconvincing. The phantoms always appear in contemporary dress, they never behave in ways that suggest earlier eras, and there is no evidence whatever to support the claim that the dead leave visible traces in the air.

HISTORY

As children we are told about the phantoms by our fathers and mothers. They in turn have been told by their own fathers and mothers, who can remember being told by their parents—our great-grandparents—when they were children. Thus the phantoms of our town are not new; they don't represent a sudden eruption into our lives, a recent change in our sense of things. We have no formal records that confirm the presence of phantoms throughout the diverse periods of our history, no scientific reports or transcripts of legal proceedings, but some of us are familiar with the second-floor Archive Room of our library, where in nineteenth-century diaries we find occasional references to "the others" or "them," without further details. Church records of the seventeenth century include several mentions of "the devil's children," which some view as evidence for the lineage of our phantoms; others argue that the phrase is so general that it cannot be cited as proof of anything. The official town history, published in 1936 on the three-hundredth anniversary of our incorporation, revised in 1986, and updated in 2006, makes no mention of the phantoms. An editorial note states that "the authors have confined themselves to ascertainable fact."

HOW WE KNOW

We know by a ripple along the skin of our forearms, accompanied by a tension of the inner body. We know because they look at us and withdraw immediately. We know because when we try to follow them, we find that they have vanished. We know because we know.

CASE STUDY #1

Richard Moore rises from beside the bed, where he has just finished the forty-second installment of a never-ending story that he tells each night to his four-year-old daughter, bends over her for a goodnight kiss, and walks quietly from the room. He loves having a daughter; he loves having a wife, a family; though he married late, at thirty-nine, he knows he wasn't ready when he was younger, not in his doped-up twenties, not in his stupid, wasted thirties, when he was still acting like some angry teenager who hated the grown-ups; and now he's grateful for it all, like someone who can hardly believe that he's allowed to live in his own house. He walks along the hall to the den, where his wife is sitting at one end of the couch, reading a book in the light of the table lamp, while the TV is on mute during an ad for vinyl siding. He loves that she won't watch the ads, that she refuses to waste those minutes, that she reads books, that she's sitting there waiting for him, that the light from the TV is flickering on her hand and upper arm. Something has begun to bother him, though he isn't sure what it is, but as he steps into the den he's got it, he's got it: the table in the side yard, the two folding chairs, the sunglasses on the tabletop. He was sitting out there with her after dinner, and he left his sunglasses. "Back in a sec," he says, and turns away, enters the kitchen, opens the door to the small screened porch at the back of the house, and walks from the porch down the steps to the backyard, a narrow strip between the house and the cedar fence. It's nine-thirty on a summer night. The sky is dark blue, the fence lit by the light from the kitchen window, the grass black here and green over there. He turns the corner of the house and comes to the private place. It's the part of the yard bounded by the fence, the side-yard hedge, and the row of three Scotch pines, where he's set up two folding chairs and a white ironwork table with a glass top. On the table lie the sunglasses. The sight pleases him: the two chairs, turned a little toward each other, the forgotten glasses, the enclosed place set off from the rest of the world. He steps over to the table and picks up the glasses: a good pair, expensive lenses, nothing flashy, stylish in a quiet way. As he lifts them from the table he senses something in the skin of his arms and sees a figure standing beside the third Scotch pine. It's darker here than at the back of the house, and he can't see her all that well: a tall, erect woman, fortyish, long face, dark dress. Her expression, which he can barely make out, seems stern. She looks at him for a moment and turns away—not hastily, as if she were frightened, but decisively, like someone who wants to be alone. Behind the Scotch pine she's no longer visible. He hesitates, steps over to the tree, sees nothing. His first impulse is to scream at her, to tell her that he'll kill her if she comes near his daughter. Immediately he forces himself to calm down. Everything

21

will be all right. There's no danger. He's seen them before. Even so, he returns quickly to the house, locks the porch door behind him, locks the kitchen door behind him, fastens the chain, and strides to the den, where on the TV a man in a dinner jacket is staring across the room at a woman with pulled-back hair who is seated at a piano. His wife is watching. As he steps toward her, he notices a pair of sunglasses in his hand.

THE LOOK

Most of us are familiar with the look they cast in our direction before they withdraw. The look has been variously described as proud, hostile, suspicious, mocking, disdainful, uncertain; never is it seen as welcoming. Some witnesses say that the phantoms show slight movements in our direction, before the decisive turning away. Others, disputing such claims, argue that we cannot bear to imagine their rejection of us and misread their movements in a way flattering to our self-esteem.

HIGHLY QUESTIONABLE

Now and then we hear reports of a more questionable kind. The phantoms, we are told, have grayish wings folded along their backs; the phantoms have swirling smoke for eyes; at the ends of their feet, claws curl against the grass. Such descriptions, though rare, are persistent, perhaps inevitable, and impossible to refute. They strike most of us as childish and irresponsible, the results of careless observation, hasty inference, and heightened imagination corrupted by conventional images drawn from movies and television. Whenever we hear such descriptions, we're quick to question them and to make the case for the accumulated evidence of trustworthy witnesses. A paradoxical effect of our vigilance is that the phantoms, rescued from the fantastic, for a moment seem to us normal, commonplace, as familiar as squirrels or dandelions.

CASE STUDY #2

Years ago, as a child of eight or nine, Karen Carsten experienced a single encounter. Her memory of the moment is both vivid and vague: she can't recall how many of them there were, or exactly what they looked like, but she recalls the precise moment in which she came upon them, one summer afternoon, as she stepped around to the back of the garage in search of a soccer ball and saw them sitting quietly in the grass. She still remembers her feeling of wonder as they turned to look at her, before they rose and went away. Now, at age fifty-six, Karen Carsten lives alone with her cat in a house filled with framed photographs of her parents, her nieces, and her late husband, who died in a car accident seventeen years ago. Karen is a high school librarian with many set routines: the TV programs, the weekend housecleaning, the twice-yearly visits in August and December to her sister's family in Youngstown, Ohio, the choir on Sunday, dinner every two weeks at the same restaurant with a friend who never calls to ask how she is. One Saturday afternoon she finishes organizing the linen closet on the second floor and starts up the attic stairs. She plans to sort through boxes of old clothes, some of which she'll give to Goodwill and some of which she'll save for her nieces, who will think of the collared blouses and floral-print dresses as hopelessly old-fashioned but who might come around to appreciating them someday, maybe. As she reaches the top of the stairs she stops so suddenly and completely that she has the sense of her own body as an object standing in her path. Ten feet away, two children are seated on the old couch near the dollhouse. A third child is sitting in the armchair with the loose leg. In the brownish light of the attic, with its one small window, she can see them clearly: two barefoot girls of about ten, in jeans and T-shirts, and a boy, slightly older, maybe twelve, blond-haired, in a dress shirt and khakis, who sits low in the chair with his neck bent up against the back. The three turn to look at her and at once rise and walk into the darker part of the attic, where they are no longer visible. Karen stands motionless at the top of the stairs, her hand clutching the rail. Her lips are dry, and she is filled with an excitement so intense that she thinks she might burst into tears. She does not follow the children into the shadows, partly because she doesn't want to upset them, and partly because she knows they are no longer there. She turns back down the stairs. In the living room she sits in the armchair until nightfall. Joy fills her heart. She can feel it shining from her face. That night she returns to the attic, straightens the pillows on the couch, smooths out the doilies on the chair arms, brings over a small wicker table, sets out three saucers and three teacups. She moves away some bulging boxes that sit beside the couch, carries off an old typewriter, sweeps the floor. Downstairs in the living room she turns on the TV, but she keeps the volume low; she's listening for sounds in the attic, even though she knows that her visitors don't make sounds.

23

She imagines them up there, sitting silently together, enjoying the table, the teacups, the orderly surroundings. Now each day she climbs the stairs to the attic, where she sees the empty couch, the empty chair, the wicker table with the three teacups. Despite the pang of disappointment, she is happy. She is happy because she knows they come to visit her every day, she knows they like to be up there, sitting in the old furniture, around the wicker table; she knows; she knows.

EXPLANATION #2

One explanation is that the phantoms *are not there*, that those of us who see them are experiencing delusions or hallucinations brought about by beliefs instilled in us as young children. A small movement, an unexpected sound, is immediately converted into a visual presence that exists only in the mind of the perceiver. The flaws in this explanation are threefold. First, it assumes that the population of an entire town will interpret ambiguous signs in precisely the same way. Second, it ignores the fact that most of us, as we grow to adulthood, discard the stories and false beliefs of childhood but continue to see the phantoms. Third, it fails to account for innumerable instances in which multiple witnesses have seen the same phantom. Even if we were to agree that these objections are not decisive and that our phantoms are in fact not there, the explanation would tell us only that we are mad, without revealing the meaning of our madness.

OUR CHILDREN

What shall we say to our children? If, like most parents in our town, we decide to tell them at an early age about the phantoms, we worry that we have filled their nights with terror or perhaps have created in them a hope, a longing, for an encounter that might never take place. Those of us who conceal the existence of phantoms are no less worried, for we fear either that our children will be informed unreliably by other children or that they will be dangerously unprepared for an encounter should one occur. Even those of us who have prepared our children are worried about the first encounter, which sometimes disturbs a child in ways that some of us remember only too well. Although we assure our children that there's nothing to fear from the phantoms, who wish only to be left alone, we ourselves are fearful: we wonder whether the phantoms are as harmless as we say they are, we wonder whether they behave differently in the presence of an unaccompanied child, we wonder whether, under certain circumstances, they might become bolder than we know. Some say that a phantom, encountering an adult and a child, will look only at the child, will let its gaze linger in a way that never happens with an adult. When we put our children to sleep, leaning close to them and answering their questions about phantoms in gentle, soothing tones, until their eyes close in peace, we understand that we have been preparing in ourselves an anxiety that will grow stronger and more aggressive as the night advances.

CROSSING OVER

The question of "crossing over" refuses to disappear, despite a history of testimony that many of us feel ought to put it to rest. By "crossing over" is meant, in general, any form of intermingling between us and them; specifically, it refers to supposed instances in which one of them, or one of us, leaves the native community and joins the other. Now, not only is there no evidence of any such regrouping, of any such transference of loyalty, but the overwhelming testimony of witnesses shows that no phantom has ever remained for more than a few moments in the presence of an outsider or given any sign whatever of greeting or encouragement. Claims to the contrary have always been suspect: the insistence of an alcoholic husband that he saw his wife in bed with *one of them*, the assertion of a teenager suspended from high school that a group of phantoms had threatened to harm him if he failed to obey their commands. Apart from statements that purport to be factual, fantasies of crossing over persist in the form of phantom-tales that flourish among our children and are half-believed by naïve adults. It is not difficult to make the case that stories of this kind reveal a secret desire for contact, though no reliable record of contact exists. Those of us who try to maintain a strict objectivity in such matters are forced to admit that a crossing of the line is not impossible, however unlikely, so that even as we challenge dubious claims and smile at fairy tales we find ourselves imagining the sudden encounter at night, the heads turning toward us, the moment of hesitation, the arms rising gravely in welcome.

CASE STUDY #3

James Levin, twenty-six years old, has reached an impasse in his life. After college he took a year off, holding odd jobs and traveling all over the country before returning home to apply to grad school. He completed his coursework in two years, during which he taught one introductory section of American History, and then surprised everyone by taking a leave of absence in order to read for his dissertation (*The Influence of Popular Culture on High Culture in Post-Civil War America, 1865-1900*) and think more carefully about the direction of his life. He lives with his parents in his old room, dense with memories of grade school and high school. He worries that he's losing interest in his dissertation; he feels he should rethink his life, maybe go the med-school route and do something useful in the world instead of wasting his time wallowing in abstract speculations of no value to anyone; he speaks less and less to his girlfriend, a law student at the University of Michigan, nearly a thousand miles away. Where, he wonders, has he taken a wrong turn? What should he do with his life? What is the meaning of it all? These, he believes, are questions eminently suitable for an intelligent adolescent of sixteen, questions that he himself discussed passionately ten years ago with friends who are now married and paying mortgages. Because he's stalled in his life, because he is eaten up with guilt, and because he is unhappy, he has taken to getting up late and going for long walks all over town, first in the afternoon and again at night. One of his daytime walks leads to the picnic grounds of his childhood. Pine trees and scattered tables stand by the stream where he used to sail a little wooden tugboat—he's always bumping into his past like that—and across the stream is where he sees her, one afternoon in late September. She's standing alone, between two oak trees, looking down at the water. The sun shines on the lower part of her body, but her face and neck are in shadow. She becomes aware of him almost immediately, raises her eyes, and withdraws into the shade, where he can no longer see her. He has shattered her solitude. Each instant of the encounter enters him so sharply that his memory of her breaks into three parts, like a medieval triptych in a museum: the moment of awareness, the look, the turning away. In the first panel of the triptych, her shoulders are tense, her whole body unnaturally still, like someone who has heard a sound in the dark. Second panel: her eyes are raised and staring directly at him. It can't have lasted for more than a second. What stays with him is something severe in that look, as if he's disturbed her in a way that requires forgiveness. Third panel: the body is half turned away, not timidly but with a kind of dignity of withdrawal, which seems to rebuke him for an intrusion. James feels a sharp desire to cross the stream and find her, but two thoughts hold him back: his fear that the

26

crossing will be unwelcome to her, and his knowledge that she has dis-appeared. He returns home but continues to see her standing by the stream. He has the sense that she's becoming more vivid in her ab-sence, as if she's gaining life within him. The unnatural stillness, the dark look, the turning away—he feels he owes her an immense apology. He understands that the desire to apologize is only a mask for his desire to see her again. After two days of futile brooding he returns to the stream, to the exact place where he stood when he saw her the first time; four hours later he returns home, discouraged, restless, and ir-ritable. He understands that something has happened to him, some-thing that is probably harmful. He doesn't care. He returns to the stream day after day, without hope, without pleasure. What's he doing there, in that desolate place? He's twenty-six, but already he's an old man. The leaves have begun to turn; the air is growing cold. One day, on his way back from the stream, James takes a different way home. He passes his old high school, with its double row of tall windows, and comes to the hill where he used to go sledding. He needs to get away from this town, where his childhood and adolescence spring up to meet him at every turn; he ought to go somewhere, do something; his long, purposeless walks seem to him the outward expression of an inner con-fusion. He climbs the hill, passing through the bare oaks and beeches and the dark firs, and at the top looks down at the stand of pine at the back of Cullen's Auto Body. He walks down the slope, feeling the steer-ing bar in his hands, the red runners biting into the snow, and when he comes to the pines he sees her sitting on the trunk of a fallen tree. She turns her head to look at him, rises, and walks out of sight. This time he doesn't hesitate. He runs into the thicket, beyond which he can see the whitewashed back of the body shop, a brilliant blue front fender lying up against a tire, and, farther away, a pickup truck driving along the street; pale sunlight slants through the pine branches. He searches for her but finds only a tangle of ferns, a beer can, the top of a pint of ice cream. At home he throws himself down on his boyhood bed, where he used to spend long afternoons reading stories about boys who grew up to become famous scientists and explorers. He summons her stare. The sternness devastates him, but draws him, too, since he feels it as a strength he himself lacks. He understands that he's in a bad way; that he's got to stop thinking about her; that he'll never stop thinking about her; that nothing can ever come of it; that his life will be harmed; that harm is attractive to him; that he'll never return to school; that he will disappoint his parents and lose his girlfriend; that none of this matters to him; that what matters is the hope of seeing once more the phantom lady who will look harshly at him and turn away; that he is weak, foolish, frivolous; that such words have no meaning for him; that he has entered a world of dark love, from which there is no way out.

MISSING CHILDREN

Once in a long while, a child goes missing. It happens in other towns, it happens in yours: the missing child who is discovered six hours later lost in the woods, the missing child who never returns, who disappears forever, perhaps in the company of a stranger in a baseball cap who was last seen parked in a van across from the elementary school. In our town there are always those who blame the phantoms. They steal our children, it is said, in order to bring them into the fold; they're always waiting for the right moment, when we have been careless, when our attention has relaxed. Those of us who defend the phantoms point out patiently that they always withdraw from us, that there is no evidence they can make physical contact with the things of our world, that no human child has ever been seen in their company. Such arguments never persuade an accuser. Even when the missing child is discovered in the woods, where he has wandered after a squirrel, even when the missing child is found buried in the yard of a troubled loner in a town two hundred miles away, the suspicion remains that the phantoms have had something to do with it. We who defend our phantoms against false accusations and wild inventions are forced to admit that we do not know what they may be thinking, alone among themselves, or in the moment when they turn to look at us, before moving away.

DISRUPTION

Sometimes a disruption comes: the phantom in the supermarket, the phantom in the bedroom. Then our sense of the behavior of phantoms suffers a shock: we cannot understand why creatures who withdraw from us should appear in places where encounters are unavoidable. Have we misunderstood something about our phantoms? It's true enough that when we encounter them in the aisle of a supermarket or clothing store, when we find them sitting on the edge of our beds or lying against a bed-pillow, they behave as they always do: they look at us and quickly withdraw. Even so, we feel that they have come too close, that they want something from us that we cannot understand, and only when we encounter them in a less-frequented place, at the back of the shut-down railroad station or on the far side of a field, do we relax a little.

EXPLANATION #3

One explanation asserts that we and the phantoms were once a single race, which at some point in the remote history of our town divided into two societies. According to a psychological offshoot of this explanation, the phantoms are the unwanted or unacknowledged portions of ourselves, which we try to evade but continually encounter; they make us uneasy because we know them; they are ourselves.

FEAR

Many of us, at one time or another, have felt the fear. For say you are coming home with your wife from an evening with friends. The porch light is on, the living room windows are dimly glowing before the closed blinds. As you walk across the front lawn from the driveway to the porch steps, you become aware of something, over there by the wild cherry tree. Then you half-see one of them, for an instant, withdrawing behind the dark branches, which catch only a little of the light from the porch. That is when the fear comes. You can feel it deep within you, like an infection that's about to spread. You can feel it in your wife's hand tightening on your arm. It's at that moment you turn to her and say, with a shrug of one shoulder and a little laugh that fools no one: "Oh, it's just one of them!"

PHOTOGRAPHIC EVIDENCE

Evidence from digital cameras, camcorders, iPhones, and old-fashioned film cameras divides into two categories: the fraudulent and the dubious. Fraudulent evidence always reveals signs of tampering. Methods of digital-imaging manipulation permit a wide range of effects, from computer-generated figures to digital clones; sometimes a slight blur is sought, to suggest the uncanny. Often the artist goes too far, and creates a hackneyed monster-phantom inspired by third-rate movies; more clever manipulators stay closer to the ordinary, but tend to give themselves away by an exaggeration of some feature, usually the ears or nose. In such matters, the temptation of the grotesque appears to be irresistible. Celluloid fraud assumes well-known forms that reach back to the era of fairy photographs: double exposures, chemical tampering with negatives, the insertion of gauze between the printing paper and the enlarger lens. The category of the dubious is harder to disprove. Here we find vague, shadowy shapes, wavering lines resembling ripples of heated air above a radiator, half-hidden forms concealed by branches or by windows filled with reflections. Most of these images can be explained as natural effects of light that have deceived the credulous person recording them. For those who crave visual proof of phantoms, evidence that a photograph is fraudulent or dubious is never entirely convincing.

CASE STUDY #4

One afternoon in late spring, Evelyn Wells, nine years old, is playing alone in her backyard. It's a sunny day; school is out, dinner's a long way off, and the warm afternoon has the feel of summer. Her best friend is sick with a sore throat and fever, but that's all right: Evvy likes to play alone in her yard, especially on a sunny day like this one, with time stretching out on all sides of her. What she's been practicing lately is roof-ball, a game she learned from a boy down the block. Her yard is bounded by the neighbor's garage and by thick spruces running along the back and side; the lowest spruce branches bend down to the grass and form a kind of wall. The idea is to throw the tennis ball, which is the color of lime Kool-Aid, onto the slanted garage roof and catch it when it comes down. If Evvy throws too hard, the ball will go over the roof and land in the yard next door, possibly in the vegetable garden surrounded by chicken wire. If she doesn't throw hard enough, it will come right back to her, with no speed. The thing to do is make the ball go almost to the top, so that it comes down faster and faster; then she's got to catch it before it hits the ground, though a one-bouncer isn't terrible. Evvy is pretty good at roof-ball—she can make the ball go way up the slope, and she can figure out where she needs to stand as it comes rushing or bouncing down. Her record is eight catches in a row, but now she's caught nine and is hoping for ten. The ball stops near the peak of the roof and begins coming down at a wide angle; she moves more and more to the right as it bounces lightly along and leaps into the air. This time she's made a mistake—the ball goes over her head. It rolls across the lawn toward the back and disappears under the low-hanging spruce branches not far from the garage. Evvy sometimes likes to play under there, where it's cool and dim. She pushes aside a branch and looks for the ball, which she sees beside a root. At the same time she sees two figures, a man and a woman, standing under the tree. They stare down at her, then turn their faces away and step out of sight. Evvy feels a ripple in her arms. Their eyes were like shadows on a lawn. She backs out into the sun. The yard does not comfort her. The blades of grass seem to be holding their breath. The white wooden shingles on the side of the garage are staring at her. Evvy walks across the strange lawn and up the back steps into the kitchen. Inside, it is very still. A faucet handle blazes with light. She hears her mother in the living room. Evvy does not want to speak to her mother. She does not want to speak to anyone. Upstairs, in her room, she draws the blinds and gets into bed. The windows are above the backyard and look down on the rows of spruce trees. At dinner she is silent. "Cat got your tongue?" her father says. His teeth are laughing. Her mother gives her a wrinkled look. At night she lies with her eyes open. She sees the man and woman standing under the tree, staring down at her. They turn their faces away. The next day, Saturday, Evvy refuses to go outside. Her mother brings orange juice, feels her forehead, takes her temperature. Outside, her father is mowing the lawn. That night she doesn't sleep. They are standing under the tree, looking at her with their shadow-eyes. She can't see their faces. She doesn't remember their clothes. On Sunday she stays in her room. Sounds startle her: a clank in the yard, a shout. At night she watches with closed eyes: the ball rolling under the branches, the two figures standing there, looking down at her. On Monday her mother takes her to the doctor. He presses the silver circle against her chest. The next day she returns to school, but after the last bell she comes straight home and goes to her room. Through the slats of the blinds she can see the garage, the roof, the dark green spruce branches bending to the grass. One afternoon Evvy is sitting at the piano in the living room. She's practicing her scales. The bell rings and her mother goes to the door. When Evvy turns to look, she sees a woman and a man. She leaves the piano and goes upstairs to her room. She sits on the throw rug next to her bed and stares at the door. After a while she hears her mother's footsteps on the stairs. Evvy stands up and goes into the closet. She crawls next to a box filled with old dolls and bears and elephants.

She can hear her mother's footsteps in the room. Her mother is knocking on the closet door. "Please come out of there, Evvy. I know you're in there." She does not come out.

CAPTORS

Despite widespread disapproval, now and then an attempt is made to capture a phantom. The desire arises most often among groups of idle teenagers, especially during the warm nights of summer, but is also known among adults, usually but not invariably male, who feel menaced by the phantoms or who cannot tolerate the unknown. Traps are set, pits dug, cages built, all to no avail. The nonphysical nature of phantoms does not seem to discourage such efforts, which sometimes display great ingenuity. Walter Hendricks, a mechanical engineer, lived for many years in a neighborhood of split-level ranch houses with backyard swing sets and barbecues; one day he began to transform his yard into a dense thicket of pine trees, in order to invite the visits of phantoms. Each tree was equipped with a mechanism that was able to release from the branches a series of closely woven steel-mesh nets, which dropped swiftly when anything passed below. In another part of town, Charles Reese rented an excavator and dug a basement-size cavity in his yard. He covered the pit, which became known as the Dungeon, with a sliding steel ceiling concealed by a layer of sod. One night, when a phantom appeared on his lawn, Reese pressed a switch that caused the false lawn to slide away; when he climbed down into the Dungeon with a high-beam flashlight, he discovered a frightened chipmunk. Others have used chemical sprays that cause temporary paralysis, empty sheds with sliding doors that automatically shut when a motion sensor is triggered, even a machine that produces flashes of lightning. People who dream of becoming captors fail to understand that the phantoms cannot be caught; to capture them would be to banish them from their own nature, to turn them into us.

EXPLANATION #4

One explanation is that the phantoms have always been here, long before the arrival of the Indians. We ourselves are the intruders. We seized their land, drove them into hiding, and have been careful ever since to maintain our advantage and force them into postures of submission. This explanation accounts for the hostility that many of us detect in the phantoms, as well as the fear they sometimes inspire in us. Its weakness, which some dismiss as negligible, is the absence of any evidence in support of it.

THE PHANTOM LORRAINE

As children we all hear the tale of the Phantom Lorraine, told to us by an aunt, or a babysitter, or someone on the playground, or perhaps by a careless parent desperate for a bedtime story. Lorraine is a phantom child. One day she comes to a tall hedge at the back of a yard where a boy and girl are playing. The children are running through a sprinkler, or throwing a ball, or practicing with a hula hoop. Nearby, their mother is kneeling on a cushion before a row of hollyhock bushes, digging up weeds. The Phantom Lorraine is moved by this picture, in a way she doesn't understand. Day after day she returns to the hedge, to watch the children playing. One day, when the children are alone, she steps shyly out of her hiding place. The children invite her to join them. Even though she is different, even though she can't pick things up or hold them, the children invent running games that all three can play. Now every day the Phantom Lorraine joins them in the backyard, where she is happy. One afternoon the children invite her into their house. She looks with wonder at the sunny kitchen, at the carpeted stairway leading to the second floor, at the children's room with the two windows looking out over the backyard. The mother and father are kind to the Phantom Lorraine. One day they invite her to a sleepover. The little phantom girl spends more and more time with the human family, who love her as their own. At last the parents adopt her. They all live happily ever after.

ANALYSIS

As adults we look more skeptically at this tale, which once gave us so much pleasure. We understand that its purpose is to overcome a child's fear of the phantoms, by showing that what the phantoms really desire is to become one of us. This of course is wildly inaccurate, since the actual phantoms betray no signs of curiosity and rigorously withdraw from contact of any kind. But the tale seems to many of us to hold a deeper meaning. The story, we believe, reveals our own desire: to know the phantoms, to strip them of mystery. Fearful of their difference, unable to bear their otherness, we imagine, in the person of the Phantom Lorraine, their secret sameness. Some go further. The tale of the Phantom Lorraine, they say, is a thinly disguised story about our hatred of the phantoms, our wish to bring about their destruction. By joining a family, the Phantom Lorraine in effect ceases to be a phantom; she casts off her nature and is reborn as a human child. In this way, the story expresses our longing to annihilate the phantoms, to devour them, to turn them into us. Beneath its sentimental exterior, the tale of the Phantom Lorraine is a dream-tale of invasion and murder.

OTHER TOWNS

When we visit other towns, which have no phantoms, often we feel that a burden has lifted. Some of us make plans to move to such a town, a place that reminds us of tall picture books from childhood. There, you can walk at peace along the streets and in the public parks, without having to wonder whether a ripple will course through the skin of your forearms. We think of our children playing happily in green backyards, where sunflowers and honeysuckle bloom against white fences. But soon a restlessness comes. A town without phantoms seems to us a town without history, a town without shadows. The yards are empty, the streets stretch bleakly away. Back in our town, we wait impatiently for the ripple in our arms; we fear that our phantoms may no longer be there. When, sometimes after many weeks, we encounter one of them at last, in a corner of the yard or at the side of the car wash, where a look is flung at us before the phantom turns away, we think: Now things are as they should be, now we can rest awhile. It's a feeling almost like gratitude.

EXPLANATION #5

Some argue that all towns have phantoms, but that only we are able to see them. This way of thinking is especially attractive to those who cannot understand why our town should have phantoms and other towns none; why our town, in short, should be an exception. An objection to this explanation is that it accomplishes nothing but a shift of attention from the town itself to the people of our town: it's our ability to perceive phantoms that is now the riddle, instead of the phantoms themselves. A second objection, which some find decisive, is that the

34

explanation relies entirely on an assumed world of invisible beings, whose existence can be neither proved nor disproved.

CASE STUDY #5

Every afternoon after lunch, before I return to work in the upstairs study, I like to take a stroll along the familiar sidewalks of my neighborhood. Thoughts rise up in me, take odd turns, vanish like bits of smoke. At the same time I'm wide open to striking impressions—that ladder leaning against the side of a house, with its shadow hard and clean against the white shingles, which project a little, so that the shingle-bottoms break the straight shadow-lines into slight zigzags; that brilliant red umbrella lying at an angle in the recycling container on a front porch next to the door; that jogger with shaved head, black nylon shorts, and an orange sweatshirt that reads, in three lines of black capital letters: EAT WELL / KEEP FIT / DIE ANYWAY. A single blade of grass sticks up from a crack in a driveway. I come to a sprawling old house at the corner, not far from the sidewalk. Its dark red paint could use a little touching up. Under the high front porch, on both sides of the steps, are those crisscross lattice panels, painted white. Through the diamond-shaped openings come pricker branches and the tips of ferns. From the sidewalk I can see the handle of an old hand mower, back there among the dark weeds. I can see something else: a slight movement. I step up to the porch, bend to peer through the lattice: I see three of them, seated on the ground. They turn their heads toward me and look away, begin to rise. In an instant they're gone. My arms are rippling as I return to the sidewalk and continue on my way. They interest me, these creatures who are always vanishing. This time I was able to glimpse a man of about fifty and two younger women. One woman wore her hair up; the other had a sprig of small blue wildflowers in her hair. The man had a long straight nose and a long mouth. They rose slowly but without hesitation and stepped back into the dark. Even as a child I accepted phantoms as part of things, like spiders and rainbows. I saw them in the vacant lot on the other side of the backyard hedge, or behind garages and toolsheds. Once I saw one in the kitchen. I observe them carefully whenever I can; I try to see their faces. I want nothing from them. It's a sunny day in early September. As I continue my walk, I look about me with interest. At the side of a driveway, next to a stucco house, the yellow nozzle of a hose rests on top of a dark green garbage can. Farther back, I can see part of a swing set. A cushion is sitting on the grass beside a three-pronged weeder with a red handle.

THE DISBELIEVERS

The disbelievers insist that every encounter is false. When I bend over and peer through the openings in the lattice, I see a slight movement, caused by a chipmunk or mouse in the dark weeds, and instantly my imagination is set in motion: I seem to see a man and two women, a long nose, the rising, the disappearance. The few details are suspiciously precise. How is it that the faces are difficult to remember, while the sprig of wildflowers stands out clearly? Such criticisms, even when delivered with a touch of disdain, never offend me. The reasoning is sound, the intention commendable: to establish the truth, to distinguish the real from the unreal. I try to experience it their way: the movement of a chipmunk behind the sunlit lattice, the dim figures conjured from the dark leaves. It isn't impossible. I exercise my full powers of imagination: I take their side against me. There is nothing there, behind the lattice. It's all an illusion. Excellent! I defeat myself. I abolish myself. I rejoice in such exercise.

YOU

You who have no phantoms in your town, you who mock or scorn our reports: are you not deluding yourselves? For say you are driving out to the mall, some pleasant afternoon. All of a sudden—it's always sudden—you remember your dead father, sitting in the living room in the house of your childhood. He's reading a newspaper in the armchair next to the lamp table. You can see his frown of concentration, the fold of the paper, the moccasin slipper half-hanging from his foot. The steering wheel is warm in the sun. Tomorrow you're going to dinner at a friend's house—you should bring a bottle of wine. You see your friend laughing at the table, his wife lifting something from the stove. The shadows of telephone wires lie in long curves on the street. Your mother lies in the nursing home, her eyes always closed. Her photograph on your bookcase: a young woman smiling under a tree. You are lying in bed with a cold, and she's reading to you from a book you know by heart. Now she herself is a child and you read to her while she lies there. Your sister will be coming up for a visit in two weeks. Your daughter playing in the backyard, your wife at the window. Phantoms of memory, phantoms of desire. You pass through a world so thick with phantoms that there is barely enough room for anything else. The sun shines on a hydrant, casting a long shadow.

EXPLANATION #6

One explanation says that we ourselves are phantoms. Arguments drawn from cognitive science claim that our bodies are nothing but artificial constructs of our brains: we are the dream-creations of electrically charged neurons. The world itself is a great seeming. One virtue of this explanation is that it accounts for the behavior of our phantoms: they turn from us because they cannot bear to witness our self-delusion.

FORGETFULNESS

There are times when we forget our phantoms. On summer afternoons, the telephone wires glow in the sun like fire. Shadows of tree branches lie against our white shingles. Children shout in the street. The air is warm, the grass is green, we will never die. Then an uneasiness comes, in the blue air. Between shouts, we hear a silence. It's as though something is about to happen, which we ought to know, if only we could remember.

HOW THINGS ARE

For most of us, the phantoms are simply there. We don't think about them continually, at times we forget them entirely, but when we encounter them we feel that something momentous has taken place, before we drift back into forgetfulness. Someone once said that our phantoms are like thoughts of death: they are always there, but appear only now and then. It's difficult to know exactly what we feel about our phantoms, but I think it is fair to say that in the moment we see them, before we're seized by a familiar emotion like fear, or anger, or curiosity, we are struck by a sense of strangeness, as if we've suddenly entered a room we have never seen before, a room that nevertheless feels familiar. Then the world shifts back into place and we continue on our way. For though we have our phantoms, our town is like your town: sun shines on the house fronts, we wake in the night with troubled hearts, cars back out of driveways and turn up the street. It's true that a question runs through our town, because of the phantoms, but we don't believe we are the only ones who live with unanswered questions. Most of us would say we're no different from anyone else. When you come to think about us, from time to time, you'll see we really are just like you.

Nominated by McSweeney's and Jay Rogoff

STATION

by MARIA HUMMEL

from POETRY

Days you are sick, we get dressed slow,
find our hats, and ride the train.
We pass a junkyard and the bay,
then a dark tunnel, then a dark tunnel.

You lose your hat. I find it. The train
sighs open at Burlingame,
past dark tons of scrap and water.
I carry you down the black steps.

Burlingame is the size of joy:
a race past bakeries, gold rings
in open black cases. I don't care
who sees my crooked smile

or what erases it, past the bakery,
when you tire. We ride the blades again
beside the crooked bay. You smile.
I hold you like a hole holds light.

We wear our hats and ride the knives.
They cannot fix you. They try and try.
Tunnel! Into the dark open we go.
Days you are sick, we get dressed slow.

Nominated by Poetry and Pamela Stewart

MR. LYTLE: AN ESSAY

by JOHN JEREMIAH SULLIVAN

from THE PARIS REVIEW

When I was twenty years old, I became a kind of apprentice to a man named Andrew Lytle, whom pretty much no one apart from his negligibly less ancient sister, Polly, had addressed except as Mister Lytle in at least a decade. She called him Brother. Or *Brutha*—I don't suppose either of them had ever voiced a terminal *r*. His two grown daughters did call him Daddy. Certainly I never felt even the most obscure impulse to call him Andrew, or "old man," or any other familiarism, though he frequently gave me to know it would be all right if I were to call him *mon vieux*. He, for his part, called me boy, and beloved, and once, in a letter, "Breath of My Nostrils." He was about to turn ninety-two when I moved into his basement, and he had not yet quite reached ninety-three when they buried him the next winter, in a coffin I had helped to make—a cedar coffin, because it would smell good, he said. I wasn't that helpful. I sat up a couple of nights in a freezing, starkly lit workshop rubbing beeswax into the boards. The other, older men—we were four altogether—absorbedly sawed and planed. They chiseled dovetail joints. My experience in woodworking hadn't gone past feeding planks through a band saw for shop class, and there'd be no time to redo anything I might botch, so I followed instructions and with rags cut from an undershirt worked coats of wax into the cedar until its ashen whorls glowed purple, as if with remembered life.

The man overseeing this vigil was a luthier named Roehm whose house stood back in the woods on the edge of the plateau. He was about six and a half feet tall with floppy bangs and a deep, grizzled mustache. He wore huge glasses. I believe I have never seen a person more tense than Roehm was during those few days. The cedar was "green"—it hadn't been properly cured. He groaned that it wouldn't behave. On some level he must have resented the haste. Lytle had lain dying for weeks; he endured a series of disorienting pin strokes. By the end they were giving him less water than morphine. He kept saying, "Time to go home," which at first meant he wanted us to take him back to his house, his real house, that he was tired of the terrible simulacrum we'd smuggled him to, in his delirium. Later, as those fevers drew together into what seemed an unbearable clarity, like a blue flame behind the eyes, the phrase came to mean what one would assume.

He had a deathbed, in other words. He didn't go suddenly. Yet although his family and friends had known for years about his wish to lie in cedar, which required that a coffin be custom made, no one had so much as played with the question of who in those mountains could do such a thing or how much time the job would take. I don't hold it against them—against us—the avoidance of duty, owing as it did to fundamental incredulity. Lytle's whole existence had for so long been essentially posthumous, he'd never risk seeming so ridiculous as to go actually dying now. My grandfather had told me once that when *he'd* been at Sewanee, in the thirties, people had looked at Lytle as something of an old man, a full sixty years before I met him. And he nursed this impression, with his talk of coming "to live in the sense of eternity," and of the world he grew up in—Middle Tennessee at the crack of the twentieth century—having more in common with Europe in the Middle Ages than with the South he lived to see. All of his peers and enemies were dead. A middle daughter he had buried long before. His only wife had been dead for thirty-four years, and now Mister Lytle was dead, and we had no cedar coffin.

But someone knew Roehm, or knew about him; and it turned out Roehm knew Lytle's books; and when they told Roehm he'd have just a few days to finish the work, he set to, without hesitation and even with a certain impatience, as if he feared to displease some unforgiving master. I see him there in the little space, repeatedly microwaving Tupperware containers full of burnt black coffee and downing them like Coca-Colas. He loomed. He was so large there hardly seemed room for the rest of us, and already the coffin lid lay on sawhorses in the center of the floor, making us sidle along the walls. At least a couple of times a night Roehm, who was used to agonizing for months over tiny, delicate instruments, would suffer a collapse, would hunch on his stool and bury his face in his hands and bellow "It's all wrong!" into the mute of his palms. My friend Sanford and I stared on. But the fourth, smaller man, a person named Hal, who'd been staying upstairs with Lytle toward the end and acting as a nurse, he knew Roehm better—now that I think of it, Hal must have been the one to tell the family about him in the first place—and Hal would put his hands on Roehm's shoulders and whisper to him to be calm, remind him how everyone understood he'd been allowed too little time, that if he wanted we could take a break. Then Roehm would smoke. I remember he gripped each cigarette with two fingertips on top, snapping it in and out of his lips the way toughs in old movies do. Sanford and I sat outside in his truck with the heater on and drank vodka from a flask he'd brought, gazing on the shed with its small bright window, barely saying a word.

Weeks later he told me a story that Hal had told him, that at seven o'clock in the morning on the day of Lytle's funeral—which strangely Roehm did not attend—Hal woke to find Roehm sitting at the foot of his and his wife's bed, repeating the words "It works," apparently to himself. I never saw him again. The coffin was art. Hardly anyone got to see it. All through the service and down the street to the cemetery it wore a pall, and when people lined up at the graveside to take turns shoveling dirt back into the pit, the hexagonal lid—where inexplicably Roehm had found a spare hour to do scrollwork—grew invisible after just a few seconds.

THERE HAD BEEN different boys living at Lytle's since not long after he lost his wife, maybe before—in any case it was a recognized if unofficial institution when I entered the college at seventeen. In former days these were mainly students whose writing showed promise, as judged by a certain well-loved, prematurely white-haired literature professor, himself a former protégé and all but a son during Lytle's long widowerhood. As years passed and Lytle declined, the arrangement came to be more about making sure someone was there all the time, someone to drive him and chop wood for him and hear him if he were to break a hip.

There were enough of us who saw it as a privilege, especially among the English majors. We were students at the University of the South, and Lytle was the South, the last Agrarian, the last of the famous "Twelve Southerners" behind *I'll Take My Stand*, a comrade to the Fugitive Poets, a friend since youth of Allen Tate and Robert Penn Warren; a mentor to Flannery O'Connor and James Dickey and Harry

Crews and, as the editor of *The Sewanee Review* in the sixties, one of the first to publish Cormac McCarthy's fiction. Bear in mind that by the mid-nineties, when I knew him, the so-called Southern Renascence in letters had mostly dwindled to a tired professional regionalism. That Lytle hung on somehow, in however reduced a condition, represented a flaw in time, to be exploited.

Not everyone felt that way. I remember sitting on the floor one night with my freshman-year suitemate, a ninety-five-pound blond boy from Atlanta called Smitty who'd just spent a miserable four years at some private academy trying to convince the drama teacher to let them do a Beckett play. His best friend had been a boy they called Tweety Bird, whose voice resembled a tiny reed flute. When I met Smitty, I asked what music he liked, and he shot back, *"Trumpets."* That night he went on about Lytle, what a grotesquerie and a fascist he was. "You know what Andrew Lytle said?" Smitty waggled his cigarette lighter. "Listen to this: 'Life is melodrama. Only art is real.'"

I nodded in anticipation.

"Don't you think that's *horrifying*?"

I didn't, though. Or I did and didn't care. Or I didn't know what I thought. I was under the tragic spell of the South, which you've either felt or haven't. In my case it was acute because, having grown up in Indiana with a Yankee father, a child exile from Kentucky roots of which I was overly proud, I'd long been aware of a nowhereness to my life. Others wouldn't have sensed it, wouldn't have minded. I felt it as a physical ache. Finally I was somewhere, there. The South . . . I loved it as only one who will always be outside it can. Merely to hear the word *Faulkner* at night brought gusty emotions. A few months after I'd arrived at the school, Shelby Foote came and read from his Civil War history. When he'd finished, a local geezer with long greasy white hair wearing a white suit with a cane stood up in the third row and asked if, in Foote's opinion, the South could have won, had such and such a general done such and such. Foote replied that the North had won "that war" with one hand behind its back. In the crowd there were gasps. It thrilled me that they cared. How could I help wondering about Lytle, out there beyond campus in his ancestral cabin, rocking before the blazing logs, drinking bourbon from heirloom silver cups and brooding on something Eudora Welty had said to him once. Whenever famous writers came to visit the school they'd ask to see him. He was from another world. I tried to read his novels, but my mind just ricocheted; they seemed impenetrably mannered. Even so, I hoped to be taken to meet him. One of my uncles had received such an invitation, in the seventies, and told me how the experience changed him, put him in touch with what's real.

The way it happened was so odd as to suggest either the involvement or the nonexistence of fate. I wasn't even a student at the time. I'd dropped out after my sophomore year, essentially in order to preempt failing out, and was living in Ireland with a friend, working in a restaurant and failing to save money. But before my departure certain things had taken place. I'd become friends with the man called Sanford, a puckish, unregenerate back-to-nature person nearing fifty, who lived alone, off the electric grid, on a nearby communal farm. His house was like something Jefferson could have invented. Spring water flowed down from an old dairy tank in a tower on top; the refrigerator had been retrofitted to work with propane canisters that he salvaged from trailers. He had first-generation solar panels on the roof, a dirt-walled root cellar, a woodstove. He showered in a waterfall. We had many memorable hallucinogenic times that did not help my grades. Sanford needed very little money, but that he made doing therapeutic massage in town, and one of his clients was none other than Andrew Lytle, who drove himself in once a week, in his yacht-sized chocolate Eldorado, sometimes in the right lane, sometimes the left, as he fancied. The cops all knew to follow him but would do so at a distance, purely to ensure he was safe. Often he arrived at Sanford's studio hours early, and anxiously waited in the car. He loved the feeling of human hands on his flesh, he said, and believed it was keeping him alive.

One day, during their session, Lytle mentioned that his current boy was about to be graduated. Sanford, who didn't know yet how badly I'd blown it at the school, or that I was leaving, told Lytle about me and gave him some stories I'd written. Or poems? Doubtless dreadful stuff—but perhaps it "showed promise." Toward the end of summer airmail letters started to flash in under the door of our hilltop apartment in Cork, their envelopes, I remember, still faintly curled from having been rolled through the heavy typewriter. The first one was dated, "Now that I have come to live in the sense of eternity, I rarely know the correct date, and the weather informs me of the day's advance, but I believe it is late August," and went on to say, "I'm presuming you will live with me here."

That's how it happened, he just asked. Actually, he didn't even ask. The fact that he was ignoring the proper channels eventually caused some awkwardness with the school. But at the time, none of that mat-

44

tered. I felt an exhilaration, the unsettling thrum of a great man's regard, and somewhere behind that the distant onrushing of fame. His letters came once, then twice a week. They were brilliantly senile, moving in and out of coherence and between tenses, between centuries. Often his typos, his poor eyesight, would produce the finest sentences, as when he wrote the affectingly commaless "This is how I protest absolutely futilely." He told me I was a writer but that I had no idea what I was doing. "This is where the older artist comes in." He wrote about the Muse, how she tests us when we're young. As our tone grew more intimate, his grew more urgent too. I must come back soon. Who knew how much longer he'd live? "No man can forestall or evade what lies in wait." There were things he wanted to pass on, things that had taken him, he said, "too long to learn." Now he'd been surprised to discover a burst of intensity left. He said not to worry about the school. "College is perhaps not the best preparation for a writer." I'd live in the basement, a guest. We'd see to our work.

It took me several months to make it back, and he grew annoyed. When I finally let myself in through the front door, he didn't get up from his chair. His form sagged so exaggeratedly into the sofa, it was as if thieves had crept through and stolen his bones and left him there. He gestured at the smoky stone fireplace with its enormous black andirons and said, "Boy, I'm sorry the wood's so poor. I had no idea I'd be alive in November." He watched as though paralyzed while I worked at building back up the fire. He spoke only to critique my form. The heavier logs at the back, to project the heat. Not too much flame. "Young men always make that mistake." He asked me to pour him some whiskey and announced flatly his intention to nap. He lay back and draped across his eyes the velvet bag the bottle had come tied in, and I sat across from him for half an hour, forty minutes. At first he talked in his sleep, then to me—the pivots of his turn to consciousness were undetectably slight, with frequent slippages. His speech was full of mutterings, warnings. The artist's life is strewn with traps. Beware "the machinations of the enemy."

"Mr. Lytle," I whispered, "who is the enemy?"

He sat up. His unfocused eyes were an icy blue. "Why, boy," he said, "the *bourgeoisie*!" Then he peered at me for a second as if he'd forgotten who I was. "Of course," he said. "You're only a baby."

I'd poured myself two bourbons during nap time and felt them somewhat. He lifted his own cup and said, "Confusion to the enemy." We drank.

45

IT WAS IDYLLIC, where he lived, on the grounds of an old Chautauqua called the Assembly, one of those rustic resorts—deliberately placed up north, or at a higher altitude—which began as escapes from the plagues of yellow fever that used to harrow the mid-Southern states. Lytle could remember coming there as a child. An old judge, they said, had transported the cabin entire up from a cove somewhere in the nineteenth century. You could still see the logs in the walls, although otherwise the house had been made rather elegant over the years. The porch went all the way around. It was usually silent, except for the wind in the pines. Besides guests, you never saw anyone. A summer place, except Lytle didn't leave.

He slept in a wide carved bed in a corner room. His life was an incessant whispery passage on plush beige slippers from bed to sideboard to seat by the fire, tracing that perimeter, marking each line with light plantings of his cane. He'd sing to himself. The Appalachian one that goes, "A haunt can't haunt a haunt, my good old man." Or songs that he'd picked up in Paris at my age or younger—"Sous les Ponts de Paris" and "Les Chevaliers de la Table Ronde." His French was superb, but his accent in English was best—that extinct mid-Southern, land-grant pioneer speech, with its tinges of the abandoned Celtic urban Northeast ("boyned" for burned) and its raw gentility.

From downstairs I could hear him move and knew where he was in the house at all times. My apartment had once been the kitchen—servants went up and down the back steps. The floor was all bare stone, and damp. And never really warm, until overnight it became unbearably humid. Cave crickets popped around as you tried to sleep, touching down with little clicks. Lots of mornings I woke with him standing over me, cane in one hand, coffee in the other, and he'd say, "Well, my lord, shall we rise and entreat Her Ladyship?" Her ladyship was the Muse. He had all manner of greetings.

For half a year we worked steadily, during his window of greatest coherence, late morning to early afternoon. We read Flaubert, Joyce, a little James, the more famous Russians, all the books he'd written about as an essayist. He tried to make me read Jung. He chopped at my stories till nothing was left but the endings, which he claimed to admire. A too-easy eloquence, was his overall diagnosis. I tried to apply his criticisms, but they were sophisticated to a degree my efforts couldn't repay. He was trying to show me how to solve problems I hadn't learned existed.

About once a day he'd say, "I may do a little writing yet, myself, if my mind holds." One morning I even heard from downstairs the slap-slap of the old electric. That day, while he napped, I slid into his room and pulled off the slipcover to see what he'd done, a single sentence of between thirty and forty words. A couple of them were hyphened out, with substitutions written above in ballpoint. The sentence stunned me. I'd come half-expecting to find an incoherent mess, and afraid that this would say something ominous about our whole experiment, my education, but the opposite confronted me. The sentence was perfect. In it, he described a memory from his childhood, of a group of people riding in an early automobile, and the driver lost control, and they veered through an open barn door, but by a glory of chance the barn was completely empty, and the doors on the other side stood wide open, too, so that the car passed straight through the barn and back out into the sunlight, by which time the passengers were already laughing and honking and waving their arms at the miracle of their own survival, and Lytle was somehow able, through his prose, to replicate this swift and almost alchemical transformation from horror to joy. I don't know why I didn't copy out the sentence—embarrassment at my own spying, I guess. He never wrote any more. But for me it was the key to the year I lived with him. What he could still do, in his weakness, I couldn't do. I started listening harder, even when he bored me.

His hair was sparse and mercury-silver. He wore a tweed jacket every day and, around his neck, a gold-handled toothpick hewn from a raccoon's sharpened bone-penis. I put his glasses onto my own face once and my hands, held just at arm's length, became big beige blobs. There was a thing on his forehead—a cyst, I assume, that had gotten out of control—it was about the size and shape of a bisected Ping-Pong ball. His doctor had offered to remove it several times, but Lytle treated it as a conversation piece. "Vanity has no claim on me," he said. He wore a gray fedora with a bluebird's feather in the band. The skin on his face was strangely young-seeming. Tight and translucent. But the rest of his body was extraterrestrial. Once a week I helped him bathe. God alone knew for how long the moles and things on his back had been left to evolve unseen. His skin was doughy. Not saggy or lumpy, not in that sense—he was hale—but fragile-feeling. He had no hair anywhere below. His toenails were of horn. After the bath he lay naked between fresh sheets, needing to feel completely dry before he dressed. All Lytles, he said, had nervous temperaments.

I found him exotic; it's probably accurate to say that I found him beautiful. The manner in which I related to him was essentially anthro-pological. Taking offense, for instance, to his more or less daily out-bursts of racism, chauvinism, anti-Semitism, class snobbery, and what I can only describe as medieval nostalgia, seemed as absurd as debating these things with a caveman. Shut up and ask him what the cave art means. The self-service and even cynicism of that reasoning are not hard to dissect at a distance of years, but I can't pretend to regret it, or that I wish I had walked away.

There was something else, something less contemptible, a voice in my head that warned it would be unfair to lecture a man with faculties so diminished. I could never be sure what he was saying, as in stating, and what he was simply no longer able to keep from slipping out of his id and through his mouth. I used to walk by his wedding picture, which hung next to the cupboard—the high forehead, the square jaw, the jug ears—and think, as I passed it, "If you wanted to contend with him, you'd have to contend with THAT man." Otherwise it was cheating.

I came to love him. Not in the way he wanted, maybe, but not in a way that was stinting. *Mon vieux.* I was twenty and believed that noth-ing as strange was liable to happen to me again. I *was* a baby. One night we were up drinking late in the kitchen and I asked him if he thought there was any hope. Like that: "Is there any hope?" He answered me quite solemnly. He told me that in the hallways at Versailles, there hung a faint, ever-so-faint smell of human excrement, "because as the cham-bermaids hurried along a tiny bit would always splash from the pots." Many years later I realized that he was half-remembering a detail from the court of Louis XV, namely that the latrines were so few and so poorly placed at the palace, the marquesses used to steal away and relieve themselves on stairwells and behind the beautiful furniture, but that night I had no idea what he meant, and still don't entirely.

"Have I shown you my incense burner?" he asked.

"Your what?"

He shuffled out into the dining room and opened a locked glass cab-inet door. He came back cradling a little three-legged pot and set it down gently on the chopping block between us. It was exquisitely painted and strewn with infinitesimal cracks. A figure of a dog-faced dragon lay coiled on the lid, protecting a green pearl. Lytle spun the object to a particular angle, where the face was darker, slightly orange-tinged. "If you'll look, the glaze is singed," he said. "From the blast, I presume, or the fires." He held it upside down. Its maker's mark was legible on the bottom, or would have been to one who read Japanese.

48

"This pot," he said, "was recovered from the Hiroshima site." A classmate of his from Vanderbilt, one of the Fugitives, had gone on to become an officer in the Marine Corps and gave it to him after the war. "When I'm dead I want you to have it," he said.

I didn't bother refusing, just thanked him, since I knew he wouldn't remember in the morning, or, for that matter, in half an hour. But he did remember. He left it to me.

Ten years later in New York City my adopted stray cat Holly Kitty pushed it off a high shelf I didn't think she could reach, and it shattered. I sat up most of the night gluing the slivers back into place.

LYTLE'S DEMENTIA began to progress more quickly. I hope it's not cruel to note that at times the effects could be funny. He insisted on calling the K-Y Jelly we used to lubricate his colostomy tube *Kye Jelly*. Finally he got confused on what it was for and appeared in my doorway one day with his toothbrush and a squeezed-out tube of the stuff. "Put *Kye* on the list, boy," he said. "We're out."

Evenings he'd mostly sit alone and rehash forty-year-old fights with dead literary enemies, performing both sides as though in a one-man play, at times yelling wildly, pounding his cane. Allen Tate, his brother turned nemesis, was by far the most frequent opponent, but it seemed in these rages that anyone he'd ever known could change into the serpent, fall prey to an obsession with power. Particularly disorienting was when the original version of the mock-battle had been between him and me. Him and the Boy. Several times, in reality, we did clash. Stood face-to-face shouting. I called him a mean old bastard, something like that; he told me I'd betrayed my gift. Later, from downstairs, I heard him say to the Boy, "You think you're not a *slave*?"

There was a day when I came in from somewhere. Polly, his sister, was staying upstairs. I loved Miss Polly's visits—everyone did. She made rum cakes you could eat yourself to death on like a goldfish. There were homemade pickles and biscuits from scratch when she came. A tiny woman with glasses so thick they magnified her eyes, her knuckles were cubed with arthritis. Who knew what she thought, or if she thought, about all the nights she'd shared with her brother and his interesting artist friends. (Once, in a rented house somewhere, she'd been forced by sleeping arrangements to lie awake in bed all night between fat old Ford Madox Ford and his mistress.) She shook her head over how the iron skillet, which their family had been seasoning in slow ovens since the Depression, would suffer at my hands. I had trouble remembering not to put it through the dishwasher. Over meals, under the chandelier with the "saltcellar" and the "salad oil," as Lytle raved about the master I might become, if only I didn't fall into this, that, or the other hubristic snare, she'd simply grin and say, "Oh, Brutha, how *exciting*."

On the afternoon in question I was coming through the security gate, entering "the grounds," as cottagers called the Assembly, and Polly passed me going the opposite way in her minuscule blue car. There was instantly something off about the encounter, because she didn't stop completely—she rolled down the window and yelled at me, but continued to idle past, going at most twenty miles per hour (the speed limit in there was twelve, I think), as if she were waving from a parade float. "I'm on my way to the store," she said. "We need [*mumble*] . . ."

"What's that?"

"BUTTAH!"

I watched with a bad feeling as she receded in the mirror. Back at the cabin, Lytle was caning around on the front porch in a panic. He waved at me as I turned into the gravel patch where we parked. "She's drunk!" he barked. "Look at this bottle, beloved. Good God, it was full this morning!"

I tried to make him tell me what had happened, but he was too antsy. He wore pajamas, black slippers without socks, a gray tweed coat, and the fedora.

"Oh, I've angered her, beloved," he said. "I've angered her."

As we sped toward the gate, he gave me the story. It was as I suspected. The same argument came up every time Polly visited, though I'd never seen it escalate so. They had family in a distant town with whom she remained on decent terms, but Lytle insisted on shunning these people and thought his little sister should, as well. It had to do with an old scandal about land, duplicity involving a will. A greedy uncle had tried to take away his father's farm. But these modern-day cousins, descendants of the rival party, they weren't pretending, as Lytle believed, not to understand why he wouldn't see them—I think they were genuinely confused. There'd been scenes. He'd stood in the doorway and denounced these people, in the highest rhetoric, "Seed of the usurper." They must have thought he was further gone mentally than he was, that when he uttered these curses he had in mind some carpetbagger from olden days, because the relatives just kept coming back, despite never having been allowed past the porch steps. Now Miss Polly had let them into the vestibule, nearly into the Court of the

Muse. Lytle viewed this as the wildest betrayal. He'd been beastly toward them, when he rose from his nap, and Polly had fled. He himself seemed shaken to remember the things he'd said.

"Mister Lytle, what did you say?"

"I told the truth" he said passionately. "I recognized the moment, that's what I did." But in the defensive thrust of his jaw there quivered something like embarrassment.

He mentions this land dispute in his "family memoir," *A Wake for the Living*, his most readable and in many ways his best book. That's perhaps an idiosyncratic opinion. There are people who've read a lot more than I have who consider his novels lost classics. But it may be precisely because of the Faustian ego that thundered above his sense of himself as a novelist that he carried a lighter burden into the memoir, and this freedom thawed in his style some of the vivacity and spontaneity that otherwise you find only in the letters. There's a scene in which he describes the morning his grandmother was shot in the throat by a Union soldier in 1863. "Nobody ever knew who he was or why he did it," Lytle writes, "he mounted a horse and galloped out of town." To the end of her long life this woman wore a velvet ribbon at her neck, fastened with a golden pin. That's how close Lytle was to the Civil War. Close enough to reach up as a child, passing into sleep, and fondle the clasp of that pin. The eighteenth century was just another generation back from there, and so on, hand to hand. This happens, I suppose, this collapsing of time, when you make it as far as your nineties. When Lytle was born, the Wright Brothers had not yet achieved a working design. When he died, Voyager II was exiting the solar system. What do you do with the coexistence of those details in a lifetime's view ? It weighed on him. The incident with his grandmother is masterfully handled:

> She ran to her nurse. The bullet had barely missed the jugular vein. Blood darkened the apple she still held in her hand, and blood was in her shoe. The enemy in the street now invaded the privacy of the house. The curious entered and stared. They confiscated the air . . . To the child's fevered gaze the long bayonets of the soldiers seemed to reach the ceiling, as they filed past her bed, staring out of boredom and curiosity.

Miss Polly passed us again. Apparently she'd changed her mind about the butter. We made a U-turn and trailed her to the cabin. Back inside

51

they embraced. She buried her face in his coat, laughing and weeping. "Oh, sister," he said, "I'm such an old fool, *goddamn* it."

I'VE WISHED AT TIMES that we had endured some meaningful falling-out. In truth he began to exasperate me in countless petty ways. He needed too much, feeding and washing and shaving and dressing, more than he could admit to and keep his pride. Anyone could sympathize, but I hadn't signed on to be his butler. One day I ran into the white-haired professor, who shared with me that Lytle had been complaining about my cooking.

Mainly, though, I'd fallen in love with a tall, nineteen-year-old half-Cuban girl from North Carolina, with freckles on her face and straight dark hair down her back. She was a class behind mine, or what would have been mine, at the school, and she could talk about books. On our second date she gave me her father's roughed-up copy of *Hunger*, the Knut Hamsun novel. I started to spend more time downstairs. Lytle became pitifully upset. When I invited her in to meet him, he treated her coldly, made some vaguely insulting remark about "Latins," and at one point asked her if she understood a woman's role in an artist's life.

There came a wickedly cold night in deep winter when she and I lay asleep downstairs, wrapped up under a pile of old comforters on twin beds we'd pushed together. By now the whole triangle had grown so unpleasant that Lytle would start drinking earlier than usual on days when he spotted her car out back, and she no longer found him amusing or, for that matter, I suppose, harmless. My position was hideous.

She shook me awake and said, "He's trying to talk to you on the thing." We had this antiquated monitor system, the kind where you depress the big silver button to talk and let it off to hear. The man hadn't mastered an electrical device in his life. At breakfast one morning, when I'd made the mistake of leaving my computer upstairs after an all-nighter, he screamed at me for "bringing the enemy into this home, into a place of work." Yet he'd become a bona fide technician on the monitor system.

"He's calling you," she said. I lay still and listened. There was a crackling.

"Beloved," he said, *"I hate to disturb you, in your slumbers, my lord. But I believe I might freeze to DEATH up here."*

"Oh, my God," I said.

"If you could just . . . lie beside me."

I looked at her. "What do I do?"

She turned away. "I wish you wouldn't go up there," she said.

"What if he dies?"

"You think he might?"

"I don't know. He's ninety-two, and he says he's freezing to death."

"*Beloved* . . .?"

She sighed. "You should probably go up there."

He didn't speak as I slipped into his bed. He fell back asleep instantly. The sheets were heavy white linen and expensive. It seemed there were shadow acres of snowy terrain between his limbs and mine. I floated off.

When I woke at dawn he was nibbling my ear and his right hand was on my genitals.

I sprang out of bed and began to hop around the room like I'd burned my finger, sputtering foul language. Lytle was already moaning in shame, fallen back in bed with his hand across his face like he'd just washed up somewhere, a piece of wrack. I should mention that he wore, as on every chill morning, a Wee Willie Winkie-style nightshirt and cap. "Forgive me, forgive me," he said.

"Jesus Christ, Mister Lytle."

"Oh, beloved . . ."

His having these desires wasn't the issue. I couldn't be that naïve. His tastes in that area were more or less an open secret. I don't know if he was gay or bisexual or pansexual or what. Those distinctions are clumsy terms in which to address the mysteries of sexuality. But on a few occasions he'd spoken about his wife in a manner that to me was movingly erotic, nothing like any self-identifying gay man I've ever heard talk about women and sex. Certainly Lytle had loved her, because it was clear how he missed her, Edna, his beautiful "squirrel-eyed gal from Memphis," whom he'd married when she was young, who was still young when she died of throat cancer.

Much more often, however, when the subject of sex came up, he would return to the idea of there having been a homoerotic side to the Agrarian movement itself. He told me that Allen Tate propositioned him once, "but I turned him down. I didn't like his smell. You see, smell is so important, beloved. To me he had the stale scent of a man who didn't take any exercise." This may or may not have been true, but it wasn't an isolated example. Later writers—including some with an interest in not playing up the issue—have noticed, for instance, Robert Penn Warren's more-than-platonic interest in Tate, when they were all at Vanderbilt together. One of the other Twelve Southerners, Stark

53

Young—he's rarely mentioned—was openly gay. Lytle professed to have carried on, as a very young man, a happy, sporadic affair with the brother of another Fugitive poet, not a well-known person. At one point the two of them fantasized about living together, on a small farm. The man later disappeared and turned up murdered in Mexico. Warren mentions him in a poem that plays with the image of the closet.

The point—the reason I risk being seen to have "outed" a man who trusted me, and was vulnerable when he did—is that you can't fully understand that movement, which went on to influence American literature for decades, without understanding that certain of the men involved in it loved one another. Most "homosocially," of course, but a few homoerotically, and some homosexually. That's where part of the power originated that made those friendships so intense, and caused the men to stay united almost all their lives, even after spats and changes of opinion, even after their Utopian hopes for the South had died. Together they produced from among them a number of good writers, and even a great one, in Warren, whom they can be seen to have lifted, as if on wing beats, to the heights for which he was destined.

Lytle himself would have beaten me with his cane and thrown me out for saying all of that. To him it was a matter for winking and nodding, frontier sexuality, fraternity brothers falling into bed with each other and not thinking much about it. Or else it was Hellenism, golden lads in the Court of the Muse. William Alexander Percy stuff. Whatever it was, I accepted it. I never showed displeasure when he wanted to sit and watch me chop wood, or when he asked me to quit showering every morning, so that he could smell me better. "I'm pert' near blind, boy," he said. "How will I find you in a fire?" Still, I'd taken for granted an understanding between us. I didn't expect him to grope me like a chambermaid.

I stayed away two nights, and then went back. When I reached the top of the steps and looked through the back-porch window, I saw him on the sofa lying asleep (or dead—I wondered every time). His hands were folded across his belly. One of them rose and hung quivering, an actor's wave; he was talking to himself. It turned out, when I cracked the door, he was talking to me.

"Beloved, now, we must forget this," he said. "I merely wanted to touch it a little. You see, I find it the most *interesting* part of the body."

Then he paused and said, "Yes," seeming to make a mental note that the phrase would do.

"I understand, you have the girl now," he continued. "Woman offers the things a man must have, home and children. And she's a lovely girl. I myself may not have made the proper choices, in that role . . ."

I closed the door and crept down to bed.

Not long after that, I moved out, both of us agreeing it was for the best. I re-enrolled at the school. They found someone else to live with him. It had become more of a medical situation by that point, at-home care. I drove out to see him every week, and I think he welcomed the visits, but things had changed. He knew how to adjust his formality by tenths of a degree, to let you know where you stood.

IT MAY BE gratuitous to remark of a ninety-two-year-old man that he began to die, but Lytle had been much alive for most of that year, fiercely so. There were some needless minor surgeries at one point, which set him back. It's funny how the living will help the dying along. One night he fell, right in front of me. He was standing in the middle room on a slippery carpet, and I was moving toward him to take a glass from his hand. The next instant he was flat on his back with a broken elbow that during the night bruised horribly, blackly. His eyes went from glossy to matte. Different people took turns staying over with him, upstairs, including the white-haired professor, whose loyalty had never wavered. I spent a couple of nights. I wasn't worried he'd try anything again. He was in a place of calm and—you could see it—preparation. His son-in-law told me he'd spoken my name the day before he died.

When the coffin was done, the men from the funeral home picked it up in a hearse. Late the same night someone called to say they'd finished embalming Lytle's body; it was in the chapel, and whenever Roehm was ready, he could come and fasten the lid. All of us who'd worked on it with him went, too. The mortician let us into a glowing side hallway off the cold ambulatory. With us was an old friend of Lytle's named Brush, who worked for the school administration, a low-built bouncy muscular man with boyish dark hair and a perpetual bowtie. He carried, as nonchalantly as he could, a bowling-ball bag, and in the bag an extremely excellent bottle of whiskey.

Brush took a deep breath, reached into the coffin, and jammed the bottle up into the crevice between Lytle's ribcage and his left arm. He quickly turned and said, "That way they won't hear it knocking around when we roll it out of the church."

Roehm had a massive electric drill in his hand. It seemed out of keeping with the artisanal methods that had gone into the rest of the job, but he'd run out of time making the cedar pegs. We stood over Lytle's body. Sanford was the first to kiss him. When everyone had, we lowered the lid onto the box, and Roehm screwed it down. Somebody wished the old man Godspeed. A eulogy that ran in the subsequent number of *The Sewanee Review* said that, with Lytle's death, "the Confederacy at last came to its end."

He appeared to me only once afterward, and that was two and a half years later, in Paris. It's not as if Paris is a city I know or have even visited more than a couple of times. He knew it well. I was coming up the stairs from the metro into the sunshine with the girl, whom I later married, on my left arm, when my senses became intensely alert to his presence about a foot and a half to my right. I couldn't look directly at him; I had to let him hang back in my peripheral vision, else he'd slip away; it was a bargain we made in silence. I could see enough to tell that he wasn't young but was maybe twenty years younger than when I'd known him, wearing the black-framed engineer's glasses he'd worn at just that time in his life, looking up and very serious, climbing the steps to the light, where I lost him.

Nominated by The Paris Review, and Karen Bender, Teresa Svoboda

HORSE LATITUDES

by KATHLEEN FLENNIKEN

from THIRD COAST

A raft of debris as large as Africa
accumulates in the Pacific gyre—

trash, plastic, rope, netting—a synthetic sea
of flotsam that will outlive us all.

Few ships enter. A windless ocean
strikes terror in the crew.

If you can't imagine
the camera pulling back, pulling back

until we see the curve of the earth,
pulling back to reveal the atmosphere's

blue glow and still not bounding
the garbage—if we can't acknowledge

the damage done—then recall your secret hurt
that churns and churns and won't

diminish—a spiral so huge,
your mind mutinies and denies it all.

Nominated by Third Coast and Linda Bierds

THAT WINTER

fiction by MIHA MAZZINI

from ECOTONE

The prisoners released before me had flown home from The Hague in airplanes sent for them by their states. I was the first one who wasn't a national hero. The guard just handed me a train ticket to Sarajevo and some pocket money for travel expenses. I greeted him with "Tot ziens" and he answered with "Tot nooit, hopelijk!"—an unsubtle indication he didn't want to see me again.

In the train I couldn't take my eyes off the window: moving, everything was moving. Houses, cities, gliding by, going away, a constant flow of change after eleven years of immobility.

Waiting for another train in Düsseldorf, I felt like a ghost returning to the world for the first time. I moved out of the way of a person talking to himself, a sure sign of madness at the time of my imprisonment, whereas now everybody had headphones and their mouths were empty of cigarettes.

After Munich the landscape got more and more orderly. Austrians took symmetry and tidiness for beauty, their windows vomiting carnations from houses built to last forever. The train entered the tunnel and came out in Slovenia. I expected to see the big steel factory, once the pride of Yugoslavia, but only one chimney still stood, covered with ads for supermarkets and foreign brands.

Nobody entered my compartment—Slovenia was now part of the EU and there were no more border policemen or customs officers in Europe. But at the Croatian border I was asked for my papers. A pair of Slovenian officers browsed my documents: "Den Haag—The International War Crimes Tribunal for crimes committed on the territory of the former Yugoslavia." They looked momentarily bewildered, until the policeman, still a kid, sucked air into his spreading chest, soaking his words in venom. I looked into his eyes and the air left him. His partner, the customs officer, elbowed him out the door. The Croat officers didn't know how to react and quickly went away; they had their own war with the Muslims and some of their heroes had been my prison buddies.

When the train stopped in Zagreb, I bought myself some newspapers. The Croats had buried one of their fascist commandants from the Second World War. In his camp they had killed at least seventy thousand people. Though he fled to Argentina after the war, escaping hanging, he had been in prison, unrepentant, for the past decade, after having finally been extradited. At the funeral the priest said the prisoner had slept peacefully throughout his life, since he knew that God had forgiven him everything.

The train entered Bosnia on the Serbian side of the country and when I offered my papers to the officers, they stood at attention, saluting me like windup toys, while they retreated backward. The staff of the small border station started walking up and down the platform, pretending to be running errands, stealing glances through my window.

I dug into the corner and shame covered me like an icy blanket.

The Sarajevo train station looked forlorn, as though no one had used it since the war began, sixteen years ago. Cigarette smoke drifted from the cafés in front of it. I waited on the abandoned platform until my bus arrived and I almost ran for it, my head lowered.

I had not called anybody in my village to let them know I was coming. The last time I had seen my former wife was in court, on the witness stand. She was talking about how she had begged me to dissolve the factory but I had beaten her into silence. I stopped listening to her. The knowledge that this must be the same lie my daughters were hearing from her dripped from my heart through my body like acid, leaving just burnt hollowness inside. For her testimony she got a change of identity and money for them to start over. I received the divorce papers in prison, signed them, and put a letter on top asking her not to ever mention me to my girls. She didn't answer.

In socialist Yugoslavia, those in power wanted to change even the hill farmers into workmen and they built factories everywhere. Every politician who had grown up in some dirt shack wanted to give his native village a factory and the people expected it; the size of the new industrial building was the measurement of the politician's status in the party. Our benefactor was a lower official in Sarajevo, so the factory was small. Like every other one, it produced something simple, so the former farmers could adapt quickly. Then capitalism discovered a work force in China adapting even faster and cheaper and the political factories fell into ruins.

I was the only person who got off the bus at the stop in my village. The walls of the factory were in ruins, the barbed wire rusty and sagging. I didn't want to look at it, but I couldn't stop. I expected memories to attack my eyes and ears, but only the wind was whispering, exhausted. A summer storm had just passed by, the wet hair of clouds still hung over a neighboring hill. Veins of tiny streams furrowed the sand on the road, and I had not yet gotten my feet wet when I was surrounded by the men who came running from the village.

I recognized them at once and at the same time was amazed that they, like me, had gotten old. Larger bellies, sagging belts, grayer hair on heads and bodies, more marks on their skin. Only the slightly soiled sleeveless T-shirts and the stubble on their faces were still the same (shaving occurred only before Sunday mass). We had received Bosnian papers in prison and the other prisoners had used their mobile phones as well, telling me the news that wasn't printed, so I had heard that Jovo had hanged himself and Milojko had died. The remaining seven stood in front of me now, only Nikola was not there.

They looked at me. Behind their backs, from the village, I could feel the looks from their wives and children, and also from those who had not been a part of our group.

I realized that my next movement would decide the kind of reception I would have.

I smiled. It felt false, mechanical, just the lengthening of the corners of my lips, but they did not notice.

There was shouting, more like roaring, slaps on my shoulders and back. The smell of unwashed bodies, of farm animals, machine oil and gasoline. Somebody took my bag for me, we walked, I was hemmed in among them. They were offering me cigarettes, I kept on refusing, and they were shouting "Europe! Europe!" in wonder. We entered Cane's Inn and the tall owner didn't hit his forehead on the doorpost like he used to do; the years had curved his spine from a bow to a question mark. The interior hadn't changed: the bar was in the corner, small and insignificant, tables occupying most of the room, for people to sit and talk. I don't know why, but in prison I had loved to browse the glossy magazines about interior decoration and I noticed that bars outside the

Balkans are different, big central monsters in the middle of the room, for lonely people to hang around them, looking at themselves in the mirror behind the bottles.

Cane brought brandy, fiery-strong, and we started drinking toasts. We were just lifting glasses in the air above us, nobody turned to the picture on the wall. It used to be Tito for decades, Miloševic afterward for a few years, and now Saint Sava, his expiry date much more lasting.

They brought a serving of lamb, the meat cold and slimy. The noise and the pouring of drinks went on and on. I did not wish to get drunk, I just sipped the surface of what was in the glass. They must have noticed, but they did not want to stop making a ruckus. If they did there would be silence and they would have to talk.

I asked them how they were, what they did, and I had to repeat myself several times before they began to talk—about being farmers again, or Pavle being a mechanic. He rubbed his dark and oily hands at the sides of his paunch, leaving only the middle of his T-shirt white, like the center of the target. They talked about the way they smuggled Chinese goods and sold them again in the three-boundary region, between Croatia, Bosnia, and Serbia, and how in this way they were getting by, slowly, getting by. They told me and then they told me again, and then once over. They kept shifting as if on the edge of a precipice. They were in danger and did not want to take the next step: asking me how I was, how it had been. And the crucial question: why had I turned myself in? They did not dare. Branimir, with his foxy face and sagging cheeks, was in a hurry to speak each time it appeared they would run out of breath. I could not recall him ever speaking so eagerly.

When there was really nothing left to say and when they had described every method of smuggling, when I had learned the contents of every market stall, they got up and accompanied me to my home. They told me they had kept watch to ensure that none of *them* had come even close. They handed me the key, I let myself in, and they did not follow me inside.

You go away for a couple of weeks and when you get back the apartment is dusty. After many years the dust has become fixed, it has stopped accumulating and just sits there, the years fly past, the particles hold their peace, only the smell which floats above them counts the days and knits them into a special stuffiness.

My wife had taken everything that could be driven away, including the washing machine where she had put my bloody clothes every morning that winter without saying anything. She did not even leave the objects that had belonged to *them*, the ones I had stolen. For a long time she made me seethe in prison, but some nights I understood that maybe she had made a good deal for my daughters, who were growing up somewhere out of these countries where history is a tool for revenge, not for learning. I felt happy for them but at the same time this was part of my punishment: what I had done I had done for them. How old had they been that winter? I thought back—three and four years old. Now they probably don't even dream in my language anymore. I try not to think of them but they're always there when my mind goes floating, in waking, before sleeping, looking out a window.

I carried everything left into a single room: an old couch, a squeaky chair, the table from the cellar that had before been good only as a workbench. I turned on the water at the mains and let it run for a long time before it was free of rust.

What now?

I went for a walk. The clouds were dragging their very last tails across the mountains. The sun that had been hot in the valley was no more than a caress up here. Behind me I heard a stifled cry of fear and when I turned I clearly saw a woman's back and the movement of her elbow as she hurried behind a corner.

Had she crossed herself, seeing a ghost?

We had burned all of the Muslim houses—every single one—and I expected to see the same blackened stumps, decaying teeth biting at the sky, as when they had taken me away, but very few ruins were left. They had begun to rebuild most of them. Concrete supporting slabs stood among the debris, with a wall or two. As if somebody was indicating that he had not given up, he was still here.

Where?

I walked past our houses and people from my group loudly and hollowly greeted me. The rest retreated. In front of me doors closed and drapes fell, and as I walked on they opened up again and I felt the looks. A short way from the village had stood the factory. I could not go that far. I turned back to Nikola's.

Bits of plaster and some tiles had fallen off his house and joined the trash in the yard. I knocked on the open door—no reply—and I stepped into the stench.

He was lying in a corner and snoring. I sat on a bench and placed my foot on one of the empty bottles. His potato-like nose had collected lots of veinlets in the intervening years, and his cheeks shook while his jaws pumped air inside, the lungs answering with a protracted whining, almost like a dying echo of the songs we used to sing at the factory.

Evening was coming on when Nikola awoke. He raised his head, it swung to and fro as though fighting more space for itself, his eyes narrowed a little and when he recognized me, he cried out.

"No! I'm not going on guard duty! NO!"

"Nikola, it's over, nobody has to do guard duty anymore."

His coughing stretched into puking until finally there was not even mucus left to fall to the floor.

"They let you out?"

"Yes."

We were silent.

He went on all fours into the next room and came back with a full bottle and swallowed almost a third in a single gulp.

"Did you meet them yet?" he asked, and waved toward the village. For the first time he looked me in the eye.

I nodded but my eyes escaped his and slipped toward the entrance.

"Why did you come back?"

I sighed and could not find any simple words.

He answered in my place: "Because you want to see how they are . . . what about you?"

"I cannot sleep," I said.

"Me too, I am never awake. Will you?" he said, offering me the bottle.

I shook my head. "If I'd had a lot of that in prison, the first year, then I would. Not now, no."

"Did you hear about Jovo? Dead!" His limp and soft body made just one surprisingly quick and savage gesture, slashing his index finger across his neck. "Milojko died, too. He just"—Nikola stabbed the fingers of both hands into his stomach and they sank into a burrow of his gut—"withered," he said, finally finding the right word. "Listen to me, boss, listen. Let me state it clear: the first option is to die. You can choose only the speed: fast or slow. The second option is to forget, like the others from our group did. But, boss, you said you can't sleep, so you're not like Cane and the others." He gestured toward the inn, but in the wrong direction. "Why are you still alive? How will you kill yourself?"

I opened my mouth to speak but he didn't let me.

"Boss, nobody wants you here. Nobody waited for you. You're a ghost, a reminder. Please, do us a favor."

Nikola seemed to want to burst out laughing, but just screeched. He bent over across the bed, I thought he was going to throw up again, but he dipped his head into a pile of trash and rummaged through it for a long while. Twitching, he turned around and flung a coil of rope in my direction, missing by a good yard.

"Did you enjoy posing as a model on your way to becoming an international star? How the fuck didn't you spot that creep photographer and shoot him!" Again he screeched and between the stumps of his teeth gleamed traces of enamel. "Commandant!" he added, as if spitting.

I could feel the hate radiating from him in my belly. I did not react and so he lost interest. He tilted the bottle and allowed it to decant into him. He threw it at the wall then, it shattered and he lay down on the bed, rolled himself into a fetus, and showed me his back.

Silence.

Socialism had wished to fertilize us, and sometimes, even into our hills, some theater troupe or other came on tour, usually an amateur one from a nearby town. Their exaggerated movements and gestures always repulsed me. But when you are locked up and cannot hope to sleep, then the day is long enough for you to remember everything, including theater performances. Do the men in our nation get drunk so often in order to show what they're feeling? They behave in the overwrought fashion of bad actors. I remembered my own drinking sessions, friendships until death after the first round that change into angry hatreds after the second one and into miraculous reconciliations after the third, then the same cycle all over. And once you are no longer someone who drinks but a drunkard, true feelings have fled and what is left is just grotesque sentimentality and, finally, bathos.

I got up and the bench sighed below me.

The house stank. Twilight was slowly eating away Nikola's body part by part, only his legs and one hand still visible. Like those bodies the earth had begun to return after that winter. Cane had mentioned them first. He said it was the same as when his Deepfreeze broke down. Except for the crows. I went to the field between the factory and the forest and *We did this?* crossed my mind for the first time. Because the ground was frozen throughout the cold months, each time we dug we hadn't been able to bury the bodies deep enough, and with the thaw, foxes and other animals had started excavating them. Remains protruded from the soil, a hand here, a leg there, a torso, a head, gnawed bones marking the way toward the trees. Crows jumped around, pick-

64

ing the meat off the bones, too full to fly, arrogantly moving just out of reach of my steps. I have always felt there was something aching in the vapors of plowed earth but this smell nauseated me. I closed my eyes and fought with my stomach.

I never saw the American photographer hidden in the forest. We later learned he'd been crossing the hills, trying to get to Sarajevo, bribing each border guard he came across and sharing a drink. When his stomach couldn't stand it anymore he asked his guide to stop the Jeep and went behind the trees, noticing the crows and following them.

The first picture he took was of me in my moment of nausea. I remember feeling disgust and horror, but in the photo, which appeared the following week in foreign newspapers, something about my face makes it look as if I'm enjoying myself.

I returned to the factory that night and told the others we must dig again and rebury. We couldn't prepare ourselves to do it until the following week, the same time the photos began to be published. Then how we dug! And we burned the bodies, taking the remains down to the valley and throwing them in the river. It wasn't that we feared foreigners. The West was impotent and weak—they did not intervene even at Srebrenica, years later. But among the bodies of Muslims, there were some of our weekend warriors as well. People who left their jobs in Serbia on Friday afternoon, took guns and drove across the border to Bosnia, robbed a house or two, killed some Muslims, and returned to work on Monday morning. Occasionally these armed men came to our village and we told them that here were just our Muslims, that they and their stuff belonged to us. Most of the intruders went away, but some had been too drunk and too courageous, and we did not want their bodies to be discovered.

The darkness took Nikola's body completely now.

I bent down to pick up the rope as I went.

The next day I went for another walk around the village as soon as I was awoken by hunger. I caught sight of Branimir bringing a heavy cardboard box around the corner of his house. When he saw me he backed away immediately, as though on a rewind button. I waited by the open trunk of his car, but he did not appear again.

In Pavle's mechanic shop—not registered, unofficial—I met only his legs. He peeked from under a vehicle, apologized that he had essential work to do, whatever I might say he would listen. I walked on.

I was the only customer at Cane's Inn. He brought me some uncut bread and put a piece of roast meat in the microwave. My glance fled to the big roasting spit which used never to stop turning. Cane flourished his dishrag as if to say: once a week or once every two weeks is nowadays quite enough. Since the war the families don't come to his inn on Sundays anymore, he said, and his eyes got big, like a hurt child's. I remembered coming here with my ex-wife and daughters and I wondered again: three and four years old that winter, do they remember anything? Do they remember me just as a presence in their childhoods, have they forgotten my face? Do they fall for a boyfriend who reminds them of me without knowing the reason? They would still be sleeping in the morning when I returned from the factory and handed stolen stuff to my wife. Sometimes somebody helped me bring in a TV or a fridge or something big from one of the Muslim houses, some days I just went to the bathroom and threw my bloody clothing on the tiles. I slept most of the day and ate supper with my family, read the girls an evening story and went back to the factory. To work, as I told them. Usually I drank a coffee with my wife in the kitchen, and I remembered now with sudden and bitter anger how she would sometimes carefully mention that we needed a new car or a video player or hi-fi, something nice she had just seen at some Muslim family's, her finger caressing the rim of the coffee cup, sending the smell into my nostrils.

I looked at the shelf in the corner. Five vases full of plastic flowers were still standing there, though dust had taken the bright colors away. During the week this had been a place for men only, but on Sundays, Cane put a vase on each table, providing a nice family setting, as he explained it. He used to sit down with every customer and drink or snack on something, in this way obeying the law of the correct innkeeper. Now he stayed behind the bar and wiped glasses. When he brought me my warmed-up food he was on the point of sitting down. A reflex of his body swung his ass toward a chair, but he caught himself, moaned a little about work, and went back behind the bar.

"Do you ever remember that winter?" I asked him.

"What?" He looked wide-eyed. "Winter?"

I pointed my finger toward the factory, just a corner of its wall was visible through the window.

"Oh . . . oh . . ."—he flapped his hand—"that's water under the bridge . . . sorry . . . you suffered . . . you are a hero . . . but for us ordinary people . . ." Droplets appeared on his forehead. He mumbled a bit more.

"Don't you have dreams?" I asked.

"No." Droplets also on his upper lip.

"No nightmares?"

"No. Please, Commandant, please! It's gone, they were different times, strange times . . . something was in the air, this won't happen again. It's like when you get a flu or something. You're not yourself . . . but then, a week, or . . . winter passes and you're your old self, healthy. Commandant, you'll destroy yourself if you won't let it go."

"Cane, don't call me 'Commandant.' You know I was just your foreman. When we . . . started this, at the factory, we started it together."

I didn't need to tell him the rest: the generals had wanted somebody to be responsible for our small unit, and it was me who became commandant.

Cane got his hurt-child eyes back: "But . . . you were the boss. I was so unimportant!" He searched for another word, then stopped abruptly. "You see! Don't mention it anymore!"

I started eating. For a while he was so tense that I expected to hear a glass crack under his hands, but he slowly calmed down and the dishrag again slid over the glasses, which he was cleaning for the second time. I finished eating and wiped my mouth and fingers with a napkin. From time to time Cane stole a nervous glance in my direction, appearing afraid of further questions.

"And what about those new houses, the renovated ones?"

He burst out in relief: "Did you see them? It's unbelievable! They could have stayed in our village, that's how it was written down in the peace agreement, but they just went and now . . . Commandant, you won't believe it. Those Muslims are like gypsies, they have settled in large numbers all over the world, but the men come here in the summers. They are here a week or two and they build walls. They sleep in the car, they bring materials from the valley up in the trunk and they build walls. That's how they spend their vacations! Their food they buy in the valley, too. They do not come to me! We get nothing from them. You will see for yourself, the first of them will arrive any day now."

He wanted to say something else, but his open mouth could not find the words.

"How much do I owe you?"

"Commandant, that's okay! Actually, we talked yesterday, if you wish we'll set up a collection campaign and help you start over. In the three-boundary district the work is great! We'll arrange a market stall for you. Just let us know: are you most interested in technical things, music, clothing? Maybe helping to traffic Chinese or Africans into Europe?"

＊　＊　＊

On my way home I stopped in front of the bare concrete pad where once Sead's house had stood. I placed my palms on the dusty surface and through the warm epidermis felt the interior cold of the building. Only a few of the Muslim inhabitants of our village had left immediately after the siege of Sarajevo started. Most of them believed, as I did, that our village would be something special, an exception, that our bonds would hold. I had gone to school with Sead, his father had taught me a trick with a coin and a dog, brotherhood and unity was the slogan of Tito's Yugoslavia. But in the summer of '92 we were at Cane's, watching the news. The Russian writer Limonov had come to visit our troops on the hills above Sarajevo and he started firing a machine gun on the city. Mother Russia was with us, the announcer said.

Cane's palm slapped the table. "Right," he said, "it's for the mushrooms."

Everybody turned toward him, our heads traveling slowly through the alcohol.

"Do they come in the fall? Do they?" Cane lifted his finger almost to the ceiling. "Do they come to our village and park on your field?" he said, pointing at Branimir, who nodded. "Do they crumple your grass? Go into our forests and pick our mushrooms? Do they sometimes even have picnics here, on that grass, and bring everything with them? Leave us nothing but damage and expenses! City people! People of Sarajevo!"

"You're right, you're right," we said, nodding.

He continued: "These city people . . . they look down on us! They think they're something more. For them we're all backwards idiots! They're like Turkish invaders. For centuries they've robbed our lands, conquered us, taken our money, bled us with taxes—those Muslims! Now revenge is ours. Cities must burn!"

I can't remember much more from that night, but soon, one by one, we became weekend warriors, occasionally for a few days on the hills above Sarajevo, until that winter when we brought the war home.

By then, half of the Muslim villagers had fled on bus convoys, begging their Serbian friends to watch over the possessions they left behind. Some of us really did look out for them. Others started slowly taking their things or even moving their houses. By that winter, the Muslims left in the village were stuck between the front lines. Some tried to go away: during the night, over the hills. We never heard from them.

Sead's father had stayed out of stubbornness. He said he had to guard the compressor in his garage. In December the compressor at Pavle's mechanic shop broke down and we came for Sead's father's. We took him to the factory. He was our first prisoner. Others followed—in The Hague, after I turned myself in, they proved five killings and seven imprisonments had happened under my command during that winter, until in the spring a humanitarian convoy evacuated the village of all remaining Muslims. I think we could have gone on beating and torturing them, because we really believed they were spies for the Muslim army, and therefore traitors. But our belief was like a balloon, we had to pump it up all the time with shouts, with frenzy, with constant movement, never stopping, never thinking. Some of our neighbors confessed. Sead's father didn't. He died after three nights of interrogations.

I walked to my house now and made a noose. One's hands never forget. The rope slid smoothly.

How many times had I pondered how the others could bear what we had done? I came to see it all from close-up; Cane had been the innkeeper, Pavle the mechanic, Branimir a farmer, and so on, then along came the idea of our great country and we did what we did. Now Cane is again the innkeeper, Pavle the mechanic, and Branimir is a salesman of Chinese goods, since it does not pay any longer to live off the land. And here I am. And was that all? Like a flu, as Cane had said, something came and infected us.

There was something escaping me that I wanted to find out before I went. Nikola's second option: to forget. Was it possible?

I had let Cane know that I would take him up on the offer of a market stall, and that we should meet that evening, all together, have something to drink and a snack, and talk about the jobs.

When I went in the inn and cheerfully said "Good evening," they raised their arms and the air expanded with relief. "Boss! Boss!" they shouted, and Cane ran up with glasses in his arms like a row of newborns.

We embraced and someone shouted loudly for music.

Cane put on a CD and for a while we just drank. Branimir began to sing quietly along with the female vocalist, sometimes too early or too late. Tears spurted from his eyes and with the palm of his hand he splashed them onto his forehead.

We embraced.

They told me about some gimmicks for selling the Chinese goods more effectively, just to Europeans, as we called those belonging to the parts of the former East that had joined the Union. You had to keep T-shirts and the inscriptions separate, and imprint them according to demand. Pavle added that you had to do the same thing with auto parts. Some clients were so unpleasant that they wanted only original ones for their money.

Even more embraces, again a song, tears, fresh glasses.

"And what about those Muslim house builders?" I asked. "What do they buy?"

Grumbles, curses, they don't do any buying, no sir!

Forgetting that he had complained to me already, Cane told me everything over, twice. There was nothing to be gotten from them.

"And is that right?" I shouted.

No, there is no justice, not anywhere on this earth!

"And is that what we fought for?"

Howls. Denials. A fresh round, down in one.

"And are we pussies to put up with the injustice they're causing us?" We are not, no!

"And will we suffer the way we've been suffering for so long?"

We shall not, no way! What they're doing to us! Shame on us!

"Will we let them trample on our heroic thousand-year-old history?" We shall not! Lead the way! Let's go!

I walked to the door and opened it wide. The men were breathing behind my back, sweaty, heated, shaking with excitement. With my arms I jammed myself against the doorposts, imprisoning them behind my back. They were stuck in that narrow room.

"What's up? What's up?" someone yelled behind me.

I turned and looked them in the eyes.

Cane was the first whose arms gave way, he began to scratch his waist. They quickly followed his example, scattering around the room, moving the tables about, straightening the tablecloths, picking their caps up off the floor—waiting for me to move away from the door.

I sat on the couch and rocked the noose between thumb and forefinger as if I was fishing. How many times before had I thought about what had happened to us, not to everybody but to enough of us in this village, in other villages, in towns? It looked like madness now and whenever I recalled the slogans that we used to shout I was always ashamed. But didn't they once, in Spain, fight war shouting "Long live death!"?

How can grown people change so that they become animals for vain, empty words? We live alongside one another until words connect our feelings and turn us into a crowd, an organism with its own needs and greed. And when the spell is broken, some people can step out of the organism with a clear conscience: it wasn't me, I'm not guilty. Nikola was wrong: there is no forgetting. People who claim they've forgotten are always reusable for another crowd.

I tossed the rope over a roof beam. I was totally at peace. I got up onto a chair and put the noose around my neck. With my left hand I checked to see whether the noose was sliding smoothly, and I was about to kick the chair.

Then a car coughed and through the window I caught sight of an old Vauxhall with British plates stopping at Sead's house. The engine died, I thought the driver's seat was empty, but the door on the right side opened and Sead emerged. He started inspecting the wall he had built the previous year. I couldn't tear my eyes away from him. From the trunk he fetched a brick, took some mortar from a small red container, spread it on, and gently put the brick in place. Over and over. He did not look around. Almost completely bald, stooping slightly, he carried brick after brick. He fixed them, overlapping, in a corner, a first row, a second, a third . . .

He was going to build a house in which nobody would ever live. A husk, a ghost reminding the torturers that even if they forgot everything, somebody else would not. What did his family think about these vacations of his, about the long journey? Did they consider him an eccentric, did they understand him?

I forgot the noose, moving my head forward to see better, and the rope tightened.

I was merely a dead cell, a flake of dandruff that had fallen off and from which there would never come any benefit. I was insignificant, I could kill myself now or later, with a rope or with alcohol. However, something else . . . something else . . . There had to be something other than Nikola's two options.

I took the noose off and jumped to the floor. I walked to the door.

I cannot, I cannot, how can I manage it?

I began to tremble and sweat, to glance toward the noose. Was it really easier to kill again than to ask forgiveness?

As I walked toward Sead I wondered what I might say to him, how I could tell him that no hour passes without my remembering that winter, that I cannot sleep, that my memories are devouring me . . .

When I reached him I could not speak.

He did not turn around. He carried on rebuilding his wall.

I fell to my knees and burst out sobbing. I wept and knelt in front of him, but Sead carried on setting bricks on his wall until he had emptied his trunk, and then he collected his tools and drove away without looking at me.

Nominated by Ecotone and David Gessner

from a translation by Tom Priestly

LAUGH

by STEPHEN DOBYNS

from AMERICAN POETRY REVIEW

for Hayden Carruth, 1921-2008

What he wished was to have his ashes flushed
down the ladies' room toilet of Syracuse City Hall,
which would so clog the pipes that the resulting
blast of glutinous broth would douse the place clean
much in the way that Heracles once flushed out
the Augean stables. After serious discussion,
his wife agreed to do the job. Such an action
was in keeping with his anarchist beginnings,
letting life come full circle and being his ultimate
say-so on the topic of individual liberty. Luckily,
or not, he then forgot, or wiser minds prevailed,
I don't know, and his ashes were packaged up
for the obligatory memorial service—probably
more than one—so the mayor and his council,
all the lackeys, flunkies, toadies and stoolies
caught up in a shit-spotted cascade down those
marble steps and into the astonished street
is an event that exists first in my imagination
and now in yours. But I'd also have you see him
in those last days in his hospital bed in Utica's
St. Luke's, wearing the ignominious blue and
flower-specked nightie the nurses call a Johnny,
stuck with more tubes than a furnace has pipes
and contraptions to check every bodily function
including the force of his farts, while his last bit

of dignity was just enough to swell that fetid bag
hanging like a golden trophy at the foot of his bed.
Blind and half-paralyzed, a bloody gauze mitten
to keep his hand from yanking out his piss-pipe,
his skin hop-scotched with scabs and splotches,
his hair and beard like the tossed off cobwebs
of a schizophrenic spider, he listened, when
those of us in the room felt certain he had fallen
into his final coma, listened as his wife read a note
from a friend who wrote how could death matter
since his prick had shuffled off its mortal coil
some years before? And he laughed, he burped out
a truncated snort, an enfeebled guffaw from fluid-packed
lungs, and those of us with him laughed
as well. Friends, to none will it come as a surprise
for me to say we're trudging toward the final dark
or that to each of us in life is given a limited
allotment of laughs. Save one, save one, to ring
death's doorbell and ease your final passage.

Nominated by American Poetry Review, Jane Hirshfield and B.J. Ward

BRIEF LIVES

fiction by PAUL ZIMMER

from THE GETTYSBURG REVIEW

> *So that the retriving of these forgotten Things from Oblivion in some sort resembles*
> *the Art of a Conjuror, who makes those walke and appeare that have layen in their*
> *graves many hundreds of yeares: and to represent as it were to the eie, the places,*
> *Customes and Fashions, that were of old Times.*
> —John Aubrey, *Brief Lives*

I've given the slip to those creeps in the geezer asylum across the road and tip-toed out the emergency exit when they thought I was taking a nap. It's Friday evening in Squires Grove, and Burkhum's Tap is crowding. I've staked myself out early at the bar and had a few Leinenkugels.

For a while I've been thinking about trying to say something to the guy sitting next to me. I want to share a few of my lives with him, but I can see he's a very tired man. I've learned to be cautious because sometimes folks get the wrong idea when I start talking to them—like they think I'm trying to make a move on them or something. So ridiculous! It should be obvious to anyone that at my age I couldn't even make an obscene phone call. It makes me feel low when people misread me like that.

When I'm discouraged, I think about throwing the whole thing over. Have I wasted my life, stuffing my brain with this horde of minibiographies? It was the one thing I could do well, and when you get as old as I am, you want just a little appreciation for what you've done.

Sometimes, I swear if I could locate the place in my brain where I've collected all these brief lives, I'd tilt my head and drain them all out through my ear hole into a bucket. Then late one night I'd sneak out of the care home and funnel the whole mess into the book drop slot of the Squires Grove library and start my life over.

But I never had the wit or strength to be a jock or a cock or a financial rock. Somehow I discovered that my only talent was for remembering the brief lives of others. I could do that, and I was a natural. When I recite these small stories to other people, it makes me feel important. Most folks don't listen, but I tell them some lives anyway. I hope maybe they'll think about it, and it might help them. It's my modest gift to people; it gives me purpose when I thought for a long time I had nothing to give.

When I was a kid, my parents were drunk and screaming at each other all the time. The cacophony went on and on until—after a particularly wounding explosion—either my mother or father would stomp out of the house. When the fugitive returned, sometimes days later, the other parent would be lurking, ready to attack with vicious insults before making their own furious exit.

I was always left to tend one wounded, intoxicated parent when I was a kid. That was their strange way of being responsible parents—they made sure they never left me *completely* alone. One of them was always *there* for me. Every evening I heated frozen dinners, and the two of us would eat in brooding silence together in the breakfast nook. Then I'd pick up the empty bottles around the house before going back to my room to read.

One summer day there was a miracle. A canny traveling salesman got his foot in the door when both my mother and father were home and only moderately lit up. Quickly he sized up our situation and, burrowing into my parents' guilt, convinced them to invest in the whole set of *Encyclopedia Britannica* for their "smart little scholar" son.

When the astonishing load of boxes arrived, we had no shelves to put them on—my parents were not good planners—so we had them stacked to one side of the front door. When the delivery people had gone away, my parents had another brutal dustup, blaming each other for this fiasco.

At first we were all intimidated by the huge stack of cartons. My parents ignored them, attending to their usual mayhem. Eventually I slit open a box and took the first volume up to my room.

I began reading from the beginning, skipping historical, scientific, and other entries to get to the brief biographies of people. I was transported by these small and great lives. The brutal sounds of my parents' slaughter faded. Other kids were happily pumping their chubby Schwinns through the streets, but I stayed in my room and stuffed my head with brief lives. It became my full-time drill, reading all those miniprofiles in the *Britannica* from *Aaron* to *Zeno*.

When I grew to be a teenager, I saved money from grocery jobs and a paper route, and bought my own set of the *Americana* encyclopedias in installments, stacking the boxes on the other side of the front door as I acquired them. I devoured all the life stories in these imposing volumes until I'd finished high school. The *Britannica* was my father, and the *Americana* was my mother—the only family I could count on.

I also spent a lot of time hanging around the racks in Iverson's Drugstore, scoping the latest news, sports, and movie magazines to get the dope on lives of prominent living people. The pharmacist finally gave up trying to shoo me away and put a stool to the side of the rack for me to sit on. Nice man.

I was ravenous for *lives*—politicians, scientists, actors, musicians, scholars, soldiers, writers, artists, clergy, entertainers, architects, thinkers, athletes, and other famous people. I wanted to know how they got into and out of this world while doing something important enough to be remembered. It is my vicarious pleasure to collect this information, and I always try to pass on some of these lives to others.

I've been drinking beer at the bar in Burkhum's for at least half an hour next to this swarthy guy, and now I've decided that I'm going to give him one of my lives. I snap my fingers at him and cock my head.

"Got it!" I say.

He gives me a wary glimmer and leans away from me as I continue. "I've been trying to figure out who you remind me of. At first I thought, Carmen Basilio, but then—maybe Vincente Minnelli or Camillo Cavour? Then it hit me for sure—you are a dead ringer for Antonio Vivaldi."

It's just after five in Burkhum's, and the place is full of weary, thirsty people. According to our town sign posted on the highway, 437 people live here, so Squires Grove is a quiet place. The grocery, pharmacy, and farmer's hardware all folded several years ago, giving way to a Super Wal-Mart built in the larger market town twenty miles up the highway. Still, there's the Mobil station, a small restaurant/motel, two garages, Burkhum's Tap, and a VFW with a World War II tank mounted in front, its cannon pointed across the highway at the nursing home where I live now.

I've grown up to be an eighty-three-year-old man, and I require assisted living. I never knew how to have a girlfriend, never married nor had the courage to risk living with someone; I just worked jobs in town and spent my spare time collecting lives.

The guy beside me in the Tap is wearing spattered bib overalls and a grimy Milwaukee Brewers cap. He's in the bar for a quick drink before heading home to his family to wash up after a hard week. He has puffy cheeks like Vivaldi's.

"You look Italian," I say. "Not many Romans in Grove." He won't look at me, doesn't chuckle at my little joke. I suppose he's heard of my reputation as a chatterbox.

But I've ducked out on those assholes in the nursing home, and now I'm on my fourth Leinenkugel. Every month or so I make a break for it and cut myself this slack. Otherwise I'd go bonkers, locked up with all those geriatrics. I've gone through three roommates, trying to tell them some of my lives. The last one attempted suicide, so now I'm assigned to a private room.

I speak loudly to my neighbor in the Tap so he can hear me over the television mounted above the bar. Other patrons are casting a wary eye.

"Vivaldi was a late seventeenth-century composer and lived halfway into the eighteenth." The guy is looking panicky, so I hurry on before he can bolt. "You may know his composition, *The Four Seasons*. Probably you've heard it on an elevator in Madison or somewhere, but Vivaldi wrote a lot of other great stuff, too—concertos, a bunch of oratorios, more than ninety operas. He wrote pieces for lute and viola da gamba and pianoforte, chorals, even songs for solo voice. He made his living teaching music in a fancy school for orphan girls. He was an ordained priest, but he was always sniffing around the young ladies and sometimes the prefects had to send him away somewhere to cool him off."

I invent these little twists in my biographies sometimes to give them some snap that folks in the Grove might relate to.

"Oh . . . yeah?" the guy says to me out of the side of his mouth. He still hasn't looked at me.

"What's your name?" I ask. "Mine's Cyril." I stick my hand out for a shake.

He's slow to respond, but at last he says, "Vern," and holds out some limp fingers for me to grasp.

"Well, Vern, let me tell you a little more that might surprise you. Vivaldi apparently had some influence on Johann Sebastian Bach. They lived around the same time, and scholars have found transcriptions of Vivaldi's music in Bach's hand. They never met, but it seems like Bach might have taken some leads from Vivaldi. Bach wrote a lot of music, and he was a sexy guy, too, but he wasn't hung up being a priest like Vivaldi. He had twenty-two kids."

Vern finally gives me a quick flash, to make sure I don't seem too dangerous, then he swishes his drink around and drains it to the cubes. It looks like a double J. D. That was my father's drink—starting around nine in the morning.

"Vivaldi was a grouchy guy," I hurry on, "he was always stewing about things. Maybe chastity made him irritable. He used to pack a knife in his cloak, and if anyone messed with him on the street in Venice, he'd back them off fast." I'm pumping this part up too, trying to make things interesting for Vern, but I see he's trying to signal Burkhum for his tab.

"I got to go see to my milking," he explains from the side of his mouth.

I hurry on, "One time Vivaldi sliced up a gondolier for shortchanging him, but they let him off without a charge because he was in the middle of composing an oratorio for the king. In those days governments sometimes gave you a little credit for being artistic."

Burkhum comes over—but before Vern can ask for his bill, I say, "Hey, Burkhum, give me another Leinie, and I'd like to buy Vern here another of whatever he's drinking." Vern relaxes just a little now. Double mixed drinks cost four big ones in the Tap, and Burkhum puts out fresh popcorn in big bowls on Friday nights.

"Maybe you don't favor music, Vern," I say. "I see you're wearing a Brewer hat. How about a little baseball? You know you look a little like Cookie Lavagetto, too?" Vern is starting to look uneasy again. Burkhum brings our drinks, and Vern takes a big pull on his double. I go on talking.

"Cookie came up with the Pirates in '34, and then was traded to Brooklyn in '37. He became the Dodger's regular third baseman in '39 and hit three hundred. But in a few years he got drafted for the war and didn't get back to baseball until '46. Mostly he warmed the bench for the Dodgers because they had Spider Jorgensen playing third. In the '47 Series against the Yankees, in the fourth game Floyd Bevans is tossing a no-hitter in the ninth, but he walks the first two guys. The Dodgers put Cookie in to pinch hit, and he smacks a double off the right field wall to ruin Bevans's no-hitter and beat the Yankees two to one. Cookie is king of Brooklyn.

"How did the Dodgers thank Lavagetto for this? They released him the next season. He'd given them everything he had. Baseball's like Russian communism. You get the red star one day, and you disappear the next."

Vern seems a little more interested in this biography, but he is still leaning away like he's expecting me to explode at any minute.

"Hey, Vern," I say. "Am I boring you? That's all I know about Cookie Lavagetto and Antonio Vivaldi. Would you like to know what I know about Alfred Sisley or Buck Clayton? Harold Stassen? Cagliostro? Sarah Teasdale? St. James the Greater? Amelita Galli-Curci? How about Sonny Tufts? Sister Kenny? Maybe you like those Italians. Cosimo dé Medici? Boom Boom Mancini? Johnny Antonelli? Amedeo Modigliani?"

But Vern is gone. He knocks his glass over making his break and spills ice cubes down the bar. Everyone's looking at me, and I feel like a backhoe on a wet clay court.

What the hell *is* wrong with me? Why do I go on gassing like this? Why can't I just stay in my room and keep my trap shut?

Because I have all this stuff in my head—I've got to let some of it out once in a while. What the hell! I'm keeper of the *lives*! But I'm like a guy who mucks out barns for a living. People stand clear of me.

Burkhum brings me the bill. "Bring me another Leinie, please," I ask him.

"That's enough today, Cyril," he says. "The nurses are going to be in here looking for you in a minute, and they're going to give me holy hell as it is."

"Well, I don't want to be a problem for you. Hey, Burkhum, did anyone ever tell you, you look like Sinclair Lewis?" Burkhum quick-steps away.

Just as I'm fixing to put on my stocking cap and leave the Tap, a guy I know from the nursing home comes in the door. His name is Nobleson. He lives in the "self-sufficient" section and can take a powder anytime he wants. He doesn't have to sneak out like I do. Nobleson checks out the crowd and sees me waving to him. He hesitates, but then heads over because he knows I've got dough and will buy him a drink.

"Nobleson," I greet him. "How're you, buddy-boy? Sit down here for a minute. What are you drinking? You know, when you were walking over here, I was thinking that you look like Arthur Godfrey?"

Nobleson knows what's up, so he steers me in a direction he favors more. "Not me," he says. "You're thinking about somebody else. I've always been told that I look like young Van Johnson."

"Now there's a guy!" I say to Nobleson.

Burkhum has approached us. "Double Old Crow on ice," Nobleson tells him.

80

"And give me another Leinie," I say.

"Crow coming up," says Burkhum, "but no Leinie for you, Cyril. You need a nap."

Burkhum is sometimes an obscenity. "Burkhum," I say to him. "You remind me of George Jeffreys. You know who he was?"

Burkhum wipes the bar in front of us, but he doesn't answer.

"He was the hanging judge for King James, the 'Bloody Assizer,' the keeper of the seal. The king's muscle. He'd swing anyone from the gallows if they mouthed off about the king. No questions asked—and no defense allowed."

"Sure, Cyril," Burkhum says. "And I'll be a bloody abettor if I give you another Leinie." Burkhum might be a prick, but I have to admit, he has some swift. He attended the university in Madison for a year when he was younger.

"But you!" I turn back to Nobleson, "You *are* a ringer for young Van Johnson."

I have to admit here though, I'm in a bit of a panic, scuffling with my gray cells, trying to come up with the goods on Johnson. I'm getting just a little rusty as I get older. I haven't thought about Van Johnson in years, and the four Leinies have addled me—but there's some Johnson stuff in there, I know it, and I can feel it beginning to shake loose—the filamentous branching of my neurons is extending. Then—aha! Bingo.

"*The Human Comedy*, now wasn't Van Johnson in that? He played a young guy going off to the Second World War. Wasn't that his first movie?" Clickety-click-click, I was on my way now. "Mickey Rooney was in it, too. And Frank McHugh. From a William Saroyan novel. Schmaltzy, but pretty good. It was okay to be a little sappy in those day."

"Let's see. What was next for Van Johnson? *Thirty Seconds Over Tokyo!* They liked him playing young soldiers. Hell of a story. Pilot gets shot down and loses his B-25. Johnson did a heap of suffering in that movie. That was a big one for him. Nobleson, you're right. You *do* look like him. He was a pretty boy."

I was buttering him up, trying to keep him sitting on his stool. "Van Johnson . . . let's see. *The Last Time I Saw Paris*, with Elizabeth Taylor. He was a soldier in that one, too. Wow! Johnson was 4-F in Hollywood during the war. All the other guys were off fighting. I'll bet he used to get more ass than a toilet seat when he was making it big. But then some folks claimed he was queer, so maybe he was working both sides of the pump."

Oh-oh! Too much. I'd gotten excited. Everyone in the bar heard that scatology. I put that last bit in just to give the story some zing. Sometimes the lives need a little help, you know—but now I'm over the top. I try to hurry on with something else. "Johnson was born in Rhode Island," I say. I think that's actually true. I pulled that out of my ratty hat. Pretty damned good for an assisted-living guy—but too late.

Burkhum is standing in front of me, and he is not impressed. He doesn't allow dirty talk in his bar. "Cyril, there's ladies in here. You're getting kind of salty. You need to go outside and breathe some cold air."

Nobleson has drained his glass and is gone. I pay the tab, pull on my stocking cap, slip into my coat, and shuffle out the door into the winter.

Hard snow is flying sideways, but I don't want to go back to that pissy room in assisted living just yet. I pull my collar up, duck my head, and walk across the parking lot to the Mobil station. A guy's pumping some lead free into his pickup, so I walk over to him. "How you doin'?" The man has his head covered in one of those button-down fur balaclavas, so I can't see his face.

"You got any money?" That's all he says. His voice is sort of spooky, coming out of that big hat. I don't answer his question, so when the gas pump snaps off, he shoves the nozzle back in the cradle, claps his arms around his sides to warm himself up, and hustles into his truck to get out of the cold. But he cranks his window part way down. "I mean it, brother," he says. "I could use a little help."

His covered face makes it hard, but I try to size him up so I can give him a life. I say, "You know, with that hat on, you look like Elisha Kent Kane." I step up to his window so he can hear me over the wind. "You probably don't know who Kane was. He was a doctor from Philly and one of the first arctic explorers. He got his party lost in the tundra in 1855, but he led them on a hike all the way out to Greenland. It took three months, and they damned near all froze to death, but he kept them plugging along and saved most of them in the end. They put his picture on a postage stamp, and there were parades and national celebrations, but you don't hear much about Elisha Kent Kane anymore."

The wind boots up hard through the gas pumps, and a tin Self-Service sign is swinging and squawking just over my head. "She's fixing to snow good," I say. I'd forgotten my scarf in Burkhum's and was starting to feel cold.

"How about it, grandpa, you going to give me a hand with my gas?" the guy asks again. His tone is tetchy and uneven. "I'm running short. Got to make it all the way to Peoria tonight."

"They're talking more than a foot of snow on the radio," I say. I'm starting to feel a little uneasy. The guy seems weird. But I still can't help myself. "That reminds me. There was this guy named Snow— C. P. Snow in the fifties and sixties, a scientist who started writing novels as a hobby, and got real deep into it. One of those real smart Brits, they made him a peer, and he was always trying to mix literary stuff with scientific in his books. It was a good shtick for a while and he cleaned up with some best sellers. Snow. Not many folks read him these days."

I can't see the balaclava guy's eyes, but I feel him watching me from the fur. I know he's wondering which wall I'd bounced off of. That's the way it is with me.

"What the fuck are you talking about?" he growls deep from his cold throat.

"Well, good luck on Peoria," I say, and make to head off. "I better get back to my room."

"Hold it, pops!" His voice snaps off and shatters like icicles from a spouting. "Get in." He's lowered his window all the way and has a pistol pointed at me.

"I'm just an old man," I say. "I don't have anything that would help you."

"Get your creaky ass into the truck!"

I make another move to walk away, but he shouts, "*Now*, geezer, or you die!"

I know he means it. I hobble around to the other side of his truck, pull the handle, and get in. "I don't know what you want, but the folks from the home are going to be looking for me," I say.

He turns on his ignition and hits the gas pedal all in one motion, and the car jumps forward. Somebody in the station flashes lights, but he doesn't stop. He's down the drive, turning fast without looking onto the highway. Snow is really flying now and beginning to mount. There must be four inches down already. He hasn't paid for his gas, and he's making fast on the slippery road out of Squires Grove with me in his passenger seat. He's a mean guy, and I'm thinking that all the lives in the world aren't going to help me now.

I watch the heavy snow twist into the windshield. We are barreling toward Freedstown through windblown drifts. "You can have all the money in my wallet," I say. "There must be about twenty-five in there." He doesn't answer. "You know, Clifford Brown was killed in snow like this. He was a great jazz trumpeter, made all kind of innovations. He was helping some motorist who got stuck in a drift, and another car going too fast slid into him and finished him."

The guy unloosens his balaclava and folds the flaps back from over his mouth. He's got a greasy black beard, and a mouth like an open cut. "Why don't you shut your fuckin' trap?" he says. He's a man who doesn't care where he goes or what he does, so long as he's getting away. He's not even going to Peoria.

There are no other cars on the road. Decent, sensible folks stay home on a night like this. You can't even see the lights of Freedstown through the blizzard. For a moment the truck starts wavering and sliding almost sideways, but he takes his foot off the gas, straightens it out of the slide, and slows down only a little. You can tell he's driven in snow like this before. He doesn't care.

I've got to do something, so I start talking again. "One time Jesse James and his brother Frank were up north raising hell in Minnesota." The guy twists in his seat, and I don't know if he's going to hit me or shoot me. To make things worse, now my groin is aching. I forgot to use the men's room in Burkhum's before I left. I have to pee. I mean I *really* have to pee.

But I keep talking. "Jesse and Frank are taking what they can get. They go into a bank in a little town, pull their guns, and have all the people up against a wall. Some women have fainted and little kids are crying. The bank clerk is moving too slow and Jesse knows he is stalling, so he tells Frank to shoot the guy in the foot just to show they mean business. Frank blows the guy's big toe off, and he's howling on the floor, but they haul him up bleeding and make him open the safe."

I can tell in the darkness that the balaclava guy is listening. I start to improve the story a little.

"There's an old man amongst the hostages, and he's not in good shape. He's gasping and clutching his chest like he's going to drop from a heart attack. Jesse sees this and he feels bad. He's partial to old guys because his father had been good to him when he was a boy."

This is whole cloth I admit—but I am out there spinning through cold darkness with this mean balaclava guy and his gun, and I have to do what I can do.

"Jesse has some mercy. He takes the old guy by his arm, leads him to the door, and—to the amazement of the people in the bank—he lets him go. Then the James boys make about finishing their business, scooping up bloody bundles of cash and running for their horses. But some of those town folks in the bank were cheering Jesse and Frank as they rode away." This last is too much of a spin.

"Get off it, you old shithead!" the guy snarls.

"I've got to pee," I say.

"What are you sayin' to me? Tough shit!"

"I'm going to do it in my pants!" I warn urgently.

"Not my problem."

"It'll get all over your upholstery."

We haven't passed another car yet, and Balaclava is whizzing down the middle of the road.

"We're the only two people in the whole county crazy enough to be out on a night like tonight," I say. "Except the sheriff. I know him. He'll be out watching for anyone speeding in this weather. By now he knows someone's skipped paying at the Mobil."

The guy thinks about this for a minute and looks into his rearview mirror. Then he says, "Bite it off, old man!" He still has his pistol on his lap.

"I've got to pee!" I try to keep quiet, but I feel it beginning to seep into my jockeys.

"What is this? Grade school?" The guy is really irritated.

"If you shoot me, I'll just bleed all over your upholstery, too."

Balaclava abruptly starts pumping his brakes, and the car is slowing down, wavering and slipping as he eases it toward the side of the highway, and it almost slides off into the berm.

Cyril, I say to myself, this is it. Now you've done it. You've recited your last brief life. But I give it one last best shot—I say to Balaclava as the storm batters around us, "You remember Neil Armstrong, the first moon walker? He was born in a little town in Ohio, and they made him commander of the first moon mission, even though he was a civilian. It was 1969. When he stepped out of the Apollo onto the moon, he said some famous stuff about taking a small step for mankind. But when he wrote a book about it later, he claimed he was really thinking—just at that very moment when he first put his foot down in the white moon dust—about his old father in a care home back in Ohio. He was remembering how the old man was always gentle to everyone and everything. He wanted to remember this so that if he came across any moon creatures, he'd know to be kind to them."

This was the wholest cloth I'd ever spun. It didn't matter. "Jesus Christ, old man!" Balaclava snaps. "*You* are from the moon." I thought he was going to laugh, but he says, "How do you shovel anything that deep?" He picks up his pistol and points it at me. "Give me your fucking wallet and get out of my truck before you start pissing on my seat."

He doesn't shoot me. I stand and watch his taillights disappear in the swirl. The snow is driving hard and horizontal, and wind is slicing. I pull my hat way down over my ears. It's ten miles between Grove and Freedstown, and I figure I'm about halfway. Out here the farms are so far in you can't even see their lights. My wet underpants are freezing solid to my groin, and my scarf is back on a stool in Burkhum's Tap.

Cyril, I say to myself, get moving. It's only five miles. I turn and start shuffling back in the direction of Grove, toward my warm, little room in the care home. Who do I start with? George Mikan? Heinrich Kuhn? The Empress Marie Louise? Bingo Binks? Catherine of Valois? Ji Chang? Siegfried Sassoon? General Alexis Kaledin? Nelly Sachs? Prince Svyatoslav of Kiev? Gorgeous George? Ségolène Royal? Thomas à Kempis? Colley Cibber? Seutonius? Édourd Vuillard? Heinrich Heine? Barbara Jordan? Marcel Cerdan?

Elisha Kent Kane. That's it. Cyril, you're on your way to Greenland. It's going to take a while.

Nominated by The Gettysburg Review and Gary Gildner,
Michael Heffernan, William Heyen

SONG

by JOHN MURILLO

from UP JUMP THE BOOGIE (Cypher Books)

I know it's wrong to stare, but it's Tuesday,
The express is going local, and this woman's

Thighs—cocoa-buttered, crossed, and stacked
To her chin—are the only beauty I think I'll see

for the next forty minutes. Not the train's
Muttering junkie, who pauses a little too long

In front of me, dozing, but never losing balance.
Not the rat we notice scurry past the closing doors,

Terrorizing the rush hour platform. Not
Even these five old Black men, harmonizing

About begging and pride, about a woman
Who won't come home. But skin, refracted

Light, and the hem's hard mysteries. I imagine
There's a man somewhere in this city, working

Up the nerve to beg this woman home, the sweet
Reconciliation of sweat on sweat, and pride

Not even afterthought. My own woman, who
I've begged sometimes not to leave, and begged

Sometimes please to leave, never has, also waits,
Uptown, in a fourth floor walk-up, in an old t-shirt

For me to make it back. She waits for me to come
Through jungles, over rivers, out from underground.

She waits, without fear, knowing no matter what,
I will make it home. And, God, there were times

I probably shouldn't have, but did. And lived
To see this day, the junkies, rats, and thighs,

And I say, praise it all. Even this ride, its every
Bump and stall, and each funky body pressed

To another, sweat earned over hours, bent over moats,
Caged in cubicles, and after it all, the pouring

Of us, like scotch, into daylight. Dusk.
Rush hour. This long trip home. Praise it all.

The dead miss out on summer. The sun
Bouncing off moving trains and a woman

To love you when you get inside. Somewhere
In this city, a man will plead for love gone,

Another chance, and think himself miserable.
He'll know, somewhere deep, he may never

Win her back. But he'll know even deeper,
That there is a kind of joy in the begging

Itself, that all songs are love songs. Blues,
Especially. Praise the knowledge. Praise

The opening and closing doors, the ascent
Into light, heat, each sidewalk square, cracks

And all, the hundred and twelve stairs between
Lobby and my woman's front door, the exact

Moment I let in this city, let out this sweat,
And come to own this mighty, mighty joy.

Nominated by Cypher Books and Martha Collins

NEPHILIM

fiction by L. ANNETTE BINDER

from ONE STORY

Freda weighed eighteen pounds when she was born. Her feet were each six inches long. At ten, she was taller than her father. Five feet eleven and one-half inches standing in her socks. I can't keep you in shoes, her mother would say, and they went to Woolworth's for men's cloth slippers. Her mother cut them open up front to leave room for Freda's toes. She'd stitch flowers in the fabric to pretty up the seams, forget-me-nots and daisies and yellow bushel roses. They sat beside the radio and listened to *The Doctor's Wife* and *Tales of the Texas Rangers* while her mother worked the needle. Some of your daddy's people are tall, she'd say. Your Aunt Mary had hands like a butcher. By God, her grip was strong.

Sometimes Freda felt her bones growing while she lay in bed. This was when the sensation was still new. Before it became as familiar as the pounding of her heart. The house was quiet except for the planes out by the base and Tishko, the Weavers' dog, who barked at the moon and stars. That dog's got a streak in him, Mr. Weaver always said. I bet he's part wolf on his momma's side.

Tishko was out there howling and the summer air was sweet and Freda's bones were pushing their way outward. Stretching her from socket to socket. There's nothing wrong with you, her mother would say. You're pretty as a Gibson Girl. You just had your growth spurt early, but Freda knew better. She knew it when she was only ten.

God was a blacksmith and her bones were the iron. He was drawing them out with a hammer. God was a spinner working the wheel and she was his silken thread. Seven feet even by the time she was sixteen and she knew all the names they called her. Tripod and eel and swizzle stick. Stork and bones and Merkel, like the triple-jointed Ragdoll who fought against the Flash. Red for the redwoods out in California. Socket like a wrench and Malibu like the car, and she took those names. She held her book bag against her chest and took them as her own.

Her house had been her parents' house. They'd bought it new when Freda was nine. A split-level built in 1951 that cost seven thousand dollars. She was thirty-seven now and sleeping in their bedroom. It had low ceilings and low doorways and she knew all the places she needed to stoop. Every three weeks she cleaned the upstairs windows by standing on the lawn. She used a bucket with hot vinegar water, she didn't mind the smell. There was a bluejay nest in the eaves up there and the birds really fouled the panes.

"Lady, what's your problem?" A little boy was standing on the sidewalk with his bike. He had a shoebox strapped to the rack behind the seat. "I never saw a person big as you."

"These bluejays are my problem," she said. "Look at the mess they're making."

"I bet they got a nest up there. My momma says they're pests."

"Where's your house?"

"We're new," he said. He pointed four doors up to where the Clevelands used to live. "We're in the yellow house, but my momma, she's gonna paint it because it's much too bright. She can't right now because of the fumes. In September I'm starting at the Bristol School. That's when I'm getting a brother."

"How do you know it won't be a girl?"

"No way," he said. "I asked my mom for a brother. And she can tell, anyhow. She gets sick in the mornings and not at night and she says only boys do that. Sometimes she's in there for hours."

Freda set her bucket down and wiped her wet hands down the front of her pants. It was May, but the air still had some bite and this boy was wearing only a pair of thin cotton shorts. She pointed to the back of his bike. "What do you have in that box?"

"I'm looking for crickets," he said. "My lizard Freddy, he's got a condition."

"I've got plenty of those," she said. "They're eating up my flowers." The waterlily tulips were done for the year, but her lady tulips were just getting started. They were red on the outside, but their insides were yellow and orange and it was like having two different gardens when they finally opened.

"You got some nice ones," he said. "You got more than Mrs. Dillman and she's out there every day." He rubbed his thumb against his jaw like somebody much older. He was wearing a T-shirt from the Freedom Train. She could see it now that she was closer. She could see his collarbones and the hollow beneath his ribs and how his legs were knobby as drumsticks and brown already from the sun.

"You want to see those birds? You want to see the babies sitting in the nest?" She held out her arms and he came to her. He should have been afraid, but he leaned his bike against her maple and walked across her lawn. She hoisted him upwards and toward the eaves, and he was all bones, this little boy. Her hands fit perfectly around his waist.

The nephilim were the children of fallen angels and ordinary women. Her mother had told her this years ago. Her mother, who was so tiny when they laid her out because she shrank as she got older. I'm five foot two and one-half, she'd say, angry if the doctors tried to round the number down, but she knew about the nephilim. She'd read about them in books. How they were giants on the earth before the coming of the floods and how they had left their bones behind. That part wasn't in the Bible, but her mother said it was true. Enormous piles of bones and the sun bleached them and they turned to rock and that's why we have the mountains. Look, she'd say, we can see them from our window and she'd point to Pikes Peak and it looked like skin, that mountain. Pink as skin when the sun hit it and not just piled-up bones.

The boy's name was Teddy Fitz. His baby sister was born that September, and every morning he walked past Freda's house on his way to school. He didn't close his jacket, not even when the wind started to blow. He wore tennis shoes in the snow. She paid him five dollars to shovel her walk. She bought him knit caps at Walgreens and thick fleece gloves, and he looked so serious while he worked. She could see in his face the man he'd become, in the set of his jaw and how his eyes slanted downwards.

Five dollars to shovel the walk and seven fifty when summer came because she couldn't push the mower. Another five to help with the bulbs the following September. She told him where to plant them so she wouldn't have to bend. Her knees were starting to go. Pretty soon she'd need a walker.

"This looks like an onion," he said, holding up one of the bulbs. "How's it gonna grow a flower?" He made holes with the dibber and set the bulbs inside and he was careful when he patted down the dirt so they wouldn't turn.

"Just wait," she said. "You'll see in April how it works." The plant was inside. It was only sleeping. It was waiting for springtime when the dirt would get warm.

He shook his head at the wheelbarrow she'd filled with bulbs. "You sure bought a lot. It'll take days to get these planted."

"I'll give you five dollars extra if you do them all today."

She sat in a mesh lawn chair and let him work. Her bones were burning again. She'd be on crutches in a few years, and the wheelchair would come next. Her internist, Dr. Spielman, brought up options. There was an operation they could try. He knew a pituitary specialist who'd had good luck with a patient in Tulsa, a man who was almost eight feet tall. The operation took out his tumor and stopped his bones from growing. Her tumor might be too big by now. Surgery might not be an option, but only the experts would know for sure. Her spine would begin to curve if they didn't do something. She'd get diabetes or high blood pressure, and eventually her heart would stop. The radiation therapy was better and surgeons more precise now than they'd ever been. She needed to be brave.

She leaned back in her chair and watched this perfect boy. He held the bulbs like they were porcelain cups and he gently laid them down. The wind was still warm when it blew and it ruffled up his blond hair. He wiped his forehead against the inside of his elbow, but he kept working because those five dollars were waiting and they'd bring him that much closer to the skateboard he wanted. She'd give him ten when he finished and not just five. She'd buy him the skateboard herself, but his mother wouldn't like it.

Anna Haining Bates was seven feet five and one-half inches at her tallest. She died the day before she would have turned forty-two. Her heart stopped while she was sleeping. Jane Bunford was another giantess. She was perfectly normal until she was eleven and took a fall from her bike. She cracked her skull against the pavement and then she started growing. Things turn in an instant, this was the lesson. Hit your head and everything changes.

The tallest man in modern days was Robert Pershing Wadlow. He was eight feet eleven inches just before he died, and when he was nine he carried his father up the stairs just to show he could. She knew this from the Guinness Book of World Records. She bought a new copy every year. How strange it would be to stand next to a man and to look him in the eye. To feel the smallness of her hands when he took them in his.

"My dad says I'm gonna be short like my mom." He sat on the bag of leaves like it was a beanbag chair. He sat right beside her and took a rest, and his nose was smudged from the dust. He'd filled five bags already just from the maple tree. "He says my sister will be taller than me when she's done growing."

Freda leaned across her mesh chair and wiped the smudge away with her thumb. "My momma was a tiny lady. Her waist was smaller than my neck." There's no knowing how things would go, she wanted to tell him. He could be a giant when he grew up. One day, he might walk on the moon. She stroked his cheek with her thumb too, but he shook himself free.

"What about your dad? He must have been pretty big."

"My dad was about as tall as yours. That just goes to show you. And how can your daddy know how big your sister'll be? She isn't even three."

"He says she's got those monkey arms."

"We're all monkeys," she said. "We all come from the same place."

"I'm no monkey." He shook his head. "Those are very dirty animals. I went to the Cheyenne Zoo last year and they were throwing poop." He got back up and finished her front yard and then started on the back. He fished the elm leaves out from her beds and all the ponderosa needles, and she followed him on her canes and stood there for a while. The canes were only temporary. Some days she didn't even need them. The canes were for when the pressure changed or when the winds started blowing. As soon as summer came, she'd walk without any problems. She just needed that dry air.

According to the Book of Enoch, the nephilim were three hundred cubits tall. Four hundred and fifty feet, give or take. That's three times higher than the Holly Sugar Building on Cascade, which was only fourteen stories. They were bigger than Barkayal and Samyaza and Akibeel and all their angel fathers, and they were always hungry. Nothing could fill them up. Not the birds or the fish or the grains in the fields, not the sand snakes or the lizards. They stripped the forests and ate the bark

94

from the trees. They turned against ordinary men when the last food was gone. They went after the newborn babies.

Teddy bought himself a skateboard with some of the money he earned. A cheap one from Target and then a nicer one from the Acme Pawnshop down on Fountain. He bought himself a bike, too. One of those Speedsters and the paint was gray and dull from the sun, but he waxed it anyway. "Just wait till I'm old enough to get my learner's permit," he said. "I've already got six hundred and thirty-four dollars." His car fund was growing each day.

His parents shouted almost every evening. Freda could hear them four doors down. Sometimes, his mother went away for a few days at a time and Teddy never said anything about it, not even when Freda asked.

He delivered the *Gazette* in the mornings and for a while he delivered the *Sun*, too. That was back in the late 1970s when the Springs still had two daily papers. He threw the papers from his bike without even slowing down. He knew just how to toss them so they landed on people's front steps and not in their flowerbeds. She waited sometimes to see him go by. She stood behind her screen door and he cycled past with an athlete's grace. What was it like to move like that, to never be still and never be tired? He stood on his pedals and pumped them hard, and the other boys were so ordinary compared to him.

The Lord ordered Michael and Raphael to kill the nephilim one by one. Crops grew again once they were gone and the trees pushed out shoots. Hunger is a terrible thing, Freda's mother had told her more than once. She knew this from her childhood in Nebraska. It's like a hot rock in your belly and you can feel it burning. The days so black you couldn't find your way from the steps to your front door. The wind blew the seeds right off the field, and days later, the alfalfa sprouted in barnyards and distant cemeteries where the seeds had scattered. Hunger has no mercy when it comes, she had said. But hunger was their burden, and they should have carried it.

He bought Mrs. Dillman's old '72 Gremlin the week he turned sixteen. It was butterscotch gold with racing stripes, and he waved at Freda when he drove by. His arm hung out the window, and he was proud as Hannibal coming over the Alps the way he raised his hand. He used cloth diapers and three coats of Mother's Wax to bring out the luster.

He installed a fancy K&N air filter and every day after school he was out there in the driveway. He rolled back and forth under the car and his sister stood beside him to hand him wrenches.

That's where he was the day his mother left. Freda saw the truck when it pulled up. Teddy brought the suitcases out to the curb, hoisted them into the bed, and he held the door for his mother. He didn't cry and he didn't wave when the truck rounded the corner. He kept on waxing his car. So many coats Freda lost count. He was still there working the diaper when the sky was dark and the driveway floodlights came on. His mother had a boyfriend, his mother was gone, and Teddy was still there working when Freda went to bed.

He painted her trim the summer before his senior year. He sanded her gutters, too, and painted them chocolate brown. He cut down a broken branch from her maple tree and brushed sealant on the open bark to keep the fungus out. Freda looked for jobs to give him because next summer he'd be gone. He was a cadet in the Junior ROTC and he'd be going away to college. Up to Boulder or Greeley or maybe to Fort Collins. He did pushups and jumping jacks on his front lawn and once his sister sat sidesaddle along his back to make the pushups harder.

He sealed the cracks in her driveway and painted her cement steps. All Freda could do was watch. She leaned on her walker like it was a banister and told him what to do. The juniper bushes needed trimming and some of her window well covers were cracked, and after he was done the house looked as nice as it did when her parents were alive and still working in the garden.

She kept her household money in a Folgers Coffee can. Teddy came inside with her and poured himself a lemonade from her pitcher while she counted out the bills. Somewhere up the street there were children shouting and the sounds of splashing water. Mrs. Dillman had an above-ground pool she filled each summer for her grandkids. Freda took ten five-dollar bills and set them on the table. Her walker scraped across the linoleum as she pulled it around. The kitchen felt so big when he was there beside her.

"I think the rubber's loose." He pointed to the bottom of her walker. "I can glue it back on for you and then it'll be real smooth." He leaned in to get a better look, and Freda caught his chin and cupped it in her hand. That face she'd known since he was little. That sad face and those eyes that slanted downwards. She wanted to remember him. He wasn't even gone yet. He was right here in her kitchen, but she was seeing him from some distant point ten or twenty years in the future. She was seeing him in her memory standing by her table. He was seventeen and in a dirty white T-shirt and his skin was pink from the sun.

In her memory she kissed him. His lips tasted like lemons. In her memory he didn't pull away. She felt so small there beside him, small as a girl when he touched her cheek. His hands were callused from the shears and all her life she'd never know anything more perfect than his breath against her skin.

Her mother said a heart at peace gives life to the body. Also, we are all small in the eyes of the Lord. Don't listen when they call you names. How could they know what it's like. She heard her mother's voice those nights when the air was still. Those summer nights when she could feel her jawbone growing. She was almost fifty and the radiation wasn't working anymore. Her teeth were starting to spread and her features were getting coarser. She didn't look in the mirror when she washed her face. She closed her eyes, but she could feel the ridge across her forehead where the skin had started to thicken. Her mother's voice came back to her after all these years. Don't be afraid, she'd said. He raises us upward. He carries us inside His palm, and sometimes Freda could feel her mother's fingers press against her cheek.

He took a pretty girl to the prom. But you already knew that's how things would go. He took a pretty girl with tiny wrists and ankles, and there were more until he found the girl who was meant for him. She wasn't the prettiest in the group, but she looked like him how her eyes slanted. She was a good three inches taller than him even in her Converse sneakers. She wore his denim jacket and he opened the car door for her and closed it again, and they drove together like they'd always been a pair.

Somebody tied Freda's feet to the ground and her hands to the wooden wheel. Somebody else worked the wheel and pulled her upwards, stretching all the muscles around her sockets. It was her companion, this feeling. She couldn't call it pain. It was the pulling she felt in her bones. Sometimes it carried her upwards, and she knew her mother was right. Sometimes it pulled her the other way. She moved downward through the dirt where her flowers had once grown, down to the rocks that would become the mountains, and she was so small beside them.

∗ ∗ ∗

All beautiful things go away. Everyone knows this is true. Their son looked like him, and he rode a bike just like him, too. They were back for the first time in years. They came to check on Grandpa Fitz. They weeded his rock beds and adjusted the sprinklers, and Teddy's wife was out there in her capris trimming back the hedges. Freda rolled closer to the window so she could see them better. That boy with eyes like his daddy and those skinny brown legs. His hair almost white from the sun. Every year it would get a little darker. And her Teddy was out there cutting the elm tree back from the power lines. His son ran circles around him and pointed to the sky and he didn't listen when Teddy shouted. His momma had to pull him away from the falling branches. Teddy was almost thirty. How could that be. He was a first lieutenant. She knew this from Mrs. Dillman's youngest daughter. In another few years he'd be a captain because anything was possible in this world. He sat up there in the branches, and his back was so straight.

He came by in the evening with a jelly jar full of flowers. Snap dragons and tiger lilies and snowfire roses. His wife had put ice cubes in the water to keep the blossoms fresh. Teddy knocked on her door, and when she didn't answer, he knocked a little louder. She could see him from the window in her living room. He was standing on the wheelchair ramp, and his boy was there beside him. He waited a good five minutes before he set the jar outside her door. He wouldn't have said anything about her jawbone or her bent fingers or how her back was shaped like an S. He would have taken her hand and knelt down to greet her, but she stayed in her spot by the window. His face was like a mirror, and it was better not to look.

Nominated by Shannon Cain, Nancy Richard, Alice Schell

ODE TO LATE MIDDLE AGE

by RICHARD CECIL

from ATLANTA REVIEW

October ought to be my favorite month.
Summer's stinging bugs are dead or sleeping;
evening chill drives loud porch-sitting neighbors
inside their heated rooms to drink and shout;
rolled-up car windows muffle thumping basses;
rock concerts in the park come to an end.
No one at work is going to blurt out,
"Let's all get together for a picnic!"
forcing me to think up lame excuses
like, *sorry, I'm allergic to fresh air*,
or *my detergent can't get grass stains out*.
Free at last from summer's hectoring—
how come you're not having a great time? —
protected from skin cancer by long sleeves
instead of slimy sunscreen, I should be
ecstatic, or, at least, satisfied.
Who cares if every day's two minutes shorter
every morning darker, slightly colder?
What difference does it make that I'm sinking
slowly toward the bottom of the year?
Artificial light and central heat
fill the slowly growing gap between
the inner and the outer weather. Autumn!
Between the last tornado and first snowstorm
the pollen count declining every day,

asthma and arthritis in remission,
sap clumping up and sinking in the ground—
no more clipping hedge and mowing lawn—
in every way but one it's the best season.
Why am I reluctant to embrace it
just because it ends so horribly?

Nominated by Atlanta Review and Maura Stanton

THREE BARTLETT PEARS

by ALICE MATTISON

from THE THREEPENNY REVIEW

MEMOIR

EDWARD, MY husband, lay in a bed with raised sides in the Medical Intensive Care Unit of Yale-New Haven Hospital. His wrists were tied to the sides of the bed, and a wide belt—in incongruous blue and green plaid—crossed his belly to keep him from sitting up. A white bandage on his nose, attached to a tube that went into his nostril, made his face hard to recognize but I could see his graying, reddish beard and pale orange eyebrows. Occasionally a nurse hung a bag of liquid on one of three poles, each holding several dripping bags. A rigid tube going into Edward's mouth was connected to a ventilator—a big blue machine—with expandable hoses. Yet another tube came out from under his white thermal blanket and led to a bag of urine. Behind his head, a screen showed numbers: pulse, blood pressure, blood oxygen level, and breathing rate.

It was Tuesday, March 24. On Sunday, Edward and I had extended our usual two-and-a-half-mile walk with our yellow dog, Gracie, next to the Mill River in East Rock Park, New Haven. A network of trails leaves the riverside and winds up a ridge toward a red cliff that gives our neighborhood a comfortable sense of limit. As we walked, I said, "Let's go up Whitney Peak." Mid-March in southern New England: the snow was gone, but it was cold. There had been little rain lately, and the trails were dry. Tips of branches were red, willow trees yellow, but I saw no other signs of spring. When the leaves came out the woods would seem larger, and it would be less obvious that we live in a city, that the park is cut by a road spiraling to the summit of East Rock, that some of the park's edges are near old factories and other industrial clutter.

Whitney Peak is one of several low summits, a short climb on a trail that intersects the one we take every day. We turned left on a third trail, and in a few minutes walked to a scrubby, rocky height from which we could see a new water treatment plant in one direction, and the town of Hamden's sprawling businesses and highways in the other. We looked around, then descended, crossed the paved road, and came to a lookout, Gracie and I going first. She's a shrewd shelter mutt, mostly yellow lab, along with something smaller and leggier. She has intense golden eyes that look conscious, like the eyes of a talking dog in a cartoon.

It was the first spring walk that could remotely be called a hike. I hurried to the edge of the lookout, giving a happy shout. Below was Lake Whitney, a reservoir. A dam and a waterfall—the turnaround place for our daily walk—were dramatic from above. I'd never realized that this spot, which we'd driven past often, was just above the place we walked to every day. Edward caught up and looked around amiably. He's an easygoing walker who emits little noises, grunts and puffs. "Fuffle!" he may say, negotiating a rough place. From the lookout we took still another trail, which soon rejoined our usual path next to the river. We were away from home just an hour and a half.

That afternoon I cleaned the kitchen. We put a photograph we bought months ago into a frame, and hung it on the wall. Edward vacuumed the house. He'd recently taken over the dusting, and was better at it than I. I heard him in the next room, talking—apparently to the dust. We ate dinner out.

Monday morning Edward said he'd had chills during the night, and now he thought he had a fever. I took his temperature with a thermometer I must have bought when our kids—three sons in their thirties—were children: 98.9. He said he'd go to work. The small nonprofit he directs argues with government, runs training programs, and does whatever else comes along that might benefit people who have a psychiatric illness, are in recovery from addiction, or are homeless. He attended an early meeting, came home and drank his usual third of a mug of coffee, and took Gracie for a short walk. We drove downtown together—he was going to his office, I to a soup kitchen where I volunteer on Mondays. On the way, he said, "I think I'm coming down with something." At one P.M. he had to run a meeting of his board of directors. When Edward is sick, he sleeps, so I encouraged him to come home and nap after the meeting, knowing he'd try to avoid that because I'd be working at home in the afternoon, and I can be grouchy about interruptions. When I got out of the car a few blocks short of the spot where he'd dropped me on other Mondays he looked bereft, which made me impatient. I wasn't ending the marriage, I just had an errand on my way to the soup kitchen.

I'm a novelist—a solitary—and the volunteer job is the one time in the work week when I'm with other people. The soup kitchen is ordinarily fascinating—because of the mix of people and a sense that it's okay to be emotionally honest there—but not on that particular Monday. Guests who were quieter than usual filled the long tables in the church hall. We had plenty of workers. I handed out plastic forks and spoons and packets of sugar or artificial sweetener, discussing with the woman handing out desserts whether people are likelier to choose pastry on the side of the tray they come to first.

I don't eat at the soup kitchen—my usual lunch is oatmeal—and I stopped downtown for a bowl of soup, then walked home, where I greeted Gracie and sat down with an apple. I took one bite and the doorbell rang. I put the apple on a shelf, opened the door, and there was my friend Lezley, who works with Edward. "We just sent Edward to the hospital," she said evenly. "Get your coat."

I'm not sure I said anything. I went into the kitchen and got my cell phone, which I mostly forget to carry. It had been plugged into its charger on the counter. We left and I locked the house. I said, "Did someone drive him there?"

"No, we called an ambulance."

"Is this like a heart attack or like flu?"

"Like flu." I couldn't imagine someone getting sick enough for an ambulance in so few hours. I was alert, oddly calm, choosing to postpone deciding how frightened to be. But Lezley ran to her van and I ran too.

During the board meeting, she reported, Edward had made less and less sense. He trembled and had chills, but refused to adjourn until a board member insisted; someone dialed 911 as he collapsed, and Lezley rushed to find me. She'd been to my house several times in the last few minutes, and had searched nearby streets.

As we drove, I phoned our son Ben, who would want to know what was happening immediately. He works nearby, and said he'd meet me at the hospital. Another son, Jacob, works in New Haven as well, but I didn't think he'd mind if I waited to phone him until I knew more. Our third son is an English professor in Ohio, and he too would be willing to wait.

Lezley dropped me off. I didn't know how frightened she was—how frightened I should have been—until much later. A uniformed guard let me in and I searched a crowded room and spotted Edward in an open cubicle. He was hooked up to an IV pole and a monitor, and beeps of varying pitches sounded. A young resident told me he had an infection. I think someone said, "Your husband is very sick." Edward was glad to see me and said he felt tired. I stood at his side, clutching my coat.

I can't remember why, after a while, I crossed the crowded room to the nurses' station. I suppose I had a question. I was distracted by something, and turned to look at a man lying on a stretcher, whose face made me take a step in his direction, when it turned into the face of my son Jacob. "What are *you* doing here?" he asked—incredulous, friendly.

I asked the same question. "I'm fine!" he said. During a lunchtime walk, Jacob had had chest pains that got worse when he walked uphill. He called his wife, a nurse, who said he'd better get himself checked out. A colleague had driven him to the hospital. The pain was gone, but he'd had blood drawn, an EKG. He'd just had an X-ray and was on his way back to his own cubicle.

A friend hearing this story the next day from our third son, Andrew, wondered how I survived. Among strangers, many of them sick, I didn't cry or panic. I added the new problem to the other one, and went back and forth from Jacob's side to Edward's. I think this coincidence seemed less strange than it might have. Somehow all rules had been suspended. I was supposed to be home, finishing my apple, checking emails and phone messages, trying to work on my novel.

Ben, waiting to ask the guard outside the ER for permission to see his father, heard the man in front of him ask about Jacob. "That's my brother's name," Ben said, and found out what had happened. If I'd checked my answering machine before Lezley arrived, I'd have heard messages about *both* emergencies. Would I have fainted? Laughed? Dropped dead?

Jacob was eventually declared, indeed, to be fine, but meanwhile the hospital had him spend the night so he could take a stress test in the morning. Edward was admitted to the medical ICU with a urinary tract infection that had spread to his blood. Ben and I followed his bed through corridors and an elevator. At the unit, we waited in a lounge that felt so distant from Edward I was afraid I'd never see him again. We'd been told a phone there would ring when we were allowed to go in, but the phone did not ring. Finally we waited at the door of the ICU until someone opened it, then demanded to see him. He was in bed. A doctor interviewed him and he answered questions clearly. Eventually we left. Edward promised me he wouldn't die in the night.

WEEKENDS, in our ordinary life, Edward is home, taking up emotional and physical space, and I don't write. I don't write much on Mondays because of the soup kitchen. Tuesdays through Fridays I write (except for one week each month that I spend on student work; I teach in a master's program at Bennington College that proceeds mostly by correspondence). My days alone are unlike other days. Edward and I walk Gracie in the morning and then he goes to work until well into the evening. I try to focus on the book I'm writing, which feels like flying slowly around something in increasingly smaller, less frantic concentric circles. Eventually I can bear to read some of what I wrote the previous day, I can decide what I need to know to write the next sentence. Then, at last, I write that sentence. Then, after another pause, another sentence. Then pages exist that I don't remember writing, I'm tired, and it's late afternoon.

Lunch is always the same. I eat oatmeal with raisins, yogurt, nuts, and cut up fruit—in the cold months an apple or a pear. Yellow Bartlett pears are what I like best, but Bosc pears are good too. Edward and I generally shop on Friday evenings, and I buy some apples and three unripe pears: greenish, plump Bartletts or elongated brown Boscs. If I buy more, I can't always eat them before they are overripe. My first oatmeal lunch of the week is on Tuesday, and usually the pears are not yet ripe, so I cut up an apple. With my oatmeal on Wednesday, Thursday, and Friday, I eat a pear.

The week Edward got sick was to be ordinary in some respects, not in others. I'd have spent Tuesday through Friday at home writing my novel except for Thursday afternoon, when I'd been invited to visit a writing program at a high school. Tuesday evening would be a reading in the Ordinary Evening Series, named for Wallace Stevens's poem "An Ordinary Evening In New Haven." Three other women and I bring writers, once a month, to the basement of a New Haven bar, and twenty or thirty people come to hear them. My friend Douglas Bauer was reading for us that Tuesday, and I planned to meet his train, then introduce his reading. We'd all have dinner later—organizers, readers, and a couple of husbands, including Edward. Doug would spend the night at our house. For breakfast we'd eat raisin scones I planned to bake when I finished writing on Tuesday.

MONDAY EVENING, still moving with stupefied calm, I said goodnight to Ben, who'd driven me home. I greeted Gracie and fed her. There was my apple, with a bite missing. I ate it. I phoned Andrew in Ohio and told him that his father and brother were both in the hospital. I listened to Lezley's increasingly tense phone messages as she searched for me, and Jacob's message about his own trip to the hospital ("I'm fine!"). I left messages for two people with whom Edward had Tuesday appointments, saying I thought he might be out of work all week. I phoned my closest friends. I wrote emails to the other Ordinary Evening organizers. I cancelled the visit to the high school. I walked the dog around the block—one of Edward's jobs—and decided I needed a cup of cocoa. Then I fell into bed with the dog's warm fur next to me, and scarcely slept. Maybe I cried, finally. After that day I cried convulsively, for minutes at a time, without warning, several times a day—at home, at Edward's bedside, in the elevator, in the hospital cafeteria. Nobody seemed to notice, which was fine.

In the morning I called our dog sitter and asked her to drop in on Gracie in the afternoons for the next two days. (After that I left notes for her, extending and extending the time. I ran out of checks to pay her, and Edward had no checks in the checkbook I found in the blood-stained pants in his hospital room, and we had forgotten to order checks. The problem seemed unsurmountable.) That Tuesday, I ate breakfast and walked Gracie. She'd been fine at night but was worried in the morning, and showed it by throwing up. Ben picked me up and we drove to the hospital. As we walked to the elevator I looked forward to telling Edward about the calls I'd made, the emails I'd written, how Gracie missed him so much she threw up. He is the person to whom I tell things.

But when we had rung the doorbell and eventually been admitted to the MICU—it always took a long time, even if you'd gone out for only a few minutes—Ben and I found Edward sedated, being looked after by a laconic nurse who was manipulating tubes and speaking only numbers. A physician's assistant and another nurse spoke to me kindly or less kindly ("Your husband is very sick") but told me only facts I already knew. Everyone seemed anxious. Edward was delirious and having trouble breathing through a face mask. Fluid he'd been given in the emergency room had leaked into his lungs. His fever was 103 degrees. The staff seemed to believe that I'd need reassurance—which they provided over and over—that delirium was not his fault.

Gradually, I learned that Edward, the world's mildest man (if you want him to get angry you have to scream at him, "You should be angry! Why aren't you angry?") had thrashed and hit at them, and it had taken four or five people to hold him down. Now, when he started to wake up, he struggled with his restraints and heaved himself in the bed. Nurses came running and held him, which agitated him more. One nurse said angrily, "We need a doctor!" They wanted permission to sedate him more heavily.

The next day a nurse told me they'd thought he was an alcoholic. "We knew *nothing*!" she said. (But why did they know nothing? Edward had told the doctor, that first night, quite a bit about himself, including his drinking habits. We'd habitually drunk one glass of wine with dinner but had stopped not long before: I because I thought wine might be giving me headaches; Edward because he's a companionable guy. I never saw that doctor again. What did he do with his knowledge?)

Now a physician's assistant told me that in "the worst case scenario" they'd put a breathing tube down Edward's throat, and minutes later they did put a breathing tube down his throat, while Ben and I were ejected. In an alcove near the elevators where cell phones worked, he called Jacob, who had been released from the hospital. Again, we rang the doorbell to beg for admission. Later, Ben went to work briefly. I went downstairs to eat and make phone calls. The cafeteria confused me, with food stations and cashiers at odd angles, and I'd set off with my tray, each time, in the wrong direction. Over the next days I figured out how to acquire a tuna sandwich or soup, how to pay. I'd eat quickly and return.

Wearing a blue gauze gown and gloves, I sat and looked at my husband. I wasn't supposed to talk to him. His pulse was high, his blood pressure low. When the nurse wasn't looking I kissed his forehead. Because of the breathing tube, even when Edward woke up briefly, he couldn't speak. He was not delirious. His closest friend appeared, having talked his way in (only immediate family were allowed). Ben returned. Jacob and his wife, Jill, came in one at a time.

Late that afternoon I asked the nurse what Edward's temperature was. "99.6."

"But that's good!" I said. Why hadn't she told me?

"Yes," she said tensely, "it's good," but her tone seemed to say, "Oh you fool, if you only understood what *isn't* good!"

But what, exactly? I was frantic for knowledge but didn't know how to get it. Still, the improved temperature made me optimistic—briefly—and while I ate my supper I left a message about it on Jacob's cell phone. By the time I went home—after the night nurse had also refused to share my optimism—I was afraid again.

MEANWHILE, THE Ordinary Evening reading happened without me. I'd planned and imagined my complicated week in so much detail that now, part of me thought it was happening as I had expected it to happen: in an alternate reality, Alice was writing, eating oatmeal, baking scones, meeting Doug at the train station, introducing his reading, putting sheets on the spare bed on our third floor. Apparently there were two Alices and one was stuck in hospital land, where there was no color except for light blue pillows, pads, and gowns, and the blue plaid restraining belts. Everything else was neutral, white or vaguely tan. Stepping from the MICU to go down to the cafeteria, I found myself staring at a visitor's red coat in the elevator. I didn't leave the hospital for ten or eleven hours a day, and the outside world, its detail and variety—its life—astonished me each evening. Somewhere in this welter, that first night, was the real Alice—clapping for Doug, eating dinner with that happy group.

Wednesday morning I noticed my three Bartlett pears, now yellow, on a plate in our kitchen. They'd be overripe soon. It was tempting to leave them, so the Alice who'd be writing her novel that morning—the one who'd be feeling toward Edward not the desperate cherishing that made my chest hurt now, but tolerant fondness, or irritation, or the pleasure of shared amusement—could cut one up and eat it on her oatmeal. But of course that pear would be right where I left it, proceeding toward rot, if I didn't eat it or take it with me. I didn't feel like eating a pear for breakfast. I cut it in quarters and put it into a small plastic bag. It would taste fine, though juice would make it sticky.

The Wednesday nurse, a man with a long ponytail, said something friendly and I burst into tears, then demanded more information, and he arranged for Ben and me to listen in on rounds. Hearing what the doctors and nurses said to one another was infinitely better than hearing the single, useless sentence they'd eventually tell me. A doctor, a young Asian-American woman, explained what they were doing and why. I began to understand that Edward's breathing problems were at least as serious as his infection. She was sober but vigorous, and for each conceivable eventuality she named a remedy. I noted that she never said, "And we wouldn't be able to do anything about *that*." Later the pony-tailed nurse looked hard at me and said, "We will get him better. He will recover fully. This is treatable." I don't think he was supposed to talk to me that way—nobody else did—but though the reassurance didn't last, it was bliss.

The bed appeared to inflate and deflate. As I stared at Edward, he would sink. (I never saw him rise.) Wednesday they let him wake up a little. They let me talk to him. Whenever he awakened, his hand would move toward the breathing tube. I'd ask, "Do you want to know what happened?" He'd nod. "You're in Yale-New Haven Hospital. You have an infection. You had trouble breathing, so they put this tube down your throat. It feels awful, but you need it now." Edward, in *his* real life, is appalled that high-tech medicine is expensive and elitist, often unavailable to people without insurance. If he could talk, I knew, he'd demand that they let him go home to his dog. As things were, he slept, wakened, reached for the tube. His blood pressure was low, supported with medication.

In the course of the morning, I ate some of the pear. I made notes in my notebook. I looked at him. Ben, a steady comfort, came and went. I ate lunch, finished the pear, had coffee, had supper. I hated leaving at night, because when I was away from Edward, I didn't know for sure he was alive. But once home, I was grateful to be there, checking phone messages and emails, eating ice cream, and going to sleep with Gracie on Edward's side of the bed.

I cut up the second pear on Thursday. A tall nurse, Amy, with earnest eyes set close together, told me that later that day they'd find out if Edward could manage without the ventilator. They had been reducing the amount of oxygen he received, but pressure from the machine still helped him breathe. If the level of oxygen in his blood didn't drop when the machine was turned off, they could remove the tube. He'd be able to talk and eat, and could bear to be awake for more than seconds at a time.

He was less sedated and more awake already, and Amy wanted to know if he could nod his head appropriately for yes and shake it for no.

109

"Is this your sister?" she shouted at Edward, pointing at me. He'd nod yes. "Do you clean toilets?" Amy shouted, trying to elicit a no. He nodded.

Her questions must have been confusing to someone barely awake. Was she asking him to clean a toilet? If it would help, of course he would. "Edward," I said, "this nurse thinks you can't shake your head no. Shake your head no for me." He did. Then I said, "I'm going to ask you questions. If the answer is yes, nod your head. If it's no, shake your head no." He looked interested and slightly amused, raising his eyebrows.

"Do we have three dogs?" I asked, and he shook his head.

"Do we have *two* dogs?" Again he shook his head.

"Do we have *one* dog?" He nodded.

"Shakes his head appropriately for yes and no," Amy said, and went to write it down. I went to lunch happy: Edward and I had had a conversation, and one that joined us and excluded the nurse. Soon they'd see if he could do without the ventilator. And his pulse and blood pressure were normal without medication. As if a peephole had been widened, I noticed that the unit he was in was twice as large as I'd thought. To get to his room I turned left when the locked door opened, but straight ahead was a similar corridor I had not seen. At lunch, I left hopeful phone messages for my friends.

In the afternoon, a respiratory therapist warned me not to be disappointed if Edward couldn't do without the machine the first time they tried, and I believed I understood the situation well enough that I would not be disappointed. She turned off the machine. Edward was awake. I encouraged him to breathe. He could bring up the oxygen in his blood, I saw from looking at the monitor, by taking deep breaths. But always, the number dropped. After a while, they turned the machine back on. The therapist told me again not to be upset.

I was upset and frightened. That afternoon he was more awake. When we were alone I said, "You're going to be all right," and Edward shook his head no. "No?" I said. "Do you think you're dying?"

He nodded. "You're not dying. You're going to be fine!" I said, but I didn't believe myself. He cried. "Don't you *dare* die," I said, but I was afraid he knew something.

That night I'd arranged for a friend to pick me up at 8:30. At 8:25 I was about to leave; Edward was asleep. Suddenly the monitor behind him began making loud noises. Red lights flashed. His pulse was 193. "Nurse!" I screamed, bursting into tears. I was afraid she'd throw me out—this was yet another new nurse—and I flattened myself into the chair. People appeared. The nurse gave orders. Edward's pulse slowed. Somebody went to check something. When things were quiet again, I ran down to the lobby to send my friend home. I went back upstairs and stayed until 10:00. They discovered Edward's potassium phosphates were low, and added another dripping plastic bag. Again, he was peaceful, sleeping. I took a taxi home, fed and walked Gracie, glumly answered cheerful messages that responded to the optimistic ones I'd left at lunchtime.

At three A.M. the phone awakened me. Edward had pulled out the breathing tube despite the hand restraints. A doctor began a methodical account of what happened next, how they tried to re-insert the tube but Edward's throat was swollen closed, what else they tried. I interrupted. "Is he alive?" I said.

"He is alive," said the doctor, and continued. After four minutes when Edward had no air, he had performed a tracheotomy. Now another doctor came to the phone; he said he'd been one of the people in the room when Edward's pulse went up, and I remembered him, a thin black man who had glanced at me kindly. He was kind again, but could tell me little. He said, "Do you have any questions?"

"What I want to know, you don't know the answer to," I said. I asked him if I should come there immediately, and he said no.

I hung up. I couldn't call anyone at three in the morning. I was afraid of the dark—I turned the light on—afraid the phone would ring again with more bad news, some additional problem I hadn't known enough to worry about. I was sure Edward was going to die—from the next setback if not from this one—and thought about what that would be like, how the life we knew had ended, how much Edward would not want to die. He always has long lists of projects, most having to do with making government more responsive and helpful to poor or disabled people, and he carries out a surprising number of them, step by step. When he takes a shower, he uses up all the hot water as he figures out a new scheme, or solves the problems that have arisen in one he's already working on, always talking to himself or to the people in his way. He was too busy to die, but the obituary pages are full of people too busy to die.

As for me, what I thought about was not how much I loved Edward—of course I loved him—but how he had been the other side of thought for so long that even though I am often alone and have frequently looked forward to times without him, it was because I assumed that sooner or later he'd be around again. With him dead, I would be only part of a person.

Toward morning it occurred to me that maybe Edward would not die. Maybe the tracheotomy would have solved that problem, and there would be no more terrifying problems. It seemed unlikely, but possible. The doctor had said he might be brain damaged. I imagined my willingness to care for a damaged Edward. Finally I slept briefly.

But when Ben and I arrived at the hospital that Friday, morning—I brought the third pear—things were not worse but better. With a tube in his neck instead of a tube down his throat, Edward looked like himself and was more comfortable. At rounds, the sober, careful doctor sounded confident. Edward's numbers were all good—pulse, blood pressure. His fever was not gone but down, and the bacteria in his blood had been identified, so he was getting a more exactly targeted antibiotic. The tracheotomy, despite the horror and risk of it, made things easier. He woke up delighted to see people. He still could not talk because all air entered and left through his neck, but he could write shakily on a pad. "Hell . . ." he wrote.

"Hell on earth?" I tried. "Helluva thing?" He waved my guesses away. Finally Ben and I deciphered the shaky writing: *hallucinations*. (Later Edward told me that space aliens had gathered around his bed, looking at him.) I noted that he had remembered the word, and almost remembered how to spell it; maybe he wasn't brain damaged. As the day progressed he wrote more and his hand shook less. Jacob came in and I thought his father wouldn't remember that he too had been in the hospital, but Edward applauded, then tapped his own chest and looked expectant. Jacob reassured him.

That Friday I noticed that the elevator reached the fifth floor quickly because there was no "4," that pictures of East Rock Park, where we walk every day, hung on the corridor wall, and that the atrium on the ground floor—an indoor space that pretends it's outdoors, with trees and skylights—contained ungainly flowers along with its sofas and tables.

I ate the third pear with my coffee, looking around the atrium. I had caught up to myself, and knew where I was—where we were. Edward was able to manage without the ventilator the next day, and was moved to a "step-down" unit, then into a regular hospital bed. A cap over the tube in his neck enabled him to talk and eat. We chose food for him from the hospital menu and I ordered it on the phone. Food tasted bad because he was on steroids for the swelling in his throat (the steroids also caused temporary diabetes), then less bad. Andrew flew from Ohio and they talked; Andrew persuaded me to go with him to a restaurant for dinner. National and world events took on detail again, and whether society should spend money on heroic medicine for a few instead of preventive care for many became, once more, an interesting moral question. When Jacob's children visited, I had lunch with them in the cafeteria, and for the first time didn't just gulp my food and hurry back. "You love the children more than me," Edward teased when I returned to his room, where he and Andrew had been discussing some complicated topic.

Now Edward was wild to go home, and the doctor was about to agree when he was diagnosed with pneumonia. One more antibiotic—his fifth—brought a new fever down, and then he did come home. The next day he had the tube removed from his neck. He slept all day each day, then not quite all day. I cooked, straightened up, walked Gracie. The weather became warmer, and forsythias and daffodils bloomed. Edward could walk several blocks, read a little, check email. I longed to write my novel, but was amazed at what I had: the sound of his grunts and sighs, his footsteps. One day we walked to an Italian market near our house and had coffee and cookies at an outside table with a yellow umbrella above it. I went inside and bought three Bosc pears, watched them get ripe, ate them for lunch with oatmeal.

Nominated by Lloyd Schwartz

MAN ON THE DUMP

by DONALD PLATT

from ALASKA QUARTERLY REVIEW

The man thrown on the garbage heap in Baghdad's Ghazaliya neighborhood
        is not Wallace Stevens's
"man on the dump." He is and is not *stanza my stone*. The photographer

        with the wide-angled lens
had to get down on his knees as if he were praying in the roadside dirt
        to shoot the man

in the sand-colored wool slacks, still crisply creased
        from the cleaners,
their pockets turned inside out. The man's hands are tied

        behind his white-shirted back
with thick black electrical wire. The bound hands, which are the center
        of the photograph, have turned

blue. Well manicured, his blue nails have been trimmed and filed down
        with an emery board.
One hand loosely clasps the other. I let my eyes detour

        to the garbage strewn around
the man — clear plastic bottles with orange tops, empty tuna fish cans,
        turquoise wrapping paper,

114

white styrofoam boxes in which something fragile must have been shipped.
                    I look away
along the long dirt highway, no traffic, along the dead power lines

                    to the block of apartment buildings
hazy on the horizon in early morning light. But my eyes always
                    return to the blue hands

of the man lying on his side, slumped over so I do not see
                    his face. Only his back,
buttocks, stout legs, and feet stripped of their shoes but still wearing

                    their expensive, beige, silk socks.
Let the atrocious images haunt us, Susan Sontag argues and urges
                    in her last book.

At sixteen I saw for the first time one of Chaim Soutine's
                    paintings of beef
carcasses. The headless body was hung upside down

                    by its hind legs
and trussed with rope to a black beam. I looked into the gutted
                    chest cavity and found

a relief map of red, ocher, and blue slashes, swirls,
                    gobs, and gouts of paint
laid down to suggest the fresh, flayed meat. The red ribcage

                    quivered against the blue
background. It was stained glass for a slaughterhouse, hell's cathedral.
                    Soutine poured buckets of blood

bought from a butcher over the carcass to keep the raw flesh
                    red. He painted it
for weeks. The stench made his neighbor vomit and call the police.

                    "Art is more
important than sanitation," Soutine insisted and persuaded them
                    to let him keep

painting. "Once I saw the village butcher slice the neck
of a bird and drain the blood
out of it," he told his biographer. "I wanted to cry out.

This cry, I always feel
it here." He patted his throat. "When I painted the beef carcass, it was still
this cry that I wanted

to liberate. I have still not succeeded." *Let the atrocious
images haunt us.*
Sontag couldn't bear to look at Titian's painting of the flaying

of Marsyas, at how
the satyr too is hung upside down from a tree. Apollo,
laurel-crowned, is gently

starting to peel back the skin below Marsyas's left nipple
with his long hunting knife.
The blood runs down Marsyas's left arm, over his bound

hands, to the ground
where a lapdog licks it up. A faun holds a wooden bucket.
Is it to collect

the blood? Or does it contain water for Marsyas to drink
so he won't faint
and will not fail to feel the pain of being flayed alive?

Under the tree, a young man
in a rose robe draws his bow over a *lira da braccio*,
early version of the viola.

String music will only partially muffle Marsyas's screams.
His panpipes hang
from a new-leafed branch. Why does sunlight turn his muscled torso

to the color of honey?
I cannot see the face of the man on the dump. He could be
Shiite or Sunni.

116

He could be the younger son of Ahmed Ali, a carpenter
        famous for making lutes.
When Ahmed went to the morgue to identify the body

        of his older son killed
a year ago, he saw holes drilled through the knee, ankle, wrist,
        and elbow joints.

His younger son, thirty years old, is missing. "I made lutes
        and sometimes
I played," says Ahmed, "but my fingers are numb now.

        I cannot play.
I want only to find my kidnapped son." Waiting for his son to return,
        Ahmed has carved

a bowl from flawed spalted wood. It holds sunlight and rotted
        persimmons
that blue flies buzz about and orbit without end.

Nominated by Alaska Quarterly Review and Jane Hirshfield

COWBOYS

fiction by SUSAN STEINBERG

from AMERICAN SHORT FICTION

There are some who say I did not kill my father.

Not technically they mean.

But the ones who say I did not kill my father are the ones who want to have sex with me.

They say I did not kill my father because they cannot have sex with a woman who killed.

What I mean is they cannot have sex with a woman who carries, like all women carry, an unbearable weight.

So they mix me another drink, they laugh, they say, You did not kill your father.

What they think they believe and what they truly believe: two different things.

I am still able to lie there nights, but I am unable to do much more than that.

Meaning I am still able to lie there nights, but I am unable to stick around in the mornings.

Meaning I am unable to lie there pretending I want what it is certain women want.

Because of this and because of that. And I cannot pretend to be anything other than the result of this and that.

When the doctor called at 4 a.m., waked me at 4 a.m. from a dream I can almost remember, something about chasing dogs in a field, something about a fence, he introduced himself as the doctor.

He said, I am Doctor Such and Such, in this uptight voice, this doctor's voice, and I laughed and said, You're who. I said, Who is this.

My brother was also on the line, and my brother was in Boston, and the doctor was in Baltimore, and I was in a place called Warrensburg, Missouri. I was in Warrensburg, Missouri, for a job I was trying to quit. When I mention Warrensburg, Missouri, people say, Where the fuck is that.

I tell them there are cowboys. I tell them there are tornadoes that can carry your house across the state. There are brown recluse spiders, I tell them, in every corner of every room. It's a shit hole, I tell them.

And there I was in it, trying my best to sleep right through it, a doctor telling me, at 4 a.m., to please be serious.

I was not always serious, and somehow the doctor already knew this, knew perhaps because I laughed when he said he was the doctor. Or he knew perhaps because my brother told him I would not be serious. Or he knew perhaps because when he told me to kill my father, I laughed again.

He did not, of course, use the word *kill*. He had another word, a series of words, a more technical way of wording.

The doctor sounded exhausted, and my brother sounded exhausted. My brother and his wife had a one-year-old boy. The boy was always crying in the background. My brother was always saying, Shh.

My brother always had circles under his eyes. They were bluish, the circles, and they made him look beaten down.

You look like dad, I said to him once.

Fuck you, he said to me more than once.

We were no longer kids and this was a serious matter. The doctor had been up all night.

Trying to save your father, he said.

To no avail, he said, and I wondered at the word *avail*, wondered if the doctor got to be a doctor because of whatever it was he had that made him use the word *avail*.

I wanted something to eat. I wanted to run downstairs in the massive house I was renting in Warrensburg, Missouri, and root through the refrigerator for the leftovers. The leftovers were in takeout containers, and I wanted to bring them up to my bed, switch on the TV, move into that blue-lit space.

The doctor said my father had flatlined several times, and I knew the word *flatlined* from my ex who had flatlined three times when we were together. He had flatlined, my ex, because he was an addict, and being an addict, as it turns out, will make one flatline. After the first flatline, my mother, a nurse, said, He'll never be the same. But he was

119

the same, as it turned out, because he flatlined again. After the third flatline, we broke up. I'd like to say we broke up because I'd had enough of his flatlining, but really he broke up with me for another woman, a thinner woman, a paler woman, the veins too vivid through her face, and she eventually flatlined too, and she eventually died from this, but he did not.

He became a firefighter.

I moved to Warrensburg, Missouri.

The whole world just went on.

The doctor said my father would be a vegetable, and upon hearing this word, I imagined a plate; I imagined vegetables on this plate.

One does not want to imagine this. One wants to imagine one's father spinning through a field, arms spread, something dynamic like that.

Even something totally made up like that.

My father would never have spun through a field.

He was mad, yes, but he was not that kind of mad. He was not that kind of happy mad. He was the other kind. He was ferocious.

And besides, what field. And where.

It was Baltimore where we all were before we all weren't, and there were no fields, just streets of nothing and more nothing, just my ex knocking on some boarded-up door, just me waiting in the car.

But here, where I was now, where I am no longer, Warrensburg, Missouri, there were fields.

The doctor said my name.

He said, Please.

My brother said my name.

I had a decision to make. I had a serious decision to make, because I was the oldest kid. Though, as stated, I was not the most serious of the two. And my serious brother with his serious boy screaming his head off in some dark room in their serious city, was waiting for me to do the right thing.

This was years ago, and I'm telling you this because the story came to me today just for no real reason, just because I happened to see a guy digging around in the trash, and I was like, You again. I was like, Get out of there. Get out my head, I was like.

And I'm telling you this, because some have been wondering why I am the way I am.

Which is to say a whirlwind.

Which is to say a lot of things.

I could not at first kill my father. I at first said no. I said, Not as long as he's still breathing.

But he isn't breathing, said the doctor.

Not technically, he said.

The doctor sounded fed up. And not fed up with the limitations of science. And not fed up with the limitations of the human body.

Meaning not fed up how I was.

A man I knew in Warrensburg, Missouri, a man I knew from the job I needed to quit, had been bitten by a brown recluse. He'd rolled over it one night in bed and got bitten in the ass. When he told me the story I laughed. I was like, Why were you naked. He was like, Wrong question. Because he was trying to tell me the bite dissolved the skin on his ass. Because he was trying to tell me that this just wasn't right.

The technical term is necrotized.

The point is I was not always serious.

No, the point is we're limited.

The doctor said, A machine is making him breathe.

He did not use the word *machine*.

I said I would have to call my mother to get her advice, and my brother said, Don't be a dumbass, and the doctor sighed in that way that the assholes I have dated since sigh when they do not get what they want.

Like the restaurant is out of chicken wings. Like the beer is flat. Like I'm trying to convince them I'm a terrible person. Like I'm already stepping into my skirt. Like I'm already reaching for the doorknob, a bigger whore than they want me to be.

They sigh and it applies pressure to the woman. And the woman is then supposed to give them what they want.

Which is to say the woman is then supposed to perform.

Which is to say the woman is then supposed to know the subtle difference between being a woman and performing one.

I said, I'm calling my mother.

My brother said, Don't.

I thought I could get her on the line. I didn't know if it would work. It involved disconnecting the call. It involved dialing her number. It involved reconnecting the call, hoping everyone was still on the line. What I mean is it involved a certain kind of trust.

The metaphor is unintentional.

I mean of disconnection.

There were many machines in the world all operating at once. All whirring and shaking at once. There are always all these machines in the world whirring and shaking and making it all go. There is always, therefore, the option of disconnection.

There is no intentional meaning in this story.

I would not subject you to intentional meaning.

I would not subject you to some grand scheme.

My mother was in Miami. Which wasn't where she should have been. But I wasn't where I should have been. No one was when you think about it. I mean when you really think about it. I don't mean anything deep about anything deep. I just mean I was confused. And yet, I disconnected, pressed some buttons, and there was my mother. And I reconnected, and there we all were.

I said, They want me to kill dad.

My mother had left my father thirty years before. There is no reason to go into the details. Suffice it to say it was his fault, as if that wasn't already clear.

As if that wasn't already totally clear.

I mean look at me.

Look at my history.

I mean I was not calling my mother because she loved my father. I was not even calling her because she was my mother. I was calling her because she was a nurse. I hoped that because she was a nurse she would tell me the right thing to do. I'm not talking morally. I'm talking medically. She knew about this. Though of course once she was wrong. I mean once she was dead wrong. I mean when my ex flatlined the first time. I mean when she said, He'll never be the same. She was of course dead wrong. I mean he was one hundred percent the same. I mean he was one hundred percent the same in every way.

Impossible, a doctor might have said.

Not impossible, I might have said.

He was a vegetable going under, a vegetable coming back.

But his heart, a doctor might have said.

I might have laughed.

I might have said something regrettable.

My mother said, What.

My brother said, Tell her.

The doctor said, He flatlined.

My mother said, You have to kill him.

She did not, of course, use these words. I don't know why I'm being so melodramatic. She used technical terms. She said, Take him off the respirator. She said, It's the right thing to do. She said, Trust me. She said, I need to go though. She said, I need to get to work. She said, I'm sorry.

And because I more often than not do the wrong thing, I said fine.

A few days later, because I was the oldest, because the decision was mine, I would donate my father's body to science. I would do this over the phone, and the conversation would be recorded. A woman would ask me questions I had not before this heard.

Do you wish to donate the lungs.

Do you wish to donate the heart.

There were other organs one doesn't think of.

There were other things besides organs.

The tissue was to go to the tissue bank.

The eyes were to go to the eye bank.

There were other things I can't remember.

But it was on the eyes, at the thought of the eyes removed from the head, the thought of the eyes going their own way, that I started to cry.

This was not about anything deep. I was not suddenly a believer of the soul. I was not suddenly a believer of anything.

It was just think about it.

And when I started to cry, the woman said, It's OK, said, Let it out, and I stopped crying and sat there, silent, and the recording just went, just recorded my breathing, the woman's breathing, the sounds of static in the phone, and minutes passed.

And I thought for some reason of a night years before, me, my father, and my brother in some fast food place. The fast food place was in a parking lot, and my brother was visiting home from college, and he was sticking his French fries into his milkshake, and I said, Sick, and he said, Fuck you, and I said, Fuck you, and he said, Try it dumbass, and I stuck a French fry into the milkshake, and it was amazing. There was something about the salty and sweet. Or the hot and cold. I don't know what it was. My father was poor then, poorer the next day, poorer the next day, poorer the next day, living in some shit hole then, like a hostel, like a hospital, like a halfway house, and my brother said he would take him to dinner. Anywhere you want, he said. My father wanted to go to the fast food place. He met us there. He was filthy. His shirt was missing buttons. He ordered two cheeseburgers. He ordered onion rings. He ordered an orange soda. He ate too fast. And watching us stick French fries into the milkshake, he said, You're both sick. But then he tried it too, and then he laughed, and then we ordered more French fries and another milkshake, and what I'm trying to say is you should try it. What I'm trying to say is. What I'm trying to say is.

I did not donate the eyes to the eye bank. At some point I said, I can't. I don't know why.

The parts that didn't go to science were burned. And no I did not want the ashes. I told the woman to send the ashes to my brother. Because my brother was a better person than I was. He was a total asshole, I told the woman, but he was still a better person than I was. I said, He's a total asshole. But in the grand scheme, I said. In the big grand scheme, I said. And I laughed, meaning I really laughed, and the recording went on, and the woman cleared her throat, and I just kept on going.

The day the ashes arrived, my brother called me and said, What the fuck, and I said, What, and he said, What the fuck, and I said Grow up.

There are no more details to tell.

There is no reason to go into the why of my father.

Or the why of madness, which I cannot answer.

Or the why of addiction, which I also cannot answer.

Or the why of poor, which I also cannot answer.

Suffice it to say it's always about a loss of something. Then a loss of some things. Then a loss of all things.

Then he was already dead, some might say.

What do you mean, I might say back.

If he had already lost everything, some might say, then he was already dead.

Yes, I might say.

Then you didn't kill him, some might say as they move toward me.

That's not the point.

Then what is.

The doctor said he was sorry for our loss.

My brother said, You did the right thing.

Then a lot of serious shit happened in a lot of serious places. My mother drove to work. The doctor flipped a switch. My brother made coffee. The sun rose somewhere, set somewhere else. A brown recluse hunched in the dust.

And the truth is I don't always leave in the mornings.

Some mornings the guy wants to get to work, and so I have to leave, but the truth is I don't want to.

Some mornings I'm still lying in their beds, and they're like, You need to leave, and I just lie there staring at their backs.

Some mornings I note the ribcage. I note the organs seething beneath the ribcage. I note the fragility of what does not, at night, seem fragile.

Some mornings I am not the whore they want me to be.

I am not the killer they want me to be.

Some mornings I try to no avail. To absolutely no avail. To no avail I try, and they get up to make coffee, and I get up and step into my skirt, and I pull on my shirt, and I walk the shortest way home.

And the woman performs happy woman on a sunny street.

The woman performs this all feels good this all feels really good.

The woman pulls it together. She pulls it tight. She further tightens that which tightens.

There were late nights he would call from a payphone, a friend's house, a hospital, a halfway house, and because it was late, and because I was not poor, and because I was not ferociously mad, but, rather, mad mad, a machine answered my phone and lied that I wasn't there eating in bed, watching TV, lied that I would return the call.

The machine would then say, Hello, stranger.

The machine would then say, It's your father, stranger.

There were voices in the background.

There was traffic in the background.

I'm OK, stranger, the machine would then say.

There was screaming in the background.

There was me in my bedroom.

Pick up the phone, the machine would say loudly.

I know you're there, the machine would say louder.

There was me turning the TV all the way up.

There was every poor soul looking downward.

There was me not believing in the soul.

There was me waiting, counting seconds, staring at the wall.

My mother said goodbye and disconnected first. Then the doctor said goodbye and disconnected. After the doctor disconnected, there was silence, but I said, Hello. I was hoping my brother was still on the line. I wanted to laugh or something. I said hello again, but my brother had disconnected too.

And before I ran downstairs to the massive kitchen that was my kitchen, I sat on the edge of my bed, still holding the phone.

I imagined the doctor arriving home that morning.

I imagined the doctor taking off his scrubs, washing his hands, and climbing into bed with his beautiful wife.

I imagined him easing into his wife's heat, the way I once eased into my ex's heat.

Before we had a sense of what came next.

Before we had a sense that something came next.

Firefighting.

Warrensburg, Missouri.

Me in my bed eating cold lo mein.

Me eating egg rolls, watching TV.

There was no grand scheme.

You have to trust me.

I would quit my job. I would leave that shit hole. I would cross the state line. I would cross another. I would cross another.

And here I am now in a different state.

And there is the man digging through the trash.

And there is the gem buried in the mess.

Listen. It was not a shit hole.

It was not that.

Call it what you will, but there were cowboys there, for God's sake, standing on corners in the biggest hats you have ever seen.

There were tornadoes that would send you into space.

There were spiders that would necrotize your ass.

There was a sky turning light. The same sky as everywhere turning light.

Call it what you will, but there I was, same as you were, under that sky.

There I was just some poor soul. Same as you.

Nominated by American Short Fiction and Lance Olsen

DECEMBER, FEVER

by JOY KATZ

from PLOUGHSHARES

A tang approaches, like the smell of snow.
Illness like a color deepens—
pale gray, thick-in-a-cloak gray, secret coat silk,
and finally the weight of rough pelts heaped on the bed.

The last enchantment of the day is tearing pages out of a book.
The paper soft and thin, like falling asleep
(a hand backstage at school smoothing my hair:
a boy named Lakamp, who became an undertaker)

My baby laughs to rip the pages.
Stays by me, does this damage.
The tearing moves like voltage through my own hands.

> *Oh mother skimming fever*

I need him to linger

> *are you still happening there, in your body?*

I just want to lie at the edge of breaking.

Yes, I am still backstage, here in my body.
The baby pulls out another page—
leaving him would come this easily.

127

I will bind myself to the thinnest sounds,
the feather coming out of the pillow.

Please keep ripping up the words.
Please don't need anything from me.

Nominated by Sharon Dolin, Kevin Prufer

HOSTS

by SUSANNE ANTONETTA

from IMAGE

MY SON AT TWELVE believes in the Greek gods. Zeus, Athena. Jin favors Poseidon and Ares but likes them all. He can tell intricate stories, like the one about Baucis and Philemon, an old couple who took in Mercury and Jupiter disguised as travelers. A thousand villagers had turned the gods away, and a thousand were punished. The old couple gave the gods all the hospitality their poverty could offer, even wiping their aged table with mint. Of course, Baucis and Philemon had a great reward: priesthoods in life, preserved together for eternity.

Jin and I have decided that he's a classical polytheist. It distinguishes him from our coastal Northwest hippie town's many New Age pagans, who believe in a loose polytheism—whales as spirits, firs as spirits, even aliens as spirits—and who he does not want to be associated with at all. In spite of his Olympian obsessions, we all go to church, and always have. I suppose he sits there and thinks his own thoughts.

We currently go to a Korean Baptist church, though my husband and I remain Catholic, because our son is Korean—adopted—and loves the church community, and so do we. We were shyly invited by Jongsu, the mother of one of Jin's taekwondo friends. My family speaks very little Korean, though we're trying to learn. The adults at this tiny church speak little English, while the kids have grown into that language and lost the old one. It's a two-tone Babel. The children have their service in English, led by a man in his twenties with a guitar. Pastor Kim also speaks to them briefly, in bits of English mixed with bits of Korean. The first week we went he told them to insert the Holy Spirit into themselves like a game cartridge, so it would become part of their operating system—*Nintendo-inmida, do Nintendo,* we heard. The kids then go into another room where they sneak candy from some occult source and play foosball.

Our service begins: women beautifully made up, in suits, with Chanel handbags and hair upswept or held back in jeweled barrettes, men in jackets.

Kituinmida, says Pastor Kim: let us pray. We've got that phrase down. Most of what he says settles in our ears as a chant, repetitive at the end of the sentence and rising in pitch, as Koreans place verbs at the last position and these generally end on vowels. Some words emerge because we know our Bible well enough—*Absalom,* the preacher said this Sunday, and while we were meant to understand we needed to behave like David, not Absalom, Absalom's was the only name I could make out. So for an hour and a half, under the track lighting, sitting in a folding chair, I thought about Absalom the wicked, who tried to take over, even betraying his father David. Who would not have welcomed gods into his home unless forced by their Olympian radiance to know them.

We hear some things in church because of borrowings from English—*crossinmida,* to do the cross, to be crucified. *Yes-su Christo.* Mostly we sit, praying and standing and bowing our heads when others do, in the hallucinatory murmur, cadence of end vowel and rising pitch, Lord and Father, *Chonim* and *Abaji.*

The Korean church members feel for us. Services run long—an hour and a half at least—and the preacher still stops at the end and gamely and haltingly tries to explain in English what he has been preaching about. We are not to be Absaloms, he tells us, though I've done nothing but try to remember all I can about Absalom or think a dreamy nothing, studying the curves and angles of *hangul,* the Korean alphabet, strung along the wall.

I want to tell him there's no need for this explanation: let everyone scoop up their children from the foosball. He has succeeded in what he wanted to do. Once Pastor Kim began gesticulating toward a TV screen set up in front of the room and I recognized Susan Boyle, improbable breakout star of *Britain's Got Talent.* I know the drill: get the congregation interested by bringing in topical things, pop culture. I have never liked hearing a priest begin with a story of the latest attention-grabbing television, or something funny his little nephew said at Thanksgiving. God may sometimes be willing to come down to our size, but we do not need to prune.

What did the gods say to Baucis and Philemon? They sat in the couple's cottage for a long time, Jupiter and Mercury, the caduceus disguised as a walking stick. With torn clothes, filthy feet, playing the role of vagrants. The gods seemed to do these things to amuse themselves. They watched as Baucis made a fire from twigs, Philemon cut a piece of fatty pork and simmered it with vegetables and potherbs. They ate olives, Ovid says, and dried figs. Did the gods mention how hot the weather had been lately, how Sparta had outrun Athens, they heard on the road, in an improbable last plunge? Baucis and Philemon, who grew their food and raised a little livestock, probably mentioned how the year had been for their crops. Ovid details the food meticulously but skips over the conversation. It's okay: the gods came for good cheer and small talk. And the couple's piety—no doubt the two asked the gods to join them in consecrating their simple meal to those whom they in fact were about to feed.

The word was in the beginning, John writes, opening salvo, necessary scrim. For the women so beautifully dressed. Korean passages on the walls we know enough of to identify the book of the Bible or the gospel author and chapter. The apostles would sleep, in the garden, in Korean.

Members of the congregation—sometimes men, but usually women—stand up from time to time, praying and crying. Some women come in before the service to pray, and they sit in metal chairs, swaying backward and forward, and keen, in a deep monotone pulled from someplace below the vocal chords and even the heart. They remind me of images of Mary, the sway picked up from a motion left in the ether, the keen a broad ontological distress.

"It seems weird at first," Katie Peach, daughter of Jongsu, confided to Jin about the keening, "but you get used to it."

My husband mentioned to me that people treat him as crazy for going to a church where he doesn't know the language. I get that reasoning; I thought it might be crazy too. The first time we went to our church—which I can't even name for you properly, because the name is written on the sign outside and in the bulletins in hangul—I expected to listen to ten minutes of language-blur, burning with self-consciousness, and flee.

But to be where we are feels more like prayer than prayer, and makes language seem an adding on your fingers, something to be used in order to be put out of the way. Saint John of the Cross wrote of God that ultimately, "even the act of prayer and communion, which was once carried on by reflections and other methods, is now wholly an act of loving." It's not new to think of mystical knowing and language as separate. It's a strange premise to take to church, with its sermon and print bulletins and writing on the wall. If we understood that the woman rising in her pleated skirt prayed for her job, it would still give little beyond the prayer of recognizing prayer: the face she hides behind her rounded oxblood nails, and her shaking shoulders. Too much knowledge reduces her cry to its smallest circumference, to all that is not-me.

At the end of our service we turn to one another and say, *I something you, I forgive you, I love you*, in Korean. I've never understood the first part, and I used to hear the formula as ending not with I love you—*saranghayo* —but with I am a person, I am only human—*saramhayo*, pretty garbled Korean it turns out, as it would mean I person you, though I confidently told my version to my husband.

Then we eat. The women have not only dressed impeccably, they have lugged in cookers full of steamed rice, spicy chicken, bulgogi, cold seaweed soup. We file into a kitchen set up with long, chipped tables, and they will not let Bruce and me fix our own plates, piling everything in bowls for us as if we're infants. They don't even believe my hot tongue. *Tashee, tashee*, I beg for more gochu jang, more pepper paste. You see, like Ovid, I can tell you everything about the food.

Sometimes my son, the happy pagan, seems to feel the need to hear my name.

Mom.

Yes?

Mom.

What?

Mom.

Jin.

Mom.

That's my name. Don't wear it out.

If I look at him I won't see a desire to tease me or bug me or much more than a half-blank look, a need to throw this verbal ball out and have me catch it. It's vital, I know, that I answer. I can say absolutely anything. He's lobbing a presence caught in that antique and comfortable sound.

Ovid included a strange touch at the end of the story of Baucis and Philemon. The gods revealed themselves slowly, causing the wine to refill itself in the bowl. When the couple realized whose presence they stood in, they threw themselves to the floor, begging apology. They had one other source of meat: a goose they had raised, improbably, to guard their hovel. They begged permission to kill the watch-goose and provide better, then took off in chase of the bird. But Ovid tells us that "quick-winged, it wore the couple out," not surprising, since he'd noted that Baucis's old breath was barely able to raise fire from her twigs. What the gods did while the old couple taxed themselves with pursuing a goose he does not say. One hopes they did not find the whole thing too funny. When the goose ran to take shelter with the gods, Jupiter and Mercury called a halt to the madness and gave the couple their reward.

How did the Romans, I wonder, read Ovid's story? Offer the best hospitality to whoever comes along, no matter how impoverished. Chase your geese. They too had a metaphoric understanding. Baucis and Philemon's story tells how to be a guest, taking what is offered kindly, not eying the fat fowl. When we mentioned how hard we have been trying to learn Korean, Jongsu insisted on teaching us, meeting us in the church dining room on Saturdays, using a children's book. *The shoe*, we read. *The kitten*. Nothing theological. She's patient with us as we do our strokes wrong, right to left or down to up rather than the opposite. It is very hard to believe she and the others want to do these things for us, as I can see it's hard for them to believe we want to be here, in the shaped silence. We are none of us gods.

Jin says the reason he believes in the pantheon is that he doesn't believe God can be everywhere. One god's not enough; he dreams of many. I get that, I tell him. It's hard to imagine. And if you can't imagine it—I don't say this—what stories you choose will trouble you anyway. That goose. Either the gods did not have the wherewithal to stop it, or it proved the vehicle by which they amused themselves at the expense of old-timers who'd laid beds for their exhaustion. Perhaps pain baffled the gods. Or joy in their creations' earnest absurdity formed a love of sorts.

I thought of Baucis and Philemon on Sunday, with women handing us plates of rice, spiced celery, bowls of soup with meat. The food drifted in all through the service: sweet-soy chili sauces, sesame oil. I can imagine the odor of spearmint rising from the table, pork cooking with rosemary and oregano. Baucis and Philemon even heated water and drew the gods a very human bath for their soiled bodies, water that, as Greeks, they might have scented with bay or juniper. I smell mint now, and do all spring and summer, and honeysuckle, roses, lily, herbs, through the night from my bed. We keep the window open when the garden comes on, sweet pour, a wordless thing, a gift of summer and of life, and of the labor of hands.

Nominated by Image

BLACK PEOPLE CAN'T SWIM

by DOUGLAS GOETSCH

from THE GETTYSBURG REVIEW

When I told Patricia how much I loved the pool at the Y,
she said, "Oh, black people can't swim,"
which made me grateful to be let in on this,
not the information, but the intimacy—
the fact that she could let fly with such a piece
of black-on-black attitude without the slightest
bit of shame or self-consciousness. We were in
a restaurant, me and five black women who had attended
Patricia's poetry reading, and who were paying
more attention than any white females I'd ever seen
to a football game on the high-definition TV.
The injured halfback in elegant street clothes
towering above the sideline interviewer
caused each woman to suck her teeth—
"That is one fine brother."
"Best thing I'll *never* have sex with."
"The lips are a little big, but homeboy still pretty."
"Why wouldn't you have sex with him?" I asked.
"'Cause he's a ho," Halle said.
"Everyone in the NFL's a ho," Cheryl and E. J. chimed in.
I looked up at the TV again, and this player,
whose name I'd known for five years, now seemed
changed into someone both simpler and deeper.
We were all toddlers, or unborn, when Martin dreamed
of little black children and little white children

going to school arm in arm. He dreamed this too:
a restaurant table where we were free to reveal
not just our true but our mysterious, irrational selves
in the presence of the other tribe without apology.
So here was Kaiasia, who had given us a lecture
on how not to pronounce her name, and who held
my arm all meal saying I was her husband.
"What was *that*?" they asked when she left.
A mystery. Earlier, on the walk over, she pulled me
away from the group into a leather shop
to show me a $200 Italian bag on layaway.
"And what did you say?"
"Nice bag."
"That's not what she wanted to hear."
"Which was?"
They eyed each other, deciding who would tell.
"Honey, when a sister shows a man something
on layaway she wants him to buy it."
"No way—" but they were all nodding, and I had to
love this country, or this ten square feet of it,
where they could tell me about men and women
and race and layaway. And I could have told them
about all the black people who swim at the Y,
though maybe they already knew
and just delighted in saying with impunity
what the vice president of the Los Angeles Dodgers
blurted out on national TV. "They don't have
the buoyancy," Al Campanis told Ted Koppel,
then promptly lost his job, and rightfully so.

Nominated by The Gettysburg Review

WE DON'T DESERVE THIS

fiction by SANDRA LEONG

from PLOUGHSHARES

The notification came on a weekend, and Jake's, in Iceland, had gotten through first. Sarah was in a desert, her cell phone wasn't working well, and she had to go back to the base to find out what was wrong.

She calls him from the landline, and he tells her as much as he knows.

"Whatever's coming, I feel I don't deserve it," he adds.

"You're breaking up," she says.

Through static, they agree to drop everything and take a week to straighten things out.

These days there aren't that many things that happen to both of them. Their children is one of them.

Ned came along their last year of med school, and, three years later, Samantha, when they were getting their MPH's. For a while they were able to make do with their postdocs' daycare consortium and a part-time nanny. They moved to New York. Then they spelled each other for the trips abroad. Jake got more of the trips than she did, and she got antsy.

The nursery was like a terrarium: babies, humidity, diaper smells, glass ceiling. Eventually, the kids went to a private school in the neighborhood, and she began working full time, which, in New York, and in that world, counts as only half time. The second shift was homework and Chinese takeout, and fights over neatness and too much soda, sibling squabbles ending in tears, listening bleary-eyed to overly inclusive accounts of incidents at school, or YouTube videos.

Meanwhile, the world burned. She kept a toe in it by working on the administrative end of public health efforts, reviewing grant proposals,

137

and envying the freedom of those who were about to travel to Viet Nam to look at the life cycles of schistosomes in the rice paddies or to study the incidence of cryptosporidium in hikers due to gannet guano encounters in the Orkneys. But mainly she wished she was able to just plain *intervene* in refugee migrations or plagues or the other holocausts that swirled around the planet.

Jake wasn't slowed down a bit. He went for it no matter what, logging all kinds of experience. When the call to Washington came, no one was surprised. And Washington didn't mean Washington. Washington meant even more travel, and more linked-in travel, and then entrée to the private sector after the burnout set in. And this time, she wasn't going to be left behind.

When the kids were nine and twelve, they dropped them at the Best boarding school. They'd been asking to be sent away anyway. No one cried.

Jake and she went, separately and together, twice around the world. They helped people. It took her very little time to hit her stride: she got a foothold in infantile diarrhea and pregnant women with AIDS. The sudden lifting of the obligation to return regularly home supplied jet fuel to their careers. They became consultants on relief efforts and vaccination campaigns and then gradually moved over into business. They joined microfinance consortiums. They raised money for charitable causes and then causes more high profile, and then less charitable and more entrepreneurial. They shook hands with Bill Gates. George Soros. Bono. Between them, they were able to save countless lives and launch countless livelihoods. They came to understand the problem of wealth-building in developing economies. And they were never shy about admitting that the Best boarding school saved their marriage.

The pristine far northern woods of New England were unassailable to direct flights and, so, not a place to visit for frivolous reasons, and not even for holidays, given how their lives had developed. They didn't see Ned and Samantha for three and a half years.

They became the sort of people of whom they used to be wary, people with a deep sense of entitlement stemming from knowledge of how unnecessary most barriers and restrictions are. They knew *others* were oppressed. They refused to be oppressed themselves. They became the kind of people who don't suffer.

It didn't begin about class. It ended up that way.

Perhaps they were poorly understood. Confusing to themselves, and their children.

Back in New York, they air out the apartment, order some Italian, and open some wine. They take advantage of the opportunity for a conjugal visit. Then, half-falling asleep, they share their worst fears. Then they sleep.

The next morning they down coffee and hit the road.

The highway is smooth and uncluttered. A heatless sun illumines the hills and casts blue shadows. The shoulders are white-edged ice.

It's odd to be driven somewhere by her husband, as if they were young marrieds on their way to a conference or a bed and breakfast. As if they were companions. Although endlessly helpful to each other, they rarely come together.

Now here they are, for the sake of their children who need them, who've been suspended. And threatened with expulsion.

"Couldn't they have postponed this till Spring?" he says. He keeps an eye out for state troopers. It's an abominably cold winter's day.

"The kids loved it there. They truly did," she says.

"Well, you couldn't just pop in all the time the way you could if they were at school in Geneva, say," he sighs, apropos of nothing.

Letters, written reports, and overproduced DVDS had been part of the contract. Parental presence had not.

She has images of Ned, in an adorable straw boater, singing "A maiden fair to see. . . ." Playing vibraphone with the percussion orchestra; delivering the opening arguments in a debate on global currency fluctuations; doing some form of dirty dancing with a thirteen-year-old. He was fifteen. Hey: sometimes she thinks she's seen more of him than parents whose sons *live* with them see.

Samantha was not much for performing yet, but she had stellar grades, ran two hard-fought but unsuccessful campaigns for class president, and never complained. A CD, images of some rather accomplished watercolors, arrived one day and gave Sarah great pleasure.

They had every reason to believe in their choice of boarding schools. They had every reason to be proud of their kids.

It's a three-hour drive from their apartment, it turns out.

"I didn't remember that it was this close" she says.

"Close?" says her husband.

139

"Would you like me to drive for a while?" she says.

He shakes his head. His back is hurting, but he wants to drive. He's large. His mane is grizzled. His features strong. She's sure he has a mistress. Several.

As for her, she's well-preserved. And what is preserved is worth preserving, if you get her drift.

She's not proud of a certain ruthlessness behind all the do-gooding, but there is nothing so wrong with ambition if you're for the causes that matter.

A whole wall of his study groans with plaques and commendations. And there are photos too, of emaciated peoples, faces speaking volumes, arms lifted in prayerful expressions of gratitude. And her? In Africa, entire tribes know her by her first name, preceded by their word for benefactress.

For a while, they exchange information about projects. She settles back. The car gulps highway. Crows settle high in bare trees.

Meetings and trips cancelled for a week. It's an odd feeling. Perhaps a pure and liberating one. Hurtling toward some sort of reckoning. Conversation ceases.

Her father came from a town in this area of the country. A town that no longer exists, where they produced hardwood hammer dulcimers.

They slow. The town sign, then a blinking yellow light, then a white church spire, anchoring and iconic. They enter the school grounds, which scream endowment, the 1850s Episcopalian chapel in the distance the size of a cathedral and site of their daughter's recent conversion to Judaism.

Late last year, she told them that she'd converted. In the thoughtful silence that ensued, she complained that they were unsupportive.

"I'm sorry if I seem unsupportive," Sarah told her. "I have to understand what it is I'm being asked to support. What do you mean that you have become *Jewish*?"

This was on Skype. If they hadn't Skyped they wouldn't have understood that Samantha had gone from atheist to Orthodox or that she now subsisted on diet coke and plain pasta, which the cafeteria made for her special without additional charge.

She's not saying it was as effective as communicating in person.

That's also how they learned that Ned was campaigning for Obama.

Preaching to the already converted of course. Jake was proud of him and, before the election, mentioned that he'd cast his absentee ballot for Obama.

140

Ned, staring into the camera, said "So what? Everyone hates you!" a retort which caught Jake by surprise. When pressed, Ned explained that investment banking was the most reviled profession on earth.

"Do you understand that I'm a doctor, not a banker?" Jake answered, peeved.

Technically, he's a doctor who came to socially conscious hedge funding via not-for-profit. They thought it was selfish of the kids, their being so critical. They're receiving a fabulous education.

They suspect that a lot of their kids' issues stem from privilege. The kids have no memory of their first apartment. The studio in the Back Bay, infested with vermin. They've never seen holes in the bottoms of their shoes. They've never had to be grateful for vaccinations or water free of mud and parasites. They've never *not* had a computer.

But Jake and Sarah have impressed upon the kids that they have *values*. And expectations: that they *find* themselves. Public Service. Or Finance. Even Art School. Something like that.

You're hard-hearted, Samantha informed her on Skype. She stared at her daughter's image. Samantha had taken to wearing her hair in braids, little blond braids.

"What do you mean?" said Jake, vigorous in his wife's defense. "At one point Mom wanted to adopt a whole raft of refugees. *We have room*, she kept saying."

"In the end it was impractical," she reminisced. "I realized: *Who would take care of them?*"

As they sit in the waiting area outside the headmistress's office they feel like schoolchildren in detention. Accustomed to visiting schools of airy thatch and newly poured concrete, she finds all this carved-wood paneling coffinlike.

They anticipate rallying around their children. They're ready to defend them with every fiber of their beings. After that they'll pull strings.

A door opens; a hand beckons.

The kids have grown. Both have entered an awkward stage. Their clothes refuse to flatter. Ned's hair does a straight-down-to-the-bridge-of-the-nose thing. Samantha, braids gone, cultivates way too many layers for a twelve-year-old. They look like plants.

Ned gives his father a stiff hug. Samantha presses herself to her mother and begins to suck her thumb, but thinks better of it.

The headmistress has the air of someone who has decided in advance not to be bullied. The school psychologist barges in. He hasn't said anything yet, but they find psychologists, especially this one, irritating. Just the beard. His stupid socks. Sue them if this is childish of them.

The kids exchange glances. It's strange seeing them in three dimensions.

The headmistress opens the meeting.

Ned and Samantha have been involved in some sort of trafficking, victimizing the children in the younger grades. They concocted a chilling Web presence, they're told. The height of manipulation, they're admonished. Apparently, the children displayed a frightening talent for the pornographic.

Sarah interrupts at that point. She doesn't think she's heard right. "Perhaps you mean the OASS?" she says.

"Organization Against Sexual Slavery," says her husband.

"They acted totally on their own," says the psychologist.

"That's commendable," says her husband. "That takes initiative."

All stare.

Nothing computes. The psychologist tells them that the trafficking is serious, and real.

"*Our* children?" they say. "Trafficked?" they say. "Trafficked in what? To what purpose?" In New England? It's insane. They feel betrayed.

The headmistress gives them a scurvy-eyed look. "Traffick*ing*," she says. And opens the dossier on her desk. There are photos. Printouts of Web pages. The photos are shocking. "Traffick*ers*" she says.

"You keep those in your desk?" Sarah says.

They're offered "details." Thus far, Ned and Samantha seem unmoved. They look at their kids. There's a disconnect.

The headmistress presents a step-by-step breakdown of the scheme. The way their children used Paypal. The way their children lured other children into their rooms with imported chocolate, took photos, doctored and posted them on a Web site, a Web site whose sophistication was top notch. There is even a musical soundtrack that they play for them, ingenious in its dull sleaziness. But that's not the half of it. The headmistress and the psychologist with the aid of a history teacher organized the sting that uncovered the conspiracy to kidnap. The front was Urban Playgrounds, an enrichment activity, a sort of reverse Fresh Air Fund; "patrons" would host overprivileged and understimulated boarding school students for weekends in the city and abroad.

The kids are sullen. They're the picture of absent contrition. It's a lot to digest.

The self-congratulatory way the operation is described is what decides them. They erupt. They tell them the charges are false, and implausible to boot. They suspect the motives of the school.

"It's all being blown out of proportion," says Ned.

"Shut up," the headmistress snaps.

"Shut up yourself," says Jake, shocked by her response.

"This could bring down the school," she says, her voice poorly modulated.

The psychologist says that it's possible the kids were apprehended before actual sales were made. But a lot of browsing had apparently taken place.

"He means our site got 200,000 hits," says Samantha.

All seem to have much more to say. But they wait first for the parents' reactions.

"You mean, this is true?" they ask their children.

"Of course not," says Ned. "Don't you see that this is *entrapment*?"

The psychologist says that, due to failure to thrive on the Endless Academic Year Plan, palliative parental attention—otherwise known as suspension—is recommended for their children and that if, after review, return is recommended, return would be only for the Finite Academic Year Plan.

Jake and Sarah are outraged. Not thriving? Not *thriving*? And what's the "Finite Academic Year Plan"?

What about the stellar report cards? What about "a maiden fair to see . . .?" What about the gallery quality watercolors?

"We feel betrayed by this school," they say.

The Headmistress says that part of the mission of Best boarding school is moral development as an integral part of intellectual. Sometimes an inadequacy cannot be compensated for.

The accusation gives them pause. Sarah blinks quick, pained tears from her eyes.

Jake is outraged. He tells them that this CYOA business reeks. He tells them their children were raised with impeccable values. Anything that happened happened on Best school's watch, as a result of Best school's slack supervision and questionable seed planting.

The psychologist tells them that their children show signs of parental neglect. Jake and Sarah announce that the school is in complete abnegation of responsibility. They're shocked that it wants to bring them into this. And Jake adds that they have no interest in participating in this kangaroo court. They are withdrawing them.

It's night. Jake keeps to the speed limit, as the trunk is inadequately battened down over hurriedly loaded cartons.

There was a clamoring for Chuck E. Cheese, and they pulled into a mall. Now, having gorged on doughy pizza and exhausted themselves running around the game room like giant toddlers, the children sleep in the back seat, blond-headed angels, smelling of sweet marinara.

Sarah confesses that she feels a bit overwhelmed.

"I hate those game-rooms too," Jake says. "I just felt like the poor things have been through so much. Like we should make it up to them, somehow."

She bristles, remembering the accusations. But then grows reflective. "But what have they been through? Nothing! It's what they're about to put *us* through that worries me."

He thinks about this. He reorients his sympathy. "I can't take any more days off. The meetings I have lined up have taken way too long to set up. We're lucky I was able to get *this* time."

She contemplates the bleak, headlight-washed highway ahead, the landscape black and invisible.

"Why did you withdraw them from the school?" she asks.

"You saw how they were treating us there," he says.

"But what will we do with them? Where will they go?"

"We'll call in some favors," he says.

"You mean you'll find a school that will take them?" She's dubious. "Another one that offers an Endless academic year?"

"We'll take them along with us in the summers," he says.

"We never even take each other along," she reminds him.

"We'll divide them up," he says. "Each of us will take one."

She contemplates his plan. "You're bluffing," she says.

"What about your parents?" he says.

"They're both dead," she reminds him.

"Oh yeah, sorry," he says. And she's perturbed by the heedlessness of all this change.

When they arrive, the children tumble from the car, rubbing their eyes. Mechanically they help load the cart that the doorman trundles to the sidewalk. Then, rendered superfluous by the adults, they stand, looking slack-jawed and numb.

"Can I have the key?" says Ned, finally. And he and Samantha disappear. Samantha drags a large pink teddy bear.

She walks alongside the cart as Jake pulls and the doorman pushes. She snags a rattle-y carton as it threatens to tip and fall. It contains empty soda bottles stuffed with rubber bands. She perches the carton on top of the trashcan on the corner.

When they get upstairs, the children have retreated to their side of the apartment and shut the dividing doors. A shower goes on. Otherwise there's the unfamiliar smell of damp socks and sneakers, the already raided pantry, the trail of clothes and candy wrappers. They left *children* and retrieved teens who no longer have anywhere to go. What was Jake thinking? A deliveryman arrives. Ned emerges, pays him, takes the bag and disappears. She tries the door to the kids' wing and finds it locked from the inside.

In bed, they lie sleepless with strange dread.

"What on earth do we do now?" she says, finally.

"Don't be so fatalistic," he says.

They talk about whether they should hire a live-in nanny for the time being. But the kids seem too old for that. Are there live-in psychotherapists?

"I hated that school psychologist," she says, remembering.

They would send any psychotherapist packing after two or three utterances.

Late into the night. Into the wee hours. They point fingers at each other for spoiling the children. Then for depriving them. They rail against Best boarding school.

From the children's wing, they hear knocking, like a renovation in progress.

In the morning, she walks to the corner and buys a dozen *pain au chocolat*. When she returns, Jake is in the shower. There is still no sign of their children. She wonders what the knocking was.

When they were young, she'd sometimes feel a jolt of panic at 9:00 p.m. She'd rush home, hoping to see them before they were put to bed. Rarely, she succeeded, squeaking in for the good night kiss. Most of the time, she returned to stillness. She'd drink in the light sound of breathing and the innocence that overtakes even the most obnoxious children during sleep. She'd look over the projects that they'd accumulated in the evening hours. Ned in particular was adept at what he called "reworking" furniture, actually taking furniture apart, and assembling the pieces into unique contraptions. Recliners tilt-a-whirled, beds spun, little leftover pieces became a series of innovative stocks and pillories for Samantha's American Girl Doll collection. Samantha didn't seem to really mind. She was a compliant child and, despite her milieu, never the most material person.

Sarah tries the door. It opens. Ned's room is first, in the hallway to the right.

They're curled, like hedgehogs, side by side. Why didn't Samantha sleep in her own bed?

Blackout shades create perpetual night. The room is populated by hulking, shrouded shapes. The kids didn't even bother removing the dust covers before they went to bed. There's a click and whir, and hum, and she starts.

After they became parents, they felt the need to do a Seven Wonders in Seven Years Challenge for their family vacations, most of which the kids, who were infants and then toddlers at the time, have no memory of. It was mainly for something for Jake and her to do while the kids were still small enough to sling around. Unfortunately, the vacation the kids remember is the seventh trip, the one to the Galapagos. After two weeks reveling in endangered life forms, all they'll ever recall is how the handlers got the month wrong and didn't show up to feed the pets. When they returned, the animals had all expired. One was still warm. It had taken them two full weeks to starve to death.

That was when Ned got them to buy him a deep freeze. That's the object that vibrates now, preserving the frost-haired bodies of Tan the pot-bellied pig, Sybil the gerbil, and some guppies whose names she doesn't recall. She remembers trying to quell Samantha's bottomless rage. At one point, exasperated, she reminded her that there were plenty of gerbils and pigs in the world, at least. That was a mistake.

She turns to leave, hand on the door, when Ned addresses her. "Do we have breakfast? From *Payard?*"

"From *Le Pain*" she says. "*Payard* went out of business."

He remains in bed as if to savor the anticipation. She leaves.

She comes out and Jake hands her a caffe latte. He goes back into the kitchen.

"Can I have one?" Samantha has appeared, making her spill. "I haven't had meat in several days."

"Don't be an idiot. Even *I* know that Jews don't have to clear meat out of their systems before they can have dairy," Ned tells her.

They're sitting, backlit and glowing in the sunny, south-facing breakfast nook, their expressions strangely weary.

"When did you start drinking coffee?" Sarah says.

Samantha looks at her, the blankness in her eyes unsettling.

The children tear into the *pain au chocolat* like castaways. Jake returns with two more lattes. He clears his throat. They strategized about this moment last night, in the dark, composing successive drafts of the lecture. He seems to decide to wing it.

"Let's close this chapter and focus on the future," he says.

"I still don't understand what hit us," she says. "I think you kids should start from the beginning and fill us in."

"It doesn't matter," Jake says. "We'll find another school."

"We'd like to hear *your* point of view," she says to the kids.

"Actually, *I* don't," Jake says. "Don't bother. No use dwelling on the past."

"The *past*?" she says. "Yesterday afternoon is the *past*?"

The children avoid their eyes. "I agree with Dad," says Samantha.

From under the silky, vegetal fringe, Ned throws his mother a glance.

The glance has a galvanizing effect. "I feel like you're trying to tell us something," Sarah says. "Something we haven't gotten yet."

"Obviously, you'll know not to tangle with the wrong people again," Jake says.

Which people? What could he mean?

"Damn straight," says Ned, his voice devoid of sarcasm.

It's all nonsense. "I want to *know*," she whines, surprising herself.

Jake is also surprised. "Give them some *privacy*," he says.

"They don't *want* privacy." She's unable to back down.

"Yes we do," the children chime.

"I trust my kids," Jake says, indicating that the discussion is closed. Ned whispers something in Samantha's ear.

Sarah's gut churns. Their goal is to maintain connectedness without any sacrifice of independence. But a yearning has infiltrated.

"Can I be excused?" asks Samantha, and the phrase pierces her.

At key moments during her deterioration, Sarah's mother used to insist on a family game of Scrabble. She would be packed and ready to be driven to the sanitarium and would suddenly announce that she refused to leave until one of them beat her. The competitions could take hours. Sarah's father was nearly always the one with the stamina and skill to finally defeat her. Once, by sheer luck, Sarah pulled it off. She was still gazing at the board, startled by her own success, when her mother collected her pocketbook and headed out the door, her father following with her suitcase. When he returned, he collapsed on the sofa, at odds with himself. Then he buried himself in his work.

Usually after six weeks or so, her mother would come back, looking rested but with no inclination to play. "It tires me out," she'd tell Sarah. And never once had Sarah asked why her mother associated Scrabble with leaving.

They check the Web and e-mail people they know. He's looking for a school. She's going through the motions. The sound of streaming video from the kids' rooms, muffled but very loud, energizes the atmosphere. Above streaming video: the occasional scream of a saw.

She tells Jake that something doesn't sit right about what they're doing. She tells him she's losing a sense of their mission. He pushes away his laptop. She reads his body language. This won't be a life-changing conversation.

"What should we do, then?" he asks.

He's toying with her. She doesn't let on that she knows. "Enroll them in public school, stay home, work locally, raise them ourselves."

He laughs, "OK," he says. He goes back to his laptop.

"I'm serious," she says.

"Forgive me," he says. "I think I'm on to something in Massachusetts." He pushes the laptop away again. "Are you sure? Why the change of heart? I thought you'd felt you'd paid your dues. I thought you wanted to prioritize your career? I thought this," and he indicates the kids' wall thrumming with noise, "drove you nuts."

"You're right," she says, feeling sick. "It's just some romantic vision of an old-fashioned family. From a bygone golden era."

"The seventies?" he says, sounding more curious than sardonic. He's already turned back to his screen.

She says she doesn't know. He isn't listening anyway. She watches him fiddling, straining over his e-mail. He announces he's got them each a spot, one at an all-girls' school, one at an all-boys' school.

She congratulates them. They kiss. She leaves the room, feeling even worse.

That night, the Shabbat, she brings home food from Zabar's. Samantha, with mysterious competence, lights candles and sings prayers. Ned eats tentatively, but with appreciation. Samantha closes her eyes in bliss. "This is the real deal," she says, with relief. "And, mom, so *festive*. You have all the holidays represented here." It's true. Sarah was inclusive in her ignorance.

Over gefilte fish, Jake announces the new school placements, and is met with stricken silence. Finally, Ned pipes up. "You mean separate us?" he says.

Jake thinks it over. "It was a feat to get any places at all," he says, finally. "Just be appreciative and we'll be fine."

"A feat," says Ned. "It took you all of half a day. If *that*."

Jake gets his back up. He says this isn't about time: it's about magnitude. Magnitude of favors called in. Due to the magnitude of the crime to begin with.

Samantha begins to cry. "So that's what this is about?" Ned says. "After all that, deep down you believe we're child-pornographers and traffickers?" Jake tells them that that obviously is not the case. If it were, he wouldn't have been able to sell the new schools on them, Board connections or no Board connections.

Ned's face wears an expression Sarah's never seen on a boy before, except perhaps in the movies. Or perhaps it only seems notable because he's *her* boy. The expression is one of injured nobility.

Jake, oblivious at best, takes his plate into the kitchen, observing that he doesn't much like Jewish food.

Sarah reaches a hand to Samantha, who is starting to dry her tears. She touches her arm. "I can't live without him," Samantha murmurs, pulling away. And, lips trembling again, she turns her expression upon her brother.

The next day, Jake, in a fine mood, returns full force to his conference calls, his calendar-massaging, his e-mails, and texts to his assistant.

"I got three days back for myself," he tells Sarah, "And I can get a fourth if the schools will allow delivery by shuttle."

Even when viewed sitting still, and from behind, his body seems to hum with ambition. She should be doing the same. But the kids' proximity awakens in her simultaneously an uncharacteristic lassitude and a perverse sort of drive. She remembers weekends when they wandered: the Circle Line, the Carousel, the English Garden, Little India, Koreatown, the Seaport, Economy Candy, Dylan's, Build-a-Bear, the American Girl Doll Flagship Store.

149

What could they do together now? Today? Before they go back to school?

In the kids' wing, it's perpetual night. The unlit hall opens into first Ned's then Samantha's room, the bathroom in between. The blackout shades are pulled. The sound of streaming video is dominant. A giant flat-screen emits the only major light.

Ned and Samantha crouch on the floor wearing headlamps, in front of them a doll in a vise. The room is furnished with unfamiliar contraptions, some the height of people, some the height of chairs.

At first, absorbed, they don't notice her. When they do, they both jump. "What are you doing here?" Ned asks.

There's a contrast between their bright faces and the dark vibe that emanates from their devices. "What do these do?" Sarah asks.

Ned offers a demonstration. Samantha protests that they're not ready. Sarah sits down in a so-called Electric Chair and is strapped in. They go back to work on the doll.

"So, is that it?" she asks. "Is that the demonstration?"

They don't seem to hear.

"A little lower," says Samantha, and there's a brief snipping noise.

"What're you doing, anyway?" Sarah says. She moves both hands, circulation unencumbered.

"An earring got loose," Samantha says, showing her the doll. "So we changed it to a double piercing."

"So what's the point of this chair?" Sarah asks.

Ned comes up to her and peers carefully at her face as if memorizing the pores. "We need you and Dad to stay put for a while," he says. He takes off his headlamp and rubs his neck. He backs away, and perches on the edge of the bed.

"What do you mean?" she says. She laughs. Both Ned and Samantha seem puzzled by this. She apologizes, but then wishes them both good luck getting their father to stay put.

They exchange a glance. She's seen them do that before.

"Call Dad," says Ned. "Get him to come in here."

"Will you unstrap me?" she says.

"No," says Ned, coming close. He punches the numbers into a phone and holds it to her ear.

Jake, in his study, answers his cell. She tells him she's in Ned's room. She tells him she needs him to come in here. She adds that he should be careful, that the kids are up to something, but by then Ned has pulled the phone away and pressed Off.

Jake seems to take forever to arrive. During that time the kids whisper to each other. She feels a certain level of misgiving.

"Can I get up now?" she asks.

"No," says Ned.

"At least tell me what's going to happen," she says.

Samantha turns to Ned. "Let's tell her," she says.

"We can't trust her," Ned replies.

Sarah takes exception to this. What has she ever done to make them not trust her? She complains to them.

"You're married to *him*, for one thing," Ned says with sudden spiteful anger.

"*Shut up*," says Samantha. "I *love* Daddy."

"That's what makes you an idiot," he says, and she pouts. He flicks his hair off his forehead. "That's what makes us *all* idiots," he says.

Sarah catches her breath. She looks at him. He sees her look.

"Did you see those pictures?" he asks. He puts his face thrillingly close.

Her heart beats. "Which?" she asks. Why is her heart doing this?

"You know which ones."

"Of the nude children?"

"Yes, of the nude children," he says. He begins to pace.

Samantha sits on the floor. "You're mean," she says, catching playfully at his ankle as he goes by.

Sarah asks them to explain. She's fascinated by her son's face.

"It was a liberation movement," Samantha says. "His idea."

"Liberation," Sarah says. She doesn't actually follow.

Ned whirls on her. "Did you really look at them?"

They're both searching her face for something. She tells them she's very bad at this kind of game. They have to be more explicit. Their faces fall. She apologizes.

After a moment, Ned looks up at her fiercely. Samantha too. "Those kids have something good," he says. Samantha nods.

Sarah asks him why the pictures were doctored.

"I was only bringing out what was already there," he says. His face is all proportion and symmetry. Disappointment, sadness, excitement and, behind the passion, the intimations of a fine and perverse intelligence. He has the fervor she's seen in certain artists.

151

"He was," says Samantha. "I saw it too."

They return to staring. Ned sinks to his knees without taking his eyes from Sarah's.

"Um. Maybe we should call Dad again," she says.

But Jake walks in, causing Ned to jump to his feet. Her husband looks around. "Whoa," he says. "Impressive. I haven't been back here in a while. What's this one for?"

Soon, he's fastened in odd-looking manacles attached to the wall.

"I see you're playing too," he says, looking over at her in the chair.

He asks the children what they wanted. "Your full attention," says Samantha, creeping a little closer.

"You have it, sweetheart," he says.

Ned drags over a hinged plank and encloses Jake's legs.

"Don't *hurt* him," says Samantha. Ned applies a padlock.

Jake reassures her that he's OK and asks again what this is all about. He strains experimentally against his confinement. Nothing gives.

"It'll hold," Ned says with satisfaction. He sits back on his haunches.

"Sarah?" says Jake.

"Yes?" she says.

He asks her to explain. She tells him she has no clue. This sets Ned pacing again.

"No clue?" he exclaims. "No *clue?* After all I've told you? You're my goddamn mother, and you have no clue."

"Whoa," says her husband. "Whoa. Language."

"We don't like boarding school," says Samantha.

"Damn straight," says Ned.

"And we're not going back," says Samantha.

"Not to any boarding school," says Ned.

"And we won't let you separate us," says Samantha.

"That's it?" says Jake.

"Yes," says Ned.

"OK, can you let me go now?" says Jake.

Ned tells him no. They all let out their breaths. Jake asks why.

"We want Mom," Ned says.

She's never seen Ned like this. She remembers tantrums in the park over a lost helium balloon or a denied request for a frozen-chemical popsicle from a stand. Tantrums were easy. All you needed were nerves of steel.

"I'm here," she says. Something about her being strapped in makes it sound like a joke.

Ned looks hurt again.

In her fingers and palms and arms she feels a shock. She screams.

"It worked," says Samantha, her hand over her mouth.

"You're *shocking* us?" Sarah says. *"Let me goddamn go."*

Jake strains at his manacles. Ned strokes his mother's cheeks. And she's not sure how it happens, but her heart goes over to his. Is this a happy ending? Lost time regained? It's hard to know. They're so resistant.

Jake is in a state. To torment him, they've placed his Blackberry on a cord. When it sounds, he lunges for it and they yank it away. From a distance, he looks at names on caller ID. He pleads to be allowed to answer. He talks about the people who need him, and their importance. Ned and Samantha seem unsurprised, the way inquisitors seem to hear only predictable circumlocution and obfuscation in the prattling of the terrorized. He talks about heads of state, their remarkable achievements. He discusses the most magnificent coastlines, the way that people need programs, and programs riches, and riches potentates, and magnates, and pooh-bahs. Ned throws a switch and Jake shrieks.

Samantha has gone out for groceries. Ned paces, a line between his brows. When she returns, they have microwaved mac and cheese.

Hours, days. The clanking of chains. Ned's high dudgeon. Samantha's tears. The humiliations of toileting. Takeout food. Jake's repetitious testimony as to the insignificance of all galaxies other than his own. Punctuating screams.

And Sarah? She's seen things too. Serene Asiatics whose smiles are like balm, children sacrificed like mosquitoes to mosquitoes. But nothing to speak of now. Not anymore. She drifts. Above. Without identity or home. She seeks definition.

And finds it in Ned. She's still fascinated by his face. His brows are like the pencil strokes of an infatuated master. His mouth's a superhero's.

Samantha seems pleased to be lackey and gofer. She returns from an outing soaked. Their diet has gone south. Kosher Oreos, kosher Doritos, kosher Coca-Cola. She chews gum nonstop and is random about the application of shocks.

What will become of them? Of them all?

Jake, grown nasty, struggles and spits when the kids come near. Sarah would say that she doesn't recognize him. But she does.

She's come to the realization that it's the father's role to be obdurate and to defy and the mother's to melt and give in. She realizes that without this maternal principle they are all as empty as ghosts, imposters proffering bags of shoddy goods. She realizes that without her children she's a Flying Dutchman, and that all that's kept her from a universe of riches is an act of self-abnegation, and the courage to suffer as all mothers and children must suffer in the absence of the ones they need and love. And to surrender herself to that suffering.

Gradually, she understands the outlines of Ned's vision. Divorce is key.

She's released. A shower feels like an orgasm.

She returns to the kids' wing, hair wrapped in a towel. Jake looks at her openmouthed. She doesn't go near him.

"Did you call the cops?" he asks.

She withers him with a glance.

"Let me go," he says.

"What for?" she says.

"So *I* can call the cops," he says.

"It'll be your word against mine," she says.

Because of the look on his face, she's glad he's still in chains.

The kids, acting like kids again, are silent. She's in charge. She presents Jake with options. He responds. Nothing he says sounds remotely like understanding. Not to mention submission. Most of what he says is insulting.

It's best they leave.

The cartons go back in the car. Her suitcase too. She calculates a safe and sobering distance and tells the doorman to go up with the set of keys in that amount of time. They drive away, Samantha sobbing.

Who knows where they'll end up? Who knows how far they'll get? She's no infant. Divorce is messy. Divorce is hell. But in defense of her children, she'll be a lioness. She's first and foremost a mother.

Nominated by Joyce Carol Oates

LOGOPHILIA

by B.H. FAIRCHILD

from NEW LETTERS

Logophilia: the falling in love with language. That's the way it begins, I believe, for obsessive readers and writers, especially poets. These are the sort of people who start reading probably at a rather early age, curled up in the big brown chair with the funky odor, oblivious to everything except the voice in their head that is someone else's voice—Dickens, maybe, or Austen, or Stephen King, who knows. They will plunge on through adolescence vaguely aware of some slight, subtle, almost imperceptible difference between themselves and their classmates—e.g., that like the character in the movie *Diner*, they feel terribly uncomfortable with the word "nuance," or that they would secretly like to be British so that they could convincingly and often use "bloody" or "wanker" in conversation. Or that they refuse to be friends with anyone who habitually employs the phrase "as it were." In adulthood, they're the sort of people who read determinedly slowly, sometimes reading the same sentence several times, often aloud, even though they understood it the first time. They can't read Shakespeare's blank verse for even five minutes without beginning to talk that way. Their list of favorite authors sometimes includes Sir Thomas Browne or Edward Dahlberg. If you asked them to name a fat word ("opprobrium," for instance) or a tall word ("lattice") or a skinny word ("weep," which is also cowardly, slightly bald, and has a girlfriend named Hermione), they would immediately know what you meant. Some become poets, many do not, though they all share the same benign disease: They have fallen in love with language.

Even though they are the best readers—meaning those who read

155

with their bodies, their senses, as well as their cerebrums—they never get the highest scores on those reading comprehension exams that are such an affliction to the language-smitten. I mean, of course, exams that inevitably include some paragraph on the economics of a South American country—say, the legendary principal exports of Peru. "One of the principal exports of Peru," the paragraph will say, "until the drought of 1957, was a flower, now considered a rarity, with the curious name of *Blue Elbow*." "*My God*," we (in particular, the poets-to-be) will exclaim internally, "*the freaking Blue Elbow! Is that beautiful or what?*" Suddenly we're imagining what it looks like, its fragrance, the look of an entire field of them, a yellow vase holding three of them beneath the delicate rays of the early morning light, or ourselves lying happily in a field of *Blue Elbow*, and DNNNNNNNN! EXAM OVER. Substandard or maybe even ridiculous score, though we didn't just read the paragraph, we were *deep inside it*; we were there with our whole bodies.

I, like many victims of logophilia, began reading early, and my mother read to me frequently, so the love of language was perhaps inevitable. But I have to think that those great teachers of reading, comic books, also had something to do with it. I remember, around the age of four, being delighted with the onomatopoeia the writers of *Captain Marvel* and *Batman* would invent for certain sounds: KAPOW, VROOM, or my favorite, POIT!, used (without any actual auditory connection I can locate) to describe something soft (the bad guy's head) bouncing off something hard (a brick wall). At a family reunion, my uncle Roy accidentally dropped a watermelon on the sidewalk: POIT! A more elevated source of logophilia at that age was surely the King James translation of the Bible. I resisted going to church. I especially hated and suffered comatose through the sermons, but the language of the King James caught my ear, all that Old Testament syntactical parallelism that would surface again in, of all places, Ginsberg's "Howl," although I couldn't recognize it at the time.

Later, when I was a teenager, there was the poetry of the oil fields (though now more a matter of metaphor than sound) often disguised as profanity: "Colder than a well digger's ass," "Colder than a witch's tit," "I whipped that bastard like a rented mule," and once during a moment of startling and pseudo-profane genius, my friend, declaring in reference to the movie star Brigitte Bardot, "I would walk on my tongue from here to Amarillo just to wash her dishes." My father, who was embarrassed by poetry and refused to read anything but nonfiction, one time just for a moment became the Prince of Language when Joe Whisnatt, a large man who for unknown reasons rode a very small motorcycle, was pulling out of the driveway. As he drove away, my father said, "You know, Whisnatt on that little bike looks like a monkey fucking a football." One Christmas when I was a boy, we received one of those unimaginably garish supersized Christmas cards all in bright metallic colors with a Christmas cliché in raised gold letters inside, and my mom said, "Good God. It looks like an invitation to a whorehouse wedding." *Merry Christmas*, I thought, *Now you're talking*. I ushered movies in high school and vividly remember Marlon Brando in the great *One-Eyed Jacks* hurling his chair across the room and screaming at Bob, "Get up, you scum-suckin' pig . . . you mention her once more and I'm goin' to tear yer arms out!" Later he calls the evil, beer-bellied Lon (bearing an uncanny resemblance to a truck driver I knew and disliked) a "tub of guts" and "gob of spit." Arguably *not* poetry, but as a blue-collar logophiliac, I admired the crude guttural beauty of those words and recall walking away from that film imagining a situation on a rig or in a honky-tonk where in the coolest possible way I might use them without somehow losing my life.

John Keats would have loved the dialogue in *One-Eyed Jacks*. I know this from his letters. He is constantly quoting lines and phrases from Shakespeare—and not necessarily the most profound or sublime ones—delighting, for instance, in Hamlet's seemingly offhand solution to the problem of a dead Polonius: "I'll lug the guts into the neighbor room." Keats thinks "lug the guts" is an absolutely marvelous locution (and so would Marlon Brando). And there is the famous story of the schoolboy Keats—after first encountering the poetry of Edmund Spenser—tramping, soaked, through wet fields to the home of his teacher, the young Cowden Clarke. Little Keats, gripping tightly a copy of *The Faerie Queene*, bunches up his shoulders to deliver the full physical impact of Spenser's lines and then adds excitedly, "What an image that is—'sea-shouldering whales.'" Typical logophilia. At an incurable stage. He might have been, in this one instance only, any young poet-to-be standing ass-deep in the Cimarron River, offering a quart bottle of Pearl beer to the stars and shouting into the wheat fields,

> *In my craft or sullen art*
> *Exercised in the still night*
> *When only the moon rages*

157

And the lovers lie abed
    With all their griefs in their arms,

stretching out the "all" like some very bad country-western singer. A
fool for language. Logophilia in the worst way.

A fool for language, and thus the foolishness in the lives of so many
poets and even their cousins, the gluttonous readers: passing up lunch
in order to spend the money on that old, beat-up copy of the Arthur
Golding *Metamorphoses* on hold at Down-And-Out Books for the last
two weeks; the rocky marriage pushed to the breaking point because
someone can't seem to remove himself from the pages of Lowell's let-
ters to Bishop long enough to fix the faucet; a certain uncontrollable
disdain for English professors who speak of the language of literature
the way an intelligent virgin might talk about sex; and in the case of the
poet, the sudden disappearance from the fifty dollar seats for *La Bo-
heme* because of the brutal compulsion to write down—quickly, im-
mediately, *now*, before she forgets it—the sudden brilliant fix for the
bad poem that will probably remain bad even after the fix. The foolish-
ness of Catullus, Li Po, Villon, Marlowe, Byron, Christina Rossetti,
Yeats, Hart Crane, Dylan Thomas, Anne Sexton, and a thousand others,
drunk on language—but without the drunkenness, that is, the logo-
philia, just solid citizens who read the newspaper and pay mortgages
and vote regularly and live sensible, organized lives.

The woman I have been sleeping with for forty-one years is taking a
bath with one of those wire contraptions bridging the sides of the tub
in order to hold her book at the proper reading angle. The book is
warped in several places, pages curled, wrinkled and, from the doorway
where I stand, looking more like a weathered shingle than a book as a
result of being knocked into the bath water several times. I recite to
her the lines from *King Henry the Fourth* that Shakespeare might have
written for a sixteenth-century version of *One-Eyed Jacks: "Thou art
violently carried away from grace: there is a devil haunts thee in the
likeness of a fat old man; a tun of man is thy companion. Why dost thou
converse with that trunk of humours, that bolting-hutch of beastliness,
that swoln parcel of dropsies, that huge bombard of sack, that stuffed
cloakbag of guts, that roasted Manningtree ox with the pudding in his
belly, that reverend vice, that grey iniquity, that father ruffian, that
vanity in years?"* And she replies, *"Oh, you mean that bawdy, fobbing,
fool-born, swag-bellied, knotty-pated lout, that whoreson knave who
denies me privacy."* Well, no, that's not what she says, though on an-

other day she might. What she says is even better, a favorite sentence from a student essay from decades ago: *In his later years, Tolstoy enjoyed walking around dressed as a pheasant.* Just a word. The wrong word in the right place. And two logophiliacs, two fools for language, lost in laughter while a book floats in the bath water.

Nominated by New Letters and Charles Harper Webb, Kirk Nesset

TRACING BACK

by ALICE FRIMAN

from THE GETTYSBURG REVIEW

In the history of reading,
there's many a cracked heart,
lost letter, stopped clock, cut wrist.
Any cursory push through poems
or stories and you could trip
over the drownings
or the heap of crushed
petticoats fluttering on the tracks.

To the bookish, I say *careful*.
What's between two covers
can creep beneath covers.
Any thief worth his prize
knows how seduction works:
ingratiation: the innocent pull
of words, that belly crawl
of language. What do you
think that first slither was,
coiling the winesap,
so lovely, our girl was forced
to write it down, there
on the underside of leaves.
Hers, to sneak past the terrible
gates, hidden in the rustle

of her figgy apron: the key
to what she didn't know yet
but would be looking for
in all her troubled incarnations.

Nominated by The Gettysburg Review and Rosellen Brown, Andrea Hollander Budy,
Stephen Corey, Marianne Boruch, Susan Terris, Carolyne Wright

ROCKAWAY

fiction by LYDIA CONKLIN

from NEW LETTERS

Dani and Laurel hit 119th, cackling and looping limbs. They've swiped a joint from Dani's mom, excavated from a wadded-up sandwich bag under a couple vibrators that could grind steel. It's only evening, and the neighbors are out like mosquitoes, pounding reggaeton and commenting on those who pass.

Dani and Laurel hold hands. Laurel leans on Dani's shoulder, even though Laurel's taller. She likes Dani's shoulder blade bumping her temple at each stride. Dani is tough but junior-sized, with long, gelled curls that stand between her and real-boyhood. Laurel is mixed race—Puerto Rican and black and a little Chinese—with an ironed spray of ponytail. There's a scar on her jaw from opening a bottle with her teeth. Sometimes tears and sweat or milky drips of moisturizer form tiny ponds in the scar. Dani monitors the ponds as they change with the light of day. She kisses them out of their beds. They're salty.

Now that it's Friday, the rules from Harlem Renaissance High School have expired, and everyone's hyper. Their classmates leer openly. Another sophomore, Andre, lunges off a fence, his teeth open to the air.

"Hey," he says, landing in their path. "How do you do it? You know, *do* it."

"What do you want?" Dani says.

"Hold on, girl. Don't get mean. I just want to get a look at you two. Wow."

"Man," Dani says. "Take a fucking picture."

"I'd love to." Andre angles his fingers into a box for his eye, snaps his tongue. "Say pussy."

"Thanks, wiseass," Dani says.

"What are you ladies up to this evening? Looking for whale barf?"

"What are you talking about?" Dani says. "You crazy?"

"Didn't you hear? Or too busy eating each other?"

"Fuck you," Dani says.

"For real, though," Andre says. "Some white boy out in Rockaway found whale barf yesterday worth eight grand. Dude: eight grand for barf. Little twerp's on the cover of *Metro*. Me and Trav thought of checking it out, but we're going to a party on Lenox instead. Hey— there's girls there. You might like it."

"Good luck with that," says Dani.

Dani and Laurel turn on St. Nicholas. There the gum is squished black eyeballs, paler and flatter the older it gets. Laurel crosses souls of pieces thrown down in 1980, new wads green and glittering with spit. Laurel spins Dani's knuckles in her hand. It's better when Dani can walk her through the neighborhood. When Laurel's alone she doesn't always watch herself, zones out on the white light that pools between the brick high rises and forgets where she's going. This gets her into trouble. A kid like Andre could get too grabby, try to coax her into how she used to be.

"Let's go somewhere," Laurel says.

"The park?" says Dani.

Morningside Park, a few steep blocks of overgrowth, is where they hook up some nights. They go up the stone steps and crouch on paths walled in by chain link fences and wild shrubs. It's evening, but summer's coming, so it's still light.

"Not the park, I guess," says Dani. "Too early."

"What about that barf?" says Laurel.

"All the way to Rockaway?" Dani says. "That's far, girl."

"I know, but think how much that shit's worth."

Maybe if Laurel got a bunch of money off barf they could even get their own place. It seems crazy for fifteen-year-olds, but their moms were eighteen when they moved into Section Eight housing across the hall from each other and started their own lives. They're going to tell their moms soon about their love, and Laurel wants to make sure they have a way out if it doesn't go over. She's seen her mom hissing *maricón* at the TV as the Wiggles jerk and jangle.

"I don't know," Dani says.

"But it could be fun looking, right?" Laurel says. "Even if Andre's just fucking with us."

"I guess," Dani says.

"Come on. Sounds crazy enough to be true. It would be sweet to have the cash, right?"

"Couldn't hurt," Dani says.

They go underground at the 125th St. A. When the train comes, without hardly noticing, they ride it through Manhattan into Brooklyn, roughhousing and kissing for an hour and a half on the plastic benches as the lamps and wires in the tunnels ride by. When the A ends, they wait for the shuttle to go even farther. In the station, Dani puts her hand on the subway bench. It comes back clammy, so they don't sit.

They board the shuttle. It leaves Brooklyn and heads into Queens. The sound of the train changes as it angles upward and catches the tracks on the bridge. Light fills the car, and they look out the window.

"I've never been to Queens," says Laurel.

"For real?" says Dani. "And you've lived here how long?"

"You know how long, dummy," says Laurel. Their moms were pregnant together, got their GEDs together, and have lived in the same building ever since. The girls shared bathwater and plastic mugs of juice, bounced around in a pair as toddlers, but after that never ran in the same crowds. They would see each other in the halls at school plenty, get babysat by each other's moms, but weren't close again until recently.

Outside the scratched subway windows the water in the bay is purple skin with weeds pricking the surface like hair. A pigeon, doused and clean, sits on a log.

"Look at it out there," says Laurel. "This is like some big fucking nature hike."

"Yo, this train goes to Far Rockaway, right?" Dani asks a man on the opposite bench. He's slouched up in a T-shirt, head wilted to the side. He has bites on his legs and ingrown hairs in his chin.

"Yup," he says, without aligning his head.

"Thanks, man," says Dani.

Laurel lies in Dani's lap. Her pupils drift and her lips un-suction and fall apart. It's funny how she spaces out like that. Dani walked by the courts at PS 125 one night in eighth grade, saw Laurel on her knees before a younger boy. Some other kids stood around, watching. The dick dropped out of Laurel's mouth as she called to Dani, but Dani didn't stop. That was a couple years back, before they fell in love.

The train crosses the bay for a long time. It's getting later, and the color of the water sinks in, a few shades behind the sky.

Dani doesn't think it's such a hot idea to tell their moms. For one thing, they might not get it. Dani's always been a little dyke to them, in a nice way or whatever, just is, but not Laurel. For another thing, Dani likes the sneaking. She likes that Laurel slips across the hall when her mom goes to bed, is gone when Dani wakes for school. Once Dani's mom came home late, cracked the door to make sure Dani was in. Laurel slunk down under the sheets to the bottom of the bed, arms wrapped around Dani's thighs, breath heating her crotch. Nothing would be that sexy if the secret's out.

"Dani," says Laurel. "Don't ever let me look like that guy." Laurel indicates the man that helped them. His shorts and T-shirt don't join, leaving out a skin sack with pink pores and a happy trail. He's been listening to them and now looks away.

"What are you talking about?" Dani says.

"Like, we're cool now, when we're kids and everything," Laurel says. "But when I get older, I'm gonna exercise all the time. I don't ever want my girl to stop wanting me."

Laurel's eyes are an urgent green. Her scar is dry. Dani wonders what would happen if she ever wanted to dump Laurel. They're in love, really, and she can't imagine it ending. But there's the option. If they tell the moms, and then Dani wanted out, she'd be stuck. The moms would give her shit for the rest of her life for hurting Laurel. Before Laurel, anytime Dani got sick of a girl clinging on her she blocked her number and IM, looked away on the street. Some of the girls got mad, hit her in public. The boys on the block gave her high-fives and winks, had her back if things got dangerous. It was the only time they respected her. Now that they sense she's settled down, they're dicks again.

"Dani. You know what I mean?" Laurel says, clutching Dani. Her nails press through Dani's shirt, emboss crescents in her skin. Dani rotates away.

"Yeah, right," she says. "How long have we been on this freaking train?"

"I don't care." Laurel lies back down.

The shuttle stops and they get off. Across the platform, there's another train ready to go right back where they came from. White kids draped in towels scoot through half-open doors. Dani and Laurel walk to the exit. The lights in their train go out. A buzzer rings, and the doors close permanently. Dani and Laurel push their stomachs through the turn-stiles and go outside.

Mixtures of people funnel through the streets. The fast-food restaurants glow competing rectangles of neon on the pavement.

"Where's the beach?" says Dani to kids eating pink meat in sandwiches.

"Down there," says one, standing. A piece of meat is tiled to his face, stuck in a dimple. As he points, it unglues, disappears in the air on its way to the sidewalk.

Dani and Laurel head down Rockaway Beach Boulevard. They turn on 25th Street, and the beach opens up ahead of them. Kids sit on driftwood posts that mark the entrance. The beach is white and soft. It's not like Brighton Beach, the only beach they've been to, where there are garbage cans every ten feet and Russian men in glossy underwear who squat in your face and chat at you.

People are out, but not many. Handfuls of children clump around bright towels and potato chips crunched into the sand.

Laurel takes off her hoodie and runs at the sea. The water hits her hard and icy, but once she's up to her waist she's okay. Her mother says if you get your pussy to a certain temperature, the rest of your body adjusts. She guesses it works.

Laurel stands in the war zone of breaking waves, half-falling with each strike. Rubber strands of seaweed tangle her wrists. She peels them off and walks through the water, out past the breaking point, where the waves are docile, wet hills. Her shoulders stay dry and feel the light. It's the golden hour, when her mom says even Harlem is like Rome. It was the golden hour when Laurel first saw Dani differently, sauntering down Lenox. Saw she was more boy than girl, a change that happened so slowly she didn't recognize it. Laurel wanted to grab Dani right there, touch her with open palms. But it took Dani awhile to get the picture. Eventually Laurel had to march across the hall, chase another girl out of Dani's bed, and slip under the covers.

"What are you doing?" Dani said. "Where's Tanya?"

"Don't give me shit," Laurel said. "You know we love each other."

Laurel puts her back to the open water and picks out Dani onshore. Her arms are crossed over her knees and she's smoking her mom's weed. A lady on meaty thighs is looking at her askance, herding her kids away.

"Hey," calls Laurel. "Don't hog that shit."

Dani's too far.

"Don't hog it," says Laurel, louder.

"What?" says Dani, cupping her ear and grinning.

Laurel realizes she's being messed with. Dani walks into the ocean, baggy jeans inflating with water. She's milking the roach, squeezing the smoke out.

"Give me some," Laurel says.

"Huh, what?" says Dani.

"Dani, fuck. Don't do that, don't."

Dani scoops up Laurel like a dazed fish. Dani weighs about thirty pounds less than Laurel, and though she is strong, she could never carry her on land. It feels sweet to lift her girl, keeping Laurel's ass and shoulders below the waterline.

"Put me down," says Laurel. She churns water into Dani's face.

"Hey," Dani says, spitting out the joint. "You ruined it."

Dani sets Laurel in the waves and she sinks, her wrecked chin going under last. As soon as she's gone she's up again, shoving Dani into a breaking wave.

"You know I can't swim, jerk," Laurel says. They return to the beach and the black sweatshirt. It looks like a burned-out fire.

Laurel takes off her tank top. Her bra is stiff, unformed to her body. She throws her arms in the sky and spins, falls on the sand. Dani pounces on her, tastes her naked stomach.

"You're gonna get us in trouble, you crazy," Dani says. "Put some clothes on."

"All right. Stop kissing me, then."

Laurel pulls on the hoodie.

"Now you're all nice and dry," Dani says. "I have to wear this shit."

"Take it off, then," says Laurel, throwing her wet shirt at Dani.

Dani and Laurel cross the beach. The sky goes fuzzy without the sun. Dani's phone dies in her pocket, letting off a hysterical chorus of beeps. The families have deserted, stuck coolers and stacked towels in their motorized wagons and settled in elsewhere. But there's still a cramped circle of people on the horizon, lit at the feet by a pale light. Dani angles their path toward the group. Maybe they know about the whale barf. Dani wants to ask them, suddenly geared up to carry it back uptown, a rich trophy from this strange day.

Laurel takes Dani's hand midswing, anchors it to her hip.

"Let's head back now," Laurel says. "Let's tell our moms tonight. If they don't accept it, fuck that. We'll figure something out. We don't need the barf."

Dani's fingers cluster and sweat in Laurel's fist.

"Come on, I'll race you," Dani says. "To those people."

Dani slips her hand out, takes off. She forgot how hard it is to run on sand. On Brighton Beach you can't run, because you'd smack into someone after about two seconds.

As she gets close, she sees the people are standing up on a hilly range of sand.

"Don't fall in," says a guy with a bagged forty.

"Huh?" says Dani.

"The hole," says the kid, dipping the bottle toward his feet.

Dani crawls up the piles. They've been pushed back from the edge of the pit so they don't sift into it. It's the biggest hole she's ever seen. There are people crowded ten feet below the beach in the tapered bottom. Crude stairs are carved in the wall, and a recess with a fire. People sit on benches of packed sand, huddle on the floor. A man with a beard of pubic hair presides.

"You ran away," says Laurel, suddenly at Dani's side.

"Come on down, girls," calls the bearded man. "We're telling ghost stories. Bwa ha ha."

Drunk faces look up at Dani and Laurel, wonky-eyed and shiny around the mouth.

"We're cool," says Laurel, backing away from the lip. "Dani, let's get out of here."

"Oh, come on," says Dani. "Don't be a pussy."

"Take the sand-case," the man says. He points to the stairs.

Dani climbs down to the flat border rimming the pit, walks to the steps. They have eroded since their original form, or else were never decently made.

"Don't hang on the walls," says the man. "The sand's getting loose."

Dani squishes her hands into the twin bladders of water in her pockets so she won't be tempted to grab the sides. She imagines the sand rushing in, the children, beer and fire sealing up underground.

"Steady," says a guy, about twenty, with clear, spiky sideburns. He reaches for Dani. She heaves down into his hands, and he swings her into the hole. Laurel rushes in behind, tripping over a tiny kid.

"Jeez," the child cries.

"Sorry, kiddy," says Laurel. She takes the kid by the wrist, hunkers down. "Didn't mean that, little bud."

"You're crazy," he says. Everyone watches, big white faces lit by the fire.

"Don't worry about him," says the pale-haired guy, cupping Laurel's shoulder. "He's an idiot. I'm Ethan, by the by."

"Thanks, Ethan. You're my hero," Laurel says. She leans into his hand.

Dani follows behind them, resists the urge to break up their little moment. Ethan clears a place for them on a sand bench.

The pubic beard finishes his story. It doesn't wind up all that scary, but Laurel crowds into Dani's armpit anyway. When it's over, people mill around the hole, talking. Turns out some of the guys woke up at dawn to start digging, worked until five or six when little kids joined to build up the stairs and fireplace. Later they'll fill it all in.

"Balls," says one guy, raw across the cheeks from the sun. "You'd think it'd be easy, but it's worse than digging."

"Yeah, dude," says Ethan. "Filling blows."

Laurel's grinning, dopey, staring at Ethan.

"Hey," Dani says. "Take a picture."

Laurel's smile unbraids, lags on her face.

"What's your deal?" she says.

"Seriously, take one." Dani skims her ass to the other side of the bench, stares Laurel down. Laurel squints, tries to read her, and then checks out.

It's the same move she pulled last week when she brought up telling the moms. Laurel had just arrived from across the hall in a ratty T-shirt and underwear. Her eyes were all bright and funny.

"Let's tell our moms tonight," she said.

"They're asleep, crazy," said Dani. "It's two a.m."

"Okay, tomorrow then."

Dani said she liked it the way things were. If anything, she said, she wanted more freedom. She asked Laurel to sleep in her own apartment that night.

"I just want to be alone this minute," she said. "It's nothing. I just don't think we should spend every freaking night together. It's like, intense, you know?"

Laurel looked stricken, then unfocused her eyes, pretended she'd vanished. By the time she was back, the conversation was over, and she was all cozy and wedged into bed. The next day, Laurel nearly blurted their secret over a hotdog snack. Dani had leapt up, shouting, pretending she'd seen a cat burglar. The moms thought she was crazy, but what could she do? She can't get trapped in some high school marriage.

People walking dogs or leaving the beach late come upon the pit and

169

join. In time, the hole settles. Burned limbs rest on the sand benches. Someone scoops handfuls from the walls and puts in tea lights. Above them is an egg of sky. The stars aren't bright, but in Harlem there are only airplanes and satellites ticking lights between the high rises.

The conversation turns on a word Dani can't catch. Finally, it travels their way.

"Did you hear about the ambergris?" Ethan asks Dani. He makes a point of looking at Laurel, sleeping in Dani's lap.

"The what?" Dani says.

"It's crazy. It's, like, whale barf."

"Oh man, yeah. That's why we came out here. What do you know about it?"

"Well, it's fossilized whale puke. It's like a bunch of yellow, lumpy junk. They make perfume with it, I guess. Someone found a piece yesterday that looked like it was snapped off. Everyone was looking for the rest today. People think some kid broke it up who didn't know what it was."

"Isn't it worth, like, a lot of money?"

"Yeah, dude," he says. "It's worth a shit ton. About fifteen or twenty bucks a gram. This kid yesterday had almost a pound. That's like eight thousand bucks. And there could be up to, like, ninety-nine more pounds somewhere."

"Damn," says Dani. "Did anyone else find any?"

"No," says Ethan. "Too bad, right? Maybe we buried it. Ha."

"Wake up," Dani says, jabbing Laurel.

Laurel opens her eyes. Yellow and orange cells of light spin, find each other, and present the scene. Dani's in her face, and she's exhausted.

"Come on," Dani says. "Let's go. We want to find that whale barf, remember?"

"What time is it?" says Laurel. Her mom sets curfew at eleven, but she doesn't usually respect it.

"I don't know," says Dani. "My phone died. Come on."

"Don't go," says Ethan, to Laurel. He turns to Dani.

"How about this: you take a walk, find that ambergris, and come back when you have it, okay?"

"Fuck you," Dani says. "Come on, Laurel."

"No," says Laurel. "I'm sleeping."

"Sure you are," says Dani. "You're really sleeping. Get up. Let's go."

"Stop," Laurel says. She pushes Dani away. "Leave me alone. I'm tired, okay?"

"I'll take care of her while you're gone," Ethan says, winking. "Don't worry about it, little butch."

The hole has emptied out. All the adults are gone, and most of the kids. Remaining are the rude child and a college kid teaching him how to extinguish the fire. Dani's phone is dead, and she doesn't know if Laurel has hers at all. If they get separated, they won't be able to get in touch.

"Okay, fine," says Dani. "Whatever. Have fun."

She goes up the steps, eroded now into a ramp. She doesn't turn to see if Ethan's surprised, if Laurel's awake.

Dani goes to the water to look for ambergris. She does it fast. She's going to fucking shove it in Ethan's face when she finds it. When she sees anything that looks promising she throws it in a pile so she won't be tricked again. The pile fills with natural sponges, jellyfish, balls of paper bags. Nothing useful. She chucks the fool's gold with increasing force. They've come all this way and now she has to look alone.

Dani digs a little with her toes. She skims the distant beach in case the ambergris really is a hundred pounds. That's bigger than her. She thinks of how she and Laurel could carry it, between the two of them, back on the shuttle over the bridge and then, going local at this hour, for fifty stops on the A train. Fifty times with the doors sliding open and Dani doesn't doubt something would fuck up, probably Laurel's doing, and they wouldn't have the barf when they reached 119th. If Laurel even leaves with her at all.

Dani smokes another joint, damp but not ruined. This one she's not supposed to have. She got it from her mom's real stash, taped to a pipe under the sink. The vibrator pot is only a decoy: shitty, stale stuff that's practically Dani's allowance. This time she actually gets high, the sky setting into black Jell-O. She shivers into it. She falls asleep.

Before it seems possible, seagulls scream, dismissing the night. The black Jell-O air turns strawberry. Dani hauls up her pants and shoves into the water, out past the salty burp of the beach. She wonders if the moms are mad they've stayed out all night, if they'll trust the girls less now.

Out at sea, a black mass pops from the water. Foam rides its back, melts off, and then it goes under. Dani supposes it could be a seal, or a manatee or something, but she hopes it's the whale. It's come back for its barf before someone steals it or fucks with it. The whale knows no one's found the ambergris, no one will, and it's taking its present

171

back. It was too easy. But then again maybe it is just too easy. The ambergris is somewhere out here, and that's the whole point.

Dani heads back to the hole. It's filled in now, and the sand rises above the rest of the beach in a hump. As soon as she sees it, Dani knows Laurel's been buried. That Ethan messed her up, then broke her body with shovelfuls of sand. She's under the beach now, naked and bent, frozen in with cans and ashes.

Dani runs inland. The sand eats her feet at each stride. She meets Ethan sitting against two shovels stuck in the ground.

"Hey," he says.

"Where's Laurel?" Dani says. She opens her stance and gathers herself for what she has to do to this fucker.

"Relax, dude," Ethan says.

"I'm not gonna relax," Dani says. "Where is she?"

Ethan laughs.

"Just hold on a second," he says. "Calm down."

Dani lurches forward, grabs Ethan's sideburns. Before they can bleed, he shakes her off.

"Jesus Christ," he says. "Are you crazy? I didn't touch her. She was a feisty little bitch, like you. You belong together."

"No shit, asshole," Dani says.

Dani kicks sand at him before she turns away. He takes it without flinching, eyes open to the grains.

Dani walks around the mound of sand and finds Laurel lying on her shirt, dry now and sugared with sand. Laurel wakes up, rolls on her back and stretches her arms so her belly shows. She spins on the sand like a dog on a smell.

"I don't think we're going to make curfew," Laurel says.

"Ha. No shit."

Dani sits on Laurel's stomach. Dani's curls are frizzy now, the gel washed out, and they hang down to form a corridor leading their faces to each other.

"Are you cool?" Dani says.

"Of course. Listen. We don't have to tell them yet."

"Okay," says Dani. "Not yet."

Dani's arms shake as she suspends over Laurel. Her muscles have rotated, and weaker ones support her now.

"How long are we going to love each other?" Dani says.

"I don't know," Laurel says. "Until we want to stop."

Dani sees that she's serious, that whether it ends or not, it will be okay. She isn't required to see Laurel beside her forever down the un-known tunnel of their futures, into marriage and maybe even two more little girls playing for fun or playing for serious.

"Let's not stop yet," says Dani.

She rolls over next to Laurel, crowding her on the bed of stiff clothes. They look at the sky together, open and blank, and don't think about anything.

Nominated by New Letters and Gary Gildner

MENDING WALL

by JANICE N. HARRINGTON

from QUIDDITY

Never carefully enough, never slowly
enough are old women lifted and lowered
into their rolling chairs. Scraped, scratched,
pierced by roughness, old women split
as easily as sun-scalded plums—

torn by uniform buttons, the loose buckle
of a flopping restraint, fingernails,
watchbands, a wedding ring's silver setting,
and a washcloth's coarse nudgings.

Nurses' aides are friction. A ward
is an obdurate, serrated edge. Injured,
the skin parts: four rips on one arm
and scabs torn again. With a cotton-swab,
the aide prods a skin flap back into place,
gently flattening the rolled edge, but still
the wound opens, the seam seeps.

On a county ward, old women wait,
holding in slack laps their mummied arms
dressed with ointment and peroxide,
paper-taped and gauzed, lined
with purpled seams and mottlings.

You learn to take the splitting skin
and seeping scabs for granted, understanding
that the body refuses, at last, to keep its wall.
The blood slows, the skin thins, a scratch
on an old woman's arm widens
into a door. Carefully, she steps through.

Nominated by Quiddity

SOLDIER OF FORTUNE

fiction by BRET ANTHONY JOHNSTON

from GLIMMER TRAIN STORIES

Her name was Holly Hensley, and except for the two years when her father was transferred to a naval base in Florida, her family lived across the street from mine. This was on Beechwood Drive, in Corpus Christi, Texas. Our parents held garage sales together, threw hurricane parties, went floundering in the shallow, bottle-green water under the causeway. If the Hensleys were working overtime and Holly was staying late for pep-squad practice—which meant grinding against Julio Chavez in the backseat of his Skylark—my mother would pick up Holly's younger brother from daycare and watch him until they got home. Sam had been born while they were living in Florida. ("My old man got one past the goalie," Holly liked to say. "There's nothing more disgusting.") In 1986, the year everything happened at the Hensley house, Sam was three. Holly was eighteen, a senior at King High School, and I was a freshman, awkward and shy and helpless with love.

Most mornings we walked to school together. Holly's hair would be wet from the shower, her eyes wide and glassy with fatigue; she'd yawn and say, "What's buzzin' cousin?" She liked to drag her fingers along the chain-link fences we passed, and to stop at Maverick Market to buy Diet Cokes and steal candy bars. I waited outside, worrying she'd get caught. We talked about what she'd do after graduation—some days she planned to enroll at the beauty college, others she wanted to dance at the Fox's Den out by the oil refineries—and about Roscoe, the collie she'd adopted in Florida. She told me how her little brother preferred her Aggie sweatshirt to his baby blanket. I invented stories of girls I'd been with, wild things named Rhonda and Mandy and Anastasia who attended different schools and who, I hoped, might make Holly jealous. Usually, she'd just bump me with her hip and say, "You're more of a slut than I am." We never talked about the rumors that she and Julio had let a crowd of kids watch them in bed at a homecoming party, or that she'd recently been spotted leaving the Sea Ranch Motel with Mr. Mitchell, the geology teacher. Even my parents had heard about Mr. Mitchell. My mother said Holly was just trying to get her parents' attention, acting out because of the new baby. My father said she was trouble and if he caught me alone with her, he'd whip my ass. But I rarely saw her after we got to campus. Holly would disappear onto the school's smoking patio, a dismal slab of concrete where stringy-haired surfers and kids with safety pins through their eyebrows loitered, and I would go find Matt Rickard.

Matt and I had been friends since elementary. We'd played on the same soccer team, joined and quit Boy Scouts together, leaned despondently against the gym bleachers and watched couples sway at the junior-high dances our parents made us attend. In our freshmen year, Matt wore sleeveless shirts and tucked the cuffs of his camouflage pants into military boots; he had a pair of fatigues for every day of the week— desert camo, woodland and blue woodland, tigerstripe and black tigerstripe. For a while, we'd been into guerilla warfare. We bought *Soldier of Fortune* magazines, made blowguns from copper tubing, slathered our faces with mud when we crept under the lacey mesquite trees behind his house. We saved our allowances for the gun expos at the Bayfront Auditorium and loaded up on Chinese throwing stars and bandoliers of blank bullets, butterfly knives and pamphlets on chokeholds, and MREs that tasted like gluey chalk. We ate meals with the forks and spoons attached to our Swiss Army knives. Over the summer, though, I'd grown bored and embarrassed by the warfare stuff—my walls had been draped with camouflage netting, and over my bed I'd had a poster of one ninja roundhousing another—but Matt still liked it so I'd recently told him he could have my cache. He was disappointed in me, I knew, as if I'd defected to the enemy, and probably the reason he hadn't yet come to collect my stuff was the hope that I'd change my mind. But I'd already packed everything into my army duffel, and each afternoon I waited for Matt to take it away. I didn't think we'd stay friends much longer.

When my father came into my room on a Friday night in early October, I thought he'd say Matt was on the porch. I was on my bed, staring at the acoustic ceiling where the ninja poster had been and listening to my stereo. My father crossed the room and lowered the volume. He wore a short-sleeved shirt and a clip-on tie; he'd just gotten off work. He gazed through my window and into the backyard.

"Is Matt here?" I asked.

"You need to take care of Holly's dog for a few days."

"Roscoe," I said.

"Make sure he has food and water. Maybe play with him a little."

I sat up on my bed. My fathers voice sounded frayed, as if I were hearing him from far away. His hands were clasped behind his back. I thought I smelled cigarette smoke on him, but then I realized it was floating down the hall from the kitchen.

"Are they heading out of town?" I asked. The Hensleys had a van and sometimes drove to Comfort or Falling Water in the Hill Country.

"Don't go over there tonight," he said. "You can just start in the morning."

"Okay," I said. A wind gusted outside. Tallow branches scraped against the side of the house.

"If the dog shits on their patio, spray it down with the hose."

"Is Mom smoking again?"

"She might be, Josh," he said and put his hand against the window. "Yes, that might be happening."

In 1986, my father worked at the naval air station—most everyone's father did, including Holly's and Matt's—but he was also moonlighting at Sears, selling radial tires and car batteries, which he blamed on Reagan. It was the year the president denied trading arms for hostages in Iran and the Space Shuttle *Challenger* exploded and Halley's Comet scorched through the sky. It was the year I loved a reckless girl, the year being around my best friend made me lonely. It was the year my mother was working at the dry-cleaning plant and trying to quit smoking. I knew she occasionally snuck cigarettes—I'd seen her in the backyard on evenings when my father was at Sears—but she hadn't smoked in our house for months. On that night in October, when the filmy scent of smoke wafted into my room, I could only think that Holly's family was moving again. The last time her father had gotten news of his transfer, they were gone within a week.

But they weren't leaving. There'd been an accident earlier that day, something involving Sam, Holly's little brother. My father only knew that Sam had been taken away in an ambulance and the Hensleys would likely spend a few nights with him at the hospital. He relayed the information in a detached tone, as if summarizing a movie he didn't want me to watch. He'd moved from the window to sit on my bed, where he looked small. He said their mail would be held and there was a key under the ceramic cow skull on their porch. I tried to remember the last time I'd seen Sam, but couldn't—maybe the previous weekend, when he and Holly drew on their driveway with colored chalk, or maybe when Mr. Hensley was watering the yard with Sam on his shoulders. In my room, my father kept dragging his hand over his face, as if trying to wake himself up. I asked if he knew how Holly was doing, and he said, "She's hurting, Josh. They're all hurting like hell."

My mother baked all night—brownies and lemon bars, biscuits and an enchilada casserole. She fried chicken and sliced vegetables and made salami-and-cheese sandwiches that she quartered into triangles. When I came into the kitchen on Saturday morning, the counter was crowded with foil-covered dishes. My mother was walleyed. She poured me a glass of orange juice and put two pieces of cold fried chicken on my plate. "Breakfast of champions," she said.

With all the foil, the kitchen was bright and strange. The table was tacky with humidity. My mother shook a cigarette from a pack, then lit it from a burner on the stove. I heard it sizzle.

"Liz called last night," she said and exhaled smoke toward the ceiling. Liz was Mrs. Hensley, Holly's mother. My mother said, "Little Sam is sedated in intensive care."

"I don't know what's happening," I said.

"He burned himself," she said. "He's scalded all over the front of his little body."

Sam, my mother explained, had woken with a fever, so Mrs. Hensley kept him home from daycare. He spent the morning watching cartoons and napping on the living-room couch. While he slept, Mrs. Hensley was cleaning the house and washing clothes, then decided to make tuna salad for lunch. She put water on to boil eggs. She checked on Sam on the couch, then stepped into the garage to put a load of laundry in the dryer. They had an attached garage, so she left the kitchen door open in case Sam woke up and called for her. She got sidetracked looking for dryer sheets and stayed out there longer than she'd intended. Then she heard her son screaming: He'd pulled the pot of boning water down onto himself.

I felt cored out, not like I was going to vomit but like I already had. I pushed my plate away. At Sam's last birthday party, my parents and I

179

had given him a toy garbage truck. Holly gave him a baseball cap that read *I Wasn't Born In Texas, But Got Here As Soon As I Could.* He'd been wearing it when Mr. Hensley watered their lawn.

My mother opened the oven, looked inside, and then closed the door. Her cigarette was in an ashtray on the counter, smoke ribboning toward the open window.

"That poor family," my mother said.

"They're behind the eightball," I said. It was a phrase my father used.

"They sure are," she said. "Liz couldn't find Holly until very late. She thought she was off with that Julio."

"She had pep-squad practice," I lied. "I saw her when I walked home."

"You did?"

"There's a game this weekend," I said. "A big one."

"Then that's a relief. I worried she was with the teacher again."

"I don't think that really happened, the stuff with Mr. Mitchell," I said.

"I know you don't, sweetheart."

I took another bite of chicken, drained my orange juice. I said, "Matt might come over today. I'm giving him all my war stuff."

"I'll leave some chicken for you two," she said. "Your father and I are taking the rest to the hospital."

"I want to go," I said.

She brought her cigarette to her lips, then stubbed it out. She said, "No, Joshie, I don't think you do."

Their house had always been nicer than ours, and bigger. Over the years, workers had renovated the Hensleys' kitchen and added two rooms on the house's backside, a study and a game room. They had a bumper-pool table, thick carpet and Saltillo tile, lights with dimmer switches, and a fireplace. "Who needs a fireplace in Corpus?" my father had said one night. He was squinting through the peephole in our front door, watching smoke rise from the Hensleys' chimney. "Don't try to be something you're not, boy," he told me, and then told me again when they bought an aboveground pool for their backyard right before Mr. Hensley was transferred to Florida. I'd assumed the transfer was a demotion or punishment, but my father said Hensley had applied for it. (By way of explanation, he'd only said, "They're Republicans, Joshie.") While they were away, the Hensleys rented the house to a

Catholic deacon and his wife, and when they returned, they paid to have new vinyl siding installed. It was gray with white and black trim, the shades of a lithograph.

Until that October weekend, I'd never been alone in their house. It seemed illicit, like when Matt and I paged through his father's *Playboys*. The darkened rooms made me anxious. I had the sense I would do something I shouldn't, the dangerous and disappointing feeling that I couldn't be trusted. Had there been a route for me to bypass the house and still reach the garage where Roscoe's food was, I would've taken it, but I didn't have their garage-door opener--their automatic door was another extravagance my father resented—so I had to cut through the kitchen. I went twice on Saturday, three times on Sunday. I moved like a thief on each visit, never lingering or touching what I didn't have to. The air in the house smelled of potpourri, cloistered and spiced, and I tried not to breathe. I averted my gaze from the familiar and mysterious artifacts of the Hensleys' lives.

And yet I couldn't keep from seeing the coffee table Mrs. Hensley had pulled over to the couch so Sam wouldn't roll off, Holly's Aggie sweatshirt spread over the cushions, little red high-top shoes upturned on the carpet. I pretended not to know the Hensleys and tried to piece together a different family based on evidence they'd left behind. *Their son is an only child*, I thought. *His parents have taken him to a swimming lesson.* Or I imagined all of the Hensleys were home and hiding, waiting for me to break or steal something. My heart pumped in my ears. I left the lights off. In the kitchen, the floor tile gleamed; Holly's father had come home briefly Friday night, mopped up the spilled water, and grabbed fresh clothes for everyone at the hospital. The copper-bottomed pot was in the sink. Four unopened cans of tuna were stacked on the counter.

In the backyard, Roscoe always barreled into my legs and knocked me sideways. He jumped as high as my shoulders and scratched my chest through my shirt and licked my hand with his warm tongue. I let him chase me around the pool, and I threw pinecones for him to catch. We wrestled in the grass the way Holly had said he liked, then I scratched the scruff of his neck until he snored. I fed him more than I should. Before school on Monday morning, maybe because I'd been hoping Holly would appear on her porch and we'd walk to school together, I opened one of the cans of tuna and let Roscoe eat it from a spoon. That evening there was diarrhea all over the patio.

At school, the story kept changing. Sam wasn't scalded, he'd drowned in the Hensleys' pool. He'd slipped on a wet floor and hit his head. His brain was swelling. He'd been hit by a car, he'd eaten roach poison. Someone claimed to have seen the geology teacher taking flowers to the hospital, and someone else said they'd been in the faculty parking lot and found him weeping in his truck. On Wednesday, Matt said he'd heard the whole thing was a lie to cover up how Sam had accidently shot himself with his father's unregistered pistol.

We were standing by the statue of a mustang, the school mascot. Matt was in his blue woodland camos. He said, "I bet it was the Luger she showed us. If it was, the kid's toast."

Shortly after she returned from Florida, Holly had taken me and Matt into her parents' bedroom and showed us her father's pistol. She'd been babysitting Sam, and we'd been climbing the retama tree in my front yard. We were wearing our camouflage with pellet rifles slung over our shoulders, pretending to be mercenaries. She'd called across the street, "Y'all want to see something cool?" The pistol was a German Parabellum 1908, a semi-automatic Luger. We'd read about them in our magazines.

"He burned himself," I told Matt. "He's sedated in intensive care, but he's going to pull through." I made up the last part. The night before, I'd asked my father about Sam and he told me to concentrate on my schoolwork and not to give Roscoe any more tuna.

"I heard he did it in the game room," Matt said. "I heard there's a gnarly bloodstain under the pool table."

"You heard from who?"

"Jeff Deyo," Matt said.

"You don't know Jeff Deyo," I said. Jeff Deyo was a red-eyed senior, a friend of Julio's who'd gotten held back. He wore the same flannel shirt every day, unbuttoned and tattered, and when I passed him in the hall, I smelled the smoker's patio.

"We've been hanging out," Matt said. "We've been getting high. If you tell, I'll kick your ass."

"You need to come get all of my gear. If you don't want it, I'll throw it away."

"Don't take it out on me just because your girlfriend's brother blew his face off."

"She's not my girlfriend," I said.

"Right," he laughed. "She's dating Mr. Mitchell and you're with Anastasia from across town."

"You're an asshole."

"Check the game room," he said. "I heard the stain looks like a pot leaf."

Later that night, Mrs. Hensley called. My father was working his shift at Sears, and I was watching television on the couch while my mother smoked beside me. After answering, my mother handed me the receiver and told me to hang up once she switched to the kitchen phone. While she made her way down the hall, I told Mrs. Hensley about Roscoe catching the pinecones I tossed. She thanked me and said Holly would call me once things calmed down with Sam. Then my mother said, "Okay, Joshie, I got it."

"Okay," I said, but I just pushed the mute button and stayed on the line. I wanted to hear if Mrs. Hensley would say anything more about Holly, if she'd mention Mr. Hensley's Luger.

"We're going to Houston," Mrs. Hensley said. "They're moving him to the burn unit at the Shriner's Hospital."

"Okay," my mother said. "Okay."

"I don't know. I don't know if it's okay."

"Are the doctors saying anything else?"

"You're going to Houston, that's what they're saying. They're saying, We can't help him here."

I checked out the game-room carpet on Saturday morning, then crept through the rest of the house that night. I knew I wouldn't find a bloodstain, just as I knew stealing through their hallways was a betrayal, but I couldn't stop myself. The moonlight canting through the blinds was bright enough in most rooms, but I also used the angle-head flashlight I'd bought at a gun expo. In the near dark, the Hensleys' house seemed smaller, not bigger, which surprised me. A fine layer of dust on the surfaces—the marble-topped dressers, the pool table's rails, the framed pictures on the walls—shone in the light, reflected it, and made me think of silt on a riverbed. Moving through their rooms gave me a jumpy, underwater feeling, as if I were swimming through the wreckage of a sunken ship, paddling from one ruined space to another. I avoided Sam's room.

And I'd told myself I wouldn't go into Holly's room, but on Sunday night I did. The moon hung low in the sky, a lurid glow seeping through her curtains and puddling on the carpet. The room smelled of lavender. I'd been in there before, but stripped of noise and electric light, the layout seemed unexpected. Her bed was made, piled high with frilly pillows and stuffed animals—open-armed bears, mostly, and a plush snake stretching the length of her mattress. Four silver-framed photos topped her vanity: Holly and Sam in an orange grove, Julio on Padre Island flexing his arms and smirking, Roscoe licking Holly's face with her eyes closed, and a picture of Holly when she was younger, eating ice cream with a fork. Green and white streamers were tacked to her closet door, and when I moved too quickly, they fluttered and startled me. She had a banana-shaped phone on her nightstand, and I began worrying it would ring. Or I thought my father would silently appear in her doorway, his eyes narrow with disgust. *Leave*, I thought. *Go home*. In my chest, my heart was wild as a trapped, frantic bird.

And yet I stayed. Outside, Roscoe trotted around the pool; his tags tinkled. Once, he started barking and I dropped to the floor and shimmied under Holly's bed. The Hensleys, I knew, had returned from Houston. I imagined Holly coming into her room and calling someone—Julio or maybe even Mr. Mitchell—to relay news about Sam. I imagined her turning off the lights and weeping and falling asleep with me under her. I considered bolting, trying to climb out the window and into the backyard, but knew I'd make too much racket. Roscoe kept barking. He was racing from one fence to another. I held my breath. I listened to phantom footfalls, the murmur of floorboards and studs behind the walls, the sad and random noises of an empty house at night. My hands were trembling, so I tucked them between my chest and the carpet. I still had the same underwater feeling, though now it was as if I were sinking, watching the surface grow blurry and distant. I waited to hit the bottom, to be discovered in the darkness.

But the lights in Holly's room never came on, and eventually Roscoe settled down. I pulled myself out from under the bed. I thought of how Matt and I used to crawl on our bellies in the brush behind his house, our faces obscured with mud. It occurred to me that while I was hiding in the Hensleys' house, he might be getting high with Jeff Deyo, and I felt suddenly and intensely alone. I had an odd sense of erasure, as if I were seeing the set for a play be dismantled. It was disorienting. And now that I'd crossed into Holly's room, I knew I'd return every night. The knowledge left me feeling resigned and melancholy, but also shot through with boldness. Before leaving, I dialed Matt's number on the banana phone, and when he answered, I didn't say a word.

My father was off from Sears that Thursday, so when he got home from the base, we mowed the Hensleys' lawns. Maybe my mother had asked him to do it, or maybe he'd gotten the idea after finishing our yard. I hoped it meant the Hensleys would return soon. As he pushed our lawnmower across the street—the engine idling, the blades scattering debris like when a Chinook lifts off—I followed him with the rake and bag of clippings.

A cold front had silvered the sky, unraveled the clouds. The air smelled briny, and every so often a wind would gust and eddy the fallen leaves. I waited for my father to announce the Hensleys were driving back from Houston, but he never did. While he swept the back patio, I said, "Maybe when Sam comes home Mom will quit smoking."

He leaned the broom against the house and fished his handkerchief out of his pocket, wiped his forehead. Roscoe was snortling along the fenceline. I looked at my shoes, flecked with cut grass.

I said, "Maybe she'll be less stressed and—"

"Josh," he interrupted, "when Sam comes home, he might not look the same. We need to start preparing ourselves for that."

I nodded and dragged the rake across the grass; the trimmings jumped like grasshoppers. I thought of the picture in the silver frame on Holly's dresser, the one of her and her brother in the orange grove. Originally, I'd assumed they were in Florida, but now I believed they might have been in the Rio Grande Valley. In the picture, they're holding hands and heading away from the camera so their faces are invisible. It had become my favorite thing in Holly's room. Since Sunday night, I'd lain on Holly's bed, opened her closet to press my nose into her clothes, even spritzed her perfume on my windbreaker so I could inhale her at home. I'd dialed every number I could think of on her banana phone—my mother at the dry cleaner, my father at the base and Sears, the secretary at King and the principal and my own house—then hung up when anyone answered. I never looked in her drawers, and I never stole anything, but every night I considered taking the orange-grove picture. I could stare at it for hours, imagining where they might go once they stepped beyond the aperture.

"He's behind the eight ball," I said.

"This kind of thing can tear up a family," my father said. "It can rip even a strong family to shreds. It's not easy to watch."

"They need our help," I said. "You're saying we need to—"

"We'll help however we can, Josh, but what I'm saying is we're not going to let them drag us into their problems."

"I understand," I said, though I didn't.

"What I'm saying is when Holly needs a shoulder to cry on, don't let it be yours."

But the Hensleys didn't come home. Mrs. Hensley, I knew, called my mother late at night every couple of days, and I kept hoping to wake up and see their van in their driveway, but it never appeared. One night, I overheard my parents talking about skin grafts and a neoprene bodysuit that would keep Sam's flesh hydrated, compressed. Their voices were hushed and somber. My father also mentioned how Mr. Hensley's sick leave and vacation days were long gone. Another night, I thought they were talking about Sam again, but they were just discussing the breakdown of talks between President Reagan and Gorbachev in Iceland. The neighborhood started getting ready for Halloween, carved pumpkins appearing on porches and cardboard witches hanging in windows, and the temperature was dropping, especially in the evenings. In Corpus, the fall is damp and glomming. I laid out a pallet of blankets for Roscoe in the garage and started pouring warm water over his food. I used the copper-bottomed pot that Holly's father had left in the sink.

I'd barely seen Matt since the day we talked about the bloodstain. He'd been skipping school a lot, and on those days when I did glimpse him in the hall, I hid behind my locker door or ducked into the bathroom. With the changing weather, he'd taken to wearing a plaid flannel shirt with his fatigues. He hung out on the smoker's patio in the mornings and afternoons. I called his house every night from Holly's banana phone and never said anything. Sometimes Matt hung up right away, others he'd lay the receiver beside a radio he'd tuned to a Tejano station, or he'd read classified ads from *Soldier of Fortune* into the phone: *The survival knife you've been waiting for, ten-inch blade and hollow compass-topped handle. Bounty hunting is legal and profitable! Silent firepower: crossbows and slingshots.* The duffel bag with all of my warfare stuff was still in my room, and though I no longer expected Matt to take it away, I also hadn't unpacked it.

So, on the morning when he waved me over to the smoker's patio and said he'd pick up the duffel that afternoon, I should have been relieved. There were a few other students on the patio, sallow-skinned seniors I'd seen with Holly, and who'd always intimidated me. I was surprised by how easily Matt fit in, saddened by it. He was wearing his tigerstripe camos, toeing out a cigarette with his combat boot. He blew smoke over his shoulder, the way my mother sometimes did, and said, "Is that cool? Jeff said he'd give me a ride."

"I threw it away," I said.

"No way," he said, his voice light with disappointment, as if I'd forgotten his birthday.

"I didn't think you were coming. I was tired of seeing it."

"That really sucks, Josh."

"And there wasn't a bloodstain," I said.

"What?"

"At Holly's house," I said. "Sam didn't shoot himself."

"That's what this is about?"

"I looked. There's no bloodstain," I said. "He burned himself with a pot of water. He'll probably have a skin graft."

Matt nodded, his eyes downcast and thoughtful. A small wind picked up, wafting the acrid smell of put-out cigarettes. I thought Matt was thinking of something kind to say about Sam. Once, when I got stung by an asp behind his house, he broke off a piece of aloe from his mother's plant and rubbed it on the wound.

Now, though, he just grinned and said, "I bet his face looks like melted cheese, all stretched and gooey. He won't need a mask for Hallowe—"

My fist connected right above Matt's temple. "Oh shit," a girl said, and a crowd of smokers cinched around us. Before Matt knew what was happening—before I knew what was happening—I'd hit him again in his mouth. Already there was blood on his teeth, in the corners of his lips. Then I was on top of him and we were falling to the patio and he was trying to cover his face with his forearms and saying, "Dude, come on, please no," and I was waiting for someone to stop me, to pull me off of him, to save both of us.

The principal called my mother at the dry cleaners to pick me up from school; he'd suspended me for three days. I expected her to be angry or embarrassed, but when I apologized to her, she said, "Oh, Joshie, we always thought Matt was a twerp."

We drove to the bayfront and sat on the seawall. Although we were out in the open—the bay seething in front of us, the docked sailboats bobbing in the marina to the west—I felt as if we were hiding, staking out a place to plot our next move. The tide heaved. Waves walloped the barnacled pylons; the dirty foam spread and dissolved. Eventually a crisp, salted wind nosed ashore and my mother scooted closer to me. I kept expecting her to light a cigarette.

"Sometimes I snoop in the Hensley house," I said.

"I know."

"You do?"

"I watch your little flashlight beam from our window," she said. "It reminds me of a fly trying to get out."

"I don't take anything," I said. "I just look."

"I know that, too."

A white gull hovered over us, then banked off and wheeled over the surf. I could hear cables clanging against hollow masts in the marina, the wind soughing through the dry palm trees that loomed along the seawall. Behind us stood the Bayfront Auditorium where the gun expos took place. My knuckles ached.

"Dad says Sam might look different when he comes home," I said.

My mother nodded. She was watching the gull. It had landed on a pylon, its head moving around in twitches.

"And he said I should stay away from Holly."

"Her life's already sewn up," she said, her gaze still trained on the gull. "Matt's is, too. And now probably Sam's."

"I don't understand," I said.

"Good," my mother said, resting her head on my shoulder. "Good, I'm glad."

Now, I think of 1986 as the year my life pivoted away from what it had been, maybe the year when all of our lives pivoted. It was the year my parents spoke in low, furtive tones and I strained to hear what they weren't saying. It was the year I surrendered the weapons of my youth—the morning after I fought Matt, I *did* throw out my duffel bag—and the year Holly Hensley shocked everyone by dropping out of school and joining the Coast Guard. This happened right after Thanksgiving. Her enlisting, I remember, was met with disillusionment and disdain—it seemed selfish and rash—but she found her footing in the military and enjoyed a distinguished career. After the Coast Guard, she moved to the army and was stationed in Hawaii, Guam, and, until her chopper went down two days ago, Afghanistan. According to the short obituary my mother just emailed me, Holly is survived by two sons and a husband, and she achieved the rank of staff sergeant. I hadn't seen her in almost twenty years. Funeral arrangements are being made in

188

Corpus. I'll send flowers, and if I can find it, I'll make a copy of the orange-grove photo and mail it to her family.

The night after I got suspended, I decided to steal that picture of Holly and her brother. I'd been lying on my bed earlier that day—my father had taken away my stereo and television privileges, and until my suspension ended, I was only allowed out of the house to feed Roscoe— and I'd thought having the orange-grove photo might quell my desire to sneak into Holly's room. I'd also started thinking Mr. Hensley would return soon, so my access to the house felt fleeting, like a journey to a foreign country—a deployment—was coming to an end. I wanted a souvenir.

The moon was full that night, lamping the Hensleys' backyard and rimming the curtains in Holly's room. Everything else lay in deep shadow; I clicked my flashlight on and off to see, and wondered if my mother was watching from across the street. I suspected she was and didn't mind. The house still smelled of potpourri, a little dank. I'd debated over grabbing another picture from Holly's parents' room to replace the one I wanted to take, but finally decided I'd just cluster the remaining three photos and hope Holly would have forgotten what had been there before. It seemed possible.

I was standing in front of her dresser, trying to visualize the most inconspicuous way to rearrange the pictures when, from behind me, I heard, "What's buzzin', cousin?"

I spun around, knocked into the dresser. The frames toppled. My heart kicked in my chest. Holly was on her bed, lying on her side among the stuffed animals. Even when I looked straight at her, her image was obscured in the dark.

"I didn't take anything," I said.

"You should have," she said. "I would."

"I just like the picture of you and Sam in the orange grove."

"I do, too," she said. "What you can't see is that the oranges are frozen solid. It was last year, right before we came back, and there was this massive cold snap that killed everything."

I clasped my hands behind my back; they were trembling again. I said, "I'm sorry for sneak—"

"We're alone here, if you're wondering," she said, shifting on the bed. "My parents are still in Houston with Sam. Julio came to get me. If I don't go back to school, I won't graduate."

"I'm suspended," I said.

"And Matt's a bloody mess."

189

"You heard?"

"I heard you were defending Sam," she said. "I almost went to your house to thank you, but then I saw the grass clippings on the carpet and figured you'd be back."

"I never looked in your drawers," I said.

"You'll do better next time," she said.

A raft of clouds floated past the moon, shrouding the room for a moment. I looked at the ceiling and couldn't see it. I could hear myself breathing.

"I wanted the orange-grove picture," I said. "I was going to steal it."

"You can't have that one, but I'll make you a copy," she said. "Want anything else?"

"I want Sam to get better."

"Me, too. He's trying. Anything else?"

"I want to know about Mr. Mitchell," I said.

Holly rolled onto her back. She tossed a stuffed white bear into the air, caught it, then did it again. She said, "I'll tell you, but you only get three wishes. You're sure this is how you want to use your last one?"

I wasn't sure of anything at that moment. I felt as if I were balancing on a precipice, and I needed to think clearly. I tried to imagine how disappointed my father would be if he knew where I was, tried to understand what my mother had meant about everyone's lives being sewn up. I thought of how Sam used Holly's sweatshirt for a blanket, and the baseball cap she'd given him for his birthday. I wondered how it would feel to live outside of Texas, what it would be like to walk through a frozen orange grove or to douse yourself with boiling water or to see your young son lying in a coma and not recognize him.

And then, like that, I understood. Before I could stop myself, I said, "He's yours, isn't he? Sam is."

Holly tossed the bear again, higher. In the air, it spiraled and looked like a silver fish flashing through murky water. She did it again, higher still. I thought she was trying to hit the ceiling I could barely see.

"That's why you went to Florida," I said. "Your parents didn't want—"

"Josh," she said.

"Yes?"

"Stop talking," she said.

"I won't tell anyone."

"Come here," Holly said, "Just come here."

I thought I would lie beside her and she would whisper the trajectory of Sam's life to me, explain who else knew her secrets and who his fa-

190

ther was. It gave me a sensation of inertia, of countless mysteries part-
ing around me like currents. But Holly offered none of this. She just
lifted the comforter and I took off my shoes and she pulled me on top
of her. We kicked her stuffed animals to the carpet, stripped off our
clothes, tangled into each other. Roscoe barked in the backyard and ran
along the fence; Holly said, "He chases possums." The house groaned.
I shivered. I thought of the Luger in her parents' bedroom and won-
dered where Matt was at that late hour. I worried my father would
come looking for me, but also felt certain my mother would run inter-
ference. Soon, Holly said, "I just want him to be okay," and started
sobbing against my chest. I was fourteen years old, scared and inexpe-
rienced and mystified by the luck of my life, and though I could think
of nothing to say, I held her close, as tight as I could. Eventually her
breathing slowed so completely I wondered if she'd gone to sleep. I
hoped so. I was wide awake, my eyes open and adjusted to the darkness.
The edges of her curtains were again framed in moonlight, and in the
shallow glow, our skin looked new and smooth and unblemished, ready
for the scars that were lying, somewhere, in ambush.

Nominated by Benjamin Percy

ORPHANAGE

by ELAINE TERRANOVA

from SALAMANDER

All day, I watched my mother: What she
could clean up, what she could
get out of the way. You know, in the rush,
in the desperation to do the laundry.

She'd wake and think, What now? Or sometimes,
I'd like to throw myself out of the window
and walk away a little dog.

It's the cold. It's the war. It's my bedroom
adjacent to theirs. Some plants
replicate as a starburst, parent plant
striking out, a hand in your face,

a clutch of fingers. I walked
with my parents past the orphanage. I looked
with longing at the empty swings

and the wide green playing field behind the gate.
The children. Where were they? Locked away
like a treasure. What was freedom then, what?

Nominated by Daniel Hoffman, Eleanor Wilner

OUR DAILY TOAST

by BRENDA MILLER

from SWEET

Today, for no good reason, I ate two slices of toasted cinnamon/raisin bread at 9:30 a.m., a mere two hours since breakfast. I slathered the first one with whipped butter, and even as I ate it I made up a reason to have another. It was that Ezekiel, biblical bread, made with sprouted grains touched by Jesus, so it couldn't be that bad for you, could it? It might even lead to a brief bout of cinnamon-scented clarity. So I toasted the second one and ate it slowly, slowly, biting off the crust first to leave a perfect round to nibble until I reached the center. The center eaten, and then there was a perfect nothingness—see? Enlightenment. And then a little nap.

Okay, I admit it: I have an unhealthy preoccupation with toast. Do I eat toast socially? Yes. Do I eat toast when alone? Yes. Do I lie about my toast consumption? Yes. Do I hide the evidence of toast consumption? Yes, Yes. Do I make up lame excuses for toast consumption? Why yes, yes I do.

My dog loves toast even more than I do, a fact that makes for an ever-ready handy reason to get out the bread sack and fire up the Sunbeam. My dog, contrary to popular belief, can be a little stand-offish at home, preferring to nap on (or under) my bed, or to disappear altogether upstairs, when her job (clearly laid out to her when she was hired) is to keep me company at all hours of the day. So, rather than endure union negotiations, sometimes I resort to bribes to get her to sit next to me on the couch. Popcorn's always a good one; as soon as the Redenbacher starts whirring, I can hear Abbe's feet scrabbling down the stairs, and then her eager face appears in the doorway to the kitchen. No matter how many times we do this, she goes into a posture of worship below the kitchen counter, staring at the popper with such intensity you'd think this billowing cloud of popped kernels really was a miracle. And as soon as those white drifts start spilling into the bowl, she jumps up on her hind legs, tail wagging, glances at me wide-eyed, tongue out as if to say: *Do you see this? Do you SEE?!*

For popcorn, my dog will jump onto the couch and put her head on my lap, eyes rolled up to watch every blessed movement of hand to mouth, and I'll feed her a few pieces, one by one. She chomps every piece with gusto, her lips wide open and smacking, a lusty girl who loves with abandon. It makes me laugh, this face, and thus I eat a lot of popcorn. And I watch a lot of TV to justify the popcorn eating, but that's another story altogether.

Toast is a different matter, makes us a little quieter in our devotions. More like communion than a tent revival. More *domestic*. Toast is thoughtful, whereas popcorn is scattered, hare-brained. Toast is private. After all you don't order a bag of toast in the movie theater (though believe me, I would love to!) Toast is something eaten in your pajamas; toast lends itself to the contemplative perusal of each bite, the way one's teeth make pretty little scallops in the surface. My dog takes the bites of crust I offer her delicately, politely, and ducks her head as she eats them, then looks up and places her nose right in my ear to say thank you. Abbe and I could eat toast all day and be very happy girls.

It occurs to me that confessing I bribe my dog for love can appear a bit pathetic. It may be just my history of love, a love that even in childhood always felt a bit like barter. You give me this, I'll give you that, and everyone's happy. Toast seems to have always hovered around the edges too: rye toast made from the fresh loaf bought at the Delicious bakery, my mother calling out, *do you want a piece of toast darling?*, a call that could always bring me back from whatever worlds I had wandered into while playing. I sat placidly at the kitchen table and ate rye toast with butter, keeping my mother company as she put away the rest of the groceries. I kept my eyes on her to see where everything went, on the look out for Mallomars and Suzie Q's. As I got older, I would make my own toast after arriving home stoned and a little giddy, the toast making the most pleasing crunch in my mouth as I posed at the window, my lips still tender from kisses. I could hear my parents turning out the light in their bedroom, able to sleep now that I was home. The smell of toast meant all their children were safe.

And even later, when I lived with one man and then another and then another, toast could allay even the most bitter arguments. When I lived with Francisco in our mildewed canvas tent at the edge of Lake Powell, we made toast on the iron skillet, a process that required patience and watchfulness and diligence. We spread it with cheap margarine, ate it in silence in the early morning cold. When I lived with Seth at Orr Springs, we made toast on a griddle pan, from loaves we made ourselves, big heavy wheat bread always a little too moist in the middle, studded with hard specks of millet. Toasting made it better, and we spread the slices with homemade apricot jam, made it something to linger over in the mornings before all the chores—wood to be chopped, leaks to be fixed, weeds to be plucked—crowded in to oppress us.

When I lived with Keith, we toasted bread at all hours of the day as we both wrote in our rooms in that little house in Green Lake. He would say, in passing, *this is my life!* and sometimes this cry meant: "I can't believe my good fortune, eating toast with you in this house on the hill!," and sometimes, if the writing weren't going so well, it meant: "I can't believe this is what my life has come to, eating toast with you in this house on the hill." But in any case, we enjoyed the toast, made with grainy, slightly sweet bread bought at the co-op down the road. Eating toast made everything good enough, for a little while at least.

For about a year I embarked on a diet (excuse me, I mean *lifestyle change*) that didn't include much bread at all, and one day I realized I hadn't used my toaster in over a month. I put it away, swept off the crumbs that had accumulated underneath, proudly announced on the Weight Watchers message board that I had committed this virtuous act. I got lots of congrats and virtual high-fives, but after a while I looked mournfully at that empty spot on the counter, my dog looked mournfully at me, and I caved. The toaster got trundled out, and I made one Thomas's Light Extra-Fiber English muffin. Then, a few days later, another. And then a piece of cinnamon toast. On the Weight Watchers board I blamed my dog, but no one bought it. I still lost 25 lbs and kept them off, but toasts of all varieties gradually wormed their way back as a daily ritual.

This daily toast doesn't often lead to epiphanies, not of the startling kind, just inaudible sighs, moments of fleeting gladness. Often I hardly notice I'm eating at all, not until my dog puts her paw on my knee, reminds me something momentous is happening: *look, toast! Do you realize you're eating toast? I could eat some of that toast.* I peel off a bit of crust, the part coated with sesame seeds, and offer it to her just out of reach, so she needs to stretch a little, showing me she wants it enough. She always does, the tip of her snout touching my fingers just for a second, and then her eyes stare into mine, holding me caught in her love as she chews and chews and chews.

Nominated by Sweet and Bruce Beasley

ROLL OUT THE FOOL

by WILLIAM TROWBRIDGE

from POEMS & PLAYS

> *St. Chrysostom formulated the most comprehensive and fundamental definition when he described The Fool or Clown as "he who gets slapped."*
> —Enid Welsford, The Fool: His Social and Literary History

In cave days, Fool mated
with the pratfall,
the hot foot, the bully's
brunt—his deadpan
so endearing when his head

met stone, he was voted
Best Victim.
The teens loved it.
Grown-ups, too.
He tamed their blood

pressure and kept
their world view cheerful
as a cannibal hoedown.
But they wanted more,
something *real*

good: no more chipped
bicuspids or routine
flesh wounds.
So they'd make him
a clubbing dummy,

spear catcher, all-day
torch, sabertooth lure.
Forest gatherings
lacked the proper tang
without a Flaming Fool,

Exploding Fool,
or—big mistake—
a Fool Frappé, which,
one snowy night,
everybody ate

like it was brain
food or something,
so now we've got
Fool in our marrow,
which explains

history, for one thing.

Nominated by Poems & Plays and Charles Harper Webb

FINAL CONCERT

by EVE BECKER

from THE GETTYSBURG REVIEW

My father sits at the edge of his bed, insisting on his shiny concert shoes. Their lack of traction on a polished floor is treacherous for a man who can no longer stand up on his own, a man who has seized and used every moment of living left to him. But the shoes are not negotiable, nor are the button-down shirt or the pants that need to be safety pinned to secure them to his wasted frame. In an hour or so, my father will find the weight of his clothes unbearable. In a few hours, my father will be dead. But first there is a final concert to play, and there is the proper attire in which to play it. I watch as my mother helps my father get into his clothing for the last time.

Earlier in the day, I held my father's mottled hand, the baggy skin flaking away, but the grip still sturdy from a lifetime of scaling the strings of his viola. For much of his career, my father was the assistant principal violist of the New York Philharmonic. "You have to know when he's going to start," my father whispered from his pillow. He took a noisy, shallow breath in, and released a long, rattling exhale. "You have to know when he wants you to play the beats."

Well, of course! I thought. *Not a black-hooded figure with a scythe, but a conductor with a baton.* "You know when to play the beats, Dad-ling," I said gently, though I hadn't been a gentle daughter.

"But you don't!" he said, with more strength than I thought he had left. He hadn't been a gentle father.

"Well, I'm not the musician," I said evenly.

He took several percussive but unhurried breaths. "It's deceptive. It begins with a rest."

"Oh. A rest." I pronounced the word lingeringly, softly. "That sounds like a good idea." My father hadn't slept for several days. His body was strung tight, and he couldn't stay still; he had plowed an agitated path between his bed and the reclining chair in the living room, going back and forth like the needle on a metronome, assisted by my mother or my sister or me. And when he no longer had the strength to get from one room to the other, he had relied on us to help him sit up in bed, lie down, sit up. All day. All night. "Do you want to rest?"

He didn't answer. His mind had drifted elsewhere. His hand was cold; I let go of it, and pulled back. The smell of death already permeated his body, and though I wanted to kiss his brow, as I had done the day before, the stench drove me away. He held the hand out in front of him and examined it. The skin under his fingernails looked bruised. His green eyes had a pale, opaque glaze to them as he slowly rotated the hand from side to side and then brought it back toward his gut. Was he already leaving his body behind like an old coat, wondering to whom this hand belonged?

I sat with him, trying to hold onto just being in his presence. As I had become more than a guest in my parents' home, my father and I had shared a comfortable closeness that had been pointedly absent from our adult relationship. My sense of the minutes floated away with him.

But then he was back. "What time is it?" He could barely get the words out, but there was a sense of urgency. "When . . . when do I play?"

"In a couple of hours, maybe," I told him.

"No!" His voice held a faint trace of power and rage that lingered like the smell of sulfur after a gun is fired. "When is it? When am I playing?" Rage was our family's stunt double for passion, for deep feeling . . . for life. To rage was to live.

"It's your concert, Dad-ling." I made my voice soothing and slow. "It can be whenever you want."

"No, it can't. I don't trust them. Who are the other players?"

"It's your concert," I repeated. "Who do you want to play with?" And then, "You're going to play beautifully. It's going to be beautiful."

He seemed to consider this. "Eve, go away," he said, not unkindly, followed by a characteristic "I'm very busy." I left him to gather the last bit of himself, to concentrate his focus.

Out in the living room, I was alone. My mother, dodging despair, was in her study, asleep. My sister had briefly relinquished the role she had carved at my father's elbow during his long illness and was off at yoga.

I sat down on the couch, next to the empty leather recliner my father had favored as he had grown weaker, and across from the piano, where a few weeks ago, my son had played for his grandfather one last time. My father had lectured Leo on the art of taking a bow. "The audience claps; they're saying 'thank you.' You acknowledge this by bowing. Never leave the stage without a gracious bow."

This was the room where we had hovered over my father all these months, while death hovered over us—unspoken, unspeakable, because to speak of it violated my father's force of will. It was maybe five or six months ago that he decided he wanted to ski again. He could barely walk. What he told me was, "I want to stand on top of the mountain."

I drove. It was the sole time he was in the passenger seat and I was behind the wheel. While he didn't get to the top of the mountain, he did stand on the peak of the bunny hill and skied down it. Once.

And he and my mother had gotten to the Cape only a month ago. Cape Cod, where he had taught me to ride waves, where he had showed Leo how to scour the bay at low tide and fill a wire basket with oysters, where the day started with a swim in the pond and ended with a sunset dinner. When they arrived, my father didn't have the strength to leave his bed. But the bed had a view of the bay. He declared he would be back—and better—when summer rolled around.

His students were still calling on his work line to schedule their next lessons.

But there was no more time left for him. I swung my legs around and stretched out on the couch. The sun glinted off the remaining sliver of the Hudson still visible between the new steel-and-glass high-rises that had gone up as my father became sicker. The diffuse, afternoon light bathed the apartment. It was silent, except for the flow of traffic so far down that it was easy to imagine it as a distant brook moving over rocks and stones to the river. I felt guiltily peaceful.

No more bearing witness to my father's dogged decision to take his meals via IV needle in his arm when his appetite died before the rest of him. No more sharing close quarters with the grief my mother and sister had claimed as an identity. I was near release from their insistent ardor that burned my oxygen. Near release from my father's orbit, with the flare of violence it had left on my adolescence. In the waning day, all that remained were the tender, complicated feelings threatening to push up through the surface of my momentary calm.

My father is almost ready. Back in the bedroom now, I ache at his tenacity, his engagement, as he asks my mother for his white shirt. He rubs the fabric gently, weakly between his fingers. He manages a shake of his head. "No. The black shirt."

I fight my tears. Of course the black shirt. He requests his tails, a fixture in the back of his closet since the philharmonic had gone from tux to the less formal suit and tie. I had little-girl memories of him wrapping his satiny cummerbund around the waistband of his trousers, fastening his bow tie, and shrugging into the jacket with the penguin tails hanging behind him like a bride's train.

My mother buttons him into the shirt he has chosen. But she eschews the satin-sided trousers that would need to be dug out of some ancient suit bag, while my father waits, hunched over on the edge of his bed. No matter. My father sees himself in his most stately clothes, rather than in his old khaki pants, pinned up, that he has worn to his last two doctor's appointments, and that my mother somehow manages to get on him for the last time. I hurt for what she will feel when she no longer needs to call up her courage and brisk efficiency. My persistent friction with her subsides in the poignancy of the moment.

Finally, she slips on the concert shoes. No socks. It is too difficult.

His legs, no power left in them, dangle down, his feet in those slippery shoes resting on the floor, marionette-like. His face is in his hands. I can see his skull through the sparse, downy wisps of hair the chemo left behind.

My father is filled with anxiety. "It's been seven months since I played," I hear him rasp through his hands. And then, "Can I do this?" He looks up. "How will I get where I'm going?" His question takes me like a sucker punch.

He waits.

I hear a key in the door. My sister drops her bag at the foot of my parents' bed and moves to position herself close by my father's side— nurse, disciple, daddy's girl. I step back, not out of kindness or deference. But at this moment, I am able to let in her tenderness, her need to protect him.

We are all here. Now he acts. Instantly. He strains to get off the bed.

"He's got a concert to play," my mother tells my sister.

"Carnegie Hall" he says, resolutely. It is where he first played when he joined the orchestra, a young man with his life ahead of him. We lift him, our arms under his arms, around his waist. He shuffles forward. We move instinctively. We know this route. He is back on the metronome track that leads to the living-room recliner. In a few precarious steps, he is off the bedroom carpet and out onto the parquet hallway floor. We can barely keep him up. And now we see how those shoes glissade against the polished wood tiles, like dull skate blades on smooth ice. We move him a few more steps down the hall, pausing at the front door of our apartment. We can't possibly get him to the reclining chair, nor even back to the bedroom.

The previous night, my father tried to get out of bed alone and fell face-first on the bathroom floor. He sports a Band-Aid on the bridge of his bruised, swollen nose. Broken, I think, though my mother can't bear to consider the possibility of one last indignity. We struggle to keep him from another fall.

My sister races to grab an armchair, which she positions where my mother and I stand, clutching my father. "Margot, go. Call for a taxi," my father instructs her. It takes all three of us to turn him around and get him seated on the snow white cushions. And now?

My father asks for his viola. "My fiddle," he calls it. My mother retrieves it, positions it on the floor in front of him as if the instrument itself is onstage. "Is my music in there?" My sister pulls a score from the side pocket of his instrument case. She places it in his hands. My mother locates his glasses and perches them on his bandaged nose.

He does what we have seen him do hundreds of times before. He leans back in his chair. He takes a breath. He licks his thumb and fore-finger deliberately. His motions are weak but so familiar. With his moistened fingers, he opens his music. He scans the two-page spread, licks his two fingers again, turns the page, and repeats the process. How often we have seen him do this without ever thinking about it. With clear vision gone, what music is he reading? What notes is he seeing, so purposeful, that for a moment, it is only him and the printed pages?

"Okay." He closes the score. "I'm ready." It is the voice I know. So tired, but deep, gravelly, and grave. In the final, brutal stages of his illness, I have fervently wished for it to be over. Now I can't bear his letting go.

My mother moves to the stereo. Through the final weeks of his illness, my father didn't listen to music. Nearly any sensory experience seemed to be too much. Sounds were too loud, lights too bright, the tangible world too saturated, perhaps too exquisite to bear. Music above all.

But my mother senses what is required now. She opens the jewel box on top of the stereo, pulls out the CD, and puts it on.

A violin sings out a gripping, declamatory phrase, supported by the bold chords of a piano, second violin, viola, and cello. My parents' home is suddenly filled with music, as it was nearly constantly before my father became ill. I feel the majestic first bars in my stomach, the clear, simple rhythm of the opening passage. My mother comes back to stand behind my father, her hands on his shoulders—holding him, bracing herself. My sister and I are on either side of his chair, sitting on the floor and clasping his hands. His viola is front and center. Schumann's Piano Quintet, opus 44 is the last piece my father will ever hear.

As the cello hands off the melody to the viola, his foot manages a few weak taps. Here is his moment; he is the voice.

We ride the mellow, honeyed sound of the viola line, the four of us. The music connects us, holds us fast in this magnificent, agonizing moment. This is a gift my father gave me, this mindful delight, and its power to bring a work of art to life—a book, a painting, this piece of music. Each note vibrates with our collective focus.

"Can you believe this?" my father says, his voice uncharacteristically subdued.

"I can't. I can't believe it," my mother replies.

It was only yesterday that my father allowed himself to consider the inevitable. "You're going to start hospice care on Monday," his oncologist had said the previous afternoon.

The last conversation I had with my father when he was fully cognizant went like this:

"Eve, how long are people on hospice care?"

I had been banging away at my computer for days, checking the signs of imminent death. The loss of appetite, the physical agitation, the purple fingernail and toenail beds, the cold extremities. "A year," I said slowly, "or six months, or a few weeks, or a few days. It depends."

He nodded. "I see."

So now he knows he is dying, and he has made short work of it. Made sure to embrace it, get right to it, do it well. If life is over, then his work is to die. He is good at working. Always has been. He has been busy. He told me so himself.

The piano, in the lower registers, introduces a passionate, urgent dance of instruments.

My father doesn't die with the final chords, though how could we not have imagined he might? Somewhere in the middle of the joyous, vibrant third movement, he says sadly, "The concert's almost over."

"It sure is," my mother echoes. She met my father sixty-two years ago, when they were young teens.

"I have to go," my father says. He strains to get out of his chair, and we help him move the few steps down the hall and back to bed.

He doesn't take the final bow.

A few hours later, I say good night to him. "I'll be back in the morning," I tell him. I kiss his forehead, trying to experience only the tender gesture, rather than the waxy feel of his skin or its odor. "If you want to leave before I get back, it's okay." He doesn't react. "It was a beautiful concert," I add.

He smiles.

I leave the apartment for the river of traffic.

Nominated by Rosellen Brown

AFTER 11 A.M.
BOMBARDMENT

by ILYA KAMINSKY

from SPILLWAY

On the balconies, sunlight, on poplars, sunlight. On my lips.
Today no one was shooting, there's just sunlight and sunlight.
A girl cuts her hair with imaginary scissors—
A girl in sunlight, a school in sunlight, a horse in sunlight.
A boy steals a pair of shoes from an arrogant man in sunlight.
I speak and I say sunlight falling inside us, sunlight.
When they shot fifty women on Tedna St.,
I sat down to write and tell you what I know:
A child learns the world by putting it in his mouth,
A boy becomes a man and a man earth.
Body, they blame you for all things and they
seek in the body what does not live in the body.

Nominated by Spillway and James Harms, Mark Irwin, Susan Terris

HOW TO FALL IN LOVE PROPERLY

fiction by JULIAN GOUGH

from A PUBLIC SPACE

Slowed a little by a stone in my shoe, I arrived in Galway City a while after dark. Galway City, the Sodom of the West! I reached the very crest of fabled Prospect Hill, to see a bolt of lightning split the sky. Its white flash outlined a dark cloud of bats against the soaring tower of Galway's greatest building, the Car-Park of the Roaches. I plunged down Prospect Hill toward the heart of the city, toward Eyre Square.

Looking behind me, I saw I had shaken off the pursuing mob.

I covered half of Eyre Square at a sprint, the next quarter of Eyre Square at a trot. I ambled through an eighth of Eyre Square, and I drifted to a halt with only a sixteenth of Eyre Square ahead of me.

A distant church bell chimed the hour of two A.M. Between the first stroke and the second, the nightclubs of Galway disgorged their contents onto the streets. A crowd milled about me; I was spun around, and around. A woman took me by the elbow, a man took a swing at me, and I spun and ducked and waltzed my way to the edge of the crowd.

There, stunned, I beheld a tremendous transparent building, lit from within with golden light. Its splendor dominated the west side of the square.

A building so vast and beautiful could only be a temple; and sure enough, through its walls of glass, I saw an enormous congregation facing a long low altar behind which a priesthood seemed busy at their rituals.

Outside it, young people milled about, many of them on their knees on the pavement, their heads bowed thoughtfully over what appeared to be modest food offerings.

Glowing a fiery red above its teeming entrance was the word SU-PERMACS. As though hypnotized, I found myself drawn inside.

And then I saw her.

A vision far ahead of me, wreathed in mist from her chip-pan: the most beautiful girl in the world. And I realized this was a chip shop the size of Killaloe Cathedral. And I realized I was in love.

I looked upon her surface, and imagined her depths. And the wild beating of my heart caused my blood to surge faster through the narrow channels of my body, so that the roar of blood in my ears deafened me, and my sight dimmed, and I grew faint.

I shall not describe her face, for its glory lay not in its geometry, nor its proportion, nor its symmetry. No. No description would convey the relevant information.

Her body was muffled under a uniform designed, by its look, for neither fashion nor comfort. Yet the way in which she inhabited her body, the way in which she deployed her face, the color and heat of the spark of life in her illuminated the temple of her flesh . . .

In a trance, I walked toward her, and bumped into a counter. Various people tried to step in front of me, poking my chest.

"A!"

"U!" they shouted.

"Q!"

I had no time for their riddles. I knocked them carefully aside, vaulted the counter, and walked to her.

"My name is Jude," I said. "I have fallen deeply in love with you at first sight."

In a voice like the whisper of silk against an angel's wing, she said, "You're taking the piss, right?"

I reassured her that I was in earnest.

"Are we on television?" she replied.

"Not to my knowledge," I said.

A selection of anxious young men in grease-spattered uniforms ceased to feed the hungry, and gathered in the aisle near us. They engaged in fierce debate in expletive-flecked undertones. Some then went back, to quell unrest among the neglected masses. At length, the eldest youth pushed forward the youngest.

The young man approached me, speckled with spots, his hair encased in a curious net.

"Please sir, please could you return to the other side of the counter, sir. Please. Sir." I looked down at him, greatly moved. No one had ever spoken to me with such politeness and evident respect before. This young man was obviously deeply spiritual, to speak with such humility to a poor Tipperary orphan such as I. A fellow far along the path to enlightenment, or indeed a high priest of some sort. Though he seemed young for such a role, I knew that in certain faiths the greatest spiritual leaders were often trained from birth. Like the Dalai Lama in Buddhism, and also the Panchen Lama, of whom I had read.

"Are you a lama?" I asked him. He very slowly backed away from me without replying. No doubt his humility forbade him from boasting of his high spiritual status. Ah, well. I returned to my conversation with the most beautiful woman I had ever seen.

Next thing I knew, my arms were pinned behind my back and I was being hurled over the counter by uniformed guardians of the peace.

"Drunk. Or high. He thought I was a sheep," the polite young man was telling them.

"Lama! Lama!" I appealed to him, as I was hustled out the door.

"Llama, sheep, whatever," said the young man. A curious crowd gathered around me.

"I love her," I tried to explain.

"Sheep shagger!" shouted someone. The crowd began to chant, "Sheep shagger!" Someone threw a curried chip. My attempts at explanation seemed only to make matters worse. The crowd closed in. I racked my mind for a clever plan.

I ran . . .

"Sheep shagger! Sheep shagger!" roared the crowd, as they pursued me down Shop Street.

The crowd, as is the way of large, running, roaring crowds, drew a crowd of its own from the after-hours drinkers, musicians, and bar staff in the pubs and clubs and alleys we passed. From The Imperial, from Garavans, from both Lower and Upper Abbeygate Street, from the Snug and Church Lane and Taaffes they came pouring. Many of these inebriated onlookers joined unsteadily in the chase. Unsure of whom it was they were chasing, many of them fought the front-runners of the chasing pack.

I made good use of this confusion to increase my lead, but soon I was slowed by a stitch in my side and the stone in my shoe. Limping, in agony, with my pursuers so close I could smell their porter breath over my shoulder, I threw myself through a narrow church gate, in search of sanctuary.

The crowd crashed to a halt against the railings behind me. Strong men held the gateposts and bulged every sinew to stop the crush pushing them through the open gate. Not a soul followed me.

"'Tis Saint Nicholas's Collegiate Church!" one cried. "He will be eaten by Protestants!"

I limped into the great church. Several old ladies and an even older gentleman looked up at me, startled. The old gentleman approached me with great caution.

Trying to remove the stone from inside the heel of my shoe, I absent-mindedly extended my right hand under my raised left knee, to shake his hand. He raised his knee and did likewise, with a great creaking of bones.

"You are a Mason!" he exclaimed with pleasure, standing on one leg.

Me, a mason? It was true I had built a short stretch of the orphanage wall, after block-laying instruction from Brother O'Driscoll, but to call me a mason seemed excessive flattery. The wall had fallen in the first high wind, leaving a gap and crushing a number of orphans.

"Why, you are a gift sent from heaven," said an old lady. "We were just saying we need a young man to be warden of Saint Nicholas's now that Ramsey has retired. But there are no God-fearing young Church of Ireland men in this parish any more, for we have stopped breeding."

Warden . . .

"What would my duties be?" I asked, interested.

"Well, to ward," said a second lady.

"And to save electricity," said a third. "And if you could play the bells now and then . . ."

"What is your name, young man?" asked the old man, dashing my hopes on the instant. Oh, curse the day the Brothers of Jesus Christ Almighty christened me after the patron saint of hopeless causes! My Catholicism revealed, I would be denied wardenship and sanctuary and be cast out to be torn limb from limb by my fellow Catholics in an orgy of both violence and irony. "And I suppose," he mused, "technically, we should also ask for a curriculum vitae, a tax clearance certificate, credit history, and two references from senior figures in the Church of Ireland community."

My dreams lay blasted. Not a one of these had I. I searched my mind for a reference from a senior figure in the Church of Ireland.

Lost in thought, I put down my left foot. Unfortunately, the stone had been stood on end, sharp point up, by my poking. It pierced my heel as I placed all my weight on it.

I spoke in tongues, put my head between my knees, lifted the foot, lost my balance, and recovered it by grabbing the old man, through his loose tweed, by the testicle, and slowly lowering my forehead to the cold stone.

I let go his testicle, raised my head, and hopped.

"Well, well, well," said the old man. "A Mason of so high a rank, and so young! You were modest earlier, with your greeting of the Fourth Rank. We may skip the formalities." He bowed low. With a creak and a groan, he removed his right shoe and tweaked, with his toes, through the cotton of his shirt, his left nipple, before handing me the keys to church, sacristy, and bell tower. He put on his shoe.

They bade me good night and left.

I took the stone from my shoe, and put it in my good pocket. It was my lucky stone. I gave the pocket a fond pat, made my way up the bell tower, and explored the store cupboards.

The contents were sparse, but sufficient for comfort. Tools, glue, oilcans, polish, an old pillow used to muffle the bells . . .

I lay on the pillow and sniffed the glue nostalgically, for it reminded me of my happy childhood in the orphanage. I drifted off to sleep, and dreamed I was a camel.

When the sun woke me next morning, I discovered that the glue had stuck my pillow firmly to my back. It would not budge. I pulled my clothes on over it. This gave me a somewhat unusual appearance. Sighing, I brushed my teeth with my travel toothbrush, in the sunny bell-tower window.

Then, of a sudden, I spied, far below me on Shop Street, the Most Beautiful Girl in the World. My heart clattered like a stick along railings.

"It is I, Jude, your admirer!" I cried, my speech somewhat impeded by toothpaste.

She looked up, and saw me.

I cannot account for what followed, unless it were that I did not look my best, hunchbacked as I was, in a bell tower, and frothing at the mouth.

She turned pale, her knees gave way, and she toppled slowly to the pavement.

My love lay there, unmoving.

Dropping my toothbrush, I leapt down the twisting wooden stairs of the bell tower. Tripping on the last landing, I tumbled the final fifty feet. Luckily, I was protected from lasting damage by the pillow glued to my back, and by my head, which between them absorbed the majority of the impacts.

Gaining the street, I hobbled to my unconscious beloved's side, in the shadow of Eason's the newsagents. I carried her limp form back to safety, to the bell tower of Saint Nicholas, a place I had already come to think of as home. I lowered her gently to the floor.

I gazed down upon her.

Her radiant face.

Her generous frontage. She no longer wore her uniform but rather a child's T-shirt sprinkled with glitter.

Her eyelids flickered, and opened. "I," she said in a voice like honey flowing from a jug of gold, "will never drink Red Bull and vodka again."

Then her eyes focused, and she leaped a foot. My appearance had not been improved by my fall. In addition to my hump and my frothing at the mouth, I had cricked my neck and was now forced to look at her entirely sideways. I abandoned my plan to play it cool.

"I love you!" I cried, perhaps too energetically, through the pain and toothpaste.

"Yuk!" she replied. She declined my offer of assistance, preferring to remove the toothpaste from her hair herself as I continued.

"I am poor, but honest. Could you find it in your heart to love me?"

She searched her heart as she backed toward the door. At the top of the stairs she found her answer: "No!"

And, overcome no doubt by womanly emotion, she sprinted downstairs in high heels, her tiny skirt inverted by the rushing wind, her skintight top failing to restrain her magnificent jiggling.

Distraught, I called from the tower as she reappeared in the church grounds below me, "Is there not a task I could perform to change your mind and win your heart?"

"Yeah, sure!" she called up as she ran, and my heart leaped like a salmon. "Get plastic surgery to look like Leonardo DiCaprio. And make a million more on . . ."

And with that tantalizing promise she was gone . . .

The first part of her request was clear, though I puzzled over the second one briefly. A million more on what? But of course! A million more on top of what I had already!

I was ecstatic, transformed. The woman I loved had set me a task.

I gazed, sideways, from my tower, at the glorious new day.

She loved me!

Nominated by A Public Space

WATCHING MY MOTHER TAKE HER LAST BREATH

by LEON STOKESBURY

from THE GEORGIA REVIEW

People ground down by what the doctors call
"acute COPD" have not much but a vacuum
left inside when the ache of that last onset
invades the hospice air. But even though
that's so, and even though there came a time
when what she wanted most was just to sail
away, the body holds some tenets of its own.
There, at the end, I saw my mother's mouth
become a perfect round, a ring, a dark hole
clearly larger than it ever seemed before—
and it strove, I thought, through the scrim
of morphine, to draw into that dim chasm
everything it could. O, let the earth be
shoveled in, it seemed to say. O, let now be
consumed into this disk of dark, this gape,
the air and every small or massive entity—
all this lonely, frightened, wanting, weary,
sad and hurting woman has throughout
her little and long life never known. And then,
the heaving ceased. And the great shroud of the sea
rolled on as it rolled five thousand years ago.

Nominated by The Georgia Review and Gibbons Ruark

THE LOBSTER MAFIA STORY

fiction by ANNA SOLOMON

from THE GEORGIA REVIEW

MY husband's funeral was a modest affair. The coffin was pine, as he would have wanted. The minister, who is new, and so young my husband would not have trusted him to pump his gas, said little. Mostly people came and went, delivering their casseroles, touching me gently. Then, at last, everyone was gone except for a small group of women who stood huddled at the front door.

"Hello, Marcie," said one, though my name is Marcella and I've never given her any reason to think I want to be called anything else.

"Hello," I said. I could not remember if she was Ginny or Janet. They were all dyed blond. All with the same gray roots. I know the women by who their husbands were—nothing more, nothing less.

"We're sorry for your loss," said another.

"Thank you."

"You should come downtown sometime," said the third, by which she meant I should sit with them on the benches outside the Saint Peter's Club. The benches are where their husbands used to sit, with my husband, after they got too old to pull traps.

"Yes," I said. "Maybe I will. Thank you."

The women watched me suspiciously. Perhaps they knew that I was lying. Or their suspicion was a cover for jealousy: my husband was the last of the gang to die. But there was something else on their faces, too, a passing terror, as if an awful noise had swept through the doorway. The look was gone the next instant—there they were, three wives contemplating me with adequate pity—but it had left behind, lingering among us, an unmistakable presence. A terrible thing our husbands did

215

together, more than twenty years ago. Another funeral, for a man we barely knew.

"Thank you for coming," I said.

Still the women didn't leave. Two of them parted slightly, revealing a tall, skinny girl of twelve or thirteen who stood, head drooping, on the step behind them. She was pulled up, and through, then pushed toward me.

"This is Emma," said the first, blondest woman. "My granddaughter. She lives down the road, with her mother. *Not* my daughter—my son's ex. Not the smartest cookie, that one, she's really not. You get my gist. In any case. I'll see that Emma visits you from time to time. You could use the company, certainly."

Behind me the old house was its usual haunted self. The woods rustled: animals getting ready for winter, wanting nothing to do with us. Emma looked shyly up at me, the whites of her eyes reminding me of a small, cold fish. I smiled.

"Come anytime, dear," I said.

She nodded, barely.

Then the wives pulled her away, fast-walk-waddled to their cars, and drove off.

Here is how I believe it happened:

At five o'clock in the morning, on February 6, 1978, four men sit in their shack on the wharf drinking rum and Coke out of Thermos caps. They listen to the forecasters on the radio saying heavy snow on the way, strong winds; one channel says blizzard; another, "historic storm." The men have heard it before, heard it all winter; one storm after another has failed to live up to expectations, left them stranded at home, feeling useless for no good reason. From the shack, at least, they can see for themselves: the warning flags in the harbor, the swell already forming, even in the cove. Four dying flashlights hang from nails, layering the men in a grisly yellow.

Or maybe the flashlights aren't dying; maybe someone's wife bought new batteries, and the men are lit too harshly, their features clownish, causing in each other unspoken bursts of fright. These men are part of a lobster gang stuck somewhere in the middle ranks of the gangs, powerful enough they can sabotage their inferiors but weak enough they need the mafia kingpins to protect them. They are the sort who never imagined being anywhere other than this middle, who at sixteen would

216

have said that washing back rum and Coke next to an electric space heater with their finest friends would mean they had achieved a place in the world. None of them imagined that they would reach this place and feel nothing.

The radio crackles. One man adjusts the dial, another the antenna. The third reaches for the rum, the fourth shakes his head: "February," he says. "Why even bother? We should be asleep right now."

The others nod in agreement, but they are lying. They don't want to be in bed next to their wives with their pale, suffering breaths. Under attics that have not been insulated, in view of traps that lie unmended in the yards. Close to the children who have grown, and the children who've not been had.

"Going to be a storm," says the man pouring the rum.

Another raises the liter of cola. "Who?"

The men hold out their caps. A gust shakes the walls, the wind already strong enough that they don't hear Tom Lanza start his motor. Instead, they feel the vibration in their feet, then his wake, soon after.

The men have plenty of reasons not to like Tom Lanza. He moved up from Rhode Island a few years before. Some outsiders make it just fine here; they accept their status, follow the rules, go humbly. But Lanza has done none of this. He refuses to join the union. He doesn't belong to any gang. He works alone and all over the place, on the edge of established territories, drawing off lobsters but quiet about it, smart and quick. He had an arrogant house built for himself, blond Italian brick with pillars. He is a bachelor.

They open the shack door just in time to see his broken stern light trembling before it disappears out into the main harbor.

That light is another thing they hate. Tom Lanza has money, but he puts nothing into his boat. The hull is peeling paint; all he has for navigation is a compass; he shits in a bucket instead of fixing his toilet. A man can be this way without a wife. Just as he can head out in any weather he wants, alone, not spreading the work around, no "Morning" when he passed their shack on the way to his boat.

Not that they would have wanted to see his smug Eye-talian face anyway. But it's the principle. The way it works, or the way it's supposed to work: nobody goes out, or everybody goes. Going out on a bad day is like stealing and showing off about it at the same time. It's an insult: the sight of his crappy boat going out to make money and the men already half-drunk, having succumbed to another alarmist forecast, and in an hour or so daylight will come. Their wives will be awake by then and listening to the radio, too, hearing the warnings. They will insist that the men come home, like children.

The men do not wonder whether for some of the women this sternness is something they have to put on, like a stiff, fancy hat.

But maybe they could manage all the pressures bearing down on them. Maybe all they would do, if things weren't about to go the way they go, is curse Lanza to the air and slump back onto their crates. They might go on with their lives; there might be no story to tell. But in that moment in the doorway, they make the mistake of looking at each other. They see their own rummed eyes in each others', and the fear there, and the shame, and the wives in the houses swinging their ankles down from the beds now, the wives with their skinny or swollen laments—and when the men turn back into the shack, they see the flashlights hanging. Then the rum bottle slips from one man's fingers, and the rum spills onto the floorboards, making a preposterous map, and the men can no longer deny how cold it is or how inadequate their space heater. One man kicks its grill, and they are off.

They follow Lanza at a distance, ten or so lengths, though it must be hard for them to judge: they are crammed onto a single boat, the pilothouse barely big enough to fit them; their breath is one raw, stupid thing. Past the breakwater Lanza opens up his engine, and they do the same, their boat nosing up, then flattening again as she gains speed. They stay behind and a little landward of Lanza. The noise of the engine drowns out any need to talk, allowing them to pretend the weather is no worse than they imagined, though it's squalling now, a light snow starting to fall. They lose sight of Lanza for seconds at a time.

He knows they're behind him. He must. Yet they're fifteen minutes out before he slows to pull a trap. They slow, too, a few lengths away, watching as he grabs the buoy and begins to pull in the line. Through the snow they can just barely make him out, but the buoy's stripes appear in flashes, orange and blue. It's one of his own, which is another thing about Tom Lanza: he's never messed with anyone else, never showed any envy. He hauls the buoy up over the rail and works the line onto his winch head; he's the only man in the harbor who hasn't gone to a hydraulic hauler. As he starts to crank the line up, the men must recognize what they haven't seen in years—the muscles and methods of their fathers, and their fathers' fathers, who worked harder than they ever will, who suffered not a single convenience.

They are close enough now that Lanza looks up. They step out of the cabin, yanking up their hoods, forearms to foreheads to keep the snow out of their eyes. Then they are close enough a man could jump from one rail to the other, close enough they could cut his line with a good knife, but Lanza—they can see his face now in his hood, its dark skin and tired eyes and lips too full for a man—smiles. And his smiling is a problem as unredeemable as his not being born here. They cannot help him any more than they can help themselves.

Lanza stops his winch. He reaches into his pilothouse for his Thermos and starts to unscrew the cap. For a minute, they think he is about to offer them coffee—he is warm, they know, from his work, whereas they are bone cold, their chests starting to quiver. The men might hope that Lanza's offering will save them. But he pours into his own cap. He pours like he can't imagine a nicer day, like he's sitting down to high tea; then he grins, tilts the cap back once to drink, and tosses the rest over the side. A gust picks up the spray and they smell coffee in the snow, Lanza's coffee in their faces. Someone throws the throttle into reverse, and they bump Lanza's boat; someone else jumps the rails. The others follow and join in, punching Lanza's face, pinning him to the deck. The waves have grown larger, slicing and tossing the boats; the wives, at home, listening to the radio, are growing angrier. The men beat Lanza bloody, and then there is no way back and no way around what they've done, and when Lanza's Thermos rolls past them, one grabs it and hits him over the head.

There is a lull in the squall, there has to be, for the men can hear Lanza's engine. They can see the charts by his wheel and his gaudy Jesus flailing, pinned to the ceiling by a thumbtack and string, and a homemade wooden shelf nailed to the wall, perfectly sized and with a hole to secure his Thermos. One man cries out. Then the wind finds its pitch again; the snow sticks to their bare hands. One of them pulls off Lanza's boots, a desperate attempt at politeness. But that only makes things worse because there, on the deck, shrouding Tom Lanza's feet, are two yellow ankle socks with little bears on them. For an instant, the socks seem like another shot at salvation—because of their brightness, or the happy bears, or because they remind the men of their mothers. Then the promise is gone and the socks are only heartbreaking. The snow is thickening fast, and the men throw Lanza over the rail.

They must move quickly now to find their boat. They were rash not to tie a rope off. Stupid. But Lanza's boat has gas, Lanza's engine works—of course. His frugality was the clever kind, the always-right kind, the kind a wife would prefer. This fact maddens them and helps them concentrate.

The lobster mafia spun Tom Lanza's death as an accident, the sort that happens all the time, no one responsible but the man himself or a dead motor or a wind changing direction without any warning. The men bribed the paper. They had cops for brothers. They did what they always do when one of the gangs cuts traps or puts water in a gas line or messes up the gears on a boat caught working their territory: they drowned the truth. This was easy because Tom Lanza was so scorned in the harbor and beyond it nearly unknown, but even easier because he died two days before the blizzard pummeled the coast from the sound all the way up to New Hampshire. It's easy to blame a man for his own death when he doesn't have enough humility to obey the weather. Five full days passed before the Coast Guard could go searching, and by the time they found Lanza's boat adrift out at Stellwagen Bank, the world was shut up under five feet of snow, quiet as a pillow.

The first time I lied was when an officer came to the door, wanting to know did I know anything about the death of a man called Tom Lanza. I didn't. Not yet. But I knew from the look on his face, a kind of long-held flinch, that even if I did, he didn't want me to tell him. Behind him, the snow glittered insanely; my back ached from days of shoveling. It was I who'd kept the back door clear, and dug out the path to the woodpile, and dug and dug, and carried logs and water and tended the stove and made our food last. The day the storm hit, my husband had fallen ill with a high fever; the morning the officer came, he was still upstairs, hot and dumb under the blankets. What that had to do with Thomas Lanza, I had no idea, but I could see from the way the man looked at me that there was likely some relation.

"Well?" he asked. He was cold, his right boot absent-mindedly kicking the step—a piece of granite cut out of the quarry two hundred years ago. He kept kicking like it might budge. He looked bewildered by my hesitation.

"No," I said. "I don't know anything."

He nodded. "You know where Bobby was in the a.m. on February six?"

I counted back, quickly, in my mind. Then I said, "Home. Like any man with half a wit about him."

* * *

Ten days after the blizzard, the roads from Rhode Island were clear enough that Tom Lanza's two sisters, his only family, were able to drive up and attend the memorial service the Fishermen's Wives Association put on for him. It was a token affair, to show respect and let the men revise their dislike for Lanza now that he was dead. There was no body, but the coffin was placed at the front of the room anyway, an unlined oak box the wives used whenever there was nothing to bury. One man stood up and said that Tom Lanza was a model of independence. Another talked about the beautiful house he'd built and how people would miss him every time they drove by. Ginny and Janet and the others were there, murmuring. I made some effort to murmur with them.

The sisters, thick women with square jaws and Lanza's tired eyes, did not speak. Afterward they waited side by side at the door while people touched them gently and left. They appeared patient—gracious—but when I pressed their hands between mine, I saw they knew that nobody had cared about their brother at all. They looked at me, and kept looking, and in their eyes was a directness so familiar to me as to be almost familial. It was as if their knowing went far beyond their brother s loneliness—as if they knew all about mine, too, and had come to remind me. They knew that I was not from here, either, that I'd grown up in Boston's North End, praying to be delivered from the crowded, garlic-stinking streets, from family, from spinsterhood, from tackiness; that when Bobby finally found me, I was grateful to him the way you are grateful when the hairdresser makes your hair into something it isn't, though you feel a little nervous, every time the wind lifts, that the style won't last.

The sisters seemed to know things they never could have known, like how, for the first couple years of our marriage, I'd watched myself as I might have watched a neighbor, had there been one close enough: I saw a wife walking softly around an old saltbox, trying not to disturb the ghosts of her husband's family, trying to love the small rooms even though they were cold and the air was thin and there was one room, the old birthing room, in which she felt strangled. She learned to cook from his mother's recipe box, plain New England food boiled or baked until everything tasted like potato. He bought her a used Ford Cortina and taught her how to drive—patiently, and without yelling—and if she came home late from running errands, he'd back his truck out the drive and let her pull in front so that he wouldn't have to wake her at four the next morning when he left for the boat.

221

These small kindnesses, these silent passings—we came to know each other in this way. The sisters knew this. They knew the disappointments, too, the daily darkness of the house, the traps lost to sabotage, the years of scarce lobsters, the wreck of a television Bobby bought me. It was the first thing I'd asked him for, that television. I wanted to look for it myself, maybe meet the women who worked in the shops, but Bobby wanted to bestow it upon me. It took him four days to find a good deal. When he finally came home with the two glittery antennae framing his face, I clapped, served our supper, then pulled him into the cold front room where he'd set up the television on a retired trap.

I made him sit in the rocker; then I approached the television like an actress in a commercial, caressing its top, oohing and ahhing. As I turned the set on and ran back toward him, Bobby opened his arms for me to sit in his lap. We waited. In the center of the black screen, a square of light appeared and grew slowly outward. After about a minute we could make out a man's hand. "Well, honey, that should be the last of it," said Dick York's voice.

"It's *Bewitched!*" I cried. I was embarrassed that I felt so moved, so in love with my husband, because of a television, but I gripped his legs and twisted around to kiss his face. Then, just as slowly as the picture had grown, it started to shrink. The studio set disappeared around the actors. Their hair was replaced by blackness. We were losing their extremities, then their faces. And then we could not see what anything was at all.

A tiny square of white. The audience went on laughing. I switched the television off and on again, then fiddled with the other dial. I unplugged it and plugged it back in. The same thing happened, the mawing open, the shrinking back. Bobby made it to the television in two strides. When he lifted it, the cord popped out from the socket, dragged behind him across the bare wood floor, then followed him, bouncing, down the basement stairs.

The sisters knew all this. Just like they knew about our annual supper out, when Bobby's steak came too raw, and his vegetables buried in pepper, and for a week after he could barely speak he was so ashamed. Bobby's pride was like that: stubborn yet uneasy, always on the edge of being devastated. He'd said something early on about raising the house's short doors and ceilings, sized to clear men from centuries past; he'd made a quiet joke about the tall sons we might have, but we never had any sons, or any daughters, either, and that added to his shame. The sisters looked at me, and that shame rose up in me like bile: each of my five miscarriages, and Bobby, refusing to stop, going on with his mechanics, night after night, and my never telling my family any of it.

Until my mother died, to keep her from visiting, I'd gone down to Boston once a month. I'd walk off the train, down Salutation Street, into the bright chaos of the old apartment, its trinkets and Marys and posters stuffing the walls, the stove flaming blue from all four burners, various aunts and uncles and cousins taking up seats and counters and floor space, and I would wonder if it was too late for me to come back. I'd thought it a poor life. But I had no children. I had no friends. Why not sit down on my mother's pink love seat (what would Bobby's ancestors do with a *love seat*?) and eat sugared nuts and argue about something with someone and then, when I was tired, lie down in my childhood bed and sleep? Why not wake up in the morning and get a job? Yet something had changed inside me, as if I had a new organ or new eyes. As if, standing in the doorway, I'd gone the black-and-white of that damaged TV: I couldn't see how to step back into the color.

I got on the train and rode back north, every time. I became a Protestant wife on a long, winding road—enduring, vigilant, content. Yet Tom Lanza's sisters looked at me as though they knew better. I let their hands go and smiled. They looked doubtful, and full of sorrow. I left.

That smile was my second lie. Not outright—I still hadn't asked my husband about Tom Lanza's death—but not entirely innocent either. Bobby's behavior was changed since the blizzard, his habits altered: he slept late and ate only toast for breakfast; all evening he sat with the paper over his knee, not reading a word. I'd turn on the radio and his face would react, but not to what was being said; he appeared to be listening to a separate current, inside his head.

I waited for the funeral to be over, and then a couple weeks longer. I waited, as he must have waited, for some indeterminate number of days to pass. It was like we'd waited, once upon a time, to discuss my miscarriages—like waiting for the right day to say out loud: *All our efforts, all our preparations, all our diligence, everything, have led to this.*

We were eating supper. Or rather I was eating and Bobby was watching me. His look of being elsewhere was accompanied by a faint expression of disgust, as though my eating were an affront to his abstinence.

I put down my fork and knife, wiped my mouth, and folded my napkin. "What happened with Tom Lanza?" I said.

Bobby stared at me.

"I'm not stupid," I said. "Besides, a cop came, asking."

"Marcella," he said.

I knew, when he said my name, that he'd helped murder the man. For years, we'd just talked. It was obvious who we were talking to.

"Bobby," I said. "What happened?"

He shifted in his chair. He'd stopped shaving, and I'd written it off as negligence, but now it struck me as his way to try to hide himself. He brought a hand to his mouth, then lowered it. I half-expected him to say, *I love you.* He wasn't a man to say that, but I thought the situation might push him to it. I thought I would tell him I loved him, too. I did. I'd grown to. I loved the care he took to clean his nails. I loved his smile, despite himself, as he enjoyed the warmth of a good cup of coffee I'd made. I loved it when he came home with his cheeks chapped, his body needing something simple, and I'd coat them in Bag Balm and cup them in my palms until the oils soaked in.

"It's got nothing to do with you," he said.

I laughed. I could see on his face that this surprised him. It surprised me, too. For all his shortcomings, he'd rarely hurt me.

"What's it got to do with?" I asked.

"Nobody." He looked at his hands.

"Your 'gang'?" My voice was tinged with nastiness now. I didn't wait for him to answer. "Your parents? Your grandparents? Your great-great-grandparents? What's it got to do with, if not with me?"

He shook his head. Beneath the bristles of his beard, his skin had gone the pale gray of the melting snow outside.

"You owe me," I said. Since the officer had come I'd been wishing the whole Tom Lanza situation would go away, but now I felt for it a sudden gratitude. I felt the license it gave me to be shocked, and angry. "You owe me," I said again, and I was thinking about the policeman, yes, and Tom Lanza's sisters, whose enemy he'd made me without my permission, but I was thinking, too, about the years I'd spent in the old hard bed with him over me, thrusting on with his hopeless hope, and I was thinking about cheapskate gifts and low water pressure and cold floors and how homesick he'd made me, how literally sick for home, for myself. And I was thinking, what if it was Tom Lanza I'd married, what if I'd lived with him inside his thick Italian-brick walls watching an Admiral color television set and drinking wine and having babies?

When Bobby told me the story—his story, an outline of a story, about the men drinking in the shack and following Lanza's boat and how it was meant to be a prank, a good scare, but how Lanza had ruined it by being the asshole that he was and then the men had lost their heads—

224

I said, "What do you mean, lost your heads? What does that even mean? And which one of you did it? Was it you? How did it happen? Tell me the *story*, Bobby."

He looked at me. He was thin, and exhausted, and ugly. "Be quiet," he said. "It's got nothing to do with you."

I stood up and hit him in the face. Clear across the jaw. Hard enough his head twisted to the right, like a bottle cap.

That must have been what he expected, because he looked less pale afterward, almost refreshed. He eyed me shyly, he ate his dinner. Certainly hitting him was what I'd most wanted to do; it was the most honest thing I'd done in years. But it didn't make me feel any better. I'd given him what he wanted. He hadn't even had to ask.

From then on, I offered only the basic necessities: food, drink, cleanliness, frugality. I grew what food I could. I took us back, in a way, though the town was moving forward, growing fast enough through the eighties and nineties that even this one-road stretch of woods began to change. New families built new houses. Public Works laid a sewer line and moved the municipal water pipes down below the frost line so that they no longer froze in the winter. Bobby and I were hooked up to those pipes, but we kept them turned off and kept on with our well, our quarter-filled baths, our little gauge by the kitchen sink that told us when we could use a little more. I'd been waiting, ever since I was thirty-eight and Bobby finally stopped trying to have a child, for us to begin living. I'd been waiting for an urge, a courage, to alter myself in some way—a special undergarment, maybe a modern haircut—or to change the house with a colorful rug, plants in the windows. But now I understood that we had been living all along—that to call the passing days and weeks and years anything but one's life was to admit to a great despair.

I sewed new curtains to look like the old ones, dark and rough as potato sacks. We kept them closed so much of the time we barely noticed a house being built at the far bend in the road, until one day there it was, fully sprung, a yellow structure that looked as if it were designed by ten different people, with a screen porch and a little turret and a round window above the door, like a ship's porthole.

I didn't know, the first time Emma came to visit by herself, that she came from the yellow house. I was eating a sandwich in the kitchen one evening, eking out the last freshness from the cold cuts from Bobby's funeral. A full week had passed, so the meat was stiff and starchy, but still I'd dressed the sandwich plainly, as I'd done for years: a scrape of mayonnaise, one leaf of lettuce. When I heard the knock, the possibility of a visitor was so foreign that for a long moment I didn't move to answer it. Instead I felt a sudden longing for mustard, and tomato, and peppers, and relish—the finely chopped sour-sweet kind in the small greenish jars.

I found Emma hunched, as she'd been at the funeral, staring down the long expanse toward her feet. She glanced up at me, then back down. She was even taller and thinner than I remembered, her face tight with concentration, and she wore a lime-green windbreaker and blue jeans, between which—due to her height—was a gap, where I could see the snail of her bellybutton. She looked, standing on the ancient block of granite in the glare of the yard light, entirely unlikely, and as if she knew herself to be so.

If I hadn't spoken, she might not have uttered a single word. She might have walked back out to the road and left me to my sandwich.

But I did. "Would you like to come in, dear?"

And she came in.

"Would you like a cookie?"

She would. The cookies, also from the funeral, had gone soft, but she ate them like a little girl, one and two and three, and when I offered her milk, she gulped it down all at once.

"Thank you," she gasped, handing me the glass.

"You're welcome." I didn't know what else to say. I was shocked still—by her entrance, by the fact of her, sitting in Bobby's chair.

"My grandmother said . . .," she trailed off.

"Yes. She told you to come. It's very kind of you."

Emma looked embarrassed. "It's not a trouble," she said, and pointed toward the east wall of the kitchen. "I live right there, on the corner."

"Corner?" I laughed. "What corner?"

"Right there." She pointed more desperately. "I can see your house from my bedroom."

"Oh." It's her mother, I thought, who calls the bend in the road a corner. She's from a city, perhaps. "You mean the yellow house?" I asked.

Emma nodded, blushing now, a rashy swath of pink from her windbreaker to her ears. She must have known what I'd seen, from my yard: a different car in her mother's driveway many mornings; men emerging, scratching their faces, blinking at the sky. Some time later three children would spill out, all different sizes and shapes, like the parts of the house. The young ones kicked each other as they waited for the bus. The tall one stood apart, her long body so still it seemed to be listening for danger all on its own.

I hadn't connected that figure with the girl I'd met at the funeral, but now she sat in front of me, flushed with shame, her wide fish-eyes on mine.

"Do you go to school, dear?" I asked. Then, realizing the cruelty of my question: "What do you like to study?"

"Math." Emma shrugged. "History."

"Do you have friends?"

A worse question. She bit her bottom lip, screwed up her face. "Sort of," she said. "I don't know." Then she smiled, suddenly mischievous. "Do you?"

I smiled back—a Cheshire cat. "Your grandmother," I blurted. "Those other ladies. A few more."

She nodded. The refrigerator went through its eight-thirty song: a soft gurgling, a few rough knocks, a long sigh.

"They say you're a witch," she said.

I stopped smiling.

"A good witch," she added.

"How kind," I said.

"I don't think you are," Emma said. "I told them that."

"Well, thank you."

But I found myself not entirely opposed to the idea. It made me feel lonely, but powerful.

"I'm sorry about your husband," Emma said.

I nodded. A tiny creek of milk ran down her chin, and I reached out with the hem of my apron, then stopped myself—the apron was not entirely clean, and it was not my place to wipe her mouth. We sat. Beyond the kitchen doorway I saw the window they carried him out through after the wake. The doors were too narrow for the coffin, so they brought it in through the window, put him inside, then passed it back out. I hadn't thought to ask how the dead get out when there is a room for birthing but none for dying. Part of me must have believed they never did. Yet there was his empty chair, with a girl in it. I was embarrassed by how strongly I wanted to touch her.

"Would you like some more milk?" I asked.

She nodded. I poured. Then, as if someone had flipped a switch in her back, Emma began to talk at a rapid clip: "I have a history report

227

due, not for another month but it's almost all our grade, I keep finding topics and they seem okay but then not, my mother thinks it's weird that I like history she says it's a sign of me not being happy, in the present I guess she means, I guess she means it's a sign of some problem in me, she wants me to go out for cheerleading or at least basketball or she wants me to be friendlier, generally, she calls it spunk, she says I've got no spunk."

She paused, looking at me, but I was too surprised to say no, no of course you've got spunk, so she went on, "So anyway I've got this project and I want to do really well on it so I can get into AP for next year—there's only two AP courses in the whole school and this is one—but first I need to find a topic."

I nodded, exhausted. "That's wonderful, dear," I said, though I knew it was inadequate. As I walked her to the door, I could see her disappointment. I could see that she'd come to visit me not only out of pity—that she needed to sit with an old woman who had nothing else to do but be with her.

But we were at the door. I couldn't see how to change that. "I hope you'll come again," I said.

Emma stepped out into the night. She turned to face me. She was hunched again, and shy. "Okay," she said. "If you want."

"Yes," I said. "I do want."

Emma looked at me strangely.

"Okay," she said, and walked home.

I quickly grew used to the circumspect beat of Emma's shoes on the gravel drive. I bought extra milk, I baked cookies. I found a recipe that called for cornflakes in place of half the flour and fretted the whole time they were in the oven, but they were *awesome*, according to Emma. She stopped knocking. She'd open the door and walk straight back to the kitchen, and there her caution would fall away. She was older than I'd guessed—fifteen, in her second year at the high school—but after she'd inhaled a dozen cookies, her cheeks were soft and bright as a young child's. She was greedy with questions:

"Mrs. Hubbard? Were you brought up religious?"

"Yes."

"Do you go to church still?"

"No."

"Do you pray?"

"I'm not sure."

"Did your parents stay married?"

"Yes."

"Did you go to college?"

"Junior college."

"What was your major?"

"Typing."

"Did you date boys?"

"Not really."

"How did you meet your husband?"

"At my younger sister's wedding."

"Was it love at first sight?"

"He was handsome."

"Did he kiss you?"

"He asked me to dance. He was a gentleman."

"So that's perfect, right, like a fairy tale?"

"Oh. I . . . Yes."

"Did you have sex before you were married?"

"I . . . no."

"See? Perfect!"

My answer about sex I regretted the moment I gave it. I didn't want Emma to hate her mother. I had some idea of what Emma was doing, why she watched my mouth as though trying to memorize my words. As I spoke I was unrolling a map she wanted, of how to become a woman with a quiet life, with a husband who leaves only when he dies. She looked at my calico dresses and aprons. She thought my life had been pure and sweet.

One night Emma arrived with a great stink—the foul, musky odor of skunk. She'd been sprayed on her way over. They must have been out at the edges of the woods, gathering the last nuts or cones or whatever they eat—there are still many things I don't know of this place—to prepare for their long nap. Emma stood twenty feet away, just inside the reach of the yard light, but I could smell her.

"I don't know what to do!" she cried.

"Tomato juice," I called back. Bobby had taught me this—a bath of tomato juice. But we'd never had to do it, and I only had one can, which was actually V8. Who knew if V8 did the trick? I could drive to the store, but I wasn't about to let Emma in my car, and I couldn't leave her. I thought to walk her back to her house, knock on the door, tell her mother to go buy the juice. But I didn't want to do that. I worried that her mother would blame me. I worried that her mother would talk to her ex-mother-in-law, Janet or Ginny, that the wives would think I'd somehow caused the problem in my witchy way, that I'd set up the skunk to spray Emma so I could keep her. Which seemed almost possible. And this much *was* true: now that she was here, looking lovely in the yard light in a way I hadn't seen her look before, her desperation lighting up her face like a full moon, her long body somehow graceful even as it jumped up and down as if to shake off the scent—I didn't want to let her go.

"Vinegar!" I cried. My mother had used vinegar for everything. Cuts, garlic, tarnish, mold, grease, tomato. If it could take out tomato, and tomato could take out skunk, maybe we were in business.

Emma offered to wait outside. I gave her one of Bobby's coats to keep her warm, and then I rushed upstairs to run the bath. Two gallons of white vinegar—all I had—and the rest water, as hot as I could run it until the pressure went low. I opened the window to call for her— "Emma!"—and nearly choked with a sudden fear that she'd left. But there were her footsteps, dashing up the stairs two at a time. There she was, at the bathroom door, dropping Bobby's coat to the floor, pulling her lime-green windbreaker up over her head. "Excuse me," I said, meaning to escape the smell and give her privacy, but Emma's shirt was already halfway up her stomach, then off altogether. She wore no brassiere. Her breasts were barely breasts. "Stay," she said, and I looked away as she took off her jeans and underwear. I wondered if she was afraid of ghosts and didn't want to be alone. I wondered if she wanted someone to see her, growing. I sat down on the closed toilet seat and looked, for the first time, at the porcelain claws that held up the tub, and I thought it strange that people of such simplicity had chosen this ornament, this wildness, for the place they washed.

"Uch," Emma said, once she'd lowered herself into the tub. "This is the grossest thing ever. This is so gross."

"I'm sorry," I said.

"It's not *your* fault."

I dared look at her now—the narrow line of her shoulders above the rim of the bath, her eyes bright still with crisis.

"Do you have a washcloth?"

"What? Oh. Yes."

Emma began to scrub herself. "Why don't you have children?" she asked, and for an instant the question came as such a surprise that I

230

heard it as a continuation of her last question—*You have a washcloth, why not children?*—and I answered it just as naturally.

"That's got nothing to do with you."

Emma flinched at the sharpness of my voice. It was the first time I'd admonished her, and I was sorry, for us both, but I knew that it was right that she saw: I was far from the perfect woman she'd conjured.

"We couldn't," I said. "I couldn't."

Emma looked up. I thought she was planning her apology. I thought she could see that the topic, along with the smell, was making me nauseous. But when she spoke, she said, "Maybe you were lucky."

"That's a terrible thing to say."

She lifted the washcloth to her left shoulder. "I was a mistake," she said. "My mother was fifteen."

I began to comprehend. "Lots of people make mistakes," I said. Then I heard what I'd said. "But later on, if they could go back, they would make them all over again. They wouldn't change anything." I spoke too brightly, wanting what I was saying to be true. I said, "They can't imagine what their lives would be without those mistakes."

"She can," Emma said. "She would change it if she could."

"How do you know?"

Emma squinted. "I just know. She wanted things. She's not what she looks like."

"Are you?"

For an instant, I caught her eye. Then Emma hunched over her knees and gave a little shiver.

"Are you cold?" I asked.

"Yes."

I tried the tap. The water wasn't back to pressure yet.

"Do you want to get out?"

"I still stink."

"We'll wait. The pressure will come back."

Emma raised an eyebrow and went back to scrubbing. The smell was diminishing, but slowly. "Yes," she said, suddenly. "I'm exactly what I look like. It would be better if I hadn't been born."

"Emma," I scolded.

"My mother would be happy. She wouldn't have had to go have more kids. She'd be a stewardess or something—something to make her *happy*. She'd get to fly all over the world."

"Don't be ridiculous," I said.

231

But Emma was only doing what I'd done for years. *If only.* If only, at our terrible dinners out, I'd told a joke; if only I'd insisted on buying the television myself; if only babies had grown inside me. If only, when Tom Lanza walked past the men's shack that morning, I had been a reason for Bobby to come home.

"Emma," I said again, but quietly.

"What." She looked at me, waiting. She'd built her own story. We all do. It's not as pitiful as it sounds. We want to know that we are real, that without us something, someone, would be different.

"I'm going to tell you something. I want you to listen."

Her teeth were chattering now. "If you're going to tell me I'll be prettier when I'm older, I've heard it before."

"No," I said. "I'm going to tell you an old story. Nobody knows it anymore. You could use it for your history report."

"I'm done with my history report."

"Then you can just have it. You can tell it to your grandmother."

Emma laughed.

"Why not?"

"She won't listen."

"Try," I said. "I bet she will."

"Okay, okay. Just tell me. I'm freezing."

"Your lips are blue."

"I know! I should go home."

"Wait." I stood. "Wait here—don't go anywhere."

"Where are you going?"

"Just wait," I said.

I moved fast down the stairs, and out into the backyard, where you can stand in the night and not know there's a house, or telephone poles, or electric wires crossing the sky just behind. The moon was big. It was easy to find the moss-grown slope of the bulkhead door, and the handle, like a rusted mushroom, waiting. I hadn't lifted anything heavy in a long while, but it felt good; it warmed me. I found Bobby's flashlight hanging on its nail and stepped down into the cellar. There was the well switch; I flipped it off. And the city water valve, which I opened, wide as it would go, before heading back out to the yard.

Across the road I could see the shapes of boys, fleeing, the night that Bobby died. *My husband died quietly in his sleep,* I'd told people. *Thank goodness,* I said, or *God bless,* depending on who I was talking to and what I expected they expected to hear. In truth, Bobby died of shock when a group of boys tried to break in through the front room window downstairs. He'd fallen asleep in his chair, as he often did. I'd covered him with a blanket and gone to bed. But a little after midnight, I woke to his shout. I heard yelping, scuffling; out the window I saw their shapes, running away. I waited. I thought Bobby would walk upstairs then. I thought I would give him that pleasure, of being the one to bear the news. He would tell me what they looked like, and try to guess whose sons or grandsons they might be, and wonder what they thought they might have found in our house to steal.

I waited. Then I went down and found him on the floor, near his chair, looking terrified. The window was open, blowing a fall wind around the room, lifting the arm covers on his mother's chair, scattering dust around the floor. If you were a man who'd done something, long ago, that you were still waiting to be punished for, it was the sort of wind that might have made you think your time had come. If you'd woken to the window creaking open and a body jumping through, followed by the fast, froggy whispers you would recognize as belonging to adolescent boys—because you'd been one, and because you'd longed to have one—then your heart might have leapt, too.

I'd told no one. To tell would have been to tell everything. But now I thought of the boys, with their secret, and how it would haunt them, as they ate, and slept, and woke, and went to school, and walked through hallways, and I thought of the women they would confess to one day, on benches or in beds, women who were now girls, like Emma, waiting to hold someone else's sorrows.

I went back in, and walked upstairs, and opened up the sink tap as fast as it would go. First the water was brown, then it turned clear, then at last the heater kicked in and the water ran hot. The pressure was strong. The water gushing up and through the old pipes made a noise like a great rain washing through. I turned off the sink, and turned on the bath, and Emma was still there, pale and long as a birch, smelling of skunk, reaching her fingers toward the hot water, asking, "So what's the story?"

Nominated by The Georgia Review

A TIBETAN MAN IN HAWLEY, MASSACHUSETTS

by PAMELA STEWART

from GHOST FARM (Pleasure Boat Studio)

Just one step off the edge into the deep
wrong place and a shoe pulls off, is lost.
Amidst twigs, leaves, mosses and stones, this shoe
cannot be found by eyes or strong hands.
Even digging into the exact place the shoe exited its foot,
farther down than the shoe could have delved,
there's no black shoe! What now?
The man stands in thick dry grasses at road's edge
and decides on the one thing children in his village
were taught to do. Slipping off
his other shoe he flings it over to where the first black shoe
must have gone. How long should he wait
for one shoe to find the other? It's August,
too hot to stand for long without flies catching in his hair.
The shoes have tongues; they should call to one another.
Its hot, but the man from Tibet will pace this roadside ditch
waiting for his shoes to rise out of the shadows.

Nominated by Pleasure Boat Studio and Collette Inez

FROM *HOUSE OF PRAYER NO. 2*

by MARK RICHARD

from THE SOUTHERN REVIEW

Sᴀʏ ʏᴏᴜ ᴀʀᴇ ᴛʜᴇ sᴘᴇᴄɪᴀʟ ᴄʜɪʟᴅ. Say one reason you are special is because there is something wrong with your legs. You cannot run. Your legs will not move fast enough. When you try to run, your hips click and pop. When you have to run a race, like at the going-away party at a doctor's house in the old town, when everyone was running toward the doctor's house that would burn completely to the ground the next year, you pretend to trip and fall and not finish the race. You avoid footraces; you avoid running at all. When something bad happens and everyone else runs away, rocks thrown through greenhouse glass, loose spikes thrown at passing caboose windows, fishing boats untethered along a riverbank, you know you will have to face whoever is coming in their anger. You learn you must never get caught.

In the new town the teachers don't say you are special like the teachers did in the old town. They use the word *slow*. And you are slow. But they also say you are slow when you are sitting at your desk unable to color the state bird. You can't get the red crayon to work on the cardinal in a way that makes the teacher happy. Your father has said to be careful about signing your name to anything, so you don't put your name on your homework. A suspicious teacher has said that if your parents are really from Louisiana, you must be able to speak French. *Oui*, you say. You try to speak with a French accent, you still try to spend your Confederate money, you still wear your father's army helmet to school. No one can understand what you are saying, and big boys from out in the county want to fight you in line to the cafeteria. They come up behind you and flip off your helmet and you have to fight them almost every day. The fighting finally stops when you break a boy's hand. When your mother finds out, she cries because she is afraid the boy is the son of a new friend of hers. You get the feeling it was selfish of you to break the boy's hand.

A good afternoon in the new town is when the school is struck twice by lightning. Everyone else starts crying when the lightning strikes the swing set first. You stand at the window. It's raining and thundering and the lightning strikes the roof, but the sun is also shining, and you heard from your father's mother that when it rains and the sun is shining, it means the Devil is beating his wife. As the big boys from the county and all the little girls cry for the mommies and the teacher is shouting for everyone to get into the cloakroom, you clap and laugh and shout, "The Devil is beating his wife! The Devil is beating his wife!" The children and teacher are afraid of your loud laughter; you can tell by their looks as they crowd into the cloakroom as you stand by the open window getting soaked by the windblown rain, the special child.

One morning you do not have to go to school. Your father does not put on his forest clothes-khaki shirt, denim jeans, snake pistol, long sheath knife, the boots with wire laces that won't burn in case he gets caught in a forest fire and has to make a run for it. He puts on a coat and a tie, and you get in the car with him. He drives you to Richmond, through swamps, low woodlands, fields turned over for peanuts and corn. Neither of you speak; there's just the tires on the corduroy road and his flying tiger class ring clicking the window when he lifts his cigarette ash to the rolled-down crack at the top. You always keep an eye out for the tiger; you never know when it may fly across your face.

Your father turns the gray sedan into a long driveway between green lawns to a place that looks like a museum. Your father signs you in, and you take an elevator upstairs. The place smells like linoleum wax and medicine and shitty diapers.

You and your father sit on folding chairs in a long dark hallway with other fathers and mothers and what an odd boy who lives in the place later calls sin spawn; children with withered legs, legs of different lengths, bent-up legs, legs in steel and leather braces, hobbling kids crying and carrying the smell of places where people live who tote water in buckets from a well and go to the bathroom in sheds out back. A lot of the people waiting have long greasy hair that needs cutting. You can tell some are missing teeth when they talk and smoke and spit in the metal trash can by the exam room door.

A woman in a white uniform comes out with a clipboard and hands it to your father. You can read the top of the paper, and you understand why you are special when you read, "Crippled Children's Hospital."

The doctor has seen your X-rays. He twists your legs and makes your hips crack and pop on the white-papered table. The doctor doesn't answer your father's questions. The doctor says he will try nails in your hips. Your father wants to know if the doctor will put the nails in your hips himself. The doctor doesn't answer your father. He says nails are the best remedy. Your father asks if there is any other remedy, and he says it in a way that makes him sound like a smartass. The doctor stares at your father and says loudly, "With or without the nails, your son will probably be in a wheelchair by the time he's thirty anyway."

To cheer you up, your father takes you to the Hollywood Cemetery where some of your heroes are buried, President Jefferson Davis, Major Generals J. E. B. Stuart and George Pickett. You and your friends have spent many afternoons playing Pickett's Charge in the park across from the Episcopal church, running into withering cannon and musket fire, and because of your legs, you are always the first casualty as the minié balls rip into your arms and throat, falling dying in the grass, sometimes crawling beneath the azalea bushes where Robert E. Lee sits astride his iron gray horse Traveller, him saying down to you sadly, *I'm sorry, I'm sorry, it was all my fault.*

After you visit the grave of the doctor who amputated Stonewall Jackson's arm and tended to Lee's heart attack on the eve of Gettysburg, you go see the big black iron dog that guards a little girl's grave. By the time you get to the grave of Jefferson Davis's five-year-old son, Joe Davis, you are ready to go home.

At the hospital they strip you naked and scrub you with tar-smelling delousing soap in a deep sink in an old tiled room full of drains even though you had a bath that morning before leaving home with your family. A nurse takes the green cardboard suitcase your mother had packed for you that morning and says she'll deliver it to your father in the reception office. It's the green cardboard suitcase you used to carry your cat in. Here are your new clothes, nice and clean, with somebody else's name in the worn waistband of the donated shorts and in the collars of the two old summer-camp shirts. One of the shirts is a good one, yellow, red, and white madras, and in the coming months you will trade for it back when it goes through the laundry and is given to someone else.

Here is the T-shirt to sleep in, here is a fresh sheet for your bed, once a week put the top sheet on the bottom, the fresh sheet on top, and here is your bed on the sun porch. The boys' ward is crowded in summer. Your bed looks out over the rigging and masts, the bars and chains of the playground swing sets. That night it will all look like shipwrecks in the gray streetlight when you turn away from the crying around you and stare out through the metal safety rails of your bed.

Your mother sat in your father's car in the parking lot earlier that afternoon nursing your baby sister because your mother's luck has changed. She's had a baby and she's going to hell. She and another lady went into the little Catholic church to put fresh flowers on the altar one Saturday afternoon, and the priest came out of the sacristy with a rope belt and Scotch on his breath. Women in culottes defiling the altar. *Whores!* The priest swung the rope belt, and in her weekly call to her own mother later in Louisiana, your mother says she has left the Church for good.

"Then you are going to hell," her mother tells her. "Good-bye." On the extension, you hear someone take a breath quickly after your grandmother says this, and you don't know if it's your mother or the long-distance operator who sometimes listens in and lives down your street in a sorrow-filled house by herself with her three children who used to be four until one drowned in the frozen pond behind the cemetery like a lot of people seem to do, including Mrs. Richardson one street over.

From your sun-porch bed that afternoon you saw your father return to the car with your green suitcase and tell your mother something, and it seemed she didn't understand, but later she was crying as she nursed your little sister.

Your father walks over to the empty playground where no one is allowed because it is not playtime and he sits in one of the swings and you watch him chain-smoke for a while until he sees your mother burping your sister and he looks at his watch. A nervous boy comes up to you and says some kid died that morning. You figure out you got the dead kid's bed. When you look out next your father is gone, there's an empty swing swinging in the swing set. In the morning you go out on the playground with all the other crippled children and you find the swing where your father sat, the smoked tobacco and cigarette butts ground into the ashy dust.

In the next days they draw your blood and take your temperature. They X-ray you some more and forget you in a hallway until suppertime.

They make you walk naked in front of an auditorium of young student doctors and nurses from a college. Walk. Run. Stop. Stand on one leg. Hop. Run some more. Also in the audience are boys your age and girls your age. They see how you can't run naked, how you can't hop naked, how you can barely walk naked. They laugh at first until they realize in a few minutes a nurse will remove their gowns and make them jump, run, walk, and hobble naked, too.

One day after lunch, instead of a nap, a nurse takes you and her purse out in front of the hospital to wait for a taxicab. The taxicab takes the two of you to a laboratory downtown. By the way the nurse pets your head, you know this is going to be bad. They give you a shot that makes you drowsy and begin to dream, but you don't fall all the way asleep. While you are drowsy and begin to dream, they lay you on your side and push long needles into your spine. Somebody in your dream is screaming.

It's you.

Later in the taxicab back to the hospital the nurse holds you in her arms like a backseat pietà, the sunlight burns your eyes, and the telephone wires hang and loop, hang and loop. In the hospital auditorium you had noticed these words painted in large letters over the stage: "Suffer the little children to come unto me."

"Who said those words?" you ask the nurse who took you to the laboratory, the nurse who sometimes sneaks Coke in your metal spout cup when everybody else gets tap water. Nurse Wilfong.

"Jesus. Jesus Christ," she says.

What kind of jerk would want little children to suffer? you wonder.

Nurse Wilfong says you're constipated. They keep track of everyone's bowel movements in a ledger. You didn't know you had to report a bowel movement while you were still walking around, if they hadn't sent you upstairs yet to let the young student doctors practice taking you apart and nailing you back together.

Nurse Wilfong wants you to drink chalky stool softener while you want to talk about what a jerk Jesus must be if that's what he said about children and suffering. It's creepy, like the older boys going around saying a kid down in North Carolina went into a department store bathroom and some man cut off his penis with a pocketknife. The older boys say it was in the newspaper.

The hospital is crowded with children from Appalachia with knees that have to be cut up and legs that have to be sawn off. They're a pretty happy bunch. They love the food so much you give them yours; you don't eat it anyway. The first night you went into the lunch-table room there was a black kid sneezing snot into his plate of food right before the blessing. The woman who ran the lunch table made everyone slide down one plate so they could squeeze you in, and you got the plate with the droplets of snot on the rim, the rest of the snot having disappeared into the stewed tomatoes and cabbage and boiled meat. The Appalachian kids start eating off your plate as soon as it's set down in front of you. One of the Appalachian kids gets sent home with a long cast on his leg, and when he comes back and they cut off the cast, they find bugs have nested in there.

The black kid who blew snot all over your food is on a respirator now. You lie awake and watch the stoplight change out on Brook Road and wonder if there was enough of something in that one spoonful of stewed tomatoes you choked down so that you'll start coughing up bloody snot yourself. The ward overflows with deformity and crying kids at night. It's been two weeks; maybe they've forgotten about you again.

Then one night they get you.

The night nurse and the night porter jerk and wheel your bed into the prison spotlight of the night nurse's desk lamp so she can better see to tie No Breakfast signs to your bed rails. The young doctors will be waiting upstairs for you in the morning. They'll make Ben or Howard or one of the other black orderlies come down and fetch you. You hope you will come back alive because everyone knows, even the little boys on the other end of the ward, that not everybody comes back from upstairs. Sometimes boys end up on a gurney covered in bloody sheets and tossed-off scrubs down in the basement waiting for a station wagon from the state to fetch you, Big Mike says. Big Mike has burns over ninety percent of his body and carries a single condom in an empty wallet. He knows things. You begin to pray to God directly, forget the creepy men's-room Christ, and you hope somebody has called your parents because sometimes they forget to do that, too.

No one tells you that you will wake up in a body cast, so it is a surprise when you wake up and you are in a cast that reaches from under your arms and goes down to your knee on one side and down to your toes on the other. You vomit a lot coming out of the anesthesia as harelip kids bang around under your bed playing cowboys. You remember trying to push yourself out of the cast like an insect molting its shell and only the searing burn of the stretching of fresh stitchery covering the hammered-in nails around one hip makes you stop.

The heat of the place in the day and the fear of roaches that might crawl down into your cast at night make it hard to sleep. The nurses put you out on the smaller sun porch that has some books that aren't worth reading, mostly schoolbooks written before World War II. For a while, there are two Jerrys. One Jerry is the guy who is called The Human Skeleton. His clothes look like scarecrow rags. He ranges around on his bed waiting for someone to come too close so he can bite them with large buckteeth. He has one large testicle that sways back and forth when he crouches at the foot of his bed, chomping at the air. Later, when you are in a wheelchair and you can sit beside his bed and feed him crayons, he lets you pet his head like a dog and he pats your arm and howls.

The other Jerry is from Appalachia. He has calm, even features and a trusting smile and the eyes of a schoolbook pioneer standing on a mountaintop leading a wagon train into a lush green valley beyond. Already the doctors have taken off one of his legs. In the daytime it doesn't seem to bother him too much. But at night, as you watch for roaches crawling along your bed rail so you can flick them off, you see Jerry in silhouette against the Brook Road streetlight, and you see him stare down at the place where his leg used to be. You pretend you are asleep. Jerry throws himself back onto his pillow and Jerry cries, and you know he is trying not to. You want to tell him that it's all right, that everyone here cries at night.

Here is a miracle—you find a game board and a box of chess pieces, none missing. You teach Jerry to play chess. At nap time, when all must be quiet, Jerry sets up the board on a small table beside his bed. He touches each of your pieces with just the tip of a finger, waiting to see if that is the piece you want to move. You nod your head. He moves the piece. You clear your throat for the number of spaces, point a finger to adjust direction.

When Jerry moves his pieces, you see he's playing a cautious defensive game. Castling confounds him. Only when he almost makes the most fatal errors do you snap your fingers and he looks up to see you tapping your temple, telling him, *Think!* You don't want to keep beating him, and he knows this and tries harder. Just when you are about to quit one afternoon, he puts you in check, and if he weren't missing a leg and you weren't flat on your back in a body cast, you'd both get up and shake hearty hands. Instead, the two of you clap without making a sound because it is nap time and all must be quiet.

On Sunday mornings, Jerry's family comes down from the mountains somewhere near Cumberland Gap. They leave their houses in the dark and drive across the state just to be with Jerry for a few hours. They stand there and hold on to his clothes as if he might float away. Jerry's family doesn't bring him anything to eat, and you know it is because they don't have anything to bring. His parents look at Jerry in his face and hold on to his clothes and Jerry looks down at the leg that he has left, and there you are across the way, with grease all over your fingers, eating a fried chicken box lunch your parents have brought, knowing Jerry's family is all hungry and will drive back across the state without stopping. Your mother has also brought you a toy with the fried chicken box lunch, a blue plastic plate and a stick. The idea is to spin the plate on the end of the stick. The first time you try to spin the blue plastic plate on the end of the stick it flies off and hits Jerry's father on the back. Jerry's father picks up the blue plastic plate and he kindly passes it back to your mother, and she smiles and hands it to you and you are ashamed.

Sundays bring the young seminarians, the practice preachers, murmuring down the hallway, doing God's work, visiting the sick in their Hush Puppies shoes. All smiles until they smell you. They can't control you around the piano wheeled out of a classroom, can't make you love Jesus, fail to threaten you with the prophet Elisha who called down she-bears to rip the forty-two little mocking children to shreds, you all laughing at the violent story with spitting harelips and cleft palates and brandishing canes and crutches, nudging the seminarians into the clutches of The Human Skeleton and brain-damaged Dennis who'll bite and strangle them, the practice preachers looking, like all visitors ultimately do, for a nurse and a quick exit.

But the men from the barber college who come to cut your hair! Clicking down the hall in polished loafers, laughing and goofing, their smiles steadfast as they round the corner and smell you, see you, mangy mongrels with overgrown bowl cuts from the hills, crew cuts from the piedmont gone to seed postsurgery, matted twists of bed-headed hair pressed against pillow twenty-four hours a day. The barbers come whistling with jokes and songs and gum, and they touch you, cradle your heads in their hands as they trim, hold you in their arms so you can safely lean over the edge of the bed in your body casts as they open your faces with their scissors, telling each crippled child who he looks like from movies and men's magazines, the barbers clipping and snipping at the dirty ropes of hair falling off the beds onto the floor for Ben the porter to sweep up.

The men from the barber college sweep the beds with little brooms from the deep pockets of their white jackets which you all keep peering into for more gum, and there is always more gum! And from the deep pockets they pull the pint flasks of cologne and cooling colored water they clap on their hands and rub around your necks and on your faces and through your hair like a blessed baptism that opens your lungs for the first time in forever with its fragrance, remembering you to a world beyond that doesn't smell like bedpans, pissed pants, dirty sheets, the deathly perfume stench of yourselves rotting in rancid plaster and body casts.

Everyone wishes the barbers came every week like the practice preachers but the barbers do not. The only good thing the practice preachers bring is the pornography, the vivid picture books of martyrs led and bound to rocks where they have their hands chopped off by laughing scoundrels. All the boys like the pictures so much the practice preachers stop bringing them. The practice preachers can't stand how you all laugh at the guys with the chopped-off hands, the way they sit with their faces turned up toward the clouds, blood gushing from their bloody stumps like broken red pipes, their hangdog tongues, their mangy shoulder-length hair, their eyes staring stupidly into heaven.

Your father is coming for you in a station wagon, the head nurse says. You say good-bye to Nurse Wilfong, who bathes you every day, you say good-bye to Big Mike, the boy with the melted face, and give him your transistor radio. You give your best friend Michael Christian, the black boy in perpetual leg braces, all of your contraband—an old Christmas tin of stale pretzels and the rubber-band slingshot metal-tipped balsa jets some Shriners had handed out that then were confiscated after everyone shot them stuck into the acoustic tile ceiling. You give The Human Skeleton a tin metal truck and the little daredevil figure that shot out of the Cracker Jack prize cannon. He breaks it the first time he fires it. You write a note to the girl on the girls' ward you talked to on the lawn when Hogan's Heroes came, Colonel Klink telling you he had a son named Mark. You tell the girl you're sorry, it's over, you're going home. The young nurse who had passed all the notes back and forth reads it and laughs and throws it away. You say good-bye to Ben the porter who always gave you a pony blanket at nap time that didn't smell like diarrhea and who always saved you a little paper cup of pineapple juice when nap time was over. You say good-bye to Jerry who now doesn't have any legs at all.

Nominated by The Southern Review and Ted Hoagland, Amanda Rea

I'M ONLY SLEEPING

by JOHN RYBICKI

from ECOTONE

Another six-pack in the tub
floating downstream
next to my bed.

I fall asleep with the light on
and a beer in hand.
It tips over

so I wake up in what
feels like my own piss.
My Jack Russell Sparky's drowsing

two feet higher at the foot of the bed
with all those clothes heaped up,
layered over Julie's hospital things:
her bathrobe and diapers and soft bottoms;
lotion for rubbing her face
and bald head.

Let go now, Johnny. The moon is writing
sweeter sentences on the water
than you anyway.

Pull the earth over you now and sleep.

Nominated by Ecotone and Rick Bass, David Kirby, David Wojahn

NUMBER STATIONS

fiction by SMITH HENDERSON

from ONE STORY

Goldsmith's mother took her own pictures of the ostrich. A man had led the bird to her door and kept it on a small chain. A sorry-looking sack of shit, she thought. The man and the bird both.

Her granddaughter caught sight of the thing and scooted outside, underneath it, and begged to climb on as soon as the man said he was selling rides. The bird dropped its head down to the girl and hung there like a pipe from under the sink, inspecting her. For five dollars the man would put her on it and take a Polaroid. He pointed to the camera slung around his neck and showed his mangled teeth in an approximate smile. The ostrich chuffed hot little clouds of breath.

"I see what this is," Goldsmith's mother said, holding closed her cardigan at her neck.

The man had taken off his cap in the manner of an older generation, holding it like reins. "I know Goldsmith," he said. "I'm Bill. I work for him? Washing dishes?"

So this was the parolee her son had hired. She pulled the girl back inside. "I'm not paying you anything for anything," she said. Her eyes all but disappeared beneath their creased and folded lids.

The girl, Charity, whined, asked please pretty please. The ostrich lifted its head and looked away, indifferent. Only seven, the girl already did not forgive herself her own crooked features and was certain that her destiny was to ride an ostrich or griffin or rainbow to her true self, who was beautiful and free. Goldsmith's mother always chided her nonsense, said that the true self was the one you were every day and no

246

other. There was no secret self waiting for you somewhere. You were you. That was it.

"I know you've been to prison," she told the man.

This intrigue silenced Charity, who slipped her grandmother's hold. But the dishwasher's face betrayed little, or there was nothing to betray. A cold front was coming in from Canada, and here was an ostrich in the front yard. A passing car slowed. The old woman fluttered her fingers for them to go on.

"Now I'll have all of Bigfork coming over. What gave you this idea?"

"Nothing give me the idea. I just had it."

"I'm not paying you anything."

"All right then." The dishwashing parolee bit his cheek and stood there waiting for her to give in or dismiss him.

"There's no point to it," she said. She uncrossed her arms. "I *would* take a picture myself," she said. "Since you're already here."

The parolee looked off so as not to show her what he thought, which was did she think he was stupid. And then that he should stay out of trouble no matter what. And finally that keeping the job her son had given him was a condition of his parole.

"All right," he said.

He lifted the girl onto the bird and held it by the chain. Charity sat on its back and swung her hair. The feathers were stiff like they'd been dipped in wax, but she didn't mind. She explained to the man about dream clouds, and asked did he know what a griffin was. The bird side-stepped. Goldsmith's mother returned from inside with a camera and snapped away. She looked up.

"It's overcast," she said. She turned on the flash, and when she took another picture, the bird reared in the silent white burst, the girl tumbling off with an abbreviated shriek.

"Whoa there," the dishwasher said, but the bird pulled back and back, pads patting the soft earth. It hopped in spurts, straining against the chain until it hove him over. His hands were chapped and cracked from all the hot water, soap, and mopping, and the chain ran bloody through them and snaked backwards jangling on the sidewalk as the ostrich sprinted away. The bird jinked into the road from tree to parked car to picket fence, and then out of sight down an alley.

The dishwasher lay on his belly, his arms slung out like a cop had ordered him there. Blocks away, a dog began to yelp at the improbable creature. Goldsmith's mother crouched over the girl and asked him what he was looking at them for.

"Is she okay?"

"Get the ostrich!" Charity yelled, rubbing her tailbone.

Bill stood, wiped his bloody hands on his pants, and ran on his stiff new boots in the direction of the sharp, astonished barks.

Goldsmith ate as he did every day, in the window booth of his restaurant, overlooking the river. Yellow leaves freckled the slow-moving water. Nearby, a pair of old ladies murmured and shot hot looks at the laughter bursting from the kitchen. It was the last day for most of the teenagers and shiftless adults who worked all summer for him. No one bought ice cream in the winter, and the restaurant could use only a few of the kids year-round. One of the girls in the kitchen shrieked, and the old ladies frowned and crushed their napkins. Goldsmith didn't mind, didn't care if the biddies were bothered. Life was short and weird.

Goldsmith wiped his mouth. Emily was across the restaurant, cleaning handprints from the display window on the ice cream freezer. He took his plate and cup to the dish tub under the coffee station, and caught her taking sips of him with her eyes. She immediately turned and checked the fudge for temperature with her pinky. She'd asked to stay on through the winter. She'd clean the greasy air vents in the kitchen. Muck out the walk-ins. Paint. Whatever. He said he'd think about it, and what he thought was she should go back to college.

The kids shushed one another at Goldsmith's appearance in the kitchen and resumed chopping, spraying the dirty dishes. The girl who shrieked went to check on the old ladies who were by now fed up and leaving. Goldsmith fetched a bread knife and a loaf of French bread, cut away the heel and then a thick slice. He plucked a hot butter knife off the pallet of steaming silverware just from the dishwasher. The door swung open and in Emily came, on cue. She idled by the stove, stirred some water set to boil for potatoes or pasta. Goldsmith took the slice of bread and the nearly scalding knife to the walk-in cooler for a ramekin of butter. The knife cooled and the softened butter snagged in cold nuggets across the bread. He leaned in the doorway of the walk-in, the refrigerated air that he paid for cooling his neck, and chewed.

She quit wearing make-up the day after he asked if she was wearing any. It had startled him to see her all painted up. She was half his age at least. Black sprigs of hair curled up and away from her head like a good time. He'd quit seeing his desires in things. There were only attributes. The freckled river, handprints on cold glass. Emily hefted the white plates. He chewed the bread and lumps of butter. She was smitten with him, there was no doubt about it.

The close-set brick houses gave way to ranchettes and at last to a field of Russian thistle. The dogs' braying had ceased or was beyond Bill's hearing and all was quiet save the gravel along the country road crunching underfoot. There was a hill he didn't want to climb and a stand of cottonwoods by the river. He scanned the thistle, picked up a stick, and beat a yellow road sign. Then he sat with his split hands dangling over his bent knees exhausted. A pickup swept by unheeding. He had no car, no one to call, save his parole officer who wouldn't help him anyway.

Bill clomped back to Goldsmith's house, and Goldsmith himself answered the door. Charity appeared behind her father in green rubber gloves, holding a slimy knife with a pumpkin seed on it.

"Bill. What can I do for you?"

"I come to talk to the lady was here earlier," he said. "She run off my bird."

"You were here earlier?"

"Yah. And the lady was here run off my bird."

"She's rocking the baby to sleep right now." Goldsmith hadn't opened the screen door and wasn't going to. "My wife's out of town."

Bill nodded that he understood. Goldsmith leaned against the jamb. "You say it run off? Was it a chicken or something?"

"An ostrich," Charity said.

Goldsmith snorted. But his daughter's face was serious. Bill was serious.

"You have an ostrich," Goldsmith said.

"Not no more I don't."

"You're saying my mother ran off an ostrich that you brought here."

"It's what happened."

"Where'd you get an ostrich?"

"Long story. Point being I don't got it now."

"Well, I doubt she meant to run it off, Bill."

"I know. I'd like to forgive her. To her face. It's just a thing I got to do."

Goldsmith looked at him a minute and then scratched his eyebrow and picked something from under the nail of the finger he had used to scratch it. Considering a counter-offer.

"What say I tell her for you?" he asked.

Bill mulled this suggestion. Charity had moved next to her father at the screen, the knife in her green clutches, looking from father to parolee to father.

"When I's inside we had group counseling, and I never seen anybody forgive anybody else for somebody else. I'd prefer to do it to her face if it's all the same to you."

"Well, like I said, she's busy."

"Maybe I could just wait."

"Bill, we're carving pumpkins this afternoon. And there's the party at the lake I got to get ready for. So."

"I can't go on account of there being liquor at it."

"I know."

"I'd like to have gone."

"I'm sorry."

"I forgive you."

A sharp laugh shot out of Goldsmith.

"Well thanks, Bill."

"No problem."

"I'll relay your message to my mother. Go on home, now." He closed the door, but it didn't latch, and the girl told Bill through the gap to keep looking, and he said he'd tried, and she just glared at him until he was uncomfortable and he left.

Goldsmith's mother put down the sleeping baby and tiptoed out. She flipped on the baby monitor in the living room, and dropped into the recliner with a finger of Beam. Goldsmith had gone to the party already. Decked out in an orange tutu and blessing everything with a duct-taped wand, Charity had kissed her Nanna on the cheek and left for her sleepover. The house was quiet save the small hum of the fridge in the kitchen.

An ice-cream truck jingle rang through the speaker. She sat up, alarmed. A voice constituted itself out of the surging static of the monitor. A man's voice, counting. *Five Whiskey Lima Nine Nine Tango.*

She lunged out of the recliner, struck her elbow on the corner of a wall on her way to the baby's room, and flung open the door. The baby stirred in the crib but did not wake. Goldsmith's mother held her breath, crept to the closet, and jerked it open. She unlatched and latched the window. There was nothing. She retreated into the hall tingling, elbow throbbing, listening.

On the monitor, the man still counted. She flipped it off and set it on the coffee table. She stepped back and watched it. She drank down the Beam. She picked up the monitor. Turned it back on. The voice counted out of order, simply reciting the numbers. *Ten Hotel Five Four Seven.* Then he said, *Alpha Juliet Nine Tango.* More numbers. *Ten Golf Five Echo.*

She turned it off. She got another Beam and downed it.

She left the room and returned with pen and paper.

The cooks smoked dope by the campfire and passed around a plinky guitar that could not be tuned. Goldsmith tested the lukewarm water in the great wooden tub not far from shore of the lake. The ice cream crew and wait staff within it drank from silver cans of beer, teased and flirted poorly at one another, and nuzzled in wet pairs. Good for them.

"Whose turn?" Goldsmith had asked.

Emily climbed out and shivered on the cold mud and pine needles. They went to the fire pit, donned the oven mitts hanging from the tree, and hefted the great pot of boiling water to the tub. Everyone splashed to the far side as they poured it in. Goldsmith and Emily dragged the pot to the lake. Emily wobbled on bare feet over the round stones. She showed him the tattoo of a triple-decker cone on her ankle in the moonlight by the water. They sunk the hissing pot into the lake and then lugged the heavy black water back to the fire.

He nodded toward the hot tub.

"Climb on in," he said.

"Are you?"

"I'm gonna stoke this fire."

Instead, she went to the cabin clutching herself on those white legs. He fed the fire and climbed into the water with the laughing, groping kids.

Four hours in that heat and he still hadn't melted away. On the bench around the tub was a whiskey that was empty and another whiskey that sat half-full. Goldsmith heaved his wet bear's girth, and the water dropped a level. The ice cream crew filled his gap. He staggered to the cabin to throw up next to it, then went in and slurped cold lake water from the cistern. Emily sat up in one of the beds and startled him into the wall.

"You scared me."

"Sorry."

"Wow," he said. "I'm drunk."

In the dark she could just be made out, by starting from her teeth.

Her face, then her neck. The whole outrageous rest of her, there on the bed. Goldsmith leaned into the air around him like he was sounding its depth in little circles.

"What I do is, I lay down for a minute," Emily said. "Concentrate on swallowing and if I don't taste that metal taste, I wait a while and sometimes I fall asleep and sometimes I can get up."

"Huh."

"Come on. Come lay down."

His steps pounded the floor. He stopped, pulled off his sopping shirt.

"Waitaminute," he said. "I'm all wet. I should put on dry clothes first."

He was about to lie down with this girl. What all would that mean? His bag was somewhere in the cabin or still out in his car or somewhere between the two, under the picnic table, in the extra tent he set up. Outside the kids splashed out of the hot tub and across the loose rocks and splashed again into the freezing lake, screaming, invincible with youth. And lust. To lie down would mean he could never be absolved. That he had completely given up. *I forgive you*, the dishwasher had said.

"I threw up."

"I could hear it."

"How old are you again?"

"Twenty-four in three days."

"I'm gonna find dry clothes and go out to the dock and drink the rest of that whiskey."

"You'll fall in the lake."

"I just might."

"I better come with."

"Yeah," he said. "You better."

The ostrich tapped the glass over the kitchen sink. Tink tink. Emily quivered hungover in Van's terrycloth robe at the table in the nook. Behind the bird's pink fuzzy head, snow fell thick and slow, then shunted sideways in the spastic gusts of wind, and then fell straight and slow again.

She had returned from the party in the brittle dawn, sneaked quietly into the house, and showered for a full hour in dread of Van and of stepping into the chill air outside the curtain. She'd slipped into Van's robe and pulled her dirty socks from the hamper. The socks smelled of campfire, and she put them on. She shuffled to the nook where the heater paid out hot and constant under the table, and worked back down the salted bile. She sweated. Felt a false fever. Then tink tink. An ostrich. She didn't question it except to question every single thing she saw. The table, the coffee ring on the table. The butter dish. The wire bowl over the sink and the brown bananas in it. Bigfork, Montana outside. The Flathead. The Continental Divide. All could be false if the bird was. She stayed put so as not to startle it or any of this possible unreality, but the bird ducked out of sight anyway.

Goldsmith and his employees had made campfires right next to Little Bitterroot Lake. The car stereo blasted from up on the dirt road until it died with the battery and headlights. And when the lake steamed in the cold, Goldsmith told Emily his secret. She held his head and snot ran out of it when he came up sheepish, glazed, and relieved to have explained everything, after he sobbed there. He said that Bill forgave him and shook with private laughter. They sat cross-legged on the dock as the pink sleeve of dawn colored the eastern horizon and the lake mist shirred white across the polished stone surface of the water. She leaned over the dock, drank handfuls, and then drove Goldsmith back to town through stoplights blinking yellow. She deposited him at his house without a word. He weaved across his yard.

Then it snowed. And now Van appeared in the doorway. He went to the sink for a glass of water.

"Have fun?"

He wasn't really asking that. She made him helpless helpless helpless. He brought her things off the mountain and from the insides of crevasses. A bandana-wrapped piece of ice that shone blue in the place he found it. A sunbleached rib bone. A purple beardtongue flower in a rusted Rainier can, both from a high meadow. She could not reciprocate these gifts, or in any case did not. Even his nightmares staged this imbalance. Mornings he rolled over under the big denim quilt and reported to her what she'd done in his sleep, how she'd slung herself like a pelt over some man. Even though Van pleaded and screamed at her, she hung and slinked her body over that man.

Van was better off not sharing the dreams. After all, she was rooting for him. Right now, drinking the water, she waited for him to make her helpless, to even things out.

"I did have fun," she said. "Goldsmith was too fucked up to drive."

He faced her.

"The boss?"

He knew damn well Goldsmith was her boss. Goldsmith was the man in his nightmares. It took effort to ignore his question, what it said.

"I wasn't, so I drove."

"Wasn't what?"

"All that drunk."

Tink tink. He looked at his empty glass. She smiled.

"There's an ostrich behind you."

"Ha."

"I swear to God, Van. Look."

He pivoted on those wonderful hips. His t-shirt lifted, revealing the twin divots of his pelvis and over that his riffled bare white stomach, and in memory she felt up his chest, the meat on his ribs, his breast, clavicle, trunk neck, and blonde-scruffed chin. He was from all over. For a time he built things where people spoke Spanish and cooked on hot rocks. There were at least fifty-seven essences in his sideburns that, could she decoct and bottle them, would heal any wound on her body, would disinfect a gut shot, would recapitate her.

"Holy shit. It is an ostrich," he said.

"Have you ever seen one in person?"

He shook his head. He couldn't stay mad. His blonde beard twinkled up his cheeks. The ostrich tink-tinked and Van leaned toward the glass and the bird cocked back in surprise.

When they opened the back door, the ostrich chittered in its tubed throat and bolted across the yard, leaving two-toed green prints in the thin snow sheeting the grass.

Van made his living measuring the glacier's recession in the national park. The melt occurred the world over. It would be Halloween soon.

Emily took his hand and said, "It snowed."

How glad that made him.

Goldsmith was a long time upstairs, waking. He'd dreamt he was boiling in a pot of water, melting like a wax model of himself, pooling pink and creamy on the surface. Where his flesh melted away, his bones shone like chrome. He'd said, "My insides are sterling." He woke with the sentiment that he had inherent value.

He laced his hands behind his throbbing head, tried to remember what day it was. He actually cherished a hangover, recovering from oblivion the current state of his life. The time from his alarm clock.

His bladder. His mutual fund yield. Where Empire Ice Cream & Restaurant stood in the ledger. The likely location of his family. It was one o'clock in the afternoon, the baby's naptime. Charity would be at her friend's house. His mother was probably tidying up and his wife was off visiting a sick friend—a dying friend—in Oregon. The woman had cancer in her marrow. My God what he'd be without them.

He couldn't remember how he got home.

Oh. Emily.

Goldsmith shuddered on knocking legs down the stairs like a man fresh from surgery. His mother sat erect at the dining room table in front of the baby monitor listening to a man's voice.

"What is that?"

X-ray Five Nine Quebec.

"I've been doing this," she said, holding up a sheet of paper on which she'd scrawled the numbers front and back. Her hair shot out from her head in shocks of gray where she had pushed her hand into it as she took the ceaseless dictation.

"Is that coffee?" he asked.

She nodded, and he sat and took her cup, sipped, and frowned at how cool it was.

"You haven't even touched it."

"*Shhh*. Listen."

She leaned towards the monitor. *Yankee Romeo Bravo*. A pipe whistle blew and then static filled the little speaker.

"I don't get it," he said.

"It started last night. On the baby monitor. It scares the hell out of me."

The monitor toned a long grim note. *Hotel Two.*

"That's just some interference. Just change the frequency."

He took it and flipped a switch.

"There. All gone."

He handed the monitor back. The heat kicked on, and the smell of stirred dust and natural gas infused the room. Outside someone scraped the sidewalk with a snow shovel, and the scraping hurt his teeth.

"I have to go in to the restaurant," he said.

She swallowed.

"Today? It's the weekend. It's snowing."

"Well Bill's there," he said and regretted it, regretted what it sounded like, like he didn't trust the man.

"I don't know about him. He came here for money, Dick. As if you don't do enough, giving a man like him a job."

Goldsmith took his throbbing head in his hands. Then he looked up at her with pink eyes that made her grimace with worry.

"Bill did his time, all right? He's not going to slit our throats."

She flinched at the image that this put in her head. She folded her hands on her lap and watched them for a moment and then put them on the table and was quiet.

"I want to know what's going on," she said.

When he didn't immediately reply, a range of answers fanned across her mind like a deck of cards. He was sick. He was dying. There were money troubles. Divorce. She had done something and he was afraid to confront her. They wanted her to move out. And as she briefly imagined awful possibilities, she met each one with relief, and there was scarcely a thing he could say that would not put her at ease, no matter how bad it might be.

"Nothing is going on," he said.

"Yes there is."

He gave her a longsuffering grin, a rage-inducing smirk he'd perfected when he was a teenager, and which, she now realized, was calculated precisely to make her irrationally angry so that he could dismiss her. The smile ostensibly said that he was listening, that he would hear her out, but he only ever wore it when he wanted to hide something, when he didn't want to say something. She realized this now. And in the past, she would have spat a whole range of useless, spiteful things, and he would have taken the abuse and given up nothing, and though she might realize she was out of control she would still say more horrible things until even she couldn't take it anymore and would at last quit. She saw the whole dynamic, how he turned her on herself.

The thought occurred to her that her son had done something awful.

"Oh Dick, what have you done?"

He stood abruptly, tottered like a drugged bear.

"When Charity gets home, just stay here. I'll call."

She searched his eyes and clutched her throat. He was her son. Her boy.

"You don't have to," she croaked. She grabbed for him, but he was already shambling for the sideboard. "I don't care what it is, Dick. I don't care!"

He dug in her purse.

"My car's still at the lake," he said, holding up her keys.

"Dick. Just wait a minute," she said, but he was out the door.

The shoveling ceased. Her car started and her son drove away. The heater quit and the vent ticked in the new quiet.

She sat for a while. Then she picked up the pen and changed the frequency back.

November Echo Echo Five.

Emily made Van drive. Flakes melted on the windshield and blew in the windows they'd rolled down to hear the ostrich's strange nickering. Snow glazed the trees, the ground, and slicked the black pavement that hissed under their tires. A tilted plastic garbage can, a pie tin in the mud, and a gap in the cedar shrubs might all have been signs of the bird's passage.

Van glanced at her.

"So you came in pretty late."

She turned up the heater.

"Go down this alley."

Van did.

"I'm not mad," he said. "It takes me a long time to fall asleep when you're out is all. I trust you, Em. It's just I don't want anything to happen."

She pointed into a yard to her right, asked him to stop.

"I'm not avoiding talking about this," she said. "But are those its prints there? In this yard?"

He leaned over her.

"Looks like 'em."

He drove to the end of the alley and turned left.

"Last night was different," she said.

"Not from my end."

"Okay. But from my end."

A woman tying closed her bathrobe jogged down from her front step, waving at them. Van stopped the car.

"You two ain't looking for Big Bird are ya?" she asked. Her husband was halfway out the door, halfway in his coat, grinning like an escapee.

"Which way?" Emily asked.

The woman pointed. Van drove on, and together they were quiet. He opened the glove box and she took out the binoculars. They crossed a bridge, and he slowed and pointed where the tracks ran along the cambered road and had crossed or gone somewhere up or down it. Or perhaps the ostrich had continued on the wet road. Van pulled into a picnic area, and Emily scanned the flats to where the creek ran away from them. She passed him the binoculars. He searched the fields and stands of trees and the mountains.

"Okay," he said. "How was it different from your end?"

He took the binoculars from his eyes.

"Goldsmith told me this . . . real bad thing."

White pinheads of snow disappeared on the windshield. She got out and slipped on wet leaves and stepped past the picnic tables to where someone had dragged an old couch, a topless coffee table, and a floor lamp. Snow had tufted the burnt armrests of the couch. She stepped onto it and looked through the binoculars into the fields across the creek. A gasoline odor rose up from the fabric. The car door opened, closed, and the fresh snow groaned under his footfalls.

"Emily."

The way he said her name, she got down. He took the binoculars. Her hands were cold and pink like she'd been stacking tubs of ice cream in the freezer. She shivered in her sweater. He opened his coat and put her hands in his armpits, and they stood like this for a while. She inhaled his sideburns.

"I want you to tell me the thing," he said, lifting her face up.

"Something else. I'll do something else."

"Em. It has to be this."

So this is Goldsmith's glacier: Six years ago and his wife gone to her parents' in Wisconsin with Charity. The restaurant was insane, lines out the door, kids crying, plates dropping and shattering, spilled drinks, squabbles in the kitchen. And he dickered all morning with the huckleberry pickers about the crop, the man-hours, and the price. He stormed out after the lunch rush for a half round, the worst back nine of his life, and shouldn't have even bothered, shanking and topping the goddamn ball like that. A personal worst. He bought a round to apologize for that display of complete incompetence, and gave Flanagan shit for being Butte Irish. Went too far. Bought another round. One more for himself. One quick last one. He trundled out into the flatiron heat of the lot—had to go back for his clubs—squeezed himself into the baking town car, and squealed out of the lot, taking side streets, halting astonished at stop signs lurching up out of the landscape like cardboard pop-ups.

He got the hang of it. Gunned the engine halfway up the block, let off, and cruised to the stop sign wheeling up at the intersection. He had the hang of it and he didn't see the girl. It was hot out and the air was lovely rushing over his bare arm out the window like he was holding up the car. He didn't see her. The air and the sun were too loud to see her. Just her arm, flung up in front of his hood and smeared away like the parked cars, the mailboxes, and the houses. He didn't really believe it until he looked in the rearview and saw her in the road, a body or just knocked out, asleep, maybe okay. The only sounds were his engine and the loud sun. The gas pedal gave under his foot, the car rolled through the intersection, and he tingled all over. He hazarded a look in the rear view. She shimmered and diminished on the hot blacktop.

He trembled home, his garage door looming up, the tires chirping to a stop. Killed the engine. Shook there. Disgorged himself from the car like an astronaut from his capsule, pulling himself into gravity. His golfer's intuition said that in forty-five minutes the black clouds bundling over the mountains would rain. A mower chortled up the block. He rushed into the house, closed the curtains, dialed and hung up on his lawyer, took hot parching swallows of Maker's Mark. He bathed his torso at the kitchen sink, and finally came to rest shirtless on a stepladder in his garage. He pressed the button and the garage door ratcheted up revealing the theater of the whole world. The small red smear on the right front bumper. His neighbor leaned back from his workbench in the garage opposite and waved. Goldsmith held up the faceted highball glass, and the man resumed planing a piece of wood. The sky disheveled over the mountains and gusted clippings of grass rose up in green dust devils. Then thick drops of rain dotted the driveway and the car. Dark sheets of it misted into garage, and the blood on the bumper, it just went away.

In the glaciers vouch testimonies of time and the secrets of weather in those times. And fitted in mirrored glasses, red parkas, and spiked boots, Van and the researchers assay the glaciers, pass through the boulders and menhirs of ice, daisy-chained, head-lamped, carefulfooted. A shifting, groaning, and dying leviathan beneath them. The audible prolapse of the world's ice uncoupling. In the narrow crevasses the melting water clinks like a child's xylophone. And from the glaring sheet Van and his colleagues draw long boles like miners of scarce iterations of blue. The one true blue. And in the dusk they make their way down in a staggered, flashing chain gang.

Last summer, he and Emily had visited a friend's cabin on Rogers Lake and the arctic grayling floated stinking on the surface because the water was too hot. In the humid morning, Van and this friend feathered the lukewarm lake in the canoe and netted twenty garbage sacks of dead fish that they emptied on the south shore for the bears and horse-flies. By noon with the sun full up, the stench choked them as they rinsed out the bags in the brothy lake. Van reeked of dead arctic fish for days, and Emily banished him to the front porch where he failed to sleep. He forgave her, but not the heat.

But for now, snow.

They followed a path off of Jewel Basin Road into the woods after the ostrich. As they walked, she told Van of Goldsmith's round confession on the dock, the bottle going back and forth between them, the false swallows she took so he might go on. How his wife came home, discovered him soused in the garage, and how her anger at that was the sum of his punishment. On the bedroom television at ten o'clock he learned that the child had died. Can you imagine? He squatted the night in the master bath. Morning, it just came. He didn't sleep for a long time. The period where he thought of nothing but death and the finality of it like a depressed teenager. Then his daughter, ceaselessly doting on her, encouraging her every outlandish dream. How he en-souled another child with his wife. The bad ratios that governed his life. How the world had come to seem in his prosperity. In each and every instance perfect nonsense.

Van dropped onto a stump. Emily stopped at the creek's edge.

"You have to get him to turn himself in."

"Van, I can't."

"You're kidding."

"I'm not."

Van was right. But it was also true that this was how he was trying to win her over, by getting her to narrow the competition. And she didn't like to think this and didn't want him to win this way, which was maybe the same thing as realizing that he wouldn't win her this way, and if he didn't, then maybe it was the way he would at last lose her.

The creek gurgled under the ice, and she didn't know if the water was freezing or the ice was melting, but it was one or the other. She pulled a tag of white skin from a cottonwood.

"Em," he said.

She put a finger to her lips. Barking. Across a fallow field she spotted the ostrich. Head pumping, it sprinted around a silo trailed by three mad dogs. It crashed into a barbwire fence, bounced up and over, and continued into the field. The dogs arrowed through the wires after.

"We have to go," she said.

Bill was washing dishes when Goldsmith came in. They nodded at each other. When Goldsmith had offered him this position, Bill had said that he would be looking for another job if Goldsmith couldn't say right then and there that he'd keep him on through the winter. Bill's parole officer didn't give two shits about seasonal fluctuations. Goldsmith started him full time, Sunday through Thursday.

Goldsmith went into his office in the basement. He came back up.

"You want a cup of coffee?" he asked.

Bill hooked the sprayer and toweled off his peeling hands.

"I could drink one."

Goldsmith returned with two cups and said, "I forgot to tell my mother that you forgave her for losing the ostrich. I'm sorry."

"It's all right."

"She was all bent about this voice coming out of the baby monitor. Just reading numbers. Probably something with Forest Service or something, huh?"

"Number stations," Bill said.

"Number stations?"

"Heard them inside," he said. "In prison," he clarified, even though he didn't need to. "Fella had a crystal radio that he powered with a potato. Used to hear them all the time."

Goldsmith thumbed the edge of his cup.

"Tell me something about prison," he said.

Bill wondered what story Goldsmith would want to hear. There was no such story. Goldsmith waited, blew on his hot coffee. There was only one story at all that the parolee could think of to tell.

They sent him to Texas for thirteen months. Never said why, just moved him. He left his cell only to eat, mandatory time in the yard, and the infirmary. He read the Bible. Especially the parts about vanity and forgiveness. All the red text, the exact words of Jesus. There were more blacks and Mexicans in Texas than he'd seen in any one place. The chiggers bit him, and the sweaty sheets gave him bedsores, and in the morning he looked like birds had been eating at him. His nightmares staged scenes of violence that put him at odds with his own sleep. He received sleeping pills from the infirmary, and they grogged him so badly that he missed all signs of the gathering riot. The bowed-up silence of the other orangemen, the parceling of the muggy yard. The silent free weights. He stood at the fence and willed thunderheads over the shivering prairie to come come come in, wet and windy. Then an orangeman flashed by and ran a pipe in the eye socket of another not five paces in front of Bill. Ripping that honed and pointed tube from the man's face, the orangeman sent red pearls into the heavy air like he was demonstrating the act for him, and Bill sprinted to the skinheads in the corner of the exploding yard, under the south tower. A bearded and inked brute met him there and turned him about to bark and jape at the paisas and blacks who fought. Canisters popped overhead and vailed down streamered with tear gas, but there was no pause in the combat. The rifles cracked from above and whole quadrants of prisoners' skulls hinged away, hearts blasted out, the orangemen diving or falling to the hardpan. Bill fainted choking on the gas. Came to sweltering and cuffed to a dead man. The storm clouds moved on.

Goldsmith had paled at this story. The parolee reckoned he'd unspooled too much. They regarded one another uncomfortably.

"What's an orangeman?" Goldsmith finally asked.

"All us prisoners. Because the jumpsuits is orange."

"How did you do it?"

"Do what now?"

"The time."

The parolee scratched his chin.

"Couldn't not," he said, and sipped his coffee.

Goldsmith's mouth pinched downward at its edges like a person about to cry, but he didn't.

"I'd like you to swab out the ice cream freezer," he said. "I'll turn it off."

Bill nodded.

"Take out all the ice cream buckets. Eat as much as you want and dump the rest. Get in there with boiled bleach water and muck it out. Walls, ceiling, everything."

The crazed dogs led Emily and Van through the field across the creek and to a frozen ditch where puce scars in the snow revealed the churned clay and dirt. The ice cracked in shards underfoot and the thin water rilled into a concrete culvert under the road. Within the black of it the barking and snarling rebounded, amplified, and carried out to Emily and Van.

"What do we do?" Emily pulled her sleeves into her fists.

"I don't think there's anything we can."

Emily kicked loose stones and stepped a little bit into the culvert. She pitched rocks into the teeming dark and shouted. A dog screamed, and the ostrich flapped in there, and Van pulled her out and onto the bank. Water splashed. Then a small dog limped out on three legs, looking back and limping up the bank past them, looking back, climbing, looking back, trotting off unevenly through the brush toward the road.

The barking was ceaseless.

The ostrich bolted from the culvert and ran up the bank opposite Emily and Van pursued by a brace of outraged curs. It crashed through the cottonwoods, low bitterbrush, over the fell trees. The dogs after. Then, in the quiet, the snow whispered down.

"Let's go home," Van said.

She shook her head.

"It's pointless, Em. We're not gonna save it."

He stood. She didn't move. He had to pull her up.

Bill's cellmate had called them *number stations*. At first they just listened for when it was a woman's voice so they could masturbate to it. After that wore off, the cellmate took down the numbers and studied them for patterns. He speculated on who acted on the messages that must be coded therein. Supposed they were spies or agents. That perhaps they worked on behalf of entities not widely known. The Illuminati. Trilateral Commission. The Elders of Zion. He envied the men and women for whom the codes were not nonsense. After a time, it was all the guy would talk about.

Then Bill found the man disassembling his radio, dropping the wires into the toilet. Bill asked why he did this. The cellmate said the number stations were depressing him and he wasn't eating or exercising. He'd never felt worse about prison. He'd discovered a ramification of humanity, a branching, he said. There were the tops, those who got the messages and carried out their secret missions. Then the regular people who had less clarity of purpose, but who were at least free. And at the bottom were prisoners like him and Bill who had no mission, nor freedom. Bill's cellmate couldn't crack the code. He knew and could spell difficult words, but this. This. If he kept listening to the number stations he swore to God he would cut his own fucking throat.

The ostrich sprinted along the spine of the hills and the dogs fell back, trotted after with lolling tongues, walked with rolling eyes, and at last gave out. The ostrich climbed out of the woods and finally stopped and panted in the treeless alien landscape.

Charity called her grandmother for a ride, but there was no car, so she walked home. Her friends didn't believe her about the ostrich, and they made fun of her orange outfit and her wand. And something about her grandmother pushing the stroller along the blacktop towards her made Charity understand that her life would be very difficult.

From the road where she saw it, the ostrich quivered against the sky like an outsized parachute ball, and downy tufts of snow like dandelion seeds, cotton candy, confectioners' sugar; and for a moment she forgot her troubles; and she would remember this was what happened right before all the sadness, when the people said the bad things about her father and took him away; and she would always feel like the ostrich or losing the ostrich was the terrific origin or at least the omen of their blooming problems; and when the old woman fetched up to her wild-eyed like the crazed harridan she would or had already become, Charity asked her did she see it, did she see the ostrich on the mountain, you know I sat on it, don't you Nanna, you took a picture, oh tell me you can see it from here.

Ice cream melted all around the kitchen. White plastic tubs of vanilla, chocolate, pink, tangerine, marbled with caramel, nuts sunken to the bottom. Bill lifted one of the great pots of boiling water when Emily entered. The windows had fogged. The sweet wet air recalled dead arctic grayling. Yesterday Goldsmith had cut a hunk of French bread, buttered it, and ate in the walk-in cooler as if no one else were there. Prep cook's hardcore blasting out of the boombox over the sink. A waitress rushing in for slices of lemon. Goldsmith chewing his bread like cud. Old, sad, terrible, and wise.

Now she'd come to see what she would do, what she would tell Goldsmith, what outlandish or tawdry thing would happen; and what happened was Bill turned to see who had come in and hooked his new boot on the duckboards. The pot tipped and the boiled water dumped onto his torso and waist before he could get out of the way, and when it was all spilled he stood in a cloud steaming off the floor and his body both. He turned full around to her. His wide arms vibrated, but his voice was steady and measured.

"Get the sprayer and turn off the hot. You gotta hose me down."

She did as she was told. She sprayed her hand, and it took forever for the water to cool. Because nothing was the right temperature. The dishwasher opened his eyes. "Go," he said, blinking furiously.

She sprayed him, and he winced. "Hold up," he said. He unbuttoned his pants and when he pulled them down, his red legs under his boxers made her cry anew. He pulled away his waistband and looked in his shorts. Grimaced at what he saw. "Go," he said.

She wiped her eyes and sprayed, and he lifted his shirt, and she shot the cold water at his chest, up and down to his feet.

"Okay stop." He bent over and a piece of skin separated on his knee like a wet paper sack as he worked his pants up over his boots. She dropped the sprayer and it dangled in the air like an ostrich neck, and the air recalled a hot lake, and she plunged her hands into a tub of peach ice cream.

"There's hot water all in these damn boots. My feet's boiling."

He unlaced the boots, grabbed the sprayer, and shot cold water into the tops of them, all the while muttering at the ceiling.

She had handfuls of ice cream melting to her forearms and she was sobbing.

"Oh dry up," he said, unlacing his boots. "It was just a accident. Hell, I've already forgiven it."

He kicked off his boots and pulled off his socks that took skin with them and then his pants and then he shoved the sprayer at her, saying to go on and get it going all over him already, but she knelt with the melting peach ice cream and slathered his legs. He gripped the sink groaning, and she took a tub down to the floor and scooped out what was cold and sweet and put it where he burned.

Nominated by Marie Helene Bertino

CASALS

by GERALD STERN

from FIVE POINTS

You could either go back to the canary
or you could listen to Bach's unaccompanied Suites
for which, in both cases, you would have the same sofa,
and you will be provided with a zigzag quilt to sleep
under and a glass-top table and great fury,
for out of those three things music comes;
nor should you sleep if even the round muscles
below the neck fall loose from their stringy moorings
for you would miss a sob and you would miss
a melody á la red canary
and á la white as well and á la canary,
perched, as the cello was, on top of a wooden box
and a small musician perched on top of the cello
and every night a church full of wild canaries.

Nominated by Christopher Buckley, Joan Murray,
Grace Schulman, B. J. Ward

MISHTI KUKUR

by DEBORAH THOMPSON

from THE IOWA REVIEW

In spite of the mange, I want to pet her. She's been lying in the powdery dirt road beside my mother-in-law's building in the Jodhpur Park area of Kolkata, India, but now she rises on her haunches as I move toward her. Distended nipples hang well below her ribcage, though there are no puppies in sight. The universal mutt, she has ears that neither stand nor droop. Her dull, short coat is brown or gray—or perhaps brindle, but this may be the effect of rivulets of dirt. Behind her every dog face, her emaciated body hovers. Like homeless humans, this dog's age is undeterminable, but I'm guessing she's younger than she looks. She harbors an odor somewhere between stale urine and putrescence. I offer the back of my hand to her parched nose.

Keep your hands to yourself, Rajiv had warned me thirteen years earlier on my first of two trips to Kolkata, back when it was still Calcutta, when we'd first gone to visit his widowed mother soon after we got married. *Don't touch stair railings, don't touch the hands of beggars* as you give them coins, and above all *do not pet the street dogs. It is not sanitary*. Rajiv had grown up in India, and had only gone westward for graduate school, where we'd met. But I, a white woman who'd never been outside North America, was ungrounded by these Calcutta streets, where stalls spilled over onto sidewalks and everyone was squeezed together. When you're so close to the bodies around you, the barriers to touch matter more. And when there's so much dirt, cleanliness becomes a moral imperative. So on my first two visits I did as I was told: I didn't touch the street dogs. I looked at them with interest, pity, disgust, and longing, while they watched me with circumspection, alert for food or danger, neither trusting nor untrusting.

Not touching Rajiv was even harder. Back home in the States, whenever we felt the brush of the other's shoulder, we instinctively slotted our arms into a tongue-and-groove fit. Some portion of my skin was almost always in contact with some of his, even if it was just a finger scrolling down a neck, a thigh nudging a thigh, a palm molding itself around a love-handle. But here in India, Rajiv told me, men and women did not touch in public. It made the nighttime touching, behind closed doors, all the more vital.

But now, on my third trip to India, Rajiv, as my mother-in-law puts it, "is no more." This time, I've returned alone to Kolkata to visit Ma, along with Rajiv's brother, Sujoy, and his wife, Joya, who are on an extended visit here for the summer. I'm still a privileged, first-world white woman, but I've been living in the liminal land of mourning, in the untouchable social space of widowhood. Grief, like culture shock, temporarily distorts the proportions of reality, skewing them into the cryptic streets of Kolkata, where nothing meets at right angles. Gradually you learn the new rules of reality and the new relations of your body to other bodies around you. Until then, grief is a trip to a third-world country. You don't belong in the privileged land of robust opulence, your home country, but where is home now? You can't find it even inside your own skin.

India would be hard for me, I knew, and India without Rajiv would be overwhelming. So I decided I'd do here what I did at home when I needed to fend off depression and anxiety: focus on the dogs. I now had three of my own—spoiled spaniel mixes who barked at paper bags, ate toilet paper off the roll, and couldn't even express their own anal glands. After Rajiv died, I'd counted on them to deliver reality in small, containable doses. Outside my house, too, I'd focus on dogs. Parties were bearable after his death only when a dog was in the house. Trips were kept from being impossibly lonely if I could find a dog to pet. When rolls of photos came back from the developer (in the days before the digital camera I got for this trip), half my pictures—I was surprised to find—featured dogs. Kolkata, I knew, would be full of dogs of all castes. I would keep my composure on this trip by studying them.

The hardest part of India would be facing my mother-in-law, whom I hadn't seen since those unreal days after Rajiv's death when, in one breath between moans, she'd thank me for my care of her son and then, in the next, tell me that if I'd fed him better, if I'd cooked fresh Indian food instead of letting him eat Chinese take-out during his last months, he might have lived. If I'd only had a hot meal waiting for him each evening of our thirteen years together, and monitored his eating better, as Joya did for Sujoy, he would never have developed colon cancer. If I'd insisted he spend less time at work and more time resting at home. If I'd given him children. If I'd been a more traditional wife. Hindered by her semi-deafness, my American accent, and the English I was confined to and which she couldn't lip-read, I don't know if Ma ever heard my attempts to defend myself.

"How is she?" I asked my brother-in-law when he picked me up from the airport, from which I'd emerged into some kind of night. We rode home through lampless streets.

Sujoy shrugged. "She never changes. India changes all around her, but always she is stuck in the past."

"Still crying all the time?"

"Crying, yelling. Brooding. Feeling sorry for herself. She wants to be pampered in her misery. Always she is wallowing, wallowing. She will try to entice you. You must not indulge her."

Ma's building was scaffolded with bamboo poles for renovations. Outside the steps I saw, through the late evening darkness, the contours of a sleeping dog, now rising from its side to observe us. For a moment its eyes caught the moonlight. Then it drooped its head back onto its front paws. I wanted to linger down there with the dog, but Sujoy was already loading my suitcases into the "lift."

Upstairs, Ma stood in the door frame, wrapped in a white cotton sari, trying not to smile. Her face seemed sunken, though her skin was smoother than I would have expected for a seventy-year-old woman who'd lost both her husband and her son. I made to kneel but she pulled me up with an *"Ah-ray!"* (the all-purpose Indian rebuke), so I moved in to hug her four-foot-eleven frame. She smelled of incense and baby powder, but below her sari blouse, I could feel sweat on the exposed skin of her back, cool and sticky. When I pulled back, she smiled, and I could see that she'd lost most of her teeth. That's what her sunkenness was: her lips clutching toothless gums. Only three teeth still stood on the lower right side. Her smile lowered. "Why you have waited so long to come visit your Ma?"

269

I tried to apologize. "*Dhannobad*." Then I realized I'd said thank you instead.

Ma ignored my failed Bengali. "Six years you have waited." She turned my face to the light. Her tongue rocked her three remaining teeth back and forth as she examined me. "Why you are looking so pulled down?"

I tried to laugh. "I *have* been on an airplane for nearly two days."

But Ma knew better. "You are looking so sickly-sickly. So many wrinkles you have gotten. You must use anti-wrinkle cream." A lightening-bolt crease formed between her eyes as she continued her inspection.

"Yes. I *must*." I failed to keep my sarcasm in check, knowing there were more imperatives to come. "I *am* forty-five years old now," I reminded Ma. But I smiled to take the edge off my petulance, and felt my crow's feet form.

She hobbled over her osteoarthritic knee as she showed me the daybed I would sleep on and where I could hang my clothes.

"Ma," Sujoy said. "You are limping. We will call doctor about your knee."

"*Ah-ray*, what doctor," Ma answered.

"Yes, we will," Sujoy said. "And you must lose weight."

"I will go up soon enough," Ma muttered to me.

In bed, after all human sounds receded, I heard a semihuman, or perhaps subhuman, sound, like a swallowed sob coming back up. Then I heard it again, and again, until it transitioned into a bark, then a yowl. It was the call not of the wild, but of the street.

Where do the street dogs go in the rain, I wondered as I dissolved into the lumpy daybed and an antimalarial medication haze. Though India was not yet into monsoon season proper, the rain came down hard that first night. Where is that mangy dog outside Ma's steps going to spend the night?

I woke up at four a.m. to the pouring rain, then drifted in and out of sentience as the rain gave way to shy bird chirps, then the brash caw of crows, and finally the bleats of street vendors. By seven a.m. I rose to the window and looked past its Art Deco grates. Barefoot dark women wrapped in bright saris bent their heads under an already drenching sunlight. Men appeared in undershirts and more drab lungis or dhotis. Both carried large loads of food or raw materials—even planks of lumber—on their heads with casual balance. A metal collector clanked his cans as he called out for more. A man on a bicycle chanted, I assumed, the prices and attributes of the live chickens he carried upside down by their legs, five in each hand. And then the car horns began, horns that would sound all day long, ruining the magic.

My brother- and sister-in-law were gone by the time I brushed my teeth with bottled water, slipped into my salwar kameez, and ventured into the common room. I poured more sterilized water into a coffee mug, popped it into the microwave, and then spooned my instant coffee into the steaming liquid. That was when Ma appeared in her billowing batik housedress, rocking from side to side to keep from bending her knees. I rose to hug her, but she stiffened. "*Ah-ray!* Still you are drinking coffee? You must not!"

"I know," I apologized, and sat back down.

"No. You must not."

Ma winced as I took a sip.

"So? They have left me," Ma stated.

"Left you?"

"Sujoy and Joya. Gone for entire day. They have things to do. They have no time for their Ma. Always they are criticizing, criticizing, I don't know what. I have my ways, they do not live here, they will leave me again." She rocked her three teeth with her tongue.

"They're only trying to help you," I said.

Ma turned a frown on me. "But, Debby, you must not drink so much coffee. It is very bad for health. Do not drink."

I tried to think about dogs as I finished the coffee, to keep Ma from killing my caffeine buzz. I was already sweating as I slipped into the kitchen to wash my mug, in spite of Ma's calling to me to leave it for the maid. "I'm going for a walk," I said, turning away.

"*Ah-ray*, in this heat!" Ma exclaimed. I closed the door on her muttering, "Always everybody is leaving me."

Outside Ma's apartment building, the mangy, crusty dog lies where I found her the night before. I extend my hand. But instead of bowing under my palm—the behavior offered by suburban U.S. dogs—she cowers back. I expected feral—a lip-drawn snarl, maybe, or a low growl—but this dog is beyond docile, almost servile. She looks up at me from a lowered head. Her dirt-caked nose twitches as if trying to catch my scent, but she will not come closer.

Not petting dogs has always been agony for me, and I have indulged in every kind of human-canine flirtation to get a dog to accept my touch.

But after Rajiv died, the need to touch fur, if not human skin, became almost mammalian, instinctual as a drive. Touch maintains your boundaries; it reminds you that you have an outline, a definition. The raw need for a defining touch, now denied, surprised me amidst my grief. Nobody, not even the grief support counselors, could have prepared me for this body hunger, the animal part of loss. Nobody warned me about the heavy emptiness of a chest no longer pressed, about the craving of skin suddenly deprived of touch, a dissolution that consumes the body like leprosy. It's not lust, exactly, or desire, or even longing; it's the way skin cries. Nobody talks about it, but widows know. Dogs know, too. It's what makes suburban dogs leap onto chests and laps against all training. It's why street dogs might, in time, forego their instinct for survival to bow their heads into a human palm.

Does everyone, not just widows, have this need for touch? Does Ma? And if so, how does she live without its fulfillment, the skin always in wait?

I will work on this dog, I decide. I will get her to trust me. For now, I just sit with her.

Over the next few days I stand as close to her as she'll let me. I squat. Without more than glancing at her, I murmur, sometimes in English, sometimes in what little Bengali I know: "*Kee-ray. To-mee kamon acho?*" (Hey you. How are you?) I take to calling her *Mishti Kukur* (Sweet Dog), careful not to accidentally slip into a similar term of endearment Rajiv and I regularly used for each other, "*Mishti Pode*" (Sweet Ass). The dog, cautiously, tolerates my presence.

"India is so spiritual," my American friends say. But they don't know my in-laws. Even Rajiv, around his mother, regressed to an ill-tempered, foot-stomping child, as they vied for dominance.

"What you have done with my plates?" Ma asks Sujoy one morning as we finish breakfast. "The ones with the sky blue petals?"

Sujoy rises to the accusation. "Gone." He dramatizes with a sweep of his hand.

"*Ah-ray?*"

"We have thrown them out, Ma. We have gifted you new plates."

"We?" Joya shouts from the bedroom. "Leave me out of it."

"But I prefer my old plates for everyday." Ma smiles defensively with flat lips.

"No. They all have chips and cracks in them. It is not sanitary."

"*Ah-ray*, not sanitary? I have used these plates for years. It is my home."

"It is not sanitary," Joya calls, concurring with her husband. "Germs can grow in the cracks."

"You hoard and hoard," Sujoy accuses her, emboldened. "We have gifted you such nice new items, but you refuse to replace. It is insulting. Yes, I would say that. It is insulting."

Ma looks to me for support, but I turn away. "What insulting?" she offers on her own. "I am an old lady on a pension. I must save. After six weeks you will leave. I am still here."

"Yes, I will leave. I will leave. Why should I stay?"

"Other widowed ladies live with their sons. I am all alone. But I will go up soon enough."

"Here we go." Sujoy throws up his hands.

"Rajiv did not treat me this way. So much disrespect you have for me. Rajiv—"

And now Sujoy is yelling in Bengali, and Ma is yelling back. I can't understand the words anymore, only the rising voices. They turn to me from time to time for affirmation, Ma especially, forgetting that I can't understand. Trying to read body language, I feel like my dogs at home, looking for a decodable sign amidst the general meaninglessness. I perk up when I can pick out a few Bengali words, just as my dogs liven with the recognition of "treat" or "walk" or "toy." But mostly I go into rest mode, mentally stretching my chin out flat against the ground, as my dogs would do when Rajiv and I argued. On those rare times that Rajiv and I fought, though, Pretzel used to flee under the dining-room table until it was over. I decide to follow his example. As I pass by Joya's bedroom, she mutters, "So much botheration all the time."

I stretch out on my daybed in the guest room with *Travelers' Tales: India*, the book I've been reading when I'm feeling particularly foreign. One writer says that for some Western sojourners, INDIA comes to stand for I'm Not Doing It Again or I'll Never Do It Again. When the fighting flares up, I vow to myself that I'll never return to India, except possibly for Ma's funeral.

Photographs of Rajiv are all over Ma's flat. Formal portraits, graduation pictures, vacation photos. He joins pictures of his father in a collage of the dead. Sujoy and Joya (of whom there are far fewer pictures displayed) criticize this shrine, saying that Ma willfully dwells in death, and morbidly refuses to look to life. That she's devoted her life to committing daily metaphorical *sati*. "You live only in the past," they scold her. "You refuse to move on. Life must go on." But they don't know widowhood and loss. They only think they do.

I like Ma's display. I'm glad to see that someone still acknowledges Rajiv's absence. The rest of India has forgotten. The relatives who come over don't refer to him. They ask me how I am "keeping," and note that I am looking "pulled down." But there's no mention of the heaviness of loss that's pulling me down. It's as if Rajiv never existed, or as if his nonexistence is unspeakable. Ma's display stands in passive-aggressive defiance.

But I don't step up to defend Ma or her shrine. Instead, at times like these, when I despair that the family is a kind of broken that can never be fixed, I resort to pulling out the photos of my Colorado dogs that I brought as part of my sanity pack. My father, before his stroke, used to be able to lower his blood pressure by imagining himself petting a golden retriever. I dream of spaniel fur.

"What are these?" Ma asks, catching me with my photos one day. "You must display."

She places my loose snapshots of Pretzel, Chappy, and Houdini around the house among the framed photos of Rajiv. She understands. We stand side by side, leaning in to look together at my spaniels. Our bare shoulders brush. Then I feel Ma pull back.

"And where are your photos of Raju? You do not travel with pictures of him? Only your dogs is it?"

Outside, the street dogs have receded into the shadows. I look for Mishti Kukur, but see no sign of her. It's so hot that even the dingy concrete buildings burn white. As I stride into the more commercial districts with their shops and stalls, I find more street life, if not liveliness, and a bit more English, at least on street signs. The vendors, shoppers, and laborers all move in measured steps. There's a certain kind of Kolkata walk, I've noticed, as if the dampness weighs everyone down. I'd congratulated myself on my first-world, well-cared-for body, but now, I notice, I'm gradually adopting this walk too, though not soon enough. Within two miles, I'm exhausted. Beyond hot and tired, I'm nauseated, and my gym-built leg muscles are cramping. I need to learn how to move with the heat rather than defy it.

The dogs have this walk too. Dogs don't run here. At most, they trot.

But more often they slink, slouched, heads bowed to the sun. "There are no puppies here," I think. Not only have I not seen a single puppy, but I've seen no dog-play, no boisterous lumbering or bounding or scrapping to relay the sheer joy of having a body.

Lunchtime hits all at once. Tiffin boxes appear as people sit along roadsides in bits of shade and heat tins of food over low flames. The workers fill their plates with rice and just enough gravy to hold the grains together as they mold balls with their fingertips. I think of the small pat of rice I take with meals to support a ladleful of curry, and realize how greedy I've been. The pace of street labor lowers as men and women alike squat over their food. Then I notice the dogs, hovering and watching the slow, steady eating of humans. My three dogs would be leaping onto laps, diving into plates; I often have to fend them off with out-thrust elbows as I try to carry a forkful to my lips. But these street dogs are calm, waiting, civil, almost as if trained.

When the eating is done and I can smell the post-meal puja incense, the dogs creep forward. Each seems to know whom to go to. Casually, humans drop leftover rice or mango peel or fish bones to their waiting dogs. Each human seems to have a different click or caw for his dog. The dogs bow gratefully into their food. I watch a cluster of three dogs, one black and two mutt-brown, feed in order of hierarchy, the black dog first.

Rajiv would have been able to tell me more about these interactions: Do the same people feed the same dogs every day? Do they give the dogs names? Do they "own" them? Or maybe the humans don't own the dogs, or the dogs the humans. Maybe there is just a kind of belonging.

Does my Mishti Kukur belong to anyone? Does anyone feed her?

As the three dogs take their last licks, two spots of white appear down the road, whiter than any white I'd seen in Kolkata, where even the pages of new books seem to wilt and yellow overnight.

These whitest white spots turn into two fluffy Chihuahua-sized dogs being walked on leashes by an Indian man in a polo shirt, flat-front pants, and Bata sandals.

"Papillons?" I ask the man, stopping him in his tracks.

"Ah, you recognize? You are the first to guess correctly. Most people say Chihuahua."

"I noticed the butterfly ears." It feels strange to speak in easy English. "They're beautiful."

"My wife's. Purebred."

The little dogs yap, and when I squat to pet them, their tails quiver. "May I?"

"Absolutely you may."

Their fur feels so soft in my fingers I could cry. How these little dogs tolerate such long fur in a place like Kolkata I can't imagine. They must get bathed often, and brushed every day. As I pet the papillons, even letting them lick my face, the three street mutts approach from behind, and sniff the butts of the purebreds, smelling the residue of privilege. But as I move to shift my hand onto the black dog's dusty head, the man shouts "*Chup!*" and mimics a karate-chop to scare off the strays. Then with a "*Challo!*" he and his unnaturally white papillons trot quickly on.

I'm beginning to identify the caste system among India's dogs, even as the country is trying to eliminate it among its humans. These two papillons are *brahmins*. I've also seen a few *ksatriya* or perhaps *shudra* service, police, and search-and-rescue dogs. There are also the *vaishya* and *shudra* rural working dogs, who guard, protect, hunt, and herd, and who, like their human counterparts, tend to be strong and lean, hungry-looking but not starving. Vastly more numerous, though, are these *dalit* dogs of the streets, literally untouchable with their mange and ticks and oozing wounds.

I walk through Kolkata's residential and commercial streets with my camera, documenting the class system of dogs, until I'm sick with heat exhaustion and dehydration.

On my way home, evening emerges in lengthening shadows. Rounding a corner, I come upon three tan dogs. Two, though mangy, are perched regally on a sand pile, as if posing for a photo. I take it. The third, who seems to have a touch of beagle in him, digs into the dirt to unearth a cool spot, then plops his belly onto it. This digging gesture contains more dogness—what I recognize as dogness—than I've seen yet in Kolkata, and I'm touched. I take his picture too, and capture his jaw relaxed into a grin. But when I step closer into their territory, one lets out a serious bark. It's the opposite of the yipping my dogs emit at my front door when the bell rings; those sounds are all energy and anxiety and excitement. This bark is calm, directed, purposeful, and efficient. I have no doubt what it means: *Do not come any nearer. Do not touch*.

I don't.

On the next block a blue heeler mix steps towards me, but as I try for his picture he trots past. "Ah-Ah!" I hear behind me, and the dog turns as I do to observe a man's hand gesture. The dog stands still for me to take the picture. Poor thing has yellow pus coming out of his eyes, and scabs across his thinning back. The man, skinny in his T-shirt and lungi, looks over my shoulder to see it in the viewfinder, then does the sideways head wag with a touch of pride and lets forth a string of Bengali, which I try to tell him I don't understand, but he only speaks louder. I smile and nod and mumble "*Jani na*" (I don't know), as Ma often does to me. Then, pointing to the dog, I ask, "Name? *Nam kee*?" But the man doesn't understand my attempt at Bengali, and makes his apologetic side-to-side head gestures when I try again. I want to ask the man if the dog is his, but don't have language. So I point to the dog, then him, then raise my eyebrows into questions. He's puzzled. Dog-you, I point, dog-you. "Ah-cha-cha," he nods. I don't know quite how my question has translated. Does he understand himself as owning the dog? Or is there simply a link between them, a hyphen, the line my finger draws from dog to man?

When I stumble back home, Mishti Kukur is waiting. I hold out my hand, and she makes to sniff it, but I can't hold back any more, and as I rush to pet her she pulls back, as if offended at my brashness. I call and chant, but she will not come closer.

The next day I realize just how much I overdid it on my reckless walk through Kolkata in the midday heat. I'm so sick that I can't go out, can barely stand to wear clothes, and take refuge in one of Ma's house-dresses. I'm even walking like her now, slumped in her batik muumuu as if weighted down by a dowager's hump. We sit together in front of the television watching Hindi serials while Ma narrates and explains the back-story intrigues. "This lady, she is very fond of this gentleman, but he does not know, and she cannot tell, because both are engaged to others. This lady here, she is an evil one, a double cross. This gentleman, he is evil too, with mustache. You just see." She shakes her head disapprovingly as the music swells.

When the serials are over and the news comes on in alternating Bengali, Hindi, English, and Sanskrit, Ma hobbles to the fridge, her large belly teetering over crackling knees. She takes out a tiffin box of gravy-soaked rice, rice she'd badgered me to finish eating at lunch when I couldn't eat any more, rice that Sujoy had yelled at Ma for storing instead of throwing out. Ma now scrapes the sticky grains onto a banana leaf. "Give this to your dog."

"My dog?"

"I see you from balcony. Poor thing must be hungry."

What else does Ma see?

"Don't tell Sujoy," she hastens. "He will go wild."

I squeeze her hand before taking the food out for Mishti Kukur. Inside this squeeze I feel the memory of another squeeze. In what would turn out to be the last few weeks of Rajiv's life, though none of us dared to think it at the time, Rajiv had taken to lying on the dining room floor with his feet up on a chair, to straighten the bones in his tumor-laden, radiated spine. His feet had become swollen from electrolyte imbalances and ached when he took off his compression socks. One day I walked in on Ma massaging Rajiv's feet in her lap as he lay below her chair, with Pretzel, our oldest dog, pressed against Rajiv's side. Ma murmured to her son as his moans lessened. Then, feeling watched, perhaps, she looked up, irrationally guilty when she saw my face, perhaps recognizing my irrational jealousy. Thirteen years of competing for Rajiv's love all concentrated into this moment as I fixed my eyes on Ma. Then she astounded me: she offered me Rajiv's feet. Wordlessly, she gave up her chair for me, positioned Rajiv's feet in my lap, and, as Pretzel repositioned himself, showed me how to squeeze in the right rhythm, her hands squeezing over mine. I had forgotten this moment until now, though I'd remembered all her scoldings.

I squeeze the banana leaf in memory as I carry it outside, where the sun has washed all life into the shade. I call out for Mishti Kukur, until I hear a rustle. She sticks her neck out from her little cove under the building, then tests a front paw. Her nose is working, registering the gravied rice, registering me. I walk away from the banana leaf, and turn my back to show her I'm not claiming it. It's hers. She edges toward it, watching me intently without making eye contact. When she gets to the pile of rice, she pulls it, leaf and all, into her own private corner under the building overhang, and eats, watching me the whole time, as if she's confused because I've violated the social structure, as if she's so settled into her untouchable status that it's become instinctual to her. When she backs into the shade, I call to her for a while, but she doesn't come back out, just watches me peripherally through crust-lined eyes.

Sujoy and Joya are out all day long now, having given up on getting along with Ma. When they leave early in the morning, to visit friends and shop and run errands for Joya's parents, they tell Ma not to wait up for them at night. They take multiple Kinley water bottles and leave. But I've been spending more time with Ma, having lowered my caffeine intake and settled into her pace. We eat dinners alone at nine p.m., when Ma gives up hope of their mealtime return.

"Why my own son cannot have dinner with his mother?" she asks one night, a few days before I am to leave. "Why is he so selfish? I tell you, Raju was not like that. Raju respected his Ma. He was not so childish."

"That's not entirely true," I offer. "Raju could be childish with you too, remember." But her deafness and her resolutely revisionist memory keep her from hearing me.

"He was a very loving boy, isn't it? Such a good boy, so loving. He never gave me any trouble."

"He loved you very much. But it's not fair to compare Raju and Sujoy."

"I have never!" Ma protests. "I do not do this thing, this compare. I have never. But I tell you, you say Raju he loved me, but Sujoy does not love me, I don't think so. But I will go up soon, and then . . ." She fills in the pause with a chin thrust as she sucks in her three teeth.

"Oh, I'm sure he loves you," I try again. "I'm sure of it. He just has a hard time expressing it. He gets frustrated. But he does love you."

"I do not think so," Ma says simply. She shakes her head, then sobs. "I don't know why, God has been so selfish, so selfish. To take both my husband and my son. Both!"

I warm her hand in mine while she cries. She looks at me through layers of wet. "I know you are feeling pain, every day I am thinking about how you are all alone. But you have not given birth to him! You don't know what it is to lose him to whom you have given birth. Nine months and ten days I have carried." She floods again, but I withdraw my hand. I know she's right, that her suffering is bigger than mine, but I do not like "this compare." She fumbles for her handkerchief.

"I have been meaning to ask you." Ma snorts back down her rush of snot. "When he was dying, Raju, he kept clawing at his wrist. Just like this. I could not figure out what. Then I saw, and I took off his wrist-watch, and he settled. What was that? I have been meaning to ask you all these years. Do you know what it means?"

I nod. "They call it the death throes. I didn't believe in it until Rajiv. It's a phase that dying people go through, where they sometimes grab at their clothes or try to throw everything off them."

"I don't know. What is it?"

"Death throes," I enunciate, separating the two words, but Ma just shakes her head.

"I don't know. He would not let me touch him. He threw off my hands. When I tried to hold him he shouted *Debby! Debby! Debby!* Thrice, just like that. You remember?"

I remember. His last words. But he did not settle after that. He struggled, fighting with his clothes, his caregivers, with death itself. The life force was so strong in him, as it is in all of us, so recalcitrant and powerful even in death. Especially in death.

Later in that endless night of Rajiv's dying, after he'd lost speech and possibly cognition, he was awake and thirsty, though unable to swallow. But when I swabbed his dry lips, he closed them around the sponge end of the swab and sucked the water—hard. I knew that the sucking instinct is one of the first a baby presents, and one of the last a body lets go of. Rajiv was going back in time, back into his animal body, before language or loss. Then I'd realized that it was Ma's turn. I'd held out the swab to her, and she offered it to her baby son, as if in her own instinctual rhythm, dipping swab after swab in water and feeding them to Rajiv's sucking mouth.

"Do you remember the mouth swabs?" I ask her now.

"How he clung to life!" Ma is crying again, heaving, and when I offer her my arms she doesn't hesitate. When I first met my mother-in-law, and when I complained about her over the years, bristling at her free-flowing advice, it had never occurred to me that I would share the most absolute moment of my life with her, the moment when, as we each held a cold hand and Pretzel stirred at his feet, Rajiv gulped in a breath, then exhaled, then waited. We waited, too, for the next gulp. Instead, his face relaxed, the muscles completely at rest. Pretzel jumped down from the bed and crawled under the futon. Ma touched her hand to her son's cheek and said, with as much simplicity as wonder, "Absolutely cold."

Now my hands press into the fat of her back, pushing her ample breasts into my training-bra-sized ones. I can feel her lungs empty and expand.

Outside a street dog is crying. Not whimpering but crying in complete dogwails: Owww-owww. I wonder if it's my Mishti Kukur. Behind this lone voice, the car horns honk on.

It's finally time to hug Ma goodbye. My suitcases are already downstairs. I offer Ma my arms, but she stays fixed. "And so, Debby, you will go back to your dogs and forget all about your Ma." When I pull her into me, the hug triggers in her a convulsion of tears. I can feel it starting from her gut, pressed against mine. "I will go up soon," she cries. "I will go up and be forgotten. You will remember your Ma? You will not forget?"

"I will miss you, Ma," I say into her right ear, the less deaf one. "I love you."

I don't know if she understands the words, but she calms some, and then pulls back to hold me by the elbows. "But Debby," she says, "you must not get any more dogs."

"You're right." I try to laugh it off, but already the word "must" is chasing away my tenderness. "I *must* not."

"No, you must not. It is too much. And also you must not let your dogs lick your face. It is unsanitary."

"Yes, Ma," I manage, approximating politeness. I know what she's doing; she's trying to mother me in the only way she knows: to treat the ones she loves as children to be scolded. And that's what I've become. Already I am determined, though the thought had not previously occurred to me, to get a fourth dog before the summer is out. And it won't be something cute and small and cuddly, like my three cocker mixes; it will be something muscular and vulpine and vital, with a sharp nose and pointed ears and drive, something tough and third-worldly. A survivor.

Ma is sobbing now, in heaves. "Be strong," Sujoy rebukes, as he and I board the lift. I wave at Ma as Sujoy closes the black metal gates and we descend below her bowing bulk.

The driver that Sujoy hired waits for me at his car with my bags as I walk around the building, calling for Mishti Kukur one last time. I need to say goodbye. I've got something special for her in my pocket. When I put on my jeans this morning, the first time I wore them since my arrival in India, I discovered a bit of Snausage in the front pocket, left over from a trip to the dog park back in Colorado. It's stale, but still smells of artificial bacon flavor. I call at Mishti Kukur's cove, and her head emerges, bowed below her shoulders. Her nose is evaluating. She makes eye contact, drops her eyes immediately, but, when I encourage her, looks straight at me. I hold out the Snausage. Her jaw drops into a tentative smile, and she pads towards me with only an instant of hesitation, as if she recognizes and even trusts me. After I hold out the Snausage, and she takes it from my hand, she retreats two steps, but only two.

"I'm gonna miss you, Mishti," I say to her. "Will you miss me?" I hold out my hand for her to sniff. She keeps several inches between us, her nose so caked with dirt I don't know how any scent molecules can get through. Then I remember the water bottle holstered in my fanny pack. I cup some water into my hand and offer it to her. She looks at it, then looks at me. I look away to show her I'm not interested, not threatening. She risks it, inches forward, stretches her pale tongue, takes a quick lap. Then another. I pour more water into my cupped left hand and, as she laps, slurping now, I set the water bottle down and touch her head with my right hand. Under my fingers, the dirt crunches as my pat turns into a stroke. *Wash your hands*, I imagine Rajiv's voice, joking and commanding. But this time I ignore it. My Mishti Kukur is starting to belong to me, and I to her.

And now I will abandon her. Will she remember me, look for me, wonder where I went? Will she find another human? Will she risk belonging again? From the car window, the first step of my long journey back to my very touchable dogs, I look at Mishti Kukur one last time. She's still waiting, watching me, as her small brown body recedes into the dirt.

We drive through streets and streets of dogs, myriads of untouchable dogs, a country full, mixing, as the landscape shifts from urban to semirural, with the rib-lined goats and cows and chickens and people. I want to feed them all, even as they recede from my alien touch, even as I fly from Kolkata to Mumbai to London to Denver and the skins of travelers get whiter and whiter, even as I am greeted at my own front door by three anxious dogs—no, not dogs, but full-grown puppies, never to mature into real adults—who jump on me wildly. When Ma was last here, in those days after Rajiv's death, she scolded them for such behavior, pushing them away with an "*Ah-ray? Bahjay kukur!*" (Bad dog!) But she is not here, and I, instead, encourage my untamable first-world dogs to bark and croon and wiggle and shake under my greedy, fur-starved fingers.

Nominated by The Iowa Review

PATRONIZED

by TARA HART

from LITTLE PATUXENT REVIEW

Dear St. Gerard, You, on the card. I am
supposed to pray to you, etcetera.
Patron saint of mothers and childbirth,
you look far too frail to bear my story.

She came much too early and I almost died
And then she did, and—damn, boy, your eyes do look kind,
but blankety blank. O dear Sainty Smoothface, what do you
know about death?

It may be you bore things—like those whips and their scorn
and you suffered with grace and you had your reward, but
earnest one, let me say something right now. I
was wheeled in, arms splayed, with a nail in my throat
and tubes in every hole until they put me out.

Let me try again. Dear St. Gerard, you are too young.
You are too delicate. You are, dare-I-say, dumb.

I can't believe that *you*, with your eyes to the sky,
is all that the Church has to give me when
I have lost everything—love, labor, lost.
Get me the round goddess, full of lines, laughter, hope,
To say *Jesus, girl, breathe,* and *I know, how I know.*

Nominated by Little Patuxent Review

THE BALLAD OF MUSHIE MOMZER

fiction by STEVE STERN

from PRAIRIE SCHOONER

My mother took a dump and out I came, more or less. It happened
like this: I was conceived when my brother Doodya, who was also my
father, sat in the privy behind the family's hovel in Vidderpol playing
with his schwantz. This is what they told me, and the Jews loved tell-
ing me at every least opportunity. My mother, fat and blind, eyeballs
like soft-boiled eggs, had lumbered into the outhouse to move her
bowels. She hoisted the skirts of her tent-sized shift to squat over the
hole, where she felt herself impaled on an alien organ as it spurted its
load. When she shrieked, Doodya opened his eyes and, bellowing like
a gelded calf himself, shoved my mother onto the outhouse floor. Then
pulling up his moleskins, he trounced through the muddy yard scat-
tering fowl, gathered his patched caftan and phylacteries from a hook,
and vanished from the earth as surely as the Ten Lost Tribes. My
mother Breyne Dobish was too bloated to show her pregnancy, and
notoriously dim, she may not even have known she was with child. But
when she finally dropped me, her husband, the hod carrier Velvel One
Lung, drove her out of the house. She went begging for a season along
the highways, but as her story had preceded her the Jews were not
inclined to be charitable—though a few generous souls insisted that
the rumor of my birth was unfounded, and from the look of me (pink
eyes, harelip, jug ears, no chin) I was more likely the child of the
demon Asmodeus, who was known to hang around privies. Eventually
my mother, infected with cholera, fell down dead in a bog, and I,
Mushie Breyne's the momzer, was sent to the poorhouse, which also
served as a foundling asylum. I dwelled there and elsewhere awhile—

some five or six decades all told—then died in desolation by my own hand.

While I lived, I was outcast even among the wretched. My earliest years were spent largely in the stableyard, pecked at and nibbled by browsing livestock though mostly ignored. I was also ignored by the humans who haunted that yard. In winter I crawled atop the stove and hugged the samovar till I was scalded; but I was often evicted from that coveted spot by other orphans, who scrambled over the sooty shelf like shipwrecked refugees clinging to a raft. I was attended to like some drooping houseplant whenever it was remembered that I required a measure of nourishment to survive, though there must have been those who questioned whether I ought to survive. Still I grew, if somewhat erratically, since my bones had the ungainly look of limbs that had been broken and improperly set. As the bastard child of an unholy union, I suppose I should have regarded myself lucky that anyone bothered to keep me alive, but I wasn't especially grateful; I never saw much advantage to having been born.

The poorhouse was a hybrid structure consisting of stable, kitchen, and dormitory loft, with a shithole out back, which my fellows were fond of reminding me was a shrine to my nativity. But little lower than the angels—as they assured us in cheder on those days when we weren't farmed out to labor (I preferred the labor)—we slept on straw pallets just above the jackasses and goats. While most of the orphans slept in a knot of pretzeled bodies for warmth, I was generally shunned for my unhappy features and the peculiar stench that emanated from my person, owing to my chronic bed-wetting. Yakov Fetser, who managed the asylum, a man whose carroty eyebrows appeared to be in flames, loaned us out to the families of the Duyanov community for a nominal fee. Our own reward, in exchange for emptying slops, sweeping sawdust, scrounging the bones, bark, and cow chips that were fed to the cook-stoves in lieu of coal, was perhaps a fistful of groats in sour milk. No wonder that, when I was old enough, I stole whatever I could from the market stalls. Never a skillful thief, however, I was commonly hauled before the elders who caned me to within an inch of my life. There were times when, as I vomited up the radish or piece of dried herring I'd bolted, I wished they had gone the extra inch.

When not indentured for the day or herded with the other boys into the tin-roofed study house, I was left to my own devices—what devices? The only pastime I had a passion for was sleep. I had no friends, since my cleft palate discouraged communication, though I was occasionally

285

pestered by Yahoodie, called the Angel, another orphan who from time to time took pity on me. He should piss green worms, the draikop; I was perfectly capable of feeling sorry for myself without anybody's help—though truth be told, the Angel's sympathy was indiscriminate. A frail, fiddle-shaped kid with a shock of ginger hair half-concealing his shaigetz-blue eyes, he was the pet of the shtetl; even the bullying butchers' apprentices indulged him for his vaunted innocence. Call it innocence if you want, but frankly I thought he was nuts.

"Mushie," he would confide; he took liberties with everyone's given name, though "Momzer" was how I was generally addressed. "Mushie, everything is alive."

Despite myself I would look around to see what he was talking about. Our town with its rat's nest houses, a quarter of them charred to cinders from former conflagrations, was sunk to its shins in mud; it reeked from the stench of slaughterhouse and tannery beneath a leaky leaden sky. Its inhabitants were no less crooked and weather-worn—such as Laibl the Kaddish, as nearly petrified as the listing tombstones he took alms to pray among; or Falik the belfer, a scarecrow upon whose head and shoulders the children perched like blackbirds en route to the beit midrash; Paltiel the wedding jester with his rancid jokes ("A Jew and a hunchback were walking past a synagogue . . .") and pious bromides; Shpindl the whore whose apiary wig was routinely snatched by the wags. There was the rattleboned Balitzer Rebbe in his long gabardine girdled with silk at the waist to separate his holy upper half from the lower, which the rebbe had no commerce with. It was therefore speculated that his organ was as shriveled as a pope's nose. They all performed their civic and liturgical functions dutifully, but could you really call them living? Then there was me, Mushie Momzer: if folks judged their own unfortunate circumstances as accidents of birth, then what of one whose very birth was an accident? Could I still lay claim to being completely alive?

"Ngh shgngh!" I spat at Yahoodie, which was as close an approximation to "Narishkeit!" as my disfigured lips allowed. Still the fool would persist in indicating miracles: a ram with a henna'd fleece and single horn, the perpetual ruby beacon of the forge. No doubt all the God-talk in cheder had addled his brain. If an early flower burst through the earth's crust in an April thaw, he took it so personally you'd have thought he'd achieved a heroic erection, the kind the older orphans—lowering their trousers—liked to flaunt in your face. Everything fueled the Angel's awe: from Torah finials to floating eiderdown to the girls with their swinging braids, their pinafores kilted in the riverbed where they washed their clothes. The more he admired, the more I resented, since everything he deemed beautiful seemed a personal affront to my ill-favored self. Especially the girls with their lilac and vinegar scent, whose tittering at my expense disturbed me in ways I couldn't yet explain. The thimblewit, he even saw living beings where there was nothing but thin air; for wandering souls, he maintained, were resident in every riven tree and polluted well.

Sometimes I goaded him: "Ngh onfen ngh . . . ," meaning, "Our town is a toilet and life a rehearsal for Gehenna." But he shrugged off my barbs, admonishing me: "Mushie, you got no imagination," as if imagination was the key. He told me that, wondrous as this world was, it was only a veil behind which was an even more wondrous world, the real Promised Land. Though it hurt me in my heart to laugh, I laughed heartily. "Ngh ngh . . . ?" meaning, "Veil? What veil? The whole earth is a splayed carcass exposed to plain sight." Another time, in a moment of weakness, I asked him amid the bedlam of the beit midrash, "Fonfen . . . ?" meaning, "So, Yahoodie, did God make me?" But I was overheard by Reb Gargl, our treble-chinned melammed with his knockwurst shnoz, his ritual garment stained with borscht or blood, who was also a seasoned interpreter of my hobbled speech. He whacked my head with a pointer and assured me, "Sometimes HaShem, may He be blessed, has his little jokes." Funny man.

It was a relief when he died, the Angel. For such a good-natured sap, you'd have thought his entrails pooped wildflowers, but in fact they refused to void anything at all. Though I seldom saw him eat—he seemed to live on the doting affections of the Duyanovers (who also plied him with sweetmeats)—he suffered from an unending constipation. "It's like the Akedah," he repined, comparing his humiliating condition to some fable he'd learned in the study house. "It's the binding of Isaac all over again in my kishkes." Eventually, when he swelled up and turned blue, Fetser called in Genendel the enema lady, who brewed some toxic concoction in her gutta-percha bag that she squeezed through a tube shoved up the Angel's ass. It turned out he'd been full of shit all along, for once the evacuation started it never stopped, and Yahoodie found himself marooned atop a rising tumulus of night soil. In the end he expelled his soul along with his insides, and as the light departed his eyes, the Angel seemed shocked to discover the secret that his sunny disposition had kept from him throughout his days. Good riddance, thought I; the burden of my existence was hard enough to bear without that flea in my ear.

Just before I was kidnapped and sold for a Cantonist conscript in place of some shopkeeper's son, a troupe of Yiddish actors passed through Duyanov. They performed on a makeshift scaffold erected over hay bales flanked by green benzine flares in Shmulke der Keziker's cow barn. The play cost a couple of kopecks at the door, but I slithered in under the splintered wall in back of the stage where the props were stored. It was a shpiel about a happy-go-lucky scamp who, for the sake of filling the village quota, is tricked by the local kahal into volunteering for the army. After a number of japes and songs—some of them scurrilous—on the part of the rag-tag company, the scamp's sweetheart dies with much hand-wringing of a broken heart, and his blind old mother, tearing her sheytl and beating her meal-sack breasts, loses her mind. Then the recruit, no longer so devil-may-care, hangs himself from a rafter by his tallis, his lolling tongue the complement to his coxcomb hair. I was interested to see that, unlike ordinary experience, make-believe did in fact make a kind of sense, which I deeply resented; I didn't like that I should be made to feel bad on account of a bunch of costumed players. Nevertheless, I was consoled by the notion that you could exit this life whenever you chose. I kept the thought in mind that, since I scarcely mattered anyway, I wouldn't be missed, and there was little I would miss in return. So I watched with insouciance as other boys my age, the sons of merchants and artisans, were solicited by marriage brokers who offered them the dowries of young girls. While I pulled my putz with a fervor usually reserved for wringing the necks of geese (a tradition that apparently ran in my family), other lads were already honoring the injunction to be fruitful and multiply. The idea of multiplying my misbegotten self was as offensive to me as it was to everyone else, and when Mendy Elefant, our resident khapper, stuffed me into a potato sack and bound it tight, "Nu," I thought, "wherever he's taking me can't be worse than here."

Not that my capture came as any real surprise: Unless you were crippled or your family had the gelt to buy your exemption, you were destined in those days of Czar Nicholas (the Jews called him Haman the Second) to fall victim to the Rekrutshina Edict. Wasn't Duyanov full of children whose fingers and toes were hacked off, their ears lopped by parents who sought to save them from the draft? They were already nine-tenths ghosts, those mutilated children—to say nothing of the ones who'd disappeared, burrowing out of sight in cellars and forest caves. You never saw them until some informer disclosed their hiding place and they were hauled off kicking and screaming to the induction center, only a few versts away in the market town of Slutsk. As for us orphans, we were viewed as a pool of ready substitutes for the sons of gentle folk.

It was the dead of winter when it happened, and I was shivering inside the sack that Mendy, a drayman in a leather apron by day, had tossed onto the bed of his horse-drawn sledge. As we rattled along the icebound highway, I felt myself nudged by other sacks wriggling in close proximity to mine, all of them sidling against one another for warmth. At one point we hit a bump and Mendy's contraption was briefly airborne, bouncing me clear out of the rackety sledge. I hit the road and rolled down an incline into a ditch that ran alongside, where I came to rest. Then it struck me that, bruised but otherwise undamaged, I was free, a concept that had little meaning since I was unable to escape the tightly lashed sack. To lie still for long, however, would mean freezing, and as there was room in the sack to raise myself into a stoop, I managed to scramble by awkward stages up the side of the ditch. While the burlap seams were wide enough to see through, the falling snow blotted out the dark landscape; still I had no option but to keep moving. I stumbled blindly forward, slipping on patches of ice and struggling back to my feet, becoming aware in my clumsy progress of sporadic laughter. As the blizzard began to abate and a full moon appeared, the laughter swelled to a noisy hilarity, and through the stretched seams I could now observe that I wasn't alone. There were other upright potato sacks in front of me toddling like nine-pins in an impromptu parade as we entered the outskirts of Slutsk, greeted by the guffaws of the gathered onlookers. It was a moment when I felt like a witness as well, as if I was watching an entertainment in which even Mushie Momzer had a part, and I came that close to laughing myself. But just as the howling of the Slutskers approached hysteria, we were scooped up by deputies of the kahal, who tossed us over their shoulders and carried us through the market arcade to the recruitment station.

They dumped us onto a tile floor that sloped toward a drain as in an abattoir, in a low-ceilinged room where a flag emblazoned with a two-headed eagle was mounted on the wall. The potato sacks, rather than unfastened (since Mendy's knots were inextricable), were slit open with knives so that we tumbled out as from a generous womb. That was

289

anyway how it was put by a boy in a crocheted skullcap with serpentine earlocks, who looked nothing at all like the Angel: this one was well fed and apple-cheeked despite the difficult journey. "This is for us our second birth," he pronounced, "only here we are born into Sitra Achra, which is the wrong side of the mirror." He talked like that, even more spookily than Yahoodie; he said we were like Joseph sold into slavery by his own brothers, but I knew he was speaking rubbish. We were nothing like Joseph, whose plight I knew from a Purim shpiel, and it galled me to hear us compared to stories in which events made a modicum of sense. In this world nothing made sense and, despite the stories they tried to force-feed us in cheder, the greatest sin was to pretend that it did. I was relieved when an officer with no face—only scar tissue like a papier-mâché mask—rose from behind the heavy desk and peremptorily stove in the kid's skull with a saber hilt. Good riddance.

There was some question in my mind as to whether my defective condition would render me ineligible for the army, but one look at the faceless officer in his frogs and epaulets dispelled my doubts. For my incapacity to answer questions intelligibly—doubly handicapped as I was by my harelip and an ignorance of the Russian tongue—I was soundly thrashed, after which I was promptly inducted into the cadet corps. More manhandling ensued as we were hustled across a courtyard, thrust into quarters where malevolent barbers shaved our heads so poorly that we resembled peeled oranges over which stray fibers lay strewn. We were draped in pocketless greatcoats that dragged on the ground, issued pants with a rough canvas lining infested with lice, coarse leather boots whose straps practically reached our hips. Further saddled with ungainly knapsacks—which contained among sundry items black dye for the mustaches we were still too callow to grow—we were dispatched in a tottering lockstep flanked by mounted soldiers over a bridge leading into the forest surrounding Slutsk. This was the point of departure for a forced march that was to take us across the frozen steppes beyond the Pale of Settlement to the garrison city of Archangelsk far to the north.

Along the way our ranks were substantially thinned. At the outset the boys that weren't crying for their mothers recited the traveler's prayer, only to be abruptly silenced by the mounted escort. Then, as if prayers were threads connecting them like marionettes to heaven, they dropped the sticks that doubled as rifles from their shoulders and crumpled to the earth. Others, rejecting the unkosher swill we were offered—mostly cabbage soup afloat with lard or a freshwater insect called a crawfish—

fell from malnourishment. Accustomed to hardship and having no convictions to constrain me, I adapted to the putrid fare. In the villages we were billeted with families who used us at least as cruelly as those to whom I was sent on eating days back in Duyanov. (Once I was housed with a lunatic who lowered me down a chimney I was supposed to purge of demons, then chased me with a brickbat for a demon myself when I emerged from the hearth covered in soot.) We were transported on one leg of the journey by a barge attached to the stern of a steamboat, but the Neva was so clogged with ice that we spent more time on the riverbank towing the boat by hawsers coiled about our waists. Some suffered from a frostbite that mercifully caused them to lose their fingers and toes, but more died outright of exposure. As the weather grew warmer, the fleas seethed in our uniforms until our skin felt as if on fire from stinging nettles, and I cursed my own instinct for survival, my apparent immunity to a medley of diseases.

By the time we reached Archangelsk, centuries later, we were a meager handful of herring-gutted Tom Thumbs; nor did the uncaulked barracks we were quartered in offer much respite from the journey's ordeal. Most of the plank beds were already occupied by older recruits, so we were forced to sleep beneath the berths, facedown so as not to inhale the bedbugs and dust. It was nearly Passover, which coincided with Easter, when the priests were especially compelled to convert us. They came into the barracks in their rosy vestments and plaited beards carrying icons. "Only submit to baptism," they enjoined us, their words translated into Yiddish by a mincing convert, "and you will no longer menstruate; your dorsal appendages will drop off and you will lose your foetor judaicus." They were accompanied by a boozy lance corporal who threatened to pound us into blood pudding if we didn't forswear our faith. Those who resisted were made to run the gauntlet, throttled with leather straps soaked in brine, forced to sweat on the seventh step of the steam bath until their brains began to boil. Some, who finally conceded to be led to the water's edge and baptized, refused—once immersed—to resurface from under the river. Some managed to drown in cauldrons of bean slops and barrels of kvass.

Ordinarily my inability to talk was deemed a virtue, but while I presented myself as a willing candidate for conversion, I couldn't make myself understood. Nasal snorting aside, I was illiterate and largely considered to be an idiot, so no one realized when I proclaimed myself geshmat: "I'm a Christian, okay?" They tortured me anyway, and when I made gestures that argued my sincerity, which included crossing myself, they thought I was mocking them and stepped up the abuse. In the face of similar persecution, some of the boys opted for kiddush ha shem, for martyrdom. They cut their own throats and hanged themselves, thus stealing my thunder, so that if only to avoid becoming a copycat, I stayed alive.

We were told that, since we were technically underage, the battalion to which we were attached would function as an academy; we would be educated and given military instruction until we reached our majority and were admitted into the regular army. But education consisted of being roused at dawn and lined up in the yard to sing hymns and recite the czar's family tree; instruction meant splashing in full battle gear about the rain-soaked parade ground for hours. Then we were issued our quarter pound of black bread with salt and sent to peel potatoes, knead dough, and clean spittoons in the officers' mess—a specialty of mine. We were assigned along with parties of convicts to dig canals and break stones for breastworks and barricades, and if ever I heard a reference to building pyramids, I spat three times. They christened us Sergei or Anastasy so that we no longer had any relation to our former identities, a relief for one who perceived himself a lump in any case. The seasons changed like moods; I was cold, I was hot, the whiskers sprouted on my chin, the fur around my parts, but did I care?

Then a Polish uprising along the western border made it necessary to deploy all available troops for active duty. I remember the Balitzer Rebbe saying that the purpose of life was to perpetuate it, but in Maykop, Krapivno, and Stawatycze an opposite corollary obtained: the purpose of life was to end as much of it as ventured into your range. Who you didn't kill, you at least tried to maim, be they soldier or civilian, and some of us—those that didn't soil themselves or faint dead away in the heat of battle—took a bisl joy in the slaughter. Myself, I felt neither joy nor fear. I already understood how this world was, so to speak, death's vestibule; so why shouldn't the earth be carpeted in corpses? I was made to dust them in quicklime, and when the charnel wind blew back in my face, I was covered in the powder myself, so that my fellows took me for a walking dead man. In combat, while my brain was befogged, my body followed its own agenda. This involved aiming my musket in the direction of the enemy and pulling the trigger, of skewering him like shashlik at close quarters on the end of my bayonet. For all I know I might have demonstrated some skill as a marksman; I believe I murdered my share of Poles, to say nothing of the Zhids who suffered collaterally at the hands of Fonya's army. After a skirmish the defeated village was torched, its population savaged, shops looted, women raped—that was the drill. I was an indifferent participant in the killing and plundering of goods, though in the violation of women I took an interest.

I was human, I had appetites, albeit they were usually limited to victuals and sleep, commodities never in any great abundance, but on occasion I had a yen for female flesh. Seeing my comrades-in-arms—Zaporozhians, Circassians, Tatars, some of them nearly as dogfaced as me—seeing them bum-basting women bent over saddle horns and the railings of galleried inns gave me ideas of my own. I dimly recalled how Yahoodie the Angel, who never touched himself (never mind the maidelehs), would talk about love: a glorious holy mystery, the poor man's tikkun olam, and so on. Curious, I chose a woman, a button-eyed girl really, with dishwater hair and a birthmark like a spider's shadow over her left cheek. She was a slip of a thing whose resistance would be negligible, and I dragged her into an alley beside a church. I shoved her down among the wagon ruts and told her, "Ngh onfen nghsh," meaning that she was my sweetheart and I cherished her forever. She responded to my overtures with an expression of dumb horror, even as I began to demonstrate my affection, lifting her petticoats and tearing her dirty drawers at the crotch. I dropped my trousers and made to implant the standard of myself, though I had to hammer away at her with my hips until her maidenhead collapsed. Then I was inside her and a star burst in my skull, the warm sparks like a school of flickering minnows swimming through my lungs and loins. The more I labored, the more she exuded her intoxicating scent of dread, and the more I loved her, feeling that my devotions were building toward some rapturous truth. I was also vaguely aware that we were surrounded by a cohort of Cossack irregulars who'd begun to cheer me on. But just when I thought I might melt or burst into flame, I was rudely separated from my neshomelah, hauled by the ankles from between her spindly thighs. Someone planted a boot-heel in my spine while the others took their turns with the girl, until she stopped screaming and went limp from exhaustion or death.

Then they told me, "Zhids got no business defiling our women." I tried to explain that I wasn't a Jew, I wasn't anything, but as usual my animal grunting went unheeded and I was further refuted by the evidence of my bald schlang. They carried me into a cottage whose rush roof was being nibbled by a horse, and swept a stiff off a table to stretch me out on. As my muddy parts were already exposed to a moth-orbited spirit lamp, the deed was soon done. The pain of the incision was superseded by the pain of the cauterization, but just before I lost consciousness, I felt them fold into the palm of my hand my own swollen beytsim. "A souvenir," said someone in the vernacular I now understood. "Just like scarlet doves' eggs." Had I not been their comrade, my testicles would have been used to replace the eyes they'd neglected to gouge from their sockets.

When I could walk again, I was released from a field hospital where I'd squirmed in delirium for an indefinite time. I was told I was fortunate the infection had left my membrum virile intact, not that I had much use for the thing anymore. The loss of my manhood was no great concern though, since I'd never judged myself much of a man in the first place, and it was good to be relieved—give or take the odd phantom spasm—of the desire for intercourse. I had little taste left now for even the most basic of needs, and there were days when I wanted for nothing on earth.

In the shtetl, years passed while time (simultaneous with the Flood and the Exodus from Egypt) stood still; whereas beyond the shtetl, out here in history, time flew, while the years were all of a piece. I was sent back to my battalion, which was transferred to another garrison somewhere in the Caucasus southeast of Kiev. There was a period of servitude and then another war, in which I figured as a cipher with blistered feet; I was a musket and ramrod in an infantry corps that belonged to a battle group that was part of a regiment attached to an artillery division joined by other divisions of grenadiers, fusiliers, sappers, and light cavalry. Our bivouacs stretched across whole valleys into the rolling uplands. Arrayed in the field with the sun glinting off of helmets and shako plates, off the polished brass of gun batteries and caissons, we sprawled like a titanic dragon with myriad scales—or so said some purple tunic soon to be shot from his steed. As a unit of the rank and file, I could be further reduced to my constituent parts: forage cap, greatcoat, chamois pants, cartridge pouch, rifle sling, entrenching tool, hobnail boots. Relieved of them, I was skin that was itself a map of historic stations: the canister burns across my belly like Cyrillic caterpillars that I'd received at Balaclava (where the British used a windmill for a missile to hit our powder magazine, the flares zigzagging upward like snakes on fire); the smallpox scars augmenting the ghastliness of my face that I'd acquired during the siege of Sevastopol. There we scuttled ships of the line to block the harbor, their lanterns extinguished like dying fireflies as they

294

sank. I saw a company of hussars fall in unison from their starved horses (which were later eaten) when their surcingles could no longer be drawn tight. Then a salvo from siege guns caused a hail of slain bodies to descend upon me where I hunkered in a redoubt on the Fedyukhin Heights. By the time I was disinterred, days had passed, and pulled from beneath that warm canopy, I was declared to have been absent without leave. Due to the general outrage over our humiliation at the hands of the British alliance, goldbricks and malingerers, or those perceived as such, were shot on the flimsiest of excuses. I was stood up against a wall and made to strip off my tattered uniform, my sodden underwear and footcloths rank as Stilton cheese. It was a frosty morning and a long moment elapsed before it was realized that my empty sac wasn't shriveled because of the cold. "He's a fucking eunuch!" they cried, regardless of the contradiction (and the secondary insult that I was circumcised)—at which point it was concluded I wasn't worth shooting. Thereafter I was regarded as a virtual slave.

Soon I was old, my wattles and wisps of beard reflected like silver drizzle in the bottom of a copper kettle licked clean of kasha. Obsolete, I was discharged from the Imperial Army with a promised pension I never received. Where would I have received it? I had no fixed abode. I wandered the roads scrounging from town to town, sleeping in study houses and barns. Once in a blue moon I stole a plum compote cooling on the sill of a peasant hut, but mostly I dug turnips in the fields and, when desperate, peeled the bark from trees like a goat. Usually the children threw stones, or at best I was treated as some harmless domestic beast and fed scraps accordingly; I was offered lentils in exchange for showing my horns and cloven hooves. What made them think I was a Jew? Meanwhile the Empire was ailing, its hamlets quarantined from typhus, inundated by floods, sows floating in the waterlogged streets like capsized dinghies; hamlets destroyed by government ukases and pogroms. On occasion, when my documents were in dispute, I was hauled into jail for a piyamnike, a vagrant, and then I would have a roof for a couple of nights. One day I entered a ruined town and saw, upheld by disciples at either elbow, a papery patriarch in a brittle capote whose vermin-ridden beard struck a chord. The chord thrummed in my aching head, its vibrations dislodging other landmarks from my dormant memory—the wooden synagogue wrecked by carpenter ants and Cossacks, the warren of the poorhouse given over to swallows' nests. Duyanov had always been something of a ghost town, but now most of the ghosts had fled. In the beit midrash, missing a wall, I inquired of the other beggars, "Nghlsh onfen ngh?" and was understood, since mine was the only question anyone ever asked.

"They went to the Promised Land," the beggars answered, explaining that to each Jew his own goldeneh medineh. Some had gone to America to become millionaires, others to Palestine to drain swamps, others sent to Siberia for fomenting the revolution that would transform Mother Russia herself into a promised land. A representative of the Society for the Resurrection of the Dead, himself a skeleton, offered me charity, which only reminded me that my tenure on earth had been for some time a post mortem affair. Anyway, I was tired. I remembered when the Angel told me about the gilgul, how if you died without having performed the 613 mitzvot (not one of which I recalled), you must return for another round. With the assurance that he was crazy, however, I rose early the next morning; I borrowed a rope from a tethered ox and tossed it over a rafter amid the debris of Shmulke der Keziker's cowbarn. I stood on a spongy scaffold erected upon rotten hay bales and, while the cock crowed and the shnorrers snored, stepped into thin air. My stringy neck stretched but didn't break when the rope went taut, so I dangled until I strangled.

Death, as it turns out, is even lonelier than life. I found myself in a dimly lit area that I took to be the backstage of a theater, though I'd never set foot in a theater before. Sandbags hung from the rigging, cables extended from catwalks like the strings of an enormous harp, their ends wrapped around belaying pins. Theatrical properties were stored against the walls: a nine-pounder unicorn battery, a cat-o'-nine-tails, a cartridge pouch, a scroll, a bandolier. There were painted flats depicting fortifications, a tilting outhouse, a village cemetery with a headstone beyond its wall, and there was a dark drop curtain that appeared opaque at first glance, but look again and it proved to be a diaphanous scrim. On the other side of the scrim a performance was in progress. I pressed my nose against the gauzy fabric and saw a spectacle illumined by a menorah's worth of radiant footlights: A beetle-browed priest assisted by devils was trying to wrest from a harried hero his immortal soul. He was a funny-looking hero, who seemed to set no great store by his soul ("What soul?"), but I knew its value, as did the rowdy audience, who mourned his persecution, grieved aloud for his apostasy, and wished he could, somehow be saved.

If I scooted left along the boards, the hero was younger, a wild orphan filching live carp from a tub in the market platz, the carp flopping out of his pants as they were lowered by elders about to lather him for his sins. The audience groaned at his punishment and laughed despite themselves at his abduction by a bogeyman in an agitated potato sack; for he was after all an antic figure, the hero, with the face of a rueful rodent. If I moved to stage right, he was older, crawling across a smoky battlefield dusted in the pollen of sunflowers, sequined in the brains of his comrades, and I thrilled with the audience to the danger and the distance he'd traveled from his quaint beginnings. I worried over his terrible wounds. But the worst of it was that I seemed to know what was coming, and wondered if his fate could be altered. Hadn't I heard that even centenarians had taken December brides and gotten children from them, sons to say kaddish for them after their passing? Scurrying back and forth along the gossamer curtain as far as the wings at either end, I sometimes overshot the production and saw the events that framed the play: the abominations of the hetman Chmelnitzki, the exiles from Spain and Jerusalem on the one side; the enormities yet to come on the other. Then the life of the hero seemed an incandescent moment fraught with possibilities, a space between past and future, as between parted waters, in which passions might culminate through exquisite suffering; and I wished I could step onto that stage and slip into his skin.

I pawed frantically at the curtain in search of a seam, a place where the fabric was worn thin enough to be torn. Eventually I located a patch no more substantial than cobweb and felt my heart drumming its martial rhythm in my chest and absent genitals. Gripping the scrim with trembling fingers, I ripped open the membrane between one world and another; I stuck my head through the hole and tumbled straightaway out of a sack onto the tiles of the recruitment center in Slutsk, where all the benighted years stretched hopelessly ahead of me.

Nominated by Prairie Schooner and Jay Rogoff

MY SKY DIARY

by CLAIRE BATEMAN

from NEW OHIO REVIEW

Because it's my book,
I will treat it however I want.
I will crack its spine, though not its spirit.
I will bend back the corners of its pages
along the margins of whose cold fronts
I will inscribe hieroglyphics,
and over whose most capacious melodic passages
I will take terrible liberties with liquid paper
whenever I crave silence.
Haven't I paid for this privilege
all those decades in the first grade,
through my retinas suffering
the mute incandescence of letters
which withheld their significance from me
as, lathered like a horse
condemned to drag his own stable behind him,
I've labored with sentences and paragraphs,
wrestling the fat green pencil
that grew quantumly heavier
as it registered each mistake?
Haven't I made perfect attendance
while all the swifter students
skipped days, weeks, even?—
they'd return from alleged bouts of flu
with gilded tans and I (HEART) TAHITI T-shirts

to find me still in the little wooden chair
I've never abandoned, even for recess?
Haven't I taken all my meals at my desk,
slept in the corner on a narrow pallet,
my pillow inhabiting the realm
beneath the ecology table whereon reside
the hamster with its cage and wheel,
and the goldfish in its pathetically cloudy tank?—
these creatures the denizens
of the far side of my heaven,
the near side being the table's
gum-studded undersurface I've nightly beheld
while I waited for sleep;
I can think of worse places
to dream, and poorer companions;
all night long, the goldfish
circumscribes its asphyxiating universe
and the hamster pants to outrun its wheel—
not unlike the way my mind
has struggled even in darkness,
tracing on wide-lined dream paper
the smudged, left-pointing loop
of a dyslexic R or P
as I've lain there under the fixed and dimly glowing
Juicy Fruit constellations of the only sky
I've personally known,
a kind of undergraduate heaven,
a nethersky I outgrew
this very day, when all at once
I mastered cursive—
the other students, the teacher, the principal,
the assistant principal, and the entire custodial staff
clustering breathlessly around me
as I swooped my Gs
and swirled the elaborate undercarriage
of the cursive Ys—
my hand was like a pale and spindly ice dancer;
I wanted to stitch it an outfit
of baby blue silk and albescently shimmering tights,
or maybe a different outfit

for every day and every night
I've spent in this classroom,
though I haven't been miserable here,
just increasingly too bulky for the chairs
and little pallet—in fact,
at this instant, I suspect I'll even mourn
my wooden sky,
since I won't immediately be ready
to write out there
in the alien weathers that await me—
little snow nocturnes,
migratory honeybee swarms with their gold auroras,
packs of feral mirages—
nevertheless, it's time for me
to venture beyond this classroom
before my dilating sleep
bursts its walls at the seams,
and in fact, to fail under such a sky
will be an honor,
even though I'll have to begin from scratch
with an entirely new alphabet
of transparent ultramarine and indigo,
and it will take me millennia
to progress from tedious tracing
to the graphomaniacal excess
my right hand assures me
I was born for.

Nominated by New Ohio Review and Thomas E. Kennedy

THE MFA/CREATIVE WRITING SYSTEM IS A CLOSED, UNDEMOCRATIC, MEDIEVAL GUILD SYSTEM THAT REPRESSES GOOD WRITING

by ANIS SHIVANI

from BOULEVARD

The comparisons to the medieval guild system are obvious, ominous, ubiquitous, irrefutable, and illuminating. Apprentices, journeymen, and masters join together in solidarity to impose control over quantity and quality of production, and enforce rigid rules to exclude outsiders. The oligarchical system sustains itself with well-told myths of internal solidarity and well-timed rituals to enhance fellow-feeling. The "craft" learned in the "workshop" is a thing of mystery, passed on from master to apprentice, a hands-on learning so precious that rules of monopoly must be imposed to prevent its dilution. They have their own religion, their annual banquet, their festival spirit. Modern creative writing program, meet your origin and fate in the medieval guild system!

Just as the guild structure was socially conservative — and hence easily superseded when the more progressive market system, flourishing along with the industrial economy, came along — so is the present MFA credentialing system. Any guild system cannot but be conservative by nature. The limitations on entry, the exaction of high entrance fees, and the social distinctions inherent in the master-journeyman-apprentice division alone dictate so. All this wouldn't matter so much — we might dismiss the system as a mere method of organization — were it not for the fact that conservativeness in organization usually results in conservativeness of product as well.

Let us try to understand how the finely tuned guild system came about in writing, explore how it operates in practice, and try to imagine conditions under which it might break up.

Just as the medieval guilds came into being as a reaction of craftsmen against the encroachments of feudal lords, to carve out a space of relative freedom for themselves, similarly modern creative writing (though early parallels such as the Iowa Writers' Workshop already existed) really took off in the 1960s, and then went into overdrive in the 1980s and 1990s. Before the 1950s, the majority of literary writers were not part of the academy; writers might sometimes teach as well, but this was not an essential condition of their identity; it was still a minority affair. The ideal was to be free of the restraint the academy, or really any institution, imposes. In 2010, literary writers not attached to the academy are so rare as to be almost nonexistent.

Why the 1960s? Why would integration of writing into academia begin to occur at the same time as the counterculture? Why not accelerated emphasis on doing it yourself? We need to think of the other side of liberalism, the mythologizing of experts and professionals, which very much went hand-in-hand with social libertarianism. The professionalization of human, spiritual, and psychic needs was very much part of the sixties scene. The AWP (Association of Writers and Writing Programs) was founded in the late 1960s, as writers clearly saw the stresses associated with being on one's own in a culture dedicated to hyperconsumerism. The late 1970s and early 1980s became really telling — with the arrival of Ronald Reagan's cowboy militarism, writers were pushed into a corner. Nobody was safe. The culture had lost its senses. The choice was made to retreat behind the barricades as protection from the masses, and to create MFA programs all over the country, where those who were scared of the easy talk of nuclear Armageddon could take permanent refuge.

As with all other institutional developments, it is easy to tell a retrospective tale of origins and growth that makes complete sense, but this has some truth to it. In brief, writers no longer wanted to be part of the market economy. If they could create a self-sufficient guild, they would be removed from its vicissitudes. The inherently conservative nature of this impulse should be more evident now. There is glory in uniting against the abusive capitalist system. Medieval guilds were endowed with the right to combine and make their own regulations — precisely this impetus is behind the MFA system's retreat from the world of unabashed capitalism (also known as "reality" in the industrialized world).

Organizationally, the parallels to the medieval guild system are everywhere. It is the rare freelancer who can shun the creative writing guild, because he would then lack social distinction. The character of the master (the creative writing teacher), as in the medieval guild, is an indispensable element. Here we notice the emphasis on "mentorship," a different tone than the prevalent attitude towards the masters (professors) in the rest of the academy, the overarching guild that accommodates the writing guild. The character of the master should be such that he brings along the apprentice (the MFA student) and even the journeyman (the writing teacher) into the rules of social solidarity upon which the system thrives.

It is not enough to learn the "craft" (the techniques of creative writing, such as "show don't tell," "write what you know," "find your own voice," "kill all your darlings," etc.) but to learn how to put yourself in the shoes of the master should the need arise. What are the ethics of the master when he is approached by an apprentice? How does he evaluate his potential to be a contributing member of the guild? If the master were indisposed, can the journeyman fill his shoes without a noticeable difference in ethical standards?

Let's get more into these standards — what exactly are they? Good conduct for medieval guild masters was extremely important for the maintenance of reputation vis-à-vis the outside world, and without this credibility the guilds would have fallen apart in no time. Freelance craftsmen would have found it easy to identify individual buyers, and the whole system would have collapsed. With the guild product, you had the guarantee of a certain quality. In terms of the character of the master/journeyman/apprentice, what you get — as a cost of removing writing from the hurly-burly world of rude market principles — is a certain tame, politically correct liberalism (universally in effect throughout the American creative writing guild now), which makes appropriate, but extremely subdued, noises about political depredations. Actually, it does not accommodate a political worldview of any consistency and significance, and so the protests are diffuse, vague, honorable, and inarticulate to the point of utter irrelevance. That is very much part of the social bargain whereby writers are "left alone" to implement their craft, as opposed to being harassed or hounded out of existence; they get their NEA and Guggenheim fellowships, and everyone is happy since the power equations in society remain undisturbed.

So we have the profession of faith, the participation in fraternity, and the declaration of oath to the principles of social conduct in the MFA guild. Along with the watered-down politically correct liberalism, the master, journeyman, and apprentice alike should express in public their modesty, their lack of divine inspiration (otherwise the system couldn't sell itself as being able to teach craft), and the predominance of sheer luck and fortuitousness in any success they've had. They should always say that their writing career just happened; it certainly wasn't planned from the very beginning. Such an attitude might scare away potential apprentices (MFA applicants) for implying very high levels of awareness, which they may not possess. The system is utterly undemocratic, once one is a member of the guild, toward the outside world, but for it to survive in today's politically correct world, it must always present itself as the quintessence of democracy (everyone can learn writing, given enough application and discipline — at least we can make you competent, we can teach you the rules of the game, we can save you years of heartache from going it alone and making avoidable mistakes).

But it is an undemocratic system from the inside, just as the medieval guild system was, despite expressions of social solidarity among the chosen fraternity. Certain über-masters (Antonya Nelson, Heather McHugh, Jorie Graham, Sharon Olds, Lan Samantha Chang, Philip Levine, Charles Baxter, Donald Hall, Marilynne Robinson, Galway Kinnell, Mark Strand, Robert Pinsky, Robert Olen Butler, Jane Hirshfield, Tim O'Brien, Tobias Wolff, etc.) exercise disproportionate control over the distribution of rewards and honors. Woe betide any journeyman, let alone an apprentice, who crosses one of them! It is easy to displease an über-master by getting too big for one's britches — by wishing to undertake political writing, for instance, or violating the narcissistic confessionalism of fiction writing or the pseudo-liberalism of the "poetry of witness" we hear so much about these days. Actually, the whole point of early workshop humiliation (masquerading as instructive peer commentary) is to weed out any such troublemakers from finishing their period of apprenticeship, so in reality outright challenges to the authority of the masters must be rare indeed. The system measures its success by the frequency of non-events.

Social distinction, like with any guild system, is rife. There are MFA programs and then there are MFA programs — the elite on the one hand, the mere go-getters and wannabes on the other. Iowa, Michigan, Columbia, NYU, Brown, Hopkins, Texas, Cornell, Irvine, Houston, etc. rule the roost. There was a great brouhaha recently about a journeyman's attempt to rank MFA programs in *Poets & Writers* magazine according to input from potential apprentices as opposed to evaluations by journeymen and masters themselves; obviously such prospective evaluation couldn't be allowed. There are those star apprentices who get recruited by agents early on, thanks to the support of concerned masters, and there are those who, no matter how hard they try, can never get such attention. There are those to whom the multicultural veneer — and this mode of expression proliferates into many social niches — comes more easily than to others, and such apprentices and journeymen find rapid and early success, toward becoming potential masters one day.

There are the MFA graduates, and then there are the MFA/PhDs — the latter a growing subset, a sure way to social distinction, and having your poetry manuscript plucked from one out of a thousand entered in a "contest." Apprentices must undergo plenty of hardship (or what substitutes for it in the unreal world of the guild) by teaching a lot of classes, and putting up with a lot of stupidity from sub-apprentices (undergraduates with an interest in writing who may one day want to be full-fledged apprentices) to prove their mettle to the masters. The guild is self-governing, and masters theoretically have equal rights. Masters may be fiercely, resentfully, insanely competitive with one another, but this may never be expressed publicly; yet it is clear to the members of the guild which masters are on the rise and which are going down. It is better to anticipate the waves of the future, to be on the good side of the ascendant masters.

The system is profoundly undemocratic when it comes to the quality of the product it engenders, and its relentless crushing of any incipient freelance competition. There is an undeclared boycott in place with the famous residencies, conferences, and awards, and non-guild members need not apply (unless they want to waste their fifty or hundred dollars in application fees). Yaddo, MacDowell, Bread Loaf, etc. among the residencies/conferences, and the well-known awards/fellowships/grants committees do not welcome outsiders. There is a de facto ban, though probably, with the minute number of writers outside the guild these days, it is something they have to worry about less and less. The same is true of the Stanford Stegner fellowship, and the Provincetown Fine

Arts Work Center fellowship, which absolutely exclude those not already privileged enough to be members of the guild. You may pay a few thousand dollars to attend Bread Loaf as a "paying contributor" and soak in the mystery surrounding the über-masters, but you may never become a scholar/fellow/waiter unless you are a certified member of the guild. Yaddo and MacDowell simply will not admit you, even if you have published well, because you will not have the necessary recommendations from über-masters to get you into such places. There is the phenomenon of the roving and repeated fellowship recipient — the few people who seem to go from Provincetown to Stanford to Ucross to Wisconsin to Virginia to everywhere else — as though to hold up to apprentices a model of the hyper-diligent medal recipient. Rather than spreading the wealth around, to concentrate so many awards in a few chosen people year after year holds up these apprentices for imitation of how to work the masters' favor.

This is all in defense of the economic aims of the guild, whose articulation can be found in *Poets & Writers*, which is a perfect chronicle of the economic principles at work. First, the quotation of first lines of recently published books (along with names of agents, editors, and publicists) by favored journeymen, then valorization of small presses and little magazines and independent bookstores as though they were the drivers of the engine rather than mere appurtenances, the inspirational stories (often from utterly marginal apprentices) to emphasize the democracy of talent, the workshop-style interpretation of a modern master by a journeyman to locate it in the tradition of craft, the interview with the editor or agent which further elaborates the "mystery" (can one learn it in workshop?) inherent in acquisition decisions, and then on to the relentless business of how to get from modest apprentice to having your book's first line be quoted at the beginning of some future issue of the magazine, i.e., the listing of contests and awards and how to send your twenty or thirty or fifty dollars to entitle yours to be one among a thousand manuscripts to be screened by journeymen and finally picked by some über-master for publication.

It might be called "restraint of trade" in modern terms, due to the monopoly of craft exercised by the guild. We are talking about a house style, a uniform product literary magazines (generally affiliated with writing programs) and so-called "independent presses" can buy without hesitation. All this churning activity is predicated on the continuous generation of the MFA house style. In fiction it means generally apolitical, domesticated narrative that remains willfully ignorant of modernism (the highbrow style doesn't work with the guild's self-presentation), leaning strongly toward the confessional, memoiristic, autobiographical, narcissistic, and plainly understood. The same qualities apply in poetry — the standard workshop poem is a narrative or associative slight effort, taking off from the quotidian, to rest in an uneasy or understated epiphany. There is also a language poetry sub-component, but this has its own utterly predictable rules (the language poets think the lyric and narrative poets are closet fascists, yet they are blind to their own brand of conservatism).

One outcome of the craft monopoly is the extreme specialization among writers. Almost nobody writes in multiple genres — you do lyrical poetry based in a particular place, or creative nonfiction dealing with illness, or surrealistic short-shorts, or hillbilly novellas, or whatever. You do not cross boundaries as a poet into fiction or vice-versa, or, horror of horrors, from poetry into criticism or fiction into criticism. "Literary" writing (choked with metaphors, abstracted from political reality, and overwritten in that peculiarly self-conscious writerly style) is set in opposition to genre writing, merely commercial writing, since part of the mystery of the guild is that it is not aiming for commercial success. Lately, however, the MFA system has started to adopt genre writing, giving it a literary twist, as an accommodation to apprentices soaked in the principles of genre writing; it had to happen sooner or later.

It is in the interest of the mystery of the guild to banish criticism altogether, and they have pretty much succeeded, reducing criticism to glowing, one hundred percent positive 700-1,200-word blurbs masquerading as reviews in the back pages of literary quarterlies, when they are allowed in at all. A new genre of "criticism" has arisen — one hesitates to call it that, since it doesn't meet the definition of criticism, but is rather hollow hagiographic appreciation (something like what criticism used to be in the pre-scientific days, before New Criticism), often written by one master in praise of another. This can be found in journals like *American Poetry Review*, and is fairly close in language and style to the "craft workshops" taught at conferences like Bread Loaf and Sewanee, getting into the nuts and bolts of fiction or poetry by popular contemporary masters without imposing any rigorous discipline of literary knowledge upon the learner.

The MFA house style is integrally connected with the conditions of production under the guild system; uniformity of product, and severe control over its amount, is essential for the guild to maintain mystery

307

about itself, and without mystery there can be no exclusion of gate-crashers. Not only is the product uniform, but its quantity must be small. Writers cannot be allowed to be prolific — Joyce Carol Oates and T.C. Boyle mess up this paradigm for everyone. Hence the MFA fetish of constant revision — as undergraduates in my day used to talk about how many all-nighters they'd pulled, apprentices, journeymen, and masters these days exaggerate the number of drafts they wrote before daring to publish the book (Twenty! Fifty! A hundred!). This is cause for bragging rights; the more drafts, the more committed the writer declares himself to execution of craft.

In the current (May/June 2010) *Poets & Writers*, Ben Percy talks about hearing from Fiona McCrae of Graywolf Press after submitting a novel; the editor wanted him to radically revise the novel, including changing the point of view and adding six different subplots. Happy to oblige, Percy accomplished the task, and then started all over again, when the editor requested further fundamental changes. The writer must never, ever complain about revision; he must only express un-qualified gratitude for it. It is the one thing that guarantees democracy of membership: genius is inspirational, it strikes when we don't expect it, it is limited to the rare elect; but revision is accessible to everyone. The guild can keep forever expanding, as long as revision keeps the upper hand. Percy begins and ends his article by talking about buying an ugly house with good bones and rebuilding it to his satisfaction; the whole piece perfectly illustrates the extended metaphor of meticulous craft practiced in workshop conditions.

But the economic aims of the MFA guild would be unrealizable with-out its social aims, which perpetuate solidarity. All the rituals of medi-eval guilds can be found in their modern versions here. There is the annual bacchanal, the AWP gathering (with almost 10,000 assembled craft practitioners), which celebrates pedagogy and publication and prestige. Here the social distinctions are manifest, among über-mas-ters, ordinary masters, preferred journeymen, struggling journeymen, and apprentices with widely divergent pedigrees of popularity. The ap-prentices, of course, constitute the overwhelming number of attendees, so the ritual gathering becomes a celebration above all of the potential of apprentices to aspire to higher levels. There is the vast bookfair at the AWP, the huge exhibition a tangible expression of production — despite harsh controls over quantity of output, the overall output is large enough to shun market forces. These days there is an explicit recognition that only poets buy other poets' work (except for Mary

Oliver and Billy Collins), and if a small number of books is sold that way, that is enough to go on. Journeymen conduct panels where they are duly modest, democratic, politically correct, and multiculturally astute. Readings accommodate every apprentice, of however modest talent — this is one of the inborn rights of apprenticeship, to be able to read to an appreciative audience.

The modern reading was initiated by Dylan Thomas and Allen Ginsberg's high performative art. To listen to a recording of Ginsberg reading "America" in 1956 is to hear the echoes of a dream that has died; gone is the revolutionary, or even anti-establishment potential of the reading; it functions these days not to stir or provoke or enlighten or anger or frustrate or cajole, but as an endorsement of the democracy of talent, and that alone. Writers as stand-up comedians, seeking desperately to hold the audience's attention, to get its love and approval, are not a pretty sight. But the ritual purpose is well-served, and it is an extension of the ultimate justification of MFA programs: this too is a space for apprentices to develop themselves without criticism of their essential identities in the company of peers, that is, removed from the tribulations of the marketplace. No major foreign writers are invited at AWP, and they're typically not part of what we think of as the national reading circuit, stopping at bookstores, universities, and auditoriums across the country. I haven't seen Gabriel Garcia Marquez or Kenzaburo Oe or Chinua Achebe as keynote speakers at AWP, have you? No, it is typically some über-master (2010: Michael Chabon) who must at all times, in front of apprentices, declaim modesty and commitment to the common religion. Note too that most of the durable writing in this country is by writers either only peripherally or not at all associated with MFA programs — Tom Perrotta, Dana Spiotta, Mohsin Hamid, Laila Halaby, Joseph O'Neill, for example — but these are not who we think of as über-masters presiding over the AWP banquet. In any event, after some success, incorporation into the guild and employment as journeyman is all but inevitable for almost everyone who has had even modest success in the marketplace; the guild is eager to remove such authentic literary writers from the marketplace as soon as possible, to eliminate the competition.

The medieval guild was deeply rooted in its local community (the rise of industrial capitalism was a nationalist movement, and precisely the locality of the guild was the merchants' bete noir); it is part of its prestige, its aura, its mystery, its honorable secrecy. MFA programs follow the local orientation. They are diligent about performing readings in the local community. Creative writers perform a number of "community" functions: teaching at local schools and prisons, organizing local festivals at a small level, and instructing adults or school children, that is, those without aspirations to becoming full-fledged apprentices, as a mark of honor. It is a necessary act of philanthropy, as is the peculiarly local flavor each major MFA program acquires over time, so that the flow of writers in and out of the program is supposed to be a boon to the community, which may come and join in appreciation of the invited masters and be a part of the ongoing celebrations from time to time.

Are there natural limits to the creative writing guild system? What are its prospects for the future, and is there any chance that the guild might collapse of its own weight? The answer seems to be that given present political and social conditions, there appear to be few natural limits to how far it can expand. The writing guild's opposition to literature departments comes in very handy — in recent years, the guild has been preferred by many who would previously have gone into the study or teaching of literature or other humanities, since the intellectual requirements (to write a memoir of illness or dysfunction, or a story, which these days is more or less indistinguishable from memoir) are minimal, compared to, say, writing a dissertation on Chaucer or Wittgenstein. So the writing guild is rapidly eating into the rest of the humanities, and at the MFA level, it is very profitable too. It somehow humanizes the whole university.

A really depressing fact is that in the last few years the MFA house style has been finding increasing acceptance among the major New York publishing houses. It is one thing to talk about a renaissance in the American short story (is there really?) confronted with stacks of unread literary journals, and another thing for major houses to put out books by journeymen who have mastered competency but lack any trace of genius; it seems another way to kill the American short story. Yet some journeymen have ascended to truly great heights recently — Wells Tower would be a good example of someone in complete mastery of the house style, who works commercially as well, because of the minimal demands he places on the reader's attention. Reading him is like taking in a horror movie of relentless brutality that leaves one feeling rather complacent because at least one possesses basic human emotions. In poetry, the talentless journeymen Michael and Matthew Dickman might be apt examples of favored stars, whom the masters — and their friends in the New York publishing and reviewing communities — have decided must ascend to the top. The inauguration of such stars comes

310

with the grandiose gestures familiar from the old Hollywood studio system (the Dickman brothers received a *New Yorker* profile). Three or four of these stars-in-the-making are necessary every year to keep hope alive among the legions of apprentices and journeymen that fame and fortune can be theirs too. The major publishers have become part of the grand bargain by accepting that so-called literary fiction has a minimal audience anyway, so they might as well go with the chosen stars (getting into the *Best New American Voices*, a celebration of workshops, pretty much guarantees a contract by a significant publisher), so that their commitment to literature may remain unquestioned, and the book in question at least generate some minimal level of sales (all those famished apprentices), awards, recognition, reviews, buzz, etc.

The medieval guild system collapsed in the end because its exclusivity, control, and mystery didn't accord well with the rise of the industrial system. It was a transitional phase between feudalism and capitalism, allowing relatively pleasant, even sometimes leisurely, space for creativity. It was a retreat from barbarism into a predetermined aesthetic zone. When a greater system, with all-embracing aspirations, came to the fore, the guild system died — although it survived in some forms, primarily the university guild, and its vestiges can be seen in labor unions. Yet recall that the MFA guild system was carved out of an already existing fully omnivorous postmodern capitalist system, so it has already, in a sense, confronted its own worst enemy (the Kennedy/Johnson/Nixon militarist/capitalist/liberal state with extreme emphasis on professionalization of all aspects of life, and its predictable even worse successors) and dealt with it. So collapse on those terms is unforeseeable. In fact, all the present trends in publishing — certainly the rise of digital publishing — herald continued strength for the MFA guild.

Again, the most important thing about this discussion is the socially conservative writing that results from the socially conservative organization of the literary writing guild. In thinking of an analogy for the medieval guildmen as they related to the Counter-Reformation, we might think of the rise of the creative writing programs at precisely the time of the Reagan ascendancy, when liberalism with a commitment to even the mildest redistributionist philosophy went into permanent retreat. A new kind of conservative writing — Raymond Carver, Ann Beattie, Jay McInerney, Bret Easton Ellis, Amy Hempel, Mary Robison — became ascendant at the time. A continuous Inquisition has been in place in American cultural life, and certainly in the writing

311

guild, ever since then, and the writing product is shaped by that. In essence, the writing guild makes it possible for apprentices to internalize the principles of the Inquisition. One is made to feel guilty and ashamed if writing compels one to move toward areas forbidden by the Inquisition. Workshop humiliation is very much part of this enforcement of Inquisition rules; it is astonishing to notice — even at the undergraduate, non-guild level — how quickly students acquire these principles of writerly conduct, and rake their fellows over the coals for the minutest transgressions ("You switched point of view in the story, you're not allowed to do that!"). One quickly becomes invested in the Inquisition; the advice manuals written by the masters convey these gently, in the guise of techniques of writing, but the social principle behind them is manifest.

Talent, in the modern writing guild, has been discounted; it is craft that counts. When the writing guild was in its infancy, thirty, forty, fifty years ago, one heard of arbitrary, cruel, even violent masters, legendary for their drinking, womanizing, and sheer idiosyncrasy. These have been snuffed out. Now the code of conduct proscribes any such flouting of the rules for even the most accomplished master. The system is in a very fine state of consolidation. All writing produced under the guild system has the dual purpose of not only functioning as writing but also as social manifesto for the guild system which produced such writing; this is the dual aspect in which we must read today's acclaimed master fiction writers and poets. The apprentice produces a "masterpiece" — a *chef d'oevre* — to pass muster and receive the license to teach — the *ius docendi* — upon conclusion of his period of training in the workshop. This signifies adherence to standards of production, and forever after, as a journeyman and perhaps as a master himself, he must not deviate from these standards. The master always retains the right of correction — the *ius corrigendi* of the medieval guilds — to guarantee quality; there is an infinitely intricate system of withholding rewards and recognition from deviants.

Nominated by Boulevard

SPELL AGAINST GODS

by PATRICK PHILLIPS

from NEW ENGLAND REVIEW

Let them be vain.
Let them be jealous.

Let them, on their own earth,
await their own heaven.

Let them know they will die.
And all those they love.

Let them, wherever
they are, be alone.

And when they call out
in prayers, in the terrible dark,

let us be present, and watching,
and silent as stars.

Nominated by New England Review

GLAD TO BE HUMAN: A
JOIE DE COEUR

by IRENE O'GARDEN

from THE TUSCULUM REVIEW

Glad to be human in the 21st century, survival licked; glad not to be selling my blood anymore or using rolled-up toilet paper for sanitary napkins. But even in those dollar-few days, I'd find a bunch of roses abandoned on the street; or once, walking up Eighth Avenue to meet my date, the strap to my only pair of shoes disintegrated, and I went into a hotel after three barefoot blocks and asked, "Do you have any shoes?" And they did, a pair of Dr. Scholl's that someone left that fit just right. Glad to be human; glad to be provided for; glad to provide for myself in faith and effort. Fun to find shoes, fun to buy them, too.

Glad to be human—for solitude and to be able to be a stranger—a gift of the 21st century, like speed and music anytime and feast upon feast of stories anytime. Glad to be human for late nights, talk and art and sex and loving and all different languages; glad to be human for words themselves, peculiar to us as paper to the wasp, as leaf to tree or song to bird—words as human as a measured square.

Glad to be human in the 21st century—where people spend lives designing, dancing, building, writing, studying their minutest fascinations, people dedicating lives to food or fashion or philosophy, creating and creating, absorbed in their work for love of it, as now they marry for love. People hungering to understand each other and their families, reading, talking, tending the earth and their dreams, and the playing of games and of sport.

Glad in the 21st century of all the mighty banquets laid: images of art of all our centuries reproduced and held in hand, writings of the writing cultures held in heart, spiritual traditions of the ages spread before us: choose, sample, compare, enjoy, discard, invent from the immense library of remembered human life! Deep feeding of consciousness. History lies on the bed, saying, *Take me, take all you wish of me, and then leave me behind; I don't mind.*

Glad to be human for the feasts of all cuisines: any day any taste in the world and invented combinations, like discovered common tastes in conversations between strangers, the mixing of cultures complementing the glorious rush of fruit and vegetable and grain, fresh and fresh, glad.

Glad to be human for the knowledge of animals and nature and material and metal and chemistry and theory, living in a living dictionary of experience and interest and curiosity; glad to know some things about my human body, of her cells and structures; glad to know about some stars; glad the mystery is infinite; glad for the burst and silence.

Glad to be living in the heart, the human heart—time for whole days spent on relationships, for soothing, for expressing pain, for pleasure, contemplation. And time and ways and means for distant friends, living in differing places, to visit, to speak—and the beauty of a letter sent received.

Glad for interiors and colors and pattern and balance and shape and movement and adornment and the way the future vapors on a loom. Glad of myriads of little helps, of zippers, paperclips, and cleverness. And of the explicit agreement in ongoing ordinary existence of plate glass.

Glad of the beauty of stones and their wisdoms, grandmothers of matter; glad of all the world, how much wider, fuller, more colorful can it be? The wild harmonic variation, rushes of beauty from all cultures differing, flood of beauty—glad to be here for this!

Glad to be safe and dry and educated and supplied and empowered and free of children; glad there are people glad to have children. Glad to choose, to help to nourish, to bless.

Glad to have coached a baby into this world, excruciating and exquisite. No sleep for 24 hours, my sister twisting in the birthing bed; her husband and I squeezing her hand, feeding her ice, our very breaths as one till salty weepy laughter chokes out of us as the red hairy head appears.

Glad to be human for all the ages that surround me always, for the precious ability to always catch sight of a baby somewhere, a toddler, and children, and the sweet pure unconsciousness of, even in anger, youth, staggering in its unknowing beauty. And the reposed beauty of lined

315

faces, relaxing into life, tendered by experience, the comfort of the presence of wisdom, with vigor yet, a beauty like a leatherbound book. And the grace of elders realized in full capacity, inspiring as centuries-old trees, the crowning loveliness of natures fulfilled, experience like rings around them of their growth, not separate into years—these feelings—but sensed around them as a life, a single mighty sheath of living over their ordinary comings and goings, sap rising and falling in them in thin streams, surrounded by the immensity of their truth.

Glad to have helped at death as well, not only the slow dangle from the hospital tubes for those I knew, but for the stranger, the old man dying alone on the southeast corner of 42nd Sreet and Ninth Avenue in NYC, to crouch at his crumpled barely moving body, hold his colding hand, tell him he did a good job with life, to feel his spirit lighten and leave, like a bird.

Glad to see the old ones with the young ones, and the middles with them both, embracing the holy hidden web, the knowledge at once forward and backward, the intentions of youth, the obligations of middle-age, the liberations of age. Joys at every stage and moment, at no time without memory, at no time without expectation—life at once like a film in a can. Much gladness that we share this, reminding each other over and over with alphabets of behavior and emotion, familiar and combined to sentences newly every day.

And glad to be human for the sake of days, that all of human history has taken place in days. The Battle of Hastings happened on a day, and so did the dancing of Fred Astaire, and all of us have days for all emotion, exploration, for being sick, recovering from travel, gathering with friends, holidays, and days for being bored, for recreation and creation—days and days and infinite days.

Glad to be human for cooking and slicing life, looking for meaning and searching and finding the missing word, the lost sock, the thrilly scary moment reaching around in your purse and not finding your wallet, rummaging, rummaging, knowing it's there, finding it under your fingers with pleasure, and finding with pleasure at last that the meaning of life's like a cell on the field of your vision, you know it is there; but each time you look it springs out of your sight, but looking at anything else, it springs back into place and you're looking right through it. Glad to be human, abundantly answered.

Hard to see the effort behind abundance here in the early 21st century: the spent backs picking berries, raw red nursing hands, the sweat of science, years of boredom for a single thought; hard to see the editor

316

tossing in her sleep, the relentless raising of children, the grinding of wheat, the servicing of machinery. But when I am spent and raw with sweat and sleeplessness, working my work, asking how can it be so hard, I remember what work it takes to bring me any single thing. My gladness of all I am brought begets gratitude, and gratitude lightens my service. And all becomes service and gladness and gratitude.

Glad for the transformations now and coming, glad for love and work and play, glad for letting go my fear to sound my song of gladness, going as it dues against prevailing currents in the thinkers of my day. Glad I learned the joy of swimming against the current in a Catskill cataract. Full strength deliberate infinity swimming, whole self pleasure challenge, young lad paddles over asking, "Do you know you're not going anywhere?" and me yessing and loving the power of current, power of body, free from having to watch where I'm going, free from having to turn around or curb my body from a pool wall, a pond curve, free from "Am I going out too far?" in salt and bobbing water, free to swim and nothing else with all myself—and a man swims over, says, "You're fighting the current," and "No," I say, "I'm enjoying it!" Whole self, full power, glad to be human.

Nominated by Sara Pritchard

THE VERANDA

fiction by FREDERIC TUTEN

from CONJUNCTIONS

—For Jill Bialosky

SHE'S ON A VERANDA fronting a beach cut short by the bandit tide. The sea beyond, its mysteries and waves, she's used to them but then again she never is. Those waves pillaging the shore each day. From time to time, she glances at the single white rose on the table. The same crystal vase as always, a different rose each day, but always from the same garden, hers. A Bach partita—winter light in a faded mirror— flows through the open French doors. She's reading Marcus Aurelius again, and again finds comfort in the obvious: To lessen the pains of living, one must diminish desire for the material world, its promises and illusions.

There is a polite rustle at the door. M, the butler—who else would it be?—with a silver pot of coffee wrapped in a linen napkin. He nods. She smiles for thanks.

M is old. He has seen her through three husbands, two who had married her for her money. The first husband died midsentence at break- fast; a sentence she had no wish for him to complete, in any case, because it concerned his allowance and the need for its substantial increase.

She was young when she first married and still young when her hus- band left her, the planet, his bespoke suits, handcrafted shoes, and the beige cashmere socks he so cherished and had kept rolled in ten cedar- lined drawers. She had come to dislike him not only because she had gradually understood that he had married her principally for her wealth but because she found his sartorial desires so conventional, like his lovemaking.

The second husband, on understanding that her wealth was not to flow endlessly into the mansion's garages, flooded with his custom-made cars, and who considered Bentleys and Rolls-Royces mere Fords, left her for an older woman who appreciated the elegant way he mixed drinks for her guests at intimate dinner parties, and who was willing to pay for his ever-increasing automotive needs.

The last husband, who was sixty-eight when they married and who made her happy well into her midforties, drowned in the same ocean she was now regarding with tenderness and fear. At breakfast one morning together, as every summer morning, he kissed her, a deep kiss on the mouth and not just a husbandly peck, then he was off for his usual swim. He waved to her from far away in the ocean and then he was gone. He was the love of her life.

He was an artist. Not very famous but not unrecognized. He was appreciated, respected, living modestly on the sale of his paintings, which unabashedly had roots in Poussin and Cézanne. Like them, he searched for the immortal structure beneath and underlying the painting in whatever subject it represented. Like them, his life was a consecration to art and a daily presence to its fulfillment. (He, however, would have been shy about such words as "consecration.") "You cannot know what the work will look like unless you show up for it" was the way he put it. He made no fuss about being dedicated to his art and he did not feel superior to those artists without similar devotion. But he did not spend time in their company either.

He lived decently and did not require much to do so—a small loft that he had bought for a song in the early sixties, in a building now the warren of billionaire condos, was all he needed and wanted for shelter and work. He had no retreat by the sea or elsewhere as had many of his colleagues. I say colleagues because he did not have friends in the full sense of the word, though he believed in the idea of friendship as found in the essays of Montaigne. He liked the idea so much that he did not attempt to injure it through experience.

He stayed in the city through the hottest summers on the deadest weekends when no one but tourists and the homeless roamed the burning streets. In the spring and into the late fall he walked to the park on the lower East River and read on a bench fronting the watery traffic of tugs and barges. A white yacht on its way to Florida or the Caribbean might pass by and someone might wave. In winter he kept in, break-

319

fasted on Irish oatmeal and coffee and then more coffee; he often skipped lunch and ate bread in torn hunks and drank coffee: two sugars, three ounces of milk. At night he dined at an Italian restaurant with so-so food on the corner of his street. It had a green awning in summer and you could sit under it in the rain.

Sometimes one of the young female assistants from his gallery found a pretext to visit him. He was friendly, solicitous, but did not mix business with sex. He imagined the resulting complications, the discomfort of going to his gallery and facing a woman he had slept with a few times but in whom he had no deeper interest. And he did not welcome the discomfort he imagined for her or the awkwardness of his circumspect dealer of fifteen years, who never mixed business with anything if he could help it.

He liked the city, he liked solitude, he liked going and coming when he wished; he liked sleeping and waking in his own bed. He liked women but mostly on a certain basis: that they did not want to live with him, did not want to have children; did not want to call him at any hour they chose to chat; that they did not like or affect to like sports; that they did not buy or urge him to buy new clothes, to get a haircut, a shave, or have his nails trimmed, though he always kept them trimmed and his face shaved and hair cut short. The women he liked did not or needed not to work. This excluded many women, even those women of leisure married to wealth because he considered their marriage a job, a fancy one without regular hours or a visible paycheck but a job nonetheless. In any case, he did not consort with married women, first out of principle—the one that has to do with not hurting people, husbands, in this case—and the other because he was selfish about his time and did not wish to waste it on clandestine arrangements and their inevitable time-consuming and emotional complications.

He liked women who read books he honored: He was snobbish about that but did not care that he might be thought so. The books one read were as telling as the friends one chose. You could be fooled or betrayed by friends but never by books. Plato, for example, always stayed faithful and always gave more than he received. Proust could be relied on for his nature descriptions, especially flowers bordering paths through luxuriant gardens. He loved gardens because of Proust but felt he need not visit any because he had seen and walked through enough of them in the Frenchman's world. He used this as an excuse to get out of visiting friends in Connecticut who prided themselves on their gardens, their endless yards of rose beds, especially.

He liked above all women who loved painting. He did not care for them as much if they liked sculpture because he did not care for sculpture, except for smallish items such as Mycenaean heads and masks from the Côte d'Ivoire, very abstract and synthetic. In short, he liked sculpture the starker and the more minimal the better. He disliked mostly everything else ever deconstructed or assembled and felt antipathy for the grand posture and thus disdained Rodin's figures in particular among the moderns. Everything, in fact, after the time of Pericles he found dreary and dead, the stuff to fill old movie palace lobbies. He once wrote in his notebook that we need not bother to fill empty space with sculpture—any natural rock formation is better than any sculpture, so, too, trees. Deserts do not need sculpture; emptiness is their point and their beauty.

About painting he had no illusions. He did not believe in its social or psychological or spiritual transformative powers. He did not believe that there is progress in art—or in civilization. All great, significant art was timeless and equal in value—in beauty. Beauty was the end and reason for all art, period.

He had few extravagances. But he would travel long distances to revisit paintings he loved and he would make, with great planning, expeditions to places holding paintings he admired. He spent two weeks alone at the Ritz Hotel in Madrid so that he could walk across the road after breakfast and before dinner to look at Velázquez's *Las Meninas*, which he considered the greatest painting ever made after the seventeenth century. His certainty about this annoyed other artists, who saw in it an inflexibility of taste that might be applied to his judging their own work. They were also put off by his unwillingness to consider that no single work of art is the "greatest." Sometimes, for fun, he would seem to concede the point and say: "Well, it is the first greatest among equals."

He once trailed a beautiful woman after seeing her studying with great intensity a painting by Picasso in a hall at the Louvre. He followed her into a room of Poussins and was pleased to see her fixed on one painting, *Echo and Narcissus*, for several full minutes. That she might have seen the affinity between the two artists intrigued him and she increased in stature and thus grew more and more beautiful by the minute. Then she seemed to take a different track altogether when she went into other rooms and gave her attention to a canvas by Perugino and then later focused on a painting by Parmigianino. He was a bit let down. It occurred to him that she was progressing or governed along no aesthetic insight or principle but merely visiting artists whose surnames began with the letter P.

He followed her to the museum's café, where she sat alone by the window facing a vast courtyard and Paris beyond. He sat at the table closest to her and took his time ordering *un grande crème* and a tartine with butter—exactly what she had requested and what finally was brought them both. She spoke to the waiter in a French from an earlier day, when words were sounded in their fullness. She would have made a great actress on the seventeenth-century stage reciting Racine or Corneille. For all that, he wasn't sure he liked the elevated, rich, over-educated, worldly, superior tone of her voice. But then he liked it—he supposed her to be French and thus she could sound as fancy and superior as she wished or why else be French? He glanced her way, hoping to make eye contact, but she had pulled a book out of her bag—expensive, smooth, trim, no frills, oxblood red, with a narrow strap—and engaged herself in its lines.

He was shy except with women, from whom he would gamble rebuff, even rebuke, to meet. His theory was that the chance of knowing an interesting woman was more important than any rejection, and since his advances were soft spoken and courteous, his politeness was met with the like or at worst with a little coldness born of natural suspicion and wariness.

"Look," he said, taking the chance that she knew English. "I understand your interest in the connection between Poussin and Picasso but I don't see your leap to Parmigianino, a fine artist but irrelevant to what connects the other two."

She gave him a long look. Almost scientific in its disinterestedness. Then in a pleasant but firm voice and in an English more beautiful than her French said: "I'm married. Happily or unhappily is another matter, but married and obedient to all its obligations and injunctions and oaths."

"Lamentably so," he answered, not sure exactly what he meant.

She drank her coffee slowly, looking at the sea, its thick swell and sullen heaviness. It covered the world. It raided its shores, carrying trees and husbands in its teeth. One day the sea would gallop over the dunes and drag her into its watery camp. But if she chose, she would not wait for it to come to carry her away and she would take a long swim from which she would never again step on shore.

She had walked into his gallery cold, looking for a watercolor by Marin and a painting by Hartley she knew were being offered there. It was an old-fashioned gallery she felt comfortable visiting because the owner kept his distance, did not make too much fanfare about his artists or their work.

The gallery specialized in early-to-mid-twentieth-century American art, thus he was in the company of Walt Kuhn, Kuniyoshi, Fairfield Porter, artists he admired although they were too tame for him, never reaching beyond the literal. He was sometimes fearful that that was also true of him, too tame, too literal, and whenever he got sufficiently worried he took the train to Philadelphia and for a full half hour stood in front of Cézanne's large *Bathers*. He would grab a sandwich in the museum's café and let his mind go nowhere, then he'd return to the painting and start absorbing it again. He would come home feeling purified and try to purge his work of the superfluous without eliminating areas that gave his painting its valuable subtext and life. He strove.

He had been approached by galleries more important and chic than his, ones that had offered him monthly stipends and lavish catalogs written by distinguished critics whose names would give added weight to his reputation, galleries that had juice in the art market and could inject oil into its machinery.

But he liked his gallery, having been invited to join it when he was still unknown; he stayed loyal to the man who had the intelligence to understand his work and to act on it—to put his money where his taste was. He found in the dealer a man not too chummy and not too remote and who quietly and successfully did his job of promoting and selling his few living artists. He liked also that his dealer always wore modest pinstripe suits and bow ties, and that he went to the Oak Room at the Plaza at five thirty every weekday and drank a dry martini and then, in nasty weather, took the Madison Ave. bus uptown to his home and to his wife of thirty years.

She bought the Marin watercolor and, undecided, put a hold on the Hartley. Then the dealer asked if she would be interested in seeing the work of an artist he had long admired and long represented and he took her into his office. He had spoken to her of this artist before but she had not made the effort to see the work. The three paintings in the dealer's office unnerved, then calmed her, as if she at last had found her map home after being lost for years in a faraway country whose language she did not understand and could never learn. Musical they

323

were, these paintings, in melancholic counterpoint with death. By what alchemy did paint become music?

She did not know who he was, had never seen his photograph, as he shunned having his face in the catalogs of his shows—there were none, in any case. His picture had never appeared in any of the art magazines she subscribed to, which, with the exception of the bulletin from the Metropolitan Museum of Art, where she was a trustee, were none.

She bought one painting, asking that she remain anonymous.

Then, two weeks later, after the first painting's music had occupied her dreams, she returned and bought another.

Weeks later, she sent the artist an unsigned note of appreciation via his gallery. He answered, through his gallery, with a handkerchief-size drawing—in the mode and friendly parody of Poussin—of a tree on fire and a medieval battlement in the distance also in flames. She withdrew, feeling the heat of his closeness and the threat of disappointment. (Better never to get too close or meet an artist whose work you admire because all artists are inferior to their work.) She wrote back thanking him politely for the drawing—and then, in a rush of feeling, added some heartfelt lines on what she loved about his work. She feared those lines would be misunderstood and open doors better left shut but she also felt that a polite mere thank you would not have expressed the fullness of her, of her emotions. She knew she was equivocating, because her letter might suggest that while her doors were shut they were also unlocked.

He responded a day later. Come, his note said, to his studio and choose a watercolor.

While the principle never to meet the artist remained true, she also wanted to meet him, if nothing else than to confirm the principle—a lie. She wanted to meet him because she wished to like him, to be moved by him, to have him move her. She wanted to believe that the untroubled purity she found in his paintings mirrored his own distinguished soul. These thoughts disturbed her for the disappointment should she ever meet him, and she was pained by her longing for someone perfect or someone whose very imperfections and failures she would find noble.

In short, after some days of indecision, she went to his loft. She had her car and chauffeur wait in the street should she decide on a quick getaway. They smiled both comfortably and uncomfortably. They chitchatted some minutes and, much to her own surprise, she asked if he lived alone.

"Lamentably," he said.

She laughed. "You seem fond of that word."

He nodded. And slyly said, "Regrettably."

"What if I said I'm still married? What would you say to that?"

"That should you leave this room, I would lament you."

"Then perhaps I won't leave."

She gave her driver the day off. He was glad and made his escape across the bridge to Astoria, Queens, where his wife and children watched TV until they went blind. She stayed there in his loft until morning, when they both went to breakfast—the scrambled eggs were cut into white strings, the bacon was undercooked and burnt at the same time, the coffee was tar hauled from a back road in Tennessee—in a dim diner by the Hudson River favored by truckers and taxi drivers and artists of that era.

"And what about God," she asked. "Where are you on that?" She was still young enough to think about and to ask such questions. In any case, she was not asking about God, she was probing to discover his blind spot, and having found none after hours of talking and finally, at 2:38 in the morning, when he said, "It's time," she followed him to his bed.

For the first several months of their years together, they divided themselves between his loft and her apartment, from whose windows they could see Central Park and the Plaza. They shared breakfast at six, after which he vanished in a taxi to his studio downtown and spent the day painting. If by seven that evening he felt not ready to leave his work, he'd phone her and they would or would not meet again for dinner, or they would or would not meet again that night, in which case he'd sleep alone but she would come downtown at six to breakfast with him at the diner with the bad food. The string eggs, burnt bacon, and tar coffee had worked into their history. Or sometimes she would appear with a full breakfast, silver service and all, her chauffeur and maid and herself toting platters and coffee pots up to her husband's loft. Then she might linger a while after they had sipped their last cup of coffee and go to his bed.

He had been painting with a new vigor and insight that his dealer recognized immediately. There was also a certain charity, a kind of generosity lacking earlier but still keeping the work within its usual reserved boundaries. "Love does its wonders," the dealer said dispassionately but with a conviction born from romantic memories of his youth, when he first met his wife.

Everything seemed in balance, so the dealer was upset when he learned that she was building a house in Montauk. "Why go out there in the first place?" the dealer asked her.

"For the calm and the air and the sea," she answered. "He's too old to spend summers broiling in the city. I'll build him a studio he won't want to leave. A place he and every other artist has ever dreamed of."

The dealer had seen artists appear from the mist and then vanish from the scene, he had seen exalted reputations fall into the mud—or, even worse, just melt away slowly into oblivion. And not always because the work had changed for the worse. The moment had changed and the artist was no longer in that moment but suddenly somewhere else, far away, in the land of the forgotten and awaiting the day to be rescued and brought home with honors.

But sometimes, their flame went out because the hungry fuel that had fed it was no longer there, and the rich life took its place. He knew artists who, when they reached the pinnacle of their art and reputation and had earned vast sums, turned out facsimiles of their earlier, hard-earned work and were more concerned with their homes, trips, social calendars, their placement at dinner parties than with anything that might have nourished their art, which coasted on its laurels.

And for that last reason the dealer said to her: "Go slow and keep the life contained, for his sake and yours."

She laughed. "Don't worry, no one will come to our dinner parties, should we ever give them, and we shall not go if ever asked."

"This is not a moralistic issue," he said. "And I'm not against money. You *know* it's not about you. I love you," he said, turning red.

"And I love you for how you were in his life and in his work from the start."

He made an exaggeratedly alarmed face and said, "Were?"

"Were, are, and always will be," she said, then repeated it.

They left on good terms. He apprehensive of what was to become of his artist; she concerned that in trying to make a gracious life for her husband she might be digging their cushioned graves.

Now he was dissolved in the sea, vanished in a soup of bones and brine. And now she was alone until the sea took her away, too, if it were the sea who one day would be her executioner. Until that time, she would remain alone with the butler, who in time would tremble and whose hand would spill the coffee and let the morning rose fall. Then, one day, he would tremble all over and, after the back and forth of hospitals, he would be gone. Then she would sit on the veranda and face the sea and listen to music, maybe some somber cello pieces from

Marais or Saint-Colombe or Bach—music on a small scale, where, atomlike, the energy of beauty compresses.

Eventually she would answer the phone and seem delighted that a friend had called to invite her to dinner. An elegant dinner with distinguished guests—an ambassador who had written a memoir, a former editor of a venerable publishing house, a novelist always mentioned for the Nobel Prize, two widows who funded the arts, a young poet who would have preferred not to be there but who understood the draw and use of powerful people—all affable and solicitous of her. The food, a poached wild salmon with sorrel, would be excellent, the wine even better. The conversation would flow with delicacy and nuance, with worldly authority. But not one word said the whole evening would approach her heart.

She would be home by eleven and sit and read in an old leather chair he had loved. The lazy cat would curl about her ankles and fall asleep. She herself would start to doze off—as she got older, fewer and fewer books held her interest. Only Proust still spoke to her, an old, intimate friend with long, twisting sentences whose fineness still absorbed her and kept her feeling grateful for his visit. She left her gardens to the gardeners, who went wild with the freedom, each planting to his own vision. Rose beds rushed against walls of blue hydrangeas, a field of yellow daffodils invaded a stand of black tulips. The grass went from tame to wild without transition. She enjoyed the anarchy and the disorder but it delivered only so much pleasure and then the excitement went flat. People also went stale quickly. The interesting ones, the ones with character and who had struggled to make their place in the world, had died. She was too tired and too far away in time to meet their replacements, if there were any.

He had left her everything. His clothes, of course, a closet full of khakis and pairs of brown loafers worn down to the heels; one pair of black shoes, soles and heels as good as new; one suit, gray pinstripe, hardly worn, made for him in London, where he had once spent a week drunk on museums; three sports jackets, two for winter, a red and green plaid for summer; two dress shirts to be adorned with a tie, the rest just blue cotton button-downs. Apart from the art, and there was little of that, she prized his notebooks, some filled with sketches like the one he had sent her years earlier and some with jottings and notes and quotes from the reading he loved.

He wrote about the *Bathers*, how he loved the awkwardness of the nude figures, the almost childish painting of their forms. As if Cézanne had set out to fail. As if he had sought through that failure a great visual truth at once obvious and occult. He quoted from a letter of Cézanne's in which he spoke about his unfinished paintings—paintings he had deliberately left unfinished, patches here and there of raw canvas as if left to be later painted. Cézanne had found truth in their incompleteness. That the empty spaces invited color, leaving the viewer to imagine that color, leaving the viewer his exciting share in the completing of the visual narrative; blank spaces suggesting also that art, like life, does not contain all the information and that it is a lie when it pretends so.

Silence, except for the churning sea. The sea is high, just some fifty yards from her, black and cold. The house, too vast for one, feeling the sea's chill, gives a shudder. She gives a shudder. Then she makes her way up the stairs to her too-large room and her too-large bed, under a too-high ceiling, and she waits for the sea—having taken from her everything else—to come crawling to her window like a bandit hungry for silver.

Nominated by Conjunctions

THEORY OF LIPSTICK

by KARLA HUSTON

from VERSE WISCONSIN

> *"Coral is far more red than her lips' red;"*
> —Shakespeare

Pot rouge, rouge pot, glosser, lip plumper, bee
stung devil's candy and painted porcelain
Fire and Ice, a vermillion bullet,
dangerous beauty lipstick, carmine death rub, history
of henna. Fact: more men get lip cancer

because they don't wear lipstick or butter,
jumble of a luminous palette with brush made
to outlast, last long, kiss off, you ruby busser,
your gilded rose bud bluster is weapon and wine.
QE's blend: cochineal mixed with egg, gum Arabic

and fig milk—alizarin crimson and lead—poison
to men who kiss women wearing lipstick, once illegal
and loathsome—then cherry jellybean licked and smeared,
then balm gloss crayon, a cocktail of the mouth
happy hour lip-o-hito, lip-arita, with pout-fashioned chaser

made from fruit pigment and raspberry cream,
a lux of shimmer-shine, lipstick glimmer, duo
in satin-lined pouch, Clara Bow glow: city brilliant
and country chick—sparkling, sensual, silks
and sangria stains, those radiant tints and beeswax liberty—

oh, kiss me now, oh, double agents of beauty
slip me essential pencils in various shades
of nude and pearl and suede, oh, bombshell lipstick,
sinner and saint, venom and lotsa sugar, lip sweet,
pucker up gelato: every pink signal is a warning.

Nominated by Verse Wisconsin and Phil Dacey

FIVE

fictions by LYDIA DAVIS

from LITTLE STAR

JUDGMENT

Into how small a space the word *judgment* can be compressed: it must fit inside the brain of a ladybug as she, before my eyes, makes a decision.

THE SKY ABOVE LOS ANGELES

The sky is always above a tract house in Los Angeles. As the day passes, the sun comes in the large window from the east, then the south, then the west. As I look out the window at the sky, I see cumulus clouds pile up suddenly in complex, pastel-colored geometrical shapes and then immediately collapse and dissolve. After this has happened a number of times in succession, at last it seems possible for me to begin painting again.

HANDEL

I have a problem in my marriage, which is that I simply do not like George Friedrich Handel as much as my husband does. It is a real barrier between us. I am envious of one couple we know, for example, who both love Handel so much they will sometimes fly all the way to Texas just to hear a particular tenor sing a part in one of his operas. By now, they have also converted another friend of ours into a lover of Handel. I am surprised, because the last time she and I talked about music, what she loved was Hank Williams. All three of them went by train to Washington, D.C., this year to hear *Giulio Cesare in Egitto*. I prefer the composers of the 19th century, and particularly Dvořák. But I'm pretty open to all sorts of music, and usually if I'm exposed to something long enough, I come to like it. But even though my husband puts on some sort of Handel vocal music almost every night, if I don't say anything to stop him, I have not come to love Handel. Fortunately, I have just found out that there is a therapist not too far from here, in Lenox, Massachusetts, who specializes in Handel-therapy, and I'm going to give her a try. (My husband does not believe in therapy and I know he would not go to a Dvořák-therapist with me even if there was one.)

HOUSEKEEPING OBSERVATION

Under all this dirt, the floor is really very clean.

SITTING WITH MY LITTLE FRIEND

Sitting with my little friend in the sunshine on the front step:
I am reading a book by Blanchot
and she is licking her leg.

Nominated by Little Star

OCEAN STATE JOB LOT

by STEPHEN BURT

from NEW OHIO REVIEW

No one is going to make
   much more of this stuff now, or ever again.

Graceless in defeat
   but beautiful, harmless and sad
on shelves that overlap like continents,

these Cookie Monster magnets, miniature
   monster trucks, scuffed multiple Elmos, banners

that say NO FEAR
   and A GRILL FOR EVERY BOY
are a feast for every sense.

Some would be bad manners
   to give or to bring home—

so many pounds of oysters, so many gallons of franks and beans . . .
                                  It is a sea

   that we discover out here,

where every piece of evidence
   has a notional price and a buyer, and we find our own
among its premises:

a hundred cans of pepper relish shaped
    like lobster pots,
a big glass pickle meant to keep coins in,

a gleaming square whose effervescent
    label promises
the taste of the Atlantic in a tin.

Nominated by New Ohio Review

PRACTICE JOURNEY

by ALBERT GOLDBARTH

from SEATTLE REVIEW

PRACTICE JOURNEY

1.

The ritzy, glitzy 24-7 exercise club—what once, in a time when neither words nor bodies were so pumped up, I would have called the "gym" and now has been termed a "mega-healthystyles emporium"—is impressive by day, on the corner here. I like especially, and I'll admit it, to look at the women (most of them so toned already, you'd think that further exercise could only be aimed at embalming those faux-tan chassis): the front of the building is almost totally glass, so that these treaders and serious buffers serve the organization as a free advertisement, even as the idea of public display is sweet to their vanity. They expose their strenuous effort and its sleeking results with obvious pride, and I (as I briskly shlep around the neighborhood for an hour—which is *my* low-rent obeisance to cardiovascular upkeep—making sure I pass this showcase building a number of times) take my part in a holistic system, and drink it all in appreciatively.

But it's really at night that the soul of the building appears. It's then that the lit front, in the midst of an otherwise dark expanse, takes on the commanding glow of a landed mothership, from some science fiction epic. And it's then, too, that the truly serious mega-health devotees appear, pumping and pounding and heave-ho lifting with such a near-religious fervor, such an expert ab-by-ab near-artistry, that Michelangelo sculpting his perfected bodies out of perfect marble comes to mind . . . except that here, in their amazing conflation, these sweat-ennobled exercisers are both the sculptor *and* the torso chiseled into exquisitude.

Their arms and legs are the dream of a dream of vigor. Their hearts are dynamos. You can see in their serious frowns, and in the care of their self-study . . . they believe, or they hope, or at moments they know: they're going to live forever.

2.

See, the thing is, we *don't* learn from history. We barely even acknowledge it. Ours isn't a culture of husbanding and treasuring memorized lists of the ancestors dozens of generations deep. "Autobiography" first entered the English language in the first decade of the nineteenth century: ever since, it's been a pellmell immediatecentric rush from me-right-now to me-in-a-minute, and there's neither time nor room—or sensibility—for consulting the formative storage cells of the past.

The disastrous "quagmire" of Vietnam is spookily part of the human-scented smoke that floats in its heavy cover over the streets of the current "quagmire" in Iraq . . . but our eyes, though they do have vision, clearly aren't visionary, and ghosts that rise from the sands and cities of Yesteryear are no part of the wavelengths that we're wired to accept. The stupidass mistakes from the first marriage happen again—thrust and feint and snicker, parry and wail and duck—in the second and third. He may be petro-wealthier this circuit around, she may be a hotter higher-packed model, but obsolescence is built in just as surely as it was the first time, and the engine is as faulty.

"Not to know what happened before one was born is always to be a child": Cicero, about 50 B.C. We're indeed that child. "Within the wind tunnels of the high-speed electronic media, the time is always now; the data blow away or shred.. . . Not only do we lose track of our own stories (who we are, where we've been, where we might be going), but our elected representatives forget why sovereign nations go to war" (Lewis H. Lapham). Go ahead: ask my students who the Axis powers were, and who the Allies. It only requires one generation of nada transmission, and then . . . anything times zero is zero.

We don't, *don't* learn from history. Our will-to-live that has the girl with her legs blown off and her right arm severed . . . wriggling, still, with her left arm and her heaved back toward the safety of a shelter: that pulse in our plasmas can't afford a backward glance. The genes themselves are the accumulated past—but they can only point toward tomorrow.

336

So Dante died, and Shakespeare died, and my father now is two dates on a stone in a city—another Jewish ghetto—of dates-encumbered stone.. . . But we *don't*, don't learn from history, and my plasmas *know*: I'm not going to die. You think I will? There's no proof, and tomorrow is out there—a pair of empty my-size shoes—waiting to be stepped into.

3.

My friend Dean is king of the rowing machine. Then Dean does reps, then Dean does reps, then Dean does reps. By now his body is super-trained into such a durable hardness that it looks as if, when anyone else might have stepped out from the tanning booth, he's stepped out from a kiln.

He takes, he says, 147 vitamins and homeopathic supplements a day. A *day*. (How many shapes? How many colors?) "I wouldn't have time," my friend John said, "to sort them out of the bottles, much less pop them down." Well Dean, I imagine, can readily afford an assistant to tend to the sorting, or what's a trust fund for?

The wealth, the steel thews . . . *of course* his lover is, as the other exercise fanatics have anointed her, the Goddess Amanda. Men and women both—I've seen this happen—part to allow her divinity easy passage through the outer doors and then into the workout space. The die-for face, the roseate glow, the voluminous tawny hair like a simoom about her . . . *all* of that, down to the two small arcs of museum-quality toes . . . but what particularly apotheosizes her from out of this group of exemplary specimens is that her perfect silhouette, no matter what the activity—jogging, squatting, grunting (beautifully) into the thrusts of martial arts—will never move within itself by a single errant wink or jiggle, it's so all-over firm. She sits and crosses her legs, and the upper thigh won't spread by a millimeter.

This is the drive-you-crazy part: both of them are likeable. Generous friends, charity work, modest in company, blah-blah-blah. Together, they really do look like a duo descended on cloud-steeds from Olympus, as done in the aureate schmaltz of a gods-besotted Renaissance painter. And looks and treasure aside (and what is no doubt sex-to-a-higher-power aside), they truly care for each other. I've known him to drive twenty miles out of his way to get her a rose. Once: "If I lost him, I'd die," she whispered to me. I looked at her—how could she say that? Neither one of them was going to die.

337

4.

"So Dante died, and Shakespeare died.. . ." So saith Albert Goldbarth. (Surely even *our* short-term memories can call up the language in section 2.) Dickinson died, and Dickens died, and every anonymous Greek and Roman poet died, and Joanne Shmoe the performance-poet-whose-near-striptease-shenanigans-with-her-famous-slither-readings-on-open-mic-night died.. . .

The problem, for one such as me, of course is in loving them and their words, in making their wisdom a perfect secular fulfillment in the way that sacred knowledge fulfills so many others.

And dammit, one after another down the line . . . they know they're going to die, and they're casting a fishily jaundiced eye at my own denial. They somehow know that my childhood was a series of dead pet dimestore turtles, and none of them—not one—is going to let me slip around what this portends on the Goldbarthian level.

Me. Even *me*? But I'm the one who conjured up a soup restaurant to be called "The Brothel." A Jewish Oz full of "menschkins." A sundries store for Arctic explorers: "Store in a Cool Dry Place." A nude dance club: "Girls Before Swine." The universe wouldn't let *me* disappear . . .! I have more of these gems, I promise! Woody Allen: "Rather than live on in the hearts and minds of my fellow man, I'd prefer to live on in my apartment."

But Keats and Chaucer and Marianne Moore and Li Po and Neruda and Whitman know that every apartment is going to be for rent again. It may be the oldest knowledge to power literature. "I sing alas for youth, alas for curst age / —the approach of one, the passing of the other." "Be young, my heart, have fun: soon other men will take / my place, and I'll be dark dust in my grave." "No return to youth / is granted by the gods to mortal men, / and no escape from death." These, anonymous lyrics from the sixth to fifth centuries B.C.

Aren't I the one who's marched into class, and looked out at the pea-row undergraduate faces, and insisted to them that poetry is the mirror we hold up to see ourselves?

5.

I've broken my arm. In the middle of writing this I've slipped on the ice like any other susceptible little old man, and broken my upper right arm and set off a chain of difficult osseous complications up through the shoulder. Housebound, can't do much, so wind up looking through a drawer of old family photographs. There's my father, younger by thirty years than I am now, with the hat and pants and smile of the 1940s, there in the afternoon light of Humboldt Park. He's newly married, the smile says. The smile can't even *think* of the heart attack and the leukemia that are waiting in ambush decades later. His own father might well be alive still.

DEATH IS HEREDITARY, I hear myself thinking, and can't even tell if my talky subconscious has stumbled upon a profundity or burbled up another easy bumperstickerism.

And I'm reading—they're ever-fascinating—about the mummies. The ancient Babylonian dead preserved by immersion in honey. British naval hero Horatio Nelson immersed by his men, at sea, in a cask of brandy. Ancient mummies recovered from the cloud forests of the Peruvian Amazon: "Even the eyeballs and genitals are preserved." The famous wrinkled Dutch bog bodies, the webs of creases still delicate and traceable on their faces. The mummies of "incorruptible" saints in certain Italian churches, holding on to their living forms with the zealotry of Ahab holding on to Moby-Dick in death. From thirteenth century Lebanon, "a four-month-old infant, preserved down to the tiny wisps of hair between her toes"—these, likely, from the kiss of the grieving mother as she bent down. Sawing off the top of one Egyptian mummy's skull: inside, a scatter of curled-up rust-red maggots, mummified too, in the resins.

When we think of the maggots, think of the flesh flies laying their miniscule clutch of eggs in the damp of the brand-new corpse's open mouth, and what the hatchlings do as they feed their way in a pack through the muscle . . . no wonder there have been times and people dedicated to keeping the body as pure of this as possible.

And here's my father, a fossil of 1940s light on its little square. And here's my arm, on a practice journey, held still in its medical mummy wrap.

6.

Because of my arm I'm not out as much. But news like this accumulates a buzz that could work its way through a buried brick bunker. No one believes it. And still, they know, it's true. And so the buzz comes with a shock, with a resistance and yet a finality, that feel as if they have force behind them enough to someday lap, in a thinner but recognizable form, at the rims of other planets.

Dean is dead of a heart attack. It turns out the genes have a very large say in our destiny, and can't be filibustered out of their determination by a hectoring speech on fitness. At the funeral his fellow gymnauts stand around like figures on the tops of trophies, well-sculpted and eerily stiff. Is there a factory flaw invisibly somewhere in *them* too?

It turns out those ancient Greek lyrics are as contemporary as any hiphop anthem or TV cereal jingle. "I cannot prolong / my life, so why / should I cry or moan?" "The rose blooms for a brief season. It fades, / and when one looks again—the rose is a briar." "Musa the singing-girl lies here mute, / who was once so witty, so much loved." "And the old-of-death will pass their wine to the newly dead / and all will drink as equals."

Dean is dead—*Dean*! Is he sacrifice enough for a while? The rest of us—are we saved?

Hey, *I'm* the one who looked at the elastically swan-throated nudes of Modigliani's, and thought of a word for those models' deaths: neck-rology. I'm working out a joke that makes sense of the punch line SQUID PRO QUO. But it will require time, a lot of time. My mind is a work in progress. *Not, not, not, not me.* Surely fate respects the rule: survival of the wittest.

Well a week chugs past, with the usual. Bills. Some half-read books. A night out with friends, maneuvering food and drink with a left-handed willingness. Students. Mail. Dreams.

And then a phone call. A spike in the buzz, that one might well have seen coming but didn't, and now what? Wordless. Now, now what? Amanda is dead of an overdose.

7.

I've broken my arm. It happens only a few months after I start my treatments for macular degeneration. They showed me the scans: there on my left eye's retinal wall was the planet Mars. I could see its lit-up orange-red tint and its polar caps and its network of canals. This meant my macula was leaking.

It's true that they numb you up well. "Do it so you could bounce a dime off the surface," I always say, and they comply. But a needle injected into your eyeball is never desirable. I've had four of those treatments now, and while they aren't guaranteed to work, they've so far created a functioning containing wall against the insidious leakage.

In a week-and-a-half I'm scheduled for my second prostate biopsy: what they call the "PSA level" was what they call "elevated" (*uh-oh*) when my annual lab work got diagnosed. I remember the first of those, five years back: they numb you up for that too, but the microcarving of microslices out of the shrieking traumatized bloody middle of you . . . is never, ever desirable.

I'm sixty, and the warranty is expired, and the rest is baby aspirin, leafy greens, and luck.

Milton was blind, and Byron was lame, and Pope was hunched and in clenches of pain every day, and Virginia Woolf combated (sometimes with success, but sometimes yielding to its suffocations) darkness of a kind that maybe Sexton knew, Jane Kenyon knew, Sylvia Plath, and Hemingway at the end.. . .

And so? Not me. Not me. Woody Allen says, "I'm a firm believer that when you're dead, naming a street after you doesn't help your metabolism."

After a month, my arm gets unwrapped. The skin is a shade of whey and the muscle is atrophied. Time for physical therapy now—three times a week, as if my body does have a future worth suffering for, and there are (the weights . . . the elastic bands . . . the pulleys . . .) years of writing left. How's this:

Two squid walk into a bar.. . .

8.

He'd think they looked too thin, this man who struggled through Depression-era hunger; he'd ask if they wanted a little nosh.

So many of us (or even most, according to some polls) think it a credible scene, my father welcoming Dean and Amanda into heaven. Not me, and not my friends. Our sense of wonder (call it "awe" or "transcendence" or "being in touch with a higher plane" or, if you want, call it "spirituality") is as great as any believer's . . . but without the supernatural involved. It's the arts that often give us access to this feeling, they really do provide the transport and the deepening of religious faith.

Without, however, an afterlife. *That's* the catch. We won't buy into the silly literality of a fairy tale, a metaphor.

And even so, our sages are here, to counsel us on days when death's demoralizing shadow slinks out of its hole and puddles across our path on its way to some engagement.

I love particularly Whitman's rousing and rhapsodic, philosophically oopy-goopy, and strategically fine-milled paean to his sense of "what's beyond," his poem "The Sleepers," in which death and sleep and night and ocean and womb and cosmic mother are so masterfully equated, are so much a part of a cyclic, recombinant process. "Why should I be afraid to trust myself to you? . . . I know not how I came of you and I know not where I go with you, but I know I came well and shall go well." There's a course I teach in which I devote twelve class-hours to the parsing of this poem.

And I teach the ancient Greek poets, so heartfelt in their adjurations to squeeze the humanistic most from the time we *do* have here—to press from it a sufficiency. "Eros, put your work clothes on. / While I live, bring flowers/ and my lovely mistress." "Being mortal / I cannot prolong / my life, so why / should I cry or moan? / Bring sweet wine, / bring my good friends. / I'll lie on a soft bed / and be lost in love." "I don't mourn those who are gone from the sweet light. / I mourn those who waste their sweet light in mourning."

There are undergraduate students I like, who trust me—as I trust them—in the back-and-forth of extracurricular banter. One day I notice a woman whose shorts and top reveal her knees and elbows to be rubbed pinkly raw, and I raise my eyebrows inquiringly. "Oh . . . rug burns from some sex last night." "Ah," pipes up the voice of my sub-conscious, "carpet diem."

9.

The corner gym was shut for a week, a sign of elegiac respect for its two most exemplary charter members. My arm is freed from its bondage on the day the gym reopens; and that night I get to pass it again, like al-ways, when I resume my walking. There it is: that lit cube, as if all of the strenuous exercise on display were converted immediately to the wattage that displays it. How could I *not* look, how could I *not* come close? Anybody would be a moth for this compelling engine-room of lonely illumination.

Out of all of them, tonight it's the ones on the rowing machines who hold my attention. The building appears to be theirs alone. Rowing . . . rowing . . . building up ohms . . . in unison, I could swear to that. Row-ing.. . .

I stand there, shadowed away, and I watch them circle their oars through the thickness of night, with such intensity, such perseverance . . . rowing.. . . I feel the block tug at its mooring. Then the rope is cast off. The neighborhood is moving, into the dark, to the stars, in a steady rhythm . . . rowing . . . into the unknown, into its current, into our fears and expectations.

342

NOTES

Heather Pringle's *The Mummy Congress*. "Preamble" in the first issue of Lewis Lapham's *Lapham's Quarterly*. Inspiration from the Greek translations of Willis Barnstone, Dudley Fitts, Richard Lattimore, Kenneth Rexroth. Wayne Zade helped with the Woody Allen quotes. Skyler Lovelace and John Crisp helped with the broken arm.

Nominated by Fleda Brown, Richard Burgin

GRACE NOTES

by NANCY MITCHELL

from GREEN MOUNTAINS REVIEW

Is that a cardinal's song so doleful
or the clock's battery wearing down?

Said she'd *try* to meet him for a drink,
but the cat curls so warm against her hip,

the hot tea has cooled just enough
to sip, the laptop sits so squarely

in her lap, and there, out the window,
what bird is it that doesn't fly upward

so much as is lifted from ground
to branch by an invisible hand?

Easier to find a four leaf clover
in a nettle patch than linen pants

on line for him- *no, not yellow,*
more a golden rod-

36 waist, he can have them
taken in when he gets thinner.

There's no finding him the shirts, too,
only blue just this side of sea breeze

as anything else will wash him out,
and *please, no three quarter sleeves.*

Like the rusted hinge of the picket
fence gate she left unlatched

coming in from getting the mail,
wings of passing geese creak.

Is their falling shit the velocity
of snow or rain or leaf?

Pines cast out shadows; further
from noon, longer the reach across the lawn.

What sense, now, in getting dressed
up, eyeliner, lipstick, without which

she's *plainer than a marsh hen.*
How the Kleenex wads flock

at her feet like small sheep grazing
the carpet. It's Phillip Glass in her ear

buds again, smearing the greens,
blurring the hours clean.

Nominated by Green Mountains Review, Dzvinia Orlowsky

FATHER OLUFEMI

fiction by TIM O'SULLIVAN

from A PUBLIC SPACE

There seemed to be a fellow feeling between the priest and bus driver, each too slight for his uniform. Father Olufemi was on the last notch of his belt, twenty-five pounds lighter after fretting and then convalescing from hip resurfacing surgery. The driver's collar was over-starched, stiff as cardboard and too wide for his thin neck. His sleeves extended to his knuckles, and his billowing shirt hid any indication of upper-body strength, but he handled Father Olufemi's heavy suitcase easily enough—bent at the knees and waist and pushed it into the luggage compartment—as if in demonstration.

"Thank you," Father Olufemi said. He squeezed the handles of his walker, flexing his uncrippled arms, and his mouth watered with a sort of envy. One forgets, until crippled again, the miracle of joints and the easy dexterity of a healthy body.

"That's his?" the driver asked Father Murphy.

Father Murphy had settled into daydreaming despondency. Startled, he took a step back from the duffel bag at his feet, and the driver took the bag onto the bus. The gloss of his black leather shoes reflected the depot's fluorescent lights at the bottom of the steps and the cabin's yellow lights at the top. That he or someone took pride in his appearance seemed to presage a safe journey

"I think he's my doppelgänger, Father Murphy."

"Doppelgänger? No, Father. Your doppelgänger? We don't accept that belief." Father Murphy placed his hand beside Father Olufemi's on the walker. "My balance," he said and shooed with his free hand at nothing in particular. "It's not fair a young man is given this and

346

I'm left to stand on my feet." For the last month, Father Olufemi had been chaperoned by the seventy-three-year-old. Left to his daydreams, the old man could have remained upright for days, not so much standing as hanging from airy thoughts. Alertness made him woozy. The day after Father Olufemi's roommate Herbert was moved to the ICU with pneumonia, Father Murphy lay for five hours in the man's bed before an orderly came for the sheets. And at the rectory of Saint Stephen's Church, where Father Olufemi moved a few days after the surgery, Father Murphy reclined whenever possible in the chair near the TV. When he had to stand, he invariably leaned against the nearest sturdy object, so Father Olufemi didn't presume Father Murphy's hand next to his was a gesture of intimacy. He patted the old man's wrist.

"I've never been to Ohio," Father Murphy said.

"I'll send you pictures."

"I'd prefer a letter. I can't hold onto photographs." Father Murphy rubbed his thumb and index finger together, and opened his void palm. "They just go, I can't find them. If you like taking photographs, include them with your letters, if you come across anything interesting."

The driver returned. "How shall we?" he said and offered his hand to Father Olufemi. They approached the bus together, two professionally dressed men in their late thirties, balding. Red hair wreathed the driver's head, which couldn't have been paler or more stubbornly non-reflective under the fluorescent lights. Father Olufemi's head was shaved, but it was obvious where his hair did and did not grow, and it did not grow almost exactly where the driver's hair did not grow. From brow to crown, the dark skin of Father Olufemi's scalp gleamed, unblemished, as if poreless.

Chandra Jackson, his visiting nurse at the rectory, hadn't missed a chance to remind Father Olufemi that bus travel in his condition was a mistake—even in the elevator ride down from his room, she'd done so—but she would have been impressed to see the driver help her former patient up the steep steps and usher him to the front aisle seat on the passenger side with more patience than most of her colleagues would have shown. She would have been satisfied he took the lives in his charge seriously and, had she been there on the floor of the depot, she would have blown Father Olufemi a kiss, like the one she'd blown him outside the rectory.

Father Murphy had witnessed the nurse's kiss. In her absence, he blew one of his own.

Father Olufemi smiled but stifled any laughter. His body was tender, doing its mystery, and he'd adopted a doctrine of stillness.

The old man's forehead crinkled as he grinned and, just like that—something clicked, his green eyes became a shade brighter—he was in a daze again. He waved and turned to go. He might have shuffled away with the walker if the driver hadn't returned and, in front of forty waiting passengers, asked whether it belonged to him. Father Murphy handed the thing over with his usual nodding deference before continuing to his car, a baby-blue Cadillac called Bertha. He was lanky. He did keep one photo in his wallet, which he'd shown to Father Olufemi. He and his sister wore lobster-emblazoned aprons some thirty years ago, standing in front of a large silver pot. In his youth, he'd been imperiously tall. He was hunched now. His wide hips reeled with each step.

Two young men took the seats across the aisle, about a foot back from Father Olufemi's seat. "I hope I haven't delayed the trip," Father Olufemi said, craning just far enough to see them. "I wanted to be early. You can see I'm moving slowly. Still, I think we're on time."

The young men didn't know what to make of his Nigerian accent. The thick-faced one in the aisle seat looked at the driver, as if for clarification, but the driver was busy trying to fit the walker into the overhead shelving.

"It's only temporary," Father Olufemi said, gesturing to the walker. "Maybe you can keep a secret. I don't plan to use it."

"Better be careful," said the one in the window seat. He had a narrow face scattered with pimples and a long snout like a weasel. His shoulder-length brown hair was pristine, well-washed and brushed, and descended to a grass-stained white T-shirt. "My mom's a nurse," he said.

"Here in Boston? It's a wonderful city. I wish I had more time to explore it."

"About an hour north of here. You wouldn't know it. She doesn't come down here for anything."

"It's peaceful here. All day out my window I saw people walking nice and slowly, and all I wanted was a long walk."

"Yeah," the young man said unconvincingly. More confidently he added, "If they gave you a walker, you'd better use it. I saw a man fall out of his hospital bed because he wouldn't let a nurse help him to the restroom. He fell on his face, broke out his teeth, and got a big bruise on his face, like a raccoon. That was my grandfather." The young man smiled nostalgically. "He died in the hospital with a big raccoon bruise on his face."

The thick-faced one had taken to watching his own hands wrestle on his lap, as if his hands were peculiar. A scar interrupted his right eyebrow, and his short-cropped black hair did nothing to hide three pink penny-sized scars on his head. He turned to Father Olufemi, his expression full of canine mistrust, and the two acknowledged—if unwittingly—the odd things people say and the odd places to which discussions lead.

"Are you going far?" Father Olufemi said.

"Not me," the thick-faced one said.

"Well, yeah," the other said. "I have a cousin in San Antonio who's got some work for me. You probably don't know where that is."

"Texas!" Father Olufemi said.

"You're not going to Texas, are you, Reverend?"

"Thank goodness, no. I don't know if I could make it that far. I'm stopping in Ohio."

The young man nodded and looked at his seatmate. The two appeared to be strangers. Still, Father Olufemi got the impression he'd interrupted their conversation. Virtually everyone he'd met in the States had asked where he was from, but the young men didn't. Just as well. There was a desperation about people who spilled their life stories onto strangers, and it was his habit to do just that.

The driver, still trying to force the walker into the overhead shelving, cursed so loudly a spray of spittle escaped his lips. Anyone could see the space was too small, but he kept trying. The walker's legs tangled in the thin netting meant to keep luggage from falling. Father Olufemi looked ahead at the brick wall of the bus depot, not wanting to provoke him, though he could see in the windshield a reflection of the man as he yanked violently and freed the walker only to slam it into the ceiling and stand there a moment, the walker held over his head, as if contemplating whether to bring it down on the priest's head—so it seemed in the windshield and so it must have appeared to others on the bus. A woman gasped. Father Olufemi crossed his arms over his head just as the flimsy metal thing crashed down into the window seat beside him. "There," the driver said. He rolled his sleeves to his elbows and for several minutes slouched in his seat on the other side of a thick pane of plastic, gripping the steering wheel—red-faced, hands thick-veined—and stared at the brick wall of the bus depot. Perhaps it had been inappropriate to accept so much assistance. When the driver peered into the rearview mirror and caught him watching, Father Olufemi turned away, back in the direction of Father Murphy's car. It was gone. Father Olufemi hadn't traveled widely He scanned the depot for a sign of the Cadillac, struck by how abruptly his new acquaintances had disappeared.

Everyone seemed excited to be setting off. The cabin was loud with conversation. They drove west out of Boston into the Berkshires, toward the Appalachians. Father Olufemi tried to sleep, but the sun shone brightly off the snow and the pain in his hip was constant. Sitting straight was the least agonizing posture. At the the rectory, Nurse Chandra Jackson had strapped his legs to an abduction pillow to prevent careless movements, and he'd felt safer knowing he couldn't kick in his sleep. He wanted now for her to appear at his seat with a tray of ugly food and a green cup of water, sit near him as she had at his bedside, and ramble about her hardships: her brother Hoby shot and killed at the age of sixteen, the family dog found hung from the lamppost a month ago, and the jobless husband she rarely saw. Father Olufemi suspected she stole stories from neighbors. How many dying men had heard her troubles and thought it all seemed a bit much, but listened if only to enjoy the movement of her lips? And then she'd say, "You should stay in Boston just another week, Father. I don't like the idea of you traveling so soon. Why are you blushing?" Father Olufemi thanked her for her concern, but he felt fine. He hadn't expected to be anxious to leave, but he was, in part to get away from Nurse Chandra Jackson. She'd developed feelings for him, he thought—or had at least become infatuated with his long eyelashes and smooth skin, which she referenced continually. "Why are you blushing, Father Olufemi? You think I have a crush on you?"

Interstate 90 was smoothly paved, the toasty cabin was a relief—since the surgery, he'd developed a fear of shivering—and God seemed to have pinned each town to the earth with half a dozen church spires. Father Olufemi leaned his head back and closed his eyes and imagined what welcome awaited him at his destination. The Catholic Diocese of Toledo had paid for his flight from Abuja to Boston, his surgery, the cost of his monthlong convalescence, the walker, and the bus ticket to Halfestus, Ohio, where he'd agreed to preside for three years over the parish of a Father Krinkle. It was probably unhealthy to imagine what his welcomers would think. He was replacing a priest accused of child molestation. He was as dark as could be and, from the photos he'd found on the Internet, the people of Halfestus were as white as could be. He'd arrive a cripple.

At least this last bit would improve. He would heal. He was growing again. His pelvis was grafting to the rough-textured backside of a titanium socket, perfectly sized to fit a titanium cap on the head of his femur. It would take months, but one day he'd stand at the pulpit and raise his arms—a man upright, his limbs deliriously functional—and proclaim, "This is the day of the Lord."

But who was this man, proclaiming? He'd never been this man. He'd never been as helpless as he was now, being carted across a foreign continent to a foreign town. He should have felt confident; Bishop Kelechi himself had recommended him for the post in Halfestus. Yet he was terribly anxious. The young men across the aisle seemed friendly enough, but he didn't intend to look in their direction for the rest of the trip. Despite a terrible thirst, each time the bus stopped at a service station and the doors opened and a wintry gust thinned the air, he failed—out of simple fearful shyness—to ask them to bring him water.

The higher the bus traveled, the more snow had accumulated until there was not a speck of green out the windows. Flailing oaks and maples were left behind; conifers stood stiff and apart like gentlemen. All the valleys and even a river two hundred feet below a bridge were white, too cold for color. He'd not imagined this much snow on Mount Everest, much less in Pennsylvania, which he'd never imagined. He wrapped his arms in a green blanket from the hospital gift shop, feeling older than his thirty-eight years, and stared at the road; behind a gray scrim the sun slipped below the horizon and left a twilight gloom so whole it was hard to imagine sunlight shining on other parts of the earth. The driver's bald pate darkened; his hands took a blue pallor from the lighted dashboard gauges.

Father Olufemi eavesdropped now and then on the conversation of the young men. The thick-faced one had just been released from Massachusetts's Walpole State Penitentiary. His family had abandoned him, he said. He spoke softly. Father Olufemi had to strain to hear. They'd all come to visit just once. He didn't know if any of them would be waiting when the bus dropped him off, and he didn't blame them. His voice became more animated when he talked about the men he'd been forced to live with for two years. He spoke of a man called Caldwell who'd begged the guards for antidepressants to help him sleep through his sentence. At night Caldwell told stories about crimes and infidelities. He'd tried to steal a motorcycle by driving it off someone's porch but didn't notice the chain connecting the motorcycle to a pipe; he woke in the yard, missing teeth, two policemen standing over him. He'd had sex with his girlfriend's mother—spun her like a top, he said, because her legs ended at the knees. The ex-convict laughed as he told the stories.

The long-haired one responded with stories of his family. His mother had been a nurse in a nursing home just about her whole life. His father constantly lent money to people he shouldn't have. His sister had married a man despite the man's near-deafness. Whereas the ex-convict had spoken softly, almost intimately, the long-haired one spoke loudly of his family's stoicism and generosity. Father Olufemi knew the young man wanted him to hear; it was a common reaction to his collar.

"I'll miss them," the long-haired one said. "I don't know my family in Texas all that well."

"Your cousin has a job for you at least," the ex-convict said. "I wish my family had a job for me."

"What did you do?"

"Delivered food to restaurants."

"I mean why did you go to prison?"

At the edge of his vision, Father Olufemi saw the ex-convict's right hand squeeze the fingers of his left hand. "I want to have dinner," the young man said. "I hope there's dinner when I get home. I haven't had time to think about what I'm doing, and that's what I need to think about." But immediately he began speaking about his time in the penitentiary again, not his own story so much as the stories of the men he'd known—the crimes they'd been caught for and the crimes they'd gotten away with, stories about their wives and girlfriends and children.

Father Olufemi prayed for the young man with great concentration, determined to make the prayer a distraction from the growing pain in his midsection, which formed like something smooth and hard with no limit to its growth. Prayer wasn't working. Ever since he was a child, Father Olufemi had liked to consider the body as something of an antenna, every bone and pound of flesh built by God to project and receive signals. But it was as if his new metal parts—the head of the femur, the socket—had ruined his connection. Not that he believed a direct communication could exist, but he'd always considered himself attuned. Now that feeling seemed childish. He unclasped his hands and gripped his biceps with bruising force, another inadequate distraction. His winsome stare induced the long-haired young man to interrupt his seatmate and ask, "Reverend, do you need assistance to the restroom?"

Father Olufemi turned. He tried to don an authentic smile, but his lip twitched.

The young man's elbow bent over his head like a question mark as he dug through his hair to scratch the back of his neck. A pink rash covered the underside of his arm. His hair was strikingly smooth and shiny.

The ex-convict stared at his lap again. What could this shy young man have done? It couldn't have been murder. Burglary perhaps, a crime less reprehensible than most. Two years seemed like a harsh punishment for burglary. Perhaps he'd stolen something valuable, a vehicle or jewelry.

"The restroom," the young man said. "Do you need help to the restroom?"

"No, no, thank you. I'll wait until the bus stops moving." Father Olufemi tried to laugh—it came out in a deep bleat. The more persistent the pain, the more nervous he became. Between the legs of the walker lay the duffel bag. He removed his Bible and placed it on his lap, if for no other reason than to seem occupied, then removed his painkillers. He popped one into his mouth and, agreeing now with Nurse Chandra Jackson that bus travel was a risky venture, he bit another in half and swallowed it. The pill-and-a-half lodged in his dry throat and descended slowly. On the highway, white divider dashes approached and, at the last moment, hurtled silently by. He tried to focus on the illusion of their movement as he waited for the pain to recede, but he couldn't concentrate. Just when his mind settled on something other than pain and remaining still, his body seemed lighter than air, a balloon, so light it might float up and whoosh through the cracked window to twirl in the bus's wake. The next moment his head became heavy, lulled and reeled delightfully from one shoulder to the other, and a string of drool descended to his chest. His eyebrows rose at the conversation of the young men and at the smells of the people and the worn upholstery and the lavatory at the rear as he half-dreamed of Nurse Chandra Jackson, who'd ironed his clothes and shaved his head the night before, so he would look nice for his new parish. The razor cleared hair and shaving cream from the right side of his head, and she rested her hand there to keep him still as she shaved the left side. Her perfume was strong, a smell like strawberry. She was telling him, again, he didn't have to travel until he was ready, and he didn't have to go anywhere he didn't want to go. He said he was more than ready to go. The razor lifted from his head in midsweep. She liked to act offended.

"You look like a wire hanger in that priest suit, Mr. Skin-and-Bones," she said. She rested her hand on his shoulder and let it linger. For an instant, the pain left his body. He felt not like a priest. Every bit of what he'd been escaped in an exhalation, and he was left without history or restriction. "You're a brave man," she said. "That town will love you."

After shaving his head, she went to work with a file on his fingernails. She sighed. "You'll never write. You'll never visit."

Ten rows back, Jason had slept through the day though his father had instructed him to wait until night. He woke occasionally to peek at his father in the window seat reading a book about World War II, and to look at the strange man across the aisle. To fight off the sun, the man had unbuttoned his shirt, exposing a doughy stomach and chest, then buttoned the shirt back up over his face so his black pelt of hair appeared where his neck should have been. As if teasing dumbstruck onlookers, he unbuttoned just the second button from the top, to let his beak of a nose stick out for air. The bottom of his shirt rose to his navel as he raised his arms, placing his hands behind his head. Soon he was snoring—a three-second inhalation and a three-second exhalation, consistent—as if his stertor were proof of proficient breathing. Throughout the day, Jason enjoyed waking occasionally to the sight of the man's nose; the sound helped him sleep in the same way the oscillating fan did at home. But after dark, when it seemed only the boy and the beak-nosed man were awake—never mind the man now wore his shirt properly—his pink face and red beak exposed under a reading light agitated the boy. And the man's giggles frightened him. At first, the sound was too soft to recognize, but it grew. He must have wanted people—or at least Jason—to hear, to think he was reacting to something in the magazine. Jason knew it was a trick. The man's gaze passed through the magazine, set on something distant. He wasn't giggling at what the words said. He giggled at his own thoughts, and each outburst began and ended without buildup or diminishment, as if a window were sliding open to an endless sound.

Jason left his seat. He knew there was an empty seat up the aisle, beside the black man in black pants and a black shirt. Since he and his father had boarded the bus in Albany, he had been interested in the man and in the metal contraption beside him. He patted the man's knee as he slid past. There was no response. "Faker," he said and climbed into the window seat, maneuvering himself between the legs of the walker. "I know you're awake." He patted the man's knee much harder.

The glare of oncoming headlights illuminated the man's long eyelashes and the ant-hole pores in his cheeks. The boy gripped the legs of the walker as if they were prison bars and screamed, "Let me out! I'm in jail. Let me out! Let me out!" A woman many rows back and the bus driver a few feet away yelled for him to quiet down. The beak-nosed man, whom no one dared to reprimand, let erupt a high-pitched giggle. If the commands of the woman and the bus driver weren't enough, the giggle was, and the boy slunk into his seat, imagining for a moment each passenger falling into a sleep so deep no one would wake no matter what madness the beak-nosed man committed.

The man sighed. Jason reached over and pinched his wrist as hard as he could, digging his fingernails into the skin. The man winced, and Jason gripped the walker's legs and said more softly, "I'm trapped! I'm in jail, and they won't let me out."

The scrape of his own manicured nails against his scalp awakened Father Olufemi to a calm, disorienting darkness. "I'm not traveling far," he muttered. In his dream someone had said, or there had been the conception, that the earth was a drop of water, there were no long journeys. The bus's destinations faced the stars at unique angles because the earth was so small, its curvature so acute. They came to the summit of a hill and drove down the other side.

"Aren't you going to ask my name?" whispered Jason.

Father Olufemi turned to find himself caught in the wide-eyed gaze of a chubby boy—about six years old.

"I'm Jason. What's your name?"

"John," Father Olufemi said, examining his wrist. He opened his mouth in a silent roar to wake his face. "Where are we?" he said, worried Halfestus had come and gone. "What time is it?"

"I'm going to Seattle to live with my mom," Jason said. "My dad's going to take me to her front porch. Then he's turning right around and going back to Albany."

"Does your father know where you are?"

Jason frowned. "He's a policeman. He's here on the bus, right near us. He's asleep now, but I can wake him up."

"You don't need to do that."

"What's that about?" Jason said, referring to the Bible on Father Olufemi's lap. Father Olufemi handed it over. Jason placed the spine between his legs and opened the book.

Father Olufemi cleared his dry throat. "It's about many things."

Jason crossed his arms and stuck out his bottom lip. "No one tells me the stories in books." He didn't look angry, only practicing anger, arranging the softer simulacra of his parents' lineaments—the dark brown eyes, the thin eyebrows—into something resembling his parents' anger. He squeezed the leather-bound book to his chest and stomach. "I can read it," he said. In the dark, he traced his fingers over the words of Leviticus 7. "It's about Goopy Goos. They landed on a planet in their spaceship. Then they took off again and landed in Seattle. They shot all the gangsters." Jason paused and pressed his finger against a word, where he'd left off. "Are you going to Seattle?" he asked.

"I'm stopping in Halfestus, Ohio."

"Hey what, Ohio?"

Father Olufemi smiled. There'd been little to glean on the Internet. He'd found the high school's website with pictures of sports teams and game schedules, a park concert series calendar from the previous summer, and pictures of sheep at a fair.

For half an hour, they passed the Bible back and forth. Father Olufemi read bits from the Book of Samuel he thought the boy would like, and Jason read a whole new rendering of ancient events, full of gangsters and guns and spaceships. Eventually, he didn't need the Bible. He closed the book and continued the story, adding Father Olufemi as a character. "The police are after you," he said. "They're coming from Alabama for you."

"No, no," Father Olufemi said. "No one is after anyone."

"They cut off all your hair because you have lice."

"No, no. I like it this way." Father Olufemi tilted his head, and Jason touched his scalp. "You see? It's very smooth. A pretty nurse in Boston shaved it."

"Did you like her?"

"I didn't know her well. Come, let's read more stories."

Jason leaned away from Father Olufemi, against the armrest. "I'm bored of that," he said, and closed his eyes.

"Are you going to sleep?" Father Olufemi said. "Jason?"

The boy smiled. His whole body shook as he held back giggles.

"You're pretending," Father Olufemi said.

But soon the boy calmed and did fall asleep, and Father Olufemi turned in the direction of the young men. The long-haired young man lay with his boot heels against the armrest and his hands cushioning his head against the window. His eyes were on Father Olufemi, as if he'd been waiting for the priest to look his way. "Found a new friend, huh?" he said. "My guy got off a while ago. Talker. Serious one. I'll get some sleep now. All I needed was this two feet of space."

Father Olufemi wanted to ask if anyone had arrived to greet the ex-convict but didn't want to show he'd been eavesdropping.

"He's finding out who his friends are. You were fast asleep. Snoring." The young man smirked. The darkness seemed to have emboldened him. "There was a big old blonde girl waiting for him. I don't get the feeling she was family. He hugged her so hard she about had to beat him away. He's home at least, I guess."

"Imagine if no one had been there," Father Olufemi said.

"Then no one would have been there—it wouldn't have happened, so it wouldn't have taken up any time at all." The young man stopped talking, perhaps thinking of the family he'd left behind. Father Olufemi couldn't help wondering whether the cousin in San Antonio had under-estimated the young man's willingness to travel so far for a job, or whether the job was really worth the trip. At a stop in western Penn-sylvania, the young man jogged into a service station and brought back a bottled water for Father Olufemi. "You were sounding a little hoarse, Reverend," he said. "Got to take care of yourself." Every other pas-senger seemed to be asleep, each headed across the country to new lives or to visit friends and family they hadn't seen for years. There was a generosity in the profession of a driver, Father Olufemi thought, even as he noticed their driver's head was disconcertingly still.

The pane of plastic behind the driver reminded Father Olufemi of Pope John Paul II's visit to Nigeria in 1998 to beatify the deceased Father Cyprian Michael Iwene Tansi. The pope arrived in the bed of a truck, surrounded by panes of plastic, and made no movements that Father Olufemi could see from an elevated platform at the back of the crowd, where he and other young clergy watched the truck inch along the dusty road. The pope clenched handles attached to the truck's cab and stooped forward, standing despite his infirmity and the white chair behind him. The rumble of a hundred thousand spectators seemed to will the vehicle's progress. There was the sense that, had he not been so stubborn, had he simply taken a seat in the white chair, the spell would have broken—the crowd would have calmed, the rumble would have ceased, the truck would have stopped. But he was a stubborn man. He scanned the multitudes, a measured smile above his rumpled chin. The plastic seemed to protect him more from the weight of the crowd's hopes than from anything else. Forever afterward Father Olufemi tried to distinguish the message in the pope's eyes. Have Courage? Have Patience? Be Good to Your People?

In the middle of the night, the driver asked everyone to return to their seats, referring to a man in the aisle speaking with a friend. The man wasn't speaking loudly. Father Olufemi would have preferred something be done about the pair of snoring passengers behind him, and he got his wish when the driver raised his voice. "Everyone please sit down!" he said, and the snoring stopped.

"I'm only stretching my legs," the man said.

"Everyone needs to be seated."

"He's not doing anything wrong," another passenger said. "You're the one being loud, and we're trying to sleep."

"Everyone needs to shut up and be seated!"

"Who are you telling to shut up?!" a deep voice said from the back of the bus.

"I'm asking all of you to please be quiet. Not you. Not her. Everyone. I'm taking you all where you need to go, and I'm trying to do so on time." He had started off in a conciliatory tone, but his own words inspired him. "I don't come to your job and harass you. Don't harass me. Go to sleep or read your books. Whatever you do, do it. Just don't behave like children." He accelerated drastically enough for the man in the aisle to fall backward. The bus listed toward the roadside, so subtly it could have been an oversight. The tires met the warning track and went a foot beyond, dangerously close to the snow and ice piled against the guardrail. All rejoinders died away as the bus drifted back to the center of the lane, veered to the warning track a second time, and again came within inches of the guardrail before righting itself. It was unclear whether the driver was showing who was in control or was suffering a nervous attack.

Each time the bus reached the edge of the roadway and the tires struck the bumps of the warning track, Father Olufemi's body went stiff with pain, and a soft grunt escaped him.

"It's okay," Jason said. He placed his hand on Father Olufemi's tensed forearm and looked up into Father Olufemi's face and gritted his teeth the way Father Olufemi was doing, as if trying to learn the expression.

The bus passed onto a bridge and struck an uneven lip. Some things were always new. Each shot of pain was powerful enough to wipe away the last, and each seemed more intense than the last. As if the pain were electricity that could be conducted through and out of his body, he grabbed the plastic armrest with one hand and squeezed the cushion near his thigh with the other. He tried surface after surface. He squeezed the blanket and the Bible, he placed his hands on his head to make a complete circuit, and finally he gripped Jason's shoulder a little harder than he should have, and Jason let out a yelp.

Father Olufemi retrieved the painkillers from his duffel bag on the floor, popped the prescribed one, then another, and a third, and washed them down with the water the young man had brought him. He concentrated again on the white hash marks and the reflectors between them, waiting for the pain to disperse and hoping the pills would calm him—his breathing—and allow him to sleep.

"I hate how slow it is," he whispered.

"How slow what is?" Jason said. The boy seemed aware of the danger as the bus listed to the side of the highway a third time, but he was already falling back asleep. "Don't worry," he said, an entirely inappropriate patience in his voice. "It's okay." And it was. The man in the aisle returned to his seat. The driver regained his senses. The bus remained in its lane and, satisfied that whatever had happened had ended, passengers quietly recounted the event and even laughed at the strangeness of it before turning their heads and closing their eyes.

The interstate was well-lit by tall lamps. In the darkness beyond, the shadowy humps of the Appalachians, like giant ocean waves, seemed to flow with infinitesimal progress east; perhaps it wasn't just an illusion of the moving bus. In the sky, an airplane's navigation lights blinked faintly. Up there, the clouds were led by the sky's currents. Between Massachusetts and Nigeria, ocean water followed the ocean's currents. And land moved too. A hundred lifetimes couldn't notice, but it moved.

The headlights came upon dark potholes. The bus shuddered over a rough patch of road and passed a blue sign with the orange shape of a roughly chiseled heart on it and the words "Welcome to Ohio: The Birthplace of Aviation." The flimsy metal walker rattled and seemed to communicate something sensible in its squeaking gibberish, and Jason murmured a response in his sleep. Father Olufemi clenched the armrests in preparation, but there was no grinding pain. He was sure there were spasms shooting through his body, powerful enough to blow the bus in two, but he couldn't feel them. Everyone remained sleeping, or at least pretended to, and he felt nothing. He half-suspected them all, including himself, of deceitfulness. The pain had to be there somewhere.

In the abstract, his pain was a productive, healing pain. His bones were growing. Again he fantasized about the pulpit. He didn't imagine the words, just himself strong, raising his arms. Perhaps there was a benefit to his weakness. Perhaps he could become a new man, he thought as he rubbed his smooth head. When he was nine years old he'd carried a smooth eyeball-sized marble in his pocket. During rainy days at Saint Vincent's Mission School, he sat beneath the veranda of the chapel rubbing his knee with one hand and kneading the marble between the thumb and fingers of the other. His knee felt damp and the polished marble, clear with a milky cataract inside, felt strangely bedewed, as if the sensations of dryness and dampness had nothing to do with water and everything to do with texture. He'd been told he was lucky to have baby skin because it meant he would age gracefully. He sat on a stool under the chapel veranda and rubbed the soft skin of his knee and kneaded the marble and watched the rain pelt the lawn and waited to see a connection between knee, marble, and lawn.

He looked down at Jason. The boy's mouth was open against the armrest. "Jason," Father Olufemi whispered.

He wanted to see where he was being taken but felt himself descending into sleep. It didn't feel like dreaming. His sleep was too complete, he was too conscious within it. He'd read that sleep was important to the collection and prioritization of memories, and now it was as if he were an archivist alone in a giant library. One would never have the time to read even a small percentage of the books, but there were few greater luxuries than a couple of hours to walk among the stacks—his pain cataloged and forgotten—and occasionally take down a tome no one had checked out for two decades.

"We can't have you thinking so much, Father Olufemi. Finish your wine and tell Mr. Geni when we will see an African pope in the Vatican." Mrs. Ogunye clapped her palms together, and a flash of light drew her guests' eyes to the large diamond on her wedding ring. "Father Olufemi is too interesting of a conversationalist to let wither in his own thoughts. You'll have to encourage him, Mr. Geni, or he'll become lost. Azi! Fill Father Olufemi's glass. We aren't relying solely on you for entertainment, Father Olufemi, but Mr. and Mrs. Geni and Mr. Ogunye and I have nearly talked each other to death. We bore each other to tears, don't we, Mrs. Geni?"

"I've had the perfect amount," Father Olufemi said. His glass was filled. He gripped it by the stem and took a swill that left wine dripping from his chin onto his white shirt. Quickly he placed the glass down but did not place it stably, and it fell toward him. A stream of wine flowed to the edge of the table and onto his lap. He stood immediately to brush himself off. Azi came with a cloth napkin, but Father Olufemi excused himself to the second-floor bathroom, which was the one he preferred. He liked how the hot water and cold water sprang from separate faucets and fed into channels, meeting and pouring into the sink before reaching a common temperature, and how the mildewed hand towels smelled of manure, and he liked the bathroom's proximity to the sleeping quarters. After washing, he entered his hosts' bedroom to peel back the covers and ran his nose an inch above the sheets and pillows, barely sniffing, waiting for the smells to rise. He smelled rubber and licorice, though neither Mr. nor Mrs. Ogunye smelled like rubber or licorice.

Back at dinner, he prayed and blessed the food, as requested. The memory of the smell entertained him throughout the meal. As Mrs. Ogunye leaned over to speak with Mrs. Geni; as Mr. Ogunye speckled his chicken with pepper, Father Olufemi, garrulous with wine, said "Rest assured," and described three Africans who'd held the papacy during Roman times, African by birth at least. He closed his eyes, concentrated, and could almost smell the Ogunyes again. The smell of a body was interesting, and the smell of bodies combined was a great thrill, like peeking not into their individual souls but into the soul of their union, a smell the lovers themselves couldn't detect. He opened his eyes and continued, "But if what you mean is the first black pope, rest assured, there will be a black pope within fifty years, within my lifetime, and within yours. I truly believe so, so strongly I almost know."

Later, he could muster no enthusiasm when Mrs. Ogunye showed the guests a chair and a painting she'd purchased that day. The colors of fabric, the pliancy of cushions, the details of chair legs and armrests—these things depended on one's mood at the instant of purchase. Or worse, these things depended on one's aesthetic. There was no mystery in the man-made. A chair was a chair. A picture hung in every house. If she could have, Mrs. Ogunye would have given up everything she was for what she wanted to be. She would have exchanged her rose-and-cowhide scent for something subtler. She would have chosen finer toes and fingers and lips and a body thirty pounds lighter so she wouldn't have to hide her outpourings of flesh under loose dresses.

"Why are you smiling, Father Olufemi?" Mrs. Ogunye said. She was possessive even in his dreams—and even of his dreams. She noticed his mind wander, pulled toward the bus's smells—the lavatory and perfumes and body odor and baby powder. She competed for his attention by raising her wine glass as if to give a toast, but she seemed to lose her words. She smiled weakly. The warmth of the dinner party was giving way to an urgency in him and in the rest of them. Even as he sat with generous and interesting people enjoying food and wine, he was traveling. White divider dashes were sweeping by. They were all traveling. Mrs. Ogunye's smile faded and she set off. From where she stood, she traveled around the world and back again as easily as turning her wrist to show her diamond.

He woke to a dark street and a red-bricked courthouse, four stories high, topped by a dome and a lit clock. It was five in the morning. One of two black cannons guarding the front steps pointed directly at Father Olufemi, its barrel topped by a bonnet of snow. He'd forgotten to revise his expectations. During the flight from Abuja, he'd imagined a church, his church, daylight, a welcoming committee, his parishioners in suits and Sunday dresses, a little girl with flowers. But the street was empty. Snow fell in clumps.

He was startled to find Jason no longer in the window seat. Had he sent the boy for water? Had the boy been in the service station when the bus departed? No, the young man had brought him water. Jason must have gone back to be with his father. Father Olufemi was sweating and shivering, and his shoulder was being shaken—by the thick-faced ex-convict, he thought, but no, that young man had left the bus hours ago. This was the other one, whose long hair descended the sides of his head like a theatre curtain.

"Is someone meeting you, Reverend?" he said.

Behind the young man, the driver frowned. "I don't have the luxury of idling."

"Are we early?" Father Olufemi said. He pushed himself up from the armrests, but after twelve hours of sitting his legs were too languid to hold any weight. He lowered himself back into his seat and rubbed his thighs.

"You should stay on the bus, Reverend," the young man said.

"Sun will be up soon," the driver said. "There will be people about. He can stay here. Or I'll let him stay on the bus one more stop to Fort Wayne, Indiana. He can find a hotel. Not much use getting a room at six or seven in the morning though."

"Don't worry," Father Olufemi said and removed a jacket from his duffel bag. "A man named Oscar will meet me. Maybe he's been delayed by the snow."

They helped him onto the sidewalk. The young man held him up as the driver retrieved his luggage and walker. All night the chill had been just outside his window and now, off the bus for the first time since Boston, it invaded every pore, even as his body felt feverishly warm. Snow melted on his hot head. The cold of the snow conducted through the wooden soles of his shoes to his feet, and beads of sweat scurried down his back.

"He's wearing a Windbreaker," the young man said.

The driver shrugged. "I can't tuck you all into bed."

"They know I'm coming," Father Olufemi said and smiled. "It will be fine."

"This place is empty," the young man said. He looked at the priest, at the driver, at the priest again, with real concern—this was no raised-voice playacting. "What if no one comes?"

"Look," the driver said and pointed down the street to an approaching figure—a young woman, they saw as she passed under a streetlight, in a man's galoshes and parka. The sleeves of the parka extended well past her hands and the zipper was undone, revealing a teal nightgown underneath. She advanced slowly, creeping, as if to take them by surprise, though they were staring at her. Father Olufemi waved, if only to allay the concerns of the other men, but she didn't notice. Her attention was fixed on each ponderous stride of her own feet. Finally, she stopped in front of them. She was an inch taller than Father Olufemi and terribly skinny. The brown of her sunken eyes seemed to have drained to the pouches underneath, and her blond-framed glasses clashed with her black hair. She wore heavy eyeliner, red lipstick, and elegant jewelry—three two-inch-long golden strands dangled from each of her ears.

Remembering a promise to begin his time in Halfestus with unmitigated cordiality, Father Olufemi hopped and pushed his walker a few feet through the snow, wincing against the pain in his hip. "Hello. Are you Oscar? I've been sent by the Diocese of Toledo to preside over Holy Trinity Church. My name is Father Olufemi." He extended his hand, but she only examined it.

"I know Oscar," she said.

That was enough for the driver. He took his seat and closed the automatic door. The long-haired young man stared out the window, disconsolate, though it was unclear why. It was strange how quickly the bus left, down Main Street, past a couple of yellow-flashing traffic lights. Father Olufemi and the young woman watched the taillights recede. When the bus was gone, she hung her head and hunched her shoulders, arms hugging her sides. She was still except for the slow clenching and unclenching of her hands within the sleeves of the parka.

"I'm happy you came," he said. "I was becoming worried."

She looked up, anxious—she didn't quite know what to do with him.

"It's only temporary," he said, referring to the walker.

Without a word, she plodded forward in her oversized galoshes as slowly as she'd arrived. She had not come to welcome him, he thought, but he abandoned his bags and followed her rather than be left alone. They turned down a side street and passed through an empty parking lot and into a park and followed a mulch path past baseball fields and swing sets.

"Are we going to Oscar?" he said.

There was not the hint of a breeze. There were no scuffling creatures in the tree branches. The only sounds were Father Olufemi's hoots of pain as he struggled to keep pace. If it weren't for the pain, he might have thought he was dreaming. Only in a dream would he be unable to keep pace with such peaceful steps. The further they traveled from the lights of the street, the darker it became. For a short time, he could make out the whites of the young woman's knobby knees. But soon he lost sight of her completely and resorted to following her tracks in the snow.

"Don't worry!" he yelled after her. "I'll be better in no time. I'm excited to be here."

Nominated by A Public Space

MEDITATION AFTER AN EXCELLENT DINNER

by MARK HALLIDAY

from COURT GREEN

All the new thinking is about not getting
squashed like a bug under the boot of time.
In this it resembles all the old
bundles of tropes and rhetorical maneuvers
on the shelves in your basement next to
Scattergories, Scrabble, Mastermind, Monopoly and Clue.
My friend this evening was all sad about
mortality and such, speaking intelligently about the new thinking,
and I daresay I cheered him up a bit by pointing out in a pithy
     fashion
how much that new thinking is not so new, and we had a chuckle
and a third martini with these exquisite Greek olives.
When I shop at Whole Foods I try to remember
we are all going to die because this makes the imported groceries
luminous with their being, you know, not forever,
and I lick my lips gently as I select my purchases.
Speaking of lips, one of my many lovers had
these naturally thick pouty lips and when she was sad
I could change her mood by sucking on her lower lip
with a throbby awareness of time, and beauty, and how
beauty has to exist in time. When I spoke of this (after sucking)
she thought I was luminous and she wriggled her small
shoulders. This was in California. So it's true
we are all going to be wiped out but before we go

there are these thick-lip moments not just luminous but
numinous (also gleaming and radiant and shining)
like when she whispered "Do me"
and I cried out *banana banana banana*.

Nominated by Court Green and Tony Hoagland, Daniel Hoffman,
Kevin Prufer, Lloyd Schwartz, Charles Harper Webb

NEVER COME BACK

fiction by ELIZABETH TALLENT

from THE THREEPENNY REVIEW

THIS WAS his life now, his real life, the thing he thought about most: his boy was in and out of trouble and he didn't know what to do.

Friday night when he got home late from the mill Daisy made him shower before supper, and he twisted the dial to its hottest setting and turned his back to the expensive showerhead whose spray never pulsed hard enough to perform the virtual massage its advertising promised— or maybe at forty-three he'd used his body too hard, its aches and pains as much a part of him now as his heart or any other organ, and he had wasted good money on an illusion. Ah well. He rubbed at mirror fog and told the dark-browed frowner (his own father!) to get ready: she'd had her Victor look. Whatever this development was, it fell somewhere between failing grade in calculus and car wreck, either of which, he knows from experience, would have been announced as soon as he walked through the door. This news, while it wasn't life or death, was bad enough that she felt she needed to lay the groundwork and had already set their places at the table and poured his beer, a habit he disliked but had never objected to and never would. As a special treat Daisy's father had let her tilt the bottle over his glass while the bubbles churned and the foam puffed like a mushroom cap sidling up from dank earth, and if she enjoyed some echo of the bliss of being in her daddy's good graces while pouring *his* beer, Sean wasn't about to deprive her of that.

Daisy told him:

Neither girl seemed very brave, yet neither seemed willing to back down. Not their own wounds but a sturdy sense of each other's being wronged had driven them to this. They had a kind of punk bravado, there on the threshold, armored in motorcycle jackets whose sleeves fell past their chipped black fingernails. A flight of barrettes had attacked their heads and seized random tufts of dirty hair. Dressed for audacity, but their pointy-chinned faces—really the same face twice—wore the stiff little mime smiles of the easily intimidated, confronting her, the tigress mother, bracing their forlorn selves as best they could, which wasn't very well at all. There was nothing to do but ask them in. As she told it to Sean, Daisy wasn't about to let them guess that A, she pitied them, and B, she understood right away there was going to be some truth in what they said. Victor's favorite sweater, needing some mending, lay across the arm of the sofa, and when one of the twins took it into her lap, talisman, claim, Daisy hardly needed to be told that girl was pregnant. As the twins took turns explaining not just one of them was in trouble, both were, an evil radiance pulsed in the corner of Daisy's right eye, the onset of a migraine.

A joke, Sean said. *Because, twins? Somebody told these girls to go to V's house and freak out his parents.*

Drinking around a bonfire and they wander deeper into the woods and they came across this mattress and it's like a sign to them. Sign is what they said. Does that sound like a joke to you? They have a word for it. Threeway. They have a word for it. Ask yourself what these girls know, what they've ever taken care of in their lives. Who's ever taken them seriously? We will. We will, now. Across the table Sean shook his head, his heavy disgust with his son failing, for once, to galvanize Daisy's defense of the boy. In the appalled harmony of their anger they traded predictions. Victor would be made to marry a twin, maybe the one whose dark eyes acquired a sheen of tears when she petted his old sweater, because she seemed the more lost. Victor would be dragged under.

"When's he get home?" Sean said.

"Away game. Not till 2 A.M." It was Daisy who would be waiting in her SUV when the bus pulled up at the high school to disgorge the sleepy jostling long-legged boys.

"So we hold off on doing anything till we hear his side of the story."

We hold off? If she hadn't loved him she would have laughed when he said that. It wasn't going to be up to them to hold off or not hold off, but if Sean was slower to accept that reality than she was, it was because he hated decisions being out of his hands.

However disgusted he'd been the night before, in the morning Sean

368

was somber, concerned, protective, everything Daisy could have wished when he sat Victor down at the kitchen table for what he called *getting the facts straight*. The reeling day-long party was true, and the bonfire, and the rain-sodden mattress in the woods where a drunken Victor had sex with both girls, though not at the same time, which was what *three-way* meant. They must have claimed that for dramatic impact, as if this thing needed more drama, or because they were so smashed events blurred together in their minds. The next several evenings were taken up with marathon phone calls—Sean asked most of the questions and wouldn't hand the receiver to Daisy even when she could tell he'd been told something especially troubling and mouthed *Give it to me!* By the following weekend they knew for sure only one twin was pregnant, though it seemed both had believed they were telling the truth when they sat on Daisy's striped couch and said the babies, plural, were due July 5th. The sweater-petting twin told Sean she had liked Victor for a long time—*years*—and had wanted to *be* with him, though not in the way it had finally happened, and when he heard this Sean coughed and his eyes got wet, but *who were those tears for?* Daisy wanted to know. *Not for his own kid, for those girls?* Questioned, Victor remembered only that they were twins. He knew it sounded bad but he wasn't sure what they looked like. Nobody was quote in love with him: that was crazy. And no, they hadn't tried to talk to him first, before coming to the house, and was that fair, that they'd assumed there was zero chance of his doing the right thing? And why was marriage the right thing if he didn't want it and whoever the girl was *she* didn't want it and it was only going to end in divorce? The twin who was pregnant had the ridiculous name of Esme, and what she asked for on the phone with Sean—patient, tolerant Sean—was not marriage but child support. If she had that she could get by, she insisted. She'd had a sonogram and she loved the alien-headed letter C curled up inside her. At their graduation dance she shed her high heels and flirted by bumping into the tuxes of various dance partners. Victor followed her into the parking lot. Below she was flatfooted and pumpkin-bellied, above she wore strapless satin, her collarbones stark as deer antlers when he backed her into an anonymous SUV hard enough their first sober kiss began with shrieks and whistles.

IN THE hushed joyous days after the baby was born Sean made a serious mistake that he blamed partly on sleep deprivation; the narrow old two-story house had hardly any soundproofing, and because Victor's and Esme's bedroom was below his and Daisy's, the baby's crying woke them all. He had stopped in the one jewelry store downtown and completely on impulse laid down his credit card for a delicate bracelet consisting of several strands of silver wound around and around each other. Though simple, the bracelet was a compelling object with a strong suggestion of narrative, as if the maker had been trying to fashion the twining, gleaming progress of several competing loves. He was the sort of husband who gets teased for not noticing her new earrings even when his wife repeatedly tucks her hair behind her ears, and any whimsical expenditure was unlike him, but he found he couldn't leave the store without it. He stopped for a beer at the Golden West, and when he got home the only light was from the kitchen where Esme sat at the table licking the filling from Oreos and washing it down with chocolate milk. Her smile hoped he would empathize with the joke of her appetite rather than scold the late-night sugar extravaganza as, he supposed, Daisy would have done, but it was the white-trash forlornness of her feast that got to Sean—the cheapness and furtiveness and excessive, teeth-aching sweetness of this stab at self-consolation. With her china-doll hair and whiter-than-white skin she was hardly the menace to their peace they had feared, only an ignorant girl who trusted neither her baby's father nor her sneaky conviction that it was she and not the grandmother who ought to be making the big decisions about the baby's care. Esme wet a forefinger and dabbed the crumbs from Daisy's tablecloth as he set the shiny box down next to her dirty plate. She said, "What is this?" and, that fast, there were tears in her eyes. She didn't believe it was for her, but she'd just understood what it would feel like if the little box *had* been hers, and this disbelief was his undoing: until those tears he had honestly had no notion of giving Esme the bracelet. He heard himself say, "Just something for the new mama." As soon as she picked the ribbon apart, even before she tipped the bracelet from its mattress of cotton, he regretted his impulsivity, but it was too late: she slid it onto her wrist and made it flash in the dim light, glancing to invite his admiration or maybe try to figure out, from his expression, what was going on. In the following days he was sorry to see that she never took it off. Luckily the household was agitated enough that nobody else noticed the bracelet, and he began to hope his mistake would have no ill consequences except for the change in Esme, whose corner-tilted eyes held his whenever he came into the room. Then, quick, she'd turn her head as if realizing this was the sort of thing that could give them away. Of course there was no *them* and not a fucking thing to give away. Sean began to blame her for his uneasiness: she had misconstrued an act of minor, impulsive charity, blown it up into something more, which had to be kept secret. The ridiculousness of her believing he was *interested* was not only troubling in its own right, it pointed to her readiness to immerse herself in fantasy, and this could be proof of some deeper instability. He didn't like being looked at like that in his own house, or keeping secrets. He was not a natural secret-keeper, but a big-boned straightforward husband. Since he'd been nineteen, a husband. Daisy came from a rough background too, her father a part-time carpenter and full-time drunk who had once burned his kids' clothes in the backyard, the boys running back into the house for more armfuls of t-shirts and shorts, disenchanted only when their dad made them strip off their cowboy pajamas and throw those in too. The first volunteer fireman on the scene dressed the boys in slickers that reached to their ankles and bundled their naked teeth-chattering sister in an old sweater that stank of crankcase oil, and to this day when Sean changes the oil in his truck he has to scrub his hands outside or Daisy will run to the bathroom to throw up.

As Esme alternated between flirtation and sullenness, he tried for kindness. This wasn't all her fault: he was helplessly responsive to vulnerability, and—he could admit it—he did have a tendency to rush in and try to fix whatever was wrong. Therefore he imitated Daisy's forbearance when Esme couldn't get even simple things right, like using hypoallergenic detergent instead of the regular kind that caused the baby to break out in a rash. The tender verbal skat of any mother cradling her baby was a language Esme didn't speak. Her hold was so tentative the baby went round-eyed and chafed his head this way and that wondering who would come to his aid. More than once Esme neglected to pick up dangerous buttons or coins from the floor. She had to be reminded to burp him after nursing and then, chastened, would sling him across her shoulder like a sack of rice. Could you even say she loved the baby? Breast-feeding might account for Esme's sleepy-eyed bedragglement and air of waiting for real life to begin, but, Daisy said, there was absolutely no justifying the girl's self-pity. Consider where she, Daisy, had come from: worse than anything this girl had gone through, but had Sean ever seen her spend whole days feeling sorry for herself, reading wedding magazines in dirty sheets, scarcely managing to crawl from bed when the baby cried? It wasn't as if she had no support. Victor was right there. Who would have believed it? He was attentive to Esme, touchingly proud of his son, and even after a long day at the mill would stay up walking the length of the downstairs hallway with the colicky child so Esme could sleep. For the first time Victor was as good as his word, and could be counted on to deal uncomplainingly with errands and show up when he'd said he would. Victor's changed ways should have mattered more to Esme, given the desolation of her childhood. Victor was *good to her*. Esme could not explain what was wrong or what she wanted, Daisy said after one conversation. She was always trying to talk to the girl, who was growing more and more restless. They could all see that, but not what was coming, because it was the kind of thing you didn't want to believe would happen in your family: Esme disappeared. Dylan was almost four and for whatever reason she had concluded that four was old enough to get by without a mother. That much they learned from her note but the rest they had to find out. She had hitchhiked to the used-car dealership on the south end of town and picked out a white Subaru station wagon; Wynn Handley, the salesman, said she negotiated pleasantly and as if she knew what she was doing and (somewhat to Wynn's surprise, you could tell) ended up with a good deal. Esme paid in cash—not that unusual in a county famed for its marijuana. She left alone—that is, there was no other man. Not as far as Wynn knew, and he was being completely forthcoming in light of the family's distress. The cash was impossible to explain, since after checking online Victor reported their joint account hadn't been touched, and they hadn't saved nearly that much anyway. Esme had no credit card, of course, making it hard to trace her. Discussion of whether they were in any way to blame and where Esme could have gone and whether she was likely to call and want to talk to her son and whether, if she called, there was any chance of convincing her to come back was carried on in hushed voices because no matter what she'd done the boy should not have to hear bad things about his mother.

WITH ESME gone, Victor began to talk about quitting the mill. The ceaseless roar was giving him tinnitus; his back hurt; there were nights he fell asleep without showering and woke already exhausted, doomed to another day just like the last, and how was he supposed to have any energy left for a four-year-old? Had Esme thought of that before she left, he wondered—that he might not be able to keep it together? No doubt his steadiness had misled her into thinking it was safe to leave, and when he remembered how easy and fond and funny and tolerant

372

he had been, anger slanted murderously through his body; and it was like anger practiced on him, got better and better at leaving him with shaking hands and a dilated sense of hatred with no nearby object; and he began to be very, very careful not to be alone with his little boy.

Dylan understood this. After nightmares he did not try his dad's room, right next to his, but padded his way through the dark house up the narrow flight of stairs to the bedroom where he slid in between Sean and Daisy. More than once his cold bare feet made accidental contact with Sean's genitals, and Sean had to capture the feet and guide them away. This left him irritably awake, needing to make the long trip to the bathroom downstairs, and when he returned the boy was still restless and Sean watched him wind a hand into Daisy's long hair and rub it against his cheek until he could sleep. Worse than jealousy was the affront to Sean's self-regard in feeling so contemptible an emotion. This was a scared little boy, this was his tight hold on safety, this was his grandfather standing by the side of the bed looking meanly down. Protectiveness toward his own flesh and blood had always been Sean's ruling principle, and if that went wrong he didn't know who he was anymore. He rose to dress for work one chilly 6 A.M. and noticed the amateur tattoos running cruelly down the boy's arm. Had an older kid got hold of him somehow, was this some kind of weird abuse, why hadn't he come running to his grandfather? Sean bent close to decipher the trail of descending letters. I LOVE YOU. Not another kid, then. Not abuse. But wasn't that bad for him, wouldn't the ink's toxins be absorbed through his skin, didn't she think that was going a little too far, inscribing her love on the boy while he did what—held his arm out bravely? Time, past time, for Sean to try to talk to Daisy, to suggest that daycare would be a good idea, or a playgroup where the boy could meet other kids. When Daisy was tired or wanted time to herself she left the boy alone with the remote, and once Sean walked in on the boy sitting cross-legged while on the screen a serial killer wrapped body parts in plastic, and how could you talk to a child after that, what could you tell him that could explain that away? All right, they could do better. He supposed most people could do better by their kids. Maybe her judgment in taking a pen to the boy's arm wasn't perfect, but was it such a bad thing to have love inscribed on your skin, whoever you were? Half the world was dying for want of that. If Daisy adored this boy he could live with her passion. More than live with it: he admired it. He admired her for being willing to begin again when she knew how it could end.

MAYBE VICTOR'S mood would have benefited from confrontation—
a kitchen-table sit-down where, with cups of reheated coffee to warm
their hands, father and son could try to get at the root of the problem—
but envisioning his own well-meaning heavy-heartedness and guessing
that Victor would take offense, Sean was inclined to ignore his son's
depression. In most cases, within a family, there was wisdom in holding
one's tongue. Except for one thing: Victor could, if he concluded his
chances were better elsewhere, take the boy with him when he left.
This gave a precarious tilt to their household, an instability whose
source was, really, Victor's fondness for appearing wronged. He came
home with elaborate tales of affronts he had suffered, but Sean knew
the foreman and doubted any unfairness had been shown Victor. When
Victor needed to vent, Sean steered clear and Daisy, rather than voicing
her true opinion—that it was time he got over Esme—calmly heard him
out. Victor could ruin his mother's peace of mind by ranting at the un-
believable fucking hopelessness of this fucking dead-end town, voice
so peeved and fanatical in its recounting of injustice that Sean, frown-
ing across the dinner table, thought he must know how ridiculous he
sounded, how almost crazy, but Victor kept on: he was only waiting for
the day when the mill closed down for good and he could pack up his
kid and his shit and get out. What were they, blind? Couldn't they see
he had no life? Did they think he could take this another fucking day?
From his chair near his dad Dylan said, "Are we going away? Are we
going away?" "No, baby boy, you're not going anywhere," said Sean, at
which Victor did the unthinkable, pulling out the gun tucked into the
back of his jeans and setting it with a chime on his dinner plate and
saying, "Then maybe this is what I should eat." Daisy said, "Sean,"
wanting him to do something, but before he could Victor pushed the
plate across the table to him and said, "No, no, no, all right, I'm sorry,
that was in front of the kid, that's taking it too far, I know I know I know,
don't ask me if I meant it because you know I don't but I swear to god,
Dad, some days it crosses my mind. But I won't. I never will." Gently
he cupped his boy's head. "I'm sorry to have scared you, Dyl. Daddy
got carried away." "I want that gun out of the house," Daisy said. Sean
had gone out into the starry night and folded the passenger seat of his
truck forward and tucked the gun into the old parka he kept there. In
bed that night Daisy turned to him, maybe needing to feel that some-
thing was still right in their life, and while he understood the impulse

374

and even shared it, he found he was picturing Esme's pointed chin, her head thrown back, her urchin hair fanned out across a filthy mattress in the woods, an image so wrong and *good* he couldn't stop breathing life into it, the visitation no longer blissfully involuntary but nursed along, fed with details; the childish lift of her upper lip as she picked at the gift-box ribbon came to him, the imagined grace of her pale body against the filthy mattress, her arms stretched overhead, her profile clean against the ropy twists of dirty hair, no she wouldn't look, she wouldn't look and he came without warning, Daisy far enough gone that momentum rocked her farther, Sean relieved when she managed the trick that mostly eluded her while also, in some far-back, disownable part of his mind, judging her climax too naked, too needful, and at the same time impersonal, since she had no idea where he was in his head, and this, her greedy solitary capacity, bothered him. In the slowed-down aftermath when their habit was to roll apart and stretch frankly and begin to talk about whatever came to mind, a brief spell, an island whose sanctity they understood, where they were truly, idly, themselves, their old selves, the secret selves which only they recognized in each other, she didn't move or speak and he continued to lie on her worrying that he was growing heavier and heavier, her panting exaggerated as if to communicate the extremity of her pleasure, and for a sorry couple of minutes he hated her. There was something offensive in her unawareness of his faithlessness. If he was faithless even in his mind he wanted it to matter and it couldn't matter unless she could intuit it and hold him accountable and by exerting herself against him, as she had a right to, make him want to come all the way back to her. That was up to her. If she couldn't do it then he might continue to be bewilderingly alone and even slightly, weirdly in love with the lost girl Esme, indefensible as that was, and astounding. Daisy squirmed companionably out from under, turned on her side, a hand below her cheek, the crook of her other arm bracing her breasts, the light of her eyes, the creases at the corners of her smile confiding, genuine, her goodness obvious, the goodness at the heart of his world, the expression on his face god knows what, but by her considering stillness she was working up to a revelation. With Daisy sex sometimes turned the keys of the secretest locks and he could never guess what was coming, since years and decades of wrongs and sorrows awaited confession, and even now, having loved her for twenty years, he could be surprised by some small flatly told story of some terrible thing that had happened when she was a kid. Damage did that, went in so deep it took long years to surface.

Tonight he had no inclination to be trusted, but could hardly stop her. "This thing's sort of been happening. Like four or five times? This thing of the phone ringing and no one being there. 'Hello.'" The *hello* was hers. "And no answer. And 'Hello.' And no answer. Somebody there, though. Somebody there."

Such a relief not to have to travel again through the charred landscape of her childhood that he almost yawned. "Kids. Messing around."

"No," she said. "Her." His expression must have been puzzled because she said, "Esme."

"Esme."

"Don't believe me then but I'm right, it was her and the last time she called I said, 'Listen to me. Are you listening?' and there was no answer and I said, 'Never come back.' I didn't know that was about to come out of my mouth, I was probably more surprised than she was. 'Never come back.'"

"And then what?"

"And then she hung up." She scratched one foot with the toes of the other. "And that's not like me. And I didn't have any right, did I?" Rueful smile. "If I'd said, 'Honey, where are you? Are you in trouble?' that would have been like me, right? And maybe she would have told me, maybe something is wrong and that girl has no where else to turn. She's the kind of girl there's not just one filthy mattress in the woods in her life, not just one fantastic fuckup, but last time she was lucky and found us, and we let her come live in our house, and we loved her, I think— did we love her?—and I think if things got bad enough for her she'd think of us and remember we were *good* to her, weren't we good to her?"

"Yes."

"Yes and now it's like I'm waiting for her to call again. Or turn up. I think that's next. She'll turn up. And I don't want her to. I never want to see that girl's face again."

He couldn't summon the energy for *I'm sure it wasn't her*, even if that was probably true. He could also have accepted Daisy's irrational conviction and addressed it with his usual calm. *Of course you're angry. Irresponsible, not just to her little boy, but to us who took her in, who cared about her—she left without a word. It's natural to be angry.*

He lay there withholding the consolation that was his part in this back-and-forth until she turned onto her back and stared at the ceiling.

I made a serious mistake with Esme once. Gave her a bracelet. If he could have said that. If he could have found a way to begin.

＊　＊　＊

DENT FIGUEREDO wasn't someone Sean thought of as a friend, but this sweet May evening they were alone in the Tip-Top, door open to the street alive with sparrow song and redolent of asphalt cooling in newly patched potholes, Dent behind the bar, Sean on his bar stool thinking about taxes, paying no attention until he heard "I want your take on this."

"My take."

"You're smart about women."

Women? But Sean nodded, and when that didn't seem to be enough, he said, "Hit me."

"See, first of all, despite her quote flawless English she utters barely a word in the airport, just looks at me like I saved her life, which you'd think I would be a sucker for but no, I'm praying *get me out of this*, ready to turn the truck around and put her on the next flight home, and like she knows what I'm on the verge of she unbuckles and slides over and you know Highway 20 twists and turns like a snake on glass, I never felt that trapped before in my life, just because this itty bitty girl has hold of my dick through my trousers and you *know* she's never done that before and I should've known that at this late date I'm not good husband material, should've lived with that but no, I had to get melty when I seen her doe-eyed picture on the Internet. Shit."

"Husband material."

"What you got to promise if you want a nice Filipina girl," Dent said. "She's some kind of born again. Dressed like a little nun, baggy skirt and these flat black worn-out shoes. No makeup. Won't hold your eye." When he catches Sean's eye he looks down and away, smiling, this imitation of girly freshness at odds with Dent's bald sunspotted pate and the patch of silvery whiskers he missed on his adam's apple, and Sean can't help laughing.

"What happens to her now?"

"Stories she tells, shit, curl your hair." Dent used his glass to print circles of wet on the bar. "America still looks good to a lot of the world, I tell you." He crouched to the refrigerator with his crippled leg stuck rigidly out behind. "She's staying in my house till I can figure out what comes next, and you should see the place, neat as a picture in a magazine. Hard little worker, I give her that. If any of my boys was unmarried I'd drag him to the altar by the scruff of his neck." He levered open

377

his beer, raising it politely. Sean shook his head. "Course before long," Dent continued, "one of them boys will shake loose.

"Meanwhile where does she sleep, this paragon?"

"Nah, Filipina."

"And you two, have you been—?"

"Ming. Cute, huh?" Dent drank from the bottle before pouring into his glass.

"Took the upstairs room for her own, cleared out years of boy shit. Jesus won't let nobody near her till there's a ring on her finger. Twenty-two and looks fifteen. That's the undernourishment."

When, sitting down to dinner that night, Sean told Daisy about the girl, she said, "You're kidding," and made him tell the entire story again, then said, amused, "Poor thing. You *know* he lied to her. And do you think he even sent his picture? He's, what, a poorly preserved sixty, a drinker, a smoker, hobbling around on that leg and he talks this child into leaving her home and her family and now he won't do the right thing?"

"He'd never seen her till she got off the plane. I think his lack of any feeling for her came as a shock. And in his defense he is leaving her alone."

"Of course he's terrified of any constraint on his drinking. Dylan Raymond, we are waiting for your father."

Dylan put down the green bean he was trailing through his gravy and said, "Why?"

"Yeah, I think that's maybe more to the point. Because she's a born again, and might start in on him."

"Is she pretty?"

"He says she has drawbacks." He bared his teeth. "Primitive dental care."

"Oh and he's George Clooney."

"But she's sweet, he says," Sean said, prolonging his bared-teeth smile. "Good natured."

Victor came to the table then in his signature ragged black t-shirt and jeans, his pale workingman's feet—which never saw the sun—bare, dark hair still dripping wet, and he stood behind Dylan, kneading the boy's shoulders. "Who're we talking about?" he wanted to know.

"My mom is pretty," Dylan announced, then waited with an air of uncertainty and daring—the kid who's said something provocative in the hope the adults will get into the forbidden subject. Victor could conceivably say, "What mom?" He could conceivably say, "You wouldn't

378

know your mom if you passed her in the street." He could conceivably say, "That bitch." Sean knew Victor to be capable of any or all of these remarks, and was relieved when Victor calmly continued to rub the boy's shoulders. Not answering was fine, given the alternatives. When Dylan began drawing in his gravy with the green bean again, his head down, he inscribed circles like those his dad was rubbing into his shoulders, in the same rhythm. How does he understand his mother's absence? Sean wondered. Surely it's hard for him that his father never mentions his mother, worrisome that nobody can say where she's gone. Daisy has not made up any tale justifying Esme's desertion. Sean understood the attraction of lying consolation; he felt it himself. The boy's relief would have been worth almost any falsehood, but Daisy had insisted that they stick with what they knew, which was virtually nothing. Daisy said, "Yes, your mother is pretty," with a sidelong glance at Victor to make sure this didn't prompt meanness from him.

Victor changed the subject: "Who were you saying was sweet?"

MING HAD no demure, closed-mouth smile, as he'd expected from an Asian girl, but a wide, flashing laugh whose shamelessness disturbed Victor, for her small teeth were separated by touching gaps, the teeth themselves incongruously short, like pegs driven hastily into the ground. The decided sweetness of her manner almost countered the daredevilish, imbecile impression made by those teeth. Seated on a slab of rock at the beach, he peeled off his socks. Flatteringly, Ming had dressed for their date—not only a dress, stockings and *high heels*—while he had worn jeans and his favorite frayed black t-shirt, but he figured this was all right, she would know from movies that American men complained about ties and jackets. Ming's poise as she stood one-legged, peeling the stocking from her sandy foot, was very pretty, and the wind wrapped her dress—navy blue printed with flying white petals—tightly around her thighs and little round butt. Her pantyhose were rolled up and tucked into a shoe, her shoes wedged into a crevice of the rock. In the restaurant earlier Victor had observed her table manners and found them wanting. It wasn't so much that she made overt mistakes as that she wasn't allowing for the grace-note pauses and frequent diversions—a smile, a little conversation—with which food is properly addressed in public, but chewed steadily with her little fox teeth. Her style overall began to seem quick and unfastidious and he was curious about what that would translate to in bed. He had been trying not to think about that because he knew from what Dent had said—first to his dad and then, when Victor called, to Victor himself—that she was a virgin, and it seemed wrong to try to guess what she'd be like, sexually, when the only right way of perceiving her was as a semi-sacred blank slate. Respect, protectiveness: he liked having these feelings as he slouched against the rock, the wind bothering his hair, the barelegged woman turning to find him smiling, smiling in return. There: the unlucky teeth. Guess what, she's human. He jumped from the rock and took her hand and they walked down the beach.

FOR NEARLY a year Victor was happier than his parents had ever known him to be, even after he was laid off from the mill for the winter. Not the time you'd want to get pregnant, but Ming did, and when she miscarried at five months, they both took it hard. "She won't get out of bed, Dad," Victor confided in a late-night call. "Won't eat, either." After work the next day Sean decided to swing by their place, a one-story clapboard cottage that suited the newlyweds fine except that it didn't have much of a yard and lacked a second bedroom for Dylan; all agreed the boy should continue living at his grandparents'. *Two birds with one stone*, in Sean's view. Not only was the continuity good for Dylan, but once she saw she wasn't going to have to negotiate for control of the boy, Daisy was free to be a kind, unintrusive mother-in-law. Privately, Sean has all along believed he is better than the other two at relating to Ming. To Daisy, Ming was the odd small immigrant solution to the riddle of Victor, the girl who had supper waiting when he got home, who considered his paycheck a prince's ransom, who tugged off his boots for him when he was tired. The miscarriage was a blow but such things happened. Ming was sturdy and would get over it. Basically Daisy was only so interested in anyone other than Dylan, and Victor—well, could you count on Victor to bring a person flowers to cheer her up? Or ice cream? Even if Ming won't eat anything else, she might try a little of the mint chocolate-chip she loves. Safeway is near their cottage, so Sean swings into the parking lot and strides in, wandering around in the slightly theatrical male confusion that says *My wife usually does all this* before finding what he wants, remembering Daisy had said they were out of greens, deciding on a sixpack of beer, too, craving a box of cigarettes when it was time to pay, that habit kicked decades ago, its urgency a symptom of his sadness about the lost baby, and bizarrely, ridiculously, he was standing in the checkout line with tears in his eyes, recognizing only then that the girl thrusting Ming's roses into the bag was Esme.

She seemed to have been trying not to catch his attention, and he wondered if she had been hoping against hope he would conclude his business and walk out without ever having noticed her. She could reasonably hope for that, he supposed: a job like hers could teach you that the vast majority of people walked through their lives unseeing. The checker was hastening the next lot of groceries down the conveyor belt, loaves of bread and boxes of cereal borne toward Esme as Sean hoisted his bags and said, "So you're back."

"Not for long."

"Not staying long, or you haven't been back long?"

Over his shoulder, to the next person: "Paper or plastic."

"You're staying with your sister?"

None of his business, her look said.

The woman behind squeezed past Sean to claim her bag, frowning at him for the inconvenience—no, he realized, she was frowning because she thought he was bothering Esme, who scratched at her wrist, then twisted a silver bracelet around, *the* bracelet, part of her repertoire of nervous gestures, because this was Esme, fidgeting, resentful, scared—smiling to cover it up but construing the mildest gestures or words as slights, taking offense with breathtaking swiftness and leaving you no way to remedy the situation. In the face of such fantastical touchiness, gracefulness became an implausible virtue—quaint, like chastity. Nonetheless he tried: "Come to see Dylan."

"Paper or plastic."

"He wonders about you, you know."

"Plastic."

To Sean, who had edged out of the aisle and stood holding his bags, she said wretchedly, "Does he?"

Sean said, though it was far from the case, "No one holds anything against you. He needs you. He's five years old."

"I know how old he is," she said. "I do."

"Or I could bring him by if that's easier."

Abruptly she stopped bagging groceries and pressed the heels of her hands to her eyelids. It was as if she'd temporarily broken with the world and was retreating to the deepest sanctuary possible in such a place. It was as if she despaired. He was sorry to have been a contributing factor, sorry to be among those she couldn't make disappear; at the same time he felt formidably in the right, and as if he was about to

381

prevail—to cut through her fears and evasiveness and self-loathing heedlessness to the brilliant revelation, from Esme to herself, of mother love, a recognition she would never be able to go back on, which would steady her and bring her to her senses and leave her grateful for the change that had begun right here and now in the checkout line at Safeway. Because lives had to change unglamorously and for the better. Because he had found her.

"Would you really do that?" Esme said.

"Yeah, I'd do that."

She tore a scrap from the edge of the bag she was filling, reached past the glaring cashier for a pen from the cup by the register, scribbled, and handed Sean the leaf of brown paper, which he had to hunt for, the next day, when it came time to call her, worrying that he'd lost it, finding it, finally, tucked far down into the pocket of the work pants he'd been wearing, but Esme wasn't there and instead he got her sister, who told him Esme would be home from work at five. Sarah was this one's name, he remembered. "You know, she said you were really nice. Kind. So I want to thank you. She might not tell you this herself but I know she can't wait to see the little guy. Me, too." Fine, they would come by around six. Sean hadn't yet broken the news of Esme's return to Daisy, much less Victor, partly for his own sake, because he wanted to conserve the energy needed to deal with Daisy's inevitable fretting and Victor's righteous anger, partly for Dylan, because he wanted the boy to meet his mother again in a relatively quiet, relatively sane atmosphere, without a lot of fireworks going off, without anyone's suggesting maybe it wasn't the best thing for the boy to spend time with a mother so irresponsible. Was there, in this secrecy, the flicker of another motive? Something like wanting to keep her to himself. Sean, driving, shook his head at this insight, and beside him Dylan asked, "Am I going to live with her now?"

"Honey, no, this is just for a little while, for you guys to see each other. You know what a visit is, right? And how it's different from *live with*? You live with us. You are going to *visit* your mom for a couple of hours. Meaning you go home after. With me. I come get you."

"What color is her hair?"

"Don't you remember? Her hair is black. Like—." He felt foolish when all he could come up with was "—well, not like any of ours."

"Not like mine."

"No, yours is brown." Sean tried to think what else Dylan wouldn't remember. "Your mom has a sister, a twin, meaning they look just alike and that'll be a little strange for you maybe, but you'll get used to it, and this sister, see, is your aunt Sarah, and this's your aunt's house I'm taking you to. Because your mom is staying there. With her sister."

Too much news for sure, and for the rest of the brief drive Dylan sucked his thumb as he hadn't for years, but Sean didn't reprimand him, just parked the truck so the two of them could study the one-story white clapboard house with the scruffy yard where a bicycle had lain on its side long enough that spears of iris had grown up through its spokes. If this had been an ordinary outing, Sean would have explained, "They built all these little houses on the west side for workers in the mill, and they don't look like much maybe but they're nice inside and the men were allowed to take home seconds from the mill and they made some beautiful cabinets in their kitchens," because he likes telling the boy bits of the history of his hometown; but he kept that lore to himself and when the boy seemed ready they climbed the front porch steps together and stood before the door. "You want to knock or should I?"

"You."

Sean used his knuckles, three light raps, and then Esme was saying through the screen to Dylan, "Hey you," smiling her pained childish smile, and Dylan couldn't help himself, he was hers, Sean saw, instantly, gloriously hers because she'd smiled and said two words. She held the door ajar and Dylan went past her into the house and he never did things like that—he was shy.

"Coming in?"

"I'll leave you two alone. To get—." *Reacquainted* would strike her as a reproach, maybe. "So you can have some time to yourselves. Just tell me when to come for him and I'll be back." He paused. "His bedtime's eight o'clock and it would be good if I got him home before that." In case he needs some settling down. He doesn't say that, or think about how he's going to keep the boy from telling her grandmother where he's been, but he'll find a way, some small bribe that will soothe the boy's need to tell all.

"Not even two hours," she said.

"It's not a great idea to feed him a lot of sugar or anything, cause then he gets kind of wired."

"I wasn't going to," she said. "I know how he is."

"It would only be natural if you wanted to give him a treat or something."

"To worm my way back into his affections."

"Not what I meant."

In her agitation she gave her wrist a punishing twist—no, she was fooling with the silver bracelet, and he suffered an emotion bruising but minor, too fleeting or odd, maybe, ever to have been named, nostalgia for a miserably wrongheaded sexual attraction. Not regret. He had repented for giving her the bracelet by bringing her kid to her. Had that really been his reason? He repeated, "Not what I meant."

"So maybe you won't believe this, I can see why you wouldn't, but I wanted to see him so bad. Only I thought you-all would for sure say no. Blame me. Not, you know, trust me. And instead you've made it easy for me and I never expected that and I don't know how to thank you, Sean, I don't, but this means everything to me, it's kind of saving my life. It's really basically saving my life." Running the sentences together, so unaccustomed was she to honesty, afraid, maybe, of the feeling of honesty, scary if you weren't used to it, and Sean reached out to lay a finger on her lips, ancient honorable gesture for *hush now*, no further explanation was necessary, he got it that to see your child again was like having your life saved, he would have felt the same way in her shoes but also chastened and rebellious confronting someone like him who was doing the real work, constantly and reliably there for the boy, and he wanted to convey the fact that none of this mattered if she was here and could give the boy a little of what he needed, a sense of his mother: but now it was Sean who was inarticulate, moved by the girl softness of her mouth, Sean whose finger rested against her lips until she jerked her head back and he was blistered by shame, the burden of impossible apology and regret shifting from her shoulders to his. He waited for her to say something direct and blaming, scathing, memorable, and when she did not he was relieved. But he wasn't fooled, either. She knew exactly what had happened and where it left them. This girl believed she now had the upper hand, but must use her leverage tactfully, however unlike her that was, if he was not to instantly deny what had taken place. What he understood was that he was in trouble here, but that she was going to collude with him because, basically, he could give her more of what she wanted. The child. His agreement was necessary for her to continue secretly seeing the child. And Sean did not know how to set any of this right, only that he needed to keep his voice down and not do any further harm—not scowl in dismay or do anything else she could construe as a sign of problems to come. He told her, "Seven-thirty then, okay? See you at seven-thirty," and she said in a voice in no way remarkable, "We'll be here."

384

*   *   *

BUT THEY were not. "She has rights," Sarah told Sean, who was in her kitchen, in a rickety chair she had pulled away from the table, saying, "She has rights," saying now, "It's wrong for him to be kept from his *mother* the way you-all have done."

For some reason, when she'd pulled the chair out for him, he'd taken it and turned it around and straddled it. Maybe he had needed to act, to take control of something, if only the chair. This is her sister—or closer than sister, twin—and he keeps his voice down. "Ask yourself why I brought him by. I'm her best friend in this mess, but what she's done is damage her own cause. This isn't gonna look good."

"To who?"

"Do you know where she's going?"

"To who won't it look good?"

Trailer trash, Daisy called the sisters once. "The thing is to make this right without having anybody else get involved."

"You're threatening me."

"I'm the opposite of threatening you. I'm saying let's work this out ourselves. You tell me where she's gone and I find her and we work it out like reasonable people and there's no need for anybody else to know she abducted a five-year-old child."

"A five-year-old. You-all opened your door and *what's in this basket? A cute little baby!* She wasn't in labor eighteen hours. She never chipped a tooth from clenching or left clawmarks on my hand. Tell me you ever even really knew she was in the house. Tell me you ever once really talked to her. Victor hit her upside the head so hard the ringing in her ear lasted a week. Do you know he said he'd kill her if she tried to leave? It was my four thousand dollars. So she ran, you know, she took the money and she ran and there was never any phone call and it kept me up a lot of nights. It wasn't the money, it was not knowing she was all right—they say twins know that but I didn't, not till I saw her again. And I never saw her look at anyone like she looks at that little boy when he says *I want to stay with you* and it's not like she planned this but after that how was she going to let him go? I'm not saying she makes great choices but you were unrealistic thinking she could give him back."

The chair wobbled as he crossed his arms on its backrest. "Maybe so. She and I need to talk about that. Work out what's best for all concerned."

"It sounds so reasonable when you say it."

"I am reasonable." He smiles. "Families need to work these things out."

"Now you're family."

"Like it or not." Still smiling.

Sarah gave in. Esme was driving north toward Arcata to go to college there. "None of you thought she was good enough for college."

An outright lie but he let it go. "How long ago did they take off?"

"Not long. She had to get her stuff. She was just throwing things into the car. Dylan helped. Laughing like they were both little kids." He continued to look at her. "Mmm. Twenty minutes maybe."

"What kind of car?"

"I don't know kinds of cars." He won't look away. "Smallish. A Toyota maybe. Green maybe." Not smiling now: he needs her to get this right. "Yeah. Green. A bumper sticker. Stop fucking something up. That really narrows it down, hunh. Trees. 'Stop Killing Ancient Trees.' Trees are her thing."

"You're sure about Arcata."

"See, she's wanted that for years, an apartment and classes and her little boy with her. Botany. Redwoods, really. Did you know that about her? She loves redwoods and there's this guy there who's famous, like *the* guy if you want to study redwoods, and she met him, and she might be going to be his research assistant this summer. She said—" But she'd told him what he needed to know and he was out the door. Lucky that it was north, the two-lane highway looping through the woods without a single exit for sixty miles and few places to pull over, lucky that after dark nobody drives this road but locals and not many of those. As long as he checks every pull-off carefully and doesn't overshoot her then it comes down to how fast he can drive, each curve with its silver-gray monoliths stepping forward while their sudden shadows revolve through the woods behind, the ellipse of shadow-swerve the mirror image of his curve, evergreen air through the window, no oncoming lights which is just as well given his recklessness, the rage he can admit now he's alone, the desire just to get his hands on her, the searing passage of his brights through the woods like the light of his mind or even his whole self gathered and concentrated into swift hunting intelligence that touches and assesses and passes on because its exclusive object is her. At this speed it's inevitable he will overtake her—nobody drives this road like this—but now he's bolted past a likely spot, a scruffy rutted crescent rimmed with trees tall enough to shade it from moonlight:

there. He brakes and runs the truck backward onto the shoulder, passing an abandoned car whose color, in the darkness, can't be discerned, and pulling in behind he reads *Stop Killing Ancient Trees*. Such fury, such concentration, and he almost missed her. An empty car. Here is his fear: that she has arranged to meet someone. That Sarah was lied to, and Arcata was a fable, and there's a guy in this somewhere, and she told him she would go away with him if she could get her kid. Nobody to be seen but when he gets out in the moonlight it was as if the air around Sean was sparkling, as if electricity flashed from his skin and glittered at the forest, as if he could convey menace even to a stone. When he checked in the back seat there was the boy curled up, sleeping in his little t-shirt and underpants with nothing over him, no blanket, not even an old sweater or jacket, and cracking the door open—its rusty hinges alarming the woods—Sean ducks into a cave of deepest oldest life-tenderness and takes the child in his arms and leans out loving the weight of him and the shampoo smell of his mussed hair. He sets him down barefoot and blinking, his underpants a triangular patch of whiteness in the moonlight, the boy as shy as if it was he who'd run away, keeping a fearful arm's length from Sean, and when Sean says, "Where's your mom?" blinking again, seeming not to trust Sean, confused and on the brink of tears and there's no time for that. That was for later. "Get in the truck," he tells the boy, "and I don't want you coming out no matter what. Your job is to stay in the truck and I don't want you getting out of that truck for any damn reason whatsoever, do you understand me?"

"I have to pee."

"Come on then."

Watching from behind Sean feels the usual solicitude at the boy's wide-legged stance. Dry weeds crackle.

"She had to go pee in the woods," he said. Solemnly: "My mom did, in the woods."

That was a new one to the boy.

Sean said, "What happened to your clothes?"

"I threw up and she made me take 'em off and throw 'em out the window cause the smell was making her sick too."

"All right, now you get in my truck and you *stay* in the truck. What did I just say?"

"*Stay* in the truck."

"What're you going to do?"

"*Stay* in the truck."

He has to boost the shivering boy up to the high seat. Sean takes the flashlight from the glovebox and checks to make sure the keys are in his pocket. He gestures for Dylan to push the lock down, first on the passenger side, then, leaning across, on the driver's. Sean nods through the window but the boy only wraps his arms around himself and twists his bare legs together, and Sean remembers the old parka stuffed down behind his seat and gestures for the boy to unlock again and leans in and says, "Look behind the seat and there's a jacket you can put on," and his flash frames twigs and brambles in sliding ovals of ghostlight, stroking the dark edge of the woods, finding the deer trail she must have followed. By now she was aware that he was coming in after her, and he took the erratic shimmer of his own agitation to mean *she* was scared, and somehow this was intolerable, that she would be scared of him, that she would not simply walk out of the woods and face him. That he is in her mind not a good man, a kind man, but instead the punisher she has always believed would come after her, and whether he wanted to cause fear or didn't want to scarcely mattered since that role was carved out ahead of him, narrow as this trail: coming into the woods after her he can't be a good man. He can't remember the last time he felt this kindled and all-over passionate, supple and brilliant, murderously *good*, and when his flash discovered her she was already running, but it took only two long strides to catch her. She broke her fall with her hands but before she could twist over onto her back he had her pinned. If she could have turned and they could have seen each other it might have calmed them both down but this way, with her back under his chest, his mouth by her ear, he was talking right to her fear-lit brain and what he said would be permanent and he felt the exhilaration of being about to drive the truth home to her, and he said *What is the matter with you* and then *You took my kid* and she said *He's not your kid* and he said *My flesh and blood* and they both waited for what she would say next to find out whether she had come to the end of defiance but she hadn't. *If you take him away I'll just come back.* Even now she could have eased them back from this brink if she had shown a little remorse and he was sorry she hadn't and said *What do I need to do to get through to you.* She thrashed as he rolled her over and her fist caught the flashlight, sending light hopping away across the ground. In the refreshed darkness he reached for her and she was screaming his name as his hands tightened to shut off her voice. Where his flashlight had rolled to a halt a cluster of hooded mushrooms stood up in awed distinctness like tiny watchers. When she clawed at his face he released her neck to hold her down by the wrists and he heard twigs breaking under her as she twisted. The twining silver bracelet imprinted itself on his palm: he could feel that, and it was enough to bring him to himself, but she did not let up, raking at his throat when he reared back, and now her despairing *Fuck you fuck you fuck you* assailed him, its echo bandied about through the woods until feeling her wrath slacken from exhaustion he rolled from her so she would know it was over and they fell quiet except for their ragged breathing, which made them what neither wanted to be, a pair, and as he sat up something nicked the back of his skull in its flight, frisking through his hair, an electrified non-contact that sang through his skull to the roots of his teeth and the retort cracked through the woods and there was the boy, five feet away, holding the gun with his legs braced wide apart. Behind him rose a fountain of sword ferns taller than he was. "Don't shoot," she said. "Listen to me, Dyl, don't shoot the gun again, okay? You need to put it down now."

He turned to Sean then to see how bad it was, what he had done, and in staring back at him Sean could feel by the contracted tensions of his face that it was a wrecked mask of disbelief and no reassurance whatsoever to the boy.

"It was a accident," the boy said. "I'm sorry if I scared you."

"Just you kneel down and put it on the ground," she said. "In the leaves—yes, just like that. That was good."

"It was a accident."

"Sweetie, I know it was." She sat up. With her face averted she said to Sean, "It could have been either of us. Did it nick you, though? Are you bleeding?"

He felt through his hair and held his hand out and they both looked: a perfect unbloodied hand stared back at them.

"A fraction of an inch," he said in a voice soft as hers had been: conspirators. "I left the damn gun in the car. Fuck, I never even checked, I was so sure it wasn't loaded. It would've been my fault and he'd've had to live with it forever."

"He doesn't have to live with it now," she said. "Or with you."

She was on her feet, collecting the flashlight, and playing through the sapling audience the light paused and she said, "Jesus," and he turned to look behind him at a young tan oak whose dove-gray bark was gashed in sharp white.

She turned from him. She told the boy, "It's okay. Look at my eyes, Dylan. Nobody's hurt. You see that, don't you? Nobody got hurt."

"You did," he said.

"Baby, I'm not hurt. Pawpaw didn't hurt me, and you know what? We're getting out of here. You're coming with me."

Dylan looked down at the gun and she said, "No, leave it." Then changed her mind. "I'm taking it," she told Sean, "because that's wisest, isn't it."

"You can't think that," Sean said.

"Tell me you're okay to be left," she said.

"A little stunned is all."

"That's three of us then."

Dylan was staring at him and Sean collected his wits to say clearly, "You know what a near miss is, don't you, Dyl? Close but not quite? That bullet came pretty close but I'm what you call unscathed. Which means fine. Are you hearing me say it didn't hurt me? Nod your head so I'm sure you understand." The boy nodded. "We're good then, right? You can see I'm good." The boy nodded.

Esme said, "We need to go, Dylan. Look at you. You're shivering."

"Where are we going?"

"Far away from here, and don't worry, it's all right if we go. Tell him now that we can go."

This was meant for Sean, and they watched as he took the full measure of what he had done and how little chance there was of her heeding what he said now: "Don't disappear with him, Esme. Don't take him away forever because of tonight. From now on my life will be one long trying to make this right to you. For him, too. Don't keep him away. My life spent making up for this. I need you to believe me. I can make this right."

"I want to believe you," she said. "I almost want to believe you."

Before he could think how to begin to answer that the mother and child were gone.

He knew enough not to go after them. He knew enough not to go after them yet.

Nominated by Threepenny Review and Jessica Roeder

FAMILY MATH

by ALAN MICHAEL PARKER

from THE KENYON REVIEW

I am more than half the age of my father,
who has lived more than twice as long
as his father, who died at thirty-six.

Once a year for four days
I am two years older than my wife,
until her birthday.

In practical terms I am three times older
than the Internet, twelve times
the age of my obsolescent computer,

eight times older than the new century
and not yet half a century old.
Impractically, here I count the nothings,

add them up to less than what I hope.
I have taught for more than half my life.
Most afternoons of teaching

follow unfinished mornings.
Yesterday I held a book seven times older
than I am. Twenty-eight hours

and a few minutes later,
I recall the smell,
a leathery, mildewed tang.

Sixteen and one-half years ago, my son
was born, which took twelve hours.
His delivery came two weeks late.

The smell in the delivery room
seemed primordial, iron in the blood,
and shit, and another kind of smell—

more abstract, if that's possible.
Twenty-six years ago I studied
abstract ideas in school, and I still don't know

what's possible. Now I teach.
My mother taught for twenty-nine years
and now she reads.

My friend remembers all he reads—
so when does he finish a book?
I can't remember when I stopped counting

on my fingers: where was I in language?
I feel older than all the wars going on,
but I'm not, some are very old.

Sadness remains the source of my politics.
In my home, very few items I own
are older than I am, and almost none I use.

We say "the wind dies down."
Is that what we mean? Lives and dies?
When babies are born, they know not

night or day. We teach them.
Tomorrow is not my birthday
but all the math will change again.

More to busy me, more to figure and record.
More to have. More to let go.

Nominated by The Kenyon Review and Tony Barnstone, Rosellen Brown,
Andrea Hollander Budy, Kevin Prufer

DARK HORSE

by LISA COUTURIER

from ORION

I WENT TO AN AUCTION last Monday. Not an auction for foreclosed homes. Not an auction for priceless art or jewelry or land. I went to the New Holland Livestock Auction in the Amish and Mennonite country of New Holland, Pennsylvania, where each week horses are sold—though I'd no intention of buying one. I know a thing or two about horses. I spend a significant amount of time with them and can groom them, bathe them, saddle them, walk them, run them on a lead, ride them, feed them, blanket them, work them in a round pen, give them medicine, soak their sore hooves, lift and stretch their hindlegs and forelegs, clean the undersides of their feet, bandage their legs, and minister to their wounds. But I could not foresee, in the spare few minutes each horse at such an auction is given to demonstrate its abilities, personality, strength, or lack thereof (whether young or old, muscled or thin), that I'd be able to determine whether any particular horse would be the one for me.

Besides, it was hard to even think at the auction. I took a seat in the large crowd of people—with the Amish men wearing straw hats, black pants, and jackets; with the Mennonite men in their black hats and suspendered pants; with the city slickers from somewhere else and the country folk from nearby; with children and their grandparents fussing over spilled sodas. People talked, laughed, visited, ate hot dogs, Amish pies, and French fries. We all sat sandwiched together in the steep, gray bleachers that formed an oval around the dirt ring in which the horses were shown, one after another, from ten a.m. until midafternoon. A "loose horse" was a horse that came into the auction ring without a

394

rider; the horses with riders were called "saddle horses." Loose horses are at a disadvantage in terms of finding a good home because even though they are often saddle broke they nonetheless sell for less without a rider atop them in the ring.

The fate of those horses that entered and exited the ring quickly—such as one thin copper-colored Thoroughbred mare I remember—seemed bleak, the implication being that the horse was barely worth the time it took to auction off. That particular Thoroughbred mare, whose long, flaxen mane and tail were braided, must have had someone who had cared enough for her to make her pretty, perhaps believing this would help sell her to a good home, where a girl might braid her once again. Her head hanging low, she slowly walked around the ring, only once, and then stepped out a side exit. If there was any bidding for her, I didn't hear or see it.

More than once the black-bearded Mennonite man running the auction—someone called him Zimmerman—asked the audience to settle down. Given the noisy crowd and the loud, stern voice of the auctioneer calling out in rapid-fire succession the back-and-forth bidding for the animals, I did not expect the saddle horses to try so hard to do well. Horses are flight animals; they flee at the unfamiliar; fear is their dominant emotion. But they are social creatures, too. They aim to please because they've learned to trust, which meant that even the strong and healthy horses, of which there were many, obediently did as they were told amid the chaos of the auction: *go forward; go back; turn left, now right; stop, immediately; go fast, go slow; stand still.* They were willing to do as asked, as they've been over the centuries—to churn the soil in our fields, to fight our battles, to run our races until their lungs bleed or their bones break. This might possibly be their last chance to perform, and they mustered up that certain nobility and courage possessed by horses, as though they had upon their backs the Navajo of long ago, the warriors who, before battle, would whisper into the ears of their horses: *Be brave and nothing will happen. We will come back safely.*

BEFORE THE AUCTION BEGAN, I had walked through the barns adjoining the auction ring where the horses stood tied to their posts. There are approximately 9 million horses in the United States, and at the auction there were two hundred of not necessarily the unwanted but surely the unlucky. Unlucky because, though I suppose going to a horse auction might sound like a day in the country—Amish food and horse-drawn buggies and all that—this particular auction is frequented by men known as "kill buyers," which, by association, makes New Holland a kill auction, one of the largest east of the Mississippi. Kill buyers (KBs) also are called "meat men"—the men who purchase horses, typically from the major kill auctions, and deliver them for slaughter, though they also visit Thoroughbred racetracks and wheel and deal with horse dealers who've secured horses elsewhere: former show horses from the hunter/jumper/ eventing/dressage worlds whose unsuspecting owners believe the dealer will place their horses in good homes; horses listed in newspaper classifieds or on Craigslist (you can find them for sale for a dollar); surplus lesson horses; horses that start out at smaller auctions, such as the Hickory Auction in Pennsylvania, the Camelot Auction in New Jersey, or any of the other nearly one hundred horse auctions scattered across the U.S. All these places are entry points for what is termed the "slaughter pipeline"; and those horses unlucky enough to stay in the pipeline eventually arrive at bigger and potentially more deadly places such as New Holland, where, the day I attended, the younger Mennonite and Amish boys managed a parade of breeds and types (drafts, minis, Quarter Horses, Thoroughbreds, Standardbreds, fit and fat and healthy horses, tired and skinny horses, carriage horses, work horses, mares and geldings and stallions and foals) by whipping in the face the more frightened horses that took longer than a few seconds to understand what they were being told to do. Of course, not just KBs attend such auctions. And the horses being sold could have many possible new homes and potential uses—with families who want a trail horse, say, or with horse trainers, or with competitive riders looking for a strong event or endurance horse. Nonetheless, by the end of the day at any number of auctions around the country, the KBs have "bid for horses against private buyers, against each other and other dealers, as well as against horse rescues," says Christy Sheidy of Another Chance 4 Horses, in Bernville, Pennsylvania. "The horses the kill buyers took could've easily been re-homed and gone on to live happy lives with families who want and appreciate them. *They were not unwanted.*"

Ultimately, kill buyers take what they need to satisfy their contracts with slaughterhouses. The day I visited New Holland, they were taking horses going for $500 or less; and though sometimes these were the young or the old, the sick or the skinny horses, it was clear that the healthy ones were preferred—the more body weight, the more money for the load. The buzz at New Holland that day was that a KB would receive about $600 from the slaughterhouse for each horse, though prices fluctuate depending on location, supply, and demand. A report quoted by a USDA slaughter statistician for that time period indicated the price of a horse at auction to be around forty-three cents per pound, but horse meat can fetch as much as fifteen dollars per pound in the retail market.

Because Americans don't eat horses, it is surprising to learn that people of other cultures do. "Horse meat became popular after World War II," says Carolyn Stull, animal welfare specialist at the School of Veterinary Medicine, University of California, Davis. It was an inexpensive protein "for lower-income people in Europe, where beef was scarce, and old or lame draft horses were processed as affordable meat." Prices have risen since World War II, but the market continues to be highly profitable for the foreign companies that process horses from the U.S. and Canada, both of which have large horse populations. In a paper concerning horse transport regulations, Stull cites the different types of horse meat various cultures prefer. For instance, the Japanese prefer draft horse meat, she writes, referencing a 1999 article titled "Horses Destined to Slaughter" (though at New Holland I heard that the Japanese and French like Quarter Horses the most because of the lean muscle mass). The Italians, cites Stull, prefer eighteen- to twenty-four-month-old horses; the French go for ten- to twelve-year-old horses; and the Swiss take the two- to three-year-olds.

There are currently no horse-slaughtering facilities in the U.S., which means horses are transported to Canada and Mexico before being put to a typically untimely death. In the 1980s there were sixteen slaughterhouses in the U.S. By 1993 there were about ten, scattered across the country—in Connecticut, Texas, Oregon, Illinois, Nebraska, and Ohio. By the fall of 2007, the last three—two in Texas and one in Illinois—were shut down by courts that upheld state laws banning horse slaughter. The fight against slaughter within the U.S. grew from outrage over the fact that ex-racehorses like Ferdinand, Kentucky Derby winner and Horse of the Year, as well as a racehorse named Exceller, who'd defeated two Triple Crown winners, had slipped through the cracks and been purchased for slaughter overseas (Exceller in Sweden in 1997, and Ferdinand in Japan in 2002). Slaughter opponents included the general public (seven in ten Americans are against it, according to Madeleine Pickens, former racehorse breeder and wife of billionaire T. Boone Pickens); a majority of the Thoroughbred racing industry; and professionals within the horse industry (trainers, riders, breeders), all of whom, once they spoke up for horses, were labeled "animal rights activists" by the proslaughter contingency as a way to discredit them.

Slaughter, however, is not banned at the federal level, and individual states that have not banned it could see new slaughterhouses opened in the future. In early 2009, a Montana state legislator, aptly named Ed Butcher, tried and failed to lure the Chinese (who eat a lot of horses) into building a plant there. But Butcher has not given up. As of March 2010, even though he decided not to run for re-election, he told a reporter for the Montana *Independent Record* that he's still "shepherding his horse slaughterhouse idea by trying to find a market." According to the *Journal of the American Veterinary Medical Association*, lawmakers in nearly a dozen states are drafting initiatives to reintroduce the possibility of slaughtering of horses in the United States. This is why slaughter opponents ceaselessly fight for the passage of the Prevention of Equine Cruelty Act of 2009 (H.R. 503 / S. 727), which would end at a national level the slaughter of horses for human consumption as well as the domestic and international transport of live horses or horseflesh for human consumption.

A new plot turn in this story is that, as of July 31, 2010, the European Union (EU) will require that horses destined for slaughter and human consumption are free from certain drugs, including many that long have been in the bodies of horses, most notably phenylbutazone (a pain reliever and anti-inflammatory commonly called "bute," which is given to an estimated 98 percent of American Thoroughbred racehorses as well as to just about any breed of horse to relieve occasional pain or swelling). Kill buyers will be required to provide a signed statement for each horse claiming that to the best of their knowledge the animal has not been treated with these particular substances. "Some kill buyers claim openly that they will simply fill in bogus forms," says John Holland, president of the Equine Welfare Alliance. The fact is, it would be impossible for KBs to tell the truth, because the horses they pick up could have had numerous owners, and it is rare for papers of any kind to travel with horses to auction, let alone an animal's lifelong medical history.

It is unlikely that this new hurdle will suddenly stop kill buyers from shipping horses across our borders, as they had been doing even before the last three U.S. slaughterhouses closed. The figures for 2009 show that horses slaughtered in Canada were sold to as many as twenty-four countries, with France, Switzerland, Japan, and Belgium receiving 92 percent of the exports. The demand from countries where horseflesh is considered a pricey delicacy is the predominant reason horses go to slaughter. Some slaughter proponents suggest that the demand is met by horses that are no longer useful to their owners and are therefore better off slaughtered than suffering starvation and neglect. Neglect does of course occur, but neglected and starving horses are not necessarily the ones chosen by the KBs, and such horses don't always make it to auction to begin with. Consider the nearly two hundred mustangs found starving—seventy-four of them already dead—at the Three Strikes Ranch in Nebraska in 2009. With such a large enticement of horseflesh, the owner of Three Strikes could have chosen to have the meat man come hither; he could've sent his neglected horses off with a KB who would've paid him for the animals. But he did not.

It is more often the case that horse owners do not wish their healthy animals an untimely death, are unaware that dealers flip their equines like real estate, and would be horrified to know that their animals had been sold into the slaughter pipeline. Bottom line: a horse is a commodity and someone is making money off of it somewhere down the road. And it is all perfectly legal, since horses are deemed livestock by the U.S. government, even though they are not part of the American food chain.

Horses in America today are used less for agricultural purposes and more for sport, competition, trail rides, and showing. They are bred and raised to be companions, not dinner entrees, which is why slaughter seems incompatible with our country's relationship to this animal. And the manner in which these horses are killed only makes it more so. Before a horse is ostensibly unconscious and hung upside down by one of its back legs, and before its throat is cut and it is bled out, the horse must enter the killbox, or knockbox, where it is shot in the head with a device called a captive bolt gun, which is a four-inch-long, retractable, nail-like instrument. The captive bolt gun does not immediately kill the horse but is meant to render it insensible to pain. According to the American Veterinary Medical Association, a captive bolt gun will work effectively under the following conditions: if it is clean and in proper working order, if the horse stands still, and if, shall we say, the gun is dead-on the right spot on the horse's forehead. These conditions are hard to ensure.

"It is a dangerous practice to equate the medical procedure of chemical euthanasia performed by a veterinarian to end an animal's life with that of a slaughterhouse worker killing an animal," says Nena Winand, a faculty member in the College of Veterinary Medicine at Cornell

University. "There are many differences. Vets monitor vitals to cause the least amount of trauma, mental or otherwise. [Slaughterhouse workers] don't take the time to monitor that the horse is dead. The horse gets hit multiple times with the captive bolt gun. We don't know that they're always insensible to pain. This treatment of horses has been going on since I was a kid, and I'm fifty-two now. The industry has never been successfully regulated. We pay taxes to monitor and enforce the humane treatment of these horses, but nothing's enforced and it never has been. Whoever says otherwise is misrepresenting the history of this industry. To say it's all perfect—well, it's just insane."

It all seems like the ultimate betrayal to a horse that likely served its owners for years and, at some point in its life, experienced human kindness. But there is not an exchange rate for kindness, while there is one for demand. In 2009 alone, demand resulted in the slaughter of 93,812 horses in Canada; of those, 56 percent were American horses; Canada's revenue was $86.9 million; and the largest importer was France, paying $27.8 million. Worth noting, in a reflective and economy-minded sort of way regarding the issue of demand, is something comedian Jon Stewart said, which was referred to by racing columnist Jay Hovdey in the *Daily Racing Form*: "There's demand for cocaine and hookers, too."

"There are two things that flourish in the dark—mushrooms and horse slaughter," said the late John Hettinger, a Thoroughbred racing legend and former member of the board of trustees of the New York Racing Association. "Most people don't know it's going on. We must deny them the darkness." To shine a light inside the darkness, various humane groups (the Humane Society of the U.S., the Humane Farming Association) have taken undercover videos inside slaughterhouses, where workers poke, whip, and beat the animals' bodies with fiberglass rods. Video from inside Mexican slaughterhouses reveals horses stabbed repeatedly with knives, which paralyzes the horse but leaves it conscious at the start of the slaughter process. The videos are exceedingly difficult to watch. In response to a Freedom of Information Act request, the USDA recently disclosed some nine hundred pages (including photos) documenting hundreds of violations of humane treatment to horses during transport to slaughter and at the American plants prior to their closings in 2007. The photos (available on Kaufmanzoning.net) depict horses with severed legs, crushed skulls, and missing eyes, as well as pregnant mares. Late-term pregnant mares, foals, blind horses, and horses who cannot stand on all four legs are not supposed to be sent to slaughter. Those animals that do make the trip are to be fed, watered, and rested. Often they are not.

"The whole thing, it's a boondoggle on the American people," said slaughter opponent and oilman T. Boone Pickens to a Chicago NBC reporter. "People that are for slaughter should be forced to go down on that kill floor."

For those of us who will never get to the kill floor, or who have not the stomach to watch the videos on YouTube, here are two short excerpts, the first from the notes of an Animal and Plant Health Inspection Investigator at eleven-twenty a.m. on April 13, 2005, at the Cavel slaughter plant in DeKalb, Illinois:

> *Eight horses were in the alleyway leading directly to the knock-box. . . . The employee who is routinely assigned to work on the kill floor, hanging the horses on the rails, was using a riding crop to whip the horse in the alleyway closest to the knock-box. This horse continued to move backward, away from the knock-box causing the other horses behind it to be overcrowded. As the whipping continued the horses in the alleyway became extremely excited. I immediately told the employee to stop but he did not listen to me. During this time, the last horse in the alleyway attempted to jump over the alleyway wall and became stuck over the top of the wall. Eventually it had flailed around enough to fall over to the other side of the wall. I went to the kill floor to find the plant manager, could not find him. . . . Meanwhile two more horses fell down in the alleyway. The first was the second horse in line to the knock-box. It had fallen forward and the horse behind it began to walk on top of it as the downed horse struggled to get up. The second horse to fall was the fourth horse in line. It had flipped over backwards due to the overcrowding and was subsequently trapped and trampled by the fifth and sixth horses in line in their excitement. . . .*

And in this statement taken from records in Cook County, Illinois, a former slaughterhouse employee testified to the following:

> *In July 1991, they were unloading one of the double-decker trucks. A horse got his leg caught in the side of the truck so*

the driver pulled the rig up and the horse's leg popped off. The
horse was still living, and it was shaking. [Another employee]
popped it on the head and we hung it up and split it open. . . .
Sometimes we would kill near 390, 370 a day. Each double-
decker might have up to 100 on it. We would pull off the dead
ones with chains. Ones that were down on the truck, we would
drag them off with chains and maybe put them in a pen or we
might drag them with an automatic chain to the knock-box.
Sometimes we would use an electric shocker to make them
stand. To get them to the knockbox, you have to shock them
. . . sometimes run them up the [anus] with the shocker. . . .
When we killed a pregnant mare, we would take the guts out
and I would take the bag out and open it and cut the cord and
put it in the trash and sometimes the baby would still be liv-
ing, and its heart would be beating, but we would put it in the
trashcan.

I'D FOUND MY WAY to New Holland with a horse rescue worker I'll call Pat. Like many people who start up rescues, Pat was a life-long rider and horse owner before opening her rescue in 2008. When I first visited her on a cold winter afternoon several weeks before the auction, I was led into a paddock of ex-racehorses rescued from nearby tracks. While we walked, Pat recounted for me the injuries that ended the horses' careers and commented on the "bottom-dweller trainers who would've sold them to the meat man" and the "good trainers who call rescues to come take them." The horses gravitated toward her, while chickens poked about and ran under the horses' legs of gold and a Labrador puppy jumped up to kiss the horses' long sculpted faces. "These are Thoroughbreds?" I asked, surprised by their calmness. "They're here for a few weeks or so, they settle in," she told me, while leaning into the horses' bellies and cooing to them. "Isn't that right?"

Pat was willing to take me to New Holland—driving us north for three hours in her 100,000-plus-mileage truck, her old trailer trailing behind us. "I need a new trailer, a new truck, fences. Everything. But it works out, somehow. It just does," she said after jump-starting the truck that morning as the sun rose and the fog settled into the foothills and roosters called in the background. We were heading to Pennsylvania to meet a man named Frank, who runs an auction in New Jersey.

"Frank is a kill buyer, plain and simple," says Anne Russek, a former

Thoroughbred racehorse trainer who trained out of Monmouth Park Racetrack in New Jersey and who worked with HBO producers on an episode of Bryant Gumbel's *Real Sports* that aired on May 12, 2008, titled "Hidden Horses." The segment was an exposé that followed the path of a four-year-old Thoroughbred bay filly named No Day Off, who raced for the last time at Mountaineer Park Racetrack in West Virginia on April 12, 2008—just one month before the program aired. *When a Thoroughbred racehorse reaches the end of its career or is simply no longer profitable on the track*, said the HBO trailer, *it is often taken directly to auction and sold for meat.*

"Frank wants to work with the rescues," says Pat. "But when he has a full load of horses, he will ship them to Canada." Pat implies, as we talk in the truck about meeting with Frank, that he has of late softened a bit. When finally I glimpse him at the auction sitting not far from us on a row of bleachers, I notice that he is older than the other KBs; he has white hair, a wide face, blue eyes, and a heather-brown, zip-up cardigan that gives him a rather grandfatherly look. Later in the day, after Frank has assisted Pat with rescuing a small pony that her daughter might like, the first thing he says to me when he learns I am writing about auctions, racing, and slaughter is: "I have an excellent attorney."

The purpose of meeting Frank at New Holland was to pick up two Thoroughbred mares, former racehorses. Thoroughbred racehorses are not supposed to end up at horse auctions, nor are they to be disposed of directly off the track with the KBs in what is euphemistically referred to as "stable to table in seven days."

"I've been involved in the Thoroughbred industry for thirty-eight years," says Russek, who is now chairperson of the Thoroughbred Celebration Horse Show series, which exclusively features off-the-track racehorses. "As much as I was involved, I never realized how many Thoroughbreds were going to slaughter. It was a secret. Everybody's dirty secret. You have to show so much identification to get onto the backstretch of a racetrack, where the horses are kept, but you show nothing to get a horse off the track. When I started working on this issue I couldn't have been more surprised by the denial. Every track said, 'It's not happening at our track.' It became very apparent to me what was happening. For instance, at a track like Belmont, where it wasn't happening so much—but then a horse loses and goes to a lower-level track and the horse starts going down. They end up at Mountaineer Park, at Charlestown, at Beulah Park, Penn National. Those are where the East Coast horses end up."

Some racetracks profess that their horses do not end up at auctions or in slaughterhouses because the tracks have instituted zero-tolerance policies for such behavior from trainers and owners. But the reality, explains Monique Koehler, founder of the Thoroughbred Retirement Foundation, is a "Thoroughbred industry made up largely of owners with only modest resources and current economics that dictate that among all owners, no matter how responsible and well-intended, only a relatively few are capable of maintaining even a single Thoroughbred once it is unable to earn its keep on the track."

Though it would not be impossible to list the policies of the nearly one hundred racetracks in the U.S., consider it safe to say that there are a good number of tracks with ostensible zero-tolerance, or "no kill," policies. These "no kill" tracks attempt to clear away their injured and their low earners through more acceptable channels—retirement, retraining and adoption, or rescue; all three options are carried out by various high- and low-budget rescue groups. One inventive effort at the Finger Lakes Racetrack involves a transition barn of sorts, called the Purple Haze Center, where horses no longer able to race are retrained and stabled on the grounds of the track until they are adopted. It is the first Thoroughbred track in the country to have an in-house adoption program that is run collaboratively between track management and horsemen. And some tracks, such as Suffolk Downs in East Boston, are connected to CANTER (the Communication Alliance to Network Thoroughbred Ex-Racehorses), a group that works with trainers to identify racehorses who need homes and lists available horses on their website.

But not all horsemen take advantage of groups like CANTER or other rescue options and, apparently, resort instead to unscrupulous practices. Russek describes a place not far from New Holland that is run by a Mennonite man. "I went there hoping to establish a relationship with him," she explained. "He told me dealers bring horses from the track saying they *must* go to slaughter because trainers don't want it known what they're doing." In other words, a dead horse is harder to trace than a horse that ends up at auction when it's not supposed to.

Take the story of Twilight Overture, a gelding who came from Thistledown, "which is a 'no-kill' track," says Nena Winand. One of the rescues alerted Thistledown's general manager that the horse had been purchased by a kill buyer at the Sugarcreek Auction in Ohio. At the request of the manager, the rescue called the KB, who, surprisingly, turned his double-decker around and returned Twilight Overture to

Sugarcreek for the rescue. Thistledown and Winand paid the KB $850 for the racehorse. "I renamed him Next Stop: Mars," says Winand. "Why? Because if you look at his record, he was in training from track to track to track. What does he think of his life? He was shipped every two weeks somewhere. Then he's on a double-decker to get his head bashed in. He's big, extremely athletic. His story epitomizes that slaughter is a convenient disposal system. This horse is very usable. There's no limit to what he can do; he's not bad-minded. It's default; it's convenient. That's why it's happening. Why would a trainer kill this horse, my horse? Because they want the 300 bucks they get for him from the kill buyer."

"Zero-tolerance at the tracks? Yeah, right. There's no enforcement," says Pat, when two weeks after our trip to New Holland I arrive at her rescue and find her all in a flurry trying to raise $1,500 to rescue three Thoroughbreds from Mountaineer Park. "The trainer wants $300 each or she's letting the meat man take them. And I need $200 each just to get them here. And I need it *now*." She scampers from the field to a stall to the computer to check in with contacts about the amount of money being raised to rescue the Thoroughbreds. "Everyone wants me to take two of them; you know, I just got those others. I don't have enough money to do it." Pat sighs, slipping in and out of various website forums and boards where people from across the country shoot messages back and forth. This is their battle—to save horses—and the computer is both their weapon and their battlefield. Pat pulls up photos of two of the Mountaineer Park horses in immediate need. One is a chestnut named Nitro, the other a black horse named I Gotta Go. Seeing their photos makes them real; and I am reminded that, as another Triple Crown season winds down—that time of year when Americans watch the fastest of the fast run their million-dollar races—thousands of the lesser-known Thoroughbreds like Nitro and I Gotta Go await their fate, having not only never made it to national television, but potentially never making it out of racing alive.

All of this sheds light on—but in the end proves nothing about—how a tall, slender, dapple-gray Thoroughbred gelding that had raced at Suffolk Downs in Boston and at Tampa Downs in Florida ended up at New Holland the morning I was there, still wearing his racing plates and standing quietly in front of me, roped to a post against a concrete wall. He already had been claimed by a KB, whom Pat would have to find and then pay more than he had paid for the gelding if she wanted to take the horse home. About a month later, I will call this kill buyer to inquire about the dapple-gray gelding. Where had the horse come from? Who'd shipped him? The KB will inform me, rather politely at first, that he is on the road with the rig and cannot give me any phone numbers. As I ask again about the journey of the dapple-gray, I picture this KB standing ringside at the auction, closest to the horses entering, along with the other KBs, all Caucasian, most in their midforties, wearing baseball caps, slouchy jackets like high-school football players, jeans, and colorful studded leather belts. Soon enough he tires of my questions.

"Who the fuck are you? Are you the horse's owner?" he rages.

"No," I answer.

"Then why the fuck are you poking your fucking nose into this?"

OF THE TWO THOROUGHBRED mares we'd planned on retrieving from Frank at the auction, one was pregnant, due imminently, so Pat had spent the weekend building a foaling stall for the mare. When I called on Sunday morning to confirm our arrangements, Pat was hammering nails into plywood with a retired neighbor who volunteers. Later that afternoon, though, Pat called back to say that the pregnant mare had been inadvertently sent off on the slaughter truck a few days earlier. It was not clear how this had happened. Despite the fact that it's against regulations, she nonetheless had been dispatched on the long trip to Canada.

Probably, said Pat, she was already dead.

At the auction, Pat leaves the bleachers frequently to track down Thoroughbreds, and while she is away, quite a few of them stream in and out of the noisy bidding ring, along with other breeds, too many to list, all in and out so fast it is hard to keep track of the numbers and prices. All of the following, which is in no way a complete list, were taken by the kill buyers:

— Thoroughbred bay gelding: $310
— Thoroughbred chestnut gelding: $325
— Palomino gelding, whipped several times by rider: $450
— Two Thoroughbred geldings, lost track of price
— Thoroughbred gelding, no price that I can hear, exits early
— Standardbred mare, leaves the ring early. On her way out, Mennonite boys whip her repeatedly in the face. Russek will tell me later that some of the Amish and Mennonite can be "truly heartless" in the way they treat their horses, an observation that is, in all but the same

words, repeated by a horse rescue worker who reported her experience at an Indiana auction on the Grateful Acres website: "The kill pen is full of Belgian draft horses, the powerful, living machinery of Amish farms. . . . [T]he Belgians in this pen are grievously and horrifyingly injured. They have been worked until they literally cannot stand any longer. . . . No matter that the animal has slaved . . . for any number of years, no matter that his swollen, oozing knee is collapsing at every forced step. Just as a broken plow would be sold to the junk man for the metal, these broken animals are sold to the kill-man for meat."

— Thoroughbred / Quarter Horse cross: $125
— Farm horse sold "as is" leaves ring early
— Paso Fino gelding, eleven years old, brown with white face: $160
— Brown and white Paint pony: $250
— Paint gelding: $360

After two hours it becomes increasingly difficult to watch, so I walk with Pat back into the barns to be with the horses, though the decision to be with the animals suddenly feels worse than staying in the bleachers. Standing so close to so many of them, looking into their faces, rubbing their bodies, listening to them eat hay, watching them watch us, I realize the emotional blackmail of the moment. There is the wish to save them all, knowing full well no one can, and that by tonight many of them will be heading to Canada, or to feedlots to be fattened up for a slaughterhouse in Canada. To the extent that one can, Pat has crossed this threshold, and her time in the barn is more goal-directed: She weaves through the lines of animals to find the Thoroughbreds. "Here's one," she yells out to me, while lifting the horse's upper lip and calling out the tattoo number for me to write down. Racehorses are required to have a tattoo inside their upper lip, which identifies the horse and links it to its registration papers. Soon enough she is off with a list of tattoos to call in to a contact waiting to help identify the racetracks to which the Thoroughbreds were last connected. Meanwhile, I scan the rows and rows of horses and ponies, looking for the copper-colored mare I'd seen earlier in the day, the one with the braided mane and tail. Pat hurries back to say she has the dapple-gray racehorse. The KB gave it over for $600. "It's a lot, but I'll train him to jump," she says. "He'll make a good jumper, and people love the dapple-grays."

People love ponies, too, Pat had said at the beginning of the auction. "They're always asking me for ponies." And so more than midway through the auction she has bought, for about $200 each, several ponies to adopt out as 4-H projects or as pony club mounts. One is a large, brown, bulldozerlike Hackney gelding she later will name Edward; another is a small gray boy just gelded and still shot up with testosterone who will be called Merry Legs; an unbroke Paint mare with one blue eye will become Maeve, or "the cause of great joy" in Gaelic. And then, finally, the gray roan Pony of the Americas (POA), who tentatively walks into the ring, scared enough that she'll barely move forward. She is led to stand near the fence by the kill buyers. Her eyes look up into the bleachers, her skin twitches when someone touches her, and the bidding begins. "Do you want that pony, Pat?" I ask.

"I don't have any money left. She's cute, though."

I raise my bidding card and so does a kill buyer. We start low, $35.

The KB raises his card for $40.

I go $45.

He goes $50; I raise for $60.

Zimmerman, the bearded Mennonite, looks up to me. I am new here, and I sense at that moment he knows it. He raises the bidding by $20.

KB agrees to $80. I go to $90. KB takes $95.

The auctioneer calls out $100. Zimmerman's dark eyes stare straight to mine. Once we get to $100 the price could keep climbing, and I am unsure what I can do; at the same time, I look at the POA. As much noise as there is around me—the old couple bickering, kids playing and laughing—it suddenly seems as if there is no sound, and I feel like the student in the classroom who everyone's looking at because I've been asked to answer a question I don't have an answer for.

I raise for $100.

Zimmerman looks at the KB. There is a pause. But the KB does not bid. It is over, suddenly, in a matter of seconds. "One hundred dollars for number 730-I," the auctioneer calls out.

I climb the stairs to the New Holland Auction office to pay for the pony I later will name Bridget and give to Pat, and I think how often I've blown a hundred dollars on a meaningless trip to Target. The cashier gives me the name and number of the person who unloaded Bridget at the auction because I request it. I am still naïve at this point and I assume her owners brought her here. I want to call them later to ask about their pony and tell them I have her now. That she is safe. "Charlie, here," the voice answers, when a few days later I call. "I don't know nothin' 'bout her, ma'am," the man says. "Bought her cheap at the Hickory Auction. I sell tack there and someone's sellin' her. So I take her. I bought her on Sunday and took her to New Holland on

Monday. Ain't gonna lie to ya ma'am, don't know nothin' 'bout her. I buy cheap horses and resell 'em. That's what I do."

Down on the auction floor, Pat is gathering up Bridget to put her in the pen with Edward, Maeve, Merry Legs, and the dapple-gray Thoroughbred. Not long after, we will meet up with Frank and transfer the mare he brought down from New Jersey. In the afternoon, when the auction is over and we are loading the horses and ponies onto Pat's trailer, around the corner will come the thin copper-colored mare with the long flaxen braids. The bones of her skinny shoulders and hips poke up from her body when she walks. She is led by a KB.

He instructs her onto his trailer. She does not move. He yanks hard on her lead rope. As thin and weak as she is, she jumps back from the trailer, her long braided mane flopping against her neck. He yells at her, harsh and fast and low, and whips her over and over in the face and on her shoulders and belly. She jumps up and throws herself against the inside wall of the trailer.

He shoves her into the horses already on the rig and they all jostle together, colliding, biting, and agitating one another. As the dust floats up and is set aglow by the afternoon sunlight streaming into the trailer, the mare stumbles. Finally, she finds a place by the window and gazes out.

Nominated by Orion

MURDER BALLAD

by JANE SPRINGER

from THE CINCINNATI REVIEW

Who made the banjo sad & wrong?
Who made the luckless girl & hell-bound boy?
Who made the ballad? The ballad, I mean—
where lovers gallop down mountain brush as though in love?
The one where all the way hooves break ground to a blood-earth scent?
Who gave the boy swift words to woo the girl from home?
(Who made the girl too pretty to leave alone?)
He locks one arm beneath her breasts as they ride on.
Maybe her apron comes undone & falls to a ditch of black-eyed Susans.
Does she dream the clouds are so much flour spilt on heavens table?

I don't know what dark county of the heart this music comes from.
I don't know where to hammer-on or to drop a thumb
to the haunted string that tells the story straight: All night Little
    Willie's dug
on Polly's grave with a silver spade & every creek they cross
makes one last splash. Though flocks of swallows loom—the one
hung in cedar now will score the girl's last thrill.
Tell me, why do I love this sawmill-tuned melancholy song
& the thud of knuckles darkening the banjo face?
Tell me how to erase the ancient, violent beauty
in the devil of not loving what we love?

Nominated by The Cincinnati Review and David Kirby

THAT STORY

fiction by JACK DRISCOLL

from THE GEORGIA REVIEW

WHEREVER my mom finds these articles I haven't a clue. All I know is that she clips them out and hands them to me to read. "Look, Fritzi, another miracle," she says, the most recent having occurred somewhere outside San Francisco.

For a good laugh I pass them along to Dieter and Brinks while we smoke in my dad's Plymouth Fury, the odometer frozen at 172,605 miles. The car is up on blocks, transmission shot and hubs painted purple. Rear risers but no tires, and snow up to both doors so we have to crawl inside, like it's an igloo or a fort, and always with some half-wrapped notion of someday firing it alive and driving hellbent away from Bethlehem. Not the one in Pennsylvania, but a town so remote you can't even locate its position on a USGS map.

And therein resides both the irony and the farthest far-flung implausibility that somebody hereabouts discovers a visage of Christ in a lint screen at the local laundromat, and that then, along with our name, we got ourselves a shrine and a destination to boot. "Imagine it," my mom says, but a million pilgrims desperate to put a knee down in this nothing town suddenly adjacent to God and heaven confounds even the dreamer in me. And yet, as misguided as such an influx sounds, it's what she's apparently banking on. Which might explain why she's hand-painting all those baby Jesus Christmas ornaments, preparing to make a fortune off the endless caravans of sinners soon to arrive here in the provinces. But she says, "Nope. Uh-uh." They're nothing more than another scheme designed to fill and quiet time. Besides, she says, each month at the diner she always manages to sell at least a few to the truckers to take home to their wives.

I hate to admit it, but a miracle is precisely what it'll take to hire a lawyer high-profile enough to enter an appeal and get my dad's sentence overturned from first-degree manslaughter to self-defense. Guilty or not, my mom maintains, when a married man slurps bar vodka from some strange woman's navel, he's going to pay a heavy price somewhere along the line. I remember how, right after the trial, she sat me down at the kitchen table and held both my hands and said, "Fritzi, listen to me. All premature deaths are wrongful deaths. But some, like this one, they're so senseless it makes them more wrong than the others. It makes them," she said, "eternally unforgivable."

Their divorce, final come May, has for a long while now been inevitable and therefore okay, I guess. Except for Bobby Bigalow, my mom's new boyfriend. Every word that falls from his loud mouth is either a rule or a sermon, and whenever he mentions my dad I can feel him present in my balled-up right fist. I know all too well that a single punch placed perfectly to the temple can kill a man, and so I afford Bobby Bigalow a wide berth. I'm only five foot six, but place a bet that I can t hoist a frozen hay bale over my head and you'll lose. Not that I'm prone to feats of strength or violence, but if he ever touches me or mistreats my mom I swear I'll take that first swing and at least rearrange his dentistry, that sneer of a smile, those tight snake lips. Maybe send him packing with a jaw wired shut and eating through a straw—though of course there's my mom to contend with, and thus the quandary.

Dieter and Brinks and me can't see him, but we know he's standing not ten yards in front of us, eyeballs straining, and so in unison we drag all the harder on our Lucky Strikes, imagining ourselves magnified behind the windshield. Tough guys you come at with a length of pipe and who leave teeth marks in the metal.

A fit father or not, my dad taught me to never take one backward step, no matter what, and for starters there's that tradition to honor and uphold. Besides, I've never been fingerprinted or booked on even a single juvenile misdemeanor charge.

Flat-out lucky is Bobby Bigalow's take, and I'd second that—but never face to face the way he'd like. He's the type, you confess anything and he dangles it in front of you like a noose. What he wants is for me to shape up, to shit-ditch what he refers to as my attitude and lack of focus, and commit to a new start before it's too late. Beginning with my friends, "those ones," as he calls them. He means tribal kids. (I'm one-quarter Ottawa on my dad's side, my hair shiny blue-black just like his. The resemblance in our face features, however, is not all that close except in the eyes—"like night minus the moon," as my mom in happier days used to proclaim.) We've grown up together, all three blood brothers, and when Dieter's snowmobile is up and running we like to shoot the glass insulators from the tops of the telephone poles with our pellet rifles. Or ding the silver dining cars mere inches below those lighted windows where couples leaning forward keep toasting their lives, the train whistle within minutes fading into the invisible distance.

Right now, we blow slow-motion smoke rings above the head of the Day-Glo dashboard Saint Christopher, perpetually open-fingered and palms up, who seems to say, "Okay, fine. But you're fifteen years old for chrissakes, and so just what, pray tell, *is* the goddamn battle plan going forward?"

It's late February and the ashtray is packed with a fat stack of Trojans, like it's a free customized in-car dispenser. We've got a bottle of Thunderbird, which Dieter scored on the reservation. Like my dad I've got no alcohol tolerance, so just a few quick hits and I envision a fig bush flowering inside Gloria Masterson's skin-tight Levi's. She's never afforded me the time of day, but there's a buffalo robe on the back seat just in case, and even the thought of it warming those impossible contours of her body accelerates my heart rate by plenty.

I can see my mom peeking out through the living room window, her hands cupped to her face like blinders. Everybody staring at everybody else, and no one advancing or uttering a single sound. A virtual standoff. Our prefab is a repo, two bedrooms and the wall so thin between them that some nights I can hear the static of my mom's nylon stockings as she undresses for bed after a double shift at the Honcho out on old Route 668, just north of the four-way stop. Out on the void, as she says, where idling, slat-sided transport trailers shake the entire parking lot like some low-grade version of the San Andreas Fault. I've seen it firsthand, the plates and silverware rattling on the Formica tables and countertops. My mom gets long hours and low pay, but jobs are tough to come by, and because we're barely hanging on she's locked in there against her long-term wishes. She's first on the seniority list, and I can't recollect when she last called in sick. Or when her credit card wasn't maxed to the hilt.

In one of the articles she gave me, a waterspout somewhere in South America spewed up coins of solid silver and gold. Not the thing you'd think to hope or wait around for, but there it is to consider, as opposed to the cash register that she tends day after day, all sticky with pitted nickels and dimes and quarters. Her dream is to someday see the Himalayas, though she's never even one time in her entire life left the state. Mark my words: Bobby Bigalow is not her ticket to anywhere you'd read about in a guidebook or travel brochure.

He's from Texas, an ex-rodeo cowboy out of Amarillo—or so he claims. He's got a slightly stooped back, so I calculate it's possible some pissed-off Brahman bull whiplashed him into early retirement a few lifetimes ago. Dieter's verdict is pisswilly on that, and Brinks agrees: Bobby Bigalow's just a self-glorified blowhard. He's got hair like General George A. Custer, wavy and blond, and I don't blame my mom for wanting company, but when the metal storm door opens and he steps back inside, I say, "Fuck him."

"And the horse he rode in on," Brinks says, though it's a Chevy Silverado he drives, and sometimes he'll rev it up real loud before he leaves, glass-packs growling, always the near side of midnight. Always after a few beers on the couch with my mom, arm around her neck or waist, and as she closes the blinds now I can see the vibrating blue waves cast by our secondhand, widescreen Sony Trinitron.

At least for the time being the arrangement isn't live-in, and so I suppress any impulse to tell my dad about what's transpired on the courtship front. I will, however, as a last resort if at some point I need his counsel. On the final Sunday of every other month is when we talk, 7:00 p.m. sharp. And it's only because he inquires that I betray my mom's whereabouts. Battalion II Bingo, I tell him. Same exact routine replayed in every single solitary conversation. "Yes, she drives herself," I say, but what I withhold is that it's also where Bobby Bigalow calls out the numbers that have sent my mom home a winner these last few times in a row. It's where they met. An omen, she says, that against all odds she and I are fated for a life of lesser burdens.

During those allotted fifteen contact minutes, my dad says her name a lot, "Laila," in ways that turn each next sentence lonelier than the last. He's never denied that trouble feeds the passions of bad men, and on the witness stand he said simply, in his own defense, that he did not, first off, consider himself to be among them, leastwise not by intention. Just some nobody, he said, with a pint in the glove box and a drinker's lack of judgment—and, no, he conceded, he was not ignorant of a record of arrests too long to overlook after a Sunday night bar fight turned deadly.

"Then you're spared now to contemplate a different life going forward," the judge said. "But for the one you've mangled thus far, Mr. Boyd, you've run your quota of last chances. For which I hereby sentence you to eighteen years in a maximum-security prison without the possibility of parole." Bars and razor wire and turrets and armed guards—that's how my dad describes the joint. The big hole, he calls it. He says piss in the chili long enough and right here's where you end up, all dulled out and dead to the entire world.

"Bum rap," Brinks says. "I ask you, where's the justice?" He means that another weekend's shot, and we're out of cigarettes, the smoke so thick inside the car that I crack the window. There's a ladder that leans against the house, and a path I keep shoveled up to the roof peak for when the motor on the rotating TV antenna seizes. Mostly all it takes is half a dozen cupped breaths and a single knuckle rap to get it started again, but I refuse to watch the tube in Bobby Bigalow's presence. Dieter, as if he's reading my mind, says, "Well, you want this waste out of the picture or what?"

The honest answer's as dumb as trying to stare down the sun. The night air is frigid and still, and as my dad sober used to say, a man's mind in winter isn't meant to be enlightened, or sought after, and any attempt then at decision making only invites grim and sorry thinking. I'm eye-level with the snowdrifts that the wind has sculpted, the temperature's double-digit at best, and it's beyond me why I say what I say, but I do, inviting trouble of a magnitude that we don't need and yet sometimes covet. I say, "Yeah, big-time," both hands locked on the Fury's steering wheel, and envision running Bobby Bigalow off the road and deep into the frozen turnip fields stretching away in all directions.

"It'd at least break the boredom," Dieter says. "There's that." He's got a deep voice and braids that sway when he walks, and every single paper he writes for English class is about the vanished nations rising up again. At school we stick close together, and if anyone wisecracks about the amulets he wears, we're a small war party to deal with. The same goes for Bobby Bigalow, who's a grown-up version of that same small-minded, small-town bully. He potshots us and takes cover behind my mom's loneliness, never smiling or offering to drive Brinks and Dieter home so they don't have to snowshoe those five miles each way just to sit in a backyard beater in the bitter cold.

"Why would anyone in his right mind do that?" Bobby Bigalow asked a few weeks back, and in my best attempt at a nasally Texas drawl, I said, "'Cause we ain't got a rowboat. That's why."

"Hah, hah, hah," he said. "Talk that bullshit and you and me, pal, we real plain and simple got us a problem to reconcile."

He leaned so close to me then that I could see the pockmarks on both his cheeks flare crimson. A grown man's glare I'd never seen fastened on a kid before, but I thought, "Hate-stare somebody else, you Lone Star loser." The only scare tactic that had ever worked on me was when my mom threatened to leave. And sometimes she did go off for a day or two, with my dad stammering in her absence, "Honest to God, Fritz. Honest to God," like it was a double vow to fix everything that had, for years, spun further and further out of control. Speeding tickets and DWIs and racking up points enough to have his license revoked ten times over. Resisting arrest, disorderly conduct, urges that over the long haul define, as my mom insists, a weak man's feverish nature.

Brinks says, "The Quonsets. Let's blindfold him and escort him there."

That's where the turnips are temporarily stored after harvest, on dirt floors cut deep like bunkers. No windows, and even in summer it's always cool, the perfect place to build our ritual fires. Shavings and sticks and just enough flame to get our knife tips glowing. Check out our inner arms and you'll witness remnants of an ancient art, the raised scars long and blade-thin and climbing almost up to our elbows.

Bobby Bigalow's got matching spur tattoos on his biceps and a silver belt buckle big as a shield. And those gaudy western shirts with fake pearl cuff and button snaps. He's a sorry-looking stand-in for anyone I might consider habitable company for my mom. She's thirty-eight, strawberry-blond and narrow-hipped, and still pretty enough for men to get the fidgets when she walks by. So, sweet-talking Bobby Bigalow into relocating somewhere else won't be an easy sell. He's already acting like a stay-around, helping himself to beers and snacks from the fridge, and sometimes shuffling the mail as if searching for something that's his.

He complains that if he doesn't time it perfectly he gets caught at the crossing gate, warning lights and bells and those freight cars throwing up sparks, and I'm halfway thinking right there's our optimum ambush spot: on the far side of the rails, so that after the sleepers and the caboose get past, there *we'd* be, the single high-beam of our snowmobile bearing down like a phantom train about to pancake his sorry ass.

Dieter's waiting on parts so he can rebuild the carburetor in auto shop. He figures by midweek. But for right now, before he and Brinks trek home, he mimics the man in Spokane whose reattached left arm at nightfall points involuntarily at the Northern Cross, according to one of my mom's articles. Not that we buy any of it, that's for sure, but it nonetheless provides us some hilarity. Holy Mary Mother of God, you lose a limb and sew it back on and all you can think to do out there under the heavens each night is reach up and thank your lucky stars?

Brinks says, "Man, if it's me I hit the casino and honk down on the lever of a thousand-dollar slot and watch the place light up like a munitions factory."

Dieter's all over that and I am, too. A little revenge for the years our dads lost to the gambling and the booze, for those declarations to change everything that ever hurt or harmed us if only they could. One summer, our faces streaked with war paint, we sent up smoke signals to the gods on our dads' behalf. If certain girls happened by, we'd turn to them and tom-tom the drums of our flat naked stomachs, hoping they'd stop and maybe dance for us.

That failed to happen, then or ever, and here we are, me and Dieter and Brinks. When we bother to attend, we each maintain a steady C-minus average in a much-lower-than-average school district so far north that the cloudlight hovering some nights turns the landscape a bluish-gray shade either gorgeous or violent, depending on your state of mind. Ours hasn't been that great of late, and to make matters worse my mom appears more and more dazed by bogus notions about Bobby Bigalow.

"He lies," I tell her. "He's a bully and a sneak." But her standard comeback is that he treats her well and that I shouldn't begrudge her another chance with a man.

"Those flank steaks," she said. "He's the one who bought them, not me. Please, don't judge him so harshly, Fritzi, inasmuch as you can't possibly know in advance how a thing might turn out in the end."

I figured she'd interject my dad as a negative example, but she didn't. Which in its own cruel way made him appear even more expendable in our lives going forward. It's as if Bobby Bigalow's got her under some spell. I've seen her turning this way and that in front of the full-length mirror, her hair down, wearing nothing but red lipstick and a slip, and making silent-still music with her hands on her hips.

Dieter says that you can crush dry gumroot and swamp irises into a fine yellowish-blue powder and boil it into a tea that forces the fork-tongued to speak the truth or else their skin pusses up and peels away. But he can't recall the exact mixture or the other herbs, and the tribe's last medicine man died long before we came into this life. And anyhow, if we wait for late spring all might be forsaken.

"We'll figure something," Brinks says as he crawls out the window, and half a dozen snowshoe-lengths later he and Dieter are out of sight. They come and go in silence, leaving no tracks or drag marks, because

417

a few weeks back we attached a horsehair tail to the ass end of the snowmobile. The two five-tined pike spears we carry with us are spoils from a raid over on Lake Tonawanda, where we war-whooped and circled the shanties to make certain nobody was inside when we finally kicked open the door. Nobody other than those nude centerfold pinups, of course, tacked to the wall and staring back at us, with their slightly parted lips all glossy and blistered in the blue flames of my dad's brush-chromed Zippo, and Brinks' and Dieter's pilfered Bics. And so go ahead and try following them across the stark windswept pastures and fields of white moose and deer and coyote, and just see how long before you're completely turned around out there where the spirit world is everywhere alive.

Here's my mom's best one yet: a capstone gets jimmied from a long-abandoned well in the Ozarks and blind lungfish cry out in the voices of angels.

"Poetic," Dieter said.

"Downright inspiring," Brinks chimed in, all crocodile with a case of the weepies. Wet-vac all the way and, right, real funny, but maybe all miracles are a matter of need and deceit—all honest Injun horseshit, as Bobby Bigalow says about Dieter and Brinks, and sometimes about me, though never when my mom's within earshot. I've seen him fingering her Christmas ornaments and eye-rolling and shaking his head. I've seen him drink milk straight from the carton and then stare at those missing children in a way that blames everyone but himself, my mom's personal savior. And mine as well, if only I'd offer up some measure of contrition and a commitment to believing in forces other than myself and my two pull-trap friends. Yeah, we've got a few illegal beaver and muskrat sets, but so what? Not that Bobby Bigalow'd know a thing about where they're at. If he did he'd turn us in first thing to Church Stoner, the C.O. who's been itching to bust us for years, but even he—who's grown up in these parts—can't track us.

But a week or so after that night in the Fury, we tracked Bobby Bigalow, and it's possible that he and my mom went dancing like she said this past Friday night, but Dieter hit seventy-five miles per hour on the snowmobile to position us at our outpost on Summit Hill. We could see the lights of town. The crisscrossing of the streets, the dull red pulse of the Grand Union sign, and Bobby Bigalow hooking a right toward that strip of drive-ins and cut-rate, off-season motels. Which merely reinforced that nothing is sacred or safe with him around. I suppose I could have waited up to interrogate my mom, but to what end other than to start my own blood throbbing? And I backed off on the attack front anyway, so as not to arouse or inflame suspicion.

Until this morning when, before boarding the school bus, I said, "It's my house, too," and she did not say back, "Of course it is," or "it always will be," like I'd anticipated. She said, "Yes, within reason," but anyone reasons this out they've identified the source of all our impending anguish and grief. She doesn't see it and no doubt won't if I don't intervene on her behalf.

"It's not an open subject, Fritzi, and I'm tired of feeling so disenchanted and god-awful all the time. I've been too long at my wit's end, but I'm dating someone now, and it's not as if they've arrived in twos and threes. Have they? I know how resentful you are, but I don't want us to face off like this all the time. And whatever happens going forward, I want you to promise not to hold it against me."

I remained silent and stone-faced. We both did, and then she said a thing I knew might someday prove to be accurate, though to hear it spoken conjured in me a consideration I hadn't until that moment ever fathomed, and hoped I'd never in a different situation have to again. She said, "If you want to blame someone, blame your father. And if he asks, you tell him the truth. That he, and he alone, is the one who led us to where we find ourselves on this very day. As crazy convoluted as it sounds, he's the one who introduced us to Bobby. Tell him that, Fritzi. And tell him that except for a man being dead, I'm glad in the end that he did."

Dieter met me as I stepped off the bus, and said, "Everything's still a go?" and I said back, "Full bore," and we both nodded. We've stashed two sickles and a roll of electrician's tape in the Fury, and the wolf headdress that he signed out from the tribe for next week's history class show-and-tell, plus a peace pipe that we've been sucking without success for residual effects.

The forecast is for a blow out of Canada. A foot or more of snow, and you watch—that'll be Bobby Bigalow's ruse to finally spend the night. And I don't mean on the couch, and I don't care to wake to that next morning, and breakfast, and the final rubble of my dad's last possessions boxed and banished to Goodwill without me even getting to go through them.

I ditched early, right after civics class, and by late morning I'd already stopped obsessing about what our civics teacher Mr. DeSclafani called a God-spot, this bay in the brain that functioned to dial back the onset of anger and treachery and revenge. I didn't raise my hand, but if I had I would have mentioned the afghan that Bobby Bigalow unfolds and drapes around my mom's shoulders just to tick me off. And how sometimes he even winks at me from right there behind the couch. In my head I hear my dad's old rant: "Give ground one time to that and you'll be doing it on a daily basis," and so it only makes sense to "bring 'em on, all comers. Every last Fo, Fuck, and Fum."

And tonight as Dieter and Brinks and I see it, we're going to right some wrongs is all. If things foul up maybe we'll move on Dieter's backup plan to screw a spigot into one of those giant wine casks we've seen stacked on the boxcars and drink our way West on the rails to the Columbia River Gorge. Out where his dad lived for a short while after a stint in the service. And where he fished for king salmon that danced on their silver tails in the froth and the sunshine, right there below what he called the great nonstop booming of the falls. Last we heard he was living outside Montreal, and I suppose someday that might be a destination for us, too. I can't legally visit *my* dad until I turn eighteen, but like Dieter says, at least there's no guesswork concerning his whereabouts.

My mom's scheduled to work a double shift, and she left wearing a polished, silver-veined quartz stone around her neck. I've never seen it before. A gift from Bobby Bigalow no doubt, who just last night complained about the lousy water pressure like somehow he owns that right. The pipes not being buried deep enough under the frost line's the problem, and so we have to let the faucet slow-drip whenever the mercury dips below fifteen degrees. Sometimes I'll place an empty upside-down ice cube tray directly under the tap in the kitchen sink just to drive him batshit. I spare him not one reminder that in my eyes he and my mom are maybe hot-wired for the short run but are destined for an abrupt chill-down.

He's clueless that Dieter and Brinks tracked him home to some doublewide off Tapico. Off Arrowhead. Off a no-name two-track that backs up to state land where the proposed hydraulic dumpster was supposed to go. All that's there is a giant hole half filled with the dead weight of ruptured appliances and bedsprings and bald tires, TVs with bullet holes through the picture tubes. Plus a few metal shopping carts that we hauled out for the caster wheels we used to build ourselves three suicide skateboards.

We've re-mapped our attack-and-capture strategy in favor of just happening to be in Bobby Bigalow's neck of the woods later tonight.

You know—to search the clearings and snow fields for a high-stepper who might teach us how to make our squaws go dumb between the bed sheets—a phrase he let slip that caused the first time I'd seen my mom flinch in his presence, her mouth muscles going taut. I wanted to say, "There. That's who he is outright. A croaker always running his lily-livered mouth and why parlay the likes of him into heartbreak? Why him?" But, they're a twosome plain and simple. And, like Brinks says, all love's a fluke either temporary or lifelong, and without incentive Bobby Bigalow ain't about to scare or bugger off anytime in our immediate future.

But, as I wait for Dieter and Brinks to pick me up, I'm *all* Indian, and the sickles are razor sharp and already taped to the insides of my wrists for a better grip. Like curved tomahawks or talons. And the wolf's skull-plate a perfect fit, my face smeared with lampblack from the inside glass of the kerosene lantern my dad always used whenever we dipped smelt in Otter Creek.

There's a full moon and the air's frostbite cold, and I remember how he said years ago, when I inquired, that he'd proposed to my mom under a meteor shower, the tracer tails so intense they turned the skyways platinum. There's Orion, the hunter. And this is the car in which my parents first dated, first kissed, and only since Bobby Bigalow does my mom, without a second's hesitation or any apparent regret, say straight-faced that it was all a colossal mistake, "a marriage so doomed and misguided." Think on that awhile like I do: I pull up short of calling her a liar, but she's nonetheless knocking a lot of careless and hurtful wrong words about.

That's a fact, and rather than let her pawn her wedding ring, last month I zinged it with my slingshot as far into the constellations as I could. And is that not, when I hear the muted roostertailing of Dieter's snowmobile up a certain draw still half a mile distant, why I roll down the car window and crawl outside without a second thought? Yes, on all fours, dressed in furs and wolf fangs and ready, finally, to move out across the frozen tundra, under the miracle of these winter stars.

"No mercy," Brinks says. He's holding a ball-and-claw table leg, and Dieter's brandishing one of the pike spears. There's no barking dog to quiet, but there is a second vehicle in Bobby's driveway. It's definitely not my mom's Cherokee, and it's parked directly in front of the pickup, which appears to be sniffing the Jeep's hind end like it's got in mind to hump it.

We're standing back a short ways from the slider. No blinds and the kitchen lighted up, but nobody's stepped into view yet. I've never seen wallpaper like this before. A jungle-clot of jonquils—all summery and yellow—and flocked here and there amid them are a few oversize roses the dark blood color of mulberries.

"Some weird shit here," Dieter whispers, and it's true that the icicles hanging halfway down in front of the glass distort this woman who appears out of nowhere like a ghost among the vines and tangles. She's stark naked, and she stops at the stove and leans over and turns her head sideways to light a cigarette from one of the front burners. Then she leans against the counter and folds her arms over her breasts like she's shy or cold, or maybe even afraid and cowering.

No one says so, but we despise Bobby Bigalow all the more when he swaggers in zipping up his pants. What I notice most, though, is the ceiling textured and flecked like ours with fake chips of mica. And how this woman is knock-kneed and shivering as the moon disappears and more snow starts to fall. It's the exact same posture I've seen my mom assume too many times—though bundled up of course. I imagine all four gas jets open full, and the oven turned on the way we always have it to survive the night whenever our furnace conks.

"It ain't his place," Brinks say. "He don't live here, Fritz. It's hers, and *now* how the fuck may I direct your call?"

The only one I'm certain owns a cellphone among us is Bobby Bigalow—some new fancy-ass gadget that takes snapshots and that he keeps holstered on his hip. I've heard it ring, though never have I seen him use or answer it. What I flash on instead is one of those old-fashioned cameras, a bellows and a black hood and that slow, hand-held explosion of gun-powdery light. This would make a one-in-a-million portrait, a classic: three armed and angry young chieftains standing side by side, the single threat of each of us tripled in the camera's eye.

"Let's dial this up or duck out of here," Dieter says, ice forming on the black buzzard and eagle feathers in his hair.

"Your call," Brinks says. "Either way." But when he passes me the wineskin it's my dad I imagine, half-drunk and fury-fisted and cleaving through the snow toward whatever door that Bobby Bigalow is about to exit.

Like father, like son, and it takes only a matter of seconds for me to calculate that weeks or months or years from now I might own up that, "Here, overtaken by rage and revenge, is where I pummeled and perhaps maimed or even killed a man." Or, "Here's where I stood with my only two friends on Earth one February night. The snow suddenly coming down so hard that a man my mom believed mattered passed unaware within ten feet of us after being with another woman. We could smell her perfume, her nakedness, his beery breath, could hear him hiss between his teeth as we watched him disappear."

Neither is a confession whose details can redeem a thing. But have I mentioned the jukebox at the Honcho? Merle Haggard and Mickey Gilley, and truckers who change dollar bills into quarters, and my mom who's destined to start humming those heart-drain tunes again real soon, one way or another, no matter what goes down here.

When I give the word we sneak away. Dieter starts the snowmobile. "Hang tight," he says, and it's as if nothing can touch us as we tear-ass into all that whiteness, flying blind and the trees coming at us out of nowhere. There's an abandoned cellar hole we somehow avoid, and then we're airborne over the not-so-high rock-face outcropping we've survived at least a hundred times. The snow's coming in waves like wings, and we rise, I swear it. Three lost-cause kids in crazy get-ups, straddling not the wide seat of a Polaris sled, but rather a bareback horse, its black tail combed shiny by the wind.

That story. The one riddled with God-spots and paybacks and love full-blown for women we might someday make giddy and, despite our best intentions, betray. Thunderbird and muscatel. Dads who've gone missing, and a mom who, against all the evidence, believes in miracles she's determined to pass along to her son.

Nominated by The Georgia Review and Marvin Bell, Jeremy Collins, Stephen Corey, Claire Davis, Nancy Richard

RUSSIANS

by DAVID RIGSBEE

from THE RED TOWER (NewSouth Books)

It wasn't the end when
my girlfriend handed me the phone
in the middle of the night and said,
"Here. Say hello to my husband."
And it wasn't the end of anything
when another grabbed the wheel at 70
and screamed, "I could pull this
right off the road right now!
I could do it *right now!*"
Those frenzies have passed
into something like the memory
of a good novel, weighted in one's lap
when the day is cleared,
and there's nothing left to do
but look in on the Russians
passing out at the feet of their superiors,
emptying their wallets into the fireplace,
throwing their brain-stuffed heads
before the locomotive of History,
rather than face the vivid memory
of errors committed when the face
was hot and stared into the eyes
of that intransigent, that other face.

Nominated by NewSouth Books and Carolyne Wright

GIRLS, AT PLAY

fiction by CELESTE NG

from BELLEVUE LITERARY REVIEW

This is how we play the game: pink means kissing; red means tongue.
Green means up your shirt; blue means down his pants. Purple means
in your mouth. Black means all the way.

We play the game at recess, and the teachers don't notice. We stand
on the playground by the flagpole, arms ringed with colored bracelets
from the drugstore, waiting. The boys come past us, in a bunch, all
elbows, laughing. They pretend not to look. We pretend not to see
them. One of them reaches out and snaps a bracelet off one of us,
breaking it like a rubber band, fast and sharp as plucking a guitar string.
He won't look back. He'll walk back the way he came, along the edge
of the football field. And whoever he picked, Angie or Carrie or Mandy,
will watch him go. After a minute she'll follow him and meet him under
the bleachers, far down the field, where the teachers can't see.

We play the game every day. In eighth grade we're too old for four-
square and tetherball and kickball. It doesn't have a name, this game,
and we don't talk about it even when we're by ourselves, after school,
the boys gone off to football or paper routes or hockey and no teachers
around. But the game has rules. You go with the boy who snaps your
bracelet. You don't pick the boy; he picks you; they're all the same to
you. You do exactly what the color prescribes, even if you hate him, like
we hate Travis Coleman whose fingernails are always grubby. No talking
other than hello. Don't tell anyone if you hate it, if his tongue feels like
a dead fish in your mouth, if his hands leave snail-trails of sweat down
your sides. No talking with the boys outside of the game. No talking
about it afterwards, no laughing, no anything, even if it's just the three

of us. Pretend it never happened. Rub the dent on your arm, the red welt where the bracelet snapped and split, until it goes away.

Ask anyone in Cleveland and they'll tell you that girls in Lakeview Heights don't play this kind of game. Maybe down in Cleveland Heights they play it, or across town on the west side. Maybe there are a few naughty girls at the high school, reapplying lipstick in the rear view mirror before they slide out of their cars and tug their miniskirts down over their thighs. But certainly not at the junior high school, where the kids still get recess, where parents still pack lunches sometimes, where Mr. Petroski the principal still comes on the P.A. every morning to lead the Pledge of Allegiance. Not in this tidy little world where there are still four-square courts and hopscotch grids painted on the blacktop. Certainly no one plays games like that here.

The other girls pretend not to know us. Their worlds are full of wholesome extracurriculars: riding lessons, field hockey practice, violin, ballet. They crowd like cattle on the playground, whispering and looking our way. Some of them say we're stupid, or high. Some of them say we don't know any better. Some call us sluts. We are the fallen women of Lakeview Heights Middle.

We aren't stupid, or high. We don't do it because we don't know better. And it isn't hormones either. If you asked us, we couldn't explain, but it has something to do with their stares. They've always stared. Because we live south of Scottsdale Avenue, where the houses are smaller and mostly rentals. Because we carry our lunches in plastic grocery bags instead of paper sacks, since crisp little paper sacks cost money and we get plastic bags free from the Sav-Mart. Because Carrie's dad works nights at the liquor store, and Mandy's mom wraps gifts at the mall customer service desk, because Angie lives with her grandmother and her parents are off in Vegas maybe, or is it L.A.? We hate the stares and we love them too and maybe that's why we play the game.

After school nobody says, "Should we stop by the drugstore today?" We just walk single-file, the automatic door half shutting between each of us, like it's saying, "All right, Angie, but not you, Carrie—all right, Carrie too, but not you, Mandy—all right, all right." We walk through the candy aisle to the back of the store, and Carrie maybe picks up a Baby Ruth to eat on the way home. Then we stroll down the toy aisle, with its neon-plastic cars and its fake Barbie dolls, the ones with fake Barbie names like Trissy, whose skin is a little too orange, whose hair is a little too blond and you can see the roots of it set in little holes. We hate them because when we were younger our moms bought us Trissy,

426

as if we couldn't tell the difference between the real thing and the cheap imitation. Sometimes we turn their boxes around so the dolls face the chipped paint on the back of the rack. Once Angie stole a black Sharpie from Mr. Hanson the gym teacher and we drew on the cellophane window of every doll, big handlebar mustaches and goatee-beards and devil-horns. On the last one, a Trissy in a frosting-pink tutu with ribbons up her legs, Angie X'd out the eyes and drew a balloon squeezing out of her mouth. It said, "I'm an ugly whore."

Today we don't mess with the dolls. We go straight to the fake jewelry and pick a pack of bracelets each. These aren't the hard plastic kind spray-painted fake gold. Those are for little girls, girls that still want to play princess. Ours are thin as spaghetti and stretchy, all different colors and a dollar for five. We take them up to the register and pay for them and while we walk home we open the bags and slide the new stack of bracelets onto our right arms and toss the empty bags onto someone's lawn. The next day we hold our arms across our bodies like we're pinning towels to our waists and wait for the boys to come by. We are ready to play the game. We are stores of iniquity with a wide, wide selection.

This is how we are when Grace moves to town.

From all the way across the blacktop we can see that everything about her is wrong. Her shirt is too big: she's tiny and it's huge and hangs down past her butt. The cuffs of her pants stop at her ankle and a band of black cotton sock shows between hem and sneaker-top. Her shoes are too new, too stiff, too blindingly white in the lunchtime sun. Even the way she stands is wrong, hands clasped behind her back, index fingers linked, like she's been told not to touch.

The other girls don't tease her, or call her names, or throw things at her. They just stand in a knot looking at her and talking loudly about other things, fingering the silver O charms around their necks that are *in* this year.

We've never seen her before but something about her looks familiar: the way she stands, heels at right angles, left toe pointing towards the girls, right toe towards the football fields where the boys are shuffling our way. Then she turns her head towards us, and we remember exactly what it's like to be her, alone and awkward on the open prairie of the playground. We know how those stares feel like blinding sunbeams, how you find yourself squinting when they hit your face. One shoulder comes up towards her ear, as if she's half shrugging, and her ridiculous T-shirt puffs in the wind and we feel tenderness welling up inside us.

We cross the asphalt and cluster around her, like mother elephants circling a calf. We shield her from the stares with our bodies. The boys drift toward the abandoned flagpole, their eyes longing after us. Without us they seem lost. One of them puts out his hand to the cold steel of the pole. *Olly-olly-oxen-free.*

"What's your name?" we say, and her face goes pink with surprise. Up close we can read her T-shirt. Under a picture of animals in the jungle it says, "If the Macaw saw what the Leopard spotted, then the Toucan can, and you can, too! SAVE THE RAINFOREST!"

"Grace," she says.

"Grace," we repeat. "Grace." We like the sound of it, the round single syllable, like a polished metal bead. A simple name, a sweet name. A name not yet corrupted into a diminutive. We wonder, for a moment, if with Grace we can be Angela, Caroline, Amanda.

"I like your bracelets," she says. We push them under our coat sleeves.

"They're nothing," we say. "Just old junk. Come sit with us. Tell us about you." We lead her over to one of the picnic tables by the pine trees where no one ever eats, because we eat in the shiny cafeteria where the tiles are painted with vegetables and fruits and the food pyramid.

She's twelve, a year younger than us, and her birthday is in July and she's in the seventh grade, Mrs. Derrick's class. She came from Ketchikan, and before that she lived in Montana, and Louisiana, and Del Norte, Colorado, and Eureka, South Dakota. "My dad works for the army," she says. "We move a lot." She's an only child. She had a dog once, a brown-and-white spaniel mutt named Goober, but he died three years ago. Her favorite food is lemon cake with chocolate icing. Her favorite color is blue. We drink in the minutiae of her life until the bell rings and it's time to go in. Grace stands and looks around, as if she's forgotten the way back into the building.

"Meet us after school," we say, and tuck a stray lock of blond behind her earlobe. Then she smiles and runs off.

That afternoon we don't go to the drugstore. We take Grace over to the Tasty-Q and buy her a chocolate-dipped cone. She's never had one before. She licks the melting ice cream from her fingers and the way she sits with her arms wrapped around her knees, trying to take up as little space as possible, you'd think she was ten.

Grace tells us that she's never lived in one place for more than six months. She's never finished a school year in the same place she started. Her father does some kind of engineering work. We know engineers build bridges, and we picture him in a trim navy worksuit with blue-prints in his hand. Her mother died of cancer when she was three. "Most days," Grace says, "I'm a latch-key kid." She doesn't say so, but we know we're the first real friends she's ever had.

At her house Grace pulls out toys—real toys, toys we had long ago, when we were still kids. We play Monopoly through the afternoons, Operation, even Candyland. We flub the Funny Bone and Charley Horse and Broken Heart operations just to feel the buzzer tingle our fingers. Weeks pass and we don't go near the flagpole. At recess we see the boys out of the corner of our eyes. Some of them move on to other things, football, kickball, skateboarding. But some keep on, as if out of habit, moving towards the flagpole like a fog and then dissipating, dis-appointed. After a while we forget to even watch them. We're busy, with Grace, because she hardly knows anything at all.

We teach her important things, like how to find the best seats in the movie theater. Asking for butter in the middle of your popcorn, not just on top. How to snap your gum. How to tell the future with straws: Tie the paper wrapper in a knot. If it breaks the thing you're thinking of will happen; if it stays knotted it won't. Grace doesn't know any of this. We give her things she's never had before: cherry Cokes, Pixy Stix, curly fries. Things we can afford on our allowances, things we forgot the joy of. We teach her the rules. Hold your breath when you pass a graveyard; punch your friend's shoulder when a VW bug drives by. Pick up a penny when it's heads up, but not tails up or you'll have bad luck. And we teach her about making wishes: on maple-tree helicopters, on cotton-wood puffs, on dandelion heads, when you see the first star at night. And on eyelashes, held on someone else's finger, the most sacred of wishes, a tiny curl bearing your most secret hopes.

"Can you wish for the same thing twice?" Grace asks one day, and we are surprised. We have never run out of things to wish for. Now we are ashamed to realize that our lives are filled with infinite longings. We pause, then nod.

"Of course you can," we say. "If you want to." That afternoon, as we roll the dice and push our pewter tokens around the board, we savor Grace—the way her hair falls over her face, the clumsiness of her movements, the artlessness of her hands. We are awed to be in the presence of someone who wants so little.

*   *   *

But it doesn't last. One Friday after school Grace is fidgety, restless. She doesn't want to play any games; she doesn't want to go out for milkshakes. Is she mad at us? we wonder. Have we done something wrong? Her T-shirt has pulled askew, and we straighten the seam along her shoulder.

"What is it?" we say. "What's bothering you? Tell us. We'll fix it." We are like fairy godmothers, wands out and eager to please. We want to preserve her lovely clumsiness, that artless, awkward smile. But she won't talk to us. She sits moping, drawing on the sole of her sneaker with a blue Bic pen.

Maybe she's just bored, we think. We suggest a movie and Grace shows a glimmer of interest. "Okay," she says. "Maybe." We open the paper and spread it on the floor. "Anything you want," we tell her.

"*Closer*," she says, jabbing at the newsprint.

We're shocked at her choice. Under Grace's finger, a quote over four half-faces reads, "Sex, Lies, and Betrayal!" Another, from *Rolling Stone*, says, "Vibrates with eroticism." For a moment we don't know what to say.

"It's rated R," we tell her. "You're too young."

"So are you," she shoots back. And we know she's right. We've seen R-rated movies dozens of times, and somehow Grace guesses this, and we feel like hypocrites, and we can't say no.

At the theater, there's no one else in line and we hop over the red velvet ropes. We look at the board, where it says *Closer* — 4:00 and smile at the pimpled clerk through the ticket-window glass and say, "The 3:50 *Polar Express*, please." Then we file into Theater 5 and sit in the back row.

"You said we were going to see *Closer*," Grace whispers. "I don't want to see this. It's for babies."

"Shush," we say. "Give us a minute. Trust us, honey, please."

The movie starts and CGI snowflakes blow across the screen. We wait five, six, seven minutes. Then we tug Grace's hand. We slip through the swinging doors one by one, so the light from the hallway doesn't attract attention, and we run across the hall into Theater 6, where Natalie Portman and Jude Law have just locked eyes.

"That's it?" Grace says afterwards. "So easy. I should have thought of it myself." She licks butter-flavored oil from her fingers and tosses the empty popcorn bag into the trash. She smiles, not at us but to herself, a little half-smile we've never seen before. It troubles us. Later we will look back to this moment and wonder if this was where we went wrong. Was this our first mistake, showing her how easy it is to sidestep her age?

The next week we're in her room playing dress-up. Grace has a box of costumes, capes and wide-brimmed hats and purple fans, and we say, you're never too old. Though it's only March, we tell her where the best neighborhoods for trick-or-treating are, who gives out whole candy bars and who just gives out boxes of raisins. Next year, we tell her, tugging clothes over our heads, we'll take her. Everything is a little small, but if we hold our breath, it still fits. We drape capes and scarves over our braceleted arms. We put on crowns and wigs and bunny ears and mug in the mirror, and it's then that we see Grace behind us. She's not wearing a costume. She's put on our clothes—Angie's little lace top and Carrie's denim skirt and Mandy's platforms—and she's looking not in the mirror but down at herself.

Grace looks up when we stop talking. But it's not until we start to take off our costumes that she looks at herself one more time and peels off our things. We snatch them up from the carpet where she's dropped them and hold them against us. They are warm as skin and they smell like Grace, and we wonder if they will have changed somehow, if they will no longer fit. But they do, and when we emerge from our shirts, Grace has pulled on her own clothing and is tossing the costumes back into the box.

When the last piece is in, Grace settles back on the carpet and says, "I look like a big old cow." She pinches the front of her T-shirt and pulls it away from her, then drops it. We watch the letters settle against the flatness of her chest in silence: POLLUTION IS A DIRTY WORD.

"Haven't you noticed?" she says. "I'm the only girl in school who wears stupid shirts like this." There's a little hole in the front, near her shoulder, and she puts her finger in and drags. The fabric rips with a noise like radio static. Through the tear we see the pale white of Grace's bra. We know that bra. It's the kind we wore years ago, the kind our mothers bought us from Sears or JC Penney, before anyone but us ever saw them, before we began to buy our own.

"You're perfect, sweetheart," we say finally. "Your shirt is fine. Don't change a thing."

But Monday Grace comes to school in a little sweater: V-necked, black, stretchy.

Soon after that Grace begins to look like a TV with the colors tuned too bright. Her cheeks glow orange, her lips are magenta, her eyes look darkish and bruised. When we press her, she admits that she's been using the watercolors from her painting kit as makeup.

We take her into the bathroom and wash her face, dyeing the washcloth in a face-shaped smudge. Then we take the makeup out of our bags and teach her to put it on. Foundation on your red spots, blush from your cheekbone to your temple. We teach her how to hold the mascara wand steady, to keep her eyes open and apply tiny coat after tiny coat. We watch her in the mirror, her elbow up like a violinist, and feel proud.

She finishes one eye, then recaps the tube and passes it back. "My dad will never buy me any of this," she says.

We look at each other, then back at Grace, whose undone eye is startlingly blue and wide, the other dark and plush as fur.

"All right," we say. "Come on."

We take her to the drugstore. We circle the store once, poking packages of diapers, rattling bags of cough drops. Then we enter the makeup aisle and pull a package of mascara from its hook. Put it somewhere it won't show, we explain. Not in your purse; if they catch you, they always look there. Put it on your body. Put it somewhere they're afraid to touch.

Each of us steals something, to show her how. Angie slides a deep red lipstick into her jeans pocket. Carrie tucks a pack of Twizzlers up the sleeve of her shirt. Mandy pops a bottle of nail polish under the tongue of her sneaker. Then finally Grace pulls the pink-and-green tube of mascara from its package and tucks it down the neckline of her sweater.

We're nervous now. We never were before, when we'd lifted perfume and fancy glitter lotion and condoms, even that time when we stole an entire bag of potato chips and a can of dip to eat in the park behind Angie's house. But this time is different somehow. Our fingers shake and our palms get damp and we wipe them on our jeans and look over at Grace, who doesn't look at us but touches the tube under her shirt with the tips of her fingers.

The clerk at the counter doesn't even look at us. He leans against the counter, turning the pages of a glossy celebrity magazine and eating M&Ms from the pocket of his smock. In the black-and-white monitor screens behind him, an old woman shakes a bottle of vitamins. A housewife pulls her toddler's hands away from the aspirin. And we stride out the automatic door, single file, Angie Carrie Mandy Grace, and walk slowly all the way across the parking lot wanting to scream, before we begin to run. We don't stop until we reach the corner and realize that Grace isn't with us. When we look back she's walking steadily towards us, looking straight ahead with a face of perfect serenity.

We never take Grace shoplifting again, but she comes to school with pinkened cheeks and reddened lips. We wonder if she's gotten an allowance now, or if her father buys it for her, or if she's just practicing what we've taught her. Sometimes we look at her, at this new creature with darkened eyes and sleek clothing, who keeps her head up in the hallways, who sees people look at her and bats her eyes and smiles. At first she looks like a stranger. But there's something familiar about her, like she's someone we saw once in a movie, or someone we knew as a child but haven't seen in years. We stare hard and screw our eyes up, trying to keep that something in focus. She's still Grace, we remind ourselves. We cling to the simple things, to Candyland, to milkshakes, to eyelash wishes. She's still our Grace.

Then one day Grace says, "Carol Ann in my English class told me you used to play some kind of game at recess."

She says it matter-of-fact but we know it's a question, a heavy one. It sinks slowly and settles on us like soot. We are unsure. Should we bluster it out? Should we lie, deny everything? We can't imagine telling her. This is something we can't bear for her to know. But when we turn back to Grace we know we've made a mistake. She's seen us exchange glances and her face closes up.

"It's nothing," we say. "Just a way to kill time. Just something stupid we did before we met you."

"All right," she says. "Don't tell me. Carol Ann said you wouldn't."

Don't listen to Carol Ann, we want to say. Forget Carol Ann. Forget about the game. Let's pretend it never happened. Let's never talk about it again. But of course it doesn't turn out that way.

Grace doesn't talk to us for eight days. During recess we sit at the picnic table, fiddling with our bracelets, watching her giggle with the other girls across the blacktop, waiting to see if she'll come back. We trace the initials there with our fingers. T.G. + A.B. J.T. + D.H 4-EVER. Generations of ancient, chaste, hand-holding love. Finally, on Friday,

Grace arrives. Her face is pale and the fingers of one hand clutch at the other. She walks slowly, like a doll might walk, legs stiff and in perfect parallel, untouching.

"I think I'm sick," she says. She doesn't sit down. "I think I might be dying."

The look on her face frightens us. How big her eyes are, how still her closed lips, as if she's been turned to wax. We forget that we were angry.

"We'll take you to the nurse," we say, stroking her shoulders, her hair. "The hospital. The emergency room." We feel her forehead for a fever. "What is it? Where do you hurt?"

"I don't hurt," she says. "I don't hurt. I just—" She touches her hand to her belly, just below the navel.

We take her to the girls' bathroom on the third floor, the one no one uses. The nurse is not needed now. Didn't you know, we keep asking her. Didn't someone explain? An aunt, the health teacher, someone? We see now the faint dark stain on Grace's skirt. We press tampons into her palm and turn her towards the handicapped stall at the end of the row. Grace looks down into her hands as if we've given her a weapon. Then she backs into the stall and shuts the door. She stays in a long time, and when she comes out she's changed into her gym pants, and she wads up the skirt and tucks it into her bookbag.

That afternoon we take her back to the drugstore. We take her into the ladies' aisle, as the sign calls it, telling her what we know. The wrapper of this kind rustles—everyone in the bathroom will hear. This kind is small enough to fit in your front pocket. She nods and listens and we're happy again, to walk her, sure-footed, through unfamiliar territory.

Then, as we head to the register, Grace stops.

"Look," she says. "Is this where you always get them?" In her hand she's got a little plastic package. Without realizing it we've led her up the toy aisle, and through the cellophane window on the package we can see the bright bracelets inside.

"Put those back," we say. We snatch the bag from Grace's hand and throw it back onto the shelf. "These aren't your style. Save your money."

"But you wear them," Grace says, and we tuck our arms behind our backs. "Why can't I?" She puts out her hand again and this time we slap it.

"Leave them alone," we say. "Forget about them."

"I'm not a baby, you know," Grace says. The pride in her voice is obvious and bleating. She pushes past us and darts out the door, and we let her go. Then we pick up the box of tampons she's dropped and

434

pay for them ourselves, and we leave them on her doorstep, swaddled in their plastic bag.

On Monday we don't see Grace before school, or in the hallways. At recess, we find her across the schoolyard, standing alone. After a minute she comes over to us, but she doesn't sit down. Her eyes look sideways, at the row of pines planted between the table and the brick wall of the school.

"I don't think we should hang out anymore," she says.

"This is about the bracelets, isn't it," we say. "About the game."

"No," she says, "no, it isn't."

We hear everything she doesn't say. She touches her forearm with her fingers and frowns. Then she looks up at us with a scowl, like we're keeping something from her, like we're evil stepmothers keeping her rightful crown under lock and key. We know, now, that we can keep nothing from her, that we will have to teach her everything we know. The girl in front of us doesn't even look like our Grace anymore. She looks like a Trissy doll: tiny clothes, perfect makeup, everything but the cartoon bubble drawn from her mouth. She looks just like us except for her bare wrists. We want to slap her, to tell her she's ungrateful.

Instead we look at her, hard.

"What do you want," we say. "Do you want to play the game?"

"Yes," she says at last. "Yes. I want to play the game."

We grab her by the shoulders and force her down. First onto her knees, then into the grass. Her shoulder hits the ground and she winces as we roll her onto her back. Then we push up our sleeves and pull off our bracelets in handfuls. They don't want to go on. They catch on the bumps of her knuckles, then the knob of her wrist, and we push harder, forcing them onto her thin arms. The rubber leaves red brush-burns against her skin, and Grace whimpers and twists. We hold her down, pressing her shoulders flat against the damp ground, pinning her legs in place with our knees. We don't look at her face. We focus on what we're doing, thinking only about the bracelets. We strip every one off our wrists and thrust them onto hers, and only when our arms are bare do we stop, our hands shaking, and step back.

Grace has stopped struggling. She sits up slowly, pushing herself up with both palms. She touches her face, then her arms, as if the bracelets are new skin she's seeing for the first time. A few crushed blades of grass cling to the back of her blouse. We reach out to brush them off, but she waves us off and gets to her feet alone. Without the bracelets, our outstretched arms look smaller, bonier, like little girls'.

We don't look her in the face. Instead we take her to the flagpole. As we cross the blacktop, the boys see us and silently follow. At first there are only a few, but by the time we reach the flagpole they are a pack. We leave Grace there alone. She stands, watching us go, her face set, her eyes wide but her mouth closed. The boys circle her, soft-footed, eyeing the bracelets on her arms. After a long, lonely winter they are lean and hungry. One reaches in and pulls off a bracelet. So does another. Another. From where we stand we hear—or think we hear—the thin spaghetti-snaps against her skin. The boys head off, one by one, toward the bleachers. Strings of colored rubber hang limp from their fingers like old, worn-out streamers.

We turn away then, and close our eyes, so we never know if Grace follows them to the bleachers or not.

Maybe she pushes them away with her hands. Maybe she holds them off with her eyes, stares till they're embarrassed to come near her. Maybe she never leaves the flagpole at all, maybe she stays standing there forever, one hand on the metal like it's home base, only she's really It. Maybe she follows them after all, as if she's in a trance, not understanding what's to come, and afterwards wipes away her mascara, which has run, with her fist.

Or maybe—and this is why we close our eyes—maybe she follows them with her head up, eyes trained on the horizon, like the day we taught her to steal. Maybe she lies down with them in the brittle grass. And when she leaves the bleachers, maybe there's a look of triumph in her eyes, as she walks back, unsquinting, into the stares at this end of the asphalt.

Nominated by Bellevue Literary Review

SILHOUETTES

by SARAH BUSSE

from THINK

Imagine it: nineteen, asleep in spring,
the upper bunk in a bay window facing the street.
Street level, and her door's been left unlocked
for a tardy roommate. Say it's 12 o'clock.

Does he pause in the lit up outer room, or glide
right through? Aimed or addled? Is he drunk?
His head so close, the light behind erases
his face to silhouette: no one to see, to tell—

But I can tell you where his hand was when I woke,
still feel the brain's confusion, "What—?" Then panic.
And then my great good luck: he ran away.
I burned circles, spinning on the carpet.

Well. More upside than down, as these things go.
I never saw him again. As far as I know.

Nominated by Antler

SEAN

by ROBERT ANTHONY SIEGEL

from HARVARD REVIEW

THE FIRST TIME I SAW SEAN, I had no idea that we would become brothers. I watched him wander through my parents' living room, with its endless supply of child-lethal bric-a-brac, then gathered my courage together and picked him up, just to be on the safe side. I was twenty-four and had no experience with toddlers. "See this," I said, holding up a little brass Buddha statue. "This is a wise man with some kind of sharp pointy crown on, so be careful."

"Yes," said Sean, taking it in his hands. He wasn't timid or shy, just limited to a small pool of words. For the most part he was silent.

"And this is Hanuman, king of the monkeys."

"Yes," he said again, taking that statue too.

Twenty-three years later, I recognize how fragile was the chain of circumstances that brought us together, how one slight alteration would have left us strangers. My mother worked for Child Welfare as an attorney prosecuting abuse and neglect cases; some months earlier, she had been assigned a case involving one of Sean's brothers, who had gone to the hospital with a broken arm of the kind that usually comes from parental yanking, and who had then gone back later with a third-degree burn from an iron. The four boys had been farmed out to different homes, and for the three oldest, those homes had become permanent. Only Sean was left. He suffered from persistent nightmares that forced him awake, screaming; a series of well-intentioned but fatally sleep-deprived people had ultimately declined to take him on permanently. The one immediately before us had reached the end of her endurance and decided she needed a break—right away. Sean was with us, I was told, for just a few days, on an emergency basis.

To be honest, I can't remember how deeply his story penetrated my post-adolescent self-absorption. My big obsession back then was trying to figure out how to write a novel in the interstices of the absurd part-time jobs (door-to-door furniture salesman, tour guide) that only a hapless recent college graduate can stumble into. I had no particular sensitivity toward little kids and no desire for a new sibling. I already had two: my brother David and sister Perrin, both of whom were away at college.

While Sean watched some cartoons on TV, I sat with my parents at the dining room table. "So you've got him for the weekend?" I asked, looking at the diaper bag, that strange, padded piece of luggage.

"The week, probably," said my mother.

"Could stretch longer," said my father.

A nervous silence. My parents looked exhausted already: two people in their mid-fifties who had lived hard lives and were not in the best physical or emotional condition. My father reached for his bottle of antidepressants and swallowed one thoughtfully, as if in preparation for the challenges ahead. But beneath the air of quiet terror there was some other feeling, something steely and certain. My parents looked like gamblers who had stumbled on a not-completely-certain-but-nevertheless-highly-probable thing, the jackpot that might make their lives good again.

I was alarmed. My parents were decidedly high maintenance. Now that David and Perrin were away, I got all the calls for help: my mother needed a lift somewhere (she didn't drive), needed me to wait in the apartment so a repairman could get in, needed me to convince my father not to do something disastrous (usually involving money). For his part, my father needed me to help him to the doctor when his back went out, or to file papers for him at court so he didn't miss a deadline (he was, like my mother, a lawyer), or he just needed company when the melancholy of daily life became too much. Both of them wanted me to listen and untangle their many complicated and vociferous disputes involving spending, housecleaning, mistakes and slights sometimes a quarter-century old.

The last few years had been especially hard on my father. He'd once been a prominent criminal defense attorney, the sort you would see interviewed on the local news about some big case, but in recent years he had been reduced to taking whatever floated his way. He now worked out of a tiny home office off the living room, with a desk covered in dirty laundry and fancy Italian shoes—he loved shoes—and a phone he never answered; he met with his clients in the McDonald's across the street.

All of this worked in Sean's favor. Common sense, caution, a respect for order, solid finances, and a full night's sleep—all the things that had stopped previous families from adopting—were not my parents' concerns. What they wanted was love, the kind of love that would propel them through their midlife confusion. Sean came that weekend and never went back; my parents filed for adoption. They lasted through a year of his nightmares and frustration tantrums, until the sheer constancy of their attention quieted the fear inside him. They took meticulous care of his asthma, and it, too, began to improve; there were fewer and fewer late night trips to the emergency room. He started to talk more, and then it became a flood. The silent little boy was now a nonstop commentator on the world around him, smart, observant, and relentlessly opinionated. I started to notice phrases reminiscent of my parents: "Who knew?" he would say, an all-purpose exclamation of surprise and satisfaction whenever an unexpected treat came his way. "Who knew?"

My mother and father seemed to relish this second chance at parenthood. Always tottering on the edge of exhaustion, overloaded with plastic grocery bags, they nevertheless looked grounded, certain of their place in the world. I remember my father pushing Sean around the neighborhood in a stroller as if he were chauffeuring a celebrity. I remember my mother at home in her nightgown cradling Sean in her arms and cooing with deep satisfaction.

Of course, they couldn't stop being feckless, either—and, to be fair, their schedules were now so complex that even the most organized people would have been overwhelmed. I still got the emergency calls, but instead of having to take care of my parents, I now had to take care of the little boy my parents were supposed to be taking care of. I complained, of course, sputtering over the phone about how important my writing time was, blaming them for preventing me from becoming a writer, but I never actually hung up on them. The truth was that the hours I spent with Sean were actually among the most genuine, human moments in a life that had become confusing and a little bit lonely. When I first took up fiction, I was under the impression that you composed a novel by pulling out a piece of paper and writing down whatever occurred to you, just as it popped into your head. But it didn't seem to actually work that way. After a couple of years of trying, the silence of the empty page had become frightening.

Taking care of Sean was something of a mystery too, but at least it felt alive. I had no idea how to entertain him at first, and my parents gave me no pointers. I took him to the park and experienced the strange slowdown that kid-time consists of, something I would have to relearn many years later when my own children were born: long, lyrical moments in which one does somersaults on the grass or plays excruciatingly cute games of peek-a-boo, only to check your watch and find that exactly two minutes have gone by, and the rest of the afternoon still stretches ahead.

Once, in that first year, I cheated and took him to the movies, a grownup movie, no less, as there were no kids' films playing nearby. It was safe enough—a romantic comedy with Tom Selleck, no violence, no sex—but looking back, I marvel at how I could have rationalized that move. Desperation, of course. I sank into the padded seat with utter relief, and the movie, at which I would have normally sneered, was bliss, simply because it did not involve pouring wet playground sand into a broken dump truck. I followed its every plot turn with such deep gratitude that I remember it all to this day. Sean was quiet enough for me to pretend that I actually thought he might be content, though when I finally looked over I found him standing in his seat, facing the back of the theater, as if the show were supposed to materialize there instead of the front. I realized then that he had never been to the movies before. "No, you watch the screen," I said, pointing. "The screen, over there."

"Why?" he asked.

"So you can see the movie." I watched him turn to dutifully stare at the giant image of Tom Selleck, and I saw the sad folly of what I was doing. "Come on," I said, "let's get some candy. We'll go to the park."

Even as a callow twenty-four-year-old, still hanging onto a long list of adolescent grievances, I started to gain some grudging appreciation for my parents: if nothing else, they had staying power.

Have I mentioned that out in the larger world, Sean is considered black and the rest of us white? That we are brothers stuck on opposite sides of that strange and contradictory classification system known as race?

When Sean was four, he seemed to realize for the first time that his skin was a different color from the rest of us. I remember a confusing

441

episode in a Chinese restaurant over the holidays, when our sister Perrin and brother David were both back from school. I'm not sure why it happened at that particular moment; it's possible that the sudden expansion of the family had left him feeling a little lost, or perhaps forgotten; in all probability, he wasn't getting much attention at dinner that night—that is, until he blurted out, "Everyone has white skin except me!"

The conversation around the table stopped. "What did you say?" asked my mother.

"Everyone has white skin except me!"

The woman I was dating at the time was Japanese. "I don't have white skin," she said, holding out her arm. "See."

"You're not *brown*," said Sean, sounding disgusted at this quibble.

"What's wrong with brown?" asked Perrin.

"I hate brown!" He didn't seem sad so much as frustrated and angry. His face quivered on the edge of tears.

We all began talking in a nervous rush, not so much to console him, I think, as to drown him out with our reassurances—reassurances meant for ourselves as well. "Brown is beautiful," said my mother. "Like chocolate."

"I wish *I* were brown," said my father.

"Brown is my favorite color," said David.

No one knew the magical words that would make this problem disappear, but then a moment later it was simply gone, as mysteriously as it came: Perrin took Sean on her lap and gave him a pile of sugar packets to play with; more food arrived for the adults; conversation resumed, though the nervousness remained, just below the surface.

Sean brought up his skin color a number of times that year. The best I could make out was that he wasn't concerned about race in the adult sense: he just wanted to look like everyone else in the family, wanted physical, visual proof that he belonged and could never be left out—a powerful hunger for a little boy who had already lost one family. All any of us could do was explain, over and over again, that looks don't make a family, knowing that this was true, and that time would prove it.

And I think it has. If Sean and I don't look alike, we certainly sound alike, much like our father, who grew up on the Lower East Side during the Great Depression and always had a bit of Borscht-belt to him. Sean and I share the same love of dumb jokes, the same penchant for grandiose plan-making, whether it's about kayaking the Atlantic or biking the continent. I was at his adoption hearing, at his big tap dance performance in summer camp, at all his school graduations. My wife and I signed him up for his first photography class, a small gift which bore extravagant fruit: photography became his college major and then his profession. He paid us back by taking the pictures at my first book party. He was at our wedding, at the hospital when our oldest child, Jonah, was born, at the *bris*—a part of every important family milestone. Seven years ago, we stood with Perrin and David beside our father's coffin; now, when I come to town, we drive out to the cemetery to visit Dad's grave and walk among the headstones, telling jokes and laughing, just as our father would have laughed if he were with us.

My worry in even mentioning race, therefore, is that I might end up misrepresenting our experience by focusing on something that is irrelevant to the fabric of our daily lives as brothers. The problem, however, is that silence would be equally distorting. For if race is a purely social construct, a figment of the collective imagination, a thing out *there*, on the street, not in *here*, within the family, it can bounce around in highly unpredictable ways and have oddly distorting effects.

Soon after Sean arrived, I took him with me to spend the day with a bunch of people at a house in Fire Island. We made a splash. He was completely outgoing, interested in everyone, full of laughter. People passed him around from arm to arm, cooing over him. Someone said to me, "This is just the most wonderful thing you're doing. You've rescued a child and given him a home. A little black boy."

That felt odd. I hated the way it flattened out the interactions between complicated individuals and turned the whole thing into an act of charity. There was no recognizing us in that. We were basically instinctual people, neither political nor principled, and more than a little selfish. "Oh no, really, it's the other way around. He's here to rescue us," I said.

"But you've changed a life."

"No, he's changed ours." I meant it, though the more calculating part of me already realized that this too would be taken as an expression of modesty and simply get me more kudos—which is why I said it, of course.

Indeed, as these encounters multiplied over the next few years, I got over my unease and started accepting the praise, then basking in it, then expecting it, even courting it, feeling miffed when it didn't come my way. I started borrowing Sean from my parents whenever I had a social occasion where I wouldn't know many people. He was perfect for backyard barbecues in Brooklyn, picnics in Central Park. With him in my arms I stood out: I was the guy with the cute little brown brother. I would carry him around the party, introducing him to all the women, and thus introducing myself in the most flattering, if contrived, light: Mr. Sensitivity, the urban saint, but also hip, because Sean was a hip little kid with his incredible smile and wonderful ringlets.

Of course, that wasn't the only type of racial interaction that we had. Soon after the trip to Fire Island, we were riding downtown on a city bus when I noticed a middle-aged white woman across the aisle, watching us very closely. Sean's asthma was acting up and he was coughing, a wet, ugly chest cough that always made me upset—I hated that he had to struggle for breath. "That's a nasty cough," said the woman.

"He's got asthma," I said, feeling obscurely accused of something, some sort of negligence—or maybe it was illegitimacy.

"He should see a doctor."

"We have medicine for it."

"Mmm" she said, looking skeptical.

From that point on, I started noticing a pattern wherever we went: older white women peering to see if Sean's coat was properly zipped, if I held his hand when we crossed the street, if I let him drink from the sippy cup he'd just dropped on the sidewalk. It took me a while to realize that they didn't see the hip older brother, Mr. Sensitivity, urban rescue hero. They assumed I was the *father*. And though I was twenty-five by then, I was the sort of baby-faced twenty-five that looked eighteen, and not particularly prosperous, either, in my repertoire of old jeans and T-shirts. Sean was still in the thrift-shop clothes my parents had inherited with him, which contained an alarming number of Michael Jackson tank tops—stuff from the bottom of the box at Goodwill. I can only imagine how these women filled in the blanks: teen parents, black and white, poor, hapless. A sort of interracial *La Bohème*, with coughing, wheezing child.

The somewhat pathetic truth is that I was secretly flattered and did nothing to dispel the impression. I guess I felt a little possessive of Sean by that point, but there was more to it: fatherhood was grown up, and nothing else about my life felt that way. I was working part time, living with a roommate, and writing nothing worth keeping or showing, but I walked a little straighter when I had him with me.

Later that first year, I got a call from my mother, who told me that an organization of African-American social workers had weighed in on Sean's adoption. Its interest wasn't Sean's case specifically, but the broader issue of adoption policy. It believed that African-American kids

444

should go to African-American families, and it asked some cogent questions: How would black children raised in white homes understand their African-American heritage? How would they learn how to navigate the difficulties of race in America without African-American role models?

I could see that they had a point; I just wanted them to make it using someone else's adoption. My parents got worried. They were receiving regularly scheduled home visits from social workers as the adoption process continued. What if policy changed and the agency started recommending against transracial adoptions? "He's half white," said my father. "Why isn't he considered white? I mean, why choose one half rather than the other?"

"Look at his skin," my mother said.

"He looks like he got a tan at the beach." That was pretty much true. Sean's biological father was African-American, but his biological mother was Caucasian. His biological half-brothers had Caucasian fathers and looked positively Nordic, with blond hair and blue eyes.

"You're not being practical," said my mother.

But my father was stuck on his point. "He's not black or white. He's a harlequin, black *and* white."

"That's idiotic."

My parents, never people much into preparation, made an effort to forestall any possible criticism. They started dressing Sean in a dashiki for big occasions, such as Passover and Yom Kippur. We all made a halfhearted effort to celebrate Kwanzaa, right after Chanukah, getting instructions from a book.

I'm not sure how much alarm the social workers would have caused if the adoption hadn't started to get a little messy for other reasons. Sean's mother had abandoned the boys in the middle of his brother's abuse case. She'd run away to Puerto Rico with a janitor from the shelter, and my parents were worried that she would return to contest his adoption. If she did, there wouldn't be a chance of winning; he would have to go back to her. My parents argued about this possibility at night when Sean was asleep, during long, circular discussions. "She let the other three go," said my father.

"She's unpredictable," said my mother.

"She won't come back."

"She might."

She didn't. What actually happened is that my mother's agency realized that Sean had been tangentially connected to the abuse case my mother had prosecuted a couple of years back, involving his brother with the broken arm. The agency brought up the possibility of what it called "the appearance of impropriety." What they were worried about was a tabloid headline something like: CITY LAWYER STEALS KID FOM MOM, LEGALLY! My mother was called in to talk to her boss, and then to her boss's boss. She was passed over for a promotion that had once looked like a sure thing, and then transferred out of the courts altogether, to a job doing paperwork. The Inspector General's office brought her up on a battery of charges, some of which were pretty far-flung—an effort to find something that would stick.

This new twist was especially frightening for my parents. Now that my father was in what was delicately called "semi-retirement," my mother's job was their primary support. But what really concerned them was the potential impact on the adoption. My father would get worked up into long, dramatic rants. "I'll never hand him over," he told me. "I'll take him and go on the lam."

"Does anyone even say *lam* anymore?" I asked, trying to lighten the mood.

"I'll change my name and drive out west. They'll never find us."

"Isn't that called kidnapping?"

"Who cares what it's called."

"What will you do for work?"

His face took on a look of exaggerated nobility. "I'll pump gas."

I couldn't help feeling that my father had been looking for reasons to go on the lam for years before Sean arrived. He often fantasized about radical personal transformation: living on a sailboat, opening a bookstore in Vermont. And yet I also understood his sense of crisis. Sean had taken root inside our hearts; whatever the law said, there was no disentangling him now.

The charges against my mother were dropped; the adoption went through. Yet a sense of insecurity stayed with us for years afterward. Would Sean have been better off in an African-American family? A younger family with more energetic parents and siblings closer in age? Part of this was a reaction to the bumpiness of the adoption process, part of it just a byproduct of who we are: overly ruminative, insecure people. But there was something more too: a sense of the willfulness of choosing a little boy still too young to choose you back. Sure, he seemed to love us, all right, but given the opportunity, would he have *chosen* us? This question, fundamentally unanswerable, was more an expression of anxiety than anything else. No one frets over the fact that biological children don't choose their families. But irrational or not, it lingered on.

Five or six years after the adoption went through, the entire family was in my parents' little Japanese station wagon, making a slow arc around the concrete island at the center of Times Square. Traffic was snarled and we crept along, only slowly becoming aware of a commotion on the center island. Someone was shouting through an old PA system, and though it was hard to make out every word, we could all understand enough to know that he was very, very angry about something. "Did you hear that?" asked Perrin. *Jew* was one of the few words that cut through the distortion.

"Roll down your window," said David.

What we saw was not what any of us expected—not a couple of neo-Nazis or Klansmen in sheets. An African-American man stood on a portable stage, a microphone in his hand. He was dressed like the Genie in *Aladdin*, in a turban, a sash, and the trademark puffy pants, and behind him stretched a line of other African-American men dressed in the same style, looking determined and scary despite the harem pants. A banner read THE TWELVE TRIBES OF ISRAEL. "The Jews have stolen everything from us," said the man with the microphone. "Not just our freedom but our identity. *We* are the true Israelites. Not them. Us!" He had a lot to say about Jewish bloodsuckers, slave masters, bankers, and pawnbrokers, but what got me was not the anti-Semitic rhetoric so much as the look on Sean's face as he listened next to me: confused, guarded, veiled, bruised.

The smart thing would have been to respond with something right away, something about how crazy these people were, how they didn't matter, how families can be black and white, Jewish and not Jewish, how they can be anything they want to be as long as the people in them love each other. Instead, we all sat very still, trying to act as if nothing were happening while we simultaneously willed the light to turn, the traffic to part so we could escape—escape, perhaps, our own fear that our belief, our instinct, wasn't in fact true, or wasn't true enough to survive the ignorance of other people.

It was Sean who finally spoke. He sat with his eyes shut, taking in the angry words from outside with an expression I can only call grave, and then he said, "They're not talking to me."

The Twelve Tribes of Israel may have been a bit of a fringe organization, but the fringe gets its emotional power, its ability to shock, be-

447

cause it is channeling, magnifying, emotional forces that already exist out in the mainstream. Step outside the door, and I'm always surprised how separate the black and white worlds can be. I think of a time on the subway not so long ago when an African-American man came through the car handing out flyers. It took a moment for me to realize that he was giving them only to African-Americans. Some glanced, others spent a little more time, but nobody seemed surprised by what they had been handed. I took one from the seat beside me and read: *The White Man Is a Demon Without a Soul.*

If I'd been there with Sean, the man with the leaflets would have had no idea that the paunchy middle-aged Jewish guy and the big brown kid in hip hop gear sitting next to each other were in fact brothers. He would have handed Sean a leaflet; he would have skipped me.

It works the other way too, of course. The 2008 presidential election was fairly contentious in the small Southern city where we now live, and the campaigning became racially charged at the margins. It pained me when I passed houses hanging confederate flags, or when a woman at the playground told me that black gangs would be unleashed downtown if Obama won. It pained me not in some abstract, principled way, but with a stab to the gut. It was as if they were trying to push me and Sean apart.

I have two children of my own now, a boy and a girl, and like most every parent I eat it up when people tell me, "He looks just like his dad," or, "She has her father's face." Phrases like that trigger a primitive sense of ownership in me, a surge of connection that is sweetly intoxicating. But I know from my brother Sean that family is not defined by blood. It is not defined by race. It is not even defined by a shared voice or way of telling a story. Family is who you choose to love. The unfathomable complexity of those two terms, *choose* and *love*, start to feel simple after a while, when you live them day by day.

Our oldest child, Jonah, was born in 1999, while we were still in New York City, in an apartment in Tribeca right beside the Hudson River. Sean was fifteen then, a big, burly teenager, already a head taller than anyone else in the family, but he held the baby with a natural, unselfconscious gentleness that I had never seen in a young man. And he was genuinely interested too: as Jonah grew, Sean would come over and play with him for hours. Eventually we hired him to do a little babysitting in the apartment, so my wife and I could get some work done, or just get some rest. He learned to feed, change, bathe, and burp, learned how to take away a breakable thing with one hand while offering a toy with the other, and in the process became such an important part of Jonah's life that the mere sight of his uncle in the doorway would make our son start to laugh and clap.

In time, we got up our courage and sent them outside together: Jonah's first foray into the world beyond the apartment without his parents. It felt momentous. I secured him in the snuggly that Sean wore on his front (have you ever seen a teenage boy comfortably wearing a snuggly?), double-checked the bottle, and then watched them disappear out the door. I remember the long wait at the window till they appeared on the street, ten stories below. I remember my wife leaning against me, watching too. I remember them crossing the Westside Highway to the river, and continuing onto the newly renovated pier, with its hot dog stand and benches. The pier was surprisingly narrow from the height of our apartment, surrounded on three sides by the muscular, glistening river, and on our side by the cityscape, with its tall buildings, its rushing cars. They were tiny figures out there, but I could see Sean's arms wrapped around Jonah in the snuggly. My brother, carrying my son.

Nominated by Harvard Review, and Karen E. Bender

THE TELEPHONE

by KATHLEEN GRABER

from THE KENYON REVIEW

> *And just as the medium obeys the voice that takes possession of him from beyond the*
> *grave, I submitted to the first proposal that came my way through the telephone.*
> —Walter Benjamin

The handmade copper phone of Austria's last emperor & the telephone
of Franz Josef. A stark Soviet-era switchboard with the buttons
of an accordion, all of its connections laid out neatly in rows

of black & white. Cranks & fiber optics. The ornate horn mouthpiece
of an operator from 1892. At the Telephone Museum this morning,
I am the only visitor. A quiet Sunday late in the summer season.

Yet the matron, as ancient as the equipment, guides me dutifully
through the displays, throwing a switch to call up an illuminated
        hologram
of a statue—where is the original?—honoring long distance.

When she sends power into the frayed, paper-coated cables
of the city's original exchange, the massive matrix begins to hum &
        click
& whir. And a long minute later—delight!—the rotary phone

beside me rings. For Benjamin, the technology is heroic.
For it has prevailed, he says, like those unfortunate infants of myth,
who, cast out into the shadowy wilderness of the back halls, surrounded

by bins of soiled linens & gas meters, emerge . . . *a consolation*
for loneliness . . . the light of a last hope. The home's benevolent king.
In a novel by George Konrád, a man attempts to explain to his daughter

why he has had so many lovers: when the clothes come off, he tells her,
everything is discovered. And, he goes on, it is, in the end, discovery
we want. Though wouldn't even the most inventive among us find—

after so much disrobing—simply more of what we already know?
Shall I celebrate the counterpoint? The nearly infinite revelatory
      potential
of a bolt of heavy silk run through the fingers of the able seamstress

or the sensuous curves of the first desktop telephone—its molded
black handset recumbent in a pair of slender chrome arms. Meaning,
once I fell in love with a beautiful voice passing through the wire.

I remember the drop of it, a man talking about something he'd read,
turning to a page with an audible rustle & breath, whispering, *Listen.
These are the lines that haunt.* It's not that the skin has no function,

only that the tongue can play so many parts. At seventeen, I was
      haunted
by those protagonists who had no interiors. Someone asks the hero,
What do you really think of me? The hero's cold reply: *I don't.* In a
      month

the phone has sounded only once. On the other end, a pre-recorded
      message
playing in a language I'll never understand. Tomorrow, I think, will be
a good day to wash the floors, though no one will visit. Solitude:
      liberation

from even the expectation of being seen. Everything I do I know I do
for myself alone. Still, I'm thinking of you just now. Perhaps you'll call.
It's a silly, outdated sentiment. Where is the glass case to hold it? And,

beside it, what shall we write? Oh, something human, something
      grand.

*Nominated by The Kenyon Review and Dan Albergotti, Renee Ashley, David Baker,
Ciaran Berry, Philip Levine, Matt Donovan, B.J. Ward, David Wojahn*

JANJAWEED WIFE

fiction by E.C. OSONDU

from THE KENYON REVIEW

When we were living in Fur, whenever my sister Nur and I did something Mother disliked, she would frighten us by invoking the name of the Janjaweed. If we whispered to ourselves in the dark as we lay on our mat at night—our same mat that smelled faintly of urine no matter how often it was put out in the sun to dry—her harsh whisper would carry into our room.

"Are you girls not going to sleep? You had better stop your whispering lest the Janjaweed hear you and carry you away on their horses and make you their wives."

Nur and I would laugh quietly to ourselves in the dark and stop our whispering. Shortly Nur would startle me with her wall-shaking snores. I would prod her on the ribs with my elbow. The snores would temporarily cease and then start again, and I would prod her once more. I would prod and prod her and would not know when I fell asleep.

I recall one occasion when Nur was chasing me around the house. We were screaming and laughing and making so much noise Mother shouted at us to stop.

"Have you people forgotten that you are girls? Good girls do not run around screeching, feet pounding *gidim, gidim, gidim* like the hooves of Janjaweed horses. Both of you had better go and sit down quietly in some corner before I marry you off to some Janjaweed so you can spend all your lives brewing tea."

Nur turned to me and said, "I do not mind brewing tea. It sounds much easier compared to gathering firewood and all the grinding and pounding of sorghum and corn on mortar and the unending trips to the water well that we have to do every day."

"God forbid," I said. "How can you say that, or don't you know that the Janjaweed are *djinns* riding on horses, and if they pick you as their wife, any day you do not brew their tea fast enough they will pluck out your heart and eat it like wicked *djinns* are wont to do?"

"You have never seen a Janjaweed with your two eyes—or have you?"

"No, but that is because they are spirits, and spirits are invisible. The day you see one you will suddenly grow giant goose bumps, catch cold, and begin to shiver. Your teeth will start to chatter and then you die and become a spirit yourself."

"God forbid," Nur said to me, her voice quivering. I thought I saw little goose bumps on her dark skin and realized that I may have frightened her. I held her hand as we both walked into the house.

We met Father sitting with his head in his hands. When he raised his head, the whites of his eyes looked as if they were covered with a thin film of blood. He looked tired, and his dark face looked even darker. Mum gestured to us with her eyes to go to our room. We ran into our room quickly, crouched behind the door, listened, and tried to hold our breaths at the same time so they would not hear us breathing fast. Father's voice sounded painful like a sore.

"Their cattle trampled our crops . . . we thought it was a mistake but they said . . . they called us slaves, sons of dogs.. . . It is the same news from different districts.. . ." *Shouk, Krindig*, he hissed, and was quiet.

2

The night they came I thought I was having one of my malaria dreams. In my *malaria dreams*, as Mum called them, I was always either being pursued by someone or something. Sometimes it was a man with a machete, or a big, black animal with two heads, or a big, fiery-eyed, dark dog snapping at my heels. Usually at the point in the dream in which the machete was about to cut my head off or the animal with two heads was about to bite off both legs, one in each mouth, or when I felt the dog's hot, fetid breath behind my legs, I would rub my eyes and wake up. Mum would be standing in front of me holding a lantern and looking worried and scared, telling me in a kind voice to go back to sleep. This night was different, though. There was fire and pounding of hooves and what appeared to be floating fire and screaming. Mum

453

swept Nur and me into her arms and Father screamed for us to run behind the house and hide. From the side of my eyes I glimpsed the Janjaweed for the first time. So they were real? They actually had horses, and their horses emitted fire through every pore. The Janjaweeds' eyes were the color of fire, and balls of fire flew out of the guns they carried. Everywhere they pointed caught fire. Our faces, our houses turned the color of fire. Father stood in front of the house. I looked at him and saw that he was no longer black; he, too, had become the color of fire. The evil ones were cursing and laughing and speaking in fast Arabic. I could hear the words they spoke: *Throw the dark-skinned slaves in the fire; let the fire lighten their skins; they are no better than firewood.*

Mother grabbed us and we began to run. We were joined by others who were screaming and running. Behind us was Abok's father, who was carrying the family's lone black sheep on his shoulder as he struggled to balance Abok on the same shoulder. I saw him stumble and fall. This would have made me laugh, but I could not laugh. We kept running, and the fire behind us grew smaller and smaller till we saw it no more.

3

Our tents at the Zagrawa Refugee Camp looked like the humps of thousands of ocher camels crouching in the sand. We all liked to call them tents, but they were not real tents. Some were merely old rags tied together; others were made of old plastic bags, while a lucky few had real tents constructed with tarpaulin. Children from whose tents smoke rose were jumping around and playing, the smoke an assurance that they would soon have something to eat. Tents like ours from which no smoke rose filled with the sullen faces of those of us waiting for our mothers to come back from where they had gone to look for firewood. Here in this camp, we were always waiting for something. We waited for Mother to come back from where she had gone to look for firewood; we waited for the meal to be cooked when we had food, but when we didn't, we waited for the trucks to bring food, then waited for the food to be distributed. When the wells were dry, we waited for the water tankers to bring water. Nur and I would always watch the road for dust rising into the air, our sign to get our buckets and water basins and go form a line and wait. Sometimes we were lucky to be among the early ones in the line, because after the first few people, the lines would scatter and the fighting would begin. I was happy that the wells had dried up, though, even though I never told Mum this. Each time I looked into the well while fetching water, I would usually see Father's head floating around in it. I would close my eyes and continue to fetch the water without looking. I never told Mother; I did not want to add to her worries. Since we had come to the camp, she had thrown silence around her like a black-colored shawl. These days she smiled only with her teeth, unlike in the past when her smile rose from her heart and I could see the three wrinkles on each corner of her eyes.

When there was still water in the well, fighting went on all day as boys and girls struggled to grab the long rope and tie it to their buckets. More water was spilled in the fight over the rope than was fetched. The strong boys helped the girls they admired to fetch water. I remember that it was while standing by the well watching the fights that I first saw Deng. I cannot talk about Deng now.

Mum did not frighten us with the Janjaweed anymore. She did not even want us to mention the word around her. The only time she had been her old self was when we came back from the office to our tent with clothes that were sent to the camp from America. The Red Cross people had made us wait as usual, and then we were told to walk to the bundle of clothes and pick one T-shirt each. Nur picked one with the inscription *I'm Loving It*; I picked one that said *Tell Me I'm Sexy*. It had a drawing of a girl with long hair and large breasts, who was pointing at her breasts and smiling. I was lucky to get a shirt that was my exact size and was very proud to wear it. I was hoping that Deng would see me wearing the shirt.

"Where do you think you are going to with the picture of that half-naked girl with a hump on her chest?" Mum shouted at me. Nur covered her mouth and began to laugh behind her fingers.

"Answer me, or has someone suddenly cut off your tongue? Or you think because your father is not here you now have the license to dress like a wayward girl? You better remove that flimsy piece of cloth and return it to wherever you got it from," she said. She walked into the inner tent where she began to blow on the firewood, her eyes quickly filling with tears, whether from the wood smoke or from her shouting at me I could not really tell.

Nur was still laughing. I turned to her and whispered that I was going to tell Mum that the inscription on her T-shirt said something bad.

"What does it say? How can you say it is saying something bad? Or is it because you love the girl with the hump on her chest?"

455

"Yours says *I'm Loving It*. What exactly are you loving? You are loving being with boys, eh?"

Mother's voice called out to us to come to help with the cooking, and we went inside the tent and began to help remove sand and dry leaves from the flour that Mum was using to prepare our evening meal.

That night the moon came out, and all over the camp there was a certain gaiety, just as if we were still in the village. In the adjoining tent, the men sat around listening to the radio. They drew closer to the radio as the crisp, clear voice of the announcer mentioned Darfur. He pronounced it *Da-Four*, and this made some of the men laugh. Mum was feeling happy, too, and she began to tell us a story.

"It was on a moonlight night like this that your father proved that he was worthy to marry me. He took more lashes than all the young men who came to ask for my hand in marriage and took the lashes without uttering a sound. In those days, before it was banned by the government in Khartoum as barbaric and a form of idol worship, it was the custom of our people that if two young men were interested in marrying a particular girl, they had to prove they were strong enough by going through an endurance test. My father told the young men that they had to prove that they could protect his precious daughter and were strong enough to protect their cattle from wild animals. There was another boy who was asking for my hand as well as your father. They both stepped out that moonlit night, their bodies covered in ashes and wearing nothing but underpants. One of the strongest men in the village was holding a long, camel-hide whip, flexing it from side to side and driving fear into the hearts of the young men. Your father was fearless and was smiling, his white teeth glowing in the moonlight. The drums began to pound and the other young man—I recall now that his name was Dau—stepped forward, and the man with the whip struck out suddenly on his back. The whip curled around him like a serpent, and the young man flinched. The drums pounded even harder and the whip continued to descend. It was at the tenth stroke of the whip that Dau cried out and raised both hands in the air. The whipping stopped. He was not allowed to cry out, and his crying out meant it was over for him.

"Your father stepped forward and the whipping started. He neither flinched nor cried out but still had the smile on his face. Even on the twenty-fourth stroke, when his back was a mass of huge welts, the smile was still on his face. The whipping stopped and your father was officially declared my husband because he had proved himself capable of protecting me. The other young man, Dau, fled the village shortly after that. He could not bear the shame, and no woman would have agreed to marry him after his disgrace. He left for the big city and later became a rich trader."

When Mother finished her story, there were tears in her eyes, and Nur and I, who would ordinarily laugh at every story, had tears in our eyes too. We went to bed thinking of our father. This was why we were more than surprised at what happened next.

Mother called Nur and me and told us to go with a few people outside the camp to search for firewood. This was a task that Mum herself was usually worried about doing. The Janjaweed patrolled the perimeter fence that surrounded the camp and often would catch girls and ride away with them on their camels into the bush and do bad things to them. Whenever Mother had to go for firewood, she would usually go with a couple of other women and a few males for protection. We were excited about leaving the camp and went with the group in search of firewood. We were not so lucky, as the wood in the area around the camp was almost all gone. We could have gone farther, but others in the group said some men on camelback had been seen riding into the bush, so we returned to camp. On our way back, Nur pulled me by my dress and began to whisper about Mum.

"Do you know why Mum sent us out of the camp? It is because she was expecting a very important visitor and she did not want us to see him. I suspect he is very ugly."

"A visitor? Who is this visitor, or has she found a husband for you at last?"

"I think she has found a husband for herself," Nur said, and covered her mouth as she laughed.

"I think she wants to wash her clothes," I said.

"If she wanted to wash her clothes, she would have told us to stay somewhere around the camp. She need not have sent us far away."

Whenever our Mum wanted to wash her only flowing, multicolored gown, she would tell Nur and me to go outside to play out of modesty. She would wash the cloth and sit naked indoors waiting for it to dry.

As we entered our tent, I smelled the strong scent of the dark green perfumed oil—*Bint el Sudan*. The smell filled the whole of our tent. It came from a fat man with folds all over his body. Every inch of him seemed to be folded in parts: his face, his arms, his cheeks. He had facial hair and a single gold tooth. He spread out his arms as Nur and I entered, and even his palms were creased and folded in many places.

"Welcome back, children. You came back so quickly and with so little wood, greet Hajj and do I need to tell you to do that? Greet like good children and thank Hajj for all the good things he has brought for us," Mum said, pointing at a rich-looking bundle lying in the tent. Nur looked at me and I looked at her. If Hajj had not been looking at us so intently through the folds of his apparently delighted eyes, we would have burst into laughter. Mum's new bride manner was hilarious. Nur and I knelt to greet Hajj, but he drew us up toward himself.

"No, no, do not kneel to greet me. The Prophet forbids it. You must never kneel in greeting before anybody from today onwards."

As he drew me toward him, I felt the folds of his plump-looking fingers graze my buttocks through my thin dress, and I flinched. I looked at Nur, but his other hand was at that very moment accidentally touching her left breast. Mum was looking down on the floor and smiling.

Hajj soon rose from his position. In rising he reminded me of an old camel, as different parts of his body heaved and seemed to jiggle.

"El Hajj, thank you for honoring our modest dwellings with your esteemed presence."

"You need not thank me at all, and you need not worry yourself further. I will take you people out of here soon," he said, his hand sweeping through the tent.

El Hajj was a big trader in the town. He already had four wives and many children. One of the gun-carrying men on horseback who rode round the camp had told him about Mother, and he had decided to take her on as something between wife and concubine. He would take us out of the camp, and we could live in a real house once more. Mum, who told us this, was ecstatic and seemed to be out of breath as she told us even more wonderful things about El Hajj. He was indeed a very holy man and had performed the pilgrimage not just once, but four times. The sand that was used to lay the foundation of his house was from the holy land of Mecca. He fasted once every week, unlike many others who waited until the holy month. Beggars from all over the town came to his gates to be fed every day. In short, Hajj was a saint in huge folds of human flesh.

We moved out of the camp to El Hajj's house. Mum was not exactly his wife, and we did not live in the main house but in a small block of two rooms that was perhaps originally built for his servants.

One night a few days later, El Hajj called me to his bedroom. The room was filled with milk-colored curtains. The bed was high and had a pole on each of the four corners. He was wearing his *djellabia* and was sitting on the edge of his bed. He was smiling as he drew me toward his huge belly. I was looking at his soft, white palms and the folds around his neck. As the soft fingers began to poke around me, they no longer felt soft. I felt like someone was poking sharp bicycle spokes into me. Everywhere he touched stung, and I began to cry.

The next day Hajj called Nur to his room, and when she came back her eyes were red.

"Did he do anything to you?" I asked Nur.

"You tell me first. Did he do anything to you?" Nur asked me.

"Should we tell Mum?" Nur asked me, though I had not answered her first question.

"I think we should go back to the camp," I said.

"Mum says he is a kind and religious man and that he is only helping us to become better Muslims."

"She is like a new bride. She no longer knows what she is doing. I think we should return to the camp," Nur said, agreeing with me.

That night as soon as it got dark, we began heading back to the camp.

When we walked into the camp, a loud ululation went up. "They have come back. They would rather be thin and free than fat but in bondage," the women sang. The elders began shouting prayers and thanking us for bringing honor to the tribe. Food in trays appeared from different tents and there was dancing and singing as the moon shone on Zagrawa Camp.

Nur looked at me as we ate, and I looked at her. We should be happy, but we were not. Father would have been so proud of us, but what about Mum? All around us men, women, and children ate and danced.

A few days later Mum came to the camp to see us. First she stood by the entrance to the camp and sent for someone to call us. People in the camp began to whisper.

"So she is now too big and important to step foot in the camp, eh?"

"Why would she not feel important? Look at all that fine jewelry around her neck."

"She should remember that she once lived here and was no better than the rest of us."

"Better to live in the poverty of this camp with my dignity intact than to be a kept woman."

The wind must have blown some of their whisperings into Mum's ears because she began to walk into the camp as we were running out to meet her. She held us and we hugged. She was crying and wiping the corners of both eyes with her shawl.

"My children, you both left me alone—your own mother that carried both of you for nine months. How could you do such a thing? I spoke with El Hajj. He said it was a misunderstanding. He only wished to draw both of you closer to him, but you misinterpreted his fatherly gesture."

We looked at each other and stared at the dusty earth.

"He is ready to make amends. He says he will give you both some time to grow closer to him."

Once again we stared at the ground.

"I saw your father in a dream."

That got our attention. We both drew closer to her.

"Your father was unhappy in the dream. He turned his face away all the while that he spoke to me. He said the only way I would ever see his face again was if I brought you all back and we all lived under the same roof. I promised him I would. You know I can't break a promise made to a departed. If I do, I, too, will die."

We both gasped. We went back to the camp and picked up our few items and returned to El Hajj's house with Mum. As we entered El Hajjs's compound, he waved at us from a distance. He had a big smile on his face.

"I told your mother that you are good children. It was a misunderstanding. This is your new home. You will both be very happy here just like your mother."

We both shivered, giant goose bumps on our skin, and walked into the house.

Nominated by Chard deNiord

THE B'S

by STEVE MYERS

from LAKE EFFECT

(for Susie)

The band's back and performing, according
   to the morning paper. Remember
weddings in the Eighties? The serial
   nuptials of Youth for Reagan—black tux,
white gown, garden variety born-again
   clergyman sucking the lifeblood
from the *Song of Songs?* It seemed possible
   no one would ever get drunk again
or fuck upright in a public cloakroom.
   Yet at every reception, after all
the Christers and buzzkills had gone, you'd
   always find a sweaty remnant, wriggling,
hip-humping, and bouncing up and down
   to *Love Shack.*
               On my bedstand, that Polaroid
of you with the beehive hairdo and green
   mascara. In the iconography
of the early Church, the hive was an emblem
   of unceasing toil for the greater good
of the community, and the drone's
   labor his gift of honor to the Queen
of Heaven, like the Cistercian I once met
   at a Scottish abbey who'd sung nine offices
and done a day's field work baling hay
   on two hour's sleep, a finger-dip of honey

461

and a cup of tea—*not bad, Mister Myers,*
　for eighty-three, he said, and went off
to knead bread.
　　　　　　I say blessed be the body,
　especially on a Sunday, when we awaken
hungry and in no hurry. When we finally
　ease apart from each other, and lie back
slick with sweat and waxen light, and breathe
　the smoke from an incense stick we'd lit
as if we were 20, and laughing, piece
　back together the lyrics to "Bushfire,"

listen to church bells calling the faithful,
　and feel the old urge to go nowhere—
the buzz in the bloodstream, the sticky sheets,
　the pollen above us, whirling in the beams.

Nominated by Lake Effect and Phil Dacey

SATAN SUN

by RAYMOND ANDREWS

from THE GEORGIA REVIEW

RESTING in peace today beneath a forest of innocent young pines just south of the town of Madison in northern Georgia is a two thousand acre tract of land known back before the coming of the atomic age's boll weevil—the cotton picking machine—as the Barnett Farm, or The Two Thousand. Owned by a Mrs. Barnett, an aging white widow whom no one on The Two Thousand had ever seen nor knew anything about except that she lived in a "Big House" cloistered somewhere in that Confederate Gray cobwebbed corner of Madison cordoned off to all non-servant blacks, this acreage during the nineteen forties was rented by *the* "Mister Charlie" Mason who chopped up the land and sowed over its red soil black sharecroppers whom he was knelt to as "Mist' Mason." But unlike the phantasmal Mrs. Barnett, Mist' Mason could be seen practically daily pulling a long trailer of dust behind his Georgia red mud splattered 1941 Plymouth sedan while racing up and down the back country rutted roads snaking in and around The Two Thousand where it was said by the land's workers that whenever looking

Note: Transcribed from an undated typescript draft of the opening chapter of a memoir titled (on its first page) both "Where Were You the Day Jackie Died"—which is typewritten and crossed out—and "Growing Up with Joe and Jackie"—which is handwritten. Some material from these pages eventually appeared, in very different form, in Andrews' The Last Radio Baby (Peachtree Publishers, 1990). The typescript is housed in the Raymond Andrews Papers at Emory University's Manuscript, Archives, and Rare Book Library, and it is published here with the permission of the literary estate of Raymond Andrews—Randy Latimer and Christopher Andrews, executors. The manuscript is printed here almost exactly as Andrews left it, with only a few incontrovertible typographical errors silently corrected. (All ellipses are in the original.) The title, "Satan Sun," was chosen by the editor and is based on a key term in the manuscript.

from the window of his speeding car out upon the respectfully bowed blacks picking cotton in the fields the only thing this white boss man ever wanted to see showing of these, *his*, niggers were their "elbows and assholes."

In the Morgan County, of which Madison (1940 population, 3,000, approximately) was county seat, of the forties it was to the advantage of a black man to "belong" to a white man of Mist' Mason's stature. For not only could the latter keep a nigger of his out of jail but if considered by the owner to be a good, Whiteman-fearing nigger who knew and accepted his place in the Dixie Dream then Mist' Mason possessed the omnipotent powers to keep him out of the big war going on at that time as well. While on the other hand any black considered to be worthless by the local hierarchy could wake up one blue Monday morning and find himself "across the pond" defending the American given rights of all the country's Mister Charlies having exercised such rights by sending his kind over there in the first place. And during these patriotic war years of the nineteen forties, in the eyes of the Southern white folks there was, next to a Northern one, nothing under God's sun more worthless than a "town nigger." Thus was the Madison town black man well represented in World War Two. Yes, it was often said, Mist' Mason could keep *his* niggers out of anything . . . 'cepting *his* debt.

The most significant effect the Depression of the 1930's had had upon the blacks of Morgan County was that it brought them work. The WPA. Not to mention providing black mothers the South over with a new name to give their newborn boy babies. Roosevelt. (Only the unhip were yet naming their male offsprings Abraham.) For as far as the Southern black of that era was concerned America had had in its history *only* two Presidents. Abraham Lincoln, the man who took away their jobs, and Franklin Delano Roosevelt, the man who gave them back, with nobody coming before or in between these two but blanks. At least nobody worthy of naming a son for.

And one family the WPA cheated the local poorhouse out of was mine, for my daddy, starting out at a whopping fifty-cents a day, began work with the Roosevelt Miracle immediately upon its happening in the area and remained with it until America's entrance into the war brought about the christening of a nearby sawmill where he got a job starting at fifteen dollars a week. The wartime money boom was on. But so was the cost of feeding a family . . . not to mention the local draft board boom which was busily snatching up *all* unowned, or "free lancing," blacks between the ages of eighteen and forty-two able to prop up their right hands long enough to be sworn in. Thus it came to pass that with the Mist' Mason security blanket dangling before the out in the cold noses of all "unclaimed" blacks, Daddy, a conscientious objector to violence of any sort conducted outside the safety of the home, commemorated Lincoln's Birthday, 1943, by selling his, Momma's, and us, the seven of an eventual ten, children's souls to Mist' Mason in exchange for political asylum from the local draft board atop thirty sharecropping acres of Barnett Farm land. Land which I was doomed to grow up on during the 1940's as a certified "Mason Nigger."

Stacked atop itself in disarray out in the middle of The Barnett Farm like a pile of discarded crates was a huge two-story frame house which from having to throw off countless coats of white paint down through the years had by the forties developed a permanent mucus gray appearance. Once the home of the unseen Barnett family and now ending its days as the quarters of Mist' Mason's appointed overseer, a redneck commoner, this formless structure was known to the "overseen" as The Big House. The overseen being those thirty odd black families ranging in sizes from two to two dozens having lived at one time or another during the forties in the fourteen clapboard shacks of one to four rooms haphazardly littering the Barnett Two Thousand. And while it was true that both my parents had grown to adulthood on their respective families' farms before leaving to get married, we children (five boys and two girls at the time of being sold into bondage and with me, just four months short of my ninth birthday, in the exact middle) weren't at all soil souled. And nor was the Mist' Mason misadventure destined to make any of us.

Listening to today's concrete sprouted youth (most of whom I've talked to on the subject not knowing the difference between "country living" and living on a farm) sends shudders through me whenever remembering back upon those nine long months each year of planting, sidling, chopping, mopping, sodaing, hoeing, bunching and, finally, picking cotton beneath that sadistic red hot Georgia sun. Rising each morning to hang by its blistering rays in a cloudless steely blue sky to oversee the dust-choking fields of baked workers below, this sun was bad. So bad that even today a lifetime later I've never forgiven it. For no matter which state, country or continent it follows me to and no matter which thermometer it registers under I'll always recognize, and detest, it as being that same ol' Georgia "Satan Sun" of my childhood.

My kind of weather then, as it is yet today, was rain. Rain, rain and let it pour baby, for rain on the tin, leaky rooftop of my family's two room Barnett Farm sharecroppers shack meant to us non-soil souled Andrews children no work in the fields. And to the continual consternation of my father we, especially the four oldest, kids would do practically *anything* to keep from tilling the soil. With feigning a major illness being the most often tried, and suspect, method used by us to keep off the field of battle. Witchcraft even came into play in our never ending efforts to wipe that sadistic grin off the face of ol' Satan Sun when we kids whenever, and wherever, finding a grasshopper would kill and immediately bury it for local superstition claimed such a ritual would bring rain within a twenty-four hour period. I don't know the official record for most grasshoppers killed and buried by one single family in one day during the forties but I feel confident that mine holds the record among America's Southern black families as I can recall on one particular grasshopper hunt alone we Andrews kids spent an entire Sunday afternoon following church trekking The Two Thousand where beneath an uneasy Satan Sun we killed and buried well over a thousand grasshoppers. In fact we exterminated so many of these insects that day that the skies overhead got so uptight that they refused to drip even a drop for fear of flooding out that end of the county if the water ever started pouring. At least that's what my oldest sister, Valaria, the family superstition historian, researcher . . . and maker . . . told the rest of us executioners several weeks later when we were yet scanning the cloudless heavens awaiting them to open up and let it all issue out.

But on those infinite spring, summer and fall days when the sky above was parched a cloudless blue and neither rain nor sickness (it being one of my other brother's or sister's turn) could save me from the fields of strife and with a mocking ol' Satan Sun believing that at long last it finally had me "whupped," was when in order to keep my sanity I would be forced into playing my trump card. The daydream. Even ol' Satan Sun himself couldn't stop the daydream from lifting me up out of the dusty cotton fields on past his leering face and over into that beautiful world where he *never* shone. For like the fabled European whom I read so much about in school in those days I, too, dreamt of someday going to that beautiful world everybody called America. And my earliest knowledge of the existence of this New World lying just the other side of the sun came via the picture show.

In those days of racial segregation of nearly all public facilities throughout the South, there was a certain type of movie theater referred to among many Southern blacks as a "laffing barrel" picture show. This was a theater whose rules forbidded laughter of any sort from its black audience who, after having sat holding in their tickle through the entire performance, following each show were permitted to go around in back of the theater where sat a huge barrel provided by a humane management for them to line up before and when came their respective turn stick their heads into and let loose with all their pentup laughter. The Madison picture show wasn't quite a laffing barrel one though it tried its damnnest to be. Situated up in the theater's nigger heaven, the balcony, were eighty-four chairs numbered in sequence from the rear to the front and at each movie performance were filled in numerical order, meaning that the person standing first in line outside the theater sat in the seat numbered one in the rear corner of the balcony and whomsoever stood twentieth outside sat in seat number twenty inside, and so forth. No random seat selecting was tolerated upstairs, nor was talking permitted On High and at any time during the performance anyone up here heard laughing before, louder or longer than the white folks sitting in the huge orchestra section spreaded out below would immediately feel the heat of the usher's flashlight caressing their throat. Yes, but to us Celluloid kooks it was just let the everloving light shine right on mother 'cause this was the only picture show in town.

The picture at the Madison changed on Monday, Wednesday, Thursday and Saturday, with no showing on Sunday at all. And by Saturday being the only day featuring a matinee, a double bill which *always* included a western, this easily made it the favorite day at the picture show for me and my colleagues, as well as for many of the grownups. The first movie I ever saw was a Tarzan film (*Tarzan Finds a Son*) which an uncle and aunt of mine took me to see when I was five. Later Daddy, when he was with the WPA, on every third month would give me fifteen cents to go into town on Saturday with my two older brothers, Harvey and Benny, and to a movie which cost a nickel, with the dime *always* going for a comic magazine, locally referred to as a "funny book." During these early Saturday afternoons at the picture show all the rage among us young, and many old, blacks was ol' badass Buck Jones. That is, until it happened. A saloon fire somewhere back East where ol' badass Buck, while sitting enjoying a glass of sarsaparilla no doubt, was called into action and, we were told, after rescuing his twentieth person went back in looking for his white hat, which he never found.

By this time the wartime money boom was getting underway and the movie prices had been jacked up from a nickel to a dime to eleven cents before shooting all the way up to a whopping fifteen cents! This meant Daddy having to shell out a quarter for my now monthly excursions into Madison where I was now being accompanied by sister Val due to Harvey and Benny having reached the ages where younger brothers dared not tread. On these monthly treks into town I *never* failed to spend my whole quarter allowance on the movies and a funny book. But not so Val, a born practical soul whose money always went for food, a loaf of white (which we called "light") bread and a jar of peanut butter. And all the way back home Val prepared and ate peanut butter sandwiches, alone, while I walked the four miles alongside her salivating over the pages of my funny book while promising my growling stomach that the next time in town rather than throwing away a whole quarter on food for thought I was going to feed it. But the next month into town it would be the same old thing, picture show and a funny book.

With the badass Buck Jones gone to chase the outlaw riders in the sky, white hatless, we adopted a new Saturday afternoon hero, Wild Bill Elliott. Besides wearing his two guns backwards, and a *black* hat, what we deep down dug about Wild Bill was after singlehandedly whupping it on a saloon full of crooks in less than three minutes flat time he would walk away, unmussed, muttering out of the side of his mouth, "I'm a peaceful man." A dove in disguise. Other two-fisted, straight-shooting, takers-of-no-shit doves on those long ago Saturday afternoons were Johnny Mack Brown (a strong rival of Wild Bill's and whom many of us mistook his middle age chubbiness for double-jointedness), Sunset Carson, Allan "Rocky" Lane (Red Ryder), Hopalong Cassidy, Buster Crabbe, Hoot Gibson, Tim Holt, Bob Livingston, The Cisco Kid, The Three Musketeers, Ken Maynard, Deadwood Dick, George O'Brien, Charles Starrett (the Durango Kid), Don "Red" Barry, Bob Steele, Russell "Lucky" Hayden, along with the "whip" boys, Whip Wilson, Lash LaRue and Zorro, plus the "singing sissies," Gene Autry, Tex Ritter and Roy Rogers. And like today's television sports announcers each cowboy had a sidekick, or "color" man, with George "Gabby" Hayes, Al "Fuzzy" St. John, Andy Devine, Raymond Hatton and Smiley "Frog" Burnette being the better known ones. While Roy Barcroft, who was whupped and killed every Saturday afternoon, was the best of the bad guys. But our real Prince of Peace remained the Peaceful Man himself, fighting Wild Bill Elliott.

Though by the time I was ten years old I had outgrown the Saturday afternoon "gunsmoke and horseshit" pictures. For by this age my interest had suddenly turned to the weekday nights movies, known among us children then as "grown folks pictures." Credit this abrupt deviation in movie morals of mine to the then very popular movie magazine.

Avid readers was my entire family. Daddy being a great reader of the newspaper, funny book, dime western, detective magazine, or anything smelling of pulp, with Momma interested mostly in women's magazines, biographies and, of course, the Bible, while we children read any and everything. But with the family's financial resources enabling us to do little more than exist, reading material was hard to come by and most of what we were able to get our hands, or eyes, on being given to us by others. With our main supplier of such second hand printed matter being an old friend of Daddy's, Mister Emerson Wale, God bless him wherever he might be, who lived in Madison where he worked in and around the homes of several white families from whose trash bins he'd gather up books, magazines and newspapers to save and give us whenever we came into town. Such voracious readers were we children that at one time there we were even happy to see Momma go into Madison to the doctor for whenever she did she never failed to come home with an armload of waiting room reading material. She would, of course, ask the doctor for these magazines but I'm sure at one point or another he must've began suspecting her of having all ten of us children just to keep something to read in the house. But perhaps our greatest coup of the printed word came the night my brother Benny and I, armed with cotton sacks and a kerosene lantern, swooped down upon the building where Madison's white boy scouts kept stored newspapers and magazines gathered up by them on war effort drives. Filling sacks to the brim with these war effort goods, Morgan County's Benedict Arnold and Vidkun Quisling slung this precious, stolen cargo over their backs and hauled it on a run the whole four miles home. Immediately following that lone successful raid, the windows and doors of this building were boarded up by the boy scouts . . . perhaps fearful that Nazi spies had been delivered by U-Boat to try and sabotage the local war effort.

Included among all this printed matter gathered up by us over the years was a liberal supply of movie magazines, all of which I began saving and with them soon replacing the funny books stored in the cardboard boxes beneath the bed where I slept along with Harvey and Benny. And it was through reading these magazines that I became interested in and started going to see the weekday nights films of such

469

"grown up" movie stars as Victor McLaglen (always good for a fight), Humphrey Bogart (more mouth than action), Alan Ladd (all action), Van Johnson (The Boy Next Door, wherever that was), Dan Duryea (Lee Marvin of the forties), George Sanders (what the English was all about), Joel McCrea (the cowboy who didn't fight), Randy Scott (the cowboy who fought dirty), Helmut Dantine (the eternal Nazi), Richard Lee (*The* Jap), Dick Powell (the tough one, not the singing one), Walter Brennan (hasn't aged a day, looked just as old then as now), Don DeFore (whom I couldn't tell from Don Taylor), Chester Morris (whom I couldn't tell from Wayne Morris), John Wayne (World War Two's most famous draft dodger) and the world's five most beautiful women, Linda Darnell, Yvonne DeCarlo, Jennifer Jones, Gail (Eyes) Russell and Gene Tierney.

The first of each month the Madison theater circulated through the mail a calendar listing by date all the pictures scheduled for local showing that month. And from this list I was allowed by my parents to select the *three* pictures I most wanted to see for the month. The war, detective-gangster-mystery and western-adventure films were the favorites of mine and Benny, who sometimes went along with me but who once entering high school became more interested in something called girl. And by each weeknight performance at the Madison beginning at seven, Benny and I in order to catch the first of the evening's two shows had to leave the fields no later than six and without stopping to eat would run the entire four miles into town in order to be in that line when those lucky "eighty-four" went marching on up those stairs to nigger heaven. What is also yet memorable about those long ago nights as well is at the ages of ten, eleven and twelve coming home alone (those times when Benny was out "girling" it) down that long pitch dark deserted country road lined by looming wind whistling ghosts, or "haints," posing by day as trees. I ran the four miles home every time, scared. Yet came my next movie night, haints or no there I would be galloping up that long dirt road into town to be in that line when they called out my number from that balcony On High.

I was destined to remain faithful to the film until the end . . . which came when I was twelve years old. Darkening earth that fatal day when in talking about my love for the picture show to Momma (herself a former child movie magazine reader) I told her that when I grew up I wanted to be a movie star, to which she replied,

"*Only* white folks are movie stars."

DOOMSDAY

MOVIE STARS WERE *WHITE*! THE *SAME* WHITE AS MADISON WHITE? IF SO THEN
THERE WAS *NO* AMERICA THE OTHER SIDE OF THE SUN. IT WAS RIGHT HERE! I'D
BEEN IN AMERICA ALL ALONG AND NEVER EVEN KNEW IT! SHIT!

True, I knew that movie star faces weren't black but on the other
hand I *never* thought of them as being white either. I somehow thought
movie stardom transcended blackness and whiteness. Yet in thinking
back about it at the time, the only black face I could recall ever seeing
on the screen with any regularity was a cat called "Shine" who appeared
only in comic shorts where he was forever being frightened by ghostly
objects, causing his eyeballs to roll and him telling his feet in a stutter-
ing voice to move, an order they always obeyed with the help of a
speeded up reel. Yet I never did see the era's super star spade, Stepin
Fetchit, who was perhaps *too* heavy for our locale.

On that DOOMSDAY Night I remember wondering if when white
mothers told their children that they weren't colored did the children
get mad and run down in the pasture in back of their house and burn
all 504 of their saved up movie magazines as I was right at that moment
doing?

This traumatic discovery that America didn't want me on its silver, lily-
white screen brought about, to say the least, an abrupt death to my love
for the movies. And also by my at the age of twelve having lost interest
in cowboys, guns, cars, reading funny books and the funny papers, and
not quite ready for the girl thing yet, this left me stranded on a day-
dream way out in the back boondocks of limbo . . . where I discovered
the world of sports.. . .

Nominated by The Georgia Review and Gary Gildner

LITTLE WET MONSTER

by CHAD SWEENEY

from AMERICAN POETRY REVIEW

for our unborn son

The cornfield winds its halo darkly
Come home my little wet monster

Time in the copper mine, time in the copper
Come darkling soon, come woe my monster

Distance shines in the ice like a flower
Come early little bornling

Before the furlight's gone from going
Come rowing soon, come wet my monster

Before the bloodtrees bramble over
Come low my rainweed monster

Come antler through the gates my thingling
Your grapes contain the houses

Unmask the stones my darkling grief
Come whole my homeward early

You alone devour the night
Gather in your teeth, my zero

You devour the night's holy sound
Come home my little wet monster

Nominated by American Poetry Review

NEVER GIVE AN INCH

by GERALD HOWARD

from TIN HOUSE

I don't suppose anyone has ever done an in-depth study of that interesting form of literary ephemera, the author dust jacket biography. But if they did, I'm sure they would notice a distinct sociological shift over the past decades. Back in the forties and fifties, the bios, for novelists at least, leaned very heavily on the tough and colorful professions and pursuits that the author had had experience in before taking to the typewriter. Popular jobs, as I recall, were circus roustabout, oil field roughneck, engine wiper, short-order cook, fire lookout, railroad brakeman, cowpuncher, gold prospector, crop duster, and long-haul trucker. Military experiences in America's recent wars, preferably combat-related, were also often mentioned. The message being conveyed was that the guy (and they were, of course, guys) who had written the book in your hand had really been around the block and seen the rougher side of life, so you could look forward to vivid reading that delivered the authentic experiential goods.

It's been a long time since an author has been identified as a one-time circus roustabout. These days such occupations have become so exotic to the average desk-bound American that they serve as fodder for cable television reality shows viz., *The Deadliest Catch*, *Dirty Jobs*, and *Ice Road Truckers*. Contemporary dust jacket biographies tend to document the author's long march through the elite institutions, garnering undergraduate and postgraduate and MFA degrees, with various prizes and publications in prestigious literary magazines all duly noted. Vocational experiences generally get mentioned only when pertinent to the subject of the novel at hand—e.g., assistant DA or clerk for a Federal judge if the book deals with crime or the intricacies of the law. Work—especially the sort of work that gets your hands dirty and that brands you as a member of the working class—no longer seems germane to our novelists' apprenticeships and, not coincidentally, is no longer easy to find in the fiction they produce. Whether one finds this scarcity something to worry about or simply a fact to be noted probably says a lot about one's class origins and prejudices.

The dignity of work and its social efficacy is one of the core tenets of our democratic creed. In the absence of inherited social privilege deriving from European feudalism, it would be the willingness to work to tame a wild continent that would define, in Hector St. John Crèvecoeur's phrase, "the American, this new man." Yet if all men are created equal, as our Declaration of Independence so ringingly declares, all men are equally defined by the social class they are born into and often seek to rise above—and nothing more inexorably marks one's class as the sort of work one does. This disjunction between the gospel of equality to which we pay lip service and the reality of social distinctions that we cannot escape makes the whole subject of class in America a tense and touchy one. Simply to bring up the subject in any context, let alone a literary one, feels discomfiting, as if some taboo were being broken or doubt being cast on our most cherished ideals (or illusions) about ourselves. As Alfred Lubrano, himself the son of a bricklayer from Bensonhurst who ascended the class ladder by way of Columbia and newspaper journalism, notes in *Limbo: Blue Collar Roots, White Collar Dreams*, "While race and gender have had their decades in the sun, however, class has been obscured and overlooked." He then quotes an economist to the effect that "people would rather talk about sex than money and money before class." In his introduction to *Class Matters*, the book that resulted from a multi-part 2004 series of articles in the *New York Times*, Bill Keller calls the subject of class "vast, amorphous, politically charged, largely unacknowledged" and describes within the paper an intense debate "between those who thought that class was the governing force in American life and those who deemed it pretty much irrelevant." Only on the planet *Times*! We can be sure that such a charged discussion did not take place over two previous gotta-get-a-Pulitzer series in the paper, on race (2000) and poverty (1993). The pump of the *Times*'s bleeding heart tends to turn off before it reaches the working stiff, one has noticed; whether this tendency extends to the way its coverage of literary matters regards fiction from and about the working class is a question worth pondering.

In any case, these blinders are of relatively recent vintage, as the postwar economic boom and the rise of a vast middle class has made it possible, even mandatory, to view American society as homogenous, socially fluid, and largely unstratified. Charles McGrath observes, however, in that same *Times* series, that "in the old days, when we were more consumed by social class, we were also more honest about it. There is an un-American secret at the heart of American culture: for a long time, it was preoccupied by class." Work and class have certainly been abiding and central preoccupations of American literature for as long as we have had writing worthy of the name. Walt Whitman, the son of a carpenter, hymned the working man and woman in his "chants democratic"; when he "hear[s] America singing," the music is made by a mechanic, a mason, a boatman, a shoemaker, a woodcutter, a girl sewing or washing, "singing with open mouths their strong melodious songs." Its vast metaphysics of good and evil aside, *Moby-Dick* portrays with minutely observed particulars the dangerous and violent work of killing whales (*The Deadliest Catch* indeed) and reducing them to whale oil and other constituent products—a pursuit that incidentally created the first great American fortunes. As the forces of industrialization, immigration, and urbanization began in earnest to transform America from a mostly rural civilization, our novelists took careful note, producing "naturalistic" works that acutely registered the class drama of these epic social and economic developments.

The protagonist of William Dean Howells's *The Rise of Silas Lapham* is a Vermont farm boy turned self-made paint magnate whose wealth cannot shield him from a disastrous collision with Boston Brahmin society. In Theodore Dreiser's *An American Tragedy*, Clyde Griffiths, a worker in a collar factory, is so desperate to rise above his class and marry the aristocratic Sondra Finchley that he is driven to murder his pregnant working-class girlfriend, for which he is condemned to death. Dreiser's grimly deterministic vision in this and other novels, as well as the almost documentary realism with which such writers as Stephen Crane, Jack London, and Upton Sinclair portrayed the lower rungs of American enterprise, put paid to the genteel tradition and left an indelible picture of American life as a Darwinian struggle in which classes and individuals are ever rising and falling.

The next turn of the literary wheel fell to the Lost Generation, a cohort that reacted against the plain naturalism of its predecessors to explore the techniques, styles, and subjects suited to the ascent of modernism. Yet even in the midst of such experimentation F. Scott Fitzgerald fashioned his own American tragedy from the attempt of a Midwestern farm boy to erase his humble origins in *The Great Gatsby*, and Sinclair Lewis anatomized with pitiless accuracy the class structure of the all-American town of Zenith in *Babbitt*. But it was the crisis of capitalism represented by the Great Depression that drew American writers to the creed of Communism as the only alternative to the bankrupt system of free enterprise, and thus the thirties became the literary decade of the worker, the figure who, as Marx had decreed, would serve as the agent of historical change.

As a result, the thirties became, in fiction, very much a star search for the writer of impeccable working-class credentials or at least the proper political point of view, the one who could produce the great proletarian novel, a much desired work of revolutionary struggle and ideological awakening. The critical arbiters of taste were all waiting for Lefty, and even Ivy League scribes were putting on proletarian airs, striding the picket lines and haring off to the Appalachians to report on the latest coal miners' strike. But little of this work, by such dusty names as Agnes Smedley (*Daughter of Earth*), Jack Conroy (*The Disinherited*), Mike Pell (*S.S. Utah*), Mary Heaton Vorse (*Strike!*), and Grace Lumpkin (*To Make My Bread*), is read today, marred as it is by formulaic plots and a hectoring political tone. Of the fiction from this period dealing with the plight of the working class, only the novels of John Steinbeck are still widely read. *Jews Without Money* by Mike Gold, the critical bullyboy of *The New Masses*, survives as a portrait of Lower East Side Jewish tenement life; James T. Farrell's Studs Lonigan trilogy serves similarly for the Irish of Chicago. Both Edward Dahlberg's *Bottom Dogs*, praised by Edmund Wilson as "a work of literature that has the stamp of a real and original gift," and Edward Anderson's *Hungry Men* offer vividly rendered portraits of American life at the economic margins unmarred by agitprop and can also be read with profit today.

And then work, at least of the physical sort, and working people pretty much disappear from American fiction for the next three decades or so. Why? We can point to the long stretch of postwar prosperity that moved millions of Americans into the middle class and off the farms and assembly lines, while bringing a measure of security and affluence to those who remained. Literary fashion played its part, as serious American fiction became more inward looking, concerned with the problems of the individual rather than those of society. Nothing remotely like the rise of the so-called Angry Young Men, an eruption of literary voices from the working class in England, occurred in this country, in part because England has a thicker working-class culture with deeper historical roots, and even more so because our working class did not have that much to be angry about, protected as it was by a still-vibrant labor movement.

Most crucially, though, the whole concept of class came to be seen as almost a choice rather than a fate, as the powerful mechanisms of the meritocracy and the vastly expanded opportunities for higher education placed millions of Americans on the escalator of social mobility. Rightly celebrated as a great democratic achievement, this development nevertheless had some downsides that only became apparent with time. The children of the working class experienced a good deal of psychic stress and social discomfort as they negotiated their passage into the formerly alien precincts of higher education and the bourgeois, white collar world. This is the subject of Alfred Lubrano's often poignant book; Richard Price, again in the *Times* series on class, wryly describes his culture shock upon arriving at Cornell, far upstate from his New York working-class neighborhood, and putting on a heavier Bronx accent than he ever had at home "to semiconsciously cultivate an exoticness about myself, probably as an ego-survival countermeasure." Meanwhile their parents began to experience their own species of alienation, as their children ascended to levels of income and achievement formerly undreamed of and their core values of thrift, self-sacrifice, hard work, and patriotism began to seem retrograde in a culture increasingly focused on consumption, leisure, and self-fulfillment. Francis Fukuyama correctly terms the upheavals of the sixties and seventies "the Great Disruption," and this is nowhere more true than in the gulf that opened up between the tradition-minded Americans famously termed "the silent majority" and the advanced youth (many of them their own children), the affluent, the left liberals, and the counterculture.

Two books first published in 1972, when that gulf hardened into what now seems like a permanent condition, provide complementary and contrasting views of the lives of working people at that tumultuous time. That they are both securely in print almost four decades later suggests that not all that much has changed. The first is *The Hidden Injuries of Class* by Richard Sennett and Jonathan Cobb, a painfully bien-pensant sociological foray into the inner world of the working class. The authors wear their compassion on their sleeves as they venture forth from Harvard Yard to interview working people in the greater

Boston area, but, to this reader at least, discordant notes of self-congratulation and condescension often intrude. They state, quite accurately, that "the terrible thing about class in our society is that it sets up a contest for dignity." This is a contest that their white working-class subjects are seen to be losing, as their ethnic enclaves dissolve, their children rise above (and look down upon) them socially, their traditional values are derided as reactionary, and the impersonal forces of finance capitalism erode their economic security. There is little of the once-vaunted "dignity of labor" to be seen in these pages, just suppurating "existential wounds" inflicted by "inner class warfare" as we work ever harder and consume at ever greater levels to heal our inner doubts about ourselves. The solidarity and fraternity that was once seen as the hallmark of working-class culture becomes an anachronism in an atomized, individualistic society. Most of the speakers struggle to articulate the reality of their situations beyond a generalized sense of bafflement, resentment, and injured pride.

All of which was no doubt there to be found, but Sennett and Cobb are blinkered and tone-deaf to the more positive aspects of working-class life that Barbara Garson found in abundance in her *All the Livelong Day*: a wised-up (if sometimes gallows) sense of humor, a toughness of spirit, and a capacity for acts of resistance both large and small. Garson had no preconceived theories or political axes to grind as she did her shoe-leather reporting to learn "how people cope with routine and monotonous work." She found much that she expected to find—"speed, stress, humiliation, monotony"—in short, exploitation. But she also discovered that, in opposition to the petty and demeaning Taylorist practices applied in the name of efficiency, "through all this the workers make a constant effort—sometimes creative, sometimes pathetic, sometimes violent—to put meaning and dignity back into their daily activity." Staunch lefty that she is, Garson can state that "there definitely is a managing class, and it is a lying class," whereas "among ordinary people I find that self-serving lies are actually quite rare"—a thirties sentiment if I ever heard one. The labor she observes in her book is most definitely alienated, yet in a lumber mill slowly being mismanaged into the ground by its new corporate owners she also observes the pride that the mill hands take not only in their manual skills but also "their class skills in sticking together to see that they got their due from the bosses." All of which serves as a useful counterweight to Sennett and Cobb's portrait of working-class demoralization, equally real and far more refreshing to contemplate.

At just about this point in our social history a major American writer emerged to put the lives of the lumpen proletariat back at the center of our literature. That writer was, of course, Raymond Carver, and there is no more authentic and important working-class hero in contemporary American fiction than he. However, if we take a closer look at how Carver and his stories were received and lionized, we may find something disturbing in the way the educated literary class chose to view him and his putative working-class characters.

Carver's working-class bona fides are unassailable. He grew up in Yakima, Washington, the son of a hard-drinking lumber-mill worker, and was raised in a close-knit milieu. He married his pregnant girlfriend, Maryann Burk, soon after graduating from high school and had two children before the age of twenty. As a self-declared "paid-in-full member of the working poor," he supported himself and his family with a series of jobs that together would add up to one of those old-school author bios—mill hand, gas station attendant, tulip picker, hospital janitor, apartment complex manager—while he struggled his way to a college degree and a stint at the Iowa Writers Workshop. Angry creditors and the specter of bankruptcy dogged Carver, as it does so many working Americans just scraping by, and he had the typical bad habits of his class, alcoholism and heavy smoking. These facts only gradually became known to the literary public as Carver's reputation grew, after he published some spectacular early stories in *Esquire* and was nominated for a National Book Award in 1977 for his first collection, *Will You Please Be Quiet, Please?* But when serious fame burst upon him in 1981 with the publication of *What We Talk About When We Talk About Love* and a much noted profile in the *New York Times Magazine*, the difficult economic row Carver had to hoe became virtually his brand, and it remains so to this day.

Carver's stories are spare modernist telegrams of despair from the ragged edges of American life, written in the plain, unadorned language of their characters, and they project a sense of spiritual defeat to equal the early Eliot. But because they are written in the stripped-down and elliptical modern style, actual social information about Carver's characters is not that easy to glean. The men are often named Vern or Earl, and they work as mechanics or door-to-door salesmen or postmen, or they declare themselves "out of work" or "between jobs" in the opening paragraph, a state not soon to be remedied. The frequency with which hunting and fishing come up suggests a general location in the American west. Carver's characters are baffled and nearly paralyzed by the conditions of their existence, often in ways that directly suggest that they suffer "the hidden injuries of class" uncovered by Sennett and Cobb; God knows their dilemmas rise to the existential. They are the literary descendants of Sherwood Anderson's isolatoes and rural misfits in *Winesburg, Ohio*, but rendered in a post-Kafka manner.

For all that this is so, one senses a rhetorical pile-on in the way Carver's characters tend to be described. Here, in fact, is Carver's own editor, Gordon Lish: "They just seem squalid. In every manifestation of human activity they seem squalid. They're like hillbillies, but hillbillies of the shopping mall. And Carver celebrates that squalor, reveals that squalor, makes poetic that squalor in a way nobody else has tried to do." It may be to the point here to note that Lish, a sophisticated Easterner, used his position of power as an editor at *Esquire* and later at Knopf to force Carver to accept radical surgery on his stories, much against his wishes. (But, I believe, much to his literary benefit. It's complicated.) As Lubrano, along with Sennett and Cobb, points out, working-class people often find themselves at a loss in dealing with the subtle strategies and verbal indirection and power games of the white-collar world, whereas middle class people learn such things as their birthright. In any case, Lish's comments, reeking of class disdain, differ only in intensity but not in kind with dozens of other socio-critical assessments. And this is emphatically not the way that Carver himself saw his characters. As he said, "Until I started reading those reviews of my work, praising me, I never felt the people I was writing about were so bad off. You know what I mean? The waitress, the bus driver, the mechanic, the hotel keeper. God, the country is filled with these people. They're good people. People doing the best they could." You could search for a long time through the body of criticism of Carver's work and not find anything as remotely generous of spirit.

But writing as powerful as Carver's has a way of totally escaping its creator's intentions, with unpredictable consequences. In Carver's case his stories spawned an entire school of American fiction known variously as minimalism or K-Mart realism. The style took hold in graduate writing programs like pinkeye in an elementary school, and soon the graduates of America's fanciest colleges were slumming at their word processors in the strip malls and trailer parks that in real life they gave the widest possible berth. Absent from this work was any hint of the compassion evident in Carver's comment. A sort of poetics emerged in which the denizens of the lower middle class were given mean and sordid lives, with only a broken and ineffectual language with which to express themselves. We've come a long way from waiting for Lefty, and not necessarily upwards.

Raymond Carver's work represents, then, a shining moment in our literary history, but it hardly provided the occasion for class solidarity, susceptible as it was to misconstrual and unconscious snobbery. His style proved easy to emulate, but his personal journey—from hard-scrabble working-class origins to the heights of American fiction—remains, if not unique, still unusual. But the Republic of Letters can still be made to behave like a literary democracy of talent. Thankfully, working-class writers of great talent and unflinching vision still manage to squeeze through the class barriers to produce work both true to their origins and to the lives that so many Americans live.

Chief among them is Russell Banks, who grew up working class in the less fashionable precincts of New England and did time as a plumber, shoe salesman, and window trimmer before his writing career took hold. One of his early works is a suite of linked stories called *Trailer Park* (1981), whose title explains itself, but his masterpiece arrived four years later in *Continental Drift* (1985), probably the most Dreiserian novel in contemporary American fiction. A closely observed tragedy of economic circumstance, the book launches two characters—a New England boiler repairman down on his luck who migrates to Florida in search of a better life, and a young woman fleeing Haiti for the same reason—on a collision course that ends shatteringly for both. (Interestingly, something of the same plot trajectory informs Andre Dubus III's Oprah-consecrated 1999 novel *House of Sand and Fog*.) Banks's subsequent novels have continued to bring stinging and important news from the margins of American life.

Larry Heinemann grew up working-class in Chicago and had the ill luck or good literary fortune to be drafted into the Army right out of high school and sent to Vietnam, where he got a grunt's eye view of that awful war. That experience gave him the raw material for his two remarkable Vietnam novels, *Close Quarters* (1977), often called the first work of fiction written by a Vietnam veteran, and the haunting *Paco's Story* (1986), which received the National Book Award. In a long praise song for his work in the *New Yorker*, Veronica Geng wrote of Heinemann that "At heart, he's a comic novelist of the post-industrial economy," and noted how his "excited feeling for the language and detail of work became a distinctive style of observation; more than that, it became a way of interpreting what he experienced in Vietnam."

Four strong women writers with roots in the rural working class have kept faith with their people. Bobbie Ann Mason emerged just shortly after Raymond Carver with her plainspoken stories of Kentucky country folk, from which she sprung, and is the other writer most often mentioned as an avatar of minimalism. Dorothy Allison's *Bastard Out of Carolina* (1992) and Carolyn Chute's *The Beans of Egypt, Maine* (1985), set in the rural South and the Maine backwoods respectively, each created a sensation upon publication and draw on a raffish and irreverent tradition of rural Americana that looks back to Erskine Caldwell and beyond. And Denise Giardina taps her family history of growing up as the daughter of a West Virginia coal miner to lend unassailable authority to her much praised historical novels, *Storming Heaven* (1987) and *The Unquiet Earth* (1992).

Finally, but hardly exhaustively, three more fiction writers of note have mined their working-class origins for novels that are redolent, in style and subject matter, of those roots. Richard Price's first two novels, *The Wanderers* (1974) and *Bloodbrothers* (1976), are tough, funny and occasionally terrifying portraits of the ethnic street and domestic life of his native borough of the Bronx. His more recent works, from *Clockers* (1992) to *Lush Life* (2008), have run more to large-canvas police procedurals, but they are still informed by the street smarts and irreverent humor that are the legacy of an earlier life spent on asphalt. The late Gilbert Sorrentino, who died in 2006, is thought of as a dauntingly experimental writer, but he remains the postmodernist you would be most likely to have a boilermaker with; novels such as *Steelwork* (1970) and *Little Casino* (2002) are almost anthropological excavations of the speech cadences and worldview of the inhabitants of the working-class enclave of Bay Ridge, Brooklyn. (I know because I grew up there.) And Richard Russo's sagas of working-class life in economically strapped upstate New York towns, most notably *Mohawk* (1986), *The Risk Pool* (1988), and *Empire Falls* (2001), are graced with the resilient humor of his sharply etched characters and are set in affectionately but precisely observed bars, diners, and workplaces that are their native habitat.

That brief survey offers a by no means complete list of contemporary fiction writers who have roots in the working class and have chosen it as their subject matter. But even augmented it would offer a slim enough roster when placed against the flood tide of novels and story collections that roll off the presses each year. As we've noted, the path to literary recognition these days runs through our most prestigious and expensive universities, and these are neither welcoming nor, increasingly, affordable places for the children of the working class. The price barriers speak for themselves, but it is the atmosphere of class privilege and a culture of secret handshake-like assumptions that may offer an even more demoralizing obstacle to the aspiring working-class writer. Former Yale professor William Deresiewicz, in a much commented-upon essay in *The American Scholar*, "The Disadvantages of an Elite Education," mounts a comprehensive attack on such institutions based on just this point. Finding himself tongue-tied before a plumber who's arrived to fix his pipes, Deresiewicz contemplates how thoroughly an extended period spent in American higher education "makes you incapable of talking to people who aren't like you." And he takes that indictment even further when he says this: "my education taught me to believe that people who didn't go to an Ivy League or equivalent school weren't worth talking to, regardless of their class." For all the brave propaganda about "diversity" in higher education, it seems that class snobbery is not only sanctioned in our ivory towers, but in certain unconscious ways encouraged and virally reproduced.

It goes without saying that the same privileged culture that produces America's novelists and short story writers staffs its publishing industry. Its denizens certainly share Deresiewicz's tied tongue when it comes to making small talk with the plumber, and they—okay, we—are a great deal more comfortable talking about a novel that deals with the wrenching problems of people in faraway Africa or China than with the struggles of our own working poor. As relatively modest as their salaries may be, people in publishing are still by birth and education and cultural assumptions members of the emerging American overclass, self-replicating and increasingly isolated from the conditions of American life outside the big cities and campus enclaves. Working-class people who pay the punishing financial price that going to college extracts these days are unlikely to be attracted to publishing, with those "relatively modest salaries" as their payoff. All of which means that voices from and on behalf of the working class have that much harder a time getting read, understood, and published. Absent some unforeseen cultural shift, they are likely to remain unfashionable.

I know that sounds pretty bleak when it comes to what I've called literary democracy. And yet the vitality and toughness of working-class life has a way of producing voices that demand to be heard. Fiction, of all the arts, is the one that has the strongest allegiance to a realistic depiction of the world as it is, however advanced the formal means by which that representation is achieved. The strongest talents in American fiction, the ones that have the most impact and durable staying power, tend to be rooted in place and local culture and informed by human struggle. Take, for instance, Ken Kesey's almost overwhelmingly powerful 1964 novel *Sometimes a Great Notion*. Kesey is best remembered today as the psychedelic superhero and culture warrior of the sixties and the author of the anti-authoritarian cult classic *One Flew Over the Cuckoo's Nest*. But Kesey was also as authentically working class as his fellow Pacific Northwesterner Carver, a son of dairy farmers who ended his gaudy days working that same family farm. *Sometimes a Great Notion* is an epic saga of a family of loggers whose slogan, in thought, word, and deed, is "never give an inch," and whose sheer cussedness brings them into conflict with the entire community. Politically incorrect (the Stampers battle *against* the union to continue delivering lumber to the local mill) and formally innovative in the manner of Faulkner's *Absalom, Absalom!* the novel is imbued with the sort of mythic American intransigence celebrated in such events as the Alamo and the Battle of the Bulge. The Stampers are too big and brawling to display an ounce of the woundedness stressed by Sennett and Cobb, but they'd find good company in the unbowed workers in *All the Livelong Day*. The book's famous master image—of patriarch Henry Stamper's severed arm mounted on his home in such a way as to give the finger—to the rising river, to the striking workers, to anyone who cares to look—may seem overdetermined to certain literary tastes. But Kesey earns his image through his undeniable vitality and authority and the reader can't help but smile.

As John Steinbeck famously wrote, in a different context, "We're the people that live. They ain't gonna wipe us out. Why, we're the people—we go on." It will be a very sad day for American literature if we ever cut ourselves finally loose from that corny but noble sentiment. A literature stratified by its subject matter and its practitioners risks become a mandarin exercise, and that would be, well, unAmerican. It behooves all of us involved in the enterprise of American fiction to make sure it doesn't happen.

Nominated by Joan Murray

CERTAINTY

by JUDITH KITCHEN

from GREAT RIVER REVIEW

1.
It is hard and round. Cylindrical.
It hides.

2.
Each morning the sun returns, now a little earlier than the day before, noticeably earlier because we live so far north, so far west. It rises in the east, from over the water, and it seems to carry with it reflections of snow on the Cascades. Light falling, rather than lifting. Tumbling down the hill that leads to the house.

3.
There are statistics.
Ask anything, there is an answer. An answer surrounded with if-thens and buts, but nevertheless assertive, resolute.

4.
Each day you wake to its presence. You reach for the bottle of pills that tells you it is there, somewhere beneath the outer skin that was prodded and poked and cut and threaded. The skin through which they insert a needle which itself inserts the poison that will kill what kills. If it kills what kills, which is what they tell you is certain.

5.
Living with certainty can be interesting. It rounds the corner just as you approach, leading you ever onward. You see nothing but its back.

6.

Here's the rub. They know. They know so much. No question retains its rising inflection. The question mark is audibly erased. They tell you what you want to know, tell you they will always tell what you want to know. So what do you want, you who think you want to face truth? What actually is it that you want?

7.

The name becomes the problem. No one wants to hear the name. Emails come with the subject heading: the dreaded c. But cancer, crab-like, walks sideways into your life, and you must learn to say its name with the clarity it deserves. You must give it its due, its place in the lexicon. You must do that, not for yourself, but for others. So they can say it back. So they can roll it on their tongues, and taste its slightly acid aftertaste, its place in their lives as well. It's the one certain thing you can do for them—give this disease its living name.

8.

Outside, the clouds roll in. It will rain in the late afternoon. Or maybe they will pass, and the sun will spotlight the tips of sails on the sound. Flickers of light, triangular, as they lift like wings on this February day. You reserve the future, knowing that you will ride out into sun or rain, and that either will be fleeting.

9.

The long held note of the coyotes. Where do they live? We see their lit eyes in the headlights as they slink past, two of them trotting into the darkness, making their way to someplace close by. Over and over, they perforate the night.

We know they are there, but where, in daylight, do they hunker down? The morning dogs do not suddenly bark; their owners sweep up the hill tethered to the leashes, and no one stops—looks around— fraught with the sense that coyotes are following. No one halts, listening for footfalls, listening for what might be breathing in the underbrush.

10.

Here's what I know: the bamboo outside the window has grown another four inches over the past two months. It is resilient. Nothing cuts it back.

11.

There is no passion in certainty. Its color is tan, the color of sand stretching itself along the beach. Sand from a distance, uniform—not the multi-grained reality it really is. This is the color of flax, or corn stubble. A nothing of a color, that persists and persists and persists.

12.

Arabic numerals, a pile of them, adding themselves, dozens upon dozens, incrementally growing by orders of ten. They march like soldiers across the page. Orderly. And punctual.

13.

Oh unlucky number, baker's dozen, oh, childhood lost to the start of it all. What would it take to return, to unbaby the body, harness the breast, become six again. Or seven, or eight. Boundless in your energy. Boundless, and bound.

Black cat, broken mirror, open umbrella. Spill of salt. Walk under a ladder, step on a crack, break your mother's back. Break your own heart. Break dance your way out of the heart and into the head. Into the thick head of silence you will wish away and away and away. Flick of the switch. Wave of the wand. Wanderlust, lusterless, less is not more.

14.

Certainty sounds like a clock, chiming the quarter hours, adding its claim to the day. Each time, a little more, until the hour announces itself, passes on into the next, and then the next. Certainty pulls out its card and places it, facedown, on the table. Turn it over. It will be exactly what you imagined. It will contain your exact specifications: name, address, phone number, date of birth, social security number, counting out its digits as though they could protect you, could put you back in place.

15.

The roots of your hair actively ache. The scalp is so certainly there, emerging as the shape of your thoughts—round, and restless.

You did not expect to encounter yourself like this. The stark expression. The round-eyed stare. The head that curves, baby round, into the crook of your upraised arm.

Even as you surprise yourself in the mirror, you realize that you recognize your head—its tidiness. You stare at your external shape because, for the life of you, you cannot find the interior. You have been turned inside out, vessel of attention, and only the bones of emotions are left. You laugh in the face of your rubble.

16.
Not yet seven a.m., the streetlight still on, Sunday creeping slowly up the hill. My dark window reflects back to me my books, lining the shelf of the night. Soon light will seep into them, and they'll tuck themselves away behind me. But for now, my books march across my glass, left to right, pages of a lifetime. I keep only those I want to die with. Only those that have spoken to me, that make of me what I've become. They define me, now, as I've defined them.

I wait for the day that they, too, will be dispensable. The day I would strip all the shelves to the bone, as though I were about to start it all over—the dipping down into someone else's mind, the coming up with a handful of salt.

17.
Each morning you forget. You touch the top of your head, and you've forgotten. And you understand that, when you remember, you will have become a part of this disease. So you wake to forgetfulness, grateful for the fact that nothing has diminished to the point of memory. White cells. Check. Red cells. Check. Markers. Check. Mark yourself checked in the mirror, checked into the day, checked over, and under, and through. Even by.

18.
Lately, I never win anything on my Bingo scratch-off cards. I have been trying not to see this as an omen. Some sort of sign that luck has abandoned me. Where does the human mind go when it thinks this way? From what primordial need for explanation? What longing of the animal to understand the stars?

19.
Workmen are building a new addition to the house across the street. Every morning, a fleet of vans pulls up. Young men wrestle with 2 x 4s, dig and trim and pour concrete. A gable has been built on the ground—something they will hoist above the new bay window. You have to imag-

488

ine light streaming in, and the outside world turning its head. What will they see that they haven't been seeing?

The doorway is new—a slice of pane at each side—so the house takes on a different guise. Wears itself well. They're saving the blossoming cherry that reaches, now, with slender fingers toward the door. Wet black bough. But today faces do not appear along its length. Today, petals are merely petals, precursor of spring, predictor of time's mercurial intellect.

20.

One drop of rain at the tip of each leaf, suspended, certain. Cautiously held in check.

21.

There is a vocabulary and you learn it. Then you learn to forget it. Adriamycin. Cytoxan. Taxol. Taxotere. Tamoxifen. Everything has an "x" in it, as though you could solve its equation. There is a vocabulary, as well, for what people will say. Your blood pressure will rise as they tell you to "think positive thoughts." If thought could cure you, you would not be sick in the first place. You do not respond well to what seems to have become adage: hold a good image in your mind.

Yet you laugh. You are in an amazingly good mood. How can you not laugh at how you resemble a plant in the mirror? A dandelion gone to seed, to be precise.

How can you not laugh at how reasonably well you feel for how you look? And the images you hold dear (though, thank god, not the ocean under a blue sky that the social worker suggested to you) are positive enough:

Benjamin at the piano;
Simon dancing;
Ian running on the beach.
You have others, if you need to call them up:
Driving Route 2 across eastern Montana;
your own young sons boarding the ferry in Salcombe;
Stan on the merry-go-round, its carved horses handsome in sunlight.
But you don't call them up—not consciously. Not in the way they prescribe. To do that would buy their pronouncements, and you refuse to do that. You will not accept the blame that comes with failure to thrive. If you thrive, it will be willpower, and willingness, and, most of all, sci-

ence. And luck. It will not be the day you gave him your love as the horse cast its wild eye backward.

22.
Five a.m. Wake to darkness. Wake to its certain demise. Walk your thirty minutes, as though the lungs were what are at stake. As though to lunge into the day, sucking in breath and swimming upstream. As though to make seamless the dream of watery flight.

23.
This is hard work. Not only the body destroying itself, but the hard long wait for it to recover. The bones ache with all their silent activities. The mouth sheds its cloak and reveals every fissure. The only thing that actually tastes good is ice-cold water. Beyond that, there are compromises you must make with the body. You must, after all, eat something.. . .

24.
When it's gone, one thing is certain. I will not miss it. The breast that turned against me, against my will. It held lovers, and babies, but most of all it got in the way of things I wanted to do. To be. Soon I can try my new image. I can fit myself into the clothes I want to wear. Tailor myself. Talk myself into what I will become. Certainly, that will happen. My hair will grow, curl I hope, and my mouth will return to its normal contours. I'll catch a glimpse of myself in the mirror and say, "I know what you look like, underneath all the hair and the clothes and the faint brush of powder." I'll know what resides in that body I'm slowly getting used to.

Even the rain carries a different light. It slants into the house, harbinger. Everything is green, a haze of moss. Daffodils push through the ground. They are urgent and unsettled, the color of sunlight, caught for a brief instant through the storm.

25.
This puzzle will be the death of me. Three feet long, one foot high, it stretches across the table as though it knows it will defeat me. Oh, there's the requisite barn, dead center, some trees, a couple of cows, but mainly it's three feet by four inches of sunflowers, blowsy in the breeze, slightly out of focus in their frantic dancing. Hundreds of them.

And three feet by three inches of variegated sky, the shades too subtle for the eye to discern until you've selected the wrong piece.

There is no ending. The pieces swim up in impossible progressions. The powers of concentration are overwhelmed. Is that the partial center of a sunflower, or part of the post in the obligatory fence? Is that stalk, or grass? In that sky shading off to the east is there a hint of darkness descending?

An American dream, made with German precision. The scene is so placid. Static. You might think the whole of a lifetime was held in the frame. Slowed to the point of contemplation. Yet when you step back, there they are—sunflowers springing into a frenzy, twisting their sunbound heads, a sari of seed and petal and stalk.

Go inside the barn, where the faint smell of hay wafts down from the rafters, and the scent of manure is, somehow, clean and replete. It's dim inside, a summer afternoon held at bay, time for a thought. Or, god forbid, image. All those days ago when you entered the barns of your childhood, awed at the height, the heft of it all. When did you stop thinking of barns? Three summers ago, on an island in Quebec, you visited a dairy farm as though you were strange to its habits. As though you didn't know stanchion and hayfork and pail. The sweet smell of sileage. The soft sounds of cows shifting in unison. As though you didn't know that all of life is memory filed in the mind: been there, done that.

I know one thing. Three days, or three weeks, I can't predict the date, the hour, that I'll pick up the final piece and place it squarely where it belongs. But when I do, it will be almost mysterious the way everything suddenly shimmies into resolution.

Nominated by Great River Review and Linda Bierds, Fleda Brown,
Jane Hirshfield, Rebecca McClanahan

THE RED CARPET

by JUAN VILLORO

from N+1 and EL MALPENSANTE

ACCORDING TO ANDY WARHOL'S MAXIM, in the future everyone will be famous for fifteen minutes. This utopia of visibility makes sense in a society of the spectacle. Mexican political culture promises happiness in the opposite way: what is important is not what is seen, but what is hidden. A life of accomplishment doesn't culminate in celebrity; it is achieved in secret. The Mexican utopia has consisted of enjoying your fifteen minutes of impunity.

For 71 years (1929–2000), the Institutional Revolutionary Party (PRI) governed without winning or losing elections. It perpetuated itself by means of an ongoing rotation of cadres that blurred the line between the public and the private, and it renewed popular hopes like a carnival barker: "If you didn't do well this time, the next Revolutionary Government will do you justice."

The Mexican mode of governance—transparency and accountability alike unknown to it—transformed our slang into a grammar of shadows. Politics was baptized *la tenebra*, political horse-trading was done in *lo oscurito*. The coming of light was dangerous; the conspirator had to act under cover of darkness, to get ahead of his adversary by rising before dawn. In his novel *La sombra del caudillo* (an impeccable portrait of the revolutionary generals who became politicians in the 1920s), Martín Luis Guzmán wrote: "He who shoots first, kills first. Indeed, the politics of Mexico, the politics of the gun, conjures only one verb: to rise early [*madrugar*]."

The exercise of power, an office of shadows, depended for almost a

492

century on the political value of inscrutability. With the end of the PRI's monopoly, the codes of the unpunished and unpunishable dissolved without being replaced by others. Welcome to a decade of chaos! Eight years after the democratic transfer of power, Mexico is a country of blood and lead.

The preeminence of violence has dissolved long-established protocols and relationships. The media have expanded their margin of freedom, but they work in an environment where telling the truth is increasingly dangerous. According to Reporters Without Borders, Mexico surpasses Iraq in its number of kidnapped and murdered journalists. In this new setting, events are confused with "pseudo-events." It's the sort of environment that would follow a shipwreck, in which the absence of principle disguises itself as prudence or "emergency measures." Political exchanges are a masquerade: the Church supports the PAN [*Partido de Acción Nacional*] in Jalisco and receives immoderate alms in return; the National Education Workers Union (the largest trade union in Latin America) offers more than a million votes to Felipe Calderón and receives posts in areas of government of such consequence as national security; corporate monopolists play out a dirty war in the media during the 2006 presidential campaign, painting the leftist candidate as a "danger to Mexico," and in return get deals that eliminate the competition. Like the Fantastic Four, the de facto powers rule from the margins. Impunity did not disappear when the PRI lost the presidency; it was dispersed in the midst of uncertainty. This has inspired a sort of nostalgia for the authoritarianism of the Official Party, who "at least knew how to steal."

In the hermetic tradition of Mexican politics, protagonists left the stage and died without making significant revelations or leaving behind compromising diaries. Nothing carried greater weight than the secret. There was no greater hierophany than the coded gesture. The journalist's mission consisted in deciphering signs that were practically esoteric. Every gesture was scrutinized like a pass in bullfighting or a pose in kabuki theater: if the president was in a good mood, he ordered huevos rancheros for breakfast on Monday; if in the same sitting he reached for the refried beans without addressing his Minister of the Interior, a cabinet change was imminent.

Political gastronomy now follows a very different course. We stand before an all-you-can-eat buffet where everyone snatches everyone else's plate, yells at the same time, and carries off his leftovers in Tupperware.

* * *

THE CRISIS IN GOVERNANCE corresponds to a crisis in the media. The executive is now incapable of determining his own information agenda. If, for seven decades, to declare was more important than to govern ("your well-being" was a promise that didn't allow for argument), now the president appears on the news for a few seconds between two assassinations, an official eye-blink amid the flying shrapnel. In this context, organized crime provides the new dominant symbolism.

The drug trade tends to act twice: in the world of events, and again in the news, where it very rarely encounters an opposing discourse. Television amplifies the horror by disseminating, in close-ups and slow motion, crimes with marks of authorship. It's possible to distinguish the "signatures" of the different cartels: some decapitate their victims, others cut out their tongues, others leave the dead in the trunks of cars, others wrap them in blankets. In some cases, criminals record their executions and send videos to the media or post them on YouTube—after a not insignificant postproduction process. The mainstream news media become the narco's late-night TV, the zone in which the offense committed in reality becomes an infomercial for terror.

The narco relies on the discourse of cruelty (*cruor*: the blood that spills, says Lyotard), in which wounds trace a sentence for the victim and a warning for the witnesses. The *jus sangui* of the narco depends on a Kafkaesque inversion of legal proceedings; the verdict is not the end but the beginning of a trial, the announcement that others might yet be called to court. "If you do not make the blood run, the law is indecipherable," Lyotard wrote about "In the Penal Colony." That is the implicit slogan of organized crime. Its words are perfectly legible. Meanwhile, the other law, "our" law, has faded.

Narcoculture expanded the radius of its influence by means of ballads, or *narcocorridos*, which are frequently paid for by their protagonists. In our atmosphere of confusion, troubadours with underworld associations enjoy the dubious glamour of criminal life, which benefits from a certain against-the-grain charisma and lays claim to "popular morality." In the *narcocorridos*, depressing accordions accompany a saga of plunder; they glorify activities that, as much as they may bring roads and electricity to poppy-growing communities, can't support all the comparisons to Robin Hood. Although it might sound fun or interesting or "authentic" to champion those who carry the *hierba mala* to the other side, *narcocorridos* belong to a sector of society that drives

10 percent of the national economy (the same percentage as petroleum) and is responsible for dozens of murders a day.

Taken as documents of the underworld, the *narcocorridos* are informative. What's strange is that they have won space on mainstream radio stations and even in some literary anthologies. In the name of a suspect multiculturalism, a few years ago a group of writers protested the fact that two *narcocorridos* had been suppressed from a textbook. In their complaint, they neglected to consider that the lyrics would be studied not in a class about contemporary issues in Mexico but in one about literature, replacing Amado Nervo or Ramón López Velarde. The narco has relied on the consent of the radio stations that it threatens or subsidizes (the terms are interchangeable) and on the anthropological solidarity of those who overinterpret crime as a manifestation of tradition.

THE SHAMELESS TENDENCY TOWARD instant gratification that characterizes modern life has allied itself, in Mexico, to "impunity." In the world of the narcos, the supremacy of the present moment plays out in a ménage à trois between fast money, advanced criminal technology, and the dominion of the secret. The past and the future, the values of tradition and of a society's long-term hopes, lose their meaning in this territory. Only the here and now exists: the opportune moment, the emporium of caprice in which you can have five wives, rent a hit man for a thousand dollars and a judge for twice that, and live at the margins of law and good taste, amid the colorful horror of Versace shirts, solid-gold giraffes, jewels resembling Amazonian insects, a $300,000 watch to tell the time, and turquoise ostrich leather boots.

As scholars like Luis Astorga and Ronaldo González Valdés have documented, fifty years ago the drug trade was regional, confined to the Mexican north. These days it involves the planetary flux of capital.

The drug trade has won cultural and informational battles in a society that hides from the problem through denial: "The *sicarios* only kill each other." More than an accepted routine or an indifferent banalization of evil, news of the underworld has produced simple distance. It's always about strangers, outlandish or faraway people. *They* must know why their throats are being slit.

Every morning the papers publish an indicator in red: the twelve beheaded in Yucatán from yesterday are replaced by the twenty-four executed today in La Marquesa national park. Nevertheless, the instinct for survival has created a mental isolation of the zones of violence. As long as "they" are the ones annihilating each other, we will be safe.

JULIO SCHERER GARCÍA, doyen of independent journalism in Mexico, recently published an illuminating book: *La Reina del Pacífico*. For months, Scherer visited Sandra Ávila Beltrán in the penitentiary where she has been held since September 28, 2007. Presented to the media as if she were the "Queen of the South" from Arturo Pérez Reverte's novel, Ávila has all the necessary traits to captivate the public imagination. She is a beautiful, strong, defiant woman, imprisoned by a weak head of state who broke his bones falling off a bicycle (a kindergartner's accident), and who is further diminished by the suits he wears (on him they all look extra-large). The Queen was irresistible prey for a president with small feet. Displaying her to the public is part of a larger propaganda strategy that has done nothing to diminish the brutal impact of the drug trade.

According to what she tells Scherer, Ávila's involvement in crime has been less direct and in a certain way more alarming than what her jailers suggest. At 44, she has never known a life outside the drug trade. She talks about the industry the way Sofia Coppola might talk about film. She had open lines of communication to all the noteworthy capos, was kidnapped by a delinquent boyfriend, has been married to two narcos (one a corrupt police commander), underwent the kidnapping of her adolescent son, has watched people die at her feet, and has had at her disposal all the parties, all the jewels, all the cars, all the mansions (each occupied only for a couple of weeks)—every excess purchasable for cash. Although she studied journalism for a semester at the Universidad Autónoma de Guadalajara, she was not familiar with Julio Scherer, the country's best-known journalist. For forty-four years she lived in a world apart, like the inmates of Biosphere 2.

Javier Marías has noted that the TV series *The Sopranos* relies on putting the private lives of gangsters on display, offering a ticket, without risk of death, inside the zone where Mafiosi are like us and have problems with their kids' schools. The narco, for his part, relies on eliminating the outside and assimilating everything to his private life: *buying* the entire residential development, the country club, the soccer stadium, the police precinct, the bubble that Sandra Ávila can inhabit. There is no need to pretend. The spectators have been bought.

The Queen of the Pacific does not appear to be the strategist of evil that the president needs her to be, but something more commonplace and awful: the consort of crime. She has lived a full and complete life without passing for a moment within the bounds of legality. The most amazing thing is not her rank within the criminal hierarchy but the fact that she has fulfilled, normally," all the obligations of the subculture into which she was born (her only grievance is not having been a man so she could have played a greater role). From girl to widow, she has traversed a path that reads like a narrative of self-actualization that years ago was exclusive to Sinaloa, home of the Pacific Cartel, but now belongs to the whole country—a narrative in which no amount of waste is reprehensible. If someone thinks that one gadget called the Rolex Oyster Perpetual Date Watch boasted enough names to satisfy the Queen, he is wrong. Sandra Ávila owned 179 of them. Such strongbox excesses are complemented by the cartels' waste of weaponry. *Sicarios* leave behind fifteen or seventeen AK-47s at the scene of a crime, proof that their arsenal is bottomless.

The narco's theatricality relies on bullets and torture, but also on this profligate weaponry and on the disguises that allow him to be a transitory member of any police force in the country. The *cartrancherels* have so thoroughly infiltrated police power that it's not surprising for them to have every kind of uniform at their disposal. What's strange is that the police, accomplices in the crime, still wear uniforms.

For his entry into public recognition, the capo needs a nickname for a passport; he can take his name from theodicy (*El Señor de los Cielos* [Lord of the Heavens]), from ranching (*Don Neto*), or from cartoons (*El Azul* [Blue Man]). The most terrible ones are those that insinuate a sort of feminine coquettishness, brutally refuted by the facts: *la Barbie* [Barbie Doll], *el Ceja Güera* [White Chick's Eyebrow].

Like superheroes, narcos don't have histories or CVs: they have legends. Their counterparts in the United States stay anonymous. In Mexico they are ubiquitous and elusive. It doesn't matter if they're in a maximum-security prison or in a mansion with a mother-of-pearl jacuzzi. They never stop working.

Curiously, the state of denial about the violence has given way to a very informed fear. To confirm that the capos are "Others," practically extraterrestrial beings, we memorize their exotic aliases and inventory their culinary habits: jaguar heart with gunpowder, lobster sprinkled with tamarind and cocaine.

The landscape has been transformed by the investment of dirty money. Any Mexican city features plenty of locations to film the death of a capo or a police commander. There, the ideal restaurant: a plastic and neon château where waitresses in miniskirts serve brontosaurus ribs, next to a Mercedes-Benz dealership and a hotel that looks like a mosque with Plexiglas cupolas. Places like Torreón or Mérida, which until recently had reputations as calm cities (because it was assumed that the narcos who built their homes there didn't use them for "work") have now also become the settings for executions.

In the new environment of fear, 10,000 companies offer security services, and close to 3,000 people have had a chip the size of a grain of rice implanted under their skin so that they can be easily located in the event of kidnapping.

On September 15, Independence Day, two grenades were tossed into a defenseless crowd in the municipal plaza of Morelia. The terrorist attack coincided with another of a virtual order: the inhabitants of Villahermosa received emails marking them as candidates for kidnapping. Crime can no longer be relegated to the tranquilizing territory of the foreign.

President Calderón came to power in a highly contentious election that divided Mexico. To demonstrate and solidify his strength, he ordered the military to patrol the country. This declaration that confrontation was thinkable provoked the cartels both to battle each other and to execute police officers. But while the corpses appeared on highways and in gutters, no financing networks were investigated, no criminal accomplices in government were detained. The last high-ranking government official to be arrested for his collusion with organized crime was Mario Villanueva, governor of Quintana Roo, who was investigated during the era of Ernesto Zedillo, the last president of the PRI. The two governments that have been in office since the democratic transfer of power have been incapable of investigating themselves and detecting the arrangements that allow the drug trade to prosper.

We have arrived at a new order of fear: we face a diffuse, delocalized war, with no notions of "front" or "rearguard," in which we can't even determine the sides of the conflict. It has become impossible to establish with a reasonable degree of certainty who belongs to the police and who is an infiltrator.

OUR PACT WITH CRIME has produced a decisive symbolic displacement. If, for decades, we protected ourselves from the violence by conceiving of it as something alien, now its influence draws ever nearer.

In the realm of art, the installation artist Rosa María Robles anticipated the resignification of fear. Her exhibition *Navajas*, shown in Culiacán, included the piece *Alfombra roja* [Red Carpet], which didn't refer to the runway where the rich and famous parade on their way to Andy Warhol's utopia, but to the bloodstained blankets of the *encobijados*, murder victims of the cartel, their bodies wrapped and dumped in this penal colony that claimed almost 5,000 victims in 2008.

The unrepeatable moment of the crime and the unlimited reach of the drug trade acquire new meaning in this installation. Robles managed to procure eight of the blankets from a police warehouse. With these she created her red carpet. Displayed in a gallery, it became a disturbing readymade. Duchamp collaborates with James Ellroy: the found object as proof of the crime. Robles staged impunity on two fronts: she put unsolved crimes before our eyes, and she proved how easy it is to penetrate the legal system and appropriate objects that ought to be guarded vigilantly.

Navajas provoked a controversy about the appropriateness of recycling criminal evidence. The real impact of the work was different: in the gallery, the blankets offered far more compelling proof than they had as evidence.

After some discussion, *Alfombra roja* was withdrawn. Rosa María Robles then dyed a blanket with her own blood. The gesture defined our Mexican moment with dramatic urgency. We all have a reason to step onto that carpet. Terror has grown simultaneously more diffuse and intimate. Before we could believe that the blood was "theirs." Now it's ours.

—*Translated from the Spanish by David Noriega*

Nominated by N+1

SPECIAL MENTION

(The editors also wish to mention the following important works published by small presses last year. Listings are in no particular order.)

POETRY

Gloss—Heidy Steidlmayer (Michigan Quarterly Review)

When I Reached into the Stomach of a Fistulated Dairy Cow: Sixth Grade Field Trip to Sonny's Dairy Barn—Anna Journey (Field)

Nightingale—Debra Allbery (The Greensboro Review & Four Way Books)

Tavern. Tavern. Church. Shuttered Tavern,—Patricia Smith (Rattle)

A Correction—Idris Anderson (Agni online)

My Life—Lynn Emanuel (from *Noose and Hook* / University of Pittsburgh Press)

Dandelions—Peter Campion (Poetry)

Elegy with Mistakes All through It—Matt Donovan (Agni)

Pantoum of the Brothel of Ruin—Patrick Donnelly (The Massachusetts Review)

Elegy—Daisy Fried (Poetry)

Anything a Box Will Hold—Bette Husted (from *At This Distance* / Wordcraft of Oregon)

Bird Watching at Night—Sherman Alexie (jubilat)

Al-A'imma Bridge—Brian Turner (Valparaiso Poetry Review & from *Phantom Noise* / Alice James Books)

Sweet Nothings—Chelsea Rathburn (Ploughshares)
from Talking Dead — Neil Rollinson (Poetry Review)
Guns 'N Roses — Austin MacRae (Barefoot Muse)
The Grass Plan — Saint James Harris Woods (Haven Chronicles)
Remission — Letitia Momirov (Healing Muse)
The End — Dora Malech (Columbia Poetry Review)
All Dressed In Green — Peter Krass (Rattle)
Why Keep at this Writing Thing — Lance Larsen (Raritan)
After A Line by Eluard — Dina Der-Havanessian (Connecticut Review)
Desert Patio— Ron Drummond (Bellevue Literary Review)
I Run Into My Father in the Form of a House — Fred Yannantuono (Hollins Critic)
To The Moon — Malachi Black (Southwest Review)
Matthew You're Leaving Again So Soon — Matthew Siegel (Ninth Letter)
At Peter Behrens' House — Jaqueline Osherow (Southwest Review)
Playbill for the Gray One — Jacquelyn Malone (Beloit Poetry Journal)
Time Pieces — Rachel Wetzsteon (New Criterion)
Plymouth on Ice — Thomas Moore (*Boltcutter* Four Hemlocks Press)

NONFICTION

Sunlight — Michael Coffey (Conjunctions)
The Gulf Between Us — Terry Tempest Williams (Orion)
Reading In A Digital Age — Sven Birkerts (American Scholar)
Celebrity Houses, Celebrity Politics — Daniel Harris (Antioch Review)
Drinking At The Fountain of Youth — Scott Ely (Kenyon Review)
A Dark Light In The West: Racism and Reconciliation — Barry Lopez (Georgia Review)
Catch and Release, Repeat — Will Jennings (River Teeth)
Venice, An Interior (1988) — Javier Marias (Threepenny Review)
Sign Here If You Exist — Jill Sisson Quinn (Ecotone)
Humor Is Not A Mood — Lynn Williams (4th Genre)
The Two Cultures of Life — Kristin Dombek (N+1)
End Of The Line — Jim Kennedy (Creative Nonfiction)
The Curse of Bigness — Christoper Ketcham (Orion)
Predatory Habits — Etay Zwick (The Point)
Bard of the Bottle — Michael White (Missouri Review)
Juventútem Meam — Gary Gildner (New Letters)

An Elliptical Essay On Violence — Ed Falco (Virginia Quarterly)
An Uncommon Friend — Grace Schulman (*First Loves*, University of Michigan Press)
Leopold and Shinner — Peggy Shinner (Colorado Review)
Lightning-Rod Man — Paul West (Agni)
My Fall Into Knowledge — Reg Saner (Georgia Review)
Across The River — Nikolina Kulidžan (The Sun)
A Hive of Mysterious Danger — Joseph Murtagh (Missouri Review)
Sway Me Smooth — Floyd Skloot (Ecotone)
Intimate Strangers — Eve Joseph (Malahat Review)

FICTION

The Jesus Lights — Donald Ray Pollock (Epoch)
The Animals of the Budapest Zoo (1944-1945) — Tamas Dobozy (Raitan)
Captivity — Daphne Tan (Shenandoah)
Witnessing — Mary Hood (Georgia Review)
The Interpreter — Mary Morris (Antioch Review)
Buckeyes — Pinckney Benedict (*Miracle Boy*, Press 53)
The Next Thing on Benefit — Castle Freeman Jr. (New England Review)
Red Ribbon Monday — Susan Straight (The Sun)
Ryan Sniffrin — Kevin Brockmeier (Tin House)
Oil & Gas — Alyson Hagy (*Ghosts of Wyoming*, Graywolf)
At Prayer Level — Marjorie Kemper (The Sun)
Adacious — Brock Adams (Sewanee Review)
Afterwards — Mark Brazaitis (Notre Dame Review)
Slipknot — Adam Stumacher (TriQuarterly)
Like Snow, Only Grayer — Mary Akers (Bellevue Literary Review)
Drunk Girl in Stilettos — Lee Martin (Georgia Review)
A People's History of Martin Zansamere — Alan Stewart Carl (Mid-Atlantic Review)
The West — Carson Mell (Electric Literature)
The Traitor of Zion — Ben Stroud (Ecotone)
Virgin — April Ayers Lawson (Paris Review)
The Mud Man — Benjamin Percy (Southern Review)
from *Glorious* — Bernice L. McFadden (Akashic Books)
Something You Can't Live Without — Matthew Neill Null (Oxford American)

A Temporary Marriage — Krys Lee (Kenyon Review)
At The National Theater — Ismet Prcic (McSweeny's)
A Space Between Rows — Elizabeth Schulte (New England Review)
The Mere Mortal — Louis B. Jones (The Sun)
My Daughter Debbie — Deb Olin Unferth (Noon)
Mr. Scary — Charles Baxter (Ploughshares)
Sister Hercule — Andrea J. Nolan (Dogwood)
After Which Everything Changed — Jane Bernstein (Confrontation)
Rip Off — Wayne Harrison (Five Chapters)
Summer Avenue — Stephen Schottenfeld (Gettysburg Review)
Troubled Youth — Poe Ballantine (The Sun)
Carry Me Home, Sisters of Saint Joseph — Marie-Helene Bertino
  (American Short Fiction)

PRESSES FEATURED IN THE PUSHCART PRIZE EDITIONS SINCE 1976

Acts
Agni
Ahsahta Press
Ailanthus Press
Alaska Quarterly Review
Alcheringa/Ethnopoetics
Alice James Books
Ambergris
Amelia
American Letters and Commentary
American Literature
American PEN
American Poetry Review
American Scholar
American Short Fiction
The American Voice
Amicus Journal
Amnesty International
Anaesthesia Review
Anhinga Press
Another Chicago Magazine
Antaeus
Antietam Review
Antioch Review
Apalachee Quarterly
Aphra
Aralia Press

The Ark
Art and Understanding
Arts and Letters
Artword Quarterly
Ascensius Press
Ascent
Aspen Leaves
Aspen Poetry Anthology
Assembling
Atlanta Review
Autonomedia
Avocet Press
The Baffler
Bakunin
Bamboo Ridge
Barlenmir House
Barnwood Press
Barrow Street
Bellevue Literary Review
The Bellingham Review
Bellowing Ark
Beloit Poetry Journal
Bennington Review
Bilingual Review
Black American Literature Forum
Blackbird
Black Renaissance Noire

Black Rooster
Black Scholar
Black Sparrow
Black Warrior Review
Blackwells Press
Bloom
Bloomsbury Review
Blue Cloud Quarterly
Blueline
Blue Unicorn
Blue Wind Press
Bluefish
BOA Editions
Bomb
Bookslinger Editions
Boston Review
Boulevard
Boxspring
Bridge
Bridges
Brown Journal of Arts
Burning Deck Press
Caliban
California Quarterly
Callaloo
Calliope
Calliopea Press
Calyx
The Canary
Canto
Capra Press
Caribbean Writer
Carolina Quarterly
Cedar Rock
Center
Chariton Review
Charnel House
Chattahoochee Review
Chautauqua Literary Journal
Chelsea
Chicago Review
Chouteau Review
Chowder Review

Cimarron Review
Cincinnati Poetry Review
City Lights Books
Cleveland State Univ. Poetry Ctr.
Clown War
CoEvolution Quarterly
Cold Mountain Press
Colorado Review
Columbia: A Magazine of Poetry and Prose
Confluence Press
Confrontation
Conjunctions
Connecticut Review
Copper Canyon Press
Cosmic Information Agency
Countermeasures
Counterpoint
Court Green
Crawl Out Your Window
Crazyhorse
Crescent Review
Cross Cultural Communications
Cross Currents
Crosstown Books
Crowd
Cue
Cumberland Poetry Review
Curbstone Press
Cutbank
Cypher Books
Dacotah Territory
Daedalus
Dalkey Archive Press
Decatur House
December
Denver Quarterly
Desperation Press
Dogwood
Domestic Crude
Doubletake
Dragon Gate Inc.
Dreamworks
Dryad Press

Duck Down Press
Durak
East River Anthology
Eastern Washington University Press
Ecotone
El Malpensante
Eleven Eleven
Ellis Press
Empty Bowl
Epiphany
Epoch
Ergo!
Evansville Review
Exquisite Corpse
Faultline
Fence
Fiction
Fiction Collective
Fiction International
Field
Fine Madness
Firebrand Books
Firelands Art Review
First Intensity
Five A.M.
Five Fingers Review
Five Points Press
Five Trees Press
The Formalist
Fourth Genre
Frontiers: A Journal of Women Studies
Fugue
Gallimaufry
Genre
The Georgia Review
Gettysburg Review
Ghost Dance
Gibbs-Smith
Glimmer Train
Goddard Journal
David Godine, Publisher
Graham House Press
Grand Street

Granta
Graywolf Press
Great River Review
Green Mountains Review
Greenfield Review
Greensboro Review
Guardian Press
Gulf Coast
Hanging Loose
Hard Pressed
Harvard Review
Hayden's Ferry Review
Hermitage Press
Heyday
Hills
Hollyridge Press
Holmgangers Press
Holy Cow!
Home Planet News
Hudson Review
Hungry Mind Review
Icarus
Icon
Idaho Review
Iguana Press
Image
In Character
Indiana Review
Indiana Writes
Intermedia
Intro
Invisible City
Inwood Press
Iowa Review
Ironwood
Jam To-day
The Journal
Jubilat
The Kanchenjuga Press
Kansas Quarterly
Kayak
Kelsey Street Press
Kenyon Review

Kestrel
Lake Effect
Latitudes Press
Laughing Waters Press
Laurel Poetry Collective
Laurel Review
L'Epervier Press
Liberation
Linquis
Literal Latté
Literary Imagination
The Literary Review
The Little Magazine
Little Patuxent Review
Little Star
Living Hand Press
Living Poets Press
Logbridge-Rhodes
Louisville Review
Lowlands Review
Lucille
Lynx House Press
Lyric
The MacGuffin
Magic Circle Press
Malahat Review
M noa
Man root
Many Mountains Moving
Marlboro Review
Massachusetts Review
McSweeney's
Meridian
Mho & Mho Works
Micah Publications
Michigan Quarterly
Mid-American Review
Milkweed Editions
Milkweed Quarterly
The Minnesota Review
Mississippi Review
Mississippi Valley Review
Missouri Review

Montana Gothic
Montana Review
Montemora
Moon Pony Press
Mount Voices
Mr. Cogito Press
MSS
Mudfish
Mulch Press
N + 1
Nada Press
Narrative
National Poetry Review
Nebraska Review
New America
New American Review
New American Writing
The New Criterion
New Delta Review
New Directions
New England Review
New England Review and Bread Loaf
        Quarterly
New Issues
New Letters
New Ohio Review
New Orleans Review
NewSouth Books
New Virginia Review
New York Quarterly
New York University Press
Nimrod
9 X 9 Industries
Ninth Letter
Noon
North American Review
North Atlantic Books
North Dakota Quarterly
North Point Press
Northeastern University Press
Northern Lights
Northwest Review
Notre Dame Review

O. ARS
O. Bl k
Obsidian
Obsidian II
Ocho
Oconee Review
October
Ohio Review
Old Crow Review
Ontario Review
Open City
Open Places
Orca Press
Orchises Press
Oregon Humanities
Orion
Other Voices
Oxford American
Oxford Press
Oyez Press
Oyster Boy Review
Painted Bride Quarterly
Painted Hills Review
Palo Alto Review
Paris Press
Paris Review
Parkett
Parnassus: Poetry in Review
Partisan Review
Passages North
Pebble Lake Review
Penca Books
Pentagram
Penumbra Press
Pequod
Persea: An International Review
Perugia Press
Per Contra
Pipedream Press
Pitcairn Press
Pitt Magazine
Pleasure Boat Studio
Pleiades

Ploughshares
Poems & Plays
Poet and Critic
Poet Lore
Poetry
Poetry Atlanta Press
Poetry East
Poetry Ireland Review
Poetry Northwest
Poetry Now
The Point
Post Road
Prairie Schooner
Prescott Street Press
Press
Promise of Learnings
Provincetown Arts
A Public Space
Puerto Del Sol
Quaderni Di Yip
Quarry West
The Quarterly
Quarterly West
Quiddity
Rainbow Press
Raritan: A Quarterly Review
Rattle
Red Cedar Review
Red Clay Books
Red Dust Press
Red Earth Press
Red Hen Press
Release Press
Republic of Letters
Review of Contemporary Fiction
Revista Chicano-Riquena
Rhetoric Review
Rivendell
River Styx
River Teeth
Rowan Tree Press
Runes
Russian *Samizdat*

Salamander

Salmagundi

San Marcos Press

Sarabande Books

Sea Pen Press and Paper Mill

Seal Press

Seamark Press

Seattle Review

Second Coming Press

Semiotext(e)

Seneca Review

Seven Days

The Seventies Press

Sewanee Review

Shankpainter

Shantih

Shearsman

Sheep Meadow Press

Shenandoah

A Shout In the Street

Sibyl-Child Press

Side Show

Sixth Finch

Small Moon

Smartish Pace

The Smith

Snake Nation Review

Solo

Solo 2

Some

The Sonora Review

Southern Poetry Review

Southern Review

Southwest Review

Speakeasy

Spectrum

Spillway

The Spirit That Moves Us

St. Andrews Press

Story

Story Quarterly

Streetfare Journal

Stuart Wright, Publisher

Sugar House Review

Sulfur

The Sun

Sun & Moon Press

Sun Press

Sunstone

Sweet

Sycamore Review

Tamagwa

Tar River Poetry

Teal Press

Telephone Books

Telescope

Temblor

The Temple

Tendril

Texas Slough

Think

Third Coast

13th Moon

THIS

Thorp Springs Press

Three Rivers Press

Threepenny Review

Thunder City Press

Thunder's Mouth Press

Tia Chucha Press

Tikkun

Tin House

Tombouctou Books

Toothpaste Press

Transatlantic Review

Triplopia

TriQuarterly

Truck Press

Tupelo Press

Turnrow

Tusculum Review

Undine

Unicorn Press

University of Chicago Press

University of Georgia Press

University of Illinois Press

University of Iowa Press
University of Massachusetts Press
University of North Texas Press
University of Pittsburgh Press
University of Wisconsin Press
University Press of New England
Unmuzzled Ox
Unspeakable Visions of the Individual
Vagabond
Vallum
Verse
Verse Wisconsin
Vignette
Virginia Quarterly Review
Volt
Wampeter Press
Washington Writers Workshop
Water-Stone
Water Table
Wave Books
West Branch

Western Humanities Review
Westigan Review
White Pine Press
Wickwire Press
Willow Springs
Wilmore City
Witness
Word Beat Press
Word-Smith
World Literature Today
Wormwood Review
Writers Forum
Xanadu
Yale Review
Yardbird Reader
Yarrow
Y-Bird
Zeitgeist Press
Zoetrope: All-Story
Zone 3
ZYZZYVA

CONTRIBUTING SMALL PRESSES FOR PUSHCART PRIZE XXXVI

A

A Cappella Zoo, 105 Harvard Ave., E., #A-1, Seattle, WA 98102
A Public Space, 323 Dean St., Brooklyn, NY 11217
Aberdeen Bay Press, 5109 Eaton Rapids Rd., Albion, MI 49224
Able Muse Review, 467 Saratoga Ave., #602, San Jose, CA 95129
ABZ Press, PO Box 2746, Huntington, WV 25757-2746
Accents Publishing, P.O. Box 910456, Lexington, KY 40591-0456
Aforementioned Productions, 70 Commercial St., 1R, Boston, MA 02109
Agni Magazine, Boston University, 236 Bay State Rd., Boston, MA 02215
Akashic Books, 232 3rd St., Ste. B404, Brooklyn, NY 11215-2712
Alaska Quarterly Review, 211 Providence Dr., ESH 208, Anchorage, AK 99508
Alice James Books, 238 Main St., Farmington, ME 04938
Alimentum, The Literature of Food, PO Box 210028, Nashville, TN 37221
Allbook Books, PO Box 562, Selden, NY 11784
The American Poetry Review, 1700 Sansom St., Ste. 800, Philadelphia, PA 19103
The American Scholar, 1606 New Hampshire Ave. NW, Washington, DC 20009
American Short Fiction, PO Box 301209, Austin, TX 78703
Amoskeag, 2500 No. River Rd., Manchester, NH 03106-1045
Ampersand Books, 5040 10th Ave. S., Gulfport, FL 33707
Ancient Paths, P.O. Box 7505, Fairfax Station, VA 22039
anderbo.com, 270 Lafayette St., Ste 1412, New York, NY 10012
Anhinga Press, P. O. Box 3665, Tallahassee, FL 32315
Anomalous Books, P.O. Box 15371, Atlanta, GA 30333
Another Chicago Magazine, P.O. Box 408439, Chicago, TL 60640
Anti-, 4237 Beethoven Ave., St. Louis, MO 63116-2503
The Antioch Review, PO Box 148, Yellow Springs, OH 45387-0148
Antrim House Books, PO Box 111, Tariffville, CT 06081
Apalachee Press, P.O. Box 10469, Tallahassee, FL 32302
Apparatus Magazine, 2200 W. Foster Ave., Unit #1, Chicago, IL 60625
Apple Valley Review, 88 South 3rd St., #336, San Jose, CA 95113
Aquarius Press, PO Box 23096, Detroit, MI 48223
The Asian American Literary Review, 1120 Cole Student Activities Bldg., College Park, MD 20740
Asia Writes, B2 L20 Psalm St., Sto. Tomas Village 4, Deparo, Kalookan City 1400, Philippines
At Length, 266 12th St., #11, Brooklyn, NY 11215
Atlanta Review, PO Box 8248, Atlanta, GA 31106
Aunt Lute Books, P.O. Box 410687, San Francisco, CA 94141

The Aurorean, P.O. Box 187, Farmington, ME 04938
Autumn House Press, 87 1/2 Westwood St., Pittsburgh, PA 15211
Autumn Sky Poetry, 5263 Artie Circle, Emmaus, PA 18049
Avery House Press, Inc., 3757 Broadway, #1E, New York, NY 10031
Axe Factory, PO Box 40691, Philadelphia, PA 19107

B

The Baffler, 200 Hampshire Street, No. 3, Cambridge, Mass 02139
Bamboo Ridge Press, PO Box 61781, Honolulu, HI 96839-1781
Banana Fish, 7740 E. Glenrosa Ave., #209, Scottsdale, AZ 85251
Barbaric Yawp, 3700 County Route 24, Russell, NY 13684
The Barefoot Muse, PO Box 115, Hainesport, NJ 08036
Barn Owl Review, Dept. of English, Univ. of Akron, Akron, OH 44325-1906
Barrelhouse, PO Box 17598, Baltimore, MD 21297-1598
Barrow Street, PO Box 1831, New York, NY 10156
Bartleby Snopes, 917 Kylemore Dr., Ballwin, MO 63021-7935
Bat City Review, Univ. of Texas, 1 University Station B 5000, Austin, TX 78712
Bayou Magazine, 2000 Lake Shore Dr., New Orleans, LA 70148
Bear Star Press, 185 Hollow Oak Dr., Cohasset, CA 95973
Beehive Press, P.O. Box 641012, Los Angeles, CA 90064
Belfire Press, Box 295, Miami MB, CANADA ROG 1HO
Bellevue Literary Review, NYU School of Medicine, 550 First Ave., New York, NY 10016
Bellingham Review, MS-9053, WWU, Bellingham, WA 98225
Beloit Poetry Journal, PO Box 151, Farmington, ME 04938
Berkeley Fiction Review, 10 B Eshleman Hall, UCB, Berkeley, CA 94720-4500
Bird & Beckett, 653 Chenery St., San Francisco, CA 94131
Birkensnake, 303 Angell St., #3, Providence, RI 02906-3233
Birmingham Poetry Review, 1517 Astre Circle, AL 35226
BkMk Press, UMKC, 5101 Rockhill Rd., Kansas City, MO 64110-2499
Black Clock, CalArts, 24700 McBean Pkwy, Valencia, CA 91355
Black Matrix Publishing, 1252 Redwood Ave., #52, Grants Pass, OR 97527-5592
Black Warrior Review, 2016 9th St., Tuscaloosa, AL 35401
Blackbird, PO Box 843082, Richmond, VA 23284-3082
Blink-Ink, P.O. Box 5, North Branford, CT 06471
Blood Lotus, 2732 N. Bremen, Unit A, Milwaukee, WI 53212
Blood Orange Review, 1495 Evergreen Ave. NE, Salem, OR 97301
The Blotter Magazine, P.O. Box 2153, Chapel Hill, NC 27515
Blue Fifth Review, 267 Lark Meadow Circle, Bluff City, TN 37618
Blue Guitar Magazine, 1616 N. Alta Mesa Dr., #33, Mesa, AZ 85205
Blue Mesa Review, UNM, MCS 03-2170, Albuquerque, NM 87131-0001
Blue Moon, 327 12th St., Davis, CA 95616
Blue Print Review, 1103 NW 11th Ave., Gainesville, FL 32601
BOA Editions, 250 North Goodman St., Ste 306, Rochester, NY 14607
Bone Bouquet, 317 Madison Ave., #520, New York, NY 10017
Boston Literary Magazine, 383 Langley Rd., #2, Newton Centre, MA 02459
Boston Review, Building E-53, Room 407, MIT, Cambridge, MA 02139
Bottom Dog Press, PO Box 425, Huron, OH 44839
Boulevard, 7507 Byron Place, 1st Floor, St. Louis, MO 63105
Bound Off, P.O. Box 821, Cedar Rapids, IA 52406-0821
Boxcar Poetry Review, 510 S. Ardmore Ave., #303, Los Angeles, CA 90020
Brain, Child, PO Box 714, Lexington, VA 24450
Brevity, 35 Avon Place, Athens, OH 45701
The Briar Cliff Review, PO Box 2100, Sioux City, IA 51104-2100
Bright Hill Press, PO Box 193, 94 Church St., Treadwell, NY 13846-0193
Brilliant Corners, Lycoming College, Williamsport, PA 17701
Broadkill Review, 104 Federal St., Milton, DE 19968
The Broadsider, P.O. Box 236, Millbrae, CA 94030
The Brooklyn Rail, 99 Commercial St., #15, Brooklyn, NY 11222

Bull Spec, P.O. Box 13146, Durham, NC 27709
Burnt Bridge, 527 Front Beach Dr., #65, Ocean Springs, MS 39564

C

Café Irreal, PO Box 87031, Tucson, AZ 85754
Caketrain Journal, PO Box 82588, Pittsburgh, PA 15218-0588
Callaloo, 4212 TAMU, Texas A&M Univ., College Station, TX 77843-4212
Calyx Inc., Box B, Corvallis, OR 97339-0539
Camas, 639 South 5th St. E., Missoula, MT 59801
The Camel Saloon, 11190 Abbotts Station Dr., Johns Creek, GA 30097
Camera Obscura, P.O. Box 2356, Addison, TX 75001
Canon Press, 205 E. 5th St., Moscow, ID 84843-2951
Carpe Articulum, P.O. Box 409, Lake Oswego, OR 97034
Casa de Snapdragon, 12901 Bryce Ave. NE, Albuquerque, NM 87112
Catlin Press, 8100 Alderwood Rd., Halfmoon Bay, BC, V0N 1Y1, Canada
Cave Wall Press, PO Box 29546, Greensboro, NC 27429-9546
Celtic Cat Publishing, 2654 Wild Fern Lane, Knoxville, TN 37931
Central Avenue Press, 5390 Fallriver Row Court, Columbia, MD 21044
Cerise Press, 2904 East Eleana Lane, Gilbert, AZ 85298-5776
Cervena Barva Press, PO Box 440357, W. Somerville, MA 02144-3222
Cezanne's Carrot, PO Box 6037, Santa Fe, NM 87502-6037
Cha, Department of English, 3/F Fung King Hey Building, Chinese University of Hong Kong, Shatin, New
    Territories, Hong Kong SAR
The Chaffey Review, 5885 Haven Ave., Rancho Cucamonga, CA 91737-3002
Chautauqua, UNC Wilmington, 601 South College Rd., Wilmington, NC 28403-5938
Chicago Poetry.com, 2626 W. Iowa, #2F, Chicago, IL 60622
The Chrysalis Reader, 1745 Gravel Hill Rd., Dillwyn, VA23936
Cider Press Review, 777 Braddock Lane, Halifax, PA 17032
Cimarron Review, Oklahoma State University, Stillwater, OK 74078
Cinnamon Press, Meirion House, Glan yr afon, Tanygrisiau, Blaenau Ffestiniog, Gwynedd, Wales,
    LL41 3SU
Cincinnati Review, Univ. of Cincinnati, PO Box 210069, Cincinnati, OH 45221-0069
Coal City Review, English Dept, University of Kansas, Lawrence, KS 66045
Cold Mountain Review, ASU — English Dept, Boone, NC 28608
The Collagist, 2779 Page Ave., Ann Arbor, MI 48104
Colorado Review, 9105 Campus Delivery, Colorado State Univ., Fort Collins, CO 80523-9105
Columbia Poetry Review, 600 South Michigan Ave., Chicago, IL 60605-1996
Common Ground Review, 40 Prospect St., #C-1, Westfield, MA 01085-1559
Concisely, 1432 W. Jonquil Terrace, #3, Chicago, IL 60626-7201
Conclave: A Journal of Character, 7144 N. Harlem Ave., #325, Chicago, IL 60631
Concrete Wolf, PO Box 1808, Kingston, WA 98346-1808
Confrontation, English Dept, C.W. Post Campus/LIU, Brookville, NY 11548
Conjunctions, Bard College, Annandale-on-Hudson, NY 12504
Connecticut Review, 501 Crescent St., New Haven, CT 06515-1355
Connecticut River Review, 53 Pearl St., New Haven, CT 06511
Conte, 32000 Campus Dr., Salisbury, MD 21804
Contrary, c/o McMahon, 1010 East 59th St., Classics 17, Chicago, IL 60637
Copper Canyon Press, PO Box 271, Port Townsend, WA 98368
Copper Nickel, D20643, P.O. Box 173364, Denver, CO 80217
Court Green, Columbia College, 600 South Michigan Ave., Chicago, IL 60605-1996
Court Jester, 7043 SE 173rd Arlington Loop, Lady Lake, FL 32162
Crab Creek Review, PO Box 1524, Kingston, WA 98346
Crab Orchard Review, SIUC, 1000 Faner Drive, Carbondale, IL 62901
Crazyhorse, College of Charleston, 66 George St., Charleston, SC 29424
Cream City Review, UW-Milwaukee, P.O. Box 413, Milwaukee, WI 53201
Creative Nonfiction, 5501 Walnut St., Ste. 202, Pittsburgh, PA 15232
Cross-Cultural Communications, 239 Wynsum Ave., Merrick, NY 11566-4725
Curbstone Press, 321 Jackson St., Willimantic, CT 06226-1738

Cutthroat, A Journal of the Arts, PO Box 2414, Durango, CO 81302
Cypher Books, 310 Bowery, New York, NY 10012

D

Dalton Publishing, 1716 Bouldin Ave., Austin, TX 78704
Daniel & Daniel Publishers, P.O. Box 2790, McKinleyville, CA 95519-2790
Dark Valentine Magazine, 4717 Ben Avenue #106, Valley Village, CA 91607
Deadly Chaps, c/o Public Restaurant, 210 Elizabeth St., New York, NY 20012
decomP, 3002 Grey Wolf Cove, New Albany, IN 47150
The Delmarva Review, PO Box 544, St. Michaels, MD 21663
Denver Quarterly, University of Denver, 2000 E Asbury, Denver, CO 80208
Diamond Point Press, 24 Wildfern Drive, Youngstown, OH 44505
The DMQ Review, 16393 Bonnie Lane, Los Gatos, CA 95032
Dog Boy, 185 Renfrew Drive, Athens, GA 30606
Dogwood, 1010 Race St., Apt 5BC, Philadelphia, PA 19107
Dragonfly Press, P.O. Box 746, Columbia, CA 95310
Drash, 2632 NE 80th St., Seattle, WA 98115-4622
Dreams & Nightmares, 1300 Kicker Rd., Tuscaloosa, AL 35404
Drunken Boat, 119 Main St., Chester, CT 06412
Dunes Review, P.O. Box 1505, Traverse City, MI 49685
DuPage Group, 23 Willabay Dr., Unit D, Williams Bay, WI 53191
Durable Goods, PO Box 282, Painted Post, NY 14870

E

Essays & Fiction, 209 Cascadilla St., Ithaca, NY 14850
The Eastern Echo, 236 King Hall, Ypsilanti, MI 48197
Echo Ink Review, 5920 Nall Ave., Ste. 301, Mission, KS 66202
Eclectic Flash, 1579 Cottonwood Bluffs Drive, Benson, AZ 85602-7514
Ecotone, UNC Wilmington, 601 S. College Rd., Wilmington, NC 28403-5938
Edge, PO Box 101, Wellington, NV 89444
Ekphrasis, PO Box 161236, Sacramento, CA 95816-1236
Electric Literature, 325 Gold St., Ste. 303, Brooklyn, NY 11201
Electrik Milk Bath Press, PO Box 833223, Richardson, TX 75083
Eleven Eleven Journal, 1111 Eighth St., S.F., CA 94107
Elkhound, PO Box 1453, Gracie Sta., New York, NY 10028
Emerson Review, 120 Boylston St., Boston, MA 02116
Emprise Review, 2100 N. Leverett Ave., #28, Fayetteville, AR 72703-2233
The Enigmatist, 104 Bronco Dr., Georgetown, TX 78633
Epiphany, 71 Bedford St., New York, NY 10014
Epoch, 251 Goldwin Smith Hall, Cornell University, Ithaca NY 14853-3201
The Equalizer, P.O. Box 272, North Bennington, VT 05257
Esopus, 64 West 3rd St., Room 210, New York, NY 10012-1021
The Evansville Review, 1800 Lincoln Ave., Evansville, IN 47722
The Evening Street Press, 7652 Sawmill Rd., #352, Dublin, OH 43016
Event, PO Box 2503, New Westminster, BC, V3L 5B2, Canada
Evermore Books, 411 S. 16th Ave., Hattiesburg, MS 39401
Exit 13, P.O. Box 423, Fanwood, NJ 07023

F

Failbetter, 2022 Grove Ave., Richmond, VA 23220
Fiction Fix, 370 Thornycroft Ave., Staten Island, NY 10312
Fiction International, SDSU, 5500 Campanile Dr., San Diego, CA 92182-6020
Field, 50 North Professor St., Oberlin, OH 44074

Fifth Wednesday Books, Inc, P.O. Box 4033, Lisle, IL 60532-9033
Final Thursday Press, UNI, English Dept., Cedar Falls, IA 50614-0502
Finishing Line Press, P.O. Box 1626, Georgetown, KY 40324
The First Line, PO Box 250382, Plano, TX 75025-0382
5 AM, Box 205, Spring Church, PA 15686
Five Chapters, 1401 Highland Ave., Louisville, KY 40204-2028
Five Points, PO Box 3970, Atlanta, GA 30302-3970
Five Star Publications, 1558 E. 19ᵗʰ St., Apt. 1K, Brooklyn, NY 11230-7225
Flatmancrooked Publishing, 3311 Franklin Blvd., Sacramento, CA 95818
The Florida Review, P.O. Box 161346, Orlando, FL 32816-1346
Fogged Clarity, PO Box 1016, Muskegon, MI 49443
Fort Hemlock Press, P.O. Box 11, Brooksville, ME 04617-0011
Fortunate Childe, 923 Sharpsburg Circle, Birmingham, AL 35213
Fortunate Daughter Press, 1105 Pumpkin Rd., Shepherdsville, KY 40165
Four Way Books, P.O. Box 535, Village Station, New York, NY 10014
Fourteen Hills, 1600 Holloway Ave., San Francisco, CA 94132
Fourth Genre, Morrill Hall, East Lansing, MI 48824-1036
Fox Chase Review, 7930 Barnes St., Apt A-7, Philadelphia, PA 19111
fractalEDGEpress, 1112 N. Ashland Ave., Chicago, IL 60622-3935
Freight Stories, PO Box 44167, Indianapolis, IN 46244
Friday Jones Publishing, 600 Cook St., Denver, CO 80206
Fringe Magazine, 93 Fox Rd., Apt 5A, Edison, NJ 08817
Fugue, University of Idaho, P.O. Box 441102, Moscow, ID 83844-1102
Fulcrum Publishing, 4690 Table Mountain Drive, Ste. 100, Golden, CO 80403

G

Gargoyle Magazine, 3819 13ᵗʰ St. N., Arlington, VA 22201-4922
Gelles-Cole Literary Enterprises, P.O. Box 341, Woodstock, NY 12498
Gemini Magazine, PO Box 1485, Onset, MA 02558
The Georgia Review, University of Georgia, Athens, GA 30602-9009
The Gettysburg Review, Gettysburg College, Gettysburg, PA 17325-1491
Gival Press, PO Box 3812, Arlington, VA 22203
Glimmer Train Press, 1211 NW Glisan St., Ste. 207, Portland, OR 97209-3054
Gloom Cupboard, 140 Marion Dr., West Orange, NJ 07052
Gold Wake Press, 5 Barry St., Randolph, MA 02368
Goose River Press, 3400 Friendship Rd., Waldoboro, ME 04572-6337
Gorsky Press, P.O. Box 42024, Los Angeles, CA 90042
Grain Magazine, Box 67, Saskatoon, SK, S7K 3K1, Canada
Graywolf Press, 250 Third Avenue No., Ste. 600, Minneapolis, MN 55401
Great River Review, Anderson Center, PO Box 406, Red Wing, MN 55066
Green Fuse Poetic Arts, 400 Vortex St., Bellvue, CO 80512-8017
Green Mountains Review, 337 College Hill, Johnson, VT 05656
The Greensboro Review, UNC Greensboro, Greensboro, NC 27402-6170
The Greensilk Journal, 1459 Redland Rd., Cross Junction, VA 22625
Grey Sparrow Press, PO Box 211664, St. Paul, MN 55121
Grist, 301 McClung Tower, Univ. of Tennessee, Knoxville, TN 37996
Groundwaters, PO Box 50, Lorane, OR 97451
Guernica, 395 Fort Washington Ave., #57, New York, NY 10033
Gulf Coast, University of Houston, Houston, TX 77204-3013

H

H.O.W. Journal, 12 Desbrosses St., New York, NY 11013
Hamilton Arts & Letters, 92 Stanley Ave., Hamilton Ontario, Canada L8P 2L3
Hampden-Sydney Poetry Review, Box 66, Hampden-Sydney, VA 23943
Harbour Publishing Co., P.O. Box 219, Madeira Park, BC V0N 2H0 Canada
Harpur Palate, PO Box 6000, Binghamton University, Binghamton, NY 13902

Harvard Review, Lamont Library, Harvard University, Cambridge, MA 02138
Hayden's Ferry Review, P.O. Box 875002, Tempe, AZ 85287-5002
The Healing Muse, 750 Fast Adams St., Syracuse, NY 13210
The Hedgehog Review, UVA, PO Box 400816, Charlottesville, VA 22904-4816
The Hell Gate Review, 24-29 19th St., Astoria, NY 11102
Heyday, P.O. Box 9145, Berkeley, CA 94709
High Coup, P.O. Box 1004, Stockbridge, MA 01262
High Desert Journal, P.O. Box 7647, Bend, OR 97708
Hobart, PO Box 1658, Ann Arbor, MI 48106
Hobble Creek Review, PO Box 3511, West Wendover, NV 89883
Hobblebush Books, 17-A Old Milford Rd., Brookline, NH 03033
The Hollins Critic, PO Box 9538, Roanoke, VA 24020
Holly Rose Review, 12 Townsend Blvd., Poughkeepsie, NY 12603
Home Planet News, PO Box 455, High Falls, NY 12440
Homestead Review, 411 Central Ave., Salinas, CA 93901
Hopewell Publications, PO Box 11, Titusville, NJ 08560
Hotel Amerika, English Dept., 600 S. Michigan Ave., Chicago, IL 60605
The Hudson Review, 684 Park Ave., New York, NY 10065
Hunger Mountain, 36 College St., Montpelier, VT 05602

I

Ibbetson Street Press, 25 School Street, Somerville, MA 02143
The Idaho Review, Boise State Univ., 1910 University Dr., Boise, ID 83725
Illuminations, College of Charleston, 66 George St., Charleston, SC 29424
Illya's Honey, PO Box 700865, Dallas, TX 75370
Image, 3307 Third Avenue West, Seattle, WA 98119
Indiana Review, 1020 E. Kirkwood Ave., Bloomington, IN 47405-7103
InDigest Magazine, 3285 33rd St., #F8, Astoria, NY 11106
Inglis House Poetry, 2600 Belmont Ave., Philadelphia, PA 19131
Inkwell, Manhattanville College, 2900 Purchase St., Purchase, NY 10577
The Iowa Review, 308 EPB, University of Iowa, Iowa City, IA 52242
Iron Horse, English Dept., Texas Tech Univ., Lubbock, TX 79409-3091
Italian Americana, 80 Washington St., Providence, RI 02903-1803

J

J Journal, 619 West 54th St., 7th Fl, NY, NY 10019
Jabberwock Review, Mississippi State Univ., Drawer E, Mississippi State, MS 39762
Jacar Press, 6617 Deerview Trail, Durham, NC 27712
Jersey Devil Press, 73 Forest St., Fl. 2, Montclair, NJ 07042
The Jewish Magazine, P.O.B. 23437, Ramot, Jerusalem, 91233, Israel
The Journal, English Dept., Ohio State Univ., 164 West 17th Ave., Columbus, OH 43210
Journal of New Jersey Poets, 214 Center Grove Rd., Randolph, NJ 07869-2086
Journal of Truth and Consequence, 618 Alto St., Santa Fe, NM 87501
Joyland, 90 Ontario St., #210, Toronto, ON M5A 3V6 Canada
Juked, 17149 Flanders St., Los Angeles, CA 91344

K

Kansas City Voices, 6045 Marrway St., Ste. 104, Mission, KS 66202
Karamu, 600 Lincoln Ave., Charleston, IL 61920
Kelsey Review, Mercer County Community College, P.O. Box B, Trenton, NJ 08690
Kenyon Review, Finn House, 102 W. Wiggin St., Gambier, OH 43022
Kerf, 883 W. Washington Blvd., Crescent City, CA 95531-8361
Kitsune Books, PO Box 1154, Crawfordville, FL 32326-1154

Knockout, 9 Nina Court SW, Isanti, MN 55040
Kore Press, PO Box 42315, Tucson, AZ 85733-2315
Kweli Journal, P.O. Box 693, New York, NY 10021

L

La Alameda Press, 9636 Guadalupe Trail NW, Alburquerque, NM 87114
The Labletter, 3712 N. Broadway, #241, Chicago, IL 60613
Lake Effect, 4951 College Drive, Erie, PA 16563-1501
Lamplighter Review, PO Box 92, Overton, TX 75684
Lapham's Quarterly, 33 Iriving Place, New York, NY 10003
Lalitamba, 110 West 86th St., Ste. 5D, New York, NY 10024
Lebanon College Press, 15 Hanover St., Lebanon, NH 03766
Lightning Strikes Press, 334 Eaton Rd., Bennington, VT 05201-9340
Lilly Press, 1848 Finch Drive, Bensalem, PA 19020
Limestone, P.O. Box 1215, University of Kentucky, Lexington, KY 40506
Lips, 7002 Blvd. East, #2-26G, Guttenberg, NJ 07093
Liquid Imagination, 7800 Loma Del Norte NE, Albuquerque, NM 87109-5419
Literal Latte, 200 e. 10th St., Ste. 240, New York, NY 10003
Literary Imagination, Oxford University Press, 2001 Evans Rd., Cary NC 27513
The Literary Review, 285 Madison Ave./M-GH2-01, Madison, NJ 07940
Little Patuxent Review, 6012 Jamina Downs, Columbia, MD 21045
Little Red Tree Publishing, 635 Ocean Avenue, New London, CT 06320
Little Star, 107 Bank St., New York, NY 10014
The Lives You Touch, P.O. Box 276, Gwynedd Valley, PA 19437-0276
Lorimer Press, PO Box 1013, Davidson, NC 28036
The Los Angeles Review, PO Box 40820, Pasadena, CA 91114
Lost Horse Press, 105 Lost Horse Lane, Sandpoint, ID 83864
Lowestoft Chronicle, 1925 Massachusetts Ave., Unit 8, Cambridge, MA 02140
Loving Healing Press Inc., 5145 Pontiac Trl, Ann Arbor, MI 48105-9279
Lumina, Sarah Lawrence College, 1 Mead Way, Bronxville, NY 10708-5999
Luna Bella Press, Inc., 55 Summerfield Ave., Somerset, MA 02725

M

The MacGuffin, 18600 Haggerty Rd., Livonia, MI 48152
Madras Press, 16 Rushmore St., Brighton, MA 02135
Magnet Magazine, 1218 Chestnut St., Ste. 508, Philadelphia, PA 19107
Magnapoets, 13300 Tecumseh Rd. E., #226, Tecumseh, Ontario N8N 4R8, Canada
Main Street Rag, P.O. Box 690100, Charlotte, NC 28227
MAKE Literary Productions, 2229 W. Iowa St., #3, Chicago, IL 60622
make/shift, PO Box 2697, Venice, CA 90294
The Malahat Review, PO Box 1700 STN CSC, Victoria BC V8W 2Y2 Canada
The Manhattan Review, 440 Riverside Dr., #38, New York, NY 10027
Manoa, English Dept, University of Hawai'i, Honolulu, HI 96822
Many Mountains Moving, 1705 Lombard St., Philadelphia, PA 19146-1518
Marco Polo, 153 Cleveland Ave., Athens, GA 30361
MARGIE, The American Journal of Poetry, PO Box 250, Chesterfield, MO 63006-0250
Marin Poetry Center, 253 Forrest Ave., Fairfax, CA 94930
The Massachusetts Review, South College 126047, Amherst, MA 01003-7140
May Fair Publishing, 3514 Mapleton Rd., Sanborn, NY 14132
Mayapple Press, 408 N. Lincoln St., Bay City, MI 48708-6653
McSweeney's Publishing, 849 Valencia, San Francisco, CA 94110
The Meadowland Review, 105 Hillside Ave., Glen Ridge, NJ 07028
Measure, University of Evansville, 1800 Lincoln Ave., Evansville, IN 47722
The Medulla Review, 612 Everett Rd., Knox, TN 37934
Melusine, 12302 Skylark Lane, Bowie, MD 20715
Memorious, 21 Endicott Ave., Apt 4, Somerville, MA 02144

Meridian, University of Virginia, PO Box 400145, Charlottesville, VA 22904-4145
Michigan Quarterly Review, 915 E. Washington St., Ann Arbor, MI 48109-1070
Mid-American Review, Bowling Green State University, Bowling Green, OH 43403
Midnight Diner, 120 Center St., Oneonta, NY 13820
Military Writers Society of America, P. O. Box 264, Bridgeville, PA 15017
Milkweed Editions, 1011 Washington Ave. So., Ste. 300, Minneapolis, MN 55415
The Minnesota Review, Carnegie Mellon University, Pittsburgh, PA 15213
Minnetonka Review, P.O. Box 386, Spring Park, MN 55384
MiPOesias, 604 Vale St., Bloomington, IL 61701-5620
Mississippi Review, 118 College Dr. #5144, Hattiesburg, MS 39406-0001
The Missouri Review, 357 McReynolds Hall, Univ. of Missouri, Columbia, MO 65211
Mobius, the Poetry Magazine, PO Box 671058, Flushing, NY 11367-1058
Modern Haiku, PO Box 33077, Santa Fe, NM 87594-3077
Moment, 4115 Wisconsin Ave. NW, Ste. 102, Washington, DC 20016
Mongrel Empire, 2302 Forest Road Cir., Norman, OK 73026-0961
Monkeybicycle, 206 Bellevue Ave., Floor 2, Montclair, NJ 07043
Moonrise Press, 8644 LeBerthon St., Sunland, CA 91040-2321
Mosaic, 5202 Old Orchard Rd., Ste 300, Skokie, IL 60077-4409
MotesBooks, 89 W. Chestnut St., Williamsburg, KY 40769
Mount Parnassus Press, 650 Delancey St., #414, San Francisco, CA 94107
Mountain Girl Press, Little Creek Books, 2195 Euclid Ave., #7, Bristol, VA 24201
Mr. Beller's Neighborhood, 270 Lafayette St., Ste 1412, New York, NY 10012
Mud Luscious Press, 2115 Sandstone Dr., Fort Collins, CO 80524
MungBeing Magazine, 1319 Maywood Ave., Upland, CA 91786
Muse-Pie Press, 73 Pennington Ave., Passaic, NJ 07055
Muzzle Magazine, 4619 N. Broadway St., Chicago, IL 60640
Mythium, 1428 N. Forbes Rd., Lexington, KY 40511
Mythopoetry Scholar, 16211 East Keymar Dr., Fountain Hills, AZ 85268
MWE, 207 W. Green Forest Dr., Cary, NC 27518

N

N + 1 Magazine, 68 Jay St., #405, Brooklyn, NY 11201
NaDa Publishing, 2515 Consuelo Lane NW, Albuquerque, NM 8710D
Narrative Magazine, 2130 Fillmore St., #233, San Francisco, CA 94115
Natural Bridge, English Department, One University Blvd., St. Louis, MO 63121
Naugatuck River Review, PO Box 368, Westfield, MA 01085
Needle, P.O. Box 1585, Louisa, VA 23093
NeoPoiesis Press, 2765 Lansdowne Rd., Victoria, BC V8R 3P6, Canada
New American Press, 2606 E. Locust St., Milwaukee, WI 53211
New American Writing, Oink! Press, 369 Molino Ave., Mill Valley, CA 94941
The New Criterion, 900 Broadway, Ste. 602, New York, NY 10003
New England Review, Middlebury College, Middlebury, VT 05753
The New Guard, P.O. Box 10612, Portland, ME 04104
New Haven Review, 352 West Rock Ave., New Haven, CT 06515
New Issues, 1903 W. Michigan Ave., Kalamazoo, MI 49008-5463
New Letters, 5101 Rockhill Rd., Kansas City, MO 64110
New Madrid, Murray State University, 7C Faculty Hall, Murray, KY 42071
New Michigan Press, 8058 E. 7th St., Tucson, AZ 85710
New Ohio Review, Ohio University, 360 Ellis Hall, Athens, OH 45701
New Orleans Review, Box 50, Loyola University, New Orleans, CA 70118
The New Orphic Review, 706 Mill St., Nelson, B.C. V1L 4S5 Canada
New Rivers Press, 1104 Seventh Avenue S., Moorhead, MN 56563
New Southerner Magazine, 375 Wood Valley Lane, Louisville, KY 40299
New Verse News, Les Belles Maisons H-11, Jl. Serpong Raya, Serpong Utara, Tangerang-Baten 15310,
    Indonesia
New York Tyrant, 676 A Ninth Ave., #153, New York, NY 10036
NewSouth Books, P.O. Box 1588, Montgomery, AL 36102
Nimrod, 800 South Tucker Dr., Tulsa, OK 74104
Ninth Letter, 608 S. Wright St., Urbana, IL 61801

Niteblade Fantasy and Horror, 11323 126th St., Edmonton, AB T5M 0R5, Canada
Noon, 1324 Lexington Ave., PMB 298, New York, NY 10128
The Normal School, 5245 N. Backer Ave., M/S PB 98, Fresno, CA 93740-8001
North American Review, Univ. of No. Iowa, 1222 West 27th St., Cedar Falls, IA 50614-0516
The North Carolina Literary Review, ECU Mailstop 555, Greenville, NC 27858-4353
North Carolina Writers' Network, P.O. Box 21591, Winston-Salem, NC 27120
North Dakota Quarterly, 276 Centennial Drive, Grand Forks, ND 58202-7209
Northwest Review, 5243 University of Oregon, Eugene, OR 97403-5243
Not One of Us, 12 Curtis Rd., Natick, MA 01760
Notre Dame Review, 840 Flanner Hall, Notre Dame, IN 46556-5639

O

OCHO, 604 Vale St., Bloomington, IL 61701
Off the Coast, PO Box 14, Robbinston, ME 04671
The Offending Adam, 1350 Kelso Dunes Ave., #426, Henderson, NV 89014-7838
Ohio University Press, 19 Circle Dr., The Ridges, Athens, OH 45701
Old Mountain Press, 2542 S. Edgewater Dr., Fayetteville, NC 28303
One for the Road, 14 Salisbury St., Little Falls, NY 13365
Old Red Kimono, 3175 Cedartown Hwy. SE, Rome, GA 30161
One Earth, 40 West 20 St., New York, NY 10011
One Small Bird Press, 3418 Harcourt Dr., Ames, IA 50010
One Story, Old American Can Factory, 232 3rd St., #A111, Brooklyn, NY 11215
Open City, 270 Lafayette St., Ste. 1412, New York, NY 10012
Open Thread, 2211 Shady Ave., Pittsburgh, PA 15201
Orchises Press, c/o Lathbury, George Mason Univ., 4400 University Dr., Fairfax, VA 22030
Original Plus, 17 High St., Maryport, Cumbria CA15 6BQ, UK
Orion Headless, 1645 Winkler Ave., Fort Myers, FL 33901
Orion Magazine, 187 Main St., Great Barrington, MA 01230
Osiris, PO Box 297, Deerfield, MA 01342
The Other Journal, 3333 East Beltline NE, Grand Rapids, MI 49525
Our Stories, 1447 Collins Ave., St. Louis, MO 63117
Out of Our, 1288 Columbus Ave., #216, San Francisco, CA 94133-1302
Overtime, PO Box 250382, Plano, TX 75025-0382
OVS Magazine, 32 Linsey Lane, Warren, NH 03279
Oxford American, 201 Donaghey Ave., Main 107, Conway, AR 72035-5001
Ozarks' Senior Living, 11 East Orange Grove, #213, Tucson, AZ 85704-5555

P

P.R.A. Publishing, PO Box 211701, Martinez, GA 30917
Painted Bride Quarterly, English Dept., 3141 Chestnut St., Philadelphia, PA 19104
Palo Alto Review, 1400 W. Villaret Blvd., San Antonio, TX 78224
Palooka, 5620 Fossil Creek Parkway, #4105, Fort Collins, CO 80525
PANK Magazine, Dept. of Humanities, 1400 Townsend Dr., Hancock, MI 49931
The Paris Review, 62 White St., New York, NY 10013
Passages North, English Dept, 1401 Presque Isle Ave., Marquette, MI 49855-5363
Paterson Literary Review, 1 College Blvd., Paterson, NJ 07505-1179
Pearl, 3030 E. Second St., Long Beach, CA 90803
PEN America, PEN American Center, 588 Broadway, Ste. 303, New York, NY 10012
Penmanship Books Poetry, 593 Yanderbilt Ave., #265, Brooklyn, NY 11238
Perugia Press, PO Box 60364, Florence, MA 01062
Petigru Review, SCWW, PO Box 7104, Columbia, SC 29202
Phrygian Press, 58-09 205th St., Bayside, NY 11364
Pieces of Someday, 1928 NE 62nd St., Seattle, WA 98115
Pill Hill Press, 343 W. 4th St., Chadron, NE 69337-2321
The Pinch, English Dept., 467 Patterson Hall, Memphis, TN 38152-3510
Ping-Pong, Henry Miller Library, Highway One, Big Sur, CA 93920

Pirene's Fountain, 3616 Glenlake Dr., Glenview, IL 60026
Pleasure Boat Studio, 201 West 89th St., New York, NY 10024
Pleiades Press, English and Philosophy, Martin 336, Warrensburg, MO 64093-5046
Ploughshares, Emerson College, 120 Boylston St., Boston, MA 02116-4624
PMS, University of Alabama, HB 213, 900 South 13th St., Birmingham, AL 35294-1260
Poems and Plays, MTSU, P. O. Box 70, Murfreesboro, TN 37132
Poet Lore, 4508 Walsh St., Bethesda, MD 20815
Poetry, 444 N. Michigan Ave., Ste. 1850, Chicago, IL 60611-4034
Poetry Center, Cleveland State Univ., 2121 Euclid Ave., Cleveland, OH 44115-2214
Poetry for the Masses, 1654 S. Volustia, Wichita, KS 67214
Poetry In the Arts Press, 5110 Avenue H, Austin, TX 78751
Poetry Kanto, 3-22-1 Kamariya-Minami, Kanazawa-Ku, Yokohama, 236-8502, Japan
Poetry Northwest, Everett Community College, 2000 Tower St., Everett, WA 98201
Poetry Review, 22 Betterton St., London WC2H 9BX, United Kingdom
Poetry South, 14000 Hwy 82 West, #5032, Itta Bena, MS 38941-1400
Poets and Artists, 604 Vale St., Bloomington, IL 61701
Poets Wear Prada, 533 Bloomfield St, 2nd Floor, Hoboken, NJ 07030
The Point, 732 S. Financial Pl., Apt 704, Chicago, IL 60605
Post Road, Boston College, 140 Commonwealth Ave., Chestnut Hill, MA 02467
POW Fast Flash Fiction, P.O. Box 395, Willoughby, OH 44096
Prairie Schooner, UNL, 201 Andrews Hall, PO Box 880334, Lincoln, NE 68588-0334
Presa Press, PO Box 792, Rockford, MI 49341
Press 53, PO Box 30314, Winston-Salem, NC 27130
Prime Number Magazine, 1853 Old Greenville Rd., Staunton, VA 24401
Prism Review, 1950 Third St., La Verne, CA 91750
Propaganda Press, P.O. Box 183, Palo Alto, CA 94302
Provincetown Arts, 650 Commercial St., Provincetown, MA 02657
A Public Space, 323 Dean St., Brooklyn, NY 11217
Puffin Circus, 442 S. Columbia Ave., Somerset, PA 15501

Q

Qarrtsiluni, P.O. Box 68, Tyrone, PA 16686
Quiddity, Benedictine University, 1500 N. Fifth St., Springfield, IL 62702
Quill and Parchment Press, 2357 Merrywood Dr., Los Angeles, CA 90046
Quote Editions, P.O. Box 1672, New York, NY 10025

R

R. L. Crow Publications, PO Box 262, Penn Valley, CA 95946
Ragazine.cc, Box 8586, Endwell, WY 13762
Raleigh Review, 1323 Duplin Rd., Raleigh, NC 27607
Ramshackle, 535 East Lawrence Rd., Lawrenceville, PA 16929
Raritan: A Quarterly Review, Rutgers, 31 Mine St., New Brunswick, NJ 08901
Rattle, 12411 Ventura Blvd., Studio City, CA 91604
The Raven Chronicles, 12346 Sand Point Way N.E., Seattle, WA 98125
Raw Art Press, 4110 Crestview Dr., Pittsburg, CA 94565
Red Fez, 5 Morningside Dr., Jacksonville, IL 62650
Red Hen Press, PO Box 40820, Pasadena, CA 91114
Red Rock Review, 3090 El Camino Rd., Las Vegas, NV 89146
Redactions, 58 South Main St., Brockport, NY 14420
Redheaded Stepchild, 62 Kilbride Dr., Pinehurst, NC 28374-8832
Redivider, Emerson College, 120 Boylston St., Boston, MA 02116
Reed Magazine, SJSU, English Dept., 1 Washington Sq., San Jose, CA 95192-0090
Referential Magazine, 8324 Highlander Court, Charlotte, NC 28269
Relief Journal, 60 W. Terra Cotta, Crystal Lake, IL 60014
The Republic of Letters, Apartado 29, Cahuita, 7032, Costa Rica
Rescue Press, 1220 E. Locust, #209, Milwaukee, WI 53212

Rhubarb Magazine, 606 - 100 Arthur St., Winnipeg, MB R3B 1H3, Canada
River Styx, 3547 Olive St., Ste. 107, St. Louis, MO 63103-1024
River Teeth, Ashland University, 401 College Ave., Ashland, OH 44805
Rougarou, PO Box 44691, Lafayette, LA 70504-4691
Ruminate, 140 N. Roosevelt Ave., Ft. Collins, CO 80521

S

The 2ndhand, 1430 Roberts Ave., Nashville, TN 37206
Saint Anne's Review, 129 Pierrepont St., Brooklyn Heights, NY 11201-2705
Salamander, 41 Temple St., Boston, MA 02114-4280
Salmagundi, Skidmore College, Saratoga Springs, NY 12866-1632
Salt Hill, English Dept., Syracuse University, Syracuse, NY 13244
The Sand Hill Review, 2284 Carmelita Drive, San Carlos, CA 94070
Santa Monica Review, 1900 Pico Blvd., Santa Monica, CA 90405-1628
The Saranac Review, 101 Broad St., Pittsburgh, NY 12901-2681
Saw Palm, 4202 E. Fowler Ave., CPR 107, Tampa, FL 33620-5550
Scapegoat Press, P.O. Box 410962, Kansas City, MO 64141
Scarletta Press, 10 South 5th Street, #1105, Minneapolis, MN 55402-1012
Schuylkill Valley Journal, 240 Golf Hills Rd., Havertown, PA 19083
Seal Press, 1700 Fourth St., Berkeley, CA 94710
The Seattle Review, University of Washington, Box 354330, Seattle, WA 98195-4330
Seems, Lakeland College, PO Box 359, Sheboygan, WI 53082-0359
The Segue Foundation, 300 Bowery, New York, NY 10012
Senses Five Press, 76 India St., #A-8, Brooklyn, NY 11222-1657
Seven Circle Press, 107 NE 43rd St., Unit B., Seattle, WA 98105
Seven Corners, 206 W. Shelbourne Dr., Apt. B, Normal, IL 61761
Seven Hills, 6508 Saylers Creek Rd., Tallahassee, FL 32309
Seven Stories Press, 140 Watts St., New York, NY 10013
Seventh Quarry, Dan-y-bryn, 74 Cwm Level Rd., Brynhyfrd, Swansea SA5 9DY, Wales, UK
Sewanee Review, University of the South, 735 University Ave., Sewanee, TN 37383
Shenandoah, Mattingly House, 2 Lee Avenue, Lexington, VA 24450-2116
The Shit Creek Review, 8241 Mountain Laurel Lane, Gaithersburg, MD 20879
Shock Totem, 107 Hovendon Ave., Brockton, MA 02302
Short Fiction Collective, 11 Woodland Ave., Tarrytown, NY 10591
Short Story, 322 Netzer Bldg., SUNY, Oneonta, NY 13820-4015
Short Story America, 66 Thomas Sumter St., Beaufort, SC 29907
Sibling Rivalry Press, 13913 Magnolia Glen, Alexander, AR 72002
Silk Road Review, 2043 College Way, Forest Grove, OR 97116-1797
Silver Boomer Books, 3301 South 14th St., Ste. 16 — PMB 134, Abilene, TX 79605
Silverfish Review Press, PO Box 3541, Eugene, OR 97403
Sixth Finch, 95 Carolina Ave., #2, Jamaica Plain, MA 02130
Sketchbook, 2115 Granberry Rd., De Ridder, LA 7063
Skyline Publications, PO Box 295, Stormville, NY 12582
Slapering Hol Press, 300 Riverside Dr., Sleepy Hollow, NY 10591
Slate: Los Angeles, 2148 1/2 Sunset Blvd., #203, Los Angeles, CA 90026
Sleet Magazine, 1846 Bohland Ave., St. Paul, MN 55116
Slice, PO Box 150029, Brooklyn, NY 11215
Slipstream, Box 2071, Niagara Falls, NY 14301
Smartish Pace, PO Box 22161, Baltimore, MD 21203
Soft Skull Press, 2117 Fourth St., Ste. D, Berkeley, CA 94710
Solstice, 38 Oakland Ave., Needham, MA 02492
Song of the San Joaquin, PO Box 1161, Modesto, CA 95353-1161
Sonora Review, English Dept., University of Arizona, Tucson AZ 85721
South Jersey Underground, 92 Dolphin Rd., Tuckerton, NJ 08087
The Southampton Review, 239 Montauk Highway, Southampton, NY 11968
The Southeast Review, English Dept, Florida State Univ., Tallahassee, FL 32306
Southern Humanities Review, 9088 Haley Center, Auburn, AL 36849-5202
Southern Poetry Review, 11935 Abercorn St., Savannah, GA 31419-1997
The Southern Review, Louisiana State University, Baton Rouge, LA 70803

Southern Women's Review, 1125 22nd St. So., Ste. 5, Birmingham, AL 35205
Southwest Review, PO Box 750374, Dallas, TX 75275-0374
specs, 1000 Holt Ave. - #2666, Winter Park, FL 32789-4499
Spillway, 11 Jordan Ave., San Francisco, CA 94118
Spire Press, 217 Thompson St., #298, New York, NY 10012
Splash of Red, 84 Asbury Ave., #1, Ocean Grove, NJ 07756
Spot Write Literary Corporation, 4729 E. Sunrise Dr., PO Box 254, Tucson, AZ 85718-4535
Star Cloud Press, 6137 East Mescal St., Scottsdale, AZ 85254-5418
Static Movement, 4 Dorsey Lane, Jaspar, GA 30143
Sterling Bridge, P.O. Box 221, Green port, NY 11944
Still, P.O. Box 1121, Berea, KY 40403
Stirring, 323 Oglewood Ave., Knoxville, TN 37917
Stone Canoe Journal, 700 University Ave., Ste. 326, Syracuse, NY 13244-2530
Stonecoast Lines, 47 Holworthy St., #2, Boston, MA 02121
Storyglossia, 1004 Commercial Ave., #1110, Anacortes, WA 98221
storySouth, UNC Greensboro, Greensboro, NC 27402-6170
The Storyteller, 2441 Washington Rd., Maynard, AR 72444
Strange Land, 26 Parnassus, San Francisco, CA 94117-4343
Straylight, 900 Wood Rd., P.O. Box 2000, Kenosha, WI 53141-2000
Stymie, 1965 Briarfield Dr. Ste. 303, Lake St. Louis, MO 63367
Sugar House Review, PO Box 17091, Salt Lake City, UT 84117
The Summerset Review, 25 Summerset Dr., Smithtown, NY 11787
The Sun, 107 North Roberson St., Chapel Hill, NC 27516
sunnyoutside, PO Box 911, Buffalo, NY 14207
Swamp Press, 15 Warwick Ave., Northfield, MA 01360
Sweet, 110 Holly Tree Lane, Brandon, FL 33511
Sycamore Review, Purdue University, 500 Oval Dr., West Lafayette, IN 47907
Synergy Press, P.O. Box 8, Flemington, NJ 08822

T

T. S. Poetry Press, 21 Belleview Ave., Ossining, NY 10562
Tampa Review, 401 W. Kennedy Blvd., Tampa, FL 33606
10 X 3 Plus, 1077 Windsor Ave., Morgantown, WV 26505
Tepppichfresser Press, 2979 N. Bremen, Apt. B, Milwaukee, WI 53212
Terrain.org, 10367 East Sixto Molina Lane, Tucson, AZ 85747
Tertulia Magazine, 623 W. Broad St., Nevada City, CA 95959
Thieves Jargon, 23-11 41st St., #2R, Astoria, NY 11105
Think Journal, PO Box 454, Downingtown, PA 19335
Third Coast, Western Michigan University, Kalamazoo, MI 49008-5331
Third Wednesday, 174 Greenside Up, Ypsilanti, MI 48197
Threepenny Review, PO Box 9131, Berkeley, CA 94709
Thumbnail Magazine, 1401 St. Edwards Dr., #174, Austin, TX 78704
Thunder House Books, P. O. Box 5183, Lutherville, MD 21094
Tidal Basin Review, 200 N Street N.W., Washington, DC 20001
Tikkun Magazine, 2342 Shattuck Ave., Ste. 1200, Berkeley, CA 94704
Tin House, PMB 280,320 7th Ave., Brooklyn, NY 11215
Tipton Poetry Journal, PO Box 804, Zionsville, IN 46077
Toasted Cheese, 44 East 13th Ave., #402, Vancouver BC V5T 4K7, Canada
Toadlily Press, PO Box 2, Chappaqua, NY 10514
Top Publications, Ltd., 12221 Merit Dr., Ste. 750, Dallas, TX 75251
The Toucan Literary Magazine, 16519 Paw Paw Ave., Orland Park, IL 60467
Trachodon, P.O. Box 1468, St. Helens, OR 97051
Traprock Books, 1330 E. 25th Ave., Eugene, OR 97403
TriQuarterly, Northwestern Univ., 339 East Chicago Ave., Evanston, IL 60611
Tryst Poetry Journal, 335 W. 49th St., Minneapolis, MN 55419
Tuesday, PO Box 1074, East Arlington, MA 02474
Tupelo Press, PO 1767, North Adams, MA 01247
Turtle Quarterly, 5431 Pleasant, Minneapolis, MN 55419

The Tusculum Review, PO Box 5113,60 Shiloh Rd., Greenville, TN 37743
A Twist of Noir, 2309 West Seventh St., Duluth, MN 55806-1536

U

U.S. 1 Poets' Cooperative, PO Box 127, Kingston, NJ 08528-0127
Umbrella, 102 West 75th St., Ste. 54, New York, NY 10023-1907
unboundCONTENT, 160 Summit St., Englewood, NJ 07631
Underground Voices, PO Box 931671, Los Angeles, CA 90093
Union Station Magazine, P.O. Box 380355, Brooklyn, NY 11238
United Shoelaces of the Mind, 463 Pandora Drive, Dayton, OH 45431
University of Arizona Press, 355 S. Euclid, Ste. 103, Tucson, AZ 85719
University of Chicago Press, 11030 South Langley Ave., Chicago, IL 60628
The University of Georgia Press, 330 Research Dr., Athens, GA 30602-4901
University of Nebraska Press, 1111 Lincoln Mall, P.O. Box 880630, Lincoln, NE 68588
University of Nevada Press, MS 0166, Reno, NV 89557-0166
University of North Texas Press, 1155 Union Circle #311336, Denton, TX 76203-5017
UNO Press, University of New Orleans Publishing, Educ. Bldg. #210, New Orleans, LA 70148
Unsaid, 3521 Pheasant Run Circle, #5, Ann Arbor, MI 48108
upstreet, PO Box 105, Richmond, MA 01254-0105

V

Vagabondage Press, P.O. Box 3563, Apollo Beach, FL 33572
Valparaiso Poetry Review, English Dept, Valparaiso Univ., Valparaiso, IN 46383
Vandalia Press, P.O. Box 6295, Morgantown, WV 26506-6295
Versal, Postbus 3865,1001 AR Amsterdam, The Netherlands
Veriditas Books, P.O. Box 968, California, MD 20619
Verse Wisconsin, P.O. Box 620216, Middleton, WI, 53562-0216
Vestal Review, 2609 Dartmouth Dr., Vestal, NY 13850
Vinyl Poetry, 814 Hutcheson Dr., Blacksburg, VA 24060
Virgogray Press, 2103 Nogales Trail, Austin, TX 78744
The Virginia Quarterly Review, 1 West Range, PO Box 400223, Charlottesville, VA 22904
Virtual Artists Collective, 540 N. Lake Shore Dr. #618, Chicago, IL 60611
VoiceCatcher, 2138 NE Hancock, Portland, OR 97212
Voices, PO Box 9076, Fayetteville, AR 72703-0018

W

Waccamaw, PO Box 261954, Conway, SC 29528-6054
Warwick Review, University of Warwick, Coventry CV4 7AL, United Kingdom
Washington Writers' Publishing House, 201 Hume Ave., Alexandria, VA 22301
Water~Stone Review, MS A1730,1536 Hewitt Ave., St. Paul, MN 55104-1284
Wayne State University Press, 4809 Woodward Ave., Detroit, MI 48201-1309
West Branch, Stadler Center for Poetry, Bucknell University, Lewisburg, PA 17837
West End Press, PO Box 27334, Albuquerque, NM 87125
The Westchester Review, Box 246H, Scarsdale, NY 10583
Western Humanities Review, Univ. of Utah - English, Salt Lake City, UT 84112
Whiskey Island Magazine, 2121 Euclid Ave., Cleveland, OH 44115
White River Press, P.O. Box 3561, Amherst, MA 01004
White Whale Review, 4219 Botanical Ave., #1-E, St. Louis, MO 631119
Wild Apples, PO Box 171, Harvard, MA 01451
Wild Goose Poetry Review, 838 4th Ave. Dr., NW, Hickory, NC 28601
Wild Ocean Press, 38 Bob Kaufman Alley, San Francisco, CA 94133
Wilderness House Literary Review, 145 Foster St., Littleton, MA 01460

Willow Springs, 501 N. Riverpoint Blvd., Ste 425, Spokane, WA 99202
Willows Wept Review, 472 Southridge Rd., Clermont, FL 34711
Wilson Quarterly, 1300 Pennsylvania Ave., NW, Washington, DC, 20004-3002
Wings Press, 627 E. Guenther, San Antonio, TX 78210
Witness, Black Mountain Institute, Box 455085, Las Vegas, NV 89154-5085
Wolfsword Press, 7144 Harlem Ave., #325, Chicago, IL 60631
The Worcester Review, 1 Ekman St., Worcester, MA 01607
Wordcraft of Oregon, P.O. Box 3235, La Grande, OR 97850
Workers Write!, PO Box 250382, Piano, TX 75025-0382
World Literature Today, 630 Parrington Oval, Ste. 110, Norman, OK 73019-4033
Write Bloody Publishing, #609, 235 East Broadway, Long Beach, CA 90802
Writecorner Press, PO Box 140310, Gainesville, FL 32614-0310
Wynterblue Publishing, P.O. Box 868, North Bay ON, P1B 8K1, Canada

X

Xenith, 2700 Pillsbury Avenue South, Apt. 1, Minneapolis, MN 55408

Y

The Yale Review, Yale University, PO Box 208243, New Haven, CT 06520
YB, P.O. Box 109, Mango Hill Post Shop, North Lakes 4509, Qld, Australia
Yellow Medicine Review, Southwest Minnesota State Univ., English Dept., 1501 State St., Marshall, MN
    56258

Z

Zahir Publishing, 315 S. Coast Highway 101, Ste. U-8, Encinitas, CA 92024
Zoetrope: All Story, 916 Kearny St., San Francisco, CA 94133
Zone 3, P.O. Box 4565, Clarksville, TN 37044
ZYZZYVA, PO Box 590069, San Francisco, CA 94159-0069

THE PUSHCART PRIZE
FELLOWSHIPS

The Pushcart Prize Fellowships Inc., a 501 (c) (3) nonprofit corporation, is the endowment for The Pushcart Prize. "Members" donated up to $249 each. "Sponsors" gave between $250 and $999. "Benefactors" donated from $1000 to $4,999. "Patrons" donated $5,000 and more. We are very grateful for these donations. Gifts of any amount are welcome. For information write to the Fellowships at PO Box 380, Wainscott, NY 11975.

FOUNDING PATRONS

The Katherine Anne Porter Literary Trust
Michael and Elizabeth R. Rea

PATRONS

Anonymous
Margaret Ajemian Ahnert
Daniel L. Dolgin & Loraine F. Gardner
James Patterson Foundation
Ellen M. Violett

BENEFACTORS

Anonymous
Ted Conklin
Bernard F. Conners
Dallas Ernst
Cedering Fox

H. E. Francis
Bill & Genie Henderson
Marina & Stephen E. Kaufman
Wally & Christine Lamb
Stacey Richter

SPONSORS

Jacob Appel
Jean M. Auel
Jim Barnes
Charles Baxter
Joe David Bellamy
Laura & Pinckney Benedict

Laure-Anne Bosselaar
Kate Braverman
Barbara Bristol
Kurt Brown
Richard Burgin
David S. Caldwell

Siv Cedering
Dan Chaon & Sheila Schwartz
James Charlton
Andrei Codrescu
Tracy Crow
Dana Literary Society
Carol de Gramont
Karl Elder
Donald Finkel
Ben and Sharon Fountain
Alan and Karen Furst
John Gill
Robert Giron
Doris Grumbach & Sybil Pike
Gwen Head
The Healing Muse
Robin Hemley
Jane Hirshfield
Helen & Frank Houghton
Joseph Hurka

Diane Johnsons
Janklow & Nesbit Asso.
Edmund Keeley
Thomas E. Kennedy
Wally & Christine Lamb
Sydney Lea
Gerald Locklin
Thomas Lux
Markowitz, Fenelon and Bank
Elizabeth McKenzie
McSweeney's
Joan Murray
Barbara and Warren Phillips
Hilda Raz
Mary Carlton Swope
Julia Wendell
Philip White
Eleanor Wilner
David Wittman
Richard Wyatt & Irene Eilers

MEMBERS

Anonymous (3)
Betty Adcock
Agni
Carolyn Alessio
Dick Allen
Russell Allen
Henry H. Allen
Lisa Alvarez
Jan Lee Ande
Ralph Angel
Antietam Review
Ruth Appelhof
Philip and Marjorie Appleman
Linda Aschbrenner
Renee Ashley
Ausable Press
David Baker
Catherine Barnett
Dorothy Barresi
Barrow Street Press
Jill Bart
Ellen Bass
Judith Baumel
Ann Beattie
Madison Smartt Bell
Beloit Poetry Journal
Pinckney Benedict
Karen Bender
Andre Bernard
Christopher Bernard
Wendell Berry
Linda Bierds
Stacy Bierlein

Bitter Oleander Press
Mark Blaeuer
Blue Lights Press
Carol Bly
BOA Editions
Deborah Bogen
Susan Bono
Anthony Brandt
James Breeden
Rosellen Brown
Jane Brox
Andrea Hollander Budy
E. S. Bumas
Richard Burgin
Skylar H. Burris
David Caliguiuri
Kathy Callaway
Janine Canan
Henry Carlile
Fran Castan
Chelsea Associates
Marianne Cherry
Phillis M. Choyke
Suzanne Cleary
Martha Collins
Ted Conklin
Joan Connor
John Copenhaven
Dan Corrie
Tricia Currans-Sheehan
Jim Daniels
Thadious Davis
Maija Devine

Sharon Dilworth
Edward J. DiMaio
Kent Dixon
John Duncklee
Elaine Edelman
Renee Edison & Don Kaplan
Nancy Edwards
M.D. Elevitch
Failbetter.com
Irvin Faust
Tom Filer
Susan Firer
Nick Flynn
Stakey Flythe Jr.
Peter Fogo
Linda N. Foster
Fugue
Alice Fulton
Eugene K. Garber
Frank X. Gaspar
A Gathering of the Tribes
Reginald Gibbons
Emily Fox Gordon
Philip Graham
Eamon Grennan
Lee Meitzen Grue
Habit of Rainy Nights
Rachel Hadas
Susan Hahn
Meredith Hall
Harp Strings
Jeffrey Harrison
Lois Marie Harrod
Healing Muse
Alex Henderson
Lily Henderson
Daniel Henry
Neva Herington
Lou Hertz
William Heyen
Bob Hicok
R. C. Hildebrandt
Kathleen Hill
Jane Hirshfield
Edward Hoagland
Daniel Hoffman
Doug Holder
Richard Holinger
Rochelle L. Holt
Richard M. Huber
Brigid Hughes
Lynne Hugo
Illya's Honey
Susan Indigo
Mark Irwin
Beverly A. Jackson

Richard Jackson
Christian Jara
David Jauss
Marilyn Johnston
Alice Jones
Journal of New Jersey Poets
Robert Kalich
Julia Kasdorf
Miriam Poli Katsikis
Meg Kearney
Celine Keating
Brigit Kelly
John Kistner
Judith Kitchen
Stephen Kopel
Peter Krass
David Kresh
Maxine Kumin
Valerie Laken
Babs Lakey
Maxine Landis
Lane Larson
Dorianne Laux & Joseph Millar
Sydney Lea
Donald Lev
Dana Levin
Gerald Locklin
Linda Lacione
Rachel Loden
Radomir Luza, Jr.
William Lychack
Annette Lynch
Elzabeth MacKierman
Elizabeth Macklin
Leah Maines
Mark Manalang
Norma Marder
Jack Marshall
Michael Martone
Tara L. Masih
Dan Masterson
Peter Matthiessen
Alice Mattison
Tracy Mayor
Robert McBrearty
Jane McCafferty
Rebecca McClanahan
Bob McCrane
Jo McDougall
Sandy McIntosh
James McKean
Roberta Mendel
Didi Menendez
Barbara Milton
Alexander Mindt
Mississippi Review

Martin Mitchell
Roger Mitchell
Jewell Mogan
Patricia Monaghan
Rick Moody
Jim Moore
James Morse
William Mulvihill
Nami Mun
Carol Muske-Dukes
Edward Mycue
Deirdre Neilen
W. Dale Nelson
Jean Nordhaus
Ontario Review Foundation
Daniel Orozco
Other Voices
Pamela Painter
Paris Review
Alan Michael Parker
Ellen Parker
Veronica Patterson
David Pearce, M.D.
Robert Phillips
Donald Platt
Valerie Polichar
Pool
Jeffrey & Priscilla Potter
Marcia Preston
Eric Puchner
Tony Quagliano
Barbara Quinn
Belle Randall
Martha Rhodes
Nancy Richard
Stacey Richter
James Reiss
Katrina Roberts
Judith R. Robinson
Jessica Roeder
Martin Rosner
Kay Ryan
Sy Safransky
Brian Salchert
James Salter
Sherod Santos
R.A. Sasaki
Valerie Sayers
Maxine Scates
Alice Schell
Dennis & Loretta Schmitz
Helen Schulman
Philip Schultz
Shenandoah
Peggy Shinner
Vivian Shipley

Joan Silver
Skyline
John E. Smelcer
Raymond J. Smith
Philip St. Clair
Lorraine Standish
Maureen Stanton
Michael Steinberg
Sybil Steinberg
Jody Stewart
Barbara Stone
Storyteller Magazine
Bill & Pat Strachan
Julie Suk
Sun Publishing
Sweet Annie Press
Katherine Taylor
Pamela Taylor
Susan Terris
Marcelle Thiébaux
Robert Thomas
Andrew Tonkovich
Pauls Toutonghi
Juanita Torrence-Thompson
William Trowbridge
Martin Tucker
Jeannette Valentine
Victoria Valentine
Hans Vandebouen Kamp
Tino Villanueva
William & Jeanne Wagner
BJ Ward
Susan Oard Warner
Rosanna Warren
Margareta Waterman
Michael Waters
Sandi Weinberg
Andrew Weinstein
Jason Wesco
West Meadow Press
Susan Wheeler
Dara Wier
Ellen Wilbur
Galen Williams
Marie Sheppard Williams
Eleanor Wilner
Irene K. Wilson
Steven Wingate
Sandra Wisenberg
Wings Press
Robert W. Witt
Margo Wizansky
Matt Yurdana
Christina Zawadiwsky
Sander Zulauf
ZYZZYVA

529

John Irving
Ha Jin
Mary Karr
Maxine Kumin
Wally Lamb
Philip Levine
Rick Moody

Joyce Carol Oates
Sherod Santos
Grace Schulman
Charles Simic
Gerald Stern
Charles Wright

CONTRIBUTORS' NOTES

RAYMOND ANDREWS (1934-1991) won the James Baldwin Prize for his first novel, *Appalachee Red*, and went on to publish five other books. His life and work were celebrated in the Fall, 2010 *Georgia Review*.

SUSAN ANTONETTA is the author of *Body Toxic* (Counterpoint), a *New York Times* Notable Book. She lives in Bellingham, Washington.

CLAIRE BATEMAN's sixth book of poems was just published by Etruscan Press. She lives in Greenville, South Carolina.

EVE BECKER teaches eighth grade English. She lives in New York.

L. ANNETTE BINDER'S work was a finalist for the 2010 Flannery O'Connor Award for Short Fiction. She is a student at the University of California, Irvine.

STEPHEN BURT's new collection of poems, *Belmont*, is forthcoming from Graywolf. He teaches at Harvard.

SARAH BUSSE co-edits *Verse Wisconsin* and has authored two chapbooks. She lives in Madison, Wisconsin.

RICHARD CECIL's *Twenty-First Century Blues* was just published. He lives in Bloomington, Indiana.

LYDIA CONKLIN is an MFA candidate at The University of Wisconsin. She has received fellowships from the McDowell Colony and Harvard.

LISA COUTURIER lives on an Agricultural Reserve in Maryland. Her first essay collection is available from Beacon Press.

LYDIA DAVIS is the author of *Collected Stories* (FSG, 2009). She has appeared in five Pushcarts since 1978.

STEPHEN DOBYNS is a poet, fiction writer, and essayist. He lives in Westerly, Rhode Island and teaches at Warren Wilson College.

JACK DRISCOLL'S second story collection, *The World of A Few Minutes Ago*, is due soon from Wayne State University Press. He teaches at Pacific University.

B.H. FAIRCHILD received fellowships from The Guggenheim Foundation, Rockefeller Foundation, and the National Endowment for the Arts. His poetry collection came out in 2009 from W.W. Norton.

KATHLEEN FLENNIKEN's *Plume* will be published by the University of Washington Press in 2012. She is editor of Floating Bridge Press.

ALICE FRIMAN latest poetry collection, *Vinculum*, is available from Louisiana State University Press. She is poet-in-residence at Georgia College and State University.

DOUGLAS GOETSCH is the editor of Jane Street Press and teaches at Oklahoma City University. He is the author of several poetry collections.

ALBERT GOLDBARTH is the author of *Budget Travel Through Time and Space*. He has been featured in nine Pushcart Prizes.

JULIAN GOUGH lives in Berlin, Germany. He is the author of the novels *Juno & Juliet* and *Jube: Level 1*.

KATHLEEN GRABER's second collection, *The Eternal City*, (Princeton University Press, 2010) was a finalist for the National Book Award and The National Book Critics Circle Award.

MARK HALLIDAY teaches at Ohio University. His fifth book of poems, *Keep This Forever*, was published by Tupelo Press.

JANICE HARRINGTON'S *Even The Hollow My Body Made Is Gone* won the A. Poulin Jr. Poetry Prize. She lives in Champaign, Illinois.

TARA HART teaches at Howard Community College in Columbia, Maryland. Her poems appeared in *The Muse, Welter* and elsewhere.

SMITH HENDERSON has been a prison guard, writer, and fellow at the Michener Center for Writers. He lives in Austin with his wife and children and is at work on a novel, stories and a screenplay.

GERALD HOWARD is an executive editor at Doubleday. He lives in Tuxedo Park, New York.

MARIA HUMMEL teaches at Stanford. Her books are the novel *Wilderness Run* and the chapbook *City of the Moon*.

KARLA HUSTON is the author of six chapbooks of poetry, most recently *An Inventory of Lost Things* (Centennial Press).

BRET ANTHONY JOHNSTON is the Director of Creative Writing at Harvard and the author of *Corpus Christi: Stories* (Random House).

ILYA KAMINSKY co-edited the *Ecco Anthology of International Poetry*. He is the author of *Dancing In Odessa* (Tupelo Press).

JOY KATZ holds a B.S. in industrial design from Ohio State University. She teaches at the University of Pittsburgh.

JUDITH KITCHEN's next book will be published by Coffee House Press in 2012. She reviews poetry for *The Georgia Review*.

SANDRA LEONG is a psychoanalyst who lives in New York. Her short fiction has appeared to *New England Review, Antioch Review, Southwest Review* and elsewhere.

ALICE MATTISON's sixth novel. *When We Argued All Night*, will be published by Harper Perennial. She lives in New Haven, Connecticut.

MIHA MAZZINI lives in Ljubljana, Slovenia. His novel *Guarding Hanna* was recently re-released by North Atlantic Books.

BRENDA MILLER is the author of *Listening Against The Stone: Selected Essays* (2011), plus two previous collections of nonfiction. She is the editor of *Bellingham Review*.

STEVEN MILLHAUSER is the author of several collections of stories. *We Others: New and Selected Stories* is forthcoming.

NANCY MITCHELL is the author of collections of poetry from Four Way Books and Cervena Barva Press. She teaches at Salisbury University in Maryland.

JOHN MURILLO teaches at Cornell University and is the author of *Up Jump The Boogie* (Cypher, 2010).

STEVE MYERS is the author of *Memory's Dog* and the chapbook *Work Site*. He lives in Center Valley, Pennsylvania.

CELESTE NG holds an MFA from the University of Michigan. Her fiction has appeared in *TriQuarterly, Subtropics* and elsewhere.

IRENE O'GARDEN has written children's books, novels and Off-Broadway scripts. Her new play, *Little Heart*, will star Amanda Plummer.

TIM O'SULLIVAN received an MFA from the Iowa Writer's Workshop. He lives in Brooklyn, New York.

E.C. OSONDU was born in Nigeria. He teaches at Providence College in Rhode Island, and is the author of *Voice of America* (Harper, 2010).

ALAN MICHAEL PARKER teaches at Davidson College. His next poetry collection is due out soon from Tupelo Press

PATRICK PHILLIPS' first book, *Chattahoochee*, won the Tufts Discovery Award, and his second, *Boy*, was published in 2008.

DONALD PLATT teaches at Purdue University. His most recent collection is *Dirt Angels* (New Issues Press, 2009).

MARK RICHARD's Pushcart selection is part of his new book just published by Doubleday.

DAVID RIGSBEE is the author of seven poetry collections and he has published critical works on Joseph Brodsky and Carolyn Kizer. Forthcoming books will be from Black Lawrence Press.

JOHN RYBICKI's third poetry collection will be published next year by Lookout Books. He teaches poetry writing to children in Detroit and Kalamazoo.

ANIS SHIVANI is the author of *Against The Workshop: Provocations, Polemics, Controversies* (Texas Review Press, 2011). He lives in Houston, Texas

ROBERT ANTHONY SIEGEL is the author of two novels. He teaches at the University of North Carolina, Wilmington.

ANNA SOLOMAN's first novel is just published by Riverhead Books. She lives in Providence, Rhode Island.

JANE SPRINGER won a Whiting Award in 2010. Her *Dear Blackbird* is available from the University of Utah Press. She teaches at Hamilton College.

SUSAN STEINBERG is the author of *Hydroplane* and *The End of Free Love*. She teaches at the University of San Francisco.

GERALD STERN has just published *Early Collected Poems: 1965-1992* (Norton, 2010). He lives in Lambertville, N.J.

STEVE STERN's most recent book is the novel *The Frozen Rabbi*. His *The Wedding Jester* won the National Jewish Book Award.

PAMELA STEWART has published several chapbooks and five volumes of poetry. She lives on a farm in Hawley, Massachusetts.

LEON STOKESBURY teaches in the writing program at Georgia State University. He is completing his fourth collection of poems.

JOHN JEREMIAH SULLIVAN's *Pulphead*. an anthology of his essays, was just published by Farrar, Straus and Giroux. He is Southern Editor for the *Paris Review*.

CHAD SWEENEY is an editor at New Issues Press. He teaches at Western Michigan University and is the author of three poetry collections and several chapbooks.

ELIZABETH TALLENT teaches creative writing at Stanford University and lives in Fort Bragg, California.

ELAINE TERRANOVA is the author of four books of poetry, Her next book, *Dames Rocket*, is due from PenStroke Press.

DEBORAH THOMPSON lives with her cat and four dogs in Fort Collins, Colorado. She teaches at Colorado State University.

WILLIAM TROWBRIDGE latest book is *Ship of Fool*, to be published by Red Hen Press. He teaches at The University of Nebraska.

FREDERIC TUTEN has published five novels, plus an interrelated book of stories, *Self Portraits: Fictions* (Norton, 2010). He lives in New York.

JUAN VILLORO is A Mexican novelist, essayist, and journalist. His most recent book is *El libro salvaje*.

PAUL ZIMMER worked in the book business for half a century. He has published nine books of poetry and two books of memoir/essays.

INDEX

The following is a listing in alphabetical order by author's last name of works reprinted in the *Pushcart Prize* editions since 1976.

541

545